Phantom Chamber

Phantom Chamber

SHATTERED LEGACY ✦ BOOK TWO

ANDREW ROWE
AND
KAYLEIGH NICOL

Podium

Podium

A Word Before We Begin . . .

The legend of Team Guiding Star Legacy continues in this second book of the Shattered Legacy series!

Andrew Rowe has graciously invited me into his expanded universe to write a series set in his world of Kaldwyn. To truly appreciate this book, a background of Andrew's Arcane Ascension series is recommended, but not necessarily required. For your reference, the appendix of this book includes character biographies, attunement images, and a list of attunements common to the Tiger Spire of Caelford, including their mana types. I hope these additions will help answer any questions you might have in regards to the setting, magic system, and characters.

For those of you familiar with Andrew Rowe's work, you may find my style of writing to be quite different. Rather than attempt to mimic Andrew's style (as we all know his feelings on mimics), I have incorporated similar elements from Andrew's other works while using my words to tell a story in his world. For consistency, I have chosen to emulate Andrew's use of brackets and italics to distinguish between telepathic communication and personal thoughts. For example, a person's thoughts *will appear in italics, like this.* A telepathic message [will be braced by brackets, like this.] A character who communicates only through telepathic speech will use different brackets <to make it immediately obvious that they are the one speaking.> Any other forms of speech, such as sign language, will be denoted in quotations and indicated in the narrative.

Just as in Andrew's other works, I use the singular "they/them" for agender and non-binary characters, as well as characters who have not had their gender determined by the narrator yet. For example: "The cloaked and hooded person shook their head."

I am deeply honored to have been invited into Andrew Rowe's expanded universe, and I am excited to share the Shattered Legacy series with all of you!

~Kayleigh Nicol

Phantom Chamber

SAGE

Seer (hand mark), Citrine

Caelford Foreign Judgment Request
   Applicant: Seiji "Sage" Hayden
   Nation of Origin: Dalenos
   Current Attunement/Location (if any): Seer, right hand
   Attunement Level (if any): Citrine
   Recommendations: Soaring Wings letter of approval, Grant of Permission extended by the Spire Affairs and Relations Bureau of Dalenos
   Reason for Judgment: I suppose my reason for seeking a Judgment from the Tiger Spire is the same as anyone else's: I want to get stronger than I am right now. But if that's the answer everyone gives, I probably need to do better than that. Wanting more strength, more power, that's an easy answer to give. The real reason behind this request is a little harder to put into words.

In short, my last climb in the Tortoise Spire ended with half of my team dying right in front of my eyes. I know that's not uncommon for climbing teams, especially with the types of challenges found on the higher floors, but this was . . . it was different. We made a mistake, I know that now, but at the time we just thought we were being clever. We didn't think we were committing heresy, and we never expected the retribution we received. Otherwise, we never—

I'm sorry, this is beginning to sound unprofessional. It's been hard for me to focus on anything for very long ever since I lost them. They weren't just my teammates. They were my friends. My family. My . . .

I *need* to get stronger. When my friends were dying in that final challenge, I was pinned down at the beginning of the fight and unable to help them at all. All I could do was retreat into this new aspect of my Seer attunement and watch them die, one by one. If I had been strong enough so that I wasn't knocked out at the start of the fight, or if my foresight had been stronger and more accurate, I could have avoided the trap altogether, or if I'd had a combat attunement, I wouldn't have been disabled so easily. I could have saved them. I *should* have saved them.

I suppose one might ask "Why apply for a foreign Judgment when there are other ways to get stronger?" and that's a fair question. For one, the memory of that last climb is simply too painful for me, and for the teammates who survived with me. Particularly Nieve, our team leader as well as my oldest friend. I don't want to downplay any grief Hane might feel, but that last climb was the first time any of us had met them, so I think it's a little different for them. But all the same, we couldn't go back to the Tortoise Spire, not after the mistake we made, and certainly not after the tragedy our fallen friends suffered there. But there's also another reason we left Dalenos: a promise.

Just before that final challenge, our healer made a discovery—one that made her want to leave the spire immediately. I wish now that we had. I can't talk about the object in detail, due to a secrecy agreement—although I guess whoever reads this form will know all about that. Suffice it to say that we found an object of great power that is currently incomplete, and it was Lani's final wish to see the object of power completed. We promised we would see it through, even though it meant leaving Dalenos. We *promised*.

If only we had ended the climb right there . . .

Would it have made a difference? I don't know. All I do know is that Aldis, Emiko, and Lani met their ends against a challenge we weren't meant to survive. The rest of us barely escaped with our lives—and with the object of power.

Sometimes I wish I'd died with them.

Now the only thing that keeps me going is my desire to see Lani's final wish fulfilled. It's the only reason I haven't given up on climbing the spires. Most days, it's the only reason I even get out of bed at all. I'm determined to see this quest through—for Lani. But I'm not strong enough. Not as I am now. I learned that lesson the hard way, and I won't go through it again. Not until I've earned a new strength—a new power—that will keep my friends safe while we seek the missing pieces of the object of power.

Please don't misunderstand: I'm proud to be a Seer. I wouldn't trade my initial attunement for anything, nor will I stop developing and training new Seer abilities and spells. I just need something else, something *more*, so I can be more than a back-row climber, shouting out attack patterns and pointing out traps and hazards. I want to *fight*. And I want to protect. And I want to honor the memory of my fallen teammates.

If that's not enough to earn a secondary attunement, then at least allow the goddess to judge me herself during my Judgment.

Thank you for your consideration.

Request Status: Approved

CHAPTER 1

NIEVE

Champion (mind mark), Citrine
??? (heart mark), Sealed

I hate that we're doing this without Sage," Nieve grumbled, pacing back and forth in front of the agreed-upon marker just outside Caelford's soaring spire. "He's the one that picked the Tiger Spire as our first delve, and he's the one who made all the arrangements through the local Soaring Wings chapter. We need him to look ahead for us, and make plans and . . . and . . . to explain that stupid report thing our team leader gave us." She paused in her pacing, glancing over at Hane, silently watching and waiting as they had been since arriving at the plinth outside the Tiger Spire. "Did you read that, by the way? I tried, but I didn't get very far."

"I learn best by experience," Hane replied placidly. They were crouched low on the balls of their feet, tucked as deeply into the shade as they could be, considering the sandstone plinth was barely wider than an outstretched hand. The plinth was topped by a carving of a skinny, long-legged racing dog, one of many animal-topped plinths that encircled the base of the spire. Apparently these plinths were used as common meeting places for one-off teams to congregate prior to entering the climber's gate. "Sage knew it was a possibility that we might be invited to join a delving team before he began his Judgment. You know as well as I do that we couldn't allow this opportunity to slip by, not when the team is headed for the vault we wanted to search. And if we don't find what we're looking for this time, Sage should be finished with his Judgment in time for our next delve."

Nieve grunted and continued pacing, not at all pacified by Hane's assurances. Second Judgments were said to be more difficult than the first—generally longer and more likely to result in injury—but since memories of Judgments faded immediately afterward, no one could say exactly how or why a second Judgment always seemed to wring a stiffer toll from those who attempted them.

There was a chance Sage might not return from his Tiger Spire Judgment.

But then again, there was always the chance that neither Nieve nor Hane would return, either.

That fact had been made abundantly clear during Team Guiding Star's final climb of the Tortoise Spire.

Nieve's heart began to race, heat rising beneath her skin; she resumed pacing so she would at least have an excuse for the sweat she felt creeping down the back of her neck.

"It looks different, doesn't it?" Hane commented, still crouched low but with their face tipped back to stare up at the spire ahead of them. "I guess I thought all the spires would look more or less the same."

Nieve halted her pacing to look back over her shoulder at the monolithic structure whose top disappeared into the clouds. Ever since she'd watched Sage disappear through the Gate of Judgment, she'd avoided looking directly at it, but that seemed a bit foolish now. It still made her guts churn uncomfortably when she pictured her best friend on his own in there.

"I remember the Judgment classes saying the spires were all a little different. Something about the god beasts, I think." Nieve shrugged. "I saw pictures of the other spires, but the only one that stuck with me was the Hydra Spire. That one was weird."

"Huh." Hane shaded their eyes against the sun. "I guess that'll be interesting to see in person, then."

Nieve considered Hane thoughtfully for a moment. They were an exceptional climber, no doubt about it, but sometimes they said things that seemed just a little off. Almost as if they had skipped the required classes prior to earning their Judgment. That would make sense for a foreigner who had been allowed to take their first Judgment in the Tortoise Spire, but by Hane's own admission, they were a Dalenos native with no history of traveling. Which meant they must have taken similar pre-Judgment classes to the ones Nieve had taken prior to being allowed through the Tortoise Spire's Judgment gate.

Right?

Regardless of their history, Hane was right: the Tiger Spire was entirely different from the Tortoise Spire. While the Tortoise Spire jutted straight up like an admonishing finger, the Tiger Spire's wider base made it look warmer somehow. Almost welcoming. The black stones of the Tortoise Spire appeared ominous and foreboding; by comparison, the reflective white blocks that made up the Tiger Spire seemed patient and inviting. Even the open space surrounding the two spires was entirely different: the Tortoise

Spire was ringed by team flags and markers, some weathered and worn from the elements while others were replaced. There were no team markers in sight outside the Tiger Spire as most teams left their return anchors at the Soaring Wings facility nearby, where climbers could receive medical attention upon their return. Instead, the Tiger Spire was ringed by small stone plinths, like the one Hane was using for shade, each one topped with a different stone-hewn animal. The one out in front of the entrance, predictably, was a large tiger sitting on its haunches.

If pressed to describe the difference between the two spires, Nieve would have said that the Tiger Spire reminded her of a stern teacher: strict but fair. She had always thought of the Tortoise Spire as a wizened old general, demanding more of her on each and every climb.

But that was only a skin-deep comparison. To Nieve, this wasn't just any spire on Kaldwyn: this was the spire where her parents had first met, the spire her father had climbed until he moved to Dalenos to start a family. This spire was a piece of the legacy left to her, a part of her history that remained mired in grief and resentment—not her own, no. She had been too young to remember the loss of her parents with any clarity. But Grandmother Mitsuki, normally warm and encouraging, still turned bitter whenever the subject of her daughter and her daughter's husband came up, so Nieve had learned not to ask questions.

Still, though. As she pressed her hand to the locket beneath her leather vest, Nieve couldn't help but wonder if the Tiger Spire had anything to do with the mysterious attunement that had appeared over her heart after her Judgment in the Tortoise Spire.

She caught Hane staring at her out of the corner of her eye and realized how odd she must have looked just then. With a deliberate huff, Nieve dropped her arm to her side and resumed pacing. She only made it three steps before she realized Hane was beckoning her in closer.

"Can you hear them here?" Hane whispered as Nieve ducked her head toward them. "You have them with you, don't you?"

The question was only confusing for a moment as Nieve realized what had happened: Hane must have thought she was speaking to Chime while gazing up at the spire. Nieve wiggled her ankle in her boot, confirming that the long, thin crystalline shard was still tucked safely inside the hidden pocket Sage had helped her design. "They're quiet right now, but I have them. They sounded pretty weak the last time I brought them here."

Hane cast a doubtful look toward the spire. "I wish we had more information about where their missing piece was. If they aren't inside the vault on the eighteenth floor, we could be wasting our time with this team."

"I hope not," Nieve grumbled, glancing up at the spire again. "It's too late to back out now."

Nieve shifted her weight until she felt the sharp tip of the crystal shard dig into the skin of her ankle as resentment pricked at the core of her being. The entity trapped inside the crystal shard had nothing to do with the tragedy that befell her team during their final climb within the Tortoise Spire, but to think of one was to think of the other. It was easier to blame the gateway crystal for delaying her personal ambition to reach the top of a spire than it was to wade through the feelings of grief, rage, and confusion each time she was forced to remember that final climb.

Yes, fulfilling her dead teammates' final wish was important, and yes, this was a good opportunity to find a new spire to climb. After god beast Genbu's general, Hogame, had pronounced her guilty of crimes against the goddess, she'd felt certain she was no longer welcome in the Tortoise Spire. But her personal desire to reach the top of a spire, to have her wish granted by that very same goddess, couldn't be put off for too long. If she missed her chance, then everything she had gone through—the people she had lost—would all be for nothing.

Can you hear me? Nieve thought loudly, directing the question at the entity inside the crystal shard. *Or do I need to stand closer to the spire?*

<I hear.> The response seemed distant and faint, as if the entity were shouting against the wind and Nieve could only make out bits and pieces of what it was saying. <Soon?>

We'll be entering the spire soon, Nieve replied, guessing that was what the gateway crystal, nicknamed Chime for convenience, was asking. *We just want to confirm that your missing piece is still where it was two days ago. Can you feel if it's moved at all?*

<I feel . . . me.> That would have been odd if Nieve wasn't already aware that they were searching for Chime's scattered bits of consciousness trapped inside broken shards of crystal. <Locked within, surrounded by objects of great power. They come and they go, always unseen. The silver eyes do not blink. So much darkness, but not alone.>

Nieve grimaced and shrugged, turning her focus to Hane rather than the crystal hidden inside her boot. "They sound pretty weak, but I think they're saying that the shard is in the same place as it was when we came here for Sage's Judgment. It still sounds like a vault to me."

Hane nodded once. "We'll just have to hope they mean the hidden vault on the eighteenth floor. Will you check with them again once we're inside?"

"I can," Nieve said doubtfully. "But I don't know if I'll get the chance to tell you once our team arrives, since we're keeping Chime a secret."

"Mm." Hane hummed thoughtfully. "It would be easier to just tell them what we're looking for, but I agree that the temptation of having any wish granted by a gateway crystal would derail the senses of most treasure-hungry climbers and delvers. If Chime tells you something important, try to make an excuse to talk to me alone. Otherwise, I'll trust your judgment."

Nieve felt a sudden pressure in her chest at that—like a steel breastplate caved in by a battering ram. Trust her judgment? No, no one should be trusting her judgment. Not when she was the one who had argued so strongly in favor of cheating to climb the Tortoise Spire faster.

Not when she had been the one to lead her teammates to their doom.

Nieve resumed pacing, each heartbeat pounding more loudly than the last one in her ears. Trying to ease her anxiety, she reminded herself that she wasn't the leader this time. No, she, Sage, and Hane had been selected to join a delving team from the climber-for-hire profiles they'd left at the local Soaring Wings administrative branch. The team leader, a young woman named Odette, had selected the three of them for their combat experience, but by the time she'd reached out to them, Sage had already entered the Judgment Gate. Nieve had wanted to wait for Sage's return, but Odette had seemed anxious to begin the delve sooner rather than later. One of the other team members had recommended a sixth, and Odette had scheduled them to begin the very next day.

Nieve had considered passing on the offer in order to wait for Sage, but the delving team's intended destination matched up too perfectly with one of the locations where Chime's missing shard might be: the vault on the eighteenth floor. The concept of a floor remaining the same for any length of time—let alone months or even years—was still difficult for Nieve to wrap her head around, so she couldn't eliminate the fear that the location of the vault might change, taking Chime's shard somewhere else entirely. The real selling point for this team was the fact that Odette had a key for the seventeenth floor, making it a short climb to the next floor. Even if they were wrong about the shard being inside the vault, it was possible the team might finish this delve before Sage even completed his Judgment.

Of course, most climbs didn't go that smoothly.

"Are you nervous?" Hane asked as Nieve passed them along her circuit.

"No," Nieve replied, a little more sharply than she intended. "The team leader said she's done this floor and the one above it before, so as long as they haven't changed, this should be a quick, easy delve. That sounds way easier than any climb in the Tortoise Spire, so why would I be nervous?"

"Because you've always climbed with the same people before," Hane said simply and without mercy. "Will this be your first climb without your friends?"

"I've climbed with you before," Nieve muttered, knowing it sounded weak. Hane was strong and reliable, but Nieve wouldn't qualify them as a friend. Even after traveling from Dalenos to Caelford by train, she still couldn't say she knew Hane very well: they had spent most of the trip either asleep or pretending to be asleep. Maybe they were just trying to give Nieve and Sage the space to grieve for their friends, but it was difficult to see Hane as respectful or caring when they made so little effort to be understood.

And honestly, maybe she was just a little nervous. Sage actually would have read the "floor summary report," as Odette called it when she hand-delivered two massive stacks of pages to Nieve and Hane. To Nieve's way of thinking, the only relevant information had been on the first page: the date, time, and location for the team to meet up prior to beginning the delve. Supposedly the rest of the pages were a summary of the challenges on the seventeenth and eighteenth floors, but the packet had been almost as thick as Nieve's fist, and studying had never been one of Nieve's strong suits. She'd made an effort, but after falling asleep while attempting to read it and knocking her tea over so that it soaked the pages, she'd given it up as hopeless. And Hane's admission of not having read it either only increased her sense of trepidation.

"I don't think it's bad to feel a little nervous," Hane said lightly. "It's a different spire with a different set of rules and expectations. Not to mention the language barrier."

"The—oh." Nieve felt her stomach sink. She hadn't even thought about the other climbers speaking Caelish; the Soaring Wings administrator they'd worked with to fill out climber-for-hire paperwork had been a native of Dalenos, and Odette had spoken Artinian when they met to discuss the delve. Did that mean the other climbers would speak Artinian? Or was Odette just particularly learned? Why hadn't Hane brought this up sooner? Nieve didn't want to climb with anyone she couldn't communicate with; that felt like a disaster in the making.

Just as Nieve was beginning to think maybe it wasn't too late to bail on this delve, Hane turned their head, eyes narrowed against the harsh sunlight.

"I think those two climbers are coming this way." Hane nodded, indicating a pair of people who appeared to be deep in conversation with each other. "Looks like they might be our new teammates."

Nieve felt her stomach churn, a sudden upwelling of nerves making her feel mildly ill. She had expected Odette to arrive first in order to make the introductions, but Nieve didn't recognize either of the two people approaching. Both wore dueling vests and leather-reinforced leggings, typical of most climbers, though the style differed a little from what Nieve was used to. If they continued along their current trajectory, their path would intersect with the skinny-dog plinth in short order. Were they actually teammates? Or was there another team that might have agreed to meet at this place and time?

As the strangers drew closer, the tone of their discussion sounded less like a conversation and more like an argument. The taller of the two lifted a hand and called a greeting that Nieve just barely recognized before the argument resumed, with the shorter of the two making an exaggerated point that had their partner rolling their eyes.

When the pair came to a halt near the plinth, the young woman crossed her arms over her chest and shifted her weight to stand at an angle, saying something that sounded roughly like a greeting. Her companion, a tall man with his head shaved bare, smiled as he met Nieve's eyes, saying something in Caelish that Nieve couldn't even begin to follow.

As Nieve exchanged a wide-eyed glance with Hane, the young woman sized up the two of them.

"Dalenos?" she asked, pointing at Hane.

"Dalenos," Nieve agreed, indicating herself as well as Hane. This wasn't the first time someone had assumed her to be Caelish based on her mixed heritage. "Sorry, I don't think either of us speaks any Caelish."

The two Caelish climbers exchanged a look that seemed both curious and mildly annoyed.

The young woman tried again. "Do you understand Valian?"

"Yes!" Nieve felt the knot in her stomach loosen. "I'm pretty good at Valian. What about you, Hane?"

"I'm okay." They shrugged. "I understand more than I speak. Valian works for me."

"So you're both from Dalenos? Odette said we'd have foreign climbers, I just assumed that meant Valians." The woman looked doubtful as she sized Nieve up again. "You don't look Dalen."

"My dad was Caelish," Nieve explained. "He died when I was young, so the only Caelish words I know are the rude ones. Er, sorry."

"Oh, that's fine." The woman waved a hand dismissively. "Valian's a common language here, so even Brick here speaks it. I'm Rose, by the way. Architect."

"Brick?" Nieve repeated, uncertain.

"It's Mason, actually. I'm a Transmuter." The tall man winked, teeth flashing white against his dark complexion. "My sister thinks it's funny to tease me, even though I'm here as a special favor to her. I heard you guys were a team of three originally."

"Yeah, we registered as a team of three, but our Seer got approved to take a Judgment and he's not back yet," Nieve explained. "We're all from Dalenos; this is our first time climbing the Tiger Spire. That's Hane, they're a Wave-walker." Nieve hooked her thumb over her shoulder, indicating Hane still crouched in the shade. "I'm Nieve. I have a Champion attunement."

A severe furrow creased Rose's forehead. "Nee-eh-vay."

Nieve blinked, startled. "Uh, what?"

"It's pronounced Nee-eh-vay," Rose repeated. "Your name. Is that how they say it in Dalenos? It's prettier in Caelish."

"Ah, I don't know, everyone's always called me Nieve." She liked the simplicity of the single syllable. Strong like a broad sword, quick like the hiss of a skate over ice. "It's what I'm used to, I guess."

"Hm." Rose looked doubtful. "I suppose that's fine elsewhere, but while you're here, there's no point in continuing to say it incorrectly."

"Not everyone cares about being correct all the time, Prickles." Mason rolled his eyes good-naturedly. "Don't mind her, she's just mad because I overslept this morning. Never mind the fact that I only just found out I was joining this delve last night."

"I'm mad because you still went out drinking after I told you that I needed you for this delve!" Rose snapped. "This is why you always rank in the lowest tier of our siblings. You don't think things through before you do them."

"If I cared about that, I'm sure my feelings would be hurt," Mason retorted. "If I stopped to think about every little thing, I'd be as stressed out and neurotic as you are. I'm fine with being ignored by our parent if it means being allowed to do what I want, when I want. You should try it sometime."

"You're going to end up getting cut off, and then you're going to come crying to me for help," Rose informed him archly. "You think I'm going to remember you when our parent chooses me as their heir?"

"Yeah, I think you will." Mason hooked his thumbs through his belt, grinning easily. "Why do you think I let you bully me into helping you all the time?"

Rose rolled her eyes and huffed hard enough to ruffle the spill of curls over one side of her forehead. "Fine. As long as you're useful, I won't let you starve." Her focus shifted sharply back to Nieve and Hane. "You're the combat veterans hired for this delve, right? Odette and I aren't fighters, and Mason's better on defense than offense."

"Yes, that's us." The whole talk about a parent and heirs was a bit mystifying to Nieve; she never would have guessed that Rose and Mason were brother and sister if they hadn't said so. Better to talk about the delve instead; at least Nieve knew where she stood there. "Just point me toward the action and give me some room. Doesn't matter if it's monsters or armies or attuned opponents, I don't back down from a fight."

"I bet you don't." Mason's gaze conveyed a little more than agreement. Nieve barely held back a grimace as he winked. "Have you been to any of the dueling grounds in Caelford yet? I'd love to take you to a tournament sometime."

Nieve snorted as she sized him up. He was taller than she was, which was enough for her to dislike him, but she had to admit that he filled out his frame well: broad chest, wide shoulders, and solid-looking enough to take a hit without going down right away even without a Transmuter's stone mana to toughen him up. His skin was so dark, it seemed to gleam in the sun. His head was shaved completely bald, but he wore a neatly trimmed goatee around his mouth. His quilted tunic was a deep green that looked good on him, but cut in the sleeveless style common among Caelford climbers. Without a shirt beneath it, his shoulders and arms were bare, showing off hard lines of muscle that flexed impressively as Nieve ran her eyes down his frame. He wore leather bracers on his forearms, possibly enchanted, but Nieve didn't bother confirming that with her Detect Aura spell—even if she did, it wouldn't tell her what type of enchantment it was, so why bother? He didn't wear a cloak and his leggings had leather armor patches sewn onto them wherever they didn't need to bend. Nieve didn't see any visible weapons, but there was something like a large quiver slung over a shoulder and across his back. Rather than arrows, the quiver was full of thick stone rods, each about half the length of a fighting staff. Surely they were weapons of some kind, but Nieve wasn't familiar with how they worked.

"Hmph." Nieve sniffed before purposefully shifting her gaze over to Rose and smiling invitingly. "That offer might actually be tempting if it came from your sister."

Rose snorted indelicately, seemingly amused as she sized up Nieve in return. "I'm not interested in duels, I'm afraid. And if you try to feed me a meathead line like the ones my brother uses, it's going to be a definite no from me. My time is too valuable to waste on meatheads."

"Meathead" wasn't a term Nieve was familiar with, but the way Rose said it, it sounded a bit like "brute" or "oaf," two words that had been applied to her on occasion, though usually laughingly among friends. It was a bit of a shame that Rose didn't seem interested: she was a good deal better-looking than her brother. She stood nearly as tall as Nieve, but slender and lean, except for a few comely curves. Her complexion was darker than Nieve's but lighter than Mason's, with a nose like a knife's edge and eyes the color of amber. Her hair was pulled tight to her skull, tied at the top so that long, bronze-colored curls spilled off the crown of her head to one side like a wave, some falling partially over her forehead. The curls themselves were actually intriguing: it looked as if the outer layer of each curl had been dyed or burnished bronze, while the inner coils were inky black. Nieve itched to touch them—curly hair was rare in Dalenos and it had always been a bit of a weakness for her. All she really wanted to do was tug one curl out straight and watch it spring back into place, but first she'd have to find a way to prove she wasn't a "meathead."

Nieve didn't see a practical weapon on Rose, like a sword or an ax, or anything to defend herself with. Instead, a thick black belt looped her waist twice, sporting neat rows of leaf-shaped throwing blades, which were great for fighting at a distance, but less so for close combat. She wore something like tool pouches secured to her leggings by belt-like straps, and her vest looked heavy, as if concealing something inside. Up close, Nieve could see the vest was made of canvas while the shirt beneath was stitched with the typical quilted protection of most dueling vests. Just like her brother, Rose didn't wear a cloak, but she did carry a low-slung backpack over one shoulder, with two bedrolls lashed to the bottom of it. Maybe she had convinced Mason to come on this climb by offering to carry his supplies for him. That seemed like something one of Nieve's own brothers would bargain for.

"Tch, nah, you don't want Prickles," Mason protested, shaking his head. "She's all thorns and sarcasm, not the kind of person you want to cuddle up with. But me, on the other hand—"

Mason was slowly moving into Nieve's space, making an exaggerated motion through his shoulders. Whether he was just flexing, or whether he intended to drop his arm over Nieve's shoulders, Nieve didn't wait to find out. When he stepped in close enough, she tilted the hilt of her sword until it jabbed him in the ribs, forcibly maintaining her space. She also gave him her best "get lost" face, which apparently needed no translation. Mason sighed heavily and backed up a step.

"Fine, fine, waste your time on Prickles, see if I care." Mason turned his sunny smile on Hane, still crouched in the slim shade of the plinth. "It's Hane, right? What's your flavor?"

Hane lifted their eyes slowly, maintaining eye contact through a long, drawn out silence. Just as the silence turned uncomfortable, Hane stated simply: "No."

Mason sighed, a pained expression on his face. "The rejection! I don't know if my heart can take it. I don't know if I can actually go through with this delve, Prickles."

"You will," his sister said, sounding bored as she checked her pockets and supplies. "And stop being so dramatic, or you'll scare off the Valian headed our way."

The mention of a "Valian" had Nieve chasing down Rose's gaze, foolishly hoping that Sage had somehow finished his Judgment already and come to join them. Her heart sank as the newcomer lifted a hand in greeting, smiling politely as he approached the skinny-dog plinth. She knew the odds of Sage finishing his Judgment so soon was unlikely, and even if he did, he would need some time to recover and learn about his new attunement, but knowing that didn't keep her from wishing otherwise. It was only after Hane's question about nerves that she realized she had never once entered a climber's gate without Sage by her side.

The Valian climber had spoken, but Nieve didn't catch the words. Neither, it seemed, had Hane, who was peering up with a quizzical look on their face. Rose started to reply, then stopped herself when she caught their blank stares.

"Sorry, I slipped." Rose gave her head a small shake. "He said hello and asked if we were all waiting for Odette. We're speaking Valian for the sake of our foreign climbers. I trust you speak Valian?"

The last part was spoken to the newcomer, who smiled as he hitched the bow hooked over his shoulder a little higher.

"What gave me away?" the newcomer asked, the notes of his voice light and playful, like petals caught in a breeze. "I'm Lief, the hired healer for this climb. Nice to meet you all."

Introductions were repeated, giving Nieve a chance to size Lief up. He stood at about her height, though she would qualify his frame as "slender" rather than "fighting fit." He had a longbow over his shoulder and a pair of quivers set over his left hip. On his right, he wore a sheathed sword, which seemed a bit odd: sure, it made sense to carry multiple weapons, but in her experience it was better to have one large weapon and multiple smaller weapons. Lief didn't appear to carry many supplies as there was only one slim satchel looped through the back of his belt, but it was also possible that the satchel was a dimensional bag, like Hane's, which would enable it to carry much more than seemed likely from its outward appearance. His clothing looked worn and practical, but still stylish with embellished colors and stitching. The cloak might have been silk by the way it played in the light breeze, and his dueling tunic was clearly quality by the intricate stitching at the pockets and seams. Typical of Valians, he wore gloves on his hands, but more stylish than practical, judging by the way they covered his palms but barely reached his wrists. Solid boots, pale leggings, and a collared, long-sleeved shirt open at the throat gave him the appearance of a rakish nobleman looking for an adventure to brag to his friends about.

While Nieve's personal interest had little to do with men, she couldn't help but notice that Lief was exceptionally pretty. His hair was a pale blond, long near the front and shorter in the back, the light breeze giving it a feathered appearance. His smile was easy and inviting, and his posture and gestures seemed open and relaxed, but it was really his eyes that were his most remarkable feature. She'd never met anyone with pale violet eyes before, and his seemed to shine with hidden intellect and perhaps a hint of humor.

Sage would like this one, Nieve thought to herself. *At least, he would if he wasn't still mourning Lani.*

Not that Nieve felt like she was finished mourning yet—she still had days when she woke up thinking about joining Emiko to watch a play, or dropping in on Lani to invite her out for a drink. When reality caught up to her thoughts, the pain felt as fresh as it had when she'd watched them die, but sulking did nothing except prolong the pain and the guilt and the regret. Unfortunately, it was hard to do anything else during long days of traveling by train, especially when sharing a cabin with someone who felt just as guilty as she did. Despite her anxiety, it was probably good that she was finally climbing again; she needed a healthy outlet for her grief, or else she'd start picking fights with strangers.

"Are you a Biomancer or a Mender?" Mason was saying to Lief, the charming smile from earlier back in place. "Where's your mark at?"

"Biomancer, and unfortunately, it's a leg attunement." Lief cast his gaze down, sighing dolefully. "I can heal minor injuries over a distance, but for anything more severe, I need to maintain contact in order to fix it."

"Feel free to put your hands on me anytime you like," Mason replied with a wink. "Any interest in spending some downtime with me during the first scenario? I'm sure we could find something fun to do."

"Ah . . ." Lief's gaze zipped down and up Mason's frame, his expression torn between amusement and consideration. "I prefer not to mix relations with climbing. I find it compromises more team dynamics than not. But I wouldn't say no if you wanted to buy me a drink sometime afterward."

Mason pouted, looking petulant over being turned down again. "No fun at all on this climb. This better be a quick run, Prickles. Otherwise, I'm not letting you bully me into going on any more climbs with you."

"We're starting one floor below the vault," Rose replied, thumbing the hilts of her throwing knives. "And there's no need to sulk. Odette still isn't here and she hasn't rejected you. Yet."

"Yeah, but Odette . . ." Mason hedged before looking around furtively. Nieve saw her at the same time Mason did, approaching from the direction of the Soaring Wings checkpoint. Nieve and Mason both lifted their hands in a far-off greeting, but as Odette returned the gesture, she dropped the heavy folder she had been carrying, causing her to scurry after the pages that tumbled free.

Mason didn't finish his thought, but he didn't have to: Nieve understood. She had only met Odette twice before, so she knew she was probably judging the young woman unfairly, but . . . there were simply too many similarities between Odette and Sage for Nieve to separate the two in her mind. And since Sage had all the sexual appeal of soggy toast, Nieve had trouble thinking of Odette as anything other than the current team leader. And even that was a shaky title at best.

Odette had a nervous manner, her eyes always darting around, her hands always fidgeting with something, her teeth always buried in her lower lip. During their first meeting, she had been more concerned about the fact that Nieve had never researched a climb before beginning it than with Nieve's successful track record as a climber. When asked about how she prepared for a climb, Nieve had listed off the supplies she generally packed the day before. Apparently packing extra cotton ponies at certain times of the month didn't count as being "properly prepared" by Odette's way of thinking.

"Sorry I'm late." Odette panted as she hurried over, clutching her folder of loose papers close to her chest with both arms. Her wide eyes jumped from face to face, confirming that she was the last to arrive. "I wanted to get here early, but then I couldn't remember our team designation, so I had to go back and check my notes, and then when I was in line to check in, I was going over all the possibilities of challenges in the first scenario in my head, and I realized I had forgotten one, but I couldn't remember which one, so I ran home again, but by then I was late, so I just grabbed the whole thing, and—and—" Odette ducked her head, almost as if she was bowing. "I'm so sorry! Is being late considered disrespectful in Dalenos? Am I supposed to kneel down as part of my apology? I am so sorry, really, I am!"

"Please don't kneel down," Nieve said quickly, more concerned about the haphazard papers cradled in Odette's arms than her tardiness. "Everyone runs late sometimes, you don't have to keep saying you're sorry."

"We've decided we're speaking Valian, by the way," Hane chimed in, startling Nieve. She hadn't even realized Odette was speaking Artinian. "I think most of us speak it fairly well. Unless you don't speak it?"

"Oh, I do. I can. Valian is good." Odette adjusted her thin, round glasses, switching to Valian as she addressed everyone. "I'm so sorry I'm late. I forgot some things, and I just—I don't think I'm used to this whole leader thing just yet."

"Don't worry about it," Lief assured her with a kind smile. "It gave us a chance to get to know one another."

"Oh, good." Odette looked relieved, smiling briefly before struggling with the unorganized mass of gathered papers grasped tightly to her chest. "Then we should take just a moment to go over—Oh no! Stop, wait!"

The papers paid her no heed as they slipped from her grasp, twisting and tumbling as the wind caught at them. Rose and Lief lunged after the closest pages while Mason twirled his hand almost lazily. Nieve felt the wind shift by the tug at her ponytail as the pages were caught by a weak cyclone, gathering them into one spot for easier collection.

"Sorry," Odette murmured, looking embarrassed as Rose stomped her boot down to pin the pages in place before dropping to a knee to gather them. She muttered softly to herself in Caelish as she began fixing the papers and putting them back into some semblance of order.

While not to Nieve's taste, Odette was kind of cute. She was shorter than Nieve, around average height with smooth dark skin and deep brown eyes that always seemed to be widened in surprise. Odette wore the tight coils of her hair combed back and gathered into a pouf at the back of her head. Like Rose, she wore a long-sleeved shirt beneath her padded dueling vest, both of which were patched with different colored fabrics, but in a way that looked artistic rather than ragged. She wore glasses like Sage did, except hers were large and round, magnifying the eyes behind the lenses. The bracer on her left wrist was leather and held tiny tools in pockets, things like scissors, a magnifying glass, sewing needles, and other useful items. The bracer on her right wrist sparkled with glass marbles, each one glowing with a magical aura to Nieve's spell-enhanced vision. There were no obvious weapons on Odette's belt, but there was a knotted cord of rings wound through her belt. Most of the rings appeared to be metal, though some looked as though they might be made of glass or wood or bone. There was no uniform size or style, though using Detect Aura revealed that each one carried an enchantment of some kind. Maybe each ring was specific to a particular spell or task? Or maybe each one carried a different sort of spell resistance for defensive purposes. It wasn't safe to wear too many active enchanted items at once, so perhaps Odette only wore a ring when she needed it, and the knotted cord was simply more convenient than searching through a pouch full of rings. Odette wore the rest of her gear in a satchel over her shoulder with a slim bedroll lashed beneath it.

"Thank you." Odette gave Rose a relieved smile as she accepted her neatened folder back, thrusting it inside her satchel before it could be caught by the wind again. "Okay, before we get started, did everyone remember to drop off their return bell anchors at the Soaring Wings administrative building? For filing, our team name was, um . . ." She checked a note tucked inside her bracer. "Greyhound 149?"

Nieve nodded yes along with everyone else. Back at the Tortoise Spire, registered climbing teams had their own banners, which team members could plant their anchors around, so everyone arrived at the same spot when exiting the spire. Here, the anchors were stored at the Soaring Wings facility nearby, close to the healing ward so that any injured climbers could receive immediate attention. It seemed a little soft to Nieve, who was used to walking off broken bones, but she couldn't deny that it was rather convenient.

"Okay, good." Odette smiled as she adjusted her glasses, a note of relief in her voice. "And did everyone read through the floor reports I prepared for you?"

There was a chorus of "Yes" that Nieve didn't join. What good did it do to study before a climb? Every spire climb was unique; reading a document as long as a book wasn't going to suddenly make the spire a safe place to be. She would figure out the challenge once she saw it, just like always.

Unfortunately, Odette didn't seem to agree.

"Um, did you both get a chance to read it?" Odette asked, a slight furrow between her brows. "Hane? Nee-eh-vay?"

Nieve grimaced at Odette's pronunciation of her name, saying it the same way Rose had said it, with three syllables instead of one. As much as she wanted to correct her, she didn't want to pick an argument before they even got inside the spire.

"I don't learn well from reading," Hane explained, tone calm and low. "My understanding is that even if certain scenarios are expected, they can still change at any time, and that even the same scenario can have different conditions for success or failure."

"That is true," Odette agreed, shifting her weight from side to side as she gazed down at the ground. "But, um, there are certain commonalities among the different challenges, which we can prepare for ahead of time, so even if the objective of the scenario changes, we won't be blindsided, so it's . . . I just think it's better to be fully prepared."

"We'll follow your lead," Nieve assured her. "We're your combat experts, just point us to where the fight is and we'll take care of it. That's how we do it at the Tortoise Spire."

"But, um . . ." Odette flicked her gaze around at the other climbers, as if looking for support. No one said anything, but Rose looked impatient with her hands resting on her hips. "Well, we have a little time. Maybe you both could read it over now? I have one copy . . . Um, did anyone else bring a copy of the notes? You two might have to share . . ."

"It's a waste of time to just sit around waiting for them to read the whole thing," Rose interjected. "Let's just summarize it and get going. I've been through this floor twice, anyway. It's not one of the harder ones."

"I made it through this scenario once before, too," Lief put in. "It shouldn't be too difficult with this team if we talk them through it."

"Yes, but . . ." Odette averted her gaze, hands twisting in front of her as she seemed to shrink. "It can still be dangerous if we get surprised. And, if we don't know what to look for, we might miss something. And then there's the next floor, the one with the vault, and there's a whole strategy for that one, too, and it's just . . . Well, this key was expensive, and we can only use it once, so . . ."

Rose blew out a breath that ruffled her burnished curls. "Okay, listen." She faced Nieve and Hane squarely, looking stern with her fists on her hips. "It's pretty straightforward, but if it'll get us started, I'll run it down for you. The seventeenth floor is a scenario that revolves around a train. It's been that way for a year now."

"Fourteen months, one week, four days," Odette corrected, her voice no higher than a whisper. Nieve had no idea why that information was relevant.

"Right," Rose agreed, though she sounded slightly exasperated. "The mission parameters vary, but there's always a mechanical failure, a mountain pass with a rockslide, and some fairly standard side quests, like trading sequences and escorts."

Hane's nose wrinkled distastefully. Nieve inwardly agreed: side quests were often a waste of time as so few of them included a combat element.

"The main objective is the point that varies," Rose continued. "Sometimes the climber team is meant to rob the train and escape from it successfully, in which case the items we steal become the treasure. Other times, the climber team is supposed to protect a valuable shipment of items, or we might be asked to find someone on the train, like a spy, or an escaped prisoner, or an Edrian defector, something like that. There's also a catastrophic failure scenario where the train will continually lose rear cars until we can fix the underlying issue, in which case we need to move the passengers and the cargo to the cars closest to the engine as quickly as possible. In those cases, our reward is given to us once we arrive at the end destination in the form of luggage given to us by a porter. Any questions?"

That sounded a lot more succinct than the stack of papers Odette had given them. Why couldn't she have just written that down instead?

"How do we know what our objective is once the scenario starts?" Hane asked.

"It depends," Odette said quietly. "If we start at a boarding station, usually we're given instructions or clues within the scenario. If we begin on the train while it's already in transit, we have to figure it out ourselves."

"That doesn't sound too combat-heavy," Nieve observed. "Is the second scenario more of a challenge?"

"Don't mistake a lack of combat for lack of a challenge," Lief suggested with a smile. "But if it's a fight you're looking for, I can assure you that you'll find it on the next floor. The treasures of the goddess are never claimed without a bit of bloodshed."

Nieve grinned: that sounded exactly like the sort of challenge she was looking for. Although Odette would probably want to discuss the vault floor in detail, too, which put a bit of a damper on the whole thing.

"There wasn't as much information on the vault in the summary you gave us," Mason pointed out, looking pointedly bored with the whole discussion. "You included the possible settings, objectives, and general labyrinth operations, but you stopped at the vault door."

"Yeah, I caught that, too," Rose said, giving Odette a pointed look. "When you asked me to come, you said you'd found one of the spire's phantom chambers, and that the entrance is through the vault. Which chamber is it? How do we open it? And how sure are you that no one else has opened it yet?"

Nieve frowned and exchanged a look with Hane. What, exactly, was a phantom chamber?

Odette shuffled her feet nervously, eyes glued to the ground. "If I'm right, it's the Vault of Shadows, and this is the first time it's been located below the twenty-fifth floor in over a decade. But how to open it . . ." She hedged, clearly anxious. "I'm sorry, but it took a lot of research, time, and travel to learn those secrets. I'm not comfortable sharing them until we reach the vault."

"We're here already," Rose pointed out. "We're all committed at this point. My concern is that we could be wasting our time on this delve. You know I've been inside the vault on the eighteenth floor before; it isn't exactly a secret among climbers. It may take a bit of work to find the vault within the labyrinth, but any team can open it once they find it, and the treasure is mostly pretty standard for the scale of the challenge. This delve isn't really worth it unless it's actually one of the phantom chambers."

"Hey, uh, sorry if this was covered in the reading, but what are the phantom chambers?" Nieve asked, curious.

"Secret vaults that appear randomly within the Tiger Spire," Lief summarized succinctly.

"Almost," Odette said at the same as Rose said, definitively, "No."

Mason yawned dramatically. "Anyone mind if I doze off? I don't need to hear this lecture again."

Rose ignored him as she launched into an explanation. "According to climber rumors collected over the past one hundred years or so, the Tiger Spire possesses five secret vaults known collectively as the phantom chambers. There's the Vault of Conquest, the Vault of Riches, the Vault of Otherwordly Metals, the Vault of Shadows, and the Armory. While many believe that finding one of these chambers is a matter of luck or divine favor, Odette is part of a team of Analysts that collects information on these vaults in order to study them, predict their locations, and figure out how to access them."

"That's, um, well . . ." Odette cringed as everyone turned to look at her. "That's all mostly correct. The team is . . . well, it is mostly Analysts, but anyone dedicated to locating and researching the chambers is welcome, it's just . . ." She coughed politely into her fist. "Not much is known for certain about these chambers; in fact, some theorize that there are only four phantom chambers instead of five, and the Vault of Conquest and the Armory are one and the same, but no one knows for sure based on the accounts and recollections of climbers who've found them, and . . . Well, of course, it depends on how reliable the source is, and, ah . . ."

"So, in essence, the phantom chambers are five—possibly four—secret vaults that appear randomly within the Tiger Spire," Lief repeated, bright smile softening any sarcastic intent.

"I think we got it," Hane said, shading their eyes against the sun.

Nieve didn't really get it, but she also didn't think more information would help her understand. Was this good for her and Hane, or was it bad? Finding a secret chamber sounded exciting, but they were supposed to be looking for Chime's missing piece. Unless Chime's crystal shard was inside one of these secret vaults? If it was, delving the Tiger Spire might take a lot longer than she'd anticipated.

Rose huffed, blowing the curls off her forehead. "Doesn't it bother anyone else that she's clearly keeping information back from the group? We've all signed on to the team, we've signed off on the loot-split, we're all sharing in the danger equally, so shouldn't we all know how to access the Vault of Shadows?"

Rose looked around expectantly as Odette mumbled and picked at her nails. Hane said nothing, but simply turned to face the spire as if anxious to get started. Nieve shrugged, not sure she would understand the information even if Odette shared it. Mason smirked at his sister's mounting impatience.

Lief hooked a thumb through his belt, his expression thoughtful. "I think it's actually very wise of Odette to hold onto the secret of the vault for now.

Otherwise, what's to stop any of us from running off and claiming it for ourselves? I'm sure she'll tell us what we need to know once we get there."

"I will, I promise," Odette agreed, nodding eagerly. "If you think I'm being unreasonable, I'm willing to take a lesser share of the loot. This is such an amazing opportunity for me to actually study one of the phantom vaults in person, that's all that really matters to me."

Rose made a face, but Mason set a hand on her shoulder before she could argue.

"Let it go, Prickles, it's not worth it," he counseled. "Even if something does happen, or if Odette is wrong, or whatever, the regular vault is still easy enough to get open, and standard treasure is enough to cover the cost of a two-floor delve. And if it works out like it's supposed to, Odette will open the super secret vault and you can pick out whatever you think will win our parent's favor. We're not losing anything except a few days' time, and I know you've been looking for an excuse to go climbing lately."

"I don't need an excuse to climb, I'm just busy with work," Rose muttered rebelliously. "I need this to be worth my time, or else I'm falling behind on orders for nothing."

"Then we should get started!" Lief clapped his hands together, smiling cheerfully. "Everyone has all their gear, right? Food, water, bedrolls, anything else you need to get through a two-floor delve?"

"Maybe we should discuss the first scenario a little more," Odette suggested timidly. "There's actually a lot more to it than Rose explained, and then there's the path to the vault, and what we should do if either scenario is different from what we expect it to be—"

"Talking isn't doing." It was a surprise to see that Hane was a few steps closer to the spire now, as if leading the team forward. "We'll handle the challenges as they come."

"They're right," Nieve agreed, hooking her hand over the hilt of her sword. "There's no way to prepare for everything, so we might as well just go for it."

Odette looked as if she wanted to protest, but Rose and Mason both wore the same hungry grin and Hane looked back expectantly. Lief appeared good-naturedly unconcerned, as if content to follow the majority.

"Okay," Odette agreed, sounding sullen. "I just wanted to make sure we were as prepared as possible. The treasure is only worth it if we're all alive to spend it later."

It took a moment for Nieve to recognize the sharp stinging behind her eyes as a sudden upswell of grief. She hadn't expected such a common climber saying to remind her that the teammates she'd lost—Aldis, Emiko, Lani— would never spend any of their cut from that last, tragic climb. Blinking back useless tears, Nieve decided to toss a few coins away at a casino once she, Sage, and Hane were ready to leave Caelford, in honor of Lani's memory.

Odette took a deep breath, adjusted the strap of her bag, then, surprisingly, she reached out to stroke the stone-carved dog, petting it from muzzle to ears. "Let's go line up at the gate, team."

Before Nieve could puzzle out a question, Odette strode off in the direction of the spire. Rose and Mason each gave the stone dog an affectionate pat before following behind her.

"Team rituals," Lief murmured, shrugging lightheartedly. "Most of the statues around this spire are worn smooth from being stroked and patted for luck."

As he spoke, he ran a hand down the dog's back, from crown to tail. A final smile, then he turned to trot after Odette and the others. Hane had already backtracked to the dog statue, their expression fading from quizzical to resigned after Lief's explanation. They traced a line from the dog's snout to the top of its head before shooting Nieve an expectant look.

The bitter flavor of grief still heavy on her tongue, Nieve determinedly tried to think of anything other than her old team's pre-climb ritual. Patting a dog statue was nothing like tugging on Emiko's hair buns, but the sentiment behind it was close enough that Nieve could almost hear Emi's playfully indignant squeal. Swallowing hard, Nieve looked away as she set her palm over the dog's head, rocking her hand back and forth as if tousling her brothers' hair. She quit abruptly, drawing her hand back sharply as she attempted to focus on the delve ahead.

"Hey." Hane spoke low and soft, dark eyes searching Nieve's. "Are you ready for this?"

Nieve raised her gaze to face the monolithic spire straight on, steeling her spirit as well as her will. She was a warrior, a fighter, the shield that stood between her teammates and danger. It didn't matter that this was an unfamiliar spire, or that her team was made up of strangers, or that she was delving rather than climbing. This was a new challenge, and Nieve didn't back down from a challenge.

But more than that, it was the first stop along the journey of finding an ancient gateway stone's missing pieces and returning them to their original form and power.

It was the first step in fulfilling the final wish of a fallen teammate. And maybe a step toward learning more about the sealed mark in the center of her chest.

Exhaling slowly, Nieve turned to Hane and nodded. "I'm ready. Let's go."

HANE

Wavewalker (leg mark), Citrine

Hane fought the urge to shuffle and fidget as they waited with their team inside the vast ground floor of the Tiger Spire. Having never attended the typical pre-Judgment classes that most Dalenos students were required to take, they hadn't expected this spire to differ so much from the one they practically considered to be their home. Sure, foreign climbers were always complaining about how long the trials of the Tortoise Spire took, but Hane thought most of them were simply impatient. Now that they were here inside the Tiger Spire, they couldn't help but wonder if they'd made a mistake in leaving Dalenos.

What if the challenges were entirely different? What if their experience didn't match up to the trials ahead? Would they be more of a hindrance to the team than an asset? Maybe they should have attempted a solo climb beginning at the first floor, just to get a feel for whatever lay ahead.

It would have been better for Hane's nerves if the team could have passed directly through the climber's gate and started their mission, but unfortunately there was a short line of teams ahead of them, each awaiting their turn at the gate. While the Tortoise Spire of Dalenos had a ground-floor climber's gate, it was almost exclusively utilized by beginner teams and foreigners who hadn't yet earned any keys to the climber gates for the higher levels. All of those gates were accessed from outside the spire, on balconies set at intervals from each other, each requiring a specific key in order for teams to gain entry. A Wayfarer was basically required to assist people in reaching the gateways corresponding to their keys, which was why so many Dalenos teams had at least one Wayfarer on their roster. Those that didn't had to pay for a Soaring Wings Wayfarer to send them to their gate. It was a little vexing, especially when the Wayfarers were busy enough that climbers had to wait in line in order to be sent to their gates, but at least the Tortoise Spire was the one that granted the Wayfarer attunement, giving Dalenos the highest population of trained Wayfarers. Hane had simply assumed that other spires utilized the same system, only with fewer Wayfarers to go around.

The Tiger Spire, it seemed, didn't have gateway balconies along its exterior. Instead, teams with a gateway key assembled at the ground-floor climber's gate and inserted the key into a keyhole next to the gateway. The gateway would then change its destination to match the key inserted into the lock, allowing the team to begin at whatever floor the key granted access to. In essence, it was a much simpler system, though Hane spotted the flaw immediately upon entering the antechamber around the open gateway.

Knights of the Soaring Wings, notable by their purple tabards and the wing-shaped guards on their swords, ringed the chamber, keeping watch over the queue of climber teams awaiting their turn to approach the gateway. Two knights kept order at the head of the line, making sure all team members were present before allowing them to step into the arc of open space in front of the gateway. Four more knights stood within arm's reach of the gateway, watching for anyone who might attempt to dart through another team's gateway. Hane wondered how many gateways had been "stolen" before the Soaring Wings put this system into effect. It didn't seem foolproof for stopping anyone truly intent on getting through a gateway they hadn't earned, but it probably served as a significant deterrent against teams attempting to steal keys from one another while waiting their turn at the gateway.

By Hane's count, there were only two teams ahead of them, so they didn't have long to wait. Even so, it was one more difference between the Tortoise Spire and the Tiger Spire, which only served to ratchet up their disquieting feelings of anticipation. As a distraction, Hane silently observed their teammates, looking for signs of nerves or fear, two of the biggest factors that played into injury or death inside a spire, in Hane's experience.

Odette had already retrieved her file folder and was fastidiously reordering the pages inside while worrying her lower lip between her teeth. It was concerning that someone so anxious was this team's leader, but really the only thing that made her the team's leader was the fact that she had organized the delve. She seemed like the type of leader that would explain the broad, overarching plan, rather than the leader that shouted orders on a battlefield. As long as Hane was allowed to accomplish their assigned tasks the way they wanted to, they could get along fine with Odette.

Rose and Mason were speaking in hushed tones—or rather, Mason was listening to Rose speaking rapidly and softly in the language Hane had only just begun to recognize as Caelish. From Rose's tone and Mason's expression, she could have been admonishing him, or giving him a list of orders, or merely going over what to expect in the scenario ahead of them. Either way, Mason looked bored with the topic, nodding occasionally while staring at Lief out of the corner of his eye. The Biomancer—who Hane assumed understood Caelish based on his earlier greeting—kept his gaze straight ahead on the gateway, a vague smile on his face as if he wasn't truly present in the moment. That indicated a level of confidence to Hane; any climber who looked that serene before a climb was either extremely skilled or delving floors that were way below their level. Only time would tell which category Lief fell into.

Out of everyone on the team, Nieve seemed the most anxious, though having climbed with her before, Hane thought they could guess at least a few of the issues that concerned her.

First was probably the fact that this was a new spire, completely different from the one she had climbed for years; that made perfect sense to Hane, as it was the same reason they felt anxious about this delve as well.

Second was most likely exactly what Nieve had confessed to before the rest of the team arrived: Sage wasn't here. Nor was anyone from her previous team except for Hane, and they had only climbed together once. She probably felt alone in a way she wasn't used to feeling. For Hane, the opposite was true: they felt uncomfortable climbing with Nieve simply because they had climbed together before. The last climb had been just long enough for Hane to get an idea of how Nieve reacted in different situations, which meant they had expectations of her. If Nieve reacted unexpectedly in the heat of battle, Hane might make a costly mistake trying to compensate for it. Better to have no expectations of their teammates, so Hane knew to wait and watch before reacting.

And finally, Hane would guess that Nieve was anxious about finding the crystalline shard that housed a piece of Chime's consciousness. From what they understood of the gateway crystal's story, the pieces they were searching for were small and translucent—not the easiest of things to search for in a spire known to shift and change at will. Even knowing approximately where the crystal shard was didn't guarantee their success: spires weren't known for being precisely linear in their progression.

Nieve shifted from foot to foot, a deep scowl on her face as she touched the locket under her protective leather vest. If Hane hadn't seen the locket while traveling, they would have guessed that Nieve had hidden Chime beneath her shirt in order to communicate with them throughout the delve. The shattered gateway crystal was currently too weak for mind-to-mind communication unless the shard that housed its consciousness was in direct contact with a person's skin, so keeping Chime inside a bag or a pouch was out of the question. Based on how Nieve shifted her weight whenever she was asked about the crystal, Hane assumed Chime was inside Nieve's left boot, hopefully protected somehow so their sharp edges didn't cut into Nieve's skin. Of course, that could simply be a clever misdirect, but Hane would be surprised if that were the case. It was nice to see that Nieve had pulled her hair back into a single ponytail at the top of her head, though. Maybe her hair catching fire last time had made her more cautious. She still wore her bright red headband over the Champion attunement centered on her forehead, but a metallic clasp kept her hair gathered in a high topknot so it didn't spill forward into her face.

The team at the gateway finished passing through and the next team was beckoned to approach. As the line shuffled forward to await their summons, Odette gasped right before shrugging off her satchel and dropping to a knee beside it.

"I completely forgot to give these out!" After a brief rustling search, Odette withdrew a handful of what appeared to be multicolored ribbons. "Here, everyone take one and tie it to your wrist or your arm, or anywhere, really. Sorry, that one's knotted, let me fix it."

"What are these?" Hane asked, examining the tangled mass closely.

"Just some simple embroidered bands. I stitch them myself." Odette tugged on the end of a sea-green ribbon, drawing it free of the tangle. The ribbon itself was barely as wide as a finger; pastel-colored threads had been stitched down its length in odd knots and whorls. Lief and Mason each accepted a ribbon as Odette freed each one from the tangle. Rose poked and prodded at the mass until she selected a black one with pink and yellow stitching. "They aren't enchanted—not really, because they don't do anything on their own—but the embroidery is actually a secret code, so I can use my attunement to locate them in case we get separated during the scenario. I use a little enchanted thread in each one so they work with my advanced tracker." She frowned as she looked up from untying the two tangled ribbons. "Do you not use location markers in Dalenos?"

"My team never did," Nieve affirmed, looking as skeptical as Hane felt. The others didn't seem as put off, though, each tying a colorful band somewhere on their person. Lief tied a simple knot around his wrist, and Mason tied his around his bicep, holding the end between his teeth to pull it tight. Rose looped hers around her neck, tying it in a neat bow like a choker. "You ever see something like this, Hane?"

"I've climbed with a few Analysts, but only one ever asked about location markers. Hers were pins, though."

"Yeah, most Analysts have their own thing," Rose supplied, using a small pocket mirror to adjust the bow of her makeshift necklace. "It depends on their craft. Odette sews, so for her, it's easiest to use embroidered bands like these."

"What's the secret?" Nieve asked, holding a red ribbon embroidered with blue and tan stitches taut between her hands. "These are just different types of knots, aren't they? How do they turn into words?"

"The stitches are like a code," Odette clarified. "Different stitches can be used to represent letters or words, or the same stitch used multiple times might represent a constellation, or a rune, or anything, really. Coding it makes it a secret, the secret itself isn't important."

"If the secret isn't important, then are we allowed to know what these codes are?" Hane asked, holding their selected ribbon by the end and trying to make sense of it. They weren't entirely sure if they were looking at the code upside down or not.

"Er, I just use the punchlines for jokes, since it doesn't really matter." Odette frowned as she squinted at the ball of ribbons in her hand. "Most of them don't translate well, sorry. Hm . . ." She picked through her handful of ribbons until she found one that tugged at the corners of her mouth. "This one works. What's the best snack to bring to a duel?"

Rose rolled her eyes and Mason snickered: apparently they had heard this one before.

"I don't know. Something poisoned?" Nieve guessed.

"A *sharp* cheese." Odette managed to look both embarrassed and pleased by the punchline's reveal.

Hane snorted before they could stop themself. A quick look around found Nieve rolling her eyes and Lief shaking his head. To hide their amusement, Hane busied themself with tying the embroidered band around their forearm, fastidiously pulling their sleeve down over it.

"Oh no, wait a minute." Odette returned the remaining tangle of bracelets to her bag and pulled out a square device with rounded edges, a little larger than one of her notebooks. "I need to save each pattern for quick recognition. Can you show me your band?"

"What does this do?" Hane asked warily. The new device appeared to be made of a lightweight ceramic with a glass screen set over a grid of squares. A series of runes was etched beneath the glass screen.

"This? This just saves the patterns and makes it easier for me to find anyone who gets lost," Odette explained. "Here, Mason, can I use yours as an example?"

"Yeah, sure." Mason held his arm steady as Odette raised the device up to the bracelet tied around his bicep. She tapped a rune below the glass before holding the device by the sides.

"Identify Pattern: Mason."

The device glowed with a soft light. Squinting through the glow, Hane saw that the light was coming from individual runes inside the grid pattern beneath the glass. Odette pressed her thumb over one of the squares, making the other runes go dim. She then tapped the same square again, this time revealing an image resembling the pattern of Mason's bracelet like a portrait in miniature.

"Okay, so now . . ." Odette held the device down low for Hane and Nieve to see. "Say if Mason gets lost inside the spire, all I have to do is . . . this." She tapped a sequence of runes along the bottom of the device, then tapped the glass over the image of Mason's bracelet. An arrow, like the needle of a compass, appeared inside the square, its tip pointed squarely at Mason. No matter how Odette moved the device, the arrow remained trained on Mason.

"Oh, I get it! Like one of those enchanted compasses, right?" Nieve asked.

"Yes, but better!" Odette looked proud of herself as she used the device to catalog Rose's embroidered band next. "Identify Pattern: Rose. Most of those compasses can only find one person, so for a team like this, you'd need six individual compasses. This device can remember each pattern individually until I clear it for new patterns. It's really convenient."

"I thought Analysts could track location markers without a compass," Hane said, still wary. "Isn't that why you made these bracelets yourself? So they would be easy for you to track?"

"Well, yes." Odette hunched her shoulders as she tapped the device, storing the image of Rose's embroidered band in the second square of the grid. "Most other Analysts make items that are exactly the same, like unique pins or rings or something, then use their tracking spell to locate that exact item." Odette looked embarrassed as she registered Nieve's bracelet to the device. "I just like making pretty things like this, and I like letting people choose the colors they want. It could be easier, but I like doing it this way."

"You make too much work for yourself," Rose informed her, tart but not unkind. "It is an interesting toy, though. Did you get it from the same Enchanter that my sister uses?"

"Oh, yes!" Odette smiled as she finished adding Hane's bracelet to the device. "Jesserah and I always go to Valia together for the latest patent releases. It's always so much fun! Did I miss anyone? I think I got—"

"Next!" the knight by the gateway called. Odette squealed and nearly dropped the device in surprise. After a quick poke at one of the runes, she stuffed it away inside her bag and hurried forward, nearly tripping over her own feet in her haste.

She showed some paperwork to the knight and confirmed that everyone present was a member of her team. After verifying the key, the knight allowed Odette to approach the gateway and set the key in the lock.

The gateway portal, an open doorway that showed nothing beyond itself but swirling black eddies of magic, seemed to ripple and pulse, reacting to the key in the lock. As Hane watched, the key slowly faded, then vanished, typical of single-use spire keys. An unexpected question occurred to Hane as they watched the key vanish in the lock: would their colored key collection from the Tortoise Spire work on any of the doors within this spire? Or did the spires use different keys in their trials?

"Ready?" Odette asked, looking back from the gateway for confirmation.

"Let's do it!" Nieve called, something close to her usual reckless grin on her face. The others probably couldn't tell, but Hane could: Nieve was nervous.

"We're good," Rose said, apparently speaking on her brother's behalf as well as her own.

"I'm all set," Lief replied cheerily, one hand holding the sash that kept his bow tied across his back.

Hane met Odette's gaze and nodded firmly. Odette nodded back, her jaw tight as she turned to face the portal again. She squared her shoulders, drew a breath, then stepped into the swirling darkness of the gateway, her body vanishing as it passed through the portal.

Hane followed close on her heels, prepared to defend the Analyst should anything attack her just inside the doorway. While the gateway transitions were always abrupt, the appearance of the scenario was surprising enough that Hane sank into a crouch, one hand reaching back for the tonfa hidden beneath their dueling vest.

Everywhere Hane looked, they were surrounded by people. People rushing, people yelling, people checking watches, people dragging luggage crates along behind them. It took a moment to identify the location as a bustling train station, and the people as travelers. The rest of the team appeared in short order, taking stock of the setting as Odette mumbled to herself in Caelish and searched her pockets.

"Ah, here!" She withdrew an envelope from an inner pocket of her vest, revealing six train tickets stamped with gold leaf foil. "Is everyone here? Yes? We're leaving from platform four, we have three private cabins reserved, and it looks like we've been hired by . . ." Odette squinted at the back of a ticket. "Keepsake Treasuries. That's all I have. Anyone else find anything for this scenario?"

Hane patted down their pockets, still feeling a bit mystified by the whole scene. The Tortoise Spire had scenario trials similar to this, but they were generally more straightforward and rarely involved searching one's pockets for clues. Something crinkled when Hane patted the hidden pocket on their sleeve, though they were certain they hadn't put anything in there before the climb. While Hane's secretive nature urged them to hide it, they tamped the instinct down and drew out a folded piece of paper.

"Here." Hane handed it to Odette rather than read it aloud. They wanted to keep their eyes up in case of trouble.

"Oh good, this looks like a mission briefing." Odette's eyes skimmed over the writing, her expression souring slowly. "Okay, not exactly a briefing, but at least it gives us our objective. It says we have three days to capture and subdue 'the target' before the train arrives at its end destination. We'll receive our payment when we deliver the target to the Keepsake Treasuries agents waiting at the station."

"Keepsake Treasuries is probably meant to represent Haven Securities," Rose pointed out, sounding distracted as she searched through her pockets. "Does it say if the target is a person, or multiple people, or if it's an object of some kind?"

"I don't think it's an object," Odette replied, scanning the note again. "It sounds like it's just one person, but that could be a misdirect. The tone of the note is that we were given a set of verbal instructions that were more detailed. We're going to have to figure out who it is we're supposed to identify and capture."

"And they have to be captured?" Nieve confirmed. "Alive, I mean?"

"A collections agency typically wants its targets alive, or else they can't pay their debts," Lief pointed out. "Although I have heard of assassination missions for this scenario, so it's a fair question."

"We'll bring them in alive," Hane declared, enduring Nieve's eye roll. "For all we know, we could be looking for a missing employee, or a corporate saboteur who needs to be questioned. If it turns out our employer wants the target dead, we can always kill them at the end of the scenario. What we can't do is bring them back to life after we've killed them."

"Taking them alive is more interesting anyway," Mason said with a grin. "Onto the more important question, though: who wants to share a private cabin with me?"

"Meathead," Rose muttered, tinkering with something made of metal. "You're in my cabin. I need you for my imbues."

"What are you imbuing?" Mason asked, exasperated. "We don't even know what we need yet."

"There are some things every team needs, Brick, and if I have the time to make them all before we get started, then I'm going to make—"

"Not to interrupt," Lief said, his tone light and easy. "But shouldn't we be having this conversation on the train? I'm not sure how much time we have before it departs."

"Oh, yes!" Odette's head whipped up, her eyes zipping back and forth until she found what she was looking for. "Platform four is that way. Let's hurry!"

In Hane's opinion, there was no need to rush: they weren't very far from the platform, and the train didn't seem all that close to departing. Rather than racing to the train in a blind panic, Hane kept their eyes out for anyone who appeared suspicious, or anyone who seemed to be watching them. Finding an unknown target among a train full of passengers was going to take some time, and Hane wanted as much information at their disposal as possible. Though it was hard to determine what was suspicious when Hane wasn't remotely familiar with the local clothing, culture, or even the language every-one seemed to be speaking.

"Welcome aboard!" A conductor greeted them cheerfully after reviewing the tickets Odette handed over. "All three of your cabins are side by side, just as requested. If you'll follow me, I will take you to them now."

Rather than gesture for everyone to follow them on board, the conduc-tor led the team along the exterior of the train, explaining that the general passenger cars were too crowded to walk through at the moment. The train cars were each painted identically with a warm brown color encompassing the row of windows along the sides and tan trim accenting the loading doors. Each car was adjoined to the next one by artful bronze gangways with waist-high railings, each separated by a gap over the heavy coupler that held the cars together. After a short walk, the conductor led them through a doorway into a beautifully decorated dining car, gleaming with polished wood, brass trim, and deep, inviting colors.

"This is our dinner car, although we serve other meals here as well," the conductor explained, leading the way through the car. "While meals are served at specific times, you are welcome here at any time. Feel free to read by a window, or hold a meeting at one of the tables. Lunch and tea times are come-as-you-please, but dinners here are a bit more formal. This car will close to guests one half hour before dinner time to allow our crew to set up, but other than that, this car will be open at all times."

The tables were all secured to the floor to prevent movement during the journey. Against the far wall was a long counter, presumably where food would be prepared. A crew member stocking a service cart with napkins and tea bags paused to smile and wave as the team passed through to the next car. A group of passengers followed a different conductor, heading for the door Hane's team had entered through. They wouldn't have been noteworthy, except for one passenger who wore an ornate longsword on their hip and walked with the precise balance of a skilled fighter.

Hane elbowed Nieve, catching her eye before jutting their chin at the sword-bearer. Her eyes narrowed as she followed their gaze.

"No shroud, but the sword has a Citrine-level enchantment on it," Nieve murmured, most likely using a spell that allowed her to see auras. "You think that's the guy we're here to capture?"

Hane shrugged; it was probably something to do with the scenario, but they couldn't simply break away from the team now. Better to mention it later, in case the others hadn't noticed it.

"This is one of two lounge cars," the conductor explained, turning to walk backward through the car. The chairs were all thick and plush, velveted in deep burgundy, giving the room a warm feel to it. "The other lounge car is just on the far side of the dinner car, though generally you'll find this lounge slightly less crowded than the other. In the mornings, you'll find breakfast foods, tea, and coffee here. Again, you are welcome here at any time, day or night. In the evenings, this also serves as one of our bar cars, so if you enjoy a spirited beverage, you'll want to come by later."

"Is it just wine?" Nieve asked, her curiosity over the swordsman seemingly behind her already. "What's that bottle up there? The purple one under the light."

"Ah, that is the prize of our collection, a twenty-year aged wine from our primary spirit provider." The conductor smiled as he folded his hands together, giving the appearance of someone who had explained this many times before. "The bottle you see there is for display purposes only, but we serve a variety of wine, mead, and ale all brewed and distilled by Twisted Roots Winery. You're sure to find something to your tastes as Twisted Roots continually innovates their flavors every season. In fact, we have some samples of their latest flavors, in case you're interested."

The conductor opened a locked wall cabinet with a small key on a wrist chain and plucked out the tiniest wine bottle Hane had ever seen. Nieve's hand seemed to swallow it as she accepted it, her face scrunching as she read the label.

"Ginger-mint honey mead?" Nieve asked, sounding skeptical. "Is this even good?"

"Everyone's tastes are different," the conductor assured her pleasantly, though Hane noted it wasn't an answer.

While Nieve examined the wine, Hane caught Mason eyeing something that wasn't on the menu—or rather, someone. A trio of passengers clustered in one corner of the car, and while Mason could have been making eyes at any one of them, Hane would have bet their share of the treasure that he had his eye on the one in the pale lavender dress with a slit up the side nearly to her hip. A wide-brimmed hat hid most of her face so that all Hane could see were crimson-painted lips pursed around the end of a long, slim cigarette holder. She and her companions stood beneath an air vent in the car's ceiling, which was more than likely an enchanted air purifier. As Mason's step lagged enough to fall behind the team, Rose looked back over her shoulder, shooting her brother a look that needed no translation. Mason made a face at her but hurried his pace to catch up.

"The next car is the galley, in which all our served food is prepared," the conductor continued, waving the team ahead of him as he held the dining car door open. "Please use the walkway along the windows to bypass the kitchen. Only staff and crew members with a badge like this can enter the restricted areas without the permission of an engineer." He held up a silver badge quickly before moving on. "Make sure to keep your tickets on you as our passengers in the general cars are not allowed to pass this way; only our private cabins and the luggage cars are past this point."

The sliding door past the gangway opened to reveal a door marked "Crew Only," along with an arrow labeled "Private Cabins" pointing along a narrow walkway that skirted the perimeter of the car. The pleasant aroma of bread baking made up for the claustrophobic passage, but only just barely. Hane didn't feel as if they could breathe again until they passed through the next outside door.

"We have three cars of private cabins, each with a shared lavatory," the conductor explained, walking backward at the head of the team again. "Out of respect for our honored guests, such as yourselves, we ask that noise in the corridors be kept to a minimum during evening and nighttime hours, whether you are on your way to the bar or returning from it. Your cabins are in the third car from this one, just this way."

Though many of the private cabins were closed up tight, a few of the doors were open, showing passengers settling in for the three-day journey. Some were hanging up clothing in wardrobes, some were asking questions of a crew member, others were cajoling children who didn't seem enthused about the prospect of sharing such a tiny space for any length of time. Hane didn't notice anyone who stood out particularly, but they observed as much as they could while following behind the conductor and the team.

"Here we are," the conductor announced brightly, holding his arms out wide as if presenting the team with an award rather than their cabins for the next three days. "You'll find a pull-cord near the door in case you require any-thing urgently. You'll find room keys on your pillows, and some refreshments available in the cabinets near the desk. Your tickets allow you access to any car of the train at any time, except for the last two cars, which are privately owned. Is there anything I can do to be of service to you all before I depart?"

"Um, can I ask you something?" Odette asked timidly. "We were hoping to run into a friend of ours who might be on this train. If we had a description of them, would you be able to help us locate them?"

"It would depend on whether your friend is traveling in the passenger cars or the private cabins," the conductor explained, seemingly used to answering such odd questions. "Obviously anyone traveling in a private cabin expects a certain amount of discretion from our staff. And, of course, that courtesy extends to all of you as well."

"Okay, then, um . . ." Odette didn't look nervous so much as she looked as if she was attempting to solve a puzzle. "Can you tell us what you know about Keepsake Treasuries? Or if anyone on board works for them, or mentioned them, or had their tickets paid for by them?"

"Oh my, you are well informed!" The conductor looked mildly surprised. "But I suppose it only makes sense, considering that your tickets were purchased by Keepsake. You must be here to provide a little extra protection, eh?"

Odette blinked, looking mystified, with Rose and Mason appearing similarly confused. Lief stepped in, smiling obsequiously as he took over the questioning of the conductor.

"Obviously that's not something we can discuss out here in the open," Lief said smoothly. "We just need to know how much your staff is aware of, in case we need your support."

"Yes, of course," the conductor replied agreeably. "I'm afraid we were told very little—I didn't even know to expect additional protection for the cargo, so I'm not sure how helpful I or any of my coworkers can be to you. All we know is that the last two cars of this train belong to Keepsake Treasuries and they are to be delivered safely to our destination. The cars have their own provisions as far as food and other supplies go, so train staff aren't even allowed to go past the final luggage car."

"Yes, good, that's what we were told, too," Lief agreed, nodding as if he wasn't learning all of this for the first time. "It's good to know we have the same information. Just to be certain, though, do you happen to know how many people are traveling in those last two cars? Or what they happen to be protecting?"

"I'm afraid I wasn't informed on that," the conductor replied, sounding disappointed. "I saw at least three people loading crates into the very last car during my pre-boarding inspection, but I don't know if those same people actually boarded, or if they were merely hired porters. The crates themselves were relatively small, though they looked delicate by the way they were carried."

"Hm." Lief tapped his chin thoughtfully. "That's more than you were supposed to see. I would keep that information to yourself for now."

"Yes, of course, I won't tell anyone else what I saw," the conductor agreed quickly, bowing very slightly at the shoulders. "Is there anything else I can do for you for now? I'm afraid the train will be departing soon and I'm needed to assist other passengers until we are underway."

"You've been very helpful, thank you for all your assistance," Lief said, still acting the part of the team leader. "If I might ask one final favor before you go: please inform your staff that if we require their assistance in protecting our employer's shipment, we will use the code phrase 'ice gold.' Anyone who hears that should follow the instructions given to them by the person who said the phrase."

"Ice gold," the conductor repeated, nodding solemnly. "Yes, I will pass along the code phrase to the staff. Thank you, good sir. And please don't hesitate to use the pull-cord in your rooms if you require immediate assistance."

The conductor departed with a final shallow bow, leaving the team alone outside their private cabins. Hane half expected Lief to take over leading the group, but instead the Biomancer looked questioningly back at Odette, as if awaiting orders.

"We should, ah . . . talk?" Odette glanced around, as if seeking out someone's approval. "Sorry, I don't normally do this. We need to, um, figure out a plan."

A plan sounded good; Hane wasn't certain what next steps to take in this scenario. There wasn't anything obvious to fight, and they were no longer certain if they were looking for a person, or protecting the cargo shipment in the last two cars. Normally in situations like this one, Hane liked to let the rest of the group solve the scenario while they went after a hidden objective on their own, but so far, Hane hadn't been able to identify any hidden objectives.

"Ice gold?" Mason asked, knocking his elbow against Lief's as the team filed into the middle of the three private cabins. "Where did that come from?"

"Just some quick thinking," Lief replied with a smile and a shrug. He leaned back against the far wall of the cabin, right beside the small window. "We might not need it, but it's nice to have the option of calling in some reinforcements."

"It's a good idea," Hane confirmed. "Especially if we need to subdue a target without involving bystanders. I'm sure the staff has access to things like ropes or manacles in case of belligerent passengers."

"Mint and ginger?" Nieve asked, still staring at the tiny wine bottle in disgust. "Who puts mint and ginger into mead? What's wrong with fruit? Or just plain honey mead?"

"As long as the ale has hops in it, I'll be fine." Rose was already clambering up to the higher bunk set into the left wall of the cabin. The ceiling was too low for her to sit upright, so she curled over in a strange hunch, pulling pouches off her belt and out of her pockets, arranging small items on the bed that Hane couldn't see from their angle.

With the cabin as small as it was, it took some shuffling and jostling for everyone to find a comfortable place to sit or stand. Odette perched on the lower bunk, drawing her knees in close to allow people to step past her. Hane sat on the desk that took up most of the right side of the cabin, folding their legs beneath them. Nieve and Mason jockeyed in front of the door for a minute, each trying to be the one standing sentinel over the only exit. Mason was both taller and broader, making him look the part of a guard more than Nieve, but Nieve's warning glower won out, chasing Mason to the other end of the room, where he slouched against the narrow wardrobe.

"Okay, did anyone else find any notes or clues on their person?" Odette began once the shuffling settled. "I think I got the tickets because I was the first one through, then Hane got the note because they were second. Who was next? Rose?"

"Nothing obvious," Rose reported tersely as she flicked open a roll of tools on the bed. "I have a lot of pockets, though. I'll let you know if I find something."

"Would any clues have appeared inside my dimensional bag?" Hane asked. "I could check, but it would take a while."

"In general, important setting information appears in obvious places, like pockets, or badges pinned to our clothing," Odette explained.

"I thought you two were experienced climbers," Mason said, skepticism heavy in his voice. "Why are you acting like this is all new?"

Nieve bristled, dividing Hane's attention between answering the question or calming her down. Luckily, Lief stepped in to answer.

"Different spires posit different types of scenarios," Lief explained, making a hand motion that suggested everyone calm down. "I've only been to the Dalenos spire once, so I might be generalizing, but I recall most of those scenarios being more battle-specific, usually with some commanding officer giving a very direct rundown. Does that sound right, Hane?"

"By a large majority, yes," Hane agreed. "There were very few scenarios like this one, where the main objective wasn't clearly spelled out. And even in the more vague scenarios, I don't recall ever receiving a clue hidden on my person."

"Yeah, same," Nieve grumbled, eyes narrowed at Mason. "We don't have these weird little playacting missions, we have combat scenarios. Defeat the army, rout the bandits, sink the other ship. Tortoise Spire scenarios are pretty clear-cut."

"Sounds easy," Mason replied with a smirk.

Hane bounded into the center of the room just as Nieve pushed away from the cabin door, snarling as she reached for Mason. Hane blocked her bodily, though they knew if Nieve wanted them to move, they would be moved.

"Stop pulling her tail, Brick," Rose called down from the upper bunk. She sounded distracted, as if she were only halfway paying attention. She appeared to be tinkering with a heavy set of goggles amid an array of large mana crystals.

"But I like watching her growl," Mason protested, grinning toothily.

"Calm down," Hane said softly, though the room was so small it likely didn't matter. "It's a misunderstanding; it's going to happen with a new team. Remember, we're the newcomers to this spire."

"Fine," Nieve spat, throwing herself back against the door with a thud that rattled the drawers and wardrobe. "Just tell me what you need me to do; I'm no good at solving puzzles."

"So no one else has any clues . . . ?" Odette asked, trailing off when no one spoke up. "Okay, so, usually the mission is either to find and subdue a target, or to protect a shipment of some kind. Considering our collective levels, as well as the fact that half of us have done this scenario before, I think we're looking at a scaled-up challenge, in which we must successfully subdue a tar-get *and* protect our employer's shipment. Does anyone else have a theory?"

"The note only told us about a target," Lief pointed out. "The shipment could be a bonus objective. Or a distraction. But I agree with the possibility that we're meant to do both."

"Even if we're supposed to, we don't have to," Mason pointed out, roll-ing his shoulders in a shrug. "We're only doing this to get up to the next floor, right? We only need to complete one objective for that. Who cares about additional treasures from this floor when the phantom vault is the real target?"

"Because we don't know if Odette's secret is really going to open a magical treasure trove instead of the standard treasury vault, meathead," Rose called down.

"Is there any chance that the person we're meant to subdue is inside one of the last two cars?" Hane asked. "I know the conductor said those last two cars are off-limits, but why would Keepsake Treasuries buy tickets for us on the same train as their shipment and tell us to stay away from it?"

"It couldn't hurt to go ask," Odette admitted with a shrug. "We're going to need to sweep the train at least once, anyway, just to check for damaged couplers, suspicious runes, and anything out of the ordinary. This is a three-day scenario and we haven't even—"

The scream of a whistle made Odette gasp in surprise. Rose scrambled to keep her tools and other equipment confined to the bed as the train lurched, jolting everyone and everything inside the cabin. Nieve pressed her hands to the walls, holding herself steady as Odette gripped the bedsheets in both hands, planting her feet down on the floor. Lief merely widened his stance, still leaning against the wall, but Mason staggered forward through the momentum, catching a jeweler's screwdriver just as it rolled off the top bunk. He handed it up to his sister, then held onto the bed frame as the *chug-chug-chug* of the engine struggled to find an even rhythm. Hane managed to maintain their seat on the desk by maintaining a light push of transference mana against the walls and ceiling of the cabin, holding themself in place as everyone else rocked and swayed.

"I don't know why that surprised me," Odette said, adjusting her glasses before patting her hair. "We all knew we'd be leaving the station soon; I should have been prepared. Anyway." She took a breath and released it slowly. "Good," Odette exhaled. "We have a plan."

"Wait, what?" Nieve asked, sounding surprised. "Did you figure out what our objective is? Did I miss something?"

"For the time being, we should assume it's both objectives," Odette said, for once sounding confident. "The capture of a target and the protection of the shipment. If we find some clues that narrow it down to one or the other, we'll figure out what to do from there. For now, let's focus on figuring out who our target might be, what Keepsake Treasuries is shipping, and keeping the engine running. But let's also be sure to keep our eyes open for additional treasure caches and side quests, like the trading sequence." Odette plucked a pencil out of her many-pocketed bracer, setting the tip against a notepad she withdrew from the inner pocket of her vest. "Who wants to do what?"

"I need some time to work on imbuing my arsenal," Rose called down from the top bunk. She was wearing her goggles over her eyes now, the lenses tinted a shadowy color that Hane couldn't see through. "Tell whoever goes to the engine to make a list of the parts in danger of failing. Oh, and I need Mason for his magic. This is our room, by the way."

"Only if I get the top bunk."

"You'll have to fight me for it, Brick."

Mason shrugged passively. "That sounds like more trouble than it's worth."

"I can try and find a way inside the Keepsake cars," Hane said, jumping in before the siblings could find something else to argue about. "Nieve can come with me to keep an eye out for our target."

"Yeah, and our cabin's that one." Nieve pointed through the left wall, indicating the next cabin over. "Hane and I are sharing."

They hadn't discussed that, but fine. Hane supposed they trusted Nieve slightly more than they trusted anyone else on this team. And maybe Nieve found it comforting to bunk with someone she already knew.

"I guess that means you and I are bunking together," Lief said mildly, meaning himself and Odette. "If that makes you uncomfortable at all, I don't mind laying my bedroll out in either of the other rooms."

"What? Oh, no, I'm—if you're fine with it, then I'm fine with it," Odette stammered as her eyes darted away from Lief's. "Um, do you mind coming with me to check on the engine? It's a little boring, since I'll just be marking down the types of gears and enchantments, but I'm a little vulnerable when I'm using my attunement, so . . ."

"Fine with me," Lief said agreeably. He stretched his arms out to the sides, arching his back away from the wall. "Are we ready to get started?"

"Not just yet," Rose ordered. "Let me just finish the last one. . . . Okay, here. Everyone take one."

Another location tracker? Hane wondered, reaching out to accept the small curved piece of metal from Rose. A glance around showed everyone but Nieve affixing the objects to one of their ears, like a little metal shell. Nieve cast a confused look over at Hane, as if they had any more of a notion of what this was than she did.

"Everyone have one? I'll test in—" Rose stopped, her hand covering the device on her ear when she noticed Hane and Nieve still holding their devices. "Oh, you don't have these in the Tortoise Spire either? It's a communication device. I just finished imbuing these so we can share information or call for help when we need it."

"So it's like an enchanted device?" Nieve asked, frowning as she examined the delicate metal object. "I don't see any runes."

"No, enchanted devices are completely different from imbued items," Rose explained with a small sniff. "Architects don't need runes or etching instruments; we can simply imbue objects with magical properties either using external mana sources, like mana crystals, or we can simulate compound mana types using dream mana. It's a great deal quicker than any standard enchantment."

"Yeah, until it runs out of mana and stops working," Mason pointed out. "Enchanted items last longer; imbues are only temporary, so things like these earpieces need to be recharged regularly. How long will these last us, Prickles?"

"That depends on a series of factors, including the mana types simulated by the dream mana, the Architect's level and finesse, and the quality of the vessel," Rose replied, as thorough as any teacher Nieve had ever come across. "These communication devices are actually enchanted to hold an imbue longer than, say, an arrowhead imbued with fire mana. Inter-team communication is always a high priority, so these are always the first imbues I create. Since these are made from pure silver and I helped work on the design myself, they're incredibly efficient, despite using dream mana to simulate both sound and communication mana. The duration of this particular imbue varies depending on how often it gets used, as well as the bleed rate, which is currently . . ." Rose paused as she squinted at a device that looked a little like a compass.

"Goddess, sis, I am begging you to stop," Mason groaned, his face buried in his palms. "Just tell us when we need to bring the communicators back to you for a recharge."

"That's what I *am* telling you," Rose retorted impatiently. "If you let me finish my calculations, I can tell you the exact second the imbues will wear off for each communicator in the order I made them."

"We need the gloss, not the grit, Prickles," Mason said firmly. "Sometime tomorrow? The day after tomorrow? Closer to breakfast, lunch, or dinner? Make it easy on us so we're not counting down the seconds."

Rose huffed, blowing away the curls that spilled over her goggles. "Tomorrow. Lunchtime. Don't forget."

"Thank the goddess," Mason muttered, securing his communication device to his ear. Shaking his head, he added to the others: "Don't ask Prickles anything unless you want to feel stupid before she gives you an annoyingly long lecture on the subject. She never learned how to give a simple answer to a simple question."

"*Some* people actually like to *learn* when they ask questions," Rose muttered petulantly. "For you newbies, this device is easy enough to work: just channel a little gray mana through the button on the peak of the device and speak out loud. The device sends your words to the rest of the team, who hear it like mind speech instead of spoken words."

"Weird," Nieve muttered, fumbling as she tried to fit the curve of the metal to her ear. "Mind-to-mind speech is easier. More direct, too, since you don't have to hear any conversations you aren't a part of."

"I tried a version like that once, but it was too complicated," Rose admitted. "Too many buttons, too many inputs, too heavy to wear comfortably. Didn't work. These may be simple, but they get the job done. Ready for a test?"

I never thought I would miss Wayfarers so much, Hane thought, resigned to securing the odd device to their ear. *It's almost as if we had it easy at the Tortoise Spire: every group had at least one person who could cast communication spells.*

The earpiece was light enough that it didn't feel too heavy on Hane's ear. The inner curve of the shell was padded with velvet, making it comfortable enough for extended wear. The metal could easily be pinched in to clamp around the shell of the ear, and a flexible wire coated in a thin layer of rubber curled under the earlobe and folded inside the ear canal, securing the device in place. Hane found its presence mildly irritating, almost entirely because the lack of symmetry made them feel off balance. They shook their head, testing the device's ability to stay put.

"Testing." Rose held her finger to the upper curve of the device on her ear. The voice inside Hane's head carried a strange, metallic vibration along with it, but the words were clear enough to be understood. Perhaps that was a result of using dream mana instead of imbuing the devices with communication and sound mana. "Testing. Does everyone hear me?"

"Yeah, I got you, Prickles." Mason held his own button down as he spoke, earning a nod from Rose as she confirmed her own unit's functionality.

"Seems to be working well for me," Lief commented.

"Me too," Odette reported.

"This is weird," Nieve said, making a face as she touched the earpiece. "You have to hold the button the whole time?"

"Only while you're talking," Rose explained. "When you finish, make sure you take your finger off the button or simply stop channeling mana into it. Try to keep messages short and to the point. If it's an emergency and you need backup, just say 'emergency' and give your location. If you hear someone call an emergency, get to them as quickly as possible."

"If you can't say your location, don't worry about it." Odette held up the enchanted tracking device she'd shown them earlier. "I can use your location markers to find you just as quickly."

"Don't get angry if I don't call any of you to join the fight." Nieve grinned hungrily, showing off her canines. "I don't like sharing."

"Well, at least call me so I can patch you up afterward," Lief advised, adjusting his bow across his back as he straightened from his slouch. "So Rose and Mason are staying here to work on gadgets, Nieve and Hane are checking out the Keepsake shipment, and Odette and I are heading up to the engine. Does anyone have anything to add to that?"

"It's probably going to take me a few hours to finish all my basic imbues," Rose reported, twisting one of the bug-eyed lenses of her goggles. As Hane watched, the tint changed from black to gold. "Oh, and I have a few blank shells that I'll need each of you to finish off for me." She directed a pointed stare at each person as she addressed them. "I'll need ice mana from Nee-eh-vay, transference from Hane, and both life and light from Lief. It'll really help me out if we can make those tonight or early tomorrow."

"How big are these shells?" Lief asked. He nodded as Rose held up a dull Sunstone mana shell. "That's no problem, just remind me later."

Hane didn't have much experience with filling mana shells, but they'd done it once or twice. As they recalled, it was a fairly simple process, especially when they were only being asked to contribute transference mana.

"I can also supply water mana, if you need it," Hane offered.

"Thanks, but my brother can help me with my water mana imbues with some cooperative spells. That way, I don't have to carry as many mana crystals with me all the time," Rose explained, hanging her goggles over a bedpost before stretching as much as the ceiling would allow. "Odette, I brought my casting equipment like you asked, but I'll need precise measurements of all the spare parts you need me to make, including angles, gauges, and fittings."

"I'll try." Odette sounded doubtful. "More likely, I'll have to sketch the shapes for you."

Rose nodded as she adjusted her other lens. "That works, too."

"What's your plan for getting inside one of the Keepsake cars?" Mason asked, looking a little smug as he directed the question at Hane and Nieve. "One of you planning to sweet-talk the guards?"

"I was going to run along the top and drop down to peek through a window first," Hane said before Nieve could say something rude. "I need to see the layout of the car before I can plan my entrance."

"Up top?" Odette asked, looking up sharply. "What do you mean, up top?"

"The roof." Hane pointed straight up. "It's easy enough for me to get up there, then I can just—"

"You can't!" Odette's eyes went wide behind her wire-rimmed glasses as her voice rose in pitch. "You can't go on top of the train! No one goes on top of the train!"

"What's wrong with that?" Nieve asked, frowning. "I was hoping I'd get a chance to brawl with someone on top of the train. Seems like it'd be a lot of fun."

"No, no, no, you can't!" Odette seemed panicked, her chest beginning to heave with short, quick breaths. "Not up top! It isn't—there's a—"

Rose swung down from the top bunk, sighing heavily as she landed beside Odette on the lower bed. She wrapped an arm around Odette's shoulders and tugged her against her side.

"You're fine, just breathe," Rose ordered, her tone at odds with the tender way she patted Odette's back. "No one's going on top of the train, Odie. Deep breaths."

She switched to speaking Caelish in a low, soothing tone while rubbing Odette's shoulders. Lief grimaced as he sidled past the bed toward Nieve and Hane, though Mason just looked amused.

"You really didn't read a word of that brief, did you?" Mason asked almost gleefully. "I've never done this scenario before, and even I know you can't go on the roof."

"What's wrong with the roof?" Hane asked, mystified by the reactions around them. "It's the fastest, most direct path in either direction. It's also the most open space for a fight, just as Nieve said."

"Yes, and in different scenarios, it works fine," Lief explained, his expression serious for once. "But in this scenario, going on the roof is almost like a trap. The scale of the challenge will spike drastically, adding monster attacks, assassins, or possible derailment. It's just not worth the trouble."

"Especially since the reward doesn't change, even if you survive," Mason added, grimacing. "Most climbers I know ring out before they make it through to the end, though."

Nieve made an aggravated noise deep in her throat as she rolled her eyes. Hane felt that same frustration like weights lashed around their ankles. It wasn't just the confinement to the inside of the train that stymied them: it was far worse to acknowledge the fact that Hane had almost ended this climb prematurely through an entirely avoidable mistake.

If only they had read that reshing brief.

"I accept your reasons, and I agree not to go on the roof of the train," Hane stated calmly, swallowing their frustration. They leaned around Lief to make eye contact with Odette. "Odette, I apologize for failing to read your report. If there is anything else I should know before we get started, I'm more than willing to listen to a summary of the scenario."

Odette sniffled as she wiped her hand beneath her eyes. She nodded, her smile tremulous. "Okay. Give me a minute and I'll tell you everything."

An hour passed by in a haze as Odette listed every single possibility that had ever been recorded by a climber completing the train scenario. Hane's attention drifted in and out despite their intention to remain focused. So much of the information Odette shared seemed entirely extraneous, such as the year the train had been made, average weather for the season, and even the migration patterns of local animals and insects. Some of it was helpful, like learning that targeting opponents on the roof of the train with weapons or spells was safe, and even ascending partway up a ladder was okay, but setting just one hand on the roof of the train would trigger the scaling difficulty.

The one interesting fact Hane learned that the train in this scenario ran on coal and steam power, instead of stored liquid mana, like the train they had ridden on from Dalenos to Caelford. Supposedly it was more efficient for shorter journeys, but it also made sense from a practical standpoint: a tank full of liquid mana would have been worth more than any treasure a floor this low could typically bestow on a climbing team. If such a prize was easy to claim, Hane imagined most teams would turn to banditry themselves, rather than actually completing the scenario.

While Odette recited the floor report from memory, Rose returned to the top bunk, where she stretched out on her stomach and resumed tinkering with metallic objects and mana crystals, one foot kicked up lazily behind her. Mason slowly slid down the length of the wardrobe until he slouched down to the floor, his eyes glazed over and a bit of drool leaking from the corner of his mouth. Lief had taken a seat at the fold-out table by the window, his chin resting in his hands as he watched the scenery roll by. Nieve leaned back against the door, rolling the tiny bottle of wine between her hands as she listened. Near the end of Odette's explanation, Hane caught her examining the label with the type of scrutiny one wore when considering swallowing poison.

"I think that's it," Odette said cheerily. "Do you have any questions?"

"No." Nieve said it at the exact moment Hane did, but hers held a quality of desperation to it rather than appreciation.

"Thank you," Hane added. "That was highly informative. I'll be sure to read the provided notes the next time I attempt a climb in this spire."

Odette smiled as she nodded. "It's pretty straightforward once you know what to expect. When we get closer to the end, I'll explain the scenario on the next floor to you."

Hane tamped down the urge to flee. "That will be helpful. Thank you."

"Let's go!" Nieve demanded, pushing herself up to her feet. "I hope sweet-talking those guards doesn't work; I need to punch something."

"We're not—I won't let her punch anyone," Hane assured Odette quickly. "We'll drop our things off in our room and begin our sweep. Thank you again."

"Hold up!" Rose ordered, objects clattering and rolling on her bunk as she shifted her weight. "I'm nearly finished here; if you can wait, then I have some neat toys that will get us a good look inside the Keepsake cars. I just need Brick to help me with a few cooperative spells, then we'll be good to go."

"Oh, that sounds good," Odette agreed. "The rest of us can get settled in our rooms, then both Nieve and Mason can keep watch for Hane and Rose. Does that work for everyone?"

The need for movement—for action—itched at Hane like wool undergarments infested with weevils, but as they no longer had a plan for approaching the Keepsake cars, it made more sense to wait. Rose was not only experienced in this particular scenario, but she seemed to have a plan as well. It chafed to be reliant on anyone other than themself, but after nearly making a critical error with the roof, Hane had to admit they were out of their depth here.

"I'm fine with that," Hane agreed, exchanging a nod with Nieve. "We'll store our gear and get ready in the next cabin. Just knock on the wall when you're ready to go."

"Got it," Rose called, already focused on her tools and trinkets again. Mason rubbed sleep from his eyes as the others filtered out into the corridor. Hane followed Nieve to the cabin on the left while Odette and Lief took the remaining cabin on the right.

"I know that was exhausting," Hane commented in a low voice, switching to Artinian speech as soon as they were alone inside their shared cabin. "But once we figure out the objectives, it should be like any other spire scenario. Until then, we just need to trust the rest of the team."

"I know," Nieve admitted, letting out a sigh as she grabbed a room key off the lower bunk. "Ugh, that stupid floor report! This is all Sage's fault. If he were here, we would have known about the roof and then we wouldn't look so dumb right now."

Hane scaled the bunk lightly, hiding a scowl just as they tucked their dimensional bag between the mattress and the wall. Maybe Nieve was used to shrugging off mistakes and passing blame, but Hane was used to being the voice of experience and caution. They spent far more time inside of the Tortoise Spire than nearly anyone else they had ever met. They thrived on adrenaline and survived by their instincts, not on classroom-taught wisdom and safety-minded trials. It was jarring to learn just how different this new spire was from the one that practically raised them. They didn't know their place here, and that realization left them feeling more than a little unsettled, like an untethered buoy, rising and plunging as the waves rolled beneath it.

As long as I keep my footing, I'll be okay, Hane told themself, acknowledging the sensations of doubt writhing in the pit of their stomach. Dangling their legs over the edge of the top bunk, they drew a sip of water from their canteen, willing their breath to stay calm and even. *Once I get a sense of this challenge, it'll all come just as naturally as the challenges in the Tortoise Spire. I just need to rely on the experience of my teammates while I adjust.*

Too bad that felt like a far more difficult challenge for Hane than defeating a lake serpent all on their own. As much as they wanted to see Chime reunited with their missing pieces of consciousness, Hane suddenly felt an upswell of doubt over leaving the familiarity of the Tortoise Spire.

NIEVE

Champion (mind mark), Citrine
??? (heart mark), Sealed

In under five minutes, Nieve knew everything there was to know about her tiny shared cabin. She opened all the drawers and cabinets, found a trash bin hidden beneath the desk, plucked lightly at the pull-cord near the door, and tested the firmness of her mattress, finding it too stiff for comfort. It didn't help that the top bunk was so low she bumped her head every time she tried to adjust her position, but it was no use complaining since the gap between the top bunk and the ceiling was even narrower. It almost made more sense to lay out a bedroll on the floor, but then she would have to pick it up each morning so it wouldn't get stepped on, and that seemed like a hassle.

After exhausting the novelty of the room, Nieve pulled the chair out from the desk and checked her sword for nicks and cracks. There weren't any, of course—she always checked her equipment prior to beginning a climb—but she had to find something to keep herself busy. She swiped her handkerchief over the steel a few times before sheathing it again and checking her war hammer. She scrubbed ineffectively at a dent on the blunt end of it for a minute before cocking her head to the side, listening intently.

"Was that a knock on the wall?"

"No." Hane was stretched out on the upper bunk, their hands folded over their stomach and their eyes closed. Had they been anyone else, Nieve would have thought it strange to catch a nap so soon inside a spire, but Hane was always quick to catch some rest whenever the opportunity presented itself.

"I thought I heard a noise," Nieve pressed.

"Something rolled into the wall," Hane explained with minimal movement. "A knock would have been louder and repeated. The walls are just thin."

"Oh." Nieve scrubbed at an imaginary speck on her hammer before tucking it away again. She looked around for something to do while she waited. There were snacks in one of the cupboards, but she wasn't hungry. If she had her travelsack, she might have hung some of her clothes up in the wardrobe, but Hane had offered to carry her personal items in their dimensional bag, so all she had were the emergency supplies on her belt. She drummed her heel against the floor until Hane cracked an eyelid to glare darkly at her. After a minute that felt like an eternity, she stood up and set one foot on the seat of the chair, unlacing her knee-length boot before lacing it up again. Then she repeated the process with the other boot.

She checked the time, sure that an hour must have passed by now. A groan escaped her when she saw it hadn't even been ten minutes yet.

"Just relax," Hane advised, still the picture of repose on the top bunk. "We'll be busy soon enough, so you might as well rest while you can."

Rest. If only it could be so simple. If only she could close her eyes to peaceful darkness, the way Hane seemed to do so easily. If only sleep came easily, if only she could nod off and simply dream as she used to. If only the darkness didn't turn into black smoke that burned the inside of her throat. If only the warmth didn't burn her skin like the splash of lava. If only she didn't hear her teammates' voices inside her head, reliving their final moments as one by one they perished in smoke and flame.

If only she'd been able to save them.

Something struck Nieve on the shoulder, causing her to stumble into the desk. She scowled up at Hane, perched on the edge of their bunk, the arm extended toward her dropping to their side as she caught her balance.

"Did you just shove me with a spell?" Nieve demanded to know.

"You weren't answering me," Hane informed her. "I called your name twice. You're squeezing that locket under your shirt."

"I—oh." Nieve acknowledged the ache on her hand as she forced herself to release the locket. "Are we ready to go? Did I miss the knock on the wall?"

"No." Hane was already stretching out to lay flat again. "If it takes longer than an hour, you and I can go on ahead. Maybe just try staring out the window if you're bored."

Bored. Nieve wished she was bored. She understood what it was to be bored, and she knew the solution to boredom was action. Boredom was easy. Grief, though . . . grief was new. Oh, she'd lost people, but never anyone close to her. Except for her parents, of course, but she'd been so young at the time that she hardly knew the meaning of the word grief. Now every time she was alone with her own thoughts, grief oozed like an open wound, excruciatingly painful while at the same time morbidly fascinating. In her head, she knew that nothing would ever change what happened—nothing would ever bring her friends back. But knowing that didn't stop her from envisioning that final fight over and over again in her mind, asking herself "what if?" as if it mattered.

And the worst part of it was the knowledge that maybe she *could* have made a difference.

Her hand was clutching her locket again, trembling slightly over the sealed mark upon her chest.

If she had remembered the words to break the seal back then, could she have saved them?

No, probably not. Whatever the attunement was, it could only be Quartz-level, and her Citrine-level Champion attunement had barely been enough to keep herself alive.

But it still would have been better if she had at least tried. Maybe there wasn't anything she could have done to save Lani and Aldis, but if she'd been just a little bit stronger, just a tiny bit faster, then maybe—just maybe—she could have saved Emi.

It was a question that plagued her every time she lay down to sleep. Every time her mind wandered. Every time she wasn't actively focused on something else. No matter how many times she told herself that nothing could change what happened, the questions circled around again, leaving trails of frustration and weakness in their wake. Sometimes it drove her to tears. Sometimes she cursed the goddess for her cruelty.

And sometimes, it made her want to long to fly into a rage and tear the nearest living being apart. Now that she was finally inside a spire again, she thought she'd have the chance to let that urge loose—but of course she'd ended up in a scenario so close to everyday life that she'd feel like a monster if she actually let herself go like that.

"You're doing it again." Hane's voice made Nieve jump. "Sage said to watch out for that. That it means you're fixating on something."

"Sage," Nieve grumbled, though thinking of him almost made her smile. Or cry. "Did he ask you to look out for me?"

"No, that's the only thing he said. I don't know what he wanted me to do about it."

The silence drew out long and thin before Nieve realized Hane was finished speaking. Sage usually had some advice to offer, and even though Nieve never took his advice, arguing with him about it often served as a distraction.

Maybe that was what she needed: a distraction.

"Maybe we could use this time to get to know each other better," Nieve suggested. "I mean, it's not like you're really asleep—"

"Because you keep waking me up."

"—and we have some time to kill," Nieve continued, undeterred. "You're officially a member of Team Guiding Star now, so we'll be climbing together for a while. It might be nice to . . . I don't know, share some climber stories, or just . . . talk."

Hane shifted onto their side, dark lashes parting to reveal a deadpan expression. "You want us to be friends, don't you?"

"Is that really so bad?" Nieve asked. "We're teammates now—more than that, we're both frontline fighters. We need to be able to rely on each other. Wouldn't that be easier if—" If they were friends. "If we trusted each other?"

"I trust you in a fight, Nieve. That should be good enough." Hane rolled onto their back again, eyes falling shut.

Frustration curled her hands into fists.

Doubt made them fall limp at her sides again.

It wasn't good enough. Not by a long shot. But why not? Hane was strong, skillful, and experienced; even on their first climb together, Nieve trusted them to watch her back in battle. But that wasn't the same sort of trust she had in Sage, or Lani, or Emiko. It wasn't even close to the amount of trust she had in Ren, a former teammate who used to fight shoulder to shoulder with her in the Tortoise Spire. The two of them had been so in sync that they didn't even need a communication spell to know what the other was thinking; they just moved on instinct, covering each other's blind spots, creating openings for one another, risking life and limb for one another.

That was it. That was the difference.

Nieve would give her sword arm to save any one of her teammates.

But she struggled to believe that Hane would do the same for her.

How do I climb with someone like that? Nieve asked herself. *How can I trust someone who won't talk to me? Who won't laugh with me? Who doesn't feel comfortable enough to be open with me?*

Am I really even sure I'd go to the same lengths for Hane as I would for Sage?

Nieve had only ever wanted to be one thing in her entire life: a spire climber. She'd wanted it ever since her grandmother first began telling her stories of her climber days, even after learning that her parents had died climbing. At first, it had just sounded heroic and exciting, like the ultimate duel, or a valiant triumph. Later, it became something more. A connection. A community. A goal.

She'd never questioned her path or her choices: Nieve was *meant* to be a climber. Her parents left their legacy team name to her, and her first team had come together so easily: Sage and Emiko signed up the moment they passed their Judgments. Then Sage had picked out the best applicants and Emiko had charmed them into joining. Back then, Nieve had assumed that the only duty of a leader was to lead the charge into battle; it wasn't until later that she understood it meant so much more than that. But by then, Lani had effectively taken over as team leader, and Nieve was happy to leave the hard stuff to her.

Guiding Star Legacy was Nieve's team, but she'd never learned how to lead it. And now, she didn't even know how to make a new team member feel welcome.

Frustration mixed with weakness, creating a new emotion that Nieve couldn't even put a name to. All she knew was that if she didn't punch something soon, she'd either throw up or burst into tears.

Hane cracked an eye open and heaved a loud sigh. "Do you just need to talk right now?"

"I don't know." Nieve shrugged. It was only then that she realized she was gripping her locket again. And drumming her heel on the floor. "Maybe. It might help."

Another deep, put-upon sigh, then Hane was sliding off the top bunk. They skirted expertly around Nieve despite the rocking of the train to perch on the desk, folding their legs neatly beneath them. An expectant stare was Nieve's only indication that Hane was ready to listen. It was only then that Nieve realized she had no idea what she wanted to say.

Nieve cleared her throat, searching for a topic of discussion that was neither too personal nor too bland. People didn't become friends by talking about the weather, after all.

"So, have you ever, ah . . ." Nieve struggled before asking the first thing that came to mind. "Have you ever led a team? Like, on a climb?"

"No."

Well, that wasn't entirely unexpected. "Have you ever wanted to?"

"I thought this was about you."

"It kind of is?" Nieve shrugged. "But I want to know more about you, too."

Hane shifted slightly. "No. I never wanted to lead a team."

"Why not?" Nieve was genuinely curious: Hane didn't like to climb with the same people, but that didn't mean they couldn't gather their own teammates for every climb instead joining other peoples' teams. Hane's reputation was well known within climbing circles of Dalenos: it would have been easy for them to assemble a new team of their own for each climb.

Hane shrugged, looking uncomfortable. "I never wanted to."

"Oh." Nieve glanced around for a place to sit before recognizing that her feeling of discomfort was coming from within. She drew a deep breath and decided to simply speak her mind. "Look, we don't have to be best friends or anything, but I think it would help us work together if we found some common ground. Something we can talk about during downtime, or while traveling. We're going to be at this for a while so . . . let's try to make it work, okay?"

Hane's eyebrows lifted in mild surprise. "I'm here. I joined the team. I'm carrying your gear in my bag. I fought by your side against the general of a god beast. Isn't that enough?"

"No, that's not—" Nieve stopped, frustrated with herself more than with Hane. "I'm not saying you're not a good teammate, I'm just saying that you're not—I mean, it's not like—it just feels . . . different. With you. You're not like—"

"I'm not like Sage," Hane said simply. "Nor do I intend to be."

"That's not what I . . . okay, maybe that's kind of what I meant." Nieve tried to order her thoughts, then gave up. Maybe she was going about this the wrong way. "I don't need you to suddenly pour out your life story to me, I just want to . . . I don't know, feel connected to you, or something. We shouldn't be strangers to each other on each new climb."

"That's what I'm used to," Hane said, shrugging. "If I'm making you uncomfortable, we don't need to stay in the same cabin. I can ask to switch with Odette or—"

"No, don't." She hadn't meant to chase Hane away; sharing a room with someone else would only widen the distance between them. Nieve dropped onto the edge of the lower bunk, one heel tapping the floor in agitation. "I know you don't want to talk, but . . . could you maybe just listen?"

Hane shifted their weight from side to side, their eyes seemingly sizing up the window as if wondering if they could fit through it. After a moment's consideration, Hane sighed and seemed to settle in, looking at Nieve expectantly.

"Thanks." This really wasn't any less uncomfortable, but maybe asking Hane questions had been the wrong way to go about this. Maybe it was better to offer something of herself first. Hane's focused gaze was more off-putting than Nieve expected, so rather than meet it, she looked away and let her gaze soften. "I, um, usually talk to Sage about this kind of stuff. Or, I used to. We were closer before we realized we were both really into Lani." A furtive glance up: Hane was still watching her with that unsettling stare. Nieve dropped her eyes again. "After that, every conversation turned into a fight, but before . . . before that, we could talk about anything. I've never even been inside a spire without him, so this . . . this all just feels wrong, and I don't know how to just make it better."

Phew! Wow, but that felt like letting steam out of a pot. Nieve wasn't entirely certain where all those words had come from—they hadn't been on

With a leg mark, Hane focused their gravity spells within their own body to help them change direction quickly or sneak up on enemies. In most cases, they preferred to use spells that relied entirely on transference mana, but that would have taken a significant amount of concentration for this task, considering how the train didn't move along a straight path, and the wind resistance was anything but consistent. The gravity spell wasn't too taxing, but as a composite mana type, it was more difficult to work with, which was why so few Wavewalkers could use it effectively.

Once Hane was close enough to the window, they chanced a look back over their shoulder. Rose was leaning over the rail, watching their progress, though there was no way she could see what Hane was doing at the window. One lens of her goggles was clear, the other a reflective silver that seemed to wink as light bounced off of it. As much as Hane wanted to ask if she was ready, they felt certain they couldn't shout loud enough to be heard over the wind without the guards inside the car hearing them. Luckily, Rose already had a solution for that.

"Whenever you see your opportunity, go for it," Rose ordered through the communication device clamped over Hane's ear. "If you need me to activate the diversion, kick your foot and get back here as fast as you can."

Hane used a hand signal for "okay" before slipping the lipstick tube out of their sleeve. They popped the cap off with their teeth, then reached out to the lowest corner of the window. Inside the car, they could see a pair of guards standing at a far window, their polearms propped casually against their shoulders. Perhaps they were taking a break, or perhaps there was simply no need to patrol constantly; either way, it worked out for Hane. They had to shake and shimmy the coil of black wire down their arm and find the end with the glass orb, straightening it slightly from its curl so it would be ready to slip through the burned hole, just as Rose had instructed.

Checking on the guards once more, Hane set the end of the lipstick tube to the corner of the window, holding the end of the black wire close at the ready. A thin trail of white smoke rose from the window, partially sheltered from the window by Hane's body. Before they reached the end of a four-count, the smoke was shredded by the slipstream as if it had never been. It was harder to fit the cord through the newly burned hole than Hane expected, due to the raised edge of molten glass and the heat of the tube itself. Hane wondered how mad Rose would be if they simply dropped the tube of lipstick, thinking she could have at least warned them that it would be hot to the touch after using it. They threaded a few inches of wire in through the window before pausing to put the cap on the lipstick, tucking it in an outside pocket so it wouldn't be pressed against their skin.

In the few moments that Hane took to secure the Kiss of Fire device, the end of the black coil began to twitch back and forth like the head of a snake. Hane chanced a glance back over their shoulder at Rose. Her lips were moving, likely directing the wire with a voice spell. When she saw Hane looking back, she waved her hand in a "keep going" sort of motion. Lifting themself up just enough on the elbows to look inside the train car, Hane began feeding more of the black wire in through the minute hole.

Through their grip on the flexible cord, Hane could feel its movement, shifting and rolling like a live animal. It was a bit unnerving, but perhaps it was just as unnerving for Rose to see Hane lying flat against the side of a train, peering through the window as if it was the skylight of a building. The guards inside the car appeared to be conversing, only occasionally glancing around the car, with their eyes always scanning the floor. That was lucky: it seemed they were more wary of the cargo than they were of an intrusion. From Hane's angle, they had a better view of the boxes across the car than the ones below the window, but hopefully the crates were arranged in a similar setup on both sides of the walkway. Any minute now, Rose should be able to direct the marble eyeball of the cord-creature between the slats of a crate and figure out what, exactly, Keepsake Treasuries was transporting.

Hane was just about to tap their communication device and ask Rose how much longer this would take, when a sharp scream cut the air. They jumped up to their hands and knees so fast that a twiggy tree branch raked along the back of their dueling vest, making them drop flat to the side of the train again. When they could look back, Rose was nowhere in sight. A peek through the windows found the guards looking around in confusion, as if wondering if they had heard something or not. Had Rose been attacked? That didn't seem likely, considering that Nieve and Mason were on guard in the luggage car, and they hadn't heard any warnings come over their communication device. Was it just Mason, come to check on their progress? Maybe he'd startled his sister, or even played a trick on her. If it was something mundane like that, then rushing back to the gangway would be a wasted effort. But if it was something more serious than that . . .

Before Hane could make up their mind—wait, or rush back to the gangway—the train car jerked unexpectedly beneath them, the sound of a loud boom following later. The guards inside the train car crashed into each other before they found their footing. Through the window on the opposite side of the car, Hane could see black smoke.

An attack? Hane guessed as they used a burst of transference mana to push themself away from the window and back toward the gangway. *But no*

*one should have gotten past Nieve and Mason without one of them calling us
through the communication devices.*

Hane dropped around the corner of the train car, their gravity spell
immediately dragging them sideways like they were falling down a pit. They
caught the rail in one hand and allowed the momentum to carry them as they
surveyed the gangway. Rose was crumpled on the steel platform, her body
twisted and rolled back against the railing as if she had been kicked there.
Her outstretched hand clutched a climbing hook, which she had somehow
managed to catch on the steel grating of the platform. Someone unfamiliar
stood over her, their boot upraised to stomp down on her hand, hard. Hane
saw the stranger's head snap up as they rounded the edge of the car, but didn't
give them a chance to react before landing a gravity-aided kick to the center
of their chest.

Gravity Return, Hane thought, closing their eyes to miss the vertigo that
occurred when the world reoriented too rapidly. As the direction they were
falling shifted, Hane coiled their feet beneath them, landing on the gangway
in a half crouch in between Rose and her attacker.

"He jumped down from the roof," Rose gasped, her voice strained as if
she'd had the breath knocked out of her. "He tried to throw me off the train.
He might be—"

"The one we need to subdue," Hane finished, sliding one tonfa out of the
harness hidden beneath their dueling tunic. "Call Nieve and Mason. Hurry."

The attacker hit the opposite rail hard enough to dent it, but he managed
to keep himself from tumbling over it. The cloak attached to his cowl was
snagged in the train's slipstream, dragging him sideways against the side of
the train. Once his footing steadied, he ripped the cowl over his head, letting the wind take it. Hane held one tonfa low behind themself, the other
arm braced to block a strike. A strong burst of transference would send the
attacker flying, but just in case this was the person the team needed to capture, Hane would have to find a way to fight in the limited space between the
two train cars.

"No one was supposed to be here," the man growled, drawing twin daggers from sheaths on either side of his belt. "I didn't mind when it was just the
girl, but where did you come from?"

Hane kept still and silent, assessing the target and waiting for them to
make the first move. Hitting the rail that hard should have hurt, but he looked
combat ready, which most likely meant he had an attunement, or at least an
enchanted item that protected him like a shroud. This wouldn't be an easy
fight, not in such a limited space while protecting Rose. If it came down to it,
Hane wouldn't hesitate to blast their opponent off the train entirely, but until

that was the only option left to them, they would do their best to hold out until Nieve arrived.

"You should run away if you want to live," the man snarled, his daggers crossed in front of him. "I'm not here on my own. The others will be here soon."

Whether he was lying or telling the truth, Hane couldn't wait any longer. They feinted with a swing of their tonfa, then swept low with their leg, hoping to knock the man flat to the gangway. He grunted and staggered, but managed to stay standing by fetching his shoulder up against the rear of the car. As he lashed out with a sideways swipe of his dagger, Hane caught the gleam of green liquid coating the edge of the blade. Poison? Possibly an Assassin attunement, then. Unless the blades were enchanted with poison. Either way, Hane preferred not to be cut by one of them.

Hane turned the next strike away with a light shove of transference mana, making the man over-rotate his next step. They heard Rose shouting behind them, as well as inside their head through the communication device: Nieve and Mason should be here soon. Unless, of course, the Assassin wasn't lying about having backup, in which case Nieve and Mason might already be preoccupied.

This time, the Assassin didn't catch his balance but fell heavily enough to make the grating tremble under foot. Hane knelt down over his shoulders, intending to strike his wrists until he dropped both poison-coated daggers.

"Stop, don't let him!" Rose shrieked, on her feet now, but grasping the railing as if it was the only thing keeping her upright. "The coupler!"

Hane barely reacted in time, sweeping their tonfa beneath the Assassin's arm and jerking it up, so the round glowing object in their hand flew up rather than striking the coupler. Afraid the object might be an incendiary device, Hane leapt backward, shielding their face with one arm while blocking Rose bodily.

"Out of my way!" Rose snarled, digging an elbow into Hane's side to move them, her other arm arcing through a throwing motion. One of the tiny knives from her belt flew from her fingertips with the speed of an arrowhead. It struck the glowing orb mid-flight and shattered it before it could break against the door of the train. Instead of heat and fire, a colorless liquid burst out of the broken orb, spraying in all directions and hissing wherever it landed.

"Acid," Hane pronounced, watching the liquid bubble and froth where it landed on metal, chewing through it like a determined termite. It had probably been meant to burn through the coupler, separating the Keepsake cars from the rest of the train. It must have been specially designed to eat through metal, because the droplets that struck Hane's sleeve and tunic fizzled quickly, leaving only colorless splotches behind.

"He has another!" Rose shouted. "Brick, get your meathead out here! We need you!"

Burst, Hane thought, sending a low wave of transference mana rolling outward from their body. The Assassin grunted as it impacted his side, tossing him roughly into the already dented rails. A second orb of acid was knocked from his hand, glittering briefly in the sunlight before the wind whisked it out of sight. Mason's voice came through the communication device, but it cut out before Hane could make sense of the words. Whatever was going on with Mason and Nieve, it seemed Hane and Rose were on their own at the moment.

Hane freed their second tonfa from under their dueling vest as the Assassin scraped himself up from the gangway. They took a step forward, cutting off the angle to the coupler without exposing themself to too much risk. They weren't as afraid of getting pushed off the train as they were of being knocked out by a rocky outcropping or a heavy tree branch. Or worse: tossed down on the track between the two cars. Hane spun one tonfa into a defensive position along their forearm while keeping the other tonfa turned out and ready to strike. It wasn't often that they fought someone who could dual-wield just as they did, especially with shorter weapons coated in poison. Without a lot of space to maneuver, Hane was reconsidering their plan to capture the Assassin alive rather than simply blast him off the side of the train.

That limited space appeared to be getting even smaller: as the Assassin slid his foot forward into an offensive position, part of the grate gave way beneath it, forcing him to quickly readjust his footing. It was only a few inches of the platform, not big enough to fall through, but other sections were turning dark and brittle. It was only a matter of time before the gangway became too unsafe to stand on.

"You gave it a good try," the Assassin said, breathless but encouraging. "You can run away now knowing you gave it your all. You're not a match for me, and you know it."

Not if I'm trying to take him alive, Hane thought, prepared for a sudden attack. Speaking to Rose, they called out: "You have anything for this?"

"Working on it," Rose replied, the sound of rummaging and rustling barely audible over the wind. "Keep him busy."

That was easier said than done. Though the Assassin held his daggers in both hands, when his eyes flicked toward the coupler, Hane moved on instinct to block it. The Assassin struck with two downward sweeping strikes, both of which Hane turned aside with their tonfa, but it left them open for the taller, broader opponent to slam their shoulder into Hane's chest, intending to knock them backward into the empty space between the cars. Expecting exactly that, Hane used their Burst spell to counter the Assassin's momentum, but they couldn't put too much force into it without slamming the Assassin through the door of the Keepsake car, so he recovered quickly, regaining his stance and attacking with precision strikes of his blades, obviously trying to score a hit rather than strike to kill. Hane blocked and spun and bobbed and weaved, careful not to yield any ground—that drop was right behind their heels and either falling or leaping out of the way would give the Assassin exactly what he wanted.

It would be easy to hop backward and land on the opposite gangway; there would be more space to maneuver without the threat of the grating crumbling beneath their feet, but Hane couldn't leave Rose alone on the platform with the Assassin. While she was more than likely trained in combat, everything she had done so far indicated that she wasn't confident in her hand-to-hand combat abilities. And jumping across the gap would give the Assassin an opportunity to separate the cars, which had to be prevented at all costs. But the longer Hane was pinned to one spot, the more likely it was that the Assassin's blades would slip through, and with the poison coating their blades, the strike didn't need to be deep in order to be fatal.

Rose moved suddenly, darting from one far corner of the gangway to the other, slapping something in the center of the Keepsake car's door as she passed it. Her eyes met Hane's as she dropped into a crouch and covered her ears.

"Get back!" she shouted, before squeezing her eyes shut. Hane leapt, crossing their tonfa in front of them to ward off strikes from the daggers as they propelled themself backward. Before they could land, they heard Rose shout: "Now!"

A wall of heat slammed into Hane's chest so hot that it singed the hairs inside their nose. Their eyes closed on instinct as their body braced for the impact they knew was coming. Their back slammed into the door of the luggage car, their shroud taking the brunt of the damage, though it did knock the wind from their chest. As they steadied their feet beneath them, they saw black smoke pouring out of the hole where the Keepsake Treasuries car door used to be. Rose, holding a cloth over her nose and mouth, darted inside the Keepsake car, vanishing behind the plume of smoke. The Assassin had been knocked flat by the explosion, his face inches away from the coupler, but he seemed far more concerned with climbing back onto the crumbling gangway than disconnecting it just now.

Their ears still ringing from the explosion, Hane leapt from the luggage gangway to the Keepsake gangway, landing on the rail for safe footing.

The more the Assassin scrambled to get up, the more the grating crumbled beneath him. Hane felt the entire platform shudder, as if it might give way any second. The Assassin seemed to think so, too, because the second he got his feet underneath him, he dove through the cabin door, the pressure of his leap making the platform creak ominously. Hane took only a second to catch their balance before leaping through the open doorway, somersaulting past the unsteady Assassin and pivoting to face him as they leapt up to their feet.

"That's the one!" Rose shouted, pointing past Hane to the Assassin. Three Keepsake guards were clustered at the rear of the car for reasons Hane didn't quite understand. Shouldn't they be defending their cargo? What was the point of striding the length of the car with weapons if they weren't prepared to use them? "He's the one who was trying to break into your car! See that?" She pointed to the black cord hanging limply through the hole Hane had burned in the window. "When we caught him trying to sneak through the window, he blew open the door with a bomb! We're here to help protect the cargo!"

"That's not—" The Assassin snarled at Rose's creative interpretation of the facts. Hane was impressed: the only person who could deny Rose's lie was the Assassin, and as he was the obvious instigator here, the guards weren't likely to believe him. "Oh, resh this. I'm out."

The Assassin swiped the air with his hand, leaving behind twisting shadows that stretched and grew, making the car as dark as night. Hane heard rushed movements, the creak of wood and nails, then the pounding rush of running footsteps. They charged through the shadows with their head ducked beneath their arm just in case the Assassin was waiting by the door to deliver a deadly slash. The shadowy veil ended abruptly at the ruined doorway of the train's car, allowing Hane to see the Assassin struggle to open the door Hane had been thrown against during the explosion. He had one wooden crate tucked under his arm and another on the gangway at his ankle, giving him a free hand to work the door handle. He glanced back in time to see Hane chasing him, then wrenched the door open with a mighty tug. With a swipe of his foot, he kicked the crate through the open doorway, barely stopping long enough to scoop it up as he ran after it.

Hane measured the distance between the doorway and the solid brass platform of the luggage car, not trusting the acid-burned one to hold their weight for a strong leap. They backed up two steps, then ran forward, soaring clear over both gangways and diving through the narrow opening of the luggage car. The Assassin had knocked several trunks into the aisle to buy himself some time to get through the next door, but Hane cleared those obstacles easily, determined to at least recover the crates from the Assassin. They read the panic on the Assassin's face as they leapt at him, but even with that warning they were unprepared for what happened next.

The Assassin hurled one of the crates directly at Hane, giving him the free hand he needed to slide the heavy outer door open. For a single crystallized moment in time, Hane considered whether it was worth dodging the box mid-flight in order to capture the Assassin before he could flee with the second crate. It would mean that whatever was inside the crate was in for a rough landing, and if it was a living being, it might not survive. They might have made a different decision if they hadn't known that Nieve and Mason were inside the very next car, but that knowledge made them secure enough to choose saving the crate over chasing the Assassin. They caught the wooden crate against their chest, cushioning it with the lightest touch of their Burst spell as possible. When they landed from their leap, the crate held protectively against their chest, the Assassin was slamming the door shut, smirking as he dropped a small red orb in between the catch and the lock. Through the tiny porthole window in the door, Hane saw the Assassin turn away and leap to the next gangway.

The crate hissed angrily in Hane's hands, confirming the presence of something alive inside of it. They set it down gently on the floor before vaulting over a tipped-over clothing trunk and tugging at the door handle. Whatever the Assassin had done to the locking mechanism had sealed it shut tight. No matter how Hane tugged at it, it wouldn't open. All they could do was keep watch and hope the Assassin didn't try to uncouple the cars again.

Luckily, uncoupling the cars no longer seemed to be a priority.

Unluckily, without the burden of a second crate, the Assassin was able to climb the iron ladder beside the train car door, ascending up to the roof. Hane's stomach dropped as they realized the Assassin would bypass Nieve and Mason entirely, getting away with the prize.

Frustrated, Hane slammed a fist against the window, knowing that even if it broke, there was no way they could fit through it, nor could they pursue over the train's roof. They watched through the window as long as they could, counting the number of times the Assassin jumped between cars until he disappeared behind a bend in the track.

NIEVE

Champion (mind mark), Citrine
??? (heart mark), Sealed

"Hey, pooch pooch pooch! That's a good little pooch. Want a treat, little pooch?"

Nieve rolled her eyes as Mason held a tiny cube of sausage up to an opening in the dog crate. A pink tongue slipped out, licking his fingers before accepting the proffered morsel.

"Can you stop talking to it like that?" Nieve asked, bored beyond all reckoning. "It's an animal, not a baby. That food might not even be good for it."

"It's meat. Dogs love meat," Mason countered. His tone reverted back to a childish lilt as he spoke through the sides of the crate. "And it makes him so happy, yes it does! Yes it does! So lonely all by himself back here, poor poochie deserves a little treaty-treat, doesn't he?"

"Treaty-treat?" Nieve repeated, her tone dry, her heel bouncing in irritation. She was sitting on a clothing trunk near the first door of the luggage car, her arms crossed over her chest as she waited for something to do other than, well, wait. "What if that dog gets sick from all that sausage? Did you think of that?"

"It's all gone, poochie, you got all of it," Mason crooned, holding his finger out for a few final licks before he straightened up and wiped his hands on his pants. "So, do you just hate dogs, or do you hate all animals?"

"I hate being bored!" Nieve kicked her heel into the floor, the resulting thud making the dog whimper and scratch at the crate. Mason shot Nieve an admonishing glare. She huffed and toyed with the hilt of her sword. "I haven't had a chance to do anything yet! Does the Tiger Spire even have combat, or is it just one long theater scene? I haven't even seen one monster!"

"There's this guy. He scared you pretty good earlier, didn't he? Didn't you, poochie?" Mason crooned at the dog crate. Nieve rolled her eyes again.

Seeming amused, Mason walked over and took a seat on a trunk opposite Nieve. "So what brought your team out to the Tiger Spire, anyway? The way you talk, I don't understand why you left Dalenos at all."

Nieve looked away, guilt colliding with her irritation. Without meaning to, she rolled her ankle to make sure Chime was still safely holstered in her boot. "We lost some people on our last climb. Good people. Friends." The truth tasted bitter in her mouth; the lie was sweeter. "It was too hard to keep climbing without them, so we decided to try the other spires. See if we could find one we like."

"Why the spires, though?" Mason asked, rolling his bare shoulders in a broad shrug. "Why not join one of the Unclaimed Lands excursions and visit a few shrines to earn some treasure? Or the elemental temples—you've got one right in Dalenos, don't you?"

"Actually, the Water Temple is . . . well, it's close by, yeah," Nieve agreed. She sighed as she reached for her locket, feeling the four engraved knots at the corners. "I have to make it to the top of a spire. I *have* to. The shrines and the temples . . . they can't give me what I want."

"What do you want?" Mason asked, his innocent-sounding question setting Nieve's defenses on edge. He shrugged again, this time only shallowly. "I know a lot of people visit the shrines and temples for magic marks, but the gateway crystals can grant other rewards, too. If you're after something specific, you just need to find the right shrine."

The latch on the train car door clicked sharply, startling the both of them to their feet before Nieve could respond.

"Oh, why, hello!" The stranger who stepped through the door seemed as surprised to see Nieve and Mason as they were to see him. The newcomer was average height, putting him well shorter than both Nieve and Mason. His skin was a light brown, but he spoke Valian, and while Nieve couldn't say exactly why, he didn't seem like a Caelford native. Maybe it was his clothing: well-made, but not overly fancy with a simple waistcoat over a button-down shirt, gray slacks, and simple brown shoes. His green newsboy cap was tipped back on his head, making his puzzled expression readily apparent. "I didn't mean to interrupt anything. I didn't know anyone was back here, ah . . . dallying, I suppose."

"No!" Nieve objected, planting her palm against Mason's chest as he started to slide his arm around her waist. She glared at him until he backed off. He was probably only playacting for the stranger, but Nieve was through playing games for whatever entity controlled this scenario. Her irritation wasn't helped by the dog's suddenly loud and obnoxious barking. She hooked her hand around her sword as she addressed the stranger. "Sorry, but there's no admittance back this way. You're going to have to turn around and head back the way you came."

"Oh, but I have a pass." The stranger frowned as they patted their pockets. "Let's see, where did I put my ticket? I didn't know I would have to show it to anyone. Did something happen back here?"

He didn't look all that dangerous, but something about him had Nieve on edge. Or maybe she was still on edge from earlier. The passenger wasn't wearing a weapon, and as he patted himself down looking for his ticket, it was clear he wasn't wearing any armor. As he twisted around to check his back pockets, she saw a walking stick tucked under his arm. With the knob shaped and colored like a green and gray marble egg, Nieve guessed it was more for form than function. The stranger seemed well balanced despite the sway and rattle of the train car.

"Some of the luggage shifted," Mason explained congenially. "We're making sure no one gets crushed during a curve in the track. We've got staff working their way forward from the second car, securing the luggage more tightly."

"Oh, I see." The stranger smiled as he produced his ticket with a flourish. "Ah, here it is! My ticket and my luggage stub. That's my dog, you see." He smiled as he held out both pieces of paper. "I just wanted to come and check on him, maybe let him stretch his legs a little. I'm afraid he knows I'm here, and that's why he's making such a fuss."

The luggage stub was stamped with a crate labeled "live," and the ticket itself did allow for luggage car access. Nieve had expected that she and Mason could turn back any passengers wishing to search through their luggage while protecting Hane and Rose on their information-gathering mission, but it was a lot harder to refuse entry to the owner of a pet than someone who just wanted to retrieve a change of shoes.

"Ah, so you're Sa'rhi Nereux," Mason said, indicating the tag secured to the outside of the dog's crate. He stepped back graciously, inviting the passenger forward, though Nieve noted how he remained in the center of the walkway so the passenger couldn't continue on through the car. "Sorry if I'm saying that wrong. I was making friends with your dog, here. He's a better conversationalist than my partner."

Nieve glared, but Sa'rhi chuckled as he dragged the crate away from the wall and crouched down beside it. "Well, thank you for keeping my little hound entertained. I'd love to keep him in my cabin, but he gets so very motion sick unless he's confined in a dark space. I'll make it up to him when we arrive at the lake, yes I will!"

Nieve rolled her eyes as Sa'rhi spoke to the dog in the same baby voice Mason used when feeding it sausage. By the way Mason watched the stranger kneel down beside the crate to open it, she wondered if he sensed something slightly off about Sa'rhi as well. That thought was dashed as Mason flashed a winning smile at the dog's owner as he leaned over the top of the crate.

"Did we meet earlier?" Mason asked smoothly. "Because I swear I recognize that smile."

"Perhaps we passed while boarding," Sa'rhi replied with a chuckle. He flipped up two brass catches and folded down a portion of the crate, allowing a small white and brown terrier to scramble out and leap into its owner's arms. "Yes, Mote, you sweet thing! I'm glad to see you, too. Not too long now, or you'll get sick, you know."

"Mote, that's a cute name!" Mason laughed as he leaned over the crate to pat the dog, though his eyes were on Sa'rhi. "Do you call him that for the little brown spots on his head?"

"Like little dust motes, yes." Sa'rhi smiled, but it wasn't the smile of someone greeting a beloved pet; it looked far more sinister than that. Nieve suddenly realized that with the crate in the middle of the walkway, she and Mason had been neatly separated. Before she could make a move, Sa'rhi's grin sharpened. "Mote, attack."

All at once the adorable terrier whipped its head around with a snarl and sunk its teeth into Mason's hand. Mason yelped and staggered backward, shaking his arm once before stopping and trying to remove the dog's teeth more carefully. Nieve reached for her sword, but the marble-topped walking stick slammed against the side of her face with stunning force. It didn't stagger her, not with enhancement mana coursing through her body, but it certainly did smart, even through her protective shroud.

"Don't make me do all the work," Sa'rhi called, barely raising his voice. "We've two brutes between us and the cargo—let's make short work of them, shall we?"

Frost Form, Nieve thought, activating the spell that made her skin as tough as ice. She wished she'd cast it sooner: by the sting in her cheek, there was going to be quite a bruise later. At least the ice that protected her numbed the pain enough that she was able to ignore it. She swept the walking stick away and reached for her sword as the car door rolled open. Two thuggish-looking men shouldered their way inside, crowding in front of Sa'rhi like a human shield.

"Careful with that one," Sa'rhi advised, pointing at Nieve with his walking stick. "A combat attunement, no doubt. Quickly now, we need to be on our way to rendezvous with Ellis."

There was someone else? Were they working with one of the guards in the Keepsake cars? If they were, then Hane and Rose could be in danger.

Nieve squared up against Sa'rhi's two goons, the dog crate blocking her retreat down the aisle.

"Mason, call the others!" Nieve ordered over the sounds of growls and Caelish curses. She would have to ask what "zakred" meant later: it sounded like a good one. "I don't know what this guy is paying you two, but I guarantee it's not worth the pain I'm about to put you through." Nieve grinned, feeling her blood sing beneath her toughened skin. "You have no idea how long I've been waiting for a fight just like this."

The space was too narrow for wide-swinging attacks, so Nieve attacked with thrusts and jabs more befitting a rapier than her katana. She half expected Sa'rhi to duck outside where it was safe, but he only set both hands atop his walking stick, smirking as his goons advanced. The closer one mirrored Nieve's stance, only without a sword. She lunged, thinking that a light graze over a sensitive area—his throat, perhaps—would be enough to scare him off that attack, but the moment her sword came within range, it was parried by a thin silvery mana construction in the shape of a rapier. This goon had to be a Shaper in order to create such an object from mana so quickly. A strong one, too, in order to use a magical construct to parry a sword made of real steel. Nieve didn't let that distract her, though—she was a trained duelist, after all, which meant she was used to defending and countering all sorts of surprises. And swords made of magic were usually weaker than swords made of steel. Before the goon could get into position to thrust, Nieve swept her blade around the magical one and slammed it sideways against the metal luggage racks. She braced her free hand against the back of her sword and, with a surge of enhancement mana strengthening her arms and chest, she shoved, hard, shattering the magical blade into sparks of light that flickered and died.

In the time it took for Nieve to disarm her first opponent, the second one had moved into position to attack. Backing up wasn't an option—her heel was already braced against the dog crate positioned across the walkway—but the second opponent appeared unarmed. Instead of reaching for a weapon, he swung hard with a meaty fist, going for the knockout hit to Nieve's temple. Nieve saw the hit coming but couldn't get her blade around in time to counter. She got her forearm up high enough to take the hit, thinking her Frost Form spell would be enough to take the hit.

The blow landed hard enough that Nieve's arm jolted painfully in its socket, the momentum nearly toppling her over the dog crate that kept her from backing away. Before she could assess the damage, the goon threw another punch, this one aimed at her stomach. Nieve pivoted to the side, meaning to pull the goon off balance, but he tracked her movement seamlessly, getting in a good, hard uppercut to her gut. Nieve slammed back against the racks of luggage but managed to keep her feet as well as her sword.

I'll feel that tomorrow, Nieve thought, getting both arms up to block the next hit. *This guy has to be a Guardian. No way he hits this hard otherwise. And why am I fighting all on my own?*

"You gonna help me or what?" Nieve shouted back to Mason. "Tell me which one you want and I'll toss you a dance partner!"

"I never thought I'd turn down a dance, but I'm afraid I have to this time." The dog's snarls had diminished into plaintive whines, but Mason still sounded pained. "You're the big bad warrior from Dalenos; this should be easy for you."

"The space is the problem," Nieve muttered, her sword held in a reverse grip as she blocked the Guardian's punches with her forearms. She could jump over the dog crate, or simply crush it under her heel, but that would put her off balance in front of two competent fighters—not to mention the one lurking behind them, smirking beneath the brim of his newsboy cap.

"We'd rather not kill anyone," Sa'rhi called out, tapping the Guardian twice with the end of his walking stick. That seemed to be a signal to stop, because the goon fell back to stand shoulder-to-shoulder with the Shaper. "All we want is to grab something from the back real quick, then you won't hear a peep out of us the rest of the trip. But corpses tend to raise questions, and we'd rather avoid that. You understand. Now, if you both could kindly step aside like the reasonable people you appear to be, we'll just be on our way."

"Ha!" Nieve sheathed her sword, bouncing lightly on her toes as she shook off her lumps. "Reasonable? What about me looks reasonable to you?"

Sa'rhi sighed loudly. "Well, be quick about it. If we toss them overboard, maybe no one will notice they're missing until later."

The Shaper advanced first, conjuring a magical blade in each hand. The right was about the length of a short sword, the left the length of a dagger. Not that it mattered much: a skilled Shaper could change the length of magical swords as they fought, making them harder to dodge or block. The shorter lengths were good for the confined space of the luggage car, and while Nieve often used ice to make her blade longer or broader, she couldn't make it shorter. Which really only left her with one option.

If the Shaper was confused by Nieve's sheathed sword, it didn't slow down his attack; he kept his dagger-length blade in a guard position while swinging the shortsword up for a downward chop, something Nieve couldn't have done without scraping the ceiling with her own sword. She watched the descent of the sword, her fists up in front of her face in a guard position. Just as the sword reached the middle of its downswing, Nieve cast the spell she'd been saving: Ice Gauntlets.

As Nieve turned her forearm to block the magical sword, conjured ice growing over her knuckles and spreading back over her fist and arm in thick layers of toughened armor, the magical blade shattered on impact, leaving the Shaper off balance to defend himself. Nieve threw a low right jab at the second blade as the Shaper fought to regain his balance. The dagger blade shattered, but the Shaper took the hit with barely a grunt. Given the chance, he likely would have conjured another blade or some other magically constructed weapon, but Nieve didn't give it to him. She stepped into his space, pummeling him with punches as she advanced, steadily driving him back toward the front of the car. Maybe if she could rattle the boss, the three of them would break and run. She hoped so, anyway: she really wanted to wrap this up so she could go check on Hane and Rose.

Sa'rhi didn't look worried though. More amused, perhaps. Or resigned. Nieve saw him sigh before he tapped his other brute and said something she couldn't quite make out. When the Shaper suddenly beat a retreat behind the Guardian, Nieve pivoted to change targets—only to see the Guardian gripping the rail of the highest luggage rack. The rack creaked and groaned as he pulled on it, metal creaking and screaming down the length of the car. Heavy trunks, suitcases, and crates lined the rack all the way back to where Mason clutched a bloodied cloth around his hand. If the luggage rack broke, the two of them would be buried in an avalanche of luggage.

"No, you don't!" Nieve kept one arm up to block anything falling from above while she hammered the Guardian's kidney, one, two, three times, hoping to force him to relinquish his grip. He snarled and let go of the rack with one hand, grabbing the closest item on a middle shelf—a suitcase—and swinging it at Nieve to drive her back. When she hit him again, he threw a bigger suitcase at her, the luggage rack screaming and creaking as it peeled away from the wall.

Plan, plan, I need a plan, Nieve thought anxiously. Freezing the rack in place might work, but that would require more finesse than conjuring a simple ice wall, and she didn't have the time to concentrate properly. She could freeze the ground and make the goon lose his footing, but that might actually bring the luggage rack down faster. The man was tall and with his arms up to grip the shelf, Nieve couldn't find an angle for a good head shot to knock him out. So what was left?

There!

The solution was the first problem: the dog crate in the middle of the walkway.

Nieve ran two steps and kicked off the box, bringing her icy gauntlets together like one massive hammer. She swung down hard, using the strength of her enhancement mana as well as her Frost Form spell. The double-fisted strike landed with the sound of an egg cracking, dazing the Guardian into releasing the luggage rack as he staggered forward, then backward, eyes wide and unfocused. When he finally dropped to the floor, still conscious but insensate, one of the luggage rack supports came loose with an ominous metallic squeal. Anything not securely fastened to the luggage rack, including small satchels and hat boxes, rained down into the aisle, making it hard to see or do anything. Nieve held her gauntlets over her head and waited for the deluge to finish. When the pummel of small items ended, the top luggage rack hung at an angle, heavier luggage containers straining against the rail as well as the straps that secured them. As the train followed a curve in the track, the metalwork groaned ominously, threatening to collapse entirely. Nieve grimaced before sweeping out a space around her on the floor with one foot while raising her gauntlets defensively.

The Guardian hadn't been knocked out, but he was having some issues with his balance, swaying back and forth with the momentum of the train. Sa'rhi sighed in exasperation as he grabbed the man's elbow to steady him. If he had a healing attunement, the Guardian would be back in the fight in no time at all: Nieve had to end it before then.

Launching herself forward with muscles aided by enhancement mana, Nieve swung her arm back, shouting as she swung for the Shaper's head. The man braced himself as he crossed his arms in front of him, leaning forward to absorb the impact of the hit. Nieve's gauntlet met with the resistance of a conjured shield, sending a rippling shockwave back through her arm to her shoulder. She set her jaw and punched again and again, trying to break the conjured shield, just as she'd broken the magical swords. Though she managed to shove the Shaper back by inches, the shield refused to give. She backed off when she began to sweat, panting as she assessed the shield's strengths.

It was far larger than the swords, taking up the width of the aisle and shielding the Shaper from head to ankle. Round and silver, it almost looked like an illusion of the moon, except that it was transparent enough that Nieve could see through it to the Shaper and his companions behind him. To hold against so many strikes, the shield had to be stronger than the conjured swords. Maybe the Shaper hadn't been fighting with his full strength the first time around, or maybe this was simply a more advanced spell than the conjured swords. Just to make sure she wasn't entirely outclassed by any of these opponents, Nieve activated her Detect Aura spell to check her opponents' shrouds.

The Shaper was Sunstone, a bright one, too, but still below Nieve's level as a Citrine. The Guardian's shroud was a nebulous red-orange color, which either made him a high Carnelian or a low Sunstone, Nieve wasn't entirely certain which. Beyond the pair of them, she could just make out a rust-red aura around their boss, confirming that Sa'rhi was also attuned, but since he had yet to display any magic, Nieve couldn't begin to guess what his attunement might be.

I think he's the one we have to capture, Nieve thought, focusing on Sa'rhi. *But just in case I'm wrong, I should try to keep them all alive.*

Nieve twitched as a loud, panicked voice came through her communication device. It sounded like Rose, but she couldn't concentrate on the words just then. In her moment of distraction, the Shaper charged forward, bracing his shoulder against the shield as he crashed headlong into Nieve. Nieve staggered off balance before shoving the shield right back and landing three rapid punches all in the dead center of the shield. It was bound to break at some point, and pounding repeatedly on the same spot seemed likely to get it there. The Shaper must have realized it too, because he shifted back a single step, taking some of the strength out of Nieve's third strike. Nieve used the opportunity to rub her ear against her shoulder until she was able to shake the communicator free: she couldn't afford the distraction just now. If it was something important, Mason could handle it.

Sa'rhi sighed loudly, checking the time on his pocket watch. "We're never going to make our rendezvous by playing defense. Hurry up and move them out of the way. You know how I hate to be late."

Nieve rushed the shield before the Shaper could come up with a new strategy. If these guys were trying to meet someone, then it was likely that Hane and Rose were in trouble. She had to hurry up and neutralize these guys so she could go protect the others. That was her job, wasn't it? Keeping everyone safe?

"Nieve, down!" Mason roared.

Nieve stepped aside, bringing her gauntlets up to protect her head. Something thin and straight zipped past her, shattering against the Shaper's shield. A second one followed in the same path of the first, allowing Nieve a better glimpse the second time around: it was a stone javelin, hurled with impressive force and precision. Nieve chanced a sharp look back at Mason, catching the wide grin on his face as he drew a stone rod from the quiver on his back and raised it into a throwing position, the shape of the rod stretching and changing into that of a javelin right before Mason let it fly. The Shaper's shield shattered at the third impact; he cried out as bits of broken stone rained down on him. Nieve darted in quickly with a punch to his gut, sending him flying backward. Sa'rhi sidestepped the limp body of his comrade before it crashed into the door and slid down into a boneless heap.

"And they came so highly recommended," Sa'rhi lamented, shaking his head. "I suppose it's true what they say: any job worth doing is worth doing yourself."

"Does that mean you're going to stay and fight?" Nieve asked, grinning. "Because I'm barely warmed up."

Sa'rhi's grin sharpened at the edges. "It's good that you're all warmed up. Because right now, I need you to turn around and subdue your comrade."

Confusion came first: why would Nieve want to fight Mason? Then the slick, slimy feeling of the command began to seep into her mind, making Nieve shake her head in revulsion.

Mind of Ice! Nieve thought rapidly, grateful that her Champion attunement had resisted the initial impulse to comply. Mind of Ice was a protective spell that locked down her thoughts, making her resistant to mind-reading spells, suggestions, and compulsions. All Champions had natural resistance to mind-altering magic, but with a mind mark, Nieve was particularly protected from them. As long as her Mind of Ice was stronger than Sa'rhi's control spell, he wouldn't be able to make her attack Mason.

But Mason, on the other hand . . .

Nieve saw the flicker of disappointment in Sa'rhi's eyes as she refused his command. His gaze tracked from her to Mason, giving Nieve a sinking feeling in her stomach. She could beat Mason in a fight, there was no doubt of that, but she didn't want to hurt him.

"Don't listen to him!" Mason shouted, clapping his hands over his ears. "Be careful, he's a Controller!"

"Yeah, I figured that out already," Nieve called back without taking her eyes off Sa'rhi. "Your trick didn't work and your guys are down. I'd love to lay you out right here, but I think our teammates need us. You want to go ahead and retreat for now?"

"If I must," Sa'rhi replied, sighing heavily. He set his hand on the Guardian's shoulder, turning him just enough to meet his eyes. "Pick up Gerrett and follow me."

The Guardian, still dazed and swaying with the movement of the train, nodded woozily. He pulled himself up by grabbing the edges of the luggage racks, making the top one groan threateningly before he staggered to his feet. Sa'rhi slid the train car door open, holding it open while the Guardian hefted the unconscious Shaper over his shoulder.

"I'll see you again before this journey is over," Sa'rhi promised, touching the brim of his hat in a mockery of respect. "Perhaps I can come up with an offer that will interest you into seeing things my way."

Nieve snorted. "Unlikely."

She held her position with her ice gauntlets raised in front of her until the train door slid shut. Only then did she allow herself to release Mind of Ice and Frost Form. Her ice gauntlets broke off her arms in chunks, crashing to the floor along with everything else that had tumbled down into the walkway.

"Watch it, coming through!" Mason barreled up the aisle, vaulting the dog crate before rushing past Nieve to get to the door. He left a trail of kicked satchels and squashed hat boxes in his wake, heedless of where he stepped. When he got to the door, he touched the handle, then jiggled it a few times. When it failed to turn and open the door, he heaved a sigh. "I locked it. Not even a conductor's key will open it until I fix it. Come on! Rose and Hane need us right now!"

"Right." Nieve shook off her spell exhaustion and shoved the dog crate back under the lowest luggage rack, clearing the biggest obstacle in the room, though it mattered little compared to the mess the Guardian had made. The sight of the dog's limp body caught her eye, conflicted feelings running through her as she glanced back at Mason's hastily bandaged hand. "Did you kill the dog?"

"Goddess, I hope not." Mason sounded guilty as he glanced down at the dog. "I didn't want to hurt it, so I made the air around its nose and mouth too thin to breathe. He passed out, but I didn't check on him after he let me go."

"We can check on him when we come back through," Nieve decided, pushing on. "We need to make sure Hane and Rose are safe first."

Mason nodded, but Nieve saw him hold his hand out toward the dog, casting a silent spell. Probably something to help him breathe. Poor creature was probably under the Controller's orders to attack. It was lucky the dog had attacked Mason instead of Nieve: she wasn't sure how she would have gotten it to let go without killing it outright. A loop of bloody bandage held a wad of gauze around Mason's hand.

"I can ice that for you," Nieve offered, pointing to his hand. "It won't heal it, but it'll take some of the pain away."

Mason considered the offer, then shook his head. "No, I want to be able to use it if I need it. We need to get to the others. Rose sounded pretty frantic over the communicator."

Oh, right, that thing. Nieve had left hers somewhere in the general rubble that cluttered the walkway. She'd have to find it later. Or not: she could always just partner with someone who understood how to use the damn thing.

Sharp winds stole Nieve's breath and tugged at her hair as she stepped out onto the platform between cars. Mason started to say something about securing the door behind them, but a flicker of movement beyond the porthole window of the next luggage car caught Nieve's eye. Someone was inside the car, walking down the aisle with their back to the window. Her sword was half drawn before Nieve recognized the person on the other side of the door.

"Hey!" Nieve shouted, barely able to hear herself over the wind and the rumble of the rails. She stepped over the gap between the platforms, shading her eyes from the sun to confirm her suspicions before tugging at the door's handle. When the door refused to budge, she pounded her fist against the circular window. "Hane!"

Was the door locked? It seemed sealed somehow. As she yanked and tugged at it, it seemed the latch would give way long before the door did. At least Hane hadn't appeared to be in any sort of danger, but why wouldn't the door open?

A slap on the window brought Nieve's focus up from the latch: Hane was shouting something on the other side of the door and pointing up at the roof of the train. The door wasn't soundproof but Nieve couldn't hear them over the roar of the wind and the rattle of the chains beneath the coupler. Was it Rose? Rose wouldn't have climbed up onto the roof, would she?

"Can you open the door?" Nieve shouted, giving it another yank. There had to be some trick that Nieve was missing; all the other doors had opened so easily. "Hane, open the door!"

"Move aside," Mason directed, stepping over the coupler. "If it's stuck, I might be able to finesse it open. Ask them if my sister's okay."

"I can't," Nieve confessed, tugging at her naked ear. "I lost my ear thing during the fight."

The motion caught Hane's attention, seemingly reminding them that they didn't have to shout through the steel door. Mason, crouched down near the door's latch with his palm pressed to the metal, frowned as Hane spoke into their communication device.

"We didn't see anyone with a crate," Mason replied, his free hand touching the device on his ear as he spoke. "We ran into some trouble, too. How is Prickles? Is she hurt?"

Nieve bounced anxiously on her heels, annoyed that she could only hear half the conversation. She'd have to find her earpiece when they went back through the luggage car, though finding it among all the spilled luggage was going to be a hassle. As long as it was taking Mason to open the door, she wished she could go back and search for it right away, but she was pretty sure Mason had said something about locking it. Now that she considered that, she realized she wasn't sure if Transmuters could cast spells on metal or not.

"Just a minute," Mason said, either to Hane or to Nieve or to the both of them. "Hane says they were ambushed by someone they believe to have an

Assassin attunement. Prickles is okay, but the Assassin got away with a crate. They said he ran off over the roof of the train."

"The roof?" Nieve repeated. "I thought we couldn't use the roof."

"Yeah, *we* can't," Mason said, dusting his hands off as he stood up. "Doesn't mean the spire constructs can't. Door was fused to the frame like it was welded shut. I got it open, but it's not my most elegant work."

It still took a strong yank to get the door open, even with Hane helping from the other side. Once it was open, it was wedged that way, allowing the wind inside to rustle the baggage and tug at the ends of the securing straps. Even so, this luggage car was in better shape than the first one: only a few trunks and crates had been shifted into the walkway, and fortunately none of them had popped open.

"The Assassin won't be far ahead," Hane said as soon as the door was open. "If we're quick, we can catch them before they find a place to hide with the crate."

"We won't catch up before he regroups with his teammates," Mason pointed out. "And tangling with an Assassin paired with a Controller isn't a match I want to take on without a healer present. What is that?" Mason pointed to a crate in the middle of the walkway. "Is that another dog crate?"

"No, that's one of the Keepsake crates," Hane explained, eyes scanning the roof of the train as if they expected to spot the Assassin up there. "The Assassin grabbed two but only got away with one. I was going to take this one back to the Keepsake car and see if it earned us any goodwill with the guards."

"Did you guys figure out what's inside?" Nieve asked, interested. It really did look like the dog crate in the first luggage car, only smaller. Maybe there was a puppy inside? That didn't make much sense, though.

"We were attacked before we could see inside any of the crates," Hane said, running their hand back through wind-tossed hair to brush it out of their eyes. "It's light, whatever it is."

"Let's take a quick peek," Mason suggested, wearing an impish grin. "It can't hurt, right? I mean, as long as we bring it back to the Keepsake car, we're not breaking any rules."

"Yeah, just a quick look," Nieve agreed, crouching down beside Mason. "We'll bring it right back. Right, Hane?"

Hane shifted their weight from side to side. They looked conflicted as if they'd rather chase after the Assassin instead. After a moment's hesitation, they rolled their shoulders in a shrug. "All right. Let's see it."

Mason turned the box around, finding the latches holding it closed. Nieve saw Hane shoot a quizzical look at the bloodied bandage on Mason's hand, but they turned their attention to the crate as Mason hinged open the lid.

Nieve barely caught a glimpse of a sleek, scaly body before the sound of the far door rolling open grabbed her attention.

"No, don't!" Rose barreled down the walkway, hair wild from the wind with soot streaked across her cheeks. She slammed her palm flat against the lid of the crate, eyes wide as she held it closed. The creature inside hissed in irritation.

"We were just looking," Mason protested. "We were going to bring it back."

"You don't understand," Rose admonished, checking the floor around the crate before flicking the latches closed. She flinched as the animal inside bumped the lid of the crate before she had it locked up again. "Hane, those polearms you saw weren't weapons—they were snake-catches."

"Snake-catches?" Nieve repeated, shooting a look up at Hane. "What are snake-catches?"

"It's a pole with a twisty hook on the end of it," Mason explained, cutting over Rose who still looked breathless. "What's the big deal? Is it one of the deadly venom ones?"

Rose shook her head, eyes still wide. "It's worse. Way worse." She glanced around quickly before looking up at Hane. "Where's the other crate? You got it, didn't you?"

Hane grimaced. "Sorry. The Assassin got away with it."

Rose hissed a word in Caelish that Nieve actually understood. She rose slowly, one hand reaching for her earpiece. "I'm calling the others in. We all need to discuss this."

CHAPTER 6

HANE

Wavewalker (leg mark), Citrine

It's been through some rough handling, but it's alive and well," Hane explained as they handed the crate over to a Keepsake guard wearing an extra gold bar on his uniform. "Can you confirm for us that there's a venomous snake in each one of these crates?"

"Not just any venomous snakes," Rose interjected with authority. "This is a shipment of ivory-crowned vipers, one of the rarest and most valuable snakes on the continent. Each one of these crates is worth ten times its weight in gold. Isn't that right, Chief Horace?"

"Yes, I'm afraid so." The chief guard looked grim as he handed off the crate to another pair of guards. He shook his head as he lifted his cap to wipe sweat from his forehead. Despite his heavy mustache, the pate beneath his cap was shiny and bald, with only a few wisps of iron-gray hair curling around his ears. "This shipment was supposed to be carried out with utmost secrecy. Keepsake Treasuries even paid for two shipments just like this one on separate trains and neither one of them was robbed. How could the Magpie know which train had the actual shipment?"

"The Magpie?" Odette asked, looking up from the notes she was taking in one of her booklets. "You already know who these bandits are?"

A loud bang made Hane twitch. They looked back over their shoulder toward the blackened and empty doorway of the train car, where Nieve and Mason were attempting to fix the door Rose had blasted open. Or rather, the door she insisted the Assassin had blasted open. Mason seemed to recognize his sister's work, though, by the dark looks he kept casting in her direction. Rose determinedly ignored him as she recovered the black coil Hane had fed through the window fewer than twenty minutes ago—another deed performed by the Assassin, according to Rose. Luckily, the guards seemed to believe her. Hane guessed that returning one of the two stolen vipers had earned at least that much goodwill.

"Well, no one's ever sure when it comes to the Magpie," Horace replied cagily. He paused as his guards confirmed that the crate Hane had recovered did, in fact, contain a live and healthy snake. They barely caught a glimpse of pearl-white scales and bony crest adorning the snake's brow before the lid was snapped shut and the latches flicked definitively closed. "All anyone really knows is that a particular thief is targeting shipments of valuable animals. We were hoping the fake shipments would have protected the real one, but it looks like they were ahead of us on this one."

"That's why we're here," Lief said, stepping in smoothly. "Keepsake Treasuries hired us to apprehend the Magpie, just in case they figured out this was the real shipment. That's how we were able to react so quickly and return this valuable snake."

That was a little much, considering that Lief had been at the other end of the train when the attempted theft occurred, but his natural charisma did seem to ease any of the guard's remaining suspicions.

"Can't say I don't appreciate the help," Horace admitted. "Just wish I'd known ahead of time. But that's Keepsake for you: the right hand doesn't know what the left hand is doing."

"Can you tell us anything about this Magpie?" Hane asked. "What they look like, or how they operate, or the type of crew they work with."

"Like I said, no one's really sure when it comes to the Magpie." Horace dabbed more sweat from his face with a handkerchief, his slim polearm—a snake-catch—resting back against his shoulder. Up close, Hane could see that the spiral tip of the pole terminated in a small hook with a blunted end. While they waited for Odette and Lief to traverse the train, Rose had explained that the tool was used for safe handling of venomous snakes, rather than as a weapon. "No one's really sure if they have an attunement or not, or what they look like, or even what happens to the animals after they steal 'em. I've even heard that there's more than one Magpie, but I don't know about that. All I know for sure is that Keepsake's internal investigation unit came up with the name 'Magpie' on account of the theft and the animal connection."

"It is a safe bet that someone who steals animals would go after ivory-crowned vipers," Rose commented, coiling her black wire around her hand. "If anything, it's surprising there's only one crew targeting a shipment this rich."

"Hey, I still don't know what's so important about these snakes," Nieve called over the wind whistling past the open doorway. She stood with her feet wide set on either side of the warped door, as if weighing it down while Mason pressed down on opposite corners, biceps bulging as he attempted to flatten it out. "Is there something special about its venom, or is it something else?"

"Ivory-crown venom is special," Odette answered, still scribbling notes in her little book. "It actively seeks out impurities in the bloodstream and body systems in order to produce a cleansing effect. When it's collected and refined, it's primarily used as the chief ingredient in Cure. You've seen those sold at climber shops, haven't you?"

Nieve's eyebrows shot up as she whistled long and low. "Those tiny vials are expensive! I never bought one because I always climbed with an Acolyte, but I know a lot of climbers who keep at least one in their med kits."

"I carry one," Rose confirmed, patting a pouch secured to her leg. "They're expensive, but it's the only curative known to purify almost any toxin entirely, no matter the delivery method. Which is better than most healers, except for Acolytes."

"I concur," Lief said, smiling ruefully. "I carry a kit with antivenins and cures for the more common toxins found in spires, but it's not exhaustive. Cure is better, but it's hard to justify the cost against upgrading armor and weapons."

Hane kept quiet, thinking of the two vials of Cure they kept in their dimensional bag. They didn't often shop in climber stores, so they didn't know the cost of a single bottle offhand. The two vials they had were taken from the supplies of fallen climbers, only one of whom had been a teammate. The other was already deceased by the time Hane found them.

"That makes this a rolling bank vault," Mason said, grunting as he sat back on his heels for a respite. "Why transport so many, though? Where are these snakes going?"

"The harvested venom isn't stable enough to ship," Horace explained. "It's easier to ship the snakes once they're old enough to start producing venom. These all came from a breeder in a secret location and we're delivering them to a lab that produces Cure. As you may have heard, breeding these particular snakes is a . . . delicate procedure."

"Why is that?" Hane asked. "Do they need a specific environment to lay their eggs?"

Rose cleared her throat like a teacher about to begin a lecture. Mason groaned loudly before resuming his efforts to straighten the door again.

"This particular snake doesn't lay eggs," Rose explained. "The female keeps the eggs inside her body until they hatch. It's called ovoviviparous birth. After the birth, the mother protects her young quite violently until they are old enough to produce their own venom. It's difficult to separate the young from the mother without being bitten while also giving the offspring enough space to grow and develop into juveniles. If they are kept in too small a space, they kill each other for resources. Too large, and the handlers can't catch them once they mature. It's a balancing act."

"Why don't people just go out and catch wild ones?" Nieve asked. "That's easier than robbing a train, isn't it?"

"Wild ivory-crowned vipers aren't as reliable as ones bred in captivity for multiple reasons," Rose enumerated, seemingly pleased to have a captive audience. "First, they are over-hunted for their venom. Plenty of people earn money by distilling their venom and making knockoff Cure products. Second, they require a very specific diet in order to produce the purifying venom. They can survive just fine by eating just about anything, but the ones that produce the highest-quality venom require a steady diet of fertilized lingen frog eggs—which are themselves quite poisonous. All that to say that while breeding and raising the snakes has its difficulties, the end result is more profitable than attempting to capture the wild ones."

"Sorry, one final question before we move on." Lief looked sheepish as he raised his hand. "If those frog eggs are necessary for these snakes to make the more potent purification venom, then has anyone tried manipulating the eggs directly, rather than feeding them to snakes?"

"It's been tried," Rose replied, throwing off a casual shrug. "So far, I don't think anyone has been successful. The conversion process isn't entirely understood, especially not for this species. Perhaps one day science will replicate the process directly from the frog eggs, but for now, we can only get it from the snakes."

"Twenty-one, twenty-two, twenty-three . . ." Odette counted under her breath, peering over the top of her glasses as she scribbled something down on her notepad. "Counting the stolen viper, you had twenty-four total? Or are there more in the other Keepsake car?"

"Just these ones here," Horace confirmed.

"Mm hm." Odette nodded, her mouth twisted to the side as she circled something in her notes. "Assuming that each snake produces a cubic half-inch of venom per day and the distilling process removes a third from the raw ingredient . . . combined with the preservatives, then the antiemetic . . . my calculations indicate that twenty-four ivory-crowned snakes would produce just under one thousand vials of Cure in a year."

"Only that many?" Nieve asked, surprised. "Then what was the point of stealing one snake? The bandits would need the whole car to make a worthwhile profit."

"He tried to run away with two," Hane reminded her. "He likely intended to grab a male and a female in order to begin his own breeding operation."

"Keepsake investigators believe the Magpie is a skilled animal handler," Horace commented. "There's never been any evidence of the animals being harmed, and there's been evidence that they use food to bribe animals into going with them, rather than more forceful methods. Some people theorize that they collect animals for a private menagerie, rather than for profit."

"If that's the case, then maybe one viper is enough," Odette murmured, tapping her pencil on her notebook. "But the Assassin was trying to uncouple the cars with acid, wasn't he? That indicates that the intent was to take the entire shipment."

"Are we sure the Assassin was working with the other three?" Mason shouted as Nieve slammed her heel repeatedly against the curled edge of the door. "That one with the dog, Sa'rhi, he said he didn't want to kill us because he was afraid of being discovered by an investigation. That doesn't sound like he was planning on getting off the train after uncoupling the cars."

"No, I'm sure they were working together," Rose said definitively. "The Assassin told us that he was expecting backup. I think he panicked when he saw he was outnumbered and grabbed the two crates just so he wouldn't return to his boss empty-handed."

"I think the logical conclusion here is that we need to capture and subdue the Magpie," Hane summarized. "From Nieve and Mason's account, it sounds like Sa'rhi is the ringleader, which probably means he's the Magpie. We need to figure out where his crew is hiding and catch them before they make another attempt to steal the cargo, or give up and flee the train."

"And return the stolen snake!" Horace added, giving Hane a pleading look. "The lab is counting on receiving a full shipment to manufacture Cure. Keepsake will take any losses out of our payment. We need you to recover that snake!"

That sounded like a bonus mission to Hane, but it seemed likely that if they found the Magpie, they would also recover the snake, so returning it would be simple enough. There were still plenty of questions, but the answers mattered less than simply completing the quest. Though there was something a little sad about so many captivity-bred snakes being shipped in tiny boxes to a distant laboratory to be used for their venom.

"Great, this is great," Odette murmured, still scribbling furiously. When she paused to look up, she withered under the incredulous stares of the Keepsake guards. "Um, I don't mean about the stolen snake, it's just . . . this has been really helpful for us. Let's, um . . ." She hedged a moment, looking around as if hoping someone would jump in and help her out. When no one did, she cleared her throat and spoke with forced authority. "Let's get the door back in place and set up some safeguards to protect this shipment from future attempts of theft or separation from the train. Once these cars are secure, maybe we could, ah . . ." Odette hesitated, then coughed into her fist. "We will formulate a plan of action."

"Aye, captain," Lief said with good humor. "How's it coming with the door, you two? I don't think I've ever seen anyone try beating a steel door back into shape before."

"Right? I'm usually the one breaking the door down in the first place," Nieve joked.

Mason sat back heavily, looking less amused as he took a long drink from his canteen. "Look, I'm trying to shape the metal, but I'm not used to working with steel in the first place, never mind steel that's been oxidized by an explosion. I can only influence one aspect of the metal at a time, and if I make it too pliable, Ribbons over here might snap it with her stompy-boots."

"Tails," Nieve corrected him, flicking one long end of her headband over her shoulder. "Ribbons sounds soft."

"Wait, are you actually shaping the metal?" Hane asked. "Do Transmuters get metal mana when they reach Citrine?"

"No," Lief said slowly, looking quizzical. "Not normally, anyway. Have you been hiding a second attunement from us, Mason?"

Despite his exhaustion, Mason managed a rakish wink at Lief. "You wanna come search me for magic marks?"

"Brick has a crystal mark from the Unclaimed Lands," Rose announced without ceremony. "It gives him access to metal mana, but he hardly trains with it at all."

"Practicing with a crystal mark is different from training an attunement, Prickles," Mason shot back at her. "And it's not like I climb all that often, so there's no reason for me to stress about training it up."

"Wait, you really have a crystal mark?" Nieve asked, incredulous. "Is that why you were talking about the gateway shrines earlier?"

"Huh? Oh, yeah." Mason had his hands pressed to the door again, forehead dripping sweat as he hunched over it. "I only challenged the Shrine of Cold Iron, but sometimes I think I'd like to go back and try a different shrine. Or maybe one of the temples. I'm not sure yet." He smirked up at Nieve, still standing on top of the battered door. "You and me, Tails, we could take on the Water Temple. Hane, you could come, too. I bet we'd have an easier time getting inside with you in the mix."

"What could you possibly need from the Water Temple?" Rose called before either Hane or Nieve could reply.

"It's not always about needing something, Prickles! Sometimes it's about the adventure."

"Maybe we can speed this along. The pair of you are distressing the guards." Lief held his arms out, like a dueling arbiter calling for a time-out. "Mason, if you like, I can give you a boost to help you channel metal mana more effectively. It would be temporary, but you'd get the door fixed faster."

"Would that work?" Mason asked doubtfully. "Crystal marks are a little different from attunements."

"I know. I'm familiar with crystal marks." Lief smiled disarmingly. "But I'm not actually changing the mark itself, I'm just altering the mana pathways to make them more efficient. It's similar to constricting or dilating blood vessels to speed or slow the flow of blood within a body. It'll go back to normal in an hour or so."

"All right." Mason shrugged. "I'll give it a try. What do I need to do?"

As Lief extended a hand to help Mason to his feet, Hane caught Nieve's eye, exchanging a significant look. Hane tapped the toe of their left foot, flicking their eyes down to Nieve's boot in a silent question. By the twist of her lips and the shake of her head, it seemed Chime still hadn't woken up yet. Was that strange? Or was that normal? It probably didn't mean anything that Mason had a crystal mark—plenty of climbers had crystal marks, after all, and even Hane could see how a Transmuter would find metal mana useful. Still, it seemed a bit of an odd coincidence. While they had never been to the Unclaimed Lands themself, the stories Hane heard were every bit as challenging and inhospitable as the spires themselves. Aside from natural hazards and the ever-present threat of monsters, the land itself seemed to reject human influence. It was mildly impressive that someone as carefree-seeming as Mason had decided to seek out a shrine just for the adventure.

Unless that wasn't the true story at all. It would have been nice to confer with Chime to see if they recognized Mason as the person who stole them from their shrine.

Although, as Hane watched Mason flirt unsuccessfully with Lief, it seemed a bit far-fetched to think that Mason could have had anything to do with Chime's broken and scattered consciousness. Not directly, anyway. And Chime themself didn't know how much time had passed since they'd been forced inside a challenger's crystal sword and used to trap other beings into unwanted contracts at the wielder's will.

"That should be it," Lief said, taking a step back from Mason as he rolled down his pant leg. Apparently the crystal mark was located on Mason's ankle. "Go on and give it a try. You should find metal shaping much easier now."

"Let's do this!" Mason flexed unnecessarily before stooping and pressing a hand to the metal door. Nieve laughed as the steel beneath her feet pressed flat into the floor. She walked along one edge, then the other, stomping down the edges as Mason did something that made the metal more malleable.

"Nice work," Rose commented, ambling over with Odette trailing behind. "But what's the plan now? You can't get it back into the frame like this: it's too big."

Mason scowled at his sister. "Why are you just saying that now? We could have propped this up in the doorway before I fixed it."

"Why do I have to come up with all the solutions?"

"Because that's like the one thing you do!"

"We can come up with a different solution for the door," Hane suggested in a low tone. "It doesn't have to be functional; it just has to serve as a barrier. It might be best to simply fuse it into the frame so it's that much harder for bandits to get inside the car."

"Fusing it would be easier than reshaping it to fit inside the track," Mason agreed bitterly. "But that platform outside isn't going to hold my weight long enough for me to fix it from the outside, and even with Lief's boost, I can't fix the platform *and* fuse the door in place."

"I can make a platform," Nieve suggested. "I make ice-bridges all the time. I'll hold it until you finish fixing the door."

"That could work," Rose agreed, nodding thoughtfully.

"Ah, I'm sorry to ask," Horace said, his gaze shifting from Rose to Mason before settling on Hane. "But if that door is sealed shut, how will you return the missing viper to us?"

"I can find a way around to the far door, or I can pass it through a window," Hane replied. "We'll try to keep you apprised of the situation, but it may be a while before we find out where the Magpie and their crew is hiding."

"It shouldn't take that long," Nieve protested, helping Mason lift the door to prop it up against the wall. "It's a train, so it's not like there are too many places to hide. The Magpie is either in a private guest cabin or one of the crew cabins, right?"

"Actually, I did notice a few, ah . . . potential hiding places on my way to the engine earlier," Odette said meekly. "But we can discuss those in a little bit. I think we should focus on keeping the cargo safe for now. Um, Hane? Could I ask a favor of you?"

"What do you need?"

Odette plucked one of the glass marbles off her bracer. Before offering it to Hane, she pinched a bit of putty out of an open belt purse and stuck it to the orb. "Can you stick this on the ceiling right above us?"

She dropped the marble into Hane's palm, where they peered at it curiously. At first glance, it appeared to be nothing more than a small sphere of glass, but upon inspection, Hane noted several tiny runes etched around the curved surface, all evenly spaced from one another. How could something this tiny be considered a trap?

There was a more important question to ask first, though.

"Does touching the ceiling count as touching the roof?"

"No, no." Odette seemed certain as she shook her head emphatically. "The ceiling is different from the roof. I've read reports of people attacking up through the ceiling without triggering the challenge scale. It's only if one of us tries to go up through the ceiling that the roof trap triggers."

"Okay." Hane was still skeptical. "But won't this trap affect the roof somehow?"

"It's a trapdoor spell." Odette beamed proudly. "It triggers after three steps: the section of roof underfoot will vanish and the person will fall into the train car. I designed it to work like the pit traps found inside spires."

Curious now, Hane had to ask: "How did you fit an entire trapdoor inside a marble?"

"It's something I've been working on with a friend of mine. I've been cataloging the mana types and runes that make up common spire traps and my friend figured out how to create the same effect by enchanting spell spheres," Odette explained, running her fingers along the rows of marbles still attached to her bracer. As she turned her wrist, it was easy to see where she had plucked off marbles to use as traps. "I don't completely understand it myself, but she says it works a bit like how a dimensional bag stores items in a state of stasis, but instead of storing an item, the sphere stores a pre-cast spell until it's activated. Most of them are pretty simple: trapdoors, smoke screens, darkness, loud noises, flashing lights, some illusions . . ."

Odette turned her wrist, pointing out different marbles as she listed their properties. Looking closely, Hane could see flecks of color in the center of each marble but couldn't differentiate one trap spell from another the way Odette apparently could. Hane squinted at a barren patch of Odette's leather bracer, their perception detecting the faintest shimmer of magic coming from the armor.

"Are the bracers enchanted, too?"

"No. Well . . . kind of." Odette flushed and shrugged. "I used a special thread enchanted with transference mana to stitch runes directly onto the leather, so the spell spheres stay in place until I remove them. Each rune creates a slight pull effect, so it's almost like the leather is magnetic. See?"

Peering closely, Hane could see the slight resistance as Odette plucked a sphere from her bracer. It didn't take a great deal of effort to remove the sphere, but it was strong enough to keep the marbles firmly in place. They weren't familiar with runes created by enchanted thread, which likely meant there was far more to it than simple stitching, but whatever else it involved lay beyond the scope of Hane's interest.

"Odie's one of the few people who can work with enchanted thread," Rose commented, watching the exchange with something akin to boredom. "Climbers commission her all the time for specialized armor enchantments. I bet you could retire from climbing and just make a living off your craft, Odette."

"That's . . . that's kind of you to say." Odette hunched into her shoulders like a turtle withdrawing into its shell. "Maybe one day? But, um . . . for now, I'm just really focused on my research."

With the novelty of the spell spheres and the embroidered runes explained, Hane glanced up to gauge the height of the ceiling, then leapt straight up, reaching above them to stick the putty side of the marble to the ceiling. When they landed, they looked to Odette for confirmation. "Will that do?"

"Yes, that should be perfect," Odette agreed. "Just let me set another tripwire trap over the door and we can be on our way."

"Uh, I'm going to seal this door in place," Mason advised her, hooking his thumb at the open doorway. "No one's going to be able to come in or out through here, so leaving a trap is a little redundant."

"Oh, right!" Odette slapped her palm against her forehead. "Let me go ahead of you so I can set this trap on the door to the luggage car. That way, I can show you all where it is so you can avoid it as you're coming through."

Mason gestured lethargically to the open doorway. "After you. I wouldn't want to seal you inside. Except for Prickles, maybe." He leered at his sister. "But then I'd feel bad for the snakes when she starts lecturing them about how to produce better venom."

Hane covered a smile behind their hand: judging by the venomous glare Rose leveled at her brother, it seemed she really could have given the vipers a lesson or two.

"You okay?" Nieve asked, frowning at Hane. "The Assassin didn't poison you, did he?"

"No," Hane said quickly, dropping their hand. "Do you need help with the ice bridge? You need to shape it around the coupler so you don't accidentally uncouple the cars."

"Yeah, I'm gonna arch the bridge up and over it," Nieve said, cracking her knuckles. She grinned as she nudged Hane with her elbow. "Are you as relieved as I am that we finally got to fight something? It felt so good to finally throw a punch again!"

"It was fine." Hane dropped back, allowing Nieve to reach the open doorway first. As much as they preferred battle-hungry Nieve to grief-stricken Nieve, Hane still wasn't comfortable with casual contact. They remembered Nieve's interactions with Sage and Emiko during their last climb in the Tortoise Spire and how often they hugged or wrestled or simply just leaned on one another. The three of them had been close—closer than most of the climbers Hane had met as a contract climber. Which was why Emiko's death had affected both Nieve and Sage so profoundly. Nieve had lost her confidence and Sage had lost his voice, his appetite, even his will at times. If it weren't for their final promise to unite Chime with their missing pieces and restore them to their proper shrine, Hane suspected neither Nieve nor Sage would have continued climbing.

That was precisely the reason Hane never wanted to be that close to anyone. They couldn't afford to let another person hold that much influence over them.

Sure, camaraderie looked nice on the surface, but it wasn't worth the fear, the anxiety, the second-guessing. And it wasn't worth the guilt that lingered long after a comrade's passing. No, better to keep one's distance. Take calculated risks. Walk away when they failed. Keep facing forward, keep getting stronger. That was what it took to survive.

Nieve looked out over the barely attached gangway, her face tightening with concentration as ice began to form beneath her feet, growing outward to arc over the train's coupler in a gentle slope before connecting to the luggage car's gangway. She let her breath go in a rush at the spell's completion, grinning as she tested the bridge with her weight.

"Good to go here!" Nieve called over her shoulder, shifting her weight to carry her forward in a glide. A slight bend in her knees took her up and over the gentle slope, and the slight drag of a turned-out toe slowed her enough to step seamlessly onto the other side. Hane waited just inside the doorway, ready to lend a hand to less competent ice skaters than Nieve.

"Oh, I can already tell this is going to be a disaster," Rose said, testing the ice with the toe of her boot. She appeared half wary, but also half amused. "Can't say I've had much opportunity to practice ice skating."

"It always looks so pretty when other people do it." Odette stood just behind Rose, eyeing the ice doubtfully. "I think I'll be happy if I make it to the far side without falling on my face."

"We'll help," Hane assured the both of them. "Just go slowly and watch your step. We won't let you fall."

Despite their assurances, Rose and Odette still appeared hesitant to step out onto the ice. After long moments of cold wind tugging at their hair,

Odette held her hand out to Rose, her smile more akin to a grimace. "Want to go together?"

"Yeah, okay." Rose's face was tight with caution as she gripped the inside of the doorway before clasping Odette's hand and easing herself onto the ice. Odette held on to the opposite side of the doorframe, squealing through a smile as her feet began to slide. Each took a moment to center themselves, eyeing the distance to the slope, then to Nieve just beyond, waiting with one arm extended to pull them across. Rose licked her lips, set her jaw, then released Odette's hand as she pushed off the end of the Keepsake car. Hane followed her onto the ice, ready to steady her if she needed it.

Rose was doing fine until she lifted her foot as if intending to step over the rising slope rather than glide over it. Her balance shifted, arms windmilling wildly as she fought to catch it. Before Hane could do anything, Odette pushed away from the train car with enough force to crash into Rose from behind. The two of them spun a half-circle, clutching each other and laughing as they fought to remain standing. Cautious steps got them turned around to face the luggage car again. Then, with a few false starts and a bit of backsliding, they charged the swell in the ice bridge at the same time, using speed and momentum to get up and over the incline. Odette's feet went out from under her and she landed on her backside with a yelp and a laugh, spinning halfway around before sliding onto the luggage car's platform. Rose fought frantically to keep her feet as she slid down from the top of the arch, but she over-corrected and nearly fell face-first onto the far platform. Nieve swept in for the rescue, catching Rose around the waist and pulling her in close before setting her down on the brass grate.

"I knew you'd fall for me eventually," Nieve said, grinning wickedly.

Rose looked flushed as she brushed her curls back from her face. "I warned you about using meathead lines on me, but considering the circumstances, I'm going to let it slide just this once."

"You can get across, right?" Lief asked Hane, once the women were safe on the far side of the bridge.

"I can," Hane assured him. "I'm just making sure everyone else gets across safely."

"That's good. I think Mason may need some help." Lief grinned as he indicated Mason with a jerk of his head. He hissed sympathetically as Odette pulled herself up using the railing; she looked to be in good spirits, but she winced as she rubbed her backside. "I think that's my cue. Watch out, I haven't done this in a while."

Lief stepped onto the ice tentatively, but he moved with gliding motions that indicated at least a passing level of competency. He skated a broad semicircle for speed before attempting to negotiate the slope in the center of the bridge. He got up and over it, but the momentum of the downslope had him going too fast and he had to catch himself against the luggage car door. Safely on the other side, he offered his hand to Odette for a healing spell.

"You got me, right?" Mason asked Hane as he eyed the ice skeptically. "I'm going to be about as graceful as Prickles was, and no offense, but you're a lot smaller than Tails over there."

"I'll manage," Hane replied. It was true: Mason was nearly twice their size, considering the difference between both of their heights and weights. But with the slide of the ice and some controlled transference mana, the size difference wouldn't matter very much. As long as Nieve stood ready to catch Mason before he crashed into the other car.

"All right, just keep me from falling while I fuse the door, okay?" Mason braced himself against the doorframe using both hands, holding himself up until he shifted his weight onto the ice. Hane circled behind him, ready to lend a hand as needed. Mason adjusted his grip, resting both palms against the side of the car before calling for the guards to place the door in its frame. It wasn't a perfect fit, but it came close enough that it didn't look as if it would be too difficult to meld the metal of the door to the metal of the frame. Hane only hoped that Lief's boost made it a quicker feat than flattening the door had been.

Mason muttered to himself in Caelish as he placed his hands on the door. One of his feet began to slip, so Hane braced it with their own, using their weight to counterbalance Mason. As they watched, the edges of the door began to blend with the frame around it. It wasn't the seamless work of a Forgemaster, but it seemed more than adequate for creating a solid barrier to protect the shipment of valuable snakes. Mason pounded on the door once, proving it was solidly in place before he carefully turned himself around, using the train as an anchor.

"Okay, so I gotta get from here to there, right?" Mason asked, nodding at the distance across the ice bridge. "Tell me this is easier than it looks."

"Not really." It would have been easier if Nieve had simply shaped her bridge around the coupler instead of over it. Her old team wouldn't have had any issues getting over the arch in the ice bridge, but her new teammates clearly weren't as familiar with using ice as a platform. "Let me get behind you and I'll push. Bend your knees and hold your hands out in front of you so you don't hit the train too hard."

"This is Prickles's fault, I know it," Mason muttered, his movements sharp and jerky as he fought to maintain his balance. Actually, spilling the acid on the gangway had been Hane's fault, but Rose's explosive certainly hadn't helped matters at all. "If we weren't on a train, I could make a stone bridge. Stone bridges aren't slippery."

"I won't let you fall. I promise." Hane stayed behind Mason as he turned to face the luggage car, placing their hands in the middle of his back. They would have preferred to push from Mason's shoulders, but he was far too tall for Hane to reach that high. In any event, they weren't pushing Mason with transference mana so much as they were pushing it through their own shroud. They just had to keep Mason steady so he didn't fall, or spin off to the side. "Ready?"

"Wait. Yeah." Mason flexed his knees slightly, arms akimbo. "Okay, push me."

Hane used a light touch of transference spread through their shroud to propel themself forward, pushing Mason ahead of them. Mason wheeled his arms once before holding himself steady. Hane felt the muscles in Mason's back clench as his feet slid up the incline of the arch in the center of the bridge, but he actually exhaled a laugh as he reached the peak. Hane let the slide carry Mason forward until he stumbled onto the luggage car platform.

"Ha! Not so bad." Mason smirked at his sister. "Better than you, anyway."

"I could have been more graceful with a little help, too," Rose retorted, sliding the door open. "Hurry up, Odette. We don't have that much time before the engine starts breaking down and it takes a while to set up all my casting equipment, never mind actually making all the parts we need."

"Sorry, sorry, one moment." Odette was on one knee, fixing one of her trap marbles to the doorframe. "Everyone's here now, right? Look at the height where I'm placing this trap. It's tripwire activated, so you need to step over it when you go through the doorway."

"What does this one do?" Hane asked.

"This one is a snare," Odette explained. "If anyone walks between the two spell spheres here, ropes will bind their legs together so that they trip and fall. I'm going to be placing other traps at the same height on all the luggage car doors."

"Can we mark it somehow?" Lief asked. "It's impossible to see the spheres from inside the car."

"I'll use an oil pen," Odette agreed, swiping her hands on her leggings. "It'll be faint, so you'll have to—whoa!"

As Odette straightened up, she stepped back just enough that her heel slipped on the edge of the ice bridge. Her leg shot out in front of her, eyes widening with fright as she fell backward. Hane lunged to catch her, but Nieve and Lief were both closer. It was a bit of a scramble as shoulders and elbows collided, but they each managed to grab one of Odette's outstretched arms and pull her back to her feet before she could fall. Her hands clutched at each of their sleeves as she caught her breath from her sudden fright.

"You're okay," Lief told her in a soothing tone. "Are you hurt? Do you want a calming spell?"

Odette shook her head, her hands still shaking as she pried them free of Lief's and Nieve's shirtsleeves. She forced out a breathy laugh before looking down to check the ground beneath her feet.

"I'm fine," she assured everyone. A tight swallow, then: "We should go. Yeah, let's—let's go."

Mason guided her over the tripwire, holding her by the shoulders to steady her. Rose followed close after, returning to the doorway with an oil pen to mark the height of the trap. Hane started to follow the others through the luggage car but stopped when they saw Nieve hanging back. At first, they thought she was planning to collapse her ice bridge, already cracking and flaking with the motion of the train, but then they noticed her expression: tight and pinched, her eyes nearly squeezed entirely shut.

"Nieve?" Hane asked, waving the others on ahead. "What is it? Are you . . ." Hane trailed off, glancing around to see if anyone had hung back before they tapped the heel of their left boot on the platform. When Nieve didn't respond, Hane raised their voice: "Nieve!"

"What?" Nieve gasped, looking startled. She looked around wide-eyed for a moment before grinding her knuckles into her temples. "Ugh, sorry, it's um . . . I can't really say."

Another furtive glance, then Hane switched to Artinian, just in case they were overheard. "Is it . . . them?"

"No, it's this—oh, wait. I mean yes. Yes, it's Chi—them." Nieve looked pained, her eyes nearly squeezed entirely shut. "It's just so loud! I can't make it stop."

"Can you power through?" Hane asked.

"Yeah," Nieve grumbled, knocking her knuckles against her head a few times. "I have to, don't I?"

"Try using one of your mental spells to see if that can help," Hane suggested, not sure if it would. "Keep up with the others. I'll stay behind and get rid of the bridge."

"The—oh, yeah. Thanks. I appreciate it." Before she stepped over the tripwire in the doorway, Nieve offered Hane a weak smile and clapped a hand on their shoulder, giving it a mild squeeze. Hane managed to bear the touch without flinching, but it left a phantom itch on their skin afterward.

Hane crouched down at the edge of the ice, placing their hands down in front of them. Ice was really just water, which was simple enough for them to work with. Water wanted to move, which made it greedily drink up the transference mana Hane fed into it. They had to work slowly, though, filling as much of the ice with transference—with motion—as possible, or else the ice could shatter into large pieces and strike the coupler as it fell. It was an easy enough spell, though, which meant Hane's mind was free to wander. While they meant to consider potential hiding places for the Magpie and their crew on the train, for some reason the sound of Odette's laughter echoed inside their mind, overlapping in ripples that made it sound like the laughter of many instead of just one.

"Hey!" The memory of a voice Hane thought they'd forgotten a lifetime ago. *"Want to chase some fireflies?"*

Childish laughter, childish games. Childish dreams severed by the stroke of a pen.

Hane squeezed their eyes shut, swallowing against the taste of bile on their tongue. Why remember any of that now? Their memories usually only surfaced in dreams, and even then, only when they spent too many nights outside a spire. A stranger's laughter shouldn't be enough to trigger such a recollection in itself, so why? Why now? Why this memory?

Hane's shoulder felt warm, tingly, like the residual effect of a harmless spell. If they turned their head, they could almost see Nieve's hand still gripping their shoulder. Their shirt still showing the marks of Nieve's friendly touch, Hane could almost see the hand of a child—of a friend—clasping their arm.

That was it: the connection. Not Odette and her laughter, but Nieve and her affectionate gesture. She probably hadn't meant anything by it—she'd been startled by a sudden pain that she couldn't share with anyone else on the team, not without violating the terms of their travel arrangements, paid for by the Dalenos government. Nieve was just a physical person; the gesture had likely been more for her own reassurance than Hane's.

But then, why had it affected them so much? They should have been able to shrug it off, like pushing Mason across the ice, or allowing a healer to cast a diagnostic spell through touch. It wasn't personal, even if Nieve did want them to become closer as teammates.

Maybe they needed to set firmer boundaries. Explain their discomfort to Nieve and ask her to respect it. Even that felt too personal, but if it kept the bitter memories vague and distant, it might just be worth it.

With a start, Hane realized they had filled the ice bridge with so much transference mana that it was beginning to vibrate the platform they perched on. With one final, evenly distributed Burst spell, the ice bridge blew apart into fragments no larger than snowflakes, the wind whipping them away before they could fall. Hane lingered a moment longer, ensuring that the coupler remained engaged before leaving the recollections behind to rejoin their current team.

Inside the luggage car, Odette attached new spell spheres to the inside of the doorway, her glasses flashing in the light as she turned her head to smile at Hane. The others were outside on the gangway, Nieve holding the sliding door open as she waited for Odette and Hane, the skin around her eyes tight as she faked a smile.

". . . locked it inside the crate when we came through earlier," Lief was saying as Hane approached. "It was groggy, but it was still alive, poor thing."

"Stupid dog," Mason muttered, one hand gripping the other. Hane had noticed the bloody bandage earlier, but Lief must have healed him at some point because the skin looked smooth and unbroken now. "We should do something to make sure Sa'rhi doesn't use it to attack us again."

"You're not going to kill him, are you?" Odette asked Mason, her eyes enlarged through the lenses of her glasses. "It's not his fault he bit you if he was under orders from a Controller."

"No, I'm not going to kill a dog," Mason said, though he still sounded resentful as he massaged a phantom pain in his hand. "I just don't want to give it back to the Controller again. Hey, Prickles! Did you ever tell me that Controllers could give orders to animals? Because I don't remember that lecture."

"It depends on the animal as well as the Controller." Rose didn't look up from rearranging her tiny throwing daggers, filling in the empty slots with knives from the back of her belt. "The way I understand it, you need different spells for different species, and just like with people, mental resistance varies. For instance, it's easier to mind-control your own pet than a pet that's loyal to someone else, especially if you're trying to make that animal turn on its owner."

"See, why can't you just give useful answers like that one?" Mason asked, striding past Rose as Odette cleared the doorway. He stepped carefully over the trap, wobbling treacherously when Rose threatened to push him. He scowled when he made it safely out onto the gangway. "What? That was a compliment!"

"It was not, you meatheaded, stone-slinging, barely literate barbarian," Rose snapped. "And for the record, I have explained mind-control spells on animals to you before. It's not my fault you weren't listening."

"What's that, Prickles?" Mason called from the next car over. "I can't hear you."

Before Rose could respond, Mason slammed the door shut. He made childish faces through the porthole window until Rose hurled one of her throwing knives at him. It struck the window with a wet splash, coating the glass in red liquid.

"What was that?" Nieve asked, looking startled. Whatever Chime was doing, it seemed it had Nieve thoroughly distracted.

"Just paint," Rose said sourly. "I use red because it looks like blood. People freak out when I hit them with one of these, even if it doesn't actually break the skin." She crossed her arms and tapped her foot, glaring down at Odette as she set a trap outside the door. "Are you planning to do that for every single door? Can you go any faster?"

"Sorry, sorry!" Odette jumped to her feet, wiping her hands off on her pants. "Um, just be careful, okay? This car is a little, um . . ."

"Wrecked," Nieve finished for her. "Oh, and I also sort of lost my earpiece in here somewhere."

"I'll help you look," Rose offered. "Since I know Odette is going to waste more time setting a trap on this door, too."

"It'll only take a minute!" Odette protested. She balked when she stepped inside the car, the spilled luggage and half-broken storage rack giving her pause. "Oh my, did this get even worse after we walked through it? It looks like Aellan ran amuck through here."

"Aellan?" Hane asked, hopping up onto the edge of the lowest luggage rack, choosing to walk along the rail than through the mess on the floor. "Is that someone from a local legend or a book?"

"No, Aellan is one of Byakko's many children," Odette replied, carefully picking her way through the clutter. "He's known for creating chaos out of order, or sowing discord within a society. Although I guess you could call that local legend, since we don't really have many confirmed accounts of him."

"Careful," Mason warned from the front of the car. "If you're not a fan of Prickles's lectures, you're not going to like it when Odie gets started on Byakko's children."

Odette's cheeks flushed with color. "I just like reading up on them, that's all. They're all so unique, with different motivations and different strengths, I just can't help but think it would be so interesting to meet one of them. Er, one of the nicer ones, I mean. Hopefully not Aellan."

Odette made a motion like flicking water off her fingertips. Strangely enough, both Rose and Mason mirrored the gesture, though they almost seemed to do it independently of Odette. Hane glanced back at Nieve, meeting her questioning gaze with their own. Lief chuckled as he slogged through the ankle-deep mass of spilled clothing and trampled satchels.

"It's a common warding gesture in Caelford when talking about the children of the god beast," Lief explained. "It's said that if you mention one of Byakko's children by name too many times, they'll get angry and interfere with your life. The flicking motion is like spraying water on a cat to make it go away."

"Does it actually work?" Nieve asked.

Hane stared at her, hoping no one else noticed the absurdity of the question.

Lief scoffed. "Even if one of Byakko's children is made of pure fire, I don't think sprinkling a little water on them is going to make them run away in fear."

"It's more superstition than anything else," Odette explained, plucking a pair of spell spheres off her bracer. "I doubt saying an entity's name would actually earn their ire, but just in case, we add the warding gesture. Isn't there something similar in Valia? A ring of iron, or something like that?"

"The ring of steel to ward against bad luck." Lief touched his hip, where his sword would be if he hadn't left it in his cabin. "That's a regional belief, but yes: after someone says something unlucky, supposedly you can prevent bad luck from befalling you by striking the steel of your sword hard enough to make it ring." To Nieve, he added, "And no, it doesn't actually work."

"So it's like a cherry blossom petal landing in your matcha?" Nieve asked. She'd made it halfway along the length of the car, and while it looked like she was searching the floor for her missing earpiece, Hane could tell she was actually holding her head, as if easing a splitting headache. "No, wait, that means good fortune, doesn't it? What's the bad one?"

Hane shrugged and they shuffled through the wreckage of spilled luggage. If they ever drank matcha beneath a cherry tree, it would have been inside a spire. That probably carried a different meaning entirely.

Rose huffed hard enough to blow the curls back from her face. "How long does it take to set a trap, Odie? Did you even consider that the mess in here practically makes this a trap as it is?"

"Oh." Odette paused in setting up her spell spheres, looking back along the cluttered car. "Sorry, it takes a while to line up the tripwire traps just right. The runes are hard to see, and if they're not lined up perfectly, then—"

"Ugh! Forget it, I'm going ahead to set up my casting equipment." Rose shoved the door open, carefully stepping over Odette and her trap. "Nieve, find your earpiece or you'll owe me a replacement. Brick, I'm going to set up my stuff on the floor, and Byakko save you if you step on anything."

"Maybe don't set things up in front of the door, then!" Mason shouted after her. Rose only stopped long enough to make a rude gesture at him before flinging the rolling door shut behind her.

"Too much yelling," Nieve muttered, kicking lazily through the detritus of luggage, her eyes downcast and barely focused. "Can we eat after this? I'm thinking of having some magpie for lunch."

"The way you said that makes me curious as to what you think a magpie actually is," Lief said with an amused grin. "Care to elaborate?"

"Tch. Everyone knows that a magpie—found it!" Nieve ducked down, genuine relief in her expression as she plucked something small and shiny from the floor. "Wow, that's a relief. I really didn't want to upset Rose over this."

"I wouldn't mind going after the Magpie right now. I have a score to settle with them." Mason curled his hand into a fist as Nieve fixed her communication device to her ear. "Can you use your attunement to locate them, Odie? It would save us the trouble of searching the whole train."

"No, it doesn't quite work like that," Odette said, her eyes narrowed and focused as she adjusted the height of a spell sphere. She lifted her glasses to rub her eyes before standing up and twisted her back from side to side. "The only reason I can find any of you if you were lost is by searching the unique pattern of your location trackers. Even if I saw the Magpie myself and identified a unique pattern that I could memorize and search for, once he took it off I'd only be tracking the item, not the person."

"We should probably sit down and strategize anyway," Hane suggested. "Didn't you say you found some things you needed to tell us?"

"Oh, yes, that's right!" Odette's knotted cord of rings clinked as she stepped over the invisible tripwire trap across the doorway. "Most of it is engine-related, but I did find a few secrets, some side quests, and maybe some hidden objectives. Let's go talk in one of the cabins. Watch your step!"

Mason and Lief followed Odette across the gangway to the next car while Nieve continued to trudge through the car. Hane stepped up beside her, hesitating only momentarily before touching the back of her hand. Nieve didn't react at all, but the moment their skin came in contact, they were assaulted by sounds so loud that they could almost be seen. It had to be Chime, reacting to some stimulus, or perhaps attempting to communicate, but Hane couldn't parse the sounds clearly enough to find a hidden message. It was like the scream of the wind mixed with blaring horn instruments, all drowned out by the reverberating boom of thunder pealing on and on. Hane very nearly drew back, but instead they grit their teeth and attempted to communicate with the shattered entity.

Chime! Hane shouted within their mind. *If you can hear me, stop! You're hurting Nieve and we don't know how to help you. Try to calm down and tell us what you need.*

If Chime heard them, they didn't answer in words, but there was a sharp ebb to the noise inside their head. The clamor didn't die off immediately, but the scream of the wind turned into something more like rain on a lake, and the blaring horns became the clatter of tin and brass striking one another. The thunder lessened, becoming more of a dull and distant rumble.

Nieve slumped as Hane drew their hand away from hers, a weak smile on her face. "Thanks," she said, pushing hair out of her face. "I kept trying to talk to them, but they just kept getting louder. At least I can hear my own thoughts again now."

"Have they said anything?" Hane asked. "Why they woke up, or why they were making that noise?"

"Nothing in words so far," Nieve explained, drawing in a breath as she straightened. "Maybe we can try talking to them after the team meeting."

"Okay," Hane agreed. "Just don't exhaust yourself. We need you if the Magpie attacks again."

Nieve chuckled bitterly. "Trust me, if I get the opportunity to punch something, I will not be holding back."

CHAPTER 7

NIEVE

Champion (mind mark), Citrine
??? (heart mark), Sealed

So, I compared the entire inventory to the logs, and found huge inconsistencies," Odette explained, flipping through one of her notebooks. She had three different ones open on the knee-high table in front of her, as well as one in her hand. "Some of the engineers admitted that they knew about a few spare parts they had left on hand, but everyone seemed shocked when I pointed out that an entire tool chest was just missing. When I tried asking who verified the supplies, they couldn't find the engineer who signed off on the logs."

"Not only that, but we found evidence that some of the enchantments on the engine parts had been tampered with as well," Lief added as Odette paused to make a note. "It doesn't look like a case of negligence; it looks like sabotage, plain and simple."

"That would imply that at least one of the engineers is on the Magpie's crew," Hane surmised. "But what does sabotaging the engine have to do with stealing the Keepsake cargo?"

It was a good question, but Nieve couldn't keep up with the conversation as the ringing in her ears crested to a peak, drowning out the voices around her. She tried to discreetly massage her temple and wait for the noise to diminish again.

Originally, Odette wanted to discuss the plan in one of the private cabins, but Rose wouldn't allow anyone inside her room while she was getting her equipment set up, and the rooms were small anyway, so someone (Nieve wasn't sure who, because the ringing in her ears had been loud then, too) had suggested holding their meeting in the lounge car, where there was more space and comfortable chairs. It was hard to focus on anything other than the noise inside her head, making it difficult to follow the conversation. She tried to participate in the discussion whenever the noise hit a low note, but she would lose the thread again whenever the pitch reached a crescendo. Hane kept shooting concerned looks at her across the table, but there wasn't anything either of them could do about it.

Not unless Nieve kicked her boot off and tossed Chime out a window.

Of course she would never do that, but it had become a fond daydream whenever the ringing tone made her vision blurry.

Chime! Nieve "shouted" from her mind, not for the first time. *Chime, stop it! Use words! Words that I can understand! Human words!*

No response, other than the wave of noise receding slightly. She used to think that meant Chime had heard her and was trying to reply, but now that hope tasted bitter on her tongue.

This can't go on, Nieve thought, only distantly aware of her teammates talking around her. *I need to hear what they're saying and I need to help strategize. There has to be some way to make this stop.*

She'd already tried using Mind of Ice, a spell that protected against mind reading and compulsion, but it had done nothing to block the sound that wasn't truly a sound. Most of her other spells involved protecting her body or conjuring ice, neither of which was helpful for dealing with an ancient entity trapped inside a shard of crystal. She did have a few spells that used mental mana, but she couldn't see how Detect Aura or Detect Mind would help her here.

If I could reach Chime's mind, like with a communication spell, maybe that would help, Nieve though miserably. *I don't know how to do that, though. Or even if I can use mental mana like that. What else does mental mana do?*

Sage would know, but Sage wasn't here. Mental mana made up the primary mana type of Sage's attunement as a Seer. He'd even helped Nieve practice the few mental mana spells she knew. She missed him intently just then—not just for his insights, but also because if he'd been here, he would have been the one listening to Chime's cacophony.

Thinking of Sage reminded Nieve of all the training sessions they'd spent together, practicing spells or trying new casting methods on familiar ones. It seemed like such a long time ago when Nieve had struggled with using her heart pathway to conjure ice or water; it came so naturally to her now.

Nieve blinked, a sudden thought occurring to her. She was terrible at practicing new spells on her own, but what if she didn't need a spell? Chime's crystalline shard was pressed against her skin, after all. Maybe all she needed was to establish a mental connection somehow; Chime should be able to do the rest from their side.

As long as this crazy idea worked.

Nieve drew a breath and concentrated, drawing her mental mana out of her mind mark. One of the first lessons any attuned person learned was how to infuse their shroud with mana, and Nieve's go-to mana type had always been enhancement for protection, though on occasion she might use water mana instead. She'd never tried filling her shroud with mental mana before, but the process was similar enough that it only took a few tries before she could sense it wrapped around her: silent and invisible, but just as present as the air she breathed.

The invisible mana suffusing her shroud caused strange auras to fade in and out of sight. Sounds seemed sharper and carried more meaning than usual. She made the mistake of glancing down at Odette's open notebooks and felt as if each word was inscribed directly on the inside of her skull—at least Odette's writing was in Caelish, so it held no meaning for Nieve.

A part of her mind wished to puzzle out the writing—she could decipher it if she only tried—but luckily she was soon distracted by a sensation that could only be described as a "tug" at her spell. The ringing sound slowly petered out as a consciousness other than her own spoke inside her mind.

<Nieve?> The gentle tinkling of wind-blown chimes filled her head—a blessed change from that infernal screaming-ring. <Is that you? Can you hear me?>

I hear you, Nieve thought, releasing the mana from her shroud. If the ringing hadn't already given her a headache, the excess mental mana would have. *What's wrong with you? Why were you making that noise? Why couldn't you hear me?*

<I hear you now.> Somehow, Chime managed to sound relieved—odd for an inhuman being that predated the arrival of the goddess on Kaldwyn. <I have been trying to find my way back to you. I was unaware of how my power might affect you.>

What do you mean, find your way back? You've been with me this whole time. Nieve rocked her boot, confirming the shard against her skin. *We've never lost contact.*

<This vessel is not myself,> Chime said, their mental voice slowly growing in strength, but mercifully not in volume. <This piece of broken sword may not have left your side, but my mind was driven far from this anchor by a touch of immensity that staggered my being as I am now.>

Really? Nieve thought back, trying to guess at what could have affected Chime so powerfully. *I could hear you just outside the spire, but after I passed through the gateway, you went silent. Is it because this is a different spire from the one we found you in?*

<No, that would not affect me so.> The notes of Chime's voice carried an echo of reflection. <I believe it occurred just as you were passing through the portal. I felt the familiar magics of transport and passage take hold, and then I felt myself seized by a vast, deep silence. As a being of sound and music and rhythm, the pure absence of anything that makes me *me* was so terrifying that my consciousness receded from it. I might even have been driven back to that accursed sword, if not for the other piece of myself hidden somewhere within this structure of power. I attempted to find my way back to you and to this vessel, but a cone of silence surrounds you still, making it difficult to find my way.>

What did that mean? A cone of silence? She hadn't noticed anything strange since entering the spire; her magic and strength all felt normal. Was Chime referring to Nieve's grief or self-doubt? That seemed unlikely, considering that doubt had been with Nieve ever since she'd recovered from her final fight in the Tortoise Spire. But then again, Sage had been Chime's primary guardian up until he began his Judgment. Was it Nieve's fault that Chime lost their way?

<As I searched for a way to return to you, a single note pierced the silence,> Chime continued. <I sensed something familiar, something calling me to return to myself. I extended what little power I could to try and break through the silence that surrounds you. It was not until your mind enveloped mine that I was able to fully return to this vessel.>

That last part likely referred to Nieve flooding her shroud with mental mana, but it still didn't explain the silence, nor whatever had helped guide Chime back to the crystal shard. Now that she knew Chime had been overpowered and scared, she felt a little selfish that she'd only meant to stop the cacophony of noise within her head.

<For that, I do apologize,> Chime said, most likely interpreting Nieve's nebulous thoughts and feelings. <I did not realize my power would affect you in that way. It was not my intent to cause you any pain or distress.>

I know you didn't, Nieve assured them. *Just, maybe try not to be so loud in the future? If I'd been in a fight, I probably would have been skewered.*

A long, low hum seemed to indicate hesitation. <It is normally so easy for sound to pierce through silence; it was distressing to learn that as I am, the silence overwhelms. Do you happen to recall the spark that called me back to you? The familiar magic that pierced the silence?>

When had the noise started? Just thinking about it brought back the shadow of a headache.

I fought a Guardian and a Shaper, Nieve thought, rubbing her forehead. *An enemy tried to mind-control me, but I resisted. I used a spell called Mind of Ice that protects me from mental spells; could that be the silence you're talk-ing about?*

Sharp, high notes denoted something like offense, but they softened quickly. <At my full power, such a spell would be far beneath my notice, but perhaps as I am now, it affects me more profoundly than I realize. I accept this as a possibility, but I do not think it was the cause.>

Okay. What else happened earlier? Now that Chime was no longer screaming inside Nieve's head, the voices of her teammates were clearer. Mason's deep, rich voice was particularly distracting, but at least it sparked a memory. *Oh! Mason has a crystal mark! He said he got it from the gateway crystal of metal and he was using a metal shaping spell earlier. Could that have been the familiar magic you felt?*

<Perhaps,> Chime allowed slowly. <I share little in common with the dominion of metal, but I would not fail to recognize the power of my own kin. It is possible that the use of such magic aided me in returning to this vessel.>

Raised voices caught Nieve's attention: she listened to her teammates long enough to get the gist of the argument. It seemed there was a potential side quest that involved changing the train's route for an unplanned stop at a remote station. Mason was arguing in favor of it, saying they could use the opportunity to fix the entire engine at once, instead of relying on the auxiliary engine. Lief argued that the reward for the side quest wasn't worth the delay. Odette seemed to want to take Lief's side, but instead of arguing, she ducked her head and scribbled in one of her notebooks, only pausing to fill in a fact or two.

Before Nieve could listen to either point long enough to take sides, Hane caught her eye, making the hand sign for "vault" subtly. Emiko had often used hand signs during spire climbs, so it was easy to recognize, but it pricked at Nieve's grief as she remembered Emiko's beaming smile whenever she used signs.

Translating Hane's signal, Nieve returned to her silent conversation with Chime.

Now that we're inside the spire, can you sense your other piece? Nieve asked. *The vault should be on the next floor, so if it's there, it should be close by.*

<I do sense a piece of myself within this structure; however, I have come to understand that physical distance means little in places such as this,> Chime replied. <While I am able to trace a straight path from our location to my other self, it is not a path you would be able to walk.>

As frustrating as that answer was, it did make a degree of sense. While Nieve understood that the floors inside spires didn't always ascend sequentially, she still found it easiest to think of them that way.

Can you tell me anything about where you are? Nieve asked, trying a different tack. *Can you see anything that might help us figure out if you're inside the vault on the next floor or not?*

<The only knowledge I can glean from my other piece is that while I was initially brought to the space of darkness and silence, the space has remained intact and unchanged in the whole time since my piece was moved there. This differs from how you found this piece of me, as the space around me changed constantly: the floors and walls would move, the magic of the environment would ebb and flow like birdsong, reshaping textures and times and patterns.>

It was strange to hear so much from Chime: they had been silent all throughout the train voyage from Dalenos, and even in the mana-saturated grounds outside the spire, they had spoken little louder than a whisper. Unfortunately, nothing they were saying could be considered "straightforward" to Nieve. <In that first spire, I could sense humans when they came close to me. I even tried connecting to them, as I did with the human who woke me in the fountain of power.> Nieve's guts clenched at the memory of Lani holding the crystal shard so tenderly, her eyes full of awe. Lani, who argued so strongly in favor of dropping everything in order to aid Chime in their quest to be whole again. Lani, who never left the spire again after that climb. <The piece of me that is here has not sensed the presence of humans in quite some time. I was beginning to fear I would never be found if no one ever sets foot in this place.>

Nieve tried not to think rude thoughts while Chime could hear her, but she couldn't help but feel Sage would have been the better person to handle this conversation. Chime was speaking as if they were in two places at once—and indeed they were—but Nieve had trouble following that type of conversation. Maybe it would have been better to let Hane carry the crystal shard on their person, but privately Nieve and Sage had agreed that until they had more than one of Chime's pieces, one of them should hold onto the shard. Outwardly, they each justified it as their desire to fulfill Lani's last wish, but Nieve couldn't help but feel it was also a matter of trust: Hane hadn't earned it yet.

<I have upset you,> Chime stated after the turbulence of confusion, frustration, guilt and doubt passed. <I am sorry I cannot be more clear. My limited interactions with humans combined with my limited memories and power make it difficult for me to understand what is expected of me.>

It's not your fault, Nieve assured them. *It would be different if you were talking to Sage. He's really good at piecing together this type of information; it's just hard for me to understand what you mean.*

A thoughtful pause. <I had similar communication issues when first learning to speak to beings such as yourself. Our forms and natures are far different from each other. Over time, I learned to adjust the way I spoke in order to be understood, but it seems likely that some of those lessons have been lost along with my memories. Perhaps if we were to speak more, it would help us understand each other better?>

That's a good idea, but I can't always stop for a conversation, Nieve replied, shifting her focus back to the discussion her team was having. She listened just long enough to hear Odette listing all the various different train routes through the mountains before returning to her conversation with Chime. *I'm sort of missing out on listening to my teammates right now by talking to you. Not to sound rude or anything. Sorry.*

<What is your team discussing right now?>

They're trying to put together a plan to finish this scenario, Nieve explained. *Once we're finished here, we move on to the next floor, where we think your missing piece might be.*

<Then that is a worthy discussion,> Chime intoned. <May I listen to the conversation?>

Nieve hesitated, glancing around at her teammates again. Only Hane caught her eye, their eyebrows pinching into a furrow that asked a silent question. Nieve longed to explain the whole long conversation to them, but asking to leave now would seem far too suspicious.

Can't you hear them? Nieve asked. *You're as close to them as I am. Or does the boot muffle the conversation?*

<As I am now, I can only perceive things that I am in contact with. I can sense concentrations of complex mana all around us, as well as the power inherent to this structure we are within, but it is not the same as seeing or hearing as you would describe it.>

So . . . how would you listen in, then? Nieve asked. *You know I can't just expose you to the other climbers; the Dalenos government is only funding our trip around the continent provided that we keep your mission a secret so you don't get stolen from us.*

<I do understand,> Chime stated. <But if you grant me permission, I can look and hear through your perceptions. I will have a better sense of when to speak to you if I know what is going on around you.>

Nieve's nerves spiked sharply before she could formulate a polite response. The first time Chime began speaking within the crystal shard, Nieve had been wary of touching them for fear of being placed under a mind-control spell. But since then, Chime had spoken to Soaring Wings administrators and a representative of the Dalenos government, and none had seemed at all affected, either magically or physically. If Chime had the ability to take control of someone's mind, surely they would have taken control of someone with greater power and authority than Nieve, wouldn't they?

That rationalization wasn't as reassuring as reminding herself of her attunement's natural ability to resist being mind-controlled. Chime's ability to sense mana concentrations was tempting, too—maybe if they looked out for spells and auras, then Nieve wouldn't have to keep using her own Detect Aura spell all the time.

Fine, I give you permission, Nieve allowed. *Do you need me to do anything?*

<No. Just shift your focus back to the discussion, and I will be with you.>

Nieve didn't feel any different as she tuned into the discussion again, though Chime's silence certainly helped her pay better attention. Not that a list of crossings and stations was all that interesting, but for some reason Odette seemed adamant about mentioning each one.

"... then the left fork takes us to Snowdrop Pass and over a trestle bridge," Odette was saying, one knee drawn up to her chest as she read a list from one of her notebooks. "And as we said before, trestle bridges hold too much potential for disaster, so we really don't want to reroute that way."

"See?" Lief pointed out emphatically. "Look, I understand the desire to complete the escort quest, I really do, but I just can't justify taking a route that would add almost a week to our schedule."

"That's all worst-case scenario," Mason protested. "There's a really good chance that we can get back on this same line even after the escort quest. We just have to—"

"I agree with Lief and Odette," Hane chimed in softly. "It would be nice to reunite the family that was separated at the train station, but nothing bad will happen to them if they have to wait for another train to take them back down the mountain. It's not just the unpredictability of the passes that concerns me, but the amount of time we would need to be stopped in order to fully fix the engine. We would have to divide our team in half, and a stopped train is much easier to rob than a moving one."

"There!" Lief thumped his hand down on the table. "An excellent point. Nieve, where do you fall on this?"

"Er . . ." Nieve didn't want to admit that she'd barely heard anything, so she defaulted to the easy answer. "I'm with Hane. It just makes more sense that way."

The crinkle of Lief's eyes told her that she hadn't entirely gotten away with being distracted, but since she'd taken Lief's side, he wasn't going to say anything about it.

"That's a majority," Lief declared, sitting back in his lounge chair. "Okay, enough about side quests. We need to talk about the main objective, which is capturing the Magpie."

"And protecting the Keepsake cargo, and fixing the engine, and protecting the train from the rockslide at the canyon," Odette added, drawing circles in her notebook. "Capturing the Magpie doesn't help us if we don't arrive safely at the station to hand him over to the authorities."

"Yes, of course," Lief agreed. "But the engine is Rose's responsibility, and the rockslide isn't until the day after tomorrow. What I meant to say was that we should focus on capturing the Magpie sooner so we're not spread too thin later."

"Why not let the Magpie and crew come to us?" Hane suggested. "We know what they're after, so setting up an ambush should be fairly simple."

"Mm . . ." Odette flipped through a few pages of notes before shaking her head. "It would be nice if it was that easy, but stepping back to look at the full picture, this Magpie bandit seems to have a few contingency plans in place. If we just set up a guard around the Keepsake cars, that leaves the engine vulnerable to further sabotage. If the train stops, they'll have a much easier time stealing all the cargo and running away. If we don't set up enough protection around the Keepsake cars, they'll just uncouple the cars and get away clean. And we can't rule out the possibility that if we delay the bandits too long, they might start attacking the passengers and crew. Finding and capturing the Magpie before that is the only surefire way to earn the maximum scenario reward."

That made sense to Nieve. Also, it sounded like a fight, so naturally she was on board with it.

"How do you propose we find the Magpie and crew?" Hane asked, more curious than argumentative. "We don't want to cause a panic among the passengers. Especially since we know they have a . . ." Hane trailed off, looking around cautiously before making the hand sign for "snake." That confused Nieve at first before she understood: not everyone liked snakes, and she could just imagine the sort of riot it would cause if passengers thought there was one loose on the train somewhere.

"Oh, I should show you the map! I can show you everything that way. Hold on." Odette stood up to free a loop of knotted cord wound around her belt. After walking her fingers along the length of the cord, she slipped her middle finger through a plain-looking metal ring without freeing it from the knot that secured it to the strand of rings. When she sat back down, the cord of rings clicked against the edge of the table, moving with her as she pressed her palms down flat on the small table. She drew a breath and closed her eyes, lifting her hands as she spoke. "Display Secrets."

A hazy mist bloomed up from the table, seemingly confined by the space between Odette's hands, twisting and writhing as it formed shapes and images. Nieve had met plenty of Illusionists before, but this looked different. Illusions intended to deceive an opponent were life-sized and often looked, smelled, and felt as real as whatever the illusion was based on. But this spell stayed small, hovering between Odette's palms, creating a small-scale version of the train made entirely of smoky mist, so that Nieve could see straight through the sides of the train and into the interior. The ring on Odette's finger gleamed softly as tiny portions of the misty train lit up with a gentle, golden glow.

"The lit areas indicate secrets or traps along the train. See this floor panel in one of the passenger cars?" The image of the train rolled over invisible tracks between Odette's hands until it stopped on a car with a bright gold spot marked in the middle of the floor. "This one comes up almost every time in this scenario, so I'm fairly certain that it leads to a secret treasure stuck in the undercarriage of the train. It's not really worth the risk in most cases, but maybe our capable Wavewalker is up to the task. And then in this car . . ." The mist-train zoomed backward until it reached the lounge car they were sitting in right now. Nieve looked for the gold mark then peered around the room, marking the spot on the wall. "It's the wine bottle on display behind the counter. I haven't taken a good look at it yet, so I don't know if it's a poison or a potion, or a message in the bottle, but I expect they won't just give it to us if we ask for it."

I could just grab it, Nieve thought, sizing up the bottle. One of the attuned staff members stood behind the counter, pouring tea into small cups for the passengers. Maybe they were stationed there to protect the bottle? But a distraction might draw them away long enough for Nieve to steal the bottle . . .

Hane coughed, drawing Nieve's attention. They shook their head, a disapproving look on their face. Nieve rolled her eyes, hiding the chagrin she felt at being caught out.

"I think the most important one is this one, inside the second luggage car." The train zoomed between Odette's hands again until she stopped it. A golden square of light illuminated one of the walls near the rear of the car. "I checked this earlier and there's nothing inside it, but it's big enough for a person to hide inside." She bit her lip as her eyes flicked up, looking first at Mason, then over at Nieve. "Well, an average-sized person, anyway. There's a few other secrets, like the sword with the Citrine-level enchantment, a porter's travelsack, a small cache behind a false wall . . ." Odette waved her right hand, rolling the mist-train along its invisible track, calling out each spot of gold as it rolled past. "The Keepsake cars show up as treasure, but as far as I can tell, that's just the cargo. Oh, there's a small secret inside the kitchen, too, but my spell doesn't show exactly where it is."

"Scenario kitchens are so reliable," Lief said with a grin. "There's almost always something hidden away in a drawer or behind the icebox."

"Yes, that's often the case, but you also have to consider that most kitchens contain traps, too," Odette advised. "Watch: Display Traps."

The smoke-train illusion remained, but the golden lights over the treasures dimmed and vanished. Glowing red marks appeared in almost every car forward of their private cabins, with at least one red glow encompassing the kitchen. "About half of the couplers are rigged to break if exposed to either pressure or magic, so to be on the safe side, avoid the couplers entirely. And then there are a few windows that will fall out of their frames when touched, a trick lock on one of the outer doors, some false rails on the platforms . . ."

"False rails?" Hane repeated, eyebrows arched. "Tell me about those."

"Oh, some of the railings on the gangways are illusions," Odette replied offhandedly. "If you try to lean on them, you'll fall off."

Nieve barked a laugh as Hane's expression became pinched. "Looks like you got lucky, eh, Hane? You're always climbing on rails and things."

"Oh!" Odette's eyes widened behind her glasses. "Oh no, I should have told you sooner! Those types of traps are common here, but you couldn't know that since you're from Dalenos, and I really *really* should have said something sooner! If anything had happened, it would be entirely my—"

"Please," Hane said, holding up a hand to forestall her. "Even if a railing gave way under me, I could still return safely to the train. It would be my own fault if I was caught off-guard by such a basic trap."

"We're all professionals here," Lief assured Odette, who looked on the verge of tears. He shot a teasing smile over at Mason, silently sulking in his chair with his arms crossed over his chest. "Well, most of us, anyway. What else should we look out for?"

Odette sniffled before waving the train forward between her hands, zipping along it to focus on the three private cars near the end. Nieve noted the red blaze on a few of the rooms, none of which belonged to anyone on the team. "I'm not entirely certain the doors to these cabins are trapped so much as they are warded against intrusion, but either way, it's safest not to try opening them. There is a possibility of losing some of our rewards at the end of this scenario if we unduly harass anyone in a private car, kill any innocent bystanders, or cause irreparable damage to the train itself. Try to keep that in mind when searching for the Magpie."

"Could our target be in one of those warded rooms?" Lief asked, leaning in closer to examine the image. "Some of the crew cars near the front are warded, too, aren't they?"

"They are," Odette agreed. "I think it's likely that the Magpie and crew are inside one of the warded rooms, but it's equally likely that they abandoned their room and left it booby-trapped behind them. If we spend all our time focusing on the warded rooms, we might miss them blending into the crowd of general passengers. It's happened to teams before."

"So what's the best strategy, then?" Hane asked.

"The best meaning the one with the most potential for a fight," Nieve added with a smirk.

Odette looked up timidly, glancing once at everyone before she pressed her palms together, snuffing out the image of the train. She shuffled wordlessly through her open notebooks until she found one containing rough sketches of gears and tools. After flipping a few pages, she revealed a series of calculations that Nieve couldn't even begin to comprehend.

"If . . . if you're asking my opinion . . ." Odette paused, looking around again as if checking to see if anyone would interrupt. "I think that—for just today!—we should set a guard on the Keepsake cars and focus on making the engine parts. Our rooms are close enough to the rear that if the cargo is attacked, we can all respond in force, but if we let the engine go for too long, the train will break down, and we'll have to split our attention between fixing the engine and protecting the cargo. Once Rose has all the parts she needs to fix the engine, we can start searching the train from back to front and roust the Magpie." She hunched into her shoulders, looking around furtively. "How does that sound to everyone?"

"What about the engine?" Hane asked. "Earlier, you said you didn't like the idea of leaving it vulnerable."

"This early on into the journey, it doesn't make sense to target the engine," Odette explained. "We're still so close to the station that a repair crew could make it out to us in no time. Whoever sabotaged the engine didn't want it to fail until the train gets deeper into the mountains, so right now is the best time to shore up that weakness."

Hane almost looked impressed as they nodded. "That makes sense. I agree with your strategy."

"I do as well," Lief concurred. "Is anyone opposed?"

"Sounds good to me," Nieve said with a shrug. "I don't mind standing guard for a while; seems like a good opportunity for a fight."

"Did it suddenly get crowded in here?" Hane asked, cringing forward in their chair as they cast a look over their shoulder. "It seems busier than before. Did something happen?"

"Oh, the dining car is closed to set up for dinner service!" Odette announced, checking the time on a pocket watch. "One of us should put our names in for a table, but before that, let's set up the guard schedule. Nieve, did you want to take the first watch? Also: where do you think is a good place to stand watch?"

"Probably at the back of the second luggage car," Nieve suggested after a moment's consideration. "That way, I can watch for anyone coming over the roof to get to the Keepsake cars. And yeah, I don't mind taking the first watch."

"I'll take one of the overnight shifts," Hane volunteered. "I have perception spells to help me once it gets dark."

"I'll split the night shift with Hane." Lief flashed a grin over the table. "If you let me take the first watch, I can boost your perception when we trade places."

Hane jerked a nod, their attention more on the milling passengers than on the team. They looked . . . nervous. Did Hane suspect the Magpie and their crew might be in the room? Nieve scanned the crowd, but no recognizable faces jumped out at her.

"Don't put Prickles down for a watch shift; she'll be casting bronzes most of the night and she'll fall asleep right after," Mason said, finally stirring from his sulk. "She's gonna put me to work, too, so I'd rather not have a shift if I can avoid it."

"I think that's okay," Odette said slowly as she wrote down the watch schedule in her notebook. "I can take the dawn shift until breakfast; after that, we'll split into teams. Half of us will go to the engine, the other half will sweep the train for the Magpie's crew. Who wants to do what?"

"I want the Magpie!" Nieve practically jumped out of her seat, hand upraised in excitement. "Put me down for the fight! I'm ready."

"You seem to have recovered," Lief observed, looking mildly surprised. "I thought you might be getting ill with how quiet you were."

"I'm fine," Nieve said quickly. Then, fearing she'd unwittingly acted suspiciously, she added: "I just had a headache. From . . . train noise."

"Uh huh." Lief looked skeptical, but also amused. "Well, next time, please feel free to ask me for a remedy spell. I know how detrimental headaches can be for someone with a mind mark."

"Thanks," Nieve muttered, feeling embarrassed.

"Okay . . ." Odette's pen continued scribbling across the page. "Who else? Magpie or engine?"

"Don't put me on the engine team," Mason begged. "I already have to put up with Prickles telling me what to do tonight, I really don't want her yelling at me tomorrow, too."

"Okay, so Mason is on the search team . . . and Rose is on the engine team, of course . . ." Odette tapped the pen against her chin for a moment. "I think I'll put myself on the engine team, too. I think I can be of more use there, with all the research I've done on this scenario."

"I'd rather not go back to the engine," Lief said with a shrug. "I hate how dirty and loud these coal-burning trains are, but I also understand if Hane wants to be on Team Magpie, as the other combat specialist on our team."

"Actually, I'll join the engine crew," Hane volunteered, much to Nieve's surprise. "If we're splitting the team, we should split the combat specialists, just in case of a surprise attack."

"That does make sense," Odette agreed. "And it puts our healer on the team more likely to see combat, which is good strategy. Okay!" Odette closed her notebook with a satisfied smile. "That was great! I'll go put our names in for a dinner table, and Nieve is heading back for the first cargo watch, correct?"

"Yeah, I'm just going to stop by my cabin real quick," Nieve said. She caught Hane's eye as the team began shuffling and stretching in their seats. "I wanted to grab my cloak in case it gets cold. Maybe some food, too, since I'll be missing dinner."

Luckily, Hane caught on quickly, rising from their chair. "I'll go with you to help you with the dimensional bag. It can be tricky to find things in there sometimes."

Nieve reached out for Chime with her thoughts, confirming the entity was still listening in through their connection. *Listen, I'm not going to have enough time to catch Hane up on everything, so if you're okay with it, I'm going to pass you to them so the two of you can talk.*

<Thank you. I appreciate that,> Chime replied. <I want you to know that I am truly grateful for all your efforts on my behalf. I know that I as I am now, I am more hindrance than help, but please know that if there is a way that I might be of use, you need only ask.>

Thanks. Nieve wasn't sure how sound magic too weak to pierce through supposed silence would be helpful, but she would keep the offer in mind. For now, she was just looking forward to not having any additional noises or voices inside her head, at least for a little while.

HANE

Wavewalker (leg mark), Citrine

I s that comfortable for you?" Hane asked, testing the flexion of their wrist and forearm.

<As this vessel lacks the ability to relate physical sensation, I do not require comfort,> Chime replied, bound to Hane's arm by a loop of bandages. <The question of comfort is best considered by yourself.>

"This works for now," Hane said, rolling down their sleeve to hide the bandages. "It's not ideal for a fight, and if someone grabs my arm for some reason, I'll have to lie and say you're a hidden knife, but that shouldn't be much of a problem."

Hane and Chime were alone in their train cabin, Nieve having left earlier to begin her watch of the Keepsake car. While Hane worked out a way to keep Chime both hidden and in contact with their skin, Chime had filled them in on their conversation with Nieve earlier. While it was disappointing that Chime couldn't confirm if their missing piece was located in the Vault of Shadows, it wasn't entirely unexpected. The best thing to do was to get through this scenario quickly and find the vault on the next floor. That, and hope the next floor was a little more straightforward than this current challenge.

<May I extend my sense through you to see and hear our surroundings?> Chime requested. <Nieve permitted it earlier, and it gave me a much better sense of what you humans perceive versus what I perceive. And I enjoyed listening to you humans strategize.>

Hane hedged a bit as they gave their armor and weapons a quick once-over, verifying that their tonfa and hidden knives and various enchanted items were all in place. "It's good that you enjoyed the planning session, but

I'm going to be searching the train for secrets and treasures, as well as possible hiding places for the Magpie's crew. I would rather practice this sort of bond in a more secure setting until I know what to expect of it."

<Oh.> How could the tinkle of a chime sound disappointed? <It was my understanding that your team would be working on a group project together.>

Chime wasn't mistaken: Hane had heard voices and movement through the wall earlier, when affixing Chime to their arm.

"Rose, Mason, and Odette are making parts for the train's engine," Hane explained. "I can't help them with that, and I don't want to be in the way."

If Chime understood, they didn't respond right away. Hane continued preparing for their surveillance of the train, tucking a pair of gloves enchanted for stealth into a hidden pocket before stashing their dimensional bag between the mattress and the wall again. Normally, physical contact with other beings felt uncomfortable to Hane, but they found they didn't mind being in contact with Chime's crystalline shard. Maybe it was because Chime was more of an object than a person, or maybe it was because the shard wasn't Chime's true form; the only thing they minded about the arrangement was how the sharp ends of the shard dug into their skin as they moved, but that wasn't Chime's fault. If anything, it was an incentive to stay hidden and not engage in any fighting during their surveillance of the train.

Out in the corridor, Hane paused outside Rose and Mason's room, cocking their head to listen for voices or sounds. Mason had joined Hane and Nieve on their way back to the rooms in order to catch his sister up on the discussion in the lounge car, but unless the room had been warded against sound, it didn't seem as if either of them were still inside the room. Odette and Lief's room seemed similarly vacant, though without knocking, Hane couldn't be entirely certain.

<There are no human mana signatures beyond either of these doors.> Chime's pronouncement caught Hane by surprise. Was Chime reading their mind? That was a little unsettling, despite how useful they found the information to be. <I cannot help but hear your surface thoughts and see your intentions. Outside of your inner dialogue, I am only able to perceive nearby concentrations of mana and sound produced by magic. I have little else to distract me from my own thoughts as I am right now.>

That explanation made sense, but it also seemed more than a little manipulative. Like Chime was trying to make Hane feel guilty over refusing to share their sight and hearing with the entity.

<My apologies. That was not my intention.>

Hane grimaced, thinking their response just in case anyone should see them and think they were talking to themself. *I'm sorry, too. I never mean to be rude, but it's difficult when you hear things as soon as I think them. Thank you for telling me the rooms are empty; information like that is really helpful. I promise that if a good opportunity to join your senses to mine comes up, we can try it. Okay?*

<Agreed.> Chime sounded a little more cheerful at that. <If I can help you by alerting you to mana concentrations, you need only ask.>

That was useful. While Hane could sense mana and enchantments through the spell Sense Mana, it wasn't as all-encompassing as Detect Aura, which was said to show the caster a person's shroud or illuminate enchanted objects. For Hane, Sense Mana usually only worked in very close proximity to a source of mana and they felt it through minute vibrations against their skin. Someone else might be able to interpret those vibrations in a way that identified the enchantment or spell, but Hane generally used it to determine if magic was present or not, and usually only when looking for false walls or hidden caches of treasure. There were likely other applications of Sense Mana, but Hane hadn't taken the time to learn them yet.

Even moving as carefully and precisely as possible, it was impossible to navigate the narrow train corridors without bumping into passengers along the way. At least when the team had been boarding, everyone had been moving in the same direction with purpose, but now that the train was underway, passengers tended to gather in small groups to gossip, laugh, and generally be in the way. It didn't help that the rocking of the train and the occasional burst of wind from outside would send everyone crashing into one another. Hane endured as stoically as possible, but inwardly they cursed the scenario with the entirety of their being.

Whatever happened to simple agility challenges? Hane wondered, waiting for a group of passengers to finish jumping from one gangway to the next. *When did every challenge turn into playacting and solving mysteries? I want my shaky platforms and colorful tiles back, please.*

If Chime heard any of that, they were wise not to respond.

Hane felt their heart contract within their chest as they rolled open the door to the lounge car. The corridors had been bad enough, but this car was packed from front to back, full of passengers waiting their turn to dine in the dinner car. There was no clear path to the opposite door and no way to navigate without unintentionally bumping elbows or pushing someone aside. It was like a scene from one of their worst nightmares.

Just as Hane was considering reversing their gravity to walk along the ceiling, a uniformed server excused themself as they shouldered their way past Hane to a group of lounge chairs centered around a low table. They wouldn't have taken further notice, but the server carried a tray of sweet-smelling tea cakes, all coated in a creamy frosting and topped with various candied fruits. They half hoped that the server would return with at least one iced cake that Hane could request of them, but they set the entire tray down on the table with a thanks to the guests there before melting into the crowd. Before they could turn away, they recognized the passenger who leaned forward to grab a cake off the tray.

"Hey, Hane!" Mason lifted a tiny tea cake topped with a candied lemon peel in a mock toast. "We're over here! Come wait with us."

It struck Hane then that this was the same circle of chairs where the team had their planning session earlier. Odette and Lief must have stayed after arranging for a dinner table, and Mason must have returned with Rose. Nieve, of course, was still on guard duty, leaving one chair open around the table.

"We have a bit of a wait until our dinner table opens up," Odette said apologetically, closing a notebook in her lap. "At least the counter here is still serving tea and snacks, so we have something to tide us over."

A part of Hane wanted to continue on through the car, certain that once they finished crossing the dinner car and the further lounge car, the rest of the train would practically seem empty by comparison. But those tiny, perfect cakes trapped them with indecision. It wasn't as if they were on a mission, they were just doing a little reconnaissance. There was nothing wrong with indulging in one simple sweet, right? But doing so would require them to sit with their teammates, which might include small talk—something Hane avoided like a cluster of shiuni.

<If I may make a request?> Chime's voice was preceded by a gentle tinkling sound—a considerate gesture so as not to startle them. <This seems a good opportunity for me to become familiar with your teammates' mana signatures. And I am also curious about the one who bears a mark gifted by my kin. Also, the shift in your tune indicates that you wish to linger here, do you not?>

Hane didn't know what they meant by "the shift in their tune," but yes, they did want to linger. The serving tray was piled with tiny tea cakes, and there was no knowing when they would have another chance to indulge like this.

You're just hoping I'll allow you to listen through me, aren't you?

<It is desired, yes.>

Fine.

Somehow, allowing Chime to extend their awareness through Hane's senses was more comfortable than conversing with their teammates. They tried not to move stiffly as they rejoined the team, taking the open seat before considering the plate of cakes. How many could they take without being remarked upon? Should they ask if the cakes needed to be divided up evenly, like treasure? Or was it like a community meal, where everyone present could simply take what they wanted? How did they choose which one to eat first?

Hane observed their teammates as discreetly as possible, attempting to figure out the current social protocol. Mason had already finished one cake and was eating a second. He had a third cake balanced on his knee. Lief finished a single cake before sitting back in his seat to listen as Rose and Odette discussed fixing the engine. Odette held a half-eaten cake in her hands, while Rose held only her steaming teacup.

"So I finished setting up all my equipment, but the room is a little small," Rose said, continuing an earlier conversation. "You got a full list of the gears that need to be replaced, right?"

"And I wrote down the enchantments on each one," Odette confirmed with a nod. "Do you want the list now, or should I give it to you later?"

Relieved that they didn't have to participate in that particular conversation, Hane eased forward and snatched a tea cake crowned with a sugared strawberry. They peeled back a layer of crinkled wax paper before taking a bite. The frosting was sweet enough to make their teeth ache, but the sponge of the cake was soft and moist. A layer of sliced strawberries was an unexpected surprise. Listening with half an ear as Rose and Odette chatted about engine parts, Hane finished the cake in three quick bites before discreetly licking the frosting off their fingers and eyeing the remaining tea cakes.

They twitched in surprise as Lief chuckled.

"It's a bit decadent, isn't it?" Lief asked with a smile. "You should try one of the citrus ones. The flavor profile is a little more balanced."

"Oh." Hane had no idea what a flavor profile was—that sounded like noble-speak. They didn't have to be told twice to take a second cake, though. On Lief's advice, they chose one topped with a curl of orange peel next. "Thanks."

"I usually prefer scones with tea," Lief continued conversationally. "I find these iced cakes too sweet sometimes."

Hane nodded in response, their mouth too full to speak. Here it was: the dreaded Small Talk Challenge. Hane should have known better than to stop for a cake; there were no rewards without challenges.

Chewing slowly, Hane considered their response. It would have been easier if either Rose or Mason initiated conversation: both of them liked to talk, which made it easy to bait them into meandering tangents. Even Odette would have been simpler to divert by asking a question related to the scenario or the floor report Hane had failed to read. But Lief . . . Lief was different. He seemed like the type of person who listened more than he spoke and knew more than he should. His easy smile looked like a mask to Hane, keeping his own secrets hidden behind those creepy-colored eyes.

It was also possible that Hane was misjudging him; Lief had been nothing but a professional climber and a considerate healer. There was no reason to mistrust Lief, and it was never a good idea to upset the healer.

Finally swallowing the bite of cake they'd been chewing, Hane searched for an acceptable topic to discuss. "You said you've completed this floor before, right? Were you with Rose or Odette on either of their previous climbs?"

"No, no, this is my first time climbing with each of you," Lief said with a cheery smile. "Odette picked my climber profile from the Soaring Wings registry. Was it the same for you and—" He paused, a conflicted look crossing his face. "I'm sorry, but is it Nieve or Nee-eh-vay? I've heard it said both ways and I would hate to say it wrong."

"Her friends and former teammates all say Nieve. To my knowledge, that's her preference," Hane explained.

"Yes, but that's not how it's said," Rose interrupted, holding her open palm toward Odette, as if placing their conversation on hold. "She doesn't have to keep saying it wrong now that she knows how to pronounce it properly."

"Who cares?" Mason protested, the words somewhat muffled by his mouthful of cake. Hane's eyes narrowed: how many cakes had he eaten already? There was icing stuck in his goatee. "It's her name! Let her say it however she wants to say it."

Rose huffed irritably. "We shouldn't encourage her to keep saying it wrong, we should help her get used to hearing the correct pronunciation. It's her heritage, she needs to accept it."

"She's gonna do what she's gonna do," Mason objected. "You need to let it go, Prickles."

"No! There is a right way to say it, and a wrong way." Rose slapped her hand on the table, startling a server who was just approaching with a pot of tea. Wide-eyed in surprise, the server backed away, finding another group of guests to serve. "It's one thing to be wrong from ignorance, and another to continue being wrong despite knowing better."

"I would like to stop discussing my colleague without her being here to defend herself," Hane said, as politely as they could manage. "I'm uncomfortable speaking on her behalf."

"This is getting a little too heated for me, too," Lief added. "Fighting over food leaves a bad taste in your mouth, don't you think?" When Rose's pursed lips suggested an argument brewing, Lief leaned across the table toward her. "You may not have noticed, but you're distressing your friend here."

Lief tipped his head toward Odette, who had sunk low in her chair, face downturned as she scribbled in her notebook. Looking over at her, Hane could see she wasn't actually writing anything, but instead was drawing a tight spiral, her pen pressing hard enough to dimple the page.

Rose sighed and looked away, adjusting her seat. "Fine. I will discuss it with Nee-eh-vay privately at a later time."

The discussion at an abrupt end, an awkward silence fell over the table. Hane finished the cake they were eating as Lief attempted to fill his teacup from a long-cold kettle. He made a face when he found only dregs remained. Hane took their time picking a tea cake, hoping someone else would break the silence. When no one did, they selected a cake topped with berries, cleared their throat, and made an attempt at some congenial small talk. "Odette, you and Rose seem quite familiar with each other. Are you old friends, or do you climb together often?"

"Oh, um . . ." Odette bit her lower lip, eyes flicking up briefly to meet Rose's gaze across the table, before fastidiously wiping her fingers clean with a handkerchief. "I don't know that we were ever . . . I mean, we knew each other. From the academy."

"We had a few introductory courses together," Rose answered, her tone slightly arch, as if still miffed from earlier. "We were grouped up for some of our mock-climb exams, but this is the first time we've been to the spire together. You did climb with my sister Jesserah once, didn't you?"

"Oh, ah, more than once." Odette looked nervous for some reason. "We were in the same apprentice program, studying lower floors together. Since we're both Analysts, we don't climb together anymore, but back then she was, um . . ."

"Lazy, but in a bossy sort of way?" Rose suggested, smirking in amusement. "It's okay, you can say it."

"Oh no, I wouldn't say—"

"I wouldn't say lazy," Mason qualified, lifting one shoulder in a shrug. "Jesserah's just impatient. She doesn't like to waste her time on the little things. You know she can handle herself in tough situations."

"I didn't say she wasn't competent," Rose retorted. "But she does like to stand back and let everyone else do the hard work, then swoop in and take the credit."

"You just don't like her because she's tied with you in second place among the siblings," Mason said, rolling his eyes. "I keep telling you, if you weren't so focused on discrediting Jesserah, you'd already be ahead of Wynsla."

"The only way anyone is beating out Wynsla is by pushing them down a bottomless pit and making it look like an accident," Rose muttered, gently swirling the dregs in her cup. "They're only the favorite because they worship Wydd the same way our parent does. They even speak as a priest of Wydd during prayer services. Seriously, how is anyone supposed to compete with that?"

"It sounds like you two come from a very complicated home life," Lief observed mildly. "Just how many siblings do you have?"

"Fourteen," Mason and Rose answered together.

"Not that we live together, or anything," Rose explained. "Our common parent never married, they just take up with lovers and support the children as they come. Some of us are full siblings, though. I have a ten-year-old sister with the same parents as me."

"That sounds . . . costly," Hane commented.

Mason rolled his shoulders in a wide shrug. "Our common parent is one of the higher nobles of Caelford. You could trace our lineage back to the royal family if you cared to. Money isn't really a problem, except for the ones who use it wrong."

"Wrong?" Odette asked timidly. "I thought your parent gave you both the start-up money you needed for your businesses?"

"They did, but we both run successful enterprises," Rose pointed out. "Well, one more successful than the other." She cast a superior look over at her brother, who only rolled his eyes as he shoved the last bite of a cake into his mouth. "It's the ones who squander their allowance that get cut off and dropped from the order of inheritance."

"Oh, I never knew that!" Odette gasped. "Jesserah told me about the competition for the inheritance, but I didn't know your parent would actually cut off any of their children!"

"It's only happened twice," Mason said, covering his mouth to talk through a mouthful. "Aishal lost everything gambling at the casino. Twice. After that, our parent refused to pay off his debts or give him any more money. Last I heard, he was working off his debt in one of the research labs funded by Haven Securities."

"Ouch." Lief shook his head. "But it makes sense if he was gambling. No one wants a gambler as their heir."

"Actually, our parent doesn't mind gambling at all," Rose corrected. "As long as we win, or cover our own losses. One of the qualities our parent values is ingenuity: it isn't enough to prove you're the best, you have to be the best in a new and unique way from anyone else."

"Ah, the quirks of a follower of Wydd," Mason sighed pedantically. "No offense, Hane."

Hane blinked, surprised. "Why would I be offended?"

Mason frowned. "Because you're a . . ." He shifted, looking embarrassed for some reason. "You're Wyddsfolk, aren't you?"

"Not all Wyddsfolk are followers of Wydd, meathead!" Rose hissed.

"No, I know, but like—" Mason waved vaguely in Hane's direction. "I don't know, you just fit the image."

Androgyny was one of Wydd's defining characteristics, and many of their followers chose to use non-gendered pronouns as a form of worship and respect, but Hane developed their sense of self independently from religion. They didn't much care for the prayer services, visages, or even the Goddess Selys, really.

"This is just how I feel comfortable," Hane explained, not for the first time. "No disrespect to Wydd, but I am who I am without faith or religion."

"See?" Rose jabbed her brother in the side with the handle of her spoon. "Don't jump to conclusions based on Wynsla and our parent, Brick. Hane doesn't owe you an explanation for how they identify."

"I didn't mean—" Mason sighed, exasperated. "Sorry, Hane. As much as I hate to admit it, Prickles is right and I shouldn't have assumed."

"I'm not offended," Hane said mildly. "But I am curious: you said two of your siblings had been cut off?"

"Yeah, Xephani." Mason's mouth twisted distastefully and Rose looked away. "She was taking ash for an edge in duels and spire climbs. When our parent found out, they disowned her."

"They didn't find out, Jesserah ratted her out," Rose muttered. "She couldn't take the competition."

"Oh, like you wouldn't have told if you'd found out first," Mason chuckled while licking icing from his fingers.

"So it's a competition, then?" Lief asked, looking from Mason to Rose. "Will only one of you inherit, or will your parent's fortune be split among the fourteen of you?"

"Oh, it's definitely a competition," Rose confirmed. "Only one of us gets to succeed the family line. If our parent died right now, it would be Wynsla. Getting ahead of them is the whole reason I'm on this climb. I need something impressive and unique to bring back home with me, and I'm hoping I'll find it in the vault on the next floor."

"Okay, but then . . ." Lief turned his gaze on Mason. "If it's a competition, why are you two so close? I thought Mason only came on this climb as a favor to Rose."

"I did," Mason said agreeably. "I don't really care about the inheritance. I have enough to get by and if I get cut off, I won't starve. But if I can help Rose win, then she'll owe me, in case I ever need anything in the future."

"It's true," Rose admitted. "There are other alliances among the siblings, it's not just us. Mason's attunement is useful for my imbues and I trust him to watch my back on spire delves. And he's not the least bit ambitious, so we get along well."

"But how certain can you really be of that?" Lief asked with a sharp-edged smile. "If one sibling already turned on another, how can you be sure that Mason isn't just waiting for you to slip so he can step over you?"

Hane hid a twitch by faking a sneeze; what kind of person thought like that?

"Because then he'd be competing against Jesserah and Wynsla all on his own, which would take time away from his incredibly busy social calendar," Rose replied dryly. "I've known Mason my whole life; he's always been satisfied with a moderate reward for the minimum amount of work possible."

"Perhaps." Lief shrugged. "But what assurances does Mason have that you'll actually repay him one day? After you inherit, how can you be held to honor your agreement?"

"You don't know Rose," Mason said with a chuckle. "She's got this scale of debts and credits in her head, and keeping it balanced is basically a compulsion for her. It's what helps her do those mana conversions as fast as she does, and how she manages her craft shop. When she owes someone, she pays up. It's like a universal constant." Mason leaned back in his chair, interlacing his fingers behind his head as he smirked. "And even if she doesn't, I haven't really lost anything I can't recover. Even if I'd rather be at home right now, I have the opportunity to strengthen my attunement and earn a little treasure for my troubles. No harm, no foul."

A brief lull in the conversation followed as Mason reached for another tea cake and Odette refilled her tea from a freshly delivered kettle. Chime's voice piped up inside Hane's mind as they considered which cake to choose next.

<Would now be an appropriate time to ask the loud one about the mark that grants him access to the dominion of metal? I can see the touch of my kin on him, but I wish to know whether he completed my kin's trial, or if my kin has been forcibly removed from their shrine, as I was.>

I can try, Hane replied, selecting a fresh cake topped with thin slices of caramelized banana. *But I think I would have heard something if the gateway crystal of metal had been relocated and forced to grant crystal marks to anyone who asked.*

It also seemed more than a little personal to ask such a question, but then again, Mason seemed like the sort of person who enjoyed talking about himself. Perhaps it wouldn't be such a difficult subject to bring up, especially if it could put Chime's mind at ease.

"So, ah . . . Mason?" Hane flinched as everyone turned to look at them. They picked at the wax paper on their cake, pretending it didn't bother them. "About your crystal mark . . . I've never been to the Unclaimed Lands, and I'm . . . curious. About the shrines and their challenges. Would you mind sharing your experience? You don't have to if you don't want to, though."

The question Hane would have considered rude and bordering on "offensive" made Mason grin as he leaned forward in his seat. "Sure thing! You know, I was talking to Nieve about the Unclaimed Lands earlier. I think every climber should take at least one excursion there; it's a totally different sort of challenge."

Rose snorted. "You didn't go on an excursion, you were escorted by a team of house guards. Did they even allow your feet to touch the ground, or did they carry you all the way to the shrine?"

Mason rolled his eyes. "That wasn't my choice, Prickles. I was only a Quartz-level Transmuter, fresh out of my Judgment. And I'm sure the extra protection was actually for the shrine map rather than for me."

"Heh." Rose smirked. "I think you may be right about that."

"Map?" Lief asked, looking interested. "You had a map to one of the shrines in the Unclaimed Lands?"

"Yeah, our parent collects them," Mason said flippantly. "It's one of their eccentricities. They normally don't like lending them out, but after I didn't get the attunement I wanted, I requested the map to the Shrine of Cold Iron as my post-Judgment gift."

Post-Judgment gift? That was an unfamiliar concept to Hane. Was that something local to Caelford, or was it a noble tradition? Rather than ask, Hane took another bite of their tea cake.

"Oh, but wait," Odette interjected. "I thought your parent gifted you both with the funds to open up your craft shops? I know your sister Jesserah got the funds for her personal library and research lab that way."

"They did," Rose agreed. "But Brick wagered his funds on returning with a crystal mark as well as the map. And I'm pretty sure the map was the higher priority. No offense, brother."

"Nah, I get it." Mason's chuckle held a touch of gallows humor in it. "Kids are easier to replace than those maps are. The maps are probably more expensive, too. They told me that if I returned without a crystal mark, I'd have to earn the funds to open my shop on my own. And if I returned without the map, then I might as well not return at all."

Odette's jaw dropped slightly. "I'm sure they were joking."

"No." The siblings said it at the same time, with almost the same inflection. Rose appeared unperturbed, calmly setting her teacup down. Mason grinned and shook his head as if he found his parent's threat amusing.

"It all worked out," Mason declared, reaching down to tap the outside of his ankle. "I earned the mark I wanted and I returned the map. And next time I take an excursion into the Unclaimed Lands, I'll go with an actual team instead of a unit of house guards."

"You plan on going back?" Odette inquired. "What crystal mark do you want next?"

"No, no mark this time. I'm happy with what I have now." Mason flashed a brilliant, perfect-toothed smile. "Don't get me wrong, I love my Transmuter attunement, but I really wanted Forgemaster, or anything with metal mana, really. Metalworking is my craft, and I love how technical it is to shape it with heat and tools, but it was so hard to bring my actual visions into reality that way. So even before I took my Judgment, I decided that I was going to ask for the shrine map if I didn't get an attunement that would allow me to work with metal."

"What was the shrine like?" Hane asked, urged on by Chime's voice inside their head. "Was it similar to completing a spire challenge?"

Mason's gaze went distant. Thoughtful. "A little? But it was different, too. I don't know how all the shrines are, but the entrance to the Shrine of Cold Iron was like the entrance of a mine. A voice told me I had to enter alone and leave all my weapons and tools outside. I guess in that way it was kind of like a Judgment."

"What about your attunement?" Hane asked. "Were you allowed to use it in the challenge?"

"Yeah, but like I said, I was a brand-new Transmuter back then." Mason leaned forward, getting into the story with hand gestures and expressions; it seemed Hane had judged his character correctly. "I only had the most basic stone sensing spells, and maybe a little more stamina and resilience. It wasn't like I could bend the shrine to my will or anything."

"You still couldn't." Rose paused mid-sip to meet her brother's scowl. "What? You think that just because you're Citrine now, you can overpower the gateway crystal of metal?"

"No, I'm saying the challenge would have been a lot easier if I'd been Citrine," Mason retorted.

<That assumption is incorrect,> Chime intoned. <The challenge is made to suit the individual's abilities. No trial should ever be easy.>

Hane decided to keep that piece of information to themself.

"Anyway," Mason continued, casting one final dirty look at his sister. "After entering the shrine, I came to this big, huge door set into a wall of stone. There were all these dark tunnels branching off in different directions, and an old-fashioned bellows and forge set up just outside the door. The voice in my head told me that I needed to forge three different keys to open three different locks on the door, and if I could do that, then I'd earn a boon from the shrine."

That actually didn't sound too terribly difficult; or at least, not all that dangerous.

"So all you had to do was mine some iron and make a few keys?" Lief asked. "That sounds almost too easy."

"Ha! Yeah, no, it was way more difficult than that." Mason laughed, eyes distant in memory. "Each key had to be made out of a specific ore that I had to go and mine myself. I think they might have been special ores, or maybe they were just magical constructs, because I only ever found one node of each type, and each one I found had a different challenge to overcome in order to mine it. Like, one was at the bottom of a subterranean lake, and I had to figure out how to mine it underwater without drowning myself." A brief chuckle at the memory. "I worked out how to mine it, but then had no idea how to actually haul it out of the water. Nearly drowned myself trying to swim with it. Finally worked out a way to wrap a net around it and drag it out. Then another was actually halfway down a pitch-black ravine, so I had to climb down to it and mine it while hanging over a lot of nothing. At least that time, I remembered to think about getting it back up, so I set up a pulley system to hoist it up. The last one . . ." Mason trailed off, the skin around his eyes tightening for an instant. Rose shot him a quizzical look, as if this was a new part of the story for her. After a beat of silence, Mason shook his head, gaze shifting away. "It was a combat challenge. That's all."

That didn't sound like all, but Hane knew better than to press when a climber got that look in their eyes. It was the haunted look of someone forced to face something they weren't ready for, or lost something they hadn't realized was important until just then.

"Wow. I never knew all that," Odette said softly. "That sounds like a huge risk to take when you could have just asked for money, like Jesserah and Rose."

"It was a good gambit," Rose said, surprisingly approving. "If only he bothered to actually train his crystal mark, he'd probably be in the second tier ranks of our siblings, instead of at the bottom."

"I got everything I need, Prickles." Mason stretched his legs out long, crossing one over the other. "I make enough money to get by, and I don't have to work all that hard. That's all I ever wanted for myself, so life is pretty good right now."

"Pardon me, honored guests." One of the servers approached the table, hands folded neatly before them. "Is this the Odette dining group of five?"

After receiving Odette's confirmation, the server continued. "Your dinner table is about to open up. You may proceed to the dining car now."

"Thank you," Odette said, hurriedly stuffing her notebooks back into various pockets. As everyone else began to stand and stretch, Hane hopped lightly to their feet.

"I'm sorry, but I don't plan on joining you for dinner," Hane explained briefly. "I was going to do some reconnaissance. Carefully."

"Oh, are you sure? You're not hungry?" Odette looked concerned, but Hane couldn't possibly eat a full meal after so many tea cakes. "Well, if you like, some of the side quests just became active. Up near the crew cabins, you should be able to find a collection quest of some sort, like finding ticket stubs, or conductor badges, something like that. Oh, and in the second passenger car, there should be a quest to find a passenger's missing belongings. The rewards are pretty small, so you don't have to do them, but just in case you want to . . ."

The request glittered in Odette's eyes. Hane sighed and shrugged.

"If I find them, I'll see what I can do. As long as it doesn't compromise the mission."

"Yes, thank you!" Odette beamed. She started to turn away, then stopped. "Oh! And please keep a look out for the beginning of the trading sequence. I can't seem to find it anywhere!"

Another quick nod. "I'll let you know."

Hane held back, waiting for the others to disappear into the crowd on their way to dinner. They would be heading that same way soon, but they wanted a little space first.

That, and the remainder of the tea cakes left behind.

NIEVE

Champion (mind mark), Citrine
??? (heart mark), Sealed

Nieve yawned as she rolled the outer door open, squinting as she stepped into the brightly lit private cabin car. The luggage cars only possessed dim lighting, which had been fine even after the sun set, but she hadn't considered how difficult it would be to traverse the chaotic carnage of the first luggage car until after Lief came to relieve her from watch duty. She'd slogged her way through, but she had a feeling she'd broken a few things along the way. Hopefully that wouldn't count against the team later on.

After her eyes adjusted to the lights in the corridor and a quick stop in the car's bathroom, Nieve pawed through her pockets for her room key, thinking she might freshen up just a little before scrounging up a warm meal. She wasn't sure if dinner was still available, but she wouldn't mind grabbing something in one of the lounge cars, especially if she could order a normal glass of red wine to go with it.

Yes, she was still upset over the ginger and mint potion gifted to her by the conductor.

Before Nieve reached the door to her room, she heard voices and clattering objects spilling into the corridor from Rose and Mason's room. With the door propped wide open in invitation, Nieve bypassed her own room in favor of checking in on her teammates.

"Hey guys," Nieve called, rapping her knuckles against the doorframe. "How are you all—whoa."

The room was both crowded and cluttered, with unfamiliar instruments and tools occupying every available inch of floor space. It looked chaotic at a glance, but gradually a pattern emerged from the chaos: all the tools, kits, pouches, and enchanted items were arranged in concentric rings, radiating outward from Rose, who sat in the dead center of the room, her legs crossed tightly beneath her. The surface of the desk was similarly cluttered, bearing stacks of notebooks, a mound of ragged-edged cloths, spools of thread, embroidery hoops, and even Odette herself. She sat at the edge of the desk, her feet planted on the seat of the chair, as if she were too afraid to touch the floor. Mason lounged on the lower bunk, his feet kicked up against the wall as he lazily rolled a stone rod between his hands.

"Oh, hi, Nieve." Odette smiled warmly. "Are you tired? If we're being too loud in here, we can move to the next room over."

"I'm not going anywhere," Rose said in a flat tone. She appeared to be weighing something on a scale, but Nieve wasn't entirely certain about that. "It would be a waste of time to move everything now. If we're being too loud, just thump on the wall."

"No, it's fine, I'm not that tired." She was more hungry than sleepy, but her curiosity was getting the better of her. "What is all of this? Is this for fixing the engine?"

"No, don't get her—"

"*This,*" Rose declared with a sweeping gesture, "is my craft."

"Started," Mason finished with a heavy sigh.

"Don't touch anything," Rose warned, ignoring her brother. "I just got everything laid out exactly where I need it, so watch where you put your feet. I've got my tools over here, molds ready to go right here, all my melt-plates primed, and my crucibles stacked and ready to go. You're welcome to stay and watch, *Nee-eh-vay,* but I won't hesitate to banish you if you knock one of my tools out of place."

Nieve pulled a face: Rose was still saying her name the Caelish way, but if she insisted on her own pronunciation, she worried that she'd lose her shot with Rose. By the way Rose looked up and paused mid-motion, she must have noticed the expression.

"I'm sorry, but *Nee-eh-vay* is the correct pronunciation, and it's common enough that I'm just used to saying it that way," Rose explained, her tone mildly softer than it usually was when giving one of her lengthy answers. "It would take the duration of the climb for me to get used to saying your name the way you prefer. If that's what you want, I will make the effort, but it might be easier for us both if you have a nickname that you don't mind being addressed by."

"Oh, sure. I get called 'Tails' a lot, if you like that better." Nieve tipped her head, letting her hair fall forward of her shoulder so she could tug on one of the ends of her headband. She shot Rose a wink and a grin as she tossed it back over her shoulder again. "But as long as it's you, I guess I don't mind the Caelish pronunciation so much."

The way Rose pinched her lips together suggested she was hiding a smile. Her gaze flicked up and down before she resumed her work, adjusting her goggles and straightening an open toolkit on the floor beside her. Nieve assessed the gear neatly arranged in nearly concentric rings, using Detect Aura to confirm that many of the items were enchanted. Even knowing that didn't help her understand what any of it did, though.

Nieve did have one slightly pressing question, though.

"Does anyone know where Hane is?"

"They said they were running reconnaissance," Odette explained. For once, she wasn't writing in one of her notebooks. She held an embroidery hoop in one hand and drew a needle through with the other, stitching a design Nieve couldn't make out. "They might do a few side quests, but they said they would be careful not to start any fights. Are you hungry? We saved some bread rolls from dinner."

Bread rolls sounded great just then, but getting the basket from Odette was a minor agility challenge. Rose watched, sharp-eyed, as Nieve edged as close as she could to the first row of tools, then bent nearly double to reach the outstretched basket of bread rolls. She managed to grab it without knocking anything out of place, but she'd broken a sweat while doing it.

"Thanks," Nieve said, cradling the basket against her chest as she leaned in the doorway. The inside of the room was hot for some reason, which was probably why the door was propped open. "I wish I could offer to help, but I'm still not too sure what all of this is."

"Prickles is casting new engine parts out of bronze," Mason explained, cutting over his sister's in-drawn breath before she could launch into a lengthy explanation. He pretended he didn't notice his sister's pointed glare as he continued: "This is all just molds and hot plates and filing tools; nothing too special. But if you get her started on it, she'll talk forever and you'll forget your question by the time she gets around to answering it. *If* she gets around to answering it."

"Ah." That was a fairly simple explanation. And now that she knew what she was looking at, she noticed the waves of heat emanating from the hot plates and recognized a few smithing tools. The explanation made the whole process seem less exotic, but the atmosphere of teammates sitting together during a lull was somehow more comforting than going out to scrounge up some food on her own. Nieve selected a bread roll and settled in against the doorframe to observe. "I've watched bladesmiths forge swords before, but it looked nothing like this. I'll stay and watch as long as I'm not in the way."

"Prepare to be lectured," Mason warned, kicking one leg over the other. "Prickles doesn't do anything without talking her audience half to death."

"Like you're any different when you're at your craft," Rose shot back. Her tone was harsh, but her movements were delicate as she fitted a tiny jeweler's screwdriver in place alongside its brethren inside a leather tool pouch. She interlaced her fingers, then cracked her knuckles with a long stretch. She twisted her neck from side to side, vertebrae popping loudly. Her gaze swept over the array of items surrounding her in rings, like ripples on a pond's surface. Rose took a deep breath, then held her hand out to Odette. "Let's see the details."

"Yes, yes. Right . . . here." Odette grabbed an open notebook, folding over herself in order to hand it to Rose without getting up. She chuckled shyly when she caught Nieve watching her. "This is actually the reason I wanted Rose to come with me on this delve. No one else can make parts like she can and then imbue them with the spells we need to keep the engine running. If I couldn't get Rose for this expedition, it wouldn't have been worth the attempt."

"What about me?" Mason asked, affronted. "I'm the other half of this process, and you didn't even ask me to join until you needed a sixth person."

"You're not integral to this process, you're just a useful shortcut," Rose said tartly as Odette looked askance, her lower lip pinched between her teeth. "And you usually decline invitations for spire delves, which is why no one asks you anymore."

"Just a shortcut, huh?" Mason leaned over the edge of his mattress, as if looking for a safe place to stand amid Rose's tools and equipment. "Guess you don't really need me, then. Think I'll go check out the bar, see if I can pick up—"

"Stop." Rose caught Mason's wrist as he reached out to sweep tools and gadgets aside. "You know I need you now. I didn't bring my full kit because I knew you'd be here. I'm ready to get started, are you?"

Mason maintained a heavy glare for a moment longer before sighing and rolling over onto his back. "Fine, fine. Let's get it done quickly so I can get a drink later. And you owe me, Prickles."

"How delightful," Rose muttered as she scanned Odette's notebook, twirling a pen in her free hand. "Did you confirm standard measurements for all engine parts, Odie? If there's a foreign metric in here, it's going to take me longer."

"I couldn't find anything about foreign parts in the engineers' manual," Odette replied promptly.

"And this sketch—" Rose turned the notebook face-out, giving Nieve a glimpse of a partially drawn circular gear with flat, blunt teeth around the outer edge. "Is this to scale?"

"I traced one of the spare parts," Odette confirmed. "I wanted to make sure I got the shape of the teeth correct."

"Good, this all looks standard enough," Rose said pensively, flipping through pages of notes. Her lips pinched into a bloodless purse, causing Odette to squirm in her seat. "This gear rack might be a problem. I didn't bring a mold this big, and combining smaller molds can cause weak spots in the cast. It might be better to have Brick reshape it directly instead of casting a new part. Did it have any nonstandard enchantments on it?"

"Um, I don't think so?" Odette looked nervous. She picked at a stitch with her needle, as if pondering its existence. "I only remember seeing runes for strength and integrity on it. It might hold up on its own?"

"Hm." Rose frowned, narrowing her eyes at the notebook. "I'll take a look at it tomorrow when we start fixing things. Hopefully it holds up that long."

"I thought we were ready to start," Mason complained, lazily twirling one of his stone rods between his hands.

"Now I'm ready," Rose said, grabbing a stack of molds and dragging it closer to herself, opening up a small space at the edge of Mason's bed. She cleared her throat once, then began reading aloud at a rapid pace. "I need five spurs, all with grade eight teeth, one size G, one size H, two size I, and one size M. After that, I need two bevels, one size E, the other size F. Make sure they fit."

Nieve could barely keep up as Rose continued listing specifications that had absolutely no meaning to her, but Mason's hands were moving almost as fast as Rose could speak, twisting off lengths of his stone rod as if it were merely clay. The shortened lengths of stone transformed and changed, turning into stone gears of varying sizes before Mason extended his hand over the side of his bed and dropped the newly formed gears into the empty space Rose created for him. Nieve found it hard not to gape as the siblings worked with a practiced rhythm, for once in perfect harmony with one another. As she watched, the stack of stone gears rose steadily higher and higher, turning into a small mound of parts. If this was all it took to make new engine parts, then what was the rest of this equipment for?

"Good notes for the imbues, Odie, but I think it'll be best if I wait until I get everything fitted into place first." Rose set the notebook facedown under her knee, so as to hold her page. "I assume we only need the imbues to last long enough to get us to our destination?"

"That should be enough to satisfy the challenge," Odette replied, her stitching resumed. "If they need to, they can get replacement parts at the station, so all we need to do is make sure this train gets there."

"What angle do you need for the bevels?" Mason asked from the bed.

Rose paused in the middle of adjusting her goggles to squint down at the notebook. "Thirty-five degrees. You can be off by a little as long as the two pieces lock teeth."

"Got it."

"I'm turning up the forges now," Rose announced, settling her goggles against her eyes and adjusting the straps behind her ears. "It's going to get warm in here, but if you're going to drink from a canteen, be careful not to spill. If the molds get too cold, the bronze will crack, and that makes me angry. You don't want me to get angry."

"I like making you angry," Mason commented, a large chunk of stone rippling and reshaping itself in his hands.

"That's because you have a poor sense of self-preservation," Rose retorted, cracking her knuckles one last time before grabbing a mold off the knee-high stack and flipping it open on the floor in front of her. Each mold was about the size of a book, and opened on hinges in the spine similar to one, too. Instead of pages, though, each side of the box held a white claylike substance, pristine and smooth until Rose grabbed a stone gear from Mason's pile, seemingly at random, then pressed it deeply into the white clay. She selected two more gears from the pile and added them to the same sheet of clay as the first, fitting them in tightly before flicking open a small leather tool roll that appeared to contain slim brass rods of varying sizes and widths, all of which were shorter than Nieve's smallest finger. Nieve watched, entranced, as Rose used a pair of tools to delicately set the brass rods in between the stone gears, then press the rod into the clay until it stuck.

"What is that for?" Nieve asked, craning her neck forward for a better view. She wished she could get closer, but after Rose's warning, she was afraid to so much as nudge something out of place.

"Hm?" Rose glanced up, both lenses on her goggles a filmy gray color. "What? The mold, or the metal?"

"The little rods." Nieve squinted, trying for a better look. "It looks like you're connecting them to the gears?"

"Oh, it's for the channels," Rose replied, resuming her work as if that answered the question. Mason must have caught her bewildered look because he chuckled and explained.

"After the mold sets, she's going to pour melted bronze in through the top," Mason explained. "The rods make channels for the bronze to fill all the wells. When you see it, it'll make sense."

"Uh huh." Nieve was beginning to doubt that: none of this really made any sense. What would her old team have done if they'd come up against a challenge like this one? Had any of them known anything about fixing train engines? Even if they had, how would they have gone about creating new gears? To her knowledge, no one on her previous team knew how to smith or how to cast, and it seemed unbelievable that every Caelford team had someone like Rose on it. Was there another way this challenge could be solved?

As Nieve pondered, Rose closed her first mold on its hinges, pressing the virgin half of the white clay down evenly over the first half, with the gears and brass rods still stuck in it. She leaned forward on her knees to press the mold closed, then flicked the latch over the seam to hold it shut. After setting it to one side, Rose grabbed the next mold and started pressing new stone gears into it, arranging them carefully to make the most of the space available.

"I got those bevels done, Prickles." Mason held an angled gear in each hand, rolling them against each other to demonstrate how the teeth interlocked. "How's that angle look to you?"

Rose looked up, adjusting one lens of her goggles until it turned yellow. With her other eye squeezed shut, Rose eyed the gears critically, then nodded and turned her lens back to gray. "Looks good. After that, you can get started on making some miter gears. Around twelve should do it, I think. All size R, so they should all fit inside one mold together."

"I hate the small ones," Mason grumbled as he drew a new stone rod from his quiver.

"Then you're going to love this," Rose said, smirking as she referred to Odette's notebook. "Two spiral bevel gears, sizes A and B."

Mason groaned loudly, expressing his displeasure. "Matching spiral bevel teeth is the worst!"

"I'm sorry," Odette murmured, as if it were her fault. "That's the most pivotal fault point. If that goes, the engineer can't engage the brakes."

Rose grunted her acknowledgment of the statement. "I'll forge two of each, then. Just in case."

"How did you learn to do all this?" Nieve asked, astounded by how seamlessly Rose went from the notebook to setting small ceramic cups on each of the hot plates, grabbing tools without looking, and examining Mason's stone gears critically before pressing them into a mold. "Is this something you train for at that fancy academy you have here?"

"What, this?" Rose looked up, confused. "No, I've been casting since I was ten. It's my craft."

"Your craft," Nieve repeated, perplexed. "Does that mean it's your job? Like something passed down through your family?"

Rose made a face, seemingly torn between answering and preparing her molds. Odette stepped in to answer.

"Rose does own a bronze casting shop and she works on commission, but not everyone makes a career of their craft," Odette explained. "Like for me, my craft is sewing. I make my own armor, the location tracking bracelets, and some other things, too. I really like making pretty things, like embroidered pillows and wall hangings." She smiled shyly, as if embarrassed. "But that's just a hobby. My primary profession is delving."

"She's being modest," Rose said without looking up from her work. "She's one of the few people trained to stitch runes using enchanted thread. Climbers commission her specially for enchantments on armor and clothing."

"I remember you saying something like that earlier, but I've never heard of enchanted thread before," Nieve admitted. "Is it just a stronger type of thread, or is it special somehow?"

"No, it's . . . ah, it's kind of embarrassing." Odette shyly held out her bracer studded with glass spheres, plucking one off to show the stitching underneath. "Enchanted thread is pretty rare and it's really hard to work with, but if you get it right, you can use it in place of enchanting runes for certain effects, like elemental resistances, or tougher armor. And some people think it's prettier than standard enchantments, and I just sort of have a knack for it, so . . ." Odette shrugged. "Like I said, it's sort of embarrassing."

"That seems pretty useful." Nieve couldn't even stitch a button, but then, things like stitching had never really interested her. "So you all just pick up these hobbies as kids and just . . . keep at 'em?"

"Caelford has a long history of crafting by hand," Mason added. He extended his hand out over the pile of stone gears and dropped a handful of tiny gears on top of it, earning a glower from Rose as the pieces scattered and rolled. "Just about everyone picks up a craft or two. We've got seasonal festivals where people show off their skills." Mason smirked as he added: "My pieces always place in the top ranks when I enter them in contests."

"That's because most of us work for a living," Rose grumbled as she closed up a mold and placed it to the side with the others. She took a moment to swipe sweat from her forehead and take a drink from her canteen. "I don't have time to sit around making pretties to enter in contests; I've got a client waitlist that's about a month long."

"It wouldn't be so long if you didn't keep letting our parent's friends jump the line," Mason replied airily. "You'd probably earn more that way, too, since you sell those pieces at cost."

Rose made a face but didn't respond. After another draught from her canteen, she picked up a small drawstring bag and tugged it open. When she upended it over her palm, shiny bronze beads spilled out with tiny clicks and clacks, filling the cup of her hand. Nieve watched, fascinated, as Rose tipped one handful into the first ceramic cup on a melt-plate, then repeated the process again and again, filling each little cup about halfway full of bronze beads.

"So, what's your craft, Mason?" Nieve asked, watching the tiny beads begin to melt. "You must be good at it if you win so many contests."

"I'm an artist," Mason boasted loftily. "People travel from all over Kaldwyn to buy my pieces. But if you ask nicely"—Mason lifted himself up on an elbow to grin and wink at Nieve— "I might make you something pretty out of the treasure we earn."

Rose blew the curls off her forehead as she removed the first mold she'd formed from the stack of closed molds. Upon opening it, she painstakingly began removing the stone gears as well as the brass rods, leaving symmetrical imprints in both sides of the white clay. "Brick's art is as worthless as he is. The only reason people pay so much for his crafts is because of our family name. If he gets disowned, his little gallery will sink faster than a stone ship."

"You're just jealous that I have the freedom to be creative, and all you do is replace mechanical parts," Mason retorted, reshaping a stone rod into a roughly roundish shape.

"Yes, I'm sure it's jealousy and not simply ambition." Using a clay-shaping tool, Rose widened a few of the channels between the gear-shaped voids within the clay, then extended one channel all the way up through the top of the mold on both sides. Once finished, she closed the mold up tight, flicking a lock along the open edge, then stood it up on its end, leaving the top of the clay and her carved channel upright. "Just don't forget that if I'm not the one who succeeds our parent, you'll end up a wastrel peddling your wares for coins and drinking your ale from the same tin cup night after night." Rose paused to check the cups on her melt-plate before calling out: "Pouring!"

Nieve started to ask what that meant, but Rose was already in motion, grabbing a pair of tongs to lift one of the ceramic cups of bronze beads from the melt-plate. Moving slowly and carefully, she tipped the crucible over the closed mold, pouring out a thin stream of molten bronze so brilliant that Nieve could only look at it so long before she had to turn her face away. After a moment or two of complete silence, Rose set the cup back on the melt-plate, refilled it with fresh bronze beads, then set the mold off to the side to cool down.

"And those are going to be the parts you use to fix the engine?" Nieve asked, still confounded by the whole process.

"Eventually," Rose confirmed, already working on plucking out the pieces of the next mold. A few of the stone gears she set aside in a small pile, but others she tossed up onto Mason's bed. He grunted the first time one rolled into his ribs, still focused on the egg-shaped stone mass between his hands, but once the pile grew larger, he reached out almost absently and reformed the bits and pieces into a long stone rod once again. "But yeah, this is basically what casting is. It's faster with Brick helping me out with the models, otherwise it takes a lot longer."

"Does that mean Mason helps out in your shop?" Nieve asked.

"Oh, no, then I'd have to pay him." Rose shook her head emphatically while Mason snickered from the bed. "Most of my commissions are fixing broken parts for antiques, or making custom decorations, so my customers bring me a sample of what they need and I use that to create a mold." Rose swiped sweat from her face with the back of her hand before lifting her goggles up like a headband. "If they don't have something I can use as a model, I'll carve a model out of wax and use that to make the impression in the clay. It's not as quick as Brick's models, but that way I don't have to put up with all his whining about how much he hates spiral bevel gears."

"Spiral bevels are hard!" Mason protested, frowning at the oddly shaped mass of stone between his hands. He'd transformed it roughly into the shape of the other gears, but something about it seemed to be frustrating him: every time grooves began to appear on the angled surface, they would suddenly smooth out and start again. Mason's foot bounced against the wall, as if agitated. "Don't tease me if you don't want the quality of your molding clay to dip. I need a compass up here, Prickles."

Rose scooped up a tool without looking and tossed it onto the bed. After a long drink of water, she sighed and adjusted her goggles over her eyes again, hands fidgeting with something on the sides to turn the lenses a deep blue color. "I pay for that clay, so you better not mess with the consistency. I keep telling you, you'd make better money if you sold that clay to other craft shops."

"Yeah, it sounds so impressive to say I make my living creating specialized dirt for people," Mason retorted, voice dripping with sarcasm. It looked as if he was using the tool Rose tossed him to measure the angle of his stone gear. He reshaped it a few times, the angle shifting from steep to shallow with each adjustment. "Talking about the intricacies of dirt is sure to help me pick up partners from bars. Thanks for the idea, sis."

"Pardon me for being practical," Rose muttered. She tapped a finger against the first mold she'd created, withdrawing it quickly as if expecting it to bite her. After a few more taps, she deemed it cool enough to lift and place it on its side. Nieve craned forward from her position in the doorway as Rose opened the mold like a book, revealing gleaming bronze gears set inside the clay.

"That didn't take long at all!" Nieve exclaimed. "Why does it take a blacksmith days to forge a single blade when they could just use a mold like that?"

"Because bronze is a much softer metal than steel," Rose explained, using a tool to lever the gears from the mold. The bronze mass came out as one piece, interconnected by the thin channels of bronze that connected the hollows prior to filling. After inspecting the gears, Rose set the entire piece between her heels and grabbed a thin file, sawing the topmost gear free of the amalgamation. "Bronze has a low melting point, which makes it quick and easy to work with, but it's also incredibly brittle and fractures easily under pressure. It's prettier than it is practical."

"Oh." Nieve frowned, considering the implications of using such a gear in something as powerful as a train engine. "Then how are these gears going to replace the parts of the engine that break?"

Rose snapped one of the connecting lines of bronze off the network of gears and dropped it in one of the crucibles heating on the melt-plate. She took a minute to sand down the spot where the line had been, leaving the surface of the gear smooth and unblemished. "That, my friend, is the whole reason I tolerate Brick for the entire duration of a delve."

Mason chuckled, shifting sideways on the mattress to hold his hand out for the first finished gear. After a moment or two, Mason set the gear down on the floor, separate from his pile of stone gears.

"Done." Mason announced, holding his hand out for the next gear Rose freed from the bronze connections. The one he'd altered looked almost entirely the same as it had when Rose handed it to him, though perhaps a bit of the brightness had gone out of it. He caught Nieve staring and grinned as he explained. "That's as hard as steel now. It'll hold for a few more full-length trips along this track—way longer than Prickles' imbues. Not that we'll be here that long."

"Oh. Is that why you wanted metal mana?" Nieve asked. "To help Rose with her casts?"

"Ha! No way, I wanted metal mana for my own craft." Mason sounded more than a little smug as he said it, as if his accomplishment was something of a rarity. Nieve hadn't known many climbers who went to the trouble of earning a crystal mark, but the topic came up often enough in climber circles that it didn't seem worth quite that much bravado. "I only help Prickles out to make her owe me. Like she owes me for coming on this delve at the last minute."

"Wait, what was your craft, again?" Nieve asked, recalling that he'd only called it "art" before.

Rather than answer immediately, Mason plucked the next bit of scrap bronze from his sister's hand, pinching it between thumb and forefinger. The gleaming bronze began to writhe and dance, shapes emerging from what had been nothing more than a thin metal stick before.

"I make jewelry," Mason explained, a fond smile overtaking his features as the bronze rippled and changed. "I've always loved working with precious metals and turning them into artforms, but there's a limit to what I could accomplish with heat and tools. I wanted more control and the ability to influence the metal into the exact shape I saw inside my head. I got pretty good at it, but it never seemed like enough to truly count as art."

The bronze in his hand transformed into a tiny, intricate rosebud, gleaming with that fresh-cast glow. While the bud was tightly furled, the thorns along the stem seemed greatly exaggerated, sharp points designed to draw blood. Rose made a face at him before taking the tiny sculpture by the bud and dropping it into one of her crucibles. Mason pouted before resuming his work on the bronze gears.

"So, wait. You went all the way to the Unclaimed Lands for a crystal mark of metal just to make jewelry?" Nieve asked, perplexed. "Isn't that a little . . . extreme?"

"It's not just jewelry, it's art," Mason said, a hint of his sister's usual firm tone creeping into his voice. "Shaping precious and rare metals is my passion, and to do it properly, I needed access to metal mana. I don't care about spire climbing, or treasure hunting, or even earning my parent's approval for the inheritance. All I want is to run my little shop in peace and maybe win a few awards at the crafting competitions."

Although she didn't truly understand it, Nieve found it impressive that Mason would work so hard to turn his hobby into a profession as well as an artform. But before she could swallow her bread roll to say that, Rose undercut the moment.

"It should be noted that Brick doesn't earn a consistent income, as I do," Rose pointed out, a touch dismissive. "I won't say he doesn't do well, but his finances can sometimes run from feast to famine on a month to month basis."

"And that's why I need you to succeed our parent," Mason said sweetly. "So I can take some time off every now and then without worrying about my budget."

Rose snorted and rolled her eyes, but it wasn't much of a protest.

"What about you, Nieve?" Odette asked, pulling a thread long through her embroidery hoop.

"Huh?" Nieve hadn't expected the question—didn't really understand what it was in reference to, either. "I don't own a shop or anything like that. I'm a professional climber."

"Oh, no, I meant: do you have any hobbies or practice any crafts?" Odette clarified, drawing a tiny pair of scissors from one of the utility pockets on her left bracer. She squinted at her thread, pulling it taut as she continued. "Or are those sorts of things discouraged in Dalenos?"

"Oh! No, not discouraged, just different, I think. We have plenty of crafters in Dalenos, but it's usually for work, rather than a hobby."

"What types of hobbies are common in Dalenos?" Rose asked, her attention mostly on her work. She was stacking the used molds near Mason's bed and gathering up the tiny gears that had scattered when he dropped them. "What do you do when you're not climbing?"

"I'm a duelist, which is kind of a hobby, I guess." Nieve usually spent most of her time between spire climbs training or dueling. That wasn't as interesting as casting bronze or making jewelry. What did her teammates do between climbs? "Poetry is really popular in Dalenos. And music. Every full moon, people host garden parties to recite poetry or play instruments and discuss nature and seasons and stuff like that. It's supposed to be reflective, but I always found it kind of boring. Oh, flower arranging is pretty big, too. Can't believe I forgot that one: I used to have to take lessons on it."

Mason snorted, covered it up, then gave up and laughed out loud. "Lessons for flower arranging? *You* did that? That's something I'd love to see."

"I wasn't very good at it," Nieve admitted frankly. "My grandmother finally let me quit after my third instructor called me hopeless and recommended I do something to channel my rambunctious energy."

"Ah," Odette nodded sagely. "Is that when you began sword training?"

"No, actually, I picked that up a little later." Nieve hedged, hesitant to spill this secret, even though it was a small one. If Sage had been here, he already would have blurted it out, so keeping it back almost felt dishonest. Still, it felt as if it cost something to admit it out loud. "I was an ice dancer."

Mason dropped a bronze gear in the middle of his chest, grunting at the impact. Odette's eyebrows climbed her forehead, and even Rose stopped her work to look up and stare.

"You were a what?" Rose asked, turning one ear forward. "I'm sorry, I believe I misheard you."

Nieve sighed heavily. "I trained and competed as an ice dancer. It was really athletic and it helped build up my endurance, but yeah. It's kind of embarrassing."

"Ice dancing is the one with music, right?" Mason asked, levering himself up on an elbow. "And the sparkly dresses, the ribbons, the fancy hair—you did all of that?"

"I did." Nieve crossed her arms over her chest, glowering down at Mason. "And I was reshing good at it, too. I placed second in my age group the last year I competed."

"I wish I could have seen that," Rose said mildly, the glow of molten bronze making her eyes sparkle. "I'm sure you were breathtaking."

"Yeah, well." Nieve shrugged, letting her arms drop to her sides. "It ended up being pretty good for me, training-wise. Especially after I got my attunement, since learning to skate wasn't new, I just had to learn to skate while wielding a sword."

"I hope I get to see that," Mason said, lying back on his bed again. "I've got this vision in my head of you twirling around in circles, hacking and slashing attackers to bits."

Nieve snorted. "It's not like that. Try twirling during a fight and someone's just gonna push you over. Jumps are pretty stupid, too—you can't change direction in midair." She hedged for a moment, then added, "Unless you're Hane."

That got a laugh from everyone. Rose sat back on her heels, dabbing sweat from her face before taking a long gulp from her canteen. Odette smiled brightly as she turned her embroidery hoop around, showing off the outline of a circular gear, like the ones Rose and Mason were making. Mason kicked one leg over the one braced against the wall while casually reaching over the edge of the bed to disturb Rose's piles of gears. Nieve grinned and finally took a seat on the floor, right in the doorway.

This is what it's supposed to be like, Nieve thought. She was almost comfortable, save for a single pang of grief that nettled her heart. She laughed as Rose slapped Mason's hand, and smiled as Odette hummed softly to herself as she selected a new spool of thread. *It's not the same as before, but this is still familiar. Still warm and supportive. Comfortable.*

It was everything she wanted to have with Hane.

The realization that she'd found what she missed most about climbing—more than the fights, more than the victories, even more than the treasures—in this room full of strangers was disconcerting at best. She knew Hane—well, probably about as well as anyone knew Hane—but she'd never felt as comfortable with them as she felt here, with people she might never see again once she left Caelford.

It was a little unsettling that Nieve felt more comfortable with these strangers than her own teammate. There had to be a way to fix that, but how? Hane was prickly and distant, and they preferred to be that way. Nieve had tried giving them space during the long journey from Dalenos to Caelford, then she'd tried the direct approach earlier. Neither had made Hane any more likely to open up, so what else was there to do?

I wish they were here to see this, Nieve thought to herself. *I want to show them what a team is supposed to be. I just wish . . .*

Actually, she wished a lot of things, but none of them were in her control. Tearing the last bread roll in half, Nieve allowed herself to revel in the camaraderie and comfort of being part of a team.

CHAPTER 10

HANE

Wavewalker (leg mark), Citrine

Standing outside the train at night was almost surreal. Hane could hear the steady rhythm of the rails and the tracks, could feel the wind knifing through them, could smell the coal that powered the steam engine, but unless they used a perception spell to enhance their vision, they couldn't see a thing. The scenery rolled by under a cover of darkness, illuminated only by the light gleaming through the windows of the train. On the platform between cars, the only light came from the round portal windows set high in the doors, making it difficult to judge where the gap between gangways was.

It was colder outside now than it had been earlier, but just then, Hane found they didn't mind. After passing through so many overcrowded cars, it was nice to take a moment and pretend they were blissfully alone. They could breathe out here without being breathed on, and they could stretch without accidentally hitting someone. No raised voices, no unwashed bodies, no clumsy boots stomping over toes. No annoying side quests to complete. Just space and breath and time.

Peace.

<You might not like it so much if you spent as much time alone as I have.>

Well, they were almost entirely alone.

I'm sorry for what happened to you, Hane replied, twisting their back from side to side. *I've spent some time alone in a spire, and sometimes it's terrifying, and other times it's not so bad. But I understand that our situations are completely different: every time I was in a spire, it was by choice, and I could leave at will. I'm sure that if my circumstances were the same as yours, I wouldn't like being alone either.*

<I didn't used to mind being alone,> Chime said conversationally. <It wasn't as if challengers visited my shrine regularly, but even if years passed without seeing another being, I never felt alone. I had the music of the world all to myself, the great orchestra of life! And now, even outside of these sky-stabbing spires, I cannot hear so much as a birdsong. I long to return home.>

I'm sorry, Hane repeated, casting Enhance Vision so they could make out the edge of the platform. *I know it probably feels slow to you, but we are trying to find your missing pieces so we can return you to your shrine. If there's anything I can do to speed this along, I welcome the advice.*

<I do not mean to criticize. I am grateful for the efforts of Nieve, Sage, and yourself.> Chime's tolls were long and sad, the tune of dejection. <I was merely lamenting my circumstances. I suppose that is not helpful to you.>

Hane didn't have a response for that; it felt too much like talking to Nieve about her doubts, fears, and grief. While it was probably necessary to talk through those feelings, such conversations made Hane incredibly uncomfortable. But looking at it from a bit of distance, how could Hane compare their discomfort with emotion to the tragedy that Chime had suffered? They weren't responsible for how Chime had been stolen from their shrine and scattered throughout the spires, but they had agreed to help. Was listening to lamentations a part of helping?

<I am sorry I was unable to aid you in that last trial,> Chime continued. <I must confess: I did not understand the purpose behind the request.>

The only purpose of side quests is for additional treasure. Hane reached inside their pocket, feeling for the metal badge they'd been gifted by a grateful conductor. *And even then, they're often not worth it.*

Not when it was a collection request to find twelve brass buttons scattered throughout two entire train cars. Apparently it was some rite of passage that new conductors all went through: senior members of the crew would steal the buttons from the new conductor's jacket and hide them. It wasn't difficult or dangerous, it was just tedious and annoying; if Hane had known the only reward was a conductor's badge, they wouldn't have accepted the request in the first place.

What I wouldn't give for a lone lake serpent, Hane thought longingly. *Or two lake serpents. Anything but scrounging under beds and through trash cans for a bunch of lousy buttons.*

Now Hane was the one lamenting their circumstances. Putting their woes aside, Hane rolled open the door to the passenger car and stepped inside. They kept one hand on the door as they waited for their eyes to adjust from the pitch blackness to the almost-too-bright light inside the car. They heard voices nearby, muffled by the partitions and doors that separated passenger compartments. Unlike the cabins at the rear of the train, these compartments were all unassigned and provided only bench-like seats and overhead luggage storage. No beds or snacks, no desks or privacy. It was the type of compartment Hane shared with Nieve and Sage on their way from Dalenos to Caelford, and they decidedly had not enjoyed it. The private cabins weren't much better—with the tiny windows, they were almost claustrophobia-inducing—but at least the door could be locked. Maybe the next time they traveled by train, they would look into the additional cost of a private cabin.

<But what about Nieve and Sage?> Chime asked. <Wouldn't they wish to travel at your side?>

They might prefer traveling together without me, Hane thought back. Their vision clear enough, they started forward along the aisle, using transference mana throughout their shroud to remain balanced despite the rocking of the train. More to change the subject than anything else, Hane asked, *Did you get a good look at our new teammates? Would you recognize them if you perceived them nearby?*

<I would.> Chime's tones became short and quick, not quite excited, but not lamentable either. <I recognize the one with the mark gifted by my kin as the one who blares as loudly as a brass trumpet, bold and straightforward, as brazen as a stallion in the spring.>

Hane nearly missed a step at the intensity of Chime's description. They were obviously talking about Mason, but as a trumpet? Or a stallion? That was a bit unusual, wasn't it?

<I will assign that one the title of Mason,> Chime stated firmly. <Which one was the discordant orchestra, with a myriad of tunes playing all at once?>

I . . . what?

<The human who sounded like many instruments playing all at once,> Chime insisted. <Most humans sound of two or three different melodies at a time, with one tune playing louder than the others. This human carried so many melodies that it was difficult to separate the tunes from one another. It was a rather intriguing chorus, though, with many sounds overlapping to become one before diverging once more. What title do I assign to that human?>

Hane thought back, trying to remember the discussion. *I thought you said Mason was the loud one? He's the one with the crystal mark.*

<Yes, but I am referring to a different human now.>

I don't know what you mean by tunes and orchestras, Hane replied. *Can you give me a physical description of who you mean?*

<It is not quite as simple as that. I am not seeing through you so much as perceiving the space around you. You may only look ahead of yourself, but

I perceive in all directions equally. If you wish me to associate a name with someone, contact with them would be the best way for me to perceive the exact person you wish to assign a title to.>

Sorry, no. As they reached out to open the outer door, Hane heard the sounds of someone being violently ill inside the bathroom. Making a face, Hane hurried outside, welcoming the distraction of the cool night air. Once again, the change in light rendered them momentarily blind, forcing them to wait until their eyes adjusted to the darkness. *Can you try describing the others as you saw them? Maybe I can guess by elimination.*

<The one of the discordant orchestra and the brazen trumpet—Mason— had the loudest auras,> Chime explained. <The other two carried softer tunes. The one who hoots and coos like a pan flute hides many secrets, but I was unable to discern the nature of those secrets. The one who struts and plucks yet never strums feels strangely out of tune and not entirely whole, like a lute with no strings, or a drum with no tension. Perhaps they are missing a limb, or some non-vital organs?>

Hane started to say no, but stopped themself; while it appeared that everyone had all their parts firmly attached, Hane couldn't be certain. There were illusions that could hide missing hands and fingers convincingly, and a prosthetic hidden beneath a sleeve or leggings would be invisible to them. And there was no way they could know if someone had all their organs or not.

I'm sorry, Chime, but I can't be sure who you mean by these descriptions. Next time, we can try working on names for the . . . sounds you hear. Hane stepped over the gap between platforms, reaching out to grab the door handle for balance. They paused before opening it, though, unable to stop the question that surfaced in their mind. *Is that how you identify all humans? By the sound of their mana, or aura, or whatever?*

<Yes. It is the truest way I have of perceiving another being,> Chime replied. <I perceive Nieve as the powerful, resonant one, though her melody has been out of tune lately.> As Chime spoke, the notes of their voice started low then swelled smoothly, as if demonstrating the sound they associated with Nieve. <The one who is missing is Sage, the one whose song should echo, yet does not. You are Hane, the one who sounds—>

Please don't tell me how I sound. The thought was more a reaction than a request. Hane yanked the door open sharply, covering the spike of adrenaline that had sped their pulse. *I know who and what I am, I don't need to be told.*

A beat of silence. Then: <I understand.>

Somehow, that only made it worse.

Luckily, Hane didn't have time to dwell on that because as soon as their eyes adjusted to the light of the car, they were confronted with a blubbering, red-faced child seated in the middle of the aisle between the passenger compartments. With the aisle as narrow as it was, the only way to avoid the child was to hop over their head entirely. Not impossible, but possibly a bit extreme.

Please don't be an escort quest, Hane thought, looking all around for a nearby parent or other authority figure before approaching the child. *Please don't be an escort quest. Anything but an escort quest.*

"Hey." Hane stopped just outside of arm's reach from the child, crouching down to be on eye level. "Are you okay? Are you lost?"

"No," the child blubbered sullenly. "But Glimmer is lost."

"Glimmer?" Hane repeated.

"Uh huh." A loud sniffle made Hane cringe. "I know I wasn't supposed to let her out, but I just wanted to play with her. And now she's—she's—"

Ah, I remember now. Hane released the breath they'd been holding. *Odette said there would be a quest to find a missing item; this must be it.*

"What does Glimmer look like?" Hane asked.

"W-will you help me find her?"

"I'll do my best." A quest reward from a child probably wasn't worth the effort, but it seemed especially cold to leave a child crying all alone. And maybe the parents would bestow the actual reward; there was no way to be sure unless they completed the quest. "Tell me about Glimmer."

"She's beautiful and shiny, with pretty blue fur," the child explained, more coherent now that they were no longer sobbing. "She likes strawberries, but only the seeds. And her eyes are black."

Hane waited a beat before asking for more details. "How big is Glimmer? Which way did she go? Does she know her name?"

"Sometimes she's this big, and sometimes she's this big." The child held both hands out wide, fingers splayed like the legs of a spider, before they pressed both palms together and interlaced their fingers. That was puzzling, but not as much as what the child said next. "She went that way, but she could be anywhere by now."

Hane followed the child's point toward the back of the car. Initially, they thought they might be looking for a cat or a small dog, but the child definitely pointed up toward the ceiling. A bird, then? That made a small amount of sense: birds could seem larger than they were by opening up their wings.

Still, Hane enhanced their vision and hearing, watching the floor as much as the ceiling and walls. They moved cautiously, gliding rather than stepping, just in case the small creature should get underfoot. It took a while to go from one end of the car to the other while moving that slowly, but at least Hane was certain they hadn't missed anything. As they approached the rear outer door, they found it blocked by two people speaking in low tones: one wearing the vest and badge of an engineer, the other wearing a long dress and a wide-brimmed hat. Hane excused themself before peering inside the vacant bathroom, looking around for the child's pet. Upon exiting, they caught the person in the hat giving them a disapproving look.

Probably because I'm acting suspiciously, Hane thought, shrugging off the look. They could stop and explain themself, but why? It probably wouldn't change anything, which made it a waste of time. Hane turned back to consider all the passenger compartments lining the walkway. Was there a way to check inside without bothering the passengers? Or maybe it was best to start in the compartment with the child's family.

Just as Hane took a step, something bright and colorful popped into existence overhead. Their first instinct was to sink into a battle-ready stance and prepare a Burst spell, but as the child shrieked "There she is, there she is!" Hane realized their mistake. By the time they looked upward, only a puff of shimmering mist remained.

Hane frowned. That wasn't typical bird behavior.

Before they could ask the child what, exactly, this pet was, a compartment door flew open and four passengers rushed out into the corridor.

"There's a bug!" one of them cried. "A large, hairy bug! Someone kill it!"

"No, it's a butterfly!" someone else protested. "One of the poisonous kind."

"Stay calm," Hane ordered, speaking firmly. They weren't a conductor or wearing anything indicative of authority, but they'd found that clear orders tended to quell panic. Sometimes. "It's a child's pet and it's not dangerous. Wait here, and I'll catch it for you."

Hane had no idea as to whether or not this creature was dangerous, but they certainly weren't going to say that in front of people already on the verge of panic. Before stepping inside the compartment, Hane slipped their stealth gloves out of an inner pocket and slipped them on. The enchantment wasn't strong enough to hide Hane from sight, but it did allow them to move silently and made their shroud undetectable to anyone using spells like Detect Aura. The gloves might not help much, but there was no reason not to give them a try. Pulling the door shut behind them, Hane eased into the compartment, scanning the ceiling and luggage rack until they spotted it.

"Beautiful, shiny, and blue." Hane nodded, as surprised as they were impressed. "The child wasn't wrong."

The creature clung to a bar along the luggage rack, wings tightly furled around itself while its nose and ears twitched wildly. Its fur was short and sky blue, which faded to periwinkle and purple along the wings. Hane couldn't blame the two passengers for thinking it a bug or a butterfly, but it was neither. It wasn't even technically an animal, but a very small monster commonly known as a blink-bat. They were mostly harmless, but they possessed the unique ability to teleport short distances, and even through solid objects. This one had to be very young if it couldn't blink through the walls of the train and escape into the wilds, but it seemed to have no trouble going through the thin partitions dividing the compartments.

"Sorry, friend," Hane whispered. The blink-bat's ears snapped together, forming a shape like a bowl. "I commend you on your escape, but it's my job to bring you back. Don't take it personally."

The blink-bat hung upside down from the luggage rack, round black eyes wide and pleading. Hane inched forward, wondering how they would capture it so it wouldn't simply teleport away. Perhaps if they could cup it between their hands, they could shape their shroud around it in a way so that it couldn't blink away. Or maybe the tiny monster was tame enough that simply taking hold of it was enough to keep it from escaping. It seemed possible, especially considering how still it stayed as Hane inched closer and closer. They reached out slowly, trying to appear as nonthreatening as possible as they moved their hands in to cup them around the blue blink-bat.

A burst of blue glitter, and then the tiny creature was gone. Hane jumped back, looking around wildly before shoving the door open and rushing back into the wall. "Did anyone see—"

Screams erupted from a compartment across the aisle. Hane just barely leapt out of the way before a door was flung open.

"There's a—"

"Harmless child's pet on the loose," Hane declared loudly and firmly. "Thank you for informing me. Please step aside and allow me to remove it for you."

Once again longing for a simple, straightforward challenge against a lake serpent, or even a sea serpent at this point, Hane ducked inside the compartment, snapping the door shut behind them. Not that it would do any good, but at least the passengers wouldn't be able to see them fumble again. This time, instead of perching on the luggage rack, the blink-bat was fluttering around the ceiling, its abdomen glowing with an ephemeral blue light.

"Oh, you're a glowing blink-bat," Hane mused. "That's why you're a pet. That's unfortunate for you, little one. Sorry about this."

Motion shaping wasn't something Hane did frequently, but in this case, it was the gentlest way to bring the creature safely within reach. A spell like Slow would send it falling to the floor, and the last thing Hane wanted was to injure the gentle monster. A spell like Burst would kill it outright. But shaping its motion so that it was drawn down from the ceiling brought it safely within reach. Before reaching up to catch it, Hane charged their shroud with transference mana. They had no idea if it would work or not, but the hope was that a heavy concentration of transference mana would interfere with the blink-bat's ability to teleport.

Hane never even got close: the blink-bat vanished in a puff of blue glitter, and judging by all the shouting and stomping in the corridor, Hane knew exactly where it had gone. By the time they threw open the compartment door, people were peering out of compartments up and down the length of the car. A few passengers were cowering on the floor while others were trying to run away. The passengers who couldn't see what was going on were shouting questions, the blink-bat started chittering loudly as it blinked from one end of the corridor to the other, and above it all Hane heard the wail of a bereft child.

"Everyone calm down." Hane didn't shout, but they did project their voice, making it sound like an order rather than a request. "The animal is harmless, but elusive. Please stay inside your compartments for now so I can catch it and return it safely to its owner."

It took a little time, but gradually the crowd dispersed. Hane didn't bother chasing after the tiny beast, but they kept an eye on it just to know where it was. The farthest it seemed able to teleport was just under three feet, though it seemed to prefer six- to twelve-inch blinks. Hopefully it would tire soon, making it all the easier to catch.

Only three people remained in the corridor, and by the way the two adults bracketed the small child, Hane guessed these were the parents. Giving the blink-bat more time to tire itself out, Hane approached the family unit.

"Sorry about this." The woman gave Hane a sympathetic look as she squeezed the child's shoulders. "We had no idea this would happen. Rui is usually so good with Glimmer, we had no idea she'd gotten loose."

"We have the crate, if that will help you." The father held out a glass box, shaped roughly like a lantern. Runes were inscribed along strips of gold at the top and bottom of the box. "It's enchanted so the little glow-bat can't jump out of it unless someone opens it." He cast an admonishing glance down at the child, who turned to sob into their mother's lap.

Glimmer wasn't a glow-bat; she was a glowing blink-bat. Somehow, Hane didn't think these people would appreciate being told the difference.

"This is what you're using to transport her?" Hane asked, examining the glass box without taking it. "Isn't it a little small?"

"No, this is more than enough for a creature that size," the father assured Hane. "Our child uses the pet as a bedside lamp and a bigger crate gives it too much space to flit away. The light only goes so far, you know."

Hane lifted their gaze to meet the father's eyes straight on. "You keep the pet inside this box all the time?"

The man's eyes narrowed and even the woman comforting the child went stiff with disapproval. "I'll have you know that that creature is not an animal, but a monster. It's lucky to be alive, never mind coddled and fed and loved. Now, will you return it to us or not?"

Hane glanced down at the sniffling child before stoically turning away, walking to the rear of the car where they had last seen the blink-bat. They no longer heard the quiet chittering, nor any shouts of surprise from the compartments they passed. Moving silently, they stepped into the open doorway of the bathroom, searching the dark room for a soft glow. It wasn't hard to spot: the tiny blue blink-bat was perched on the sink faucet, hanging from a clawed wing as it lapped at a droplet of water.

"Thirsty?" Hane asked, lips quirking as those ears perked in their direction once more. "Here, friend. I have some water for you."

The blink-bat watched, intrigued, as Hane conjured an orb of water to hover just above their palm. This type of shaping was difficult, but not terribly strenuous. What was difficult was drawing the water orb into two halves and shaping each half into a deep, hollow bowl. Hane held their breath as they slid forward, bringing the two water bowls around on either side of the blink-bat. The rodent-like nose twitched, black eyes wary, then a tiny tongue flicked out to taste the conjured water. A few more licks kept it distracted while Hane gently brought the water bowls together, forming a cage of water around the blue-furred blink-bat. It took a great deal of concentration to walk while keeping the water cage thick enough that the blink-bat would have trouble teleporting through it, but at least Hane didn't have far to go.

They didn't even look back at the family unit as they flicked open the latch on the door with a push of transference mana, then slid it open with their foot. They let the door slide all the way shut behind them before they released the shape of the water prison, letting the cutting wind carry it away in a stream. Only the blink-bat was left in their open palm, nose wiggling adorably as it peered up at Hane with inquisitive eyes.

"If their child needs a bedside lamp, then they can get a bedside lamp," Hane informed the tiny monster. "You are not a bedside lamp."

The blink-bat cocked its head from side to side almost thoughtfully before it curled a tiny wing-claw around Hane's finger and sniffed the air. A sudden puff of blue glitter, then the blink-bat was gone.

A low, throaty chuckle had Hane reaching for a tonfa. They whirled around on the platform, shocked to find that they weren't alone. The woman from earlier—the one with the broad hat—was standing against the rail holding a long-stemmed cigarette holder. The burning ember illuminated a gleaming red smile.

"That's a kind thing you did," she said in a low voice. "But they won't thank you for it."

Embarrassed, Hane quickly tucked their tonfa away. "I didn't do it for any thanks."

A long, slow, smoky exhale, stolen by the train's slipstream. "We never do, do we?"

That was a little cryptic. And possibly the start of a new side quest. Rather than ask what she meant, Hane hopped to the next platform, intent on returning to their room. They really should try and get a little sleep before they relieved Lief on guard duty.

For a low-combat scenario, they'd had their share of excitement for the day.

NIEVE

Champion (mind mark), Citrine
??? (heart mark), Sealed

H ello?" Nieve called, thumping her fist against the door. "Anyone in there? Hello!"

She waited a moment, listening through the door before shrugging and taking a step back. Most of the private cabins in this car had been empty, and the few that weren't contained grumpy passengers who had maybe enjoyed the lounge car's bar a little too thoroughly the night before. It felt too early for Nieve to be awake, too, as she'd stayed up fairly late watching Rose create a wide variety of gears, rods, and even specialized tools in order to fix the engine.

Not that she regretted it at all; she was beginning to enjoy the way Rose said her name. She'd very nearly asked Hane to switch teams with her for the day, just to stay close to Rose, but in the end, the potential for a fight won out over any potential flirting. Which meant her morning so far had consisted of knocking on doors.

At least that was the last one, Nieve thought as she covered a yawn. Hopefully Mason or Lief found something, but it seemed unlikely as Nieve had heard nothing through her communication device. She rolled open the outside door of the train car, lazily shouldering it wide enough to pass through. *Maybe if I get to the lounge car first, I can grab some breakfast while I wait for Mason and Lief. That'll wake me up a little.*

Nieve and Mason had split the task of checking the private cabins for the Magpie's crew while Lief, wearing a special badge Hane had earned from a side quest, headed to the kitchen. He'd seemed particularly cheery about it, but Nieve had been too tired at the time to question it. It was only later she'd realized that he'd probably claimed the kitchen in order to snack as he searched.

Clever pretty-boy, Nieve thought, more amused than upset. *I hope he doesn't find anything; I need to tease someone.*

As she passed through the final car of private cabins, Nieve heard sounds of distress coming from one of the rooms. She stopped and listened, hoping an enemy hadn't gotten the drop on Mason while he'd been searching this car. Maybe they'd taken his earpiece so he couldn't call for help. He could be hurt, or dying, or—

Nieve drew back from the door sharply as the sound on the other side became clear: retching. Now that she really looked at it, she realized she was standing outside the door to the bathroom.

Probably not Mason, Nieve determined, taking another step back. Mason had seemed slow and sleepy during the brief strategy meeting that morning, but not ill. No, this was likely one more passenger who had overindulged at the bar the night before.

<I can confirm that the one called Mason is not on the other side of this door,> Chime pronounced. The crystal shard was once again safely ensconced in Nieve's boot. Hane had seemed almost relieved when they returned them to Nieve after their watch shift ended. <The mana signature I sense here does not quite seem human, but more of an echo of a human. Many of the mana signatures here are like this one.>

Spire constructs, Nieve thought by way of explanation. *They're not real-real, like us. They're like really advanced illusions.*

Sage would have gone into more detail, but that was how Nieve commonly thought of the spire simulacra.

Before she could continue any further, the bathroom door came open, revealing a pale-faced and wobbly passenger who appeared surprised to see her. "Oh, I'm sorry. Were you waiting? You might want to try a different bathroom; this one is . . . well, just trust me."

"No, sorry, I was just passing by." Nieve tried not to make a face as she edged past. "Feel better!"

"Ugh, I've felt awful ever since I got on this train," the passenger moaned. Nieve hesitated, torn between sympathy and disgust. "I get terrible motion sickness whenever I travel. I haven't been able to eat anything since we left the station."

"Uh huh." Nieve longed to run away. Why did she need this nameless person's life story? Still, it felt rude to walk away from someone so clearly in distress. "Do you want me to find a conductor for you? I bet they have someone on staff who can help with motion sickness."

"It doesn't work," the passenger said miserably. "Medicine and healing magic settle my stomach for a little while, but then the nausea always comes back."

"Er, sorry." Nieve edged further away. "I hope you start to feel better soon, or—"

"If only I had something to drink!" the passenger bemoaned, slumping against the doorway. "Something with some flavor to get this taste out of my mouth, but mild so it's not terrible when I—when I—"

Nieve turned away, scrunching up her face as the passenger wheeled away to retch. As much as she longed to run away, she felt obligated to wait.

"I can share some of my water," Nieve offered when the passenger finished washing their face. "If you think that would help."

"No, I have plenty of water." The passenger indicated the sink, which operated on a foot pump to draw water from a hidden receptacle. "I need something tasty that won't make me feel worse than I already do."

"Er . . ." Nieve made a show of searching her pockets, fully expecting to come up empty. To her surprise, she found the sample wine bottle given to her by the conductor upon boarding. "I have this? I mean, I wouldn't drink it. It might actually make you sicker, but—"

"I'll take anything," the passenger begged. "Please?"

"Here. Just don't say I didn't warn you."

Her good deed complete, Nieve started fast-walking to the exit. Mason and Lief were probably both waiting for her by now, but at least she no longer felt hungry.

"Oh, wow, this is great!" the passenger called after her. "Ginger honey mint? This might as well be medicine!"

Nieve groaned as she halted her step, grudgingly turning around. "I probably should have told you that it's wine. I know it doesn't look like it because of the size and the weird flavors, but—"

"I have to thank you!" The pale-faced passenger lurched into the corridor, clutching the tiny wine bottle in one hand as they patted themself down in search of something. "This is exactly what I needed! You have no idea how grateful I am."

"That's okay!" Nieve insisted, holding her hands up defensively as she backed away. "Really, your good health is the only—"

"Here!" The passenger smiled as they presented Nieve with a well-loved book. The paper cover had been folded over so often that the image appeared faded, the spine was cracked, and the pages were yellow. It looked like one of Sage's favorite old books. "It's my favorite. I brought it to read on the train, but every time I open it, I—" The passenger snapped their mouth closed, expression becoming strained.

"You really don't have to do that," Nieve insisted, reeling backward. "I'm not much of a reader, and I don't really have the time anyway, and I'd hate to take it from you."

A few deep breaths, then the look of urgency left the passenger's face. "Please take it? I'd feel terrible if I couldn't give you anything in return for the wine. And the more I think about it, the more I realize that reading it might be what's making me ill."

"Oh, ah, um . . . well, I guess so." More to be finished with the interaction than anything, Nieve accepted the book. She pinched it between her thumb and forefinger, concerned that the passenger's illness might be catching. After one final expression of gratitude, the passenger shuffled back to the bathroom.

Nieve turned and ran to the end of the car, throwing open the outer door to get outside.

"Ugh, gross," she muttered, examining the book at a safe distance. Interactions with spire simulacra didn't normally last that long or include that level of detail unless it was meant to be important, but Nieve couldn't see what was special about this old book. It looked like a travel account of a fisherwoman, traveling from lake to river to stream in search of a particular fish from an old legend. Definitely not something Nieve would enjoy. Just to be certain, she checked for messages written inside the cover, then flipped through the pages, searching for anything hidden inside. "Oh, well. Maybe someone else on the team wants it."

Tucking the book under her arm, Nieve hopped the coupler and continued on her way to the lounge car.

It was still early enough that the car wasn't crowded, but a fair amount of people were already present, sipping their morning tea and enjoying a selection of pastries. Before Nieve could flag down a server, Mason caught her eye with a lazy wave. He was lounging against the service counter, looking livelier than he had first thing that morning. Perhaps the teacup at his elbow had something to do with that.

"Hey. You find anything?"

"Nope. You?"

"Nah." Mason drained his teacup, sighing loudly in satisfaction. "Did you happen to see Lief in the kitchen car?"

"No, I didn't try passing through the kitchen." Nieve looked around the car, studying the faces of the passengers. "Do you see anyone familiar here?"

"I've been watching, but nothing suspicious here." Mason beckoned a server with a gesture. "You should grab something to eat while you can. Depending on how big the kitchen is, it might take Lief a while to—"

As he spoke, the lounge door rolled open, admitting a pleased-looking Valian with wind-ruffled hair.

"I was wrong. Sorry, Nieve."

"Hello again." Lief's eyes danced as he approached the pair of them at the counter. "I can already tell by your faces you didn't find anything."

"Nope," Mason agreed.

"Just a very sick passenger," Nieve said, making a face.

"Yeah, I passed by there, too." Mason grimaced. "That's a little too much detail for me."

"I wonder if it's the same passenger I healed yesterday," Lief mused. "They were complaining of motion sickness. The spell should have worked, but they didn't look any better when I left them."

Nieve shrugged. "They wanted something to drink, so I gave them that weird wine sample. I got this. Think it's important?"

Mason and Lief leaned in close to examine the book.

"I'm not familiar with it," Mason said, giving up quickly. "Prickles might know something about it. You know, since she knows everything."

"The art on this tree is really detailed," Lief pointed out. "There could be an image hidden in it. Does anything jump out at you?"

Nieve hadn't really looked at the cover beyond reading the title. The image depicted a fisherwoman sitting at the base of an old tree, a frothing stream running past her boots as she set a worm to the hook. The tree hadn't seemed all that remarkable, but now that she really looked at it, she couldn't help but think she'd seen that image before.

Nieve looked up sharply, eyes narrowing at the bottle of wine on display behind the counter—the one Odette said contained a secret. "There. Isn't that the same tree on the label of the bottle?"

"Huh!" Mason looked impressed. "What does that mean?"

Nieve snorted, trying to cover a laugh. She gave up and guffawed loudly, earning a few scandalized stares from nearby passengers. The fit of mirth passed quickly, Nieve shaking her head at herself as she tucked the book inside one of her belt purses.

"What was that?" Lief asked, amused.

"Nothing," Nieve assured him. "It's just that, one of my friends is going to laugh really hard when I tell him that I tripped and fell into a trading sequence."

"Oh, I think you're right!" Lief arched his eyebrows. "Odette was concerned about finding that yesterday. I'm sure she'll be relieved when she learns we started it. Is anyone going to ask me what I found?"

Nieve eyed him suspiciously. "You better have saved me a piece if you found any magpie."

The corner of Lief's mouth twitched in a barely suppressed grin. "No, I did not. And I continue to wonder what you think a magpie is. I believe I did find the hidden secret, though: look."

With an unnecessary flourish, he opened his fist, revealing a tiny silver key on a chain just large enough to wear around a wrist. Nieve frowned as she examined it.

"Isn't that the key to the sample wine cabinet?" she asked. "What would we need that for?"

"I don't know, but it seems at least as useful as this badge was." Lief plucked the badge from his collar, tucking both it and the key into a pocket. "If the sample wine started the trading sequence, maybe we need the key to the cabinet in case we need to start over."

It seemed as good an explanation as any. As the three of them conferred, Nieve managed to grab a cold pastry with apple and cinnamon baked inside it. Not exactly the meal she'd been hoping for, but now that the three of them were finished with their assignments, it was time to move on.

"And we're sure that none of these guests are the Magpie or their goons in disguise?" Lief asked, glancing around the room. "I imagine the Magpie must be a master of disguise if Keepsake Treasuries doesn't even have a description of him."

"We both saw him yesterday and I've been watching for a while." Mason rolled his shoulders through a shrug. "The only one neither of us would recognize is the Assassin."

Nieve activated Detect Aura, scanning the room for anyone bearing a shroud. The only people of note were two servers, each surrounded by a crimson-colored shroud. "Unless the Magpie is wearing something to hide his shroud, he's not in here."

"All right. Moving on, then." Lief smiled brightly as he led the way to the door.

"Someone seems sprightly this morning," Mason observed, grinning as he followed. "Or are you just glad you got to search the kitchen like you wanted?"

"Why were you so insistent about searching the kitchen?" Nieve asked. "Is there something special about kitchens in this spire?"

"It's not just this spire," Lief assured her. He held open the outside door, allowing Nieve and Mason out onto the platform. "Kitchens are just great places to search in general. You can almost always find a hidden treasure or a secret tucked away inside a kitchen, and if you get ambushed, there's tons of handy weapons lying around, like iron skillets, knives, and melon ballers. But even if you don't find anything at all—"

"You can still grab a snack," Mason said with a wide grin. "What'd you find? Anything good?"

"Let's just say I happen to know the tea cakes for this afternoon are cinnamon flavored," Lief replied with a smirk. Before Nieve could open the door to the dining car, Lief motioned for her to wait. "Remember, if you do spot the Magpie or anyone on his crew, point them out to me so I can use a spell to memorize their mana signature. That way, I'll be able to find them even if they use a disguise."

"Yeah, yeah," Nieve agreed. They had agreed it was better not to start a fight, especially in public areas where civilians might get hurt, but Nieve was secretly hoping for a fight. She rolled the door to the dining car open, revealing it to be moderately busier than the lounge car. With Detect Aura still active, Nieve scanned the crowd for shrouds and enchanted items.

"Don't forget that we're searching for a Controller," Mason warned, trailing in behind Nieve. "I don't know if you guys got special training to protect yourselves, but I'm warning you now: if it looks like you're mind-controlled, I will knock you out, and I won't be sorry for it."

"Fair enough," Lief agreed, eyeing the size difference between himself and Mason. "I have a few tricks of my own, but I'm going to take 'playing along' off that list right now. How about you, dear Champion?"

"My attunement gives me a natural resistance." Nieve tapped the headband that hid her attunement mark. "And I have protection spells that can help as well. Not that you could knock me out if you tried, Mason."

"It might take me a few tries," Mason said, grinning cheerfully. "I'm just letting you know what's going to happen."

"There are a lot of people here," Lief commented, scanning the room slowly. "How can you be sure the Magpie isn't here? Supposedly he's been a thorn in the side of this version of Haven Securities for a while now; that means he must be good at hiding in plain sight, doesn't it?"

"I'm checking for shrouds," Nieve explained, moving slowly through the car. She stopped each time she spotted someone cloaked in a shroud, scanning their features to verify they weren't Sa'rhi in disguise. She wouldn't be able to tell if anyone were using an advanced illusion, though, so it wasn't a foolproof system.

"I'm not gonna forget the face of a guy who set his dog on me," Mason grumbled. "We should make a plan, like you two come at him head on and I'll sneak up behind him. I want to beat him with his own walking stick."

Nieve snickered at the mental image but didn't let it distract her as she wended her way through the crowd.

"You don't have any natural resistance to mind control, do you?" Lief commented. "If you'll allow me, I have a preventative spell I can place over your mind to protect it from influence."

"Yeah, sure." Mason shrugged, stopping so Lief could cast his spell. "I'm not completely helpless, but since we don't know how strong the Magpie is, it's probably better this way."

Lief touched a finger to Mason's brow, murmuring the words "Clarity of Thought" as Nieve blinked off her Detect Aura spell and rubbed her eyes.

"None of the Magpie's crew are here," she announced. "Let's keep going so I can steal the Magpie's stick before Mason gets his hands on it."

"Oh, are we competing?" Mason asked gleefully. "I'll bet you one share of my loot that I get that stick before you do."

"You wanna bet? Then make it interesting." Nieve grinned, remembering former wagers among teammates while tamping down a tide of grief. "Winner gets to pick one treasure from the loser's cut."

"Deal!"

"Settle down, you two," Lief sighed, walking ahead of Nieve and Mason. He crossed the gangways to the second lounge car first, tugging the door open as he spoke. "Remember, we're not looking for a fight. We're just searching the team out for later."

"We're just having a little fun," Nieve retorted, stepping through the door Lief held open. "Look, it's not as if we're going to find the Magpie just sitting out in the—"

She stopped herself as she spotted Sa'rhi seated at the service counter, smiling cheerily as he wiggled his fingers in a greeting.

"Open," Nieve finished, sighing heavily. Activating Detect Aura, she scanned the lounge car for the auras of the Shaper and the Guardian. This lounge was far more crowded than the first one had been, which meant a lot of potential collateral damage.

"I take it that's one of them?" Lief asked, mimicking the Magpie's wave.

"That one was the leader," Mason whispered. "The one we're assuming is the Magpie."

Sa'rhi lifted a teacup in a mock toast before beckoning Nieve and the others over. He clearly wasn't even attempting to escape notice, sitting out in the open wearing nearly the same outfit as the day before, including the green newsboy cap. In fact, the stolen snake crate sat on the bar at his elbow, almost as if he had been waiting for Nieve and her team to find him.

"It's gotta be a trap," Nieve said, failing to spot even a single other shroud aside from the Magpie's. "Should we call the others?"

"No, they said it would take hours to get the engine fully repaired," Lief replied, speaking softly. "Let's try and give them as much time as possible. Maybe he just wants to talk to us."

"Or it's a trap," Mason countered. "He could have his goons on the roof, ready to drop down and attack us. Or he could set the—" Mason looked around sharply, then lowered his voice to a whisper. "The ivory-crowned critter loose to start a panic."

Just the thought of someone screaming "Snake!" in such a crowded space was enough to make Nieve nervous, never mind if there was a real, live snake slithering around people's ankles. An ambush would be just as bad: if a fight broke out here, there would be no way to avoid collateral damage.

"I don't see their bodyguards," Nieve said, still scanning the crowded room with Detect Aura. "The only person who looks like a threat is the one with the sword, but I can't see a shroud around them."

"I think Odie's notes mentioned that guy," Mason suggested, following Nieve's gaze. "That might be a different challenge entirely."

"Let's hope so," Lief said dryly. "Let's keep an eye on them in case they get mind-controlled. Nieve, do you see anything in that corner near the far door? I thought I sensed something when we entered, but it's gone now."

Nieve put her back to Mason, trusting him to keep watch as she narrowed her focus to the spot Lief indicated. There was a curiously empty stretch of space near the door, enough for a person or two to crowd into, but despite the sway and stagger of the crowd, the space remained open. After a moment of searching, Nieve gave up and shrugged.

"Maybe someone spilled something there and no one wants to step in it," she reasoned. "I don't see anything with Detect Aura."

Lief nodded, though he cast one final look over at the door before turning squarely to face the Magpie. "Then I suppose we should find out what he wants from us."

"And try to get the crate back," Mason added. "If we can get it without a fight, I mean."

I'll just grab him if it looks like he's up to something, Nieve thought to herself. *Most Controllers are at a physical disadvantage, and he can't mind-control me. This scenario will be that much closer to being complete once we have this bandit tied up and secured.*

"Hello again," Sa'rhi said, smiling broadly once they all stood close enough for casual conversation. He hooked an elbow casually over a corner of the crate, looking a touch too smug for someone who had run away from his last fight. His weighted walking stick was tucked beneath one of his suspenders, the polished marble gleaming in the sunlight pouring through the windows. His eyes skipped over Nieve and Mason before landing on Lief. "We didn't meet earlier. I'm calling myself Sa'rhi on this little exploit. Not that I happened to catch either of your friends' names."

"What's in a name isn't important here," Lief quipped with a smile every bit as easy as Sa'rhi's. "Or at least, not as important as what you have there."

"Oh?" Sa'rhi seemed to be enjoying himself as he sipped tea from a delicate-looking cup. "Since you came looking for it, I'll assume you already know what Keepsake is transporting, as well as why they're transporting such cargo. If you will give me a moment to explain my side of the story, I will return this stolen property to you as a sign of good faith."

"That's not even a bargain," Nieve growled, one hand on her sword, though she doubted she'd have the room to draw it. To her companions, she added, "We can just take it from him. It's not like he can stop us in a room this crowded."

"Oh, I wouldn't be so sure." Sa'rhi flashed a grin. "While I might not be a match for any of you, we are currently surrounded by about sixty people all without attunements of their own, so while my influence might not work on you, it will work on all of them."

Nieve flinched, more for failing to see the dilemma herself than its implications. She would hate to have to fight her way through mind-controlled bystanders, nor could she stand by and watch if Sa'rhi gave orders for every person in the car to jump off the side of the train. A room this crowded was practically a bomb and Sa'rhi was the fuse.

"We have some time to listen," Lief said, leaning up against the counter. He gestured lazily to the server behind the counter, waving them over as he spoke to Sa'rhi. "But at the end, we'll be taking that crate from you and returning it to where it belongs. One way or another." As the server approached, he gave her a winning smile and added: "Some tea, please. Any flavor is fine; just make sure it's ice gold."

The server looked almost stunned for a moment, but then she nodded and moved away to comply with Lief's request. Nieve didn't blame her: it sounded as though Lief had said "ice gold" instead of "ice cold." Even that was an odd request: the weather wasn't so warm that cold tea was warranted.

"The crate should not have been removed in the first place, so my apologies for that," Sa'rhi confessed once the server was out of earshot. "Ellis does not comprehend the depths of my intentions, but that is not his fault. I did take the liberty of making sure our little guest was unharmed." He laid his hand flat on top of the crate before peering up at Nieve and Mason questioningly. "Do you happen to know if the other crate was safely returned? Ellis admitted to a bit of . . . rough handling."

"It's alive," Nieve answered, keeping her voice low. "And back where it belongs."

"How noble of you," Sa'rhi returned dryly. "And Mote? You didn't harm my dog, did you?"

"The one that nearly took my hand off?" Mason thumped his fist down on the countertop, earning a few disapproving glares from nearby passengers.

He ignored them in favor of looming intimidatingly over Sa'rhi. "He's fine, but you won't be if you don't start talking."

"Yes, yes." Sa'rhi gave a put-upon sigh while turning his teacup delicately. "I've been after this cargo for quite some time now, so I suppose I should have accounted for additional security beyond Keepsake's own guards, but I didn't expect a full team of attuned. I hope you're being well compensated." Sa'rhi smirked at each of them, but it faded as he traced his fingers over the crate, a gesture that was almost a caress. "You are aware of the fate in store for these poor creatures?"

"They're going to a laboratory that distills the primary ingredient necessary to brew Cure potions," Lief answered. "Admirable work, if you ask me. I wouldn't want to be the one handling these things day in and day out."

"Interesting," Sa'rhi commented. "You consider the conditions for the humans, but not for the animals. Do you have any idea what it takes to milk a snake for its venom?"

"Oh, please." Mason rolled his eyes. "You're worried about the *snakes*? What about all the people minding their own business when a snake comes up and bites them? You think those people should just die?"

"Snakes don't just attack without reason," Sa'rhi countered, his eyes suddenly hard. "They only bite when they feel threatened, like when someone wanders too close to their nest, or across their sunning spot, where there's no place to hide. A little care goes a long way in preventing snake bites."

"So everyone should just walk with their heads down?" Mason asked skeptically.

"In a perfect world, yes." Sa'rhi shrugged coolly. "Or everyone could use a walking stick to tap the ground ahead of them, so that innocent snakes aren't caught off guard and frightened. But I'll allow that keeping common antivenins stocked in medical clinics is warranted, as mistakes do happen. But consider: antivenin for common snake bites is easy to come by. Easy enough that once one vial is used for treatment, all a potion-maker needs to do is capture one snake that produces that specific venom, milk it for a few days, then release it once again. That's just about as balanced as it gets: one human saved, one snake milked. One for one."

"That's assuming the bite victim knows exactly what kind of snake bit them," Lief pointed out. "As I understand it, most people are more concerned with running away than noting the exact color, pattern, and head shape of the snake that bit them. Using Cure made from ivory-crown venom is the safest way to save someone from an unknown venom."

"I agree with you on that point," Sa'rhi allowed. "But it could still follow the one-for-one logic: each time a clinic uses a bottle of Cure, one ivory-crown viper could be collected, harvested, and released. Instead, hundreds of these vipers are bred to live out their lives in captivity, eating only toxic frog eggs and forcibly milked of venom every day for the rest of their miserable, sunless existence. All of that so humans don't have to worry about noticing whether they were bitten by a racer-back python or a diamond-belly cobra. Producing Cure isn't even about saving lives: it's about profits. Why else would it be marketed to adventurers at all? It should be regulated through clinics and hospitals, and administered only by trained medics and healers. Anyone who wishes to go haring off into the wilds needs to do their own research and carry the appropriate antivenins along with them. It's as simple as that."

"Wait a minute," Nieve said slowly, failing to follow the thief's logic. "I thought you were stealing the snakes so you could sell your own black market Cure potions. But if you don't agree with using them for their venom, then why are you trying to steal these snakes?"

"Oh, I get it now." Lief groaned, rolling his eyes exaggeratedly. "The Magpie hasn't been stealing animals for profit; he's been stealing them to set them free. You consider yourself some sort of savior for these creatures."

"I do." Sa'rhi looked perplexed by Lief's reaction. "Milking snakes for their venom isn't entirely painless, you know. And these snakes can live just fine without eating those toxic frog eggs to produce their venom. They shouldn't have to live their lives trapped in glass cages, waiting for the next time they get grabbed up, their mouths forced open so that the venom can be expressed from their glands. They should be caught, milked, and released, just like any other snake used for antivenin production."

"Look, these aren't just any other snakes," Mason pointed out. "And what you're saying doesn't even make sense: only ivory-crowns raised on a strict diet produce venom pure enough to be made into Cure. A wild-caught one isn't guaranteed to have the right venom."

"If people stop relying on Cure as a venom catch-all and instead rely on specific antivenins, then there won't be such a need for pure ivory-crown venom," Sa'rhi replied tartly. "And right now, there is more Cure available on the market than all the other antivenins combined. That's quite a stockpile to move through while people are properly educated on preventing snake bites, or identifying the snakes common to their locales."

"I still feel like I'm missing something here," Nieve commented, shaking her head. "But now that he's told us his evil plans, can we just capture him already?"

"I haven't even gotten to my proposal yet," Sa'rhi objected. "Listen: the plan was to disconnect the Keepsake cars and redirect them onto another track via a hidden engine. And then yes, my plan—in the long run—was to release the cargo in a location I picked out specifically for this population. The environment won't be affected by the sudden influx of ivory-crowns, and there's enough food and water to support them. You can rest assured that I've taken every precaution for introducing these sheltered animals to their native habitat."

"This sounds more like a justification than a proposal," Mason pointed out.

"More to the point, how were you planning on paying your goons if you were never planning to manufacture Cure?" Lief asked, plucking at the edges of his gloves. "It seems at least one of them thought using the snakes for profit was the objective of this merry little jaunt."

"Funds are not my issue. My people would still be adequately paid without the exploitation of animals," Sa'rhi replied somewhat sharply. "As to the proposal portion of my explanation: I have activists waiting to take possession of the cargo once my team delivers it. If you will allow my people to disconnect the last two cars without interference, I will surrender myself to you and your employer with nary a fight, nor a complaint." Sa'rhi flashed a cunning smile at the three of them. "You can't tell me that's not a fair trade. The living cargo gets released, safe and unharmed, and you get the prestige of bringing in the notorious Magpie."

"You can't really expect us to trust you," Nieve said sourly. "After the cargo detaches from the train, there's no reason for you to keep to your end of the bargain. I can't believe you'd willingly give yourself up just to save a few snakes."

"It's principle over profit, my dear," Sa'rhi explained with a sigh. "I don't steal animals to use them; I steal them to free them, or to protect them from exploitation. If Keepsake wishes to charge me for my crimes, then I will gladly testify to my ideals in open court. You would be surprised how sympathetic my cause is among common folk and nobility alike."

"Morality aside, theft is still theft," Lief pointed out, smiling as the server returned to set a cup of tea down in front of him. He gestured for the others to wait as he made a note on a small piece of paper, folded it, and handed it over to the server. "Send the bill to my cabin, please. You may add whatever tip you believe to be fair." With that handled, Lief turned his attention back to the Magpie. "That cargo isn't just bought and paid for; those creatures only exist because they were bred for a specific purpose. The point is moot: without the need for Cure, these animals wouldn't even be here in the first place. You're not saving something that was poached from the wild, you're releasing animals that have never even seen the outdoors."

"Which is why they will be gradually introduced to living in the wild until they acclimate," Sa'rhi replied, checking a pocket watch. "I'm afraid our time draws short. Do we have an accord?"

Nieve felt more conflicted than she thought she would. Capturing the Magpie was the mission objective, and he was offering himself up to them willingly—with the caveat that the team allow the cargo to be stolen from their employer. Would that count against them at the end of this challenge? Or was the cargo outside of their objective? Resh, but Nieve missed the simplicity of beating a villain into submission!

"I have an alternate proposal," Lief said thoughtfully. "Surrender to us right now, and we will discuss the issue of the cargo with the rest of our team before we make our decision. We can even be nice enough to let you speak with one of your goons to relay any plan changes once we have you secured under our watch."

"That puts me at too much of a disadvantage, I'm afraid." Sa'rhi sighed as he set his empty tea cup down with a clack. "But I understand you need time to discuss my offer with your teammates. They passed through here just over an hour ago, correct?"

Nieve felt her stomach twist unpleasantly as Sa'rhi hooked a thumb over his shoulder.

"Three of them, right?" Sa'rhi continued. "Two women and the lithe one all in black? Ellis went after them the moment you showed your faces in here."

Mason's face went tight, though he didn't allow his focus to waver from Sa'rhi. "That's your Assassin, right? They handled him once, they can take him again."

"Well, he was surprised last time. That won't happen again." Sa'rhi lifted a hand, calling the nearest server over—a different one than the one who had served Lief. "I'm finished with my tea. Thank you so much, it was lovely. Would you mind looking after this for me?" Before Nieve could react, Sa'rhi pushed the crate across the counter, into the server's hands. "Treat it gently, but don't let these three have it for any reason."

"Stop!" Nieve lunged at the same time that Lief and Mason hurled themselves across the counter, reaching futilely after the crate as the server backed away wide-eyed with fright. Nieve grabbed for Sa'rhi rather than the box, but before she secured her grip, the weighted end of his walking stick impacted her ribs, once, twice, before hitting the inside of her elbow and knocking her arm away, allowing him to duck beneath her grip to escape. Nieve started to follow, only to find the end of the walking stick thrust between her ankles, making her stumble into the crowd of passengers. By the time she found her feet, Sa'rhi was nearly at the gangway door.

As if he felt her eyes on him, Sa'rhi stopped and looked back over his shoulder, winking conspiratorially before raising his voice and addressing the crowd at large.

"Stop those three people," Sa'rhi ordered, pointing at Nieve, Lief, and Mason. "They're thieves trying to steal from me! They'll steal from all of you if they aren't stopped."

Nieve snarled and lunged, fighting her way through the crowd to grab him, but before she got very far, no fewer than four people hung from her shoulders and arms, preventing her from going any farther. Mason was similarly accosted, pinned against the service counter by three passengers and a server carrying . . . were those manacles? Why would a server have manacles? How could she have gotten them so quickly?

Lief jumped atop the counter, his expression vexed as he watched the Magpie exit the car, all while dancing away from the hands that sought to grab him. His hand hovered over his quiver of arrows, his strung bow held in his opposite hand before he shook his head, giving up his shot. "He's heading back toward the Keepsake cars. You two go after him. I'll get the crate."

"Get off me!" Nieve growled, slamming her body from side to side, shaking off the bystanders roped into this mess. She didn't want to actually hurt any of them—they were only mind-controlled, after all—but she couldn't just let Sa'rhi get away, either. "That's enough! Let go of me, or I'll drop you all like flies."

It was threatening the innocent bystanders that made Nieve realize she needed more than brawn to win this fight. She let the spell protecting her thoughts fade, giving herself a wider latitude to come up with a plan. Even without Frost Form, the people clinging to her weren't all that heavy, but the crush of humanity within the train car was enough to keep her from moving quickly. The first order of business had to be getting free of the people who held her.

Nieve freed one arm from the passenger who gripped it, then set her shoulder against the crowd, shoving her way through, despite the hands that grabbed at her and the one or two people clinging to her back. There was even a child wrapped around her boot, forcing her to step with care, lest she hurt them. The progress was slow, and when she finally arrived at the car door, she found it blocked by a large passenger holding what looked like a fire ax.

"I don't want to hurt you, but I will," Nieve warned, lifting a pair of looped arms off her shoulders. "Are you going to move? No? Then consider this your final warning."

Nieve grabbed the fire ax by the handle, holding the passenger's eyes as she directed as much enhancement mana into her fist as possible. The hardened handle creaked, then splintered, the heavy ax head falling free and landing on the passenger's foot—thankfully on the dull end, rather than the blade, but it still made him howl and scream all the same.

"I did warn you," Nieve grumbled, grabbing him by the shoulder and pushing him aside. She stooped to remove the child from her ankle, tossing them gently into the arms of someone trying to grab her. Nieve ripped the door open before yanking her hair out of a woman's grip. "Mason!"

"Behind!" Mason gave the hair-puller a shove before stumbling out onto the gangway. He helped Nieve slam it shut behind them, earning a few more yelps of pain from hastily withdrawn fingers and hands.

"Hurry!" Nieve hopped to the next gangway, swaying as the train rounded a curve. "He can't be too far ahead."

"Go!" Mason held the car door shut with his shoulder, one hand raised to the communication device on his ear. "I'll catch up after I call the others."

"Right." Nieve dashed through the dining car door, nearly crashing directly into a crew member wearing the apron of a server.

"Oh! Excuse me, kind guest!" The server's eyes were wide with surprise, but she kept her tone light and welcoming. "I'm informing any passengers that this car is scheduled to—"

"There he is!" Nieve snarled, pushing past the server. Sa'rhi was already at the door at the far end of the car. "Stop him! Grab him! Wait, wait, what was that code phrase again?"

Nieve wracked her brain for the code phrase that would get the staff to listen to her. Before she could remember it, Sa'rhi winked and flicked the brim of his cap then ducked out the far door. Nieve charged after him, dodging tables and leaping over chairs. The car was surprisingly empty now, compared to how busy it was only minutes ago. Only a few crew members stared at her in the same bewilderment as she cursed and chased after the thief. It was frustrating that she couldn't remember the code phrase to request their assistance, but at least Sa'rhi hadn't mind-controlled anyone into getting in Nieve's way this time.

Nieve burst through the dining car door just in time to see Sa'rhi duck out of sight beyond the next door. She caught her breath for just a moment, preparing herself to tackle another lounge car full of mind-controlled people, then hurled herself across the gap to the next gangway. She heard Sa'rhi's voice loud and clear the moment she pulled the door open, but she didn't hear what he said until the door slammed shut behind her. Sa'rhi whirled around, grinning at her as he clapped his hands together.

"Let's dance!" Sa'rhi proclaimed before lighting off for the far door. Nieve started after him, only to huff in surprise as someone crashed into her side, laughing and whirling to the steps of a dance Nieve didn't recognize.

Well, at least this is better than making them attack me, Nieve thought, dodging out of the way of an enthusiastic pair of dancers.

Whatever orders Sa'rhi had given prior to Nieve's entrance had the passengers in a riot of uncoordinated movements. Some clasped partners tight to their sides in an intimate and broad-sweeping waltz, while others joined hands in a circle, singing loudly as they crowded inward before jumping back and skipping around in a ring. Others rocked to a silent beat only they could hear while some danced like performers on a stage. The results were so scattered and chaotic that Nieve found herself dodging and ducking more than actually chasing. Someone tried to catch her around the waist and pull her into a dance, but she shoved them away with a hand over their face. The ring of dancers surrounded her, laughing merrily as they pressed in on all sides before swinging wide once more. Nieve ducked beneath their clasped hands, running almost blindly for the door. After this car, there was only the galley, then three cars of private cabins, most of which had been deserted earlier. All she had to do was get through here, then Sa'rhi was as good as caught.

By the time Nieve broke through the dancers and made her way outside, Sa'rhi was nowhere in sight. Undaunted, Nieve raced through the empty corridor, hoping Sa'rhi had been foolish enough to try cutting through the kitchen. If he had, catching him on the far side would be no trouble. Before exiting the galley car, Nieve thrust open the door to the kitchen, just in case Sa'rhi was hiding in order to double back. Finding nothing more than startled cooks standing at prep stations and stoves, Nieve dashed across the gangway to the first car of private cabins. Before she could yank the door open, a flash of motion caught her eye. She spun around, grabbing the hilt of her sword as she sank into a ready position, knees bent to spring, elbows out to guard.

Sa'rhi was just clearing the ladder outside the car door, smirking as he looked back over his shoulder, one hand holding the cap to his head against the wind. He blew a kiss at her, then lowered his head and ran into the wind. Nieve snarled before jumping back to the galley car, halfway up the ladder before the door beside her crashed open.

"Where are you—whoa, wait!" Mason grabbed Nieve's belt, holding her back from reaching the roof. "We can't go up there. And that's the wrong way, isn't it?"

"Sa'rhi went that way!" Nieve argued, pointing with the hand that had failed to grab onto the roof. "He's headed to the front of the train. We have to catch him!"

"Not along the roof!" Mason declared firmly. Nieve made a face, but she allowed him to pull her down to the gangway. "I told Prickles and the others about the Assassin. When we get a chance, we'll tell them about the Magpie, too. Let's try and catch up."

"Back the way we came," Nieve groaned, frustrated about having to fight her way through two cars of mind-controlled passengers once again.

"Yeah, but at least we can meet up with Lief and make sure he got the crate," Mason called, retreating through the galley car. Just outside the lounge car, Mason drew one of his stone rods and reshaped it into a long, thin staff. Inside, there were fewer people dancing than before, but still enough to hinder their progress. Mason used his staff to divert dancers out of his way, using firm but gentle sweeping motions. Deciding that was as good an idea as any, Nieve took her sheathed sword from her belt and grew ice along it to create a rod similar to Mason's, moving people aside to create an aisleway for the two of them. A good number of people seemed to have broken free of the mind-control order and sat or stood along the walls, catching their breath and gulping down glasses of water. Hopefully the spell would break entirely before anyone grew too exhausted.

Outside once again, Nieve only caught a breath of fresh air before catching sight of Sa'rhi's heel vanishing over the top of the car.

"There!" she gasped, pointing. "The wind on top of the train is slowing him down. We can get ahead of him if—"

Mason was already leaping over the gangway and reaching for the dining car door. He missed his grip as the door slid open of its own accord, his momentum sending him stumbling into Lief, who had to fumble to hold onto the snake crate while keeping his own balance. Nieve grit her teeth against the urge to leap for the ladder and scale to the roof again—it felt so restraining to be bound to the inside of the train!

"What's going on?" Lief asked once he and Mason were steady on the gangway. "I thought you were chasing Sa'rhi."

"He doubled back!" Nieve pointed. "He's on top of the train and heading for the engine.

Without wasting another breath, Lief shoved the snake crate into Mason's arms and shook his bow off his shoulder. He leapt over to the gangway on Nieve's side and spun around, setting an arrow to the bow. Nieve gripped a brass rail as the train swayed around a curve in the track. She could just make out Sa'rhi leaping to the roof of the next car, though he was definitely moving slowly against the wind. Lief exhaled as he sighted, drawing the fletching of the arrow back to his cheek.

"I've got him," Lief said, voice barely above a whisper. The fine bones on the back of his hand twitched, but before he could release, the sound of a door rolling open nearby made him jump in surprise. The arrow went flying harmlessly out over the canyon below.

Lief cursed as a train crew member stepped out onto the gangway beside Mason, the car door snapping shut behind her. She seemed surprised to see them all standing outside, but she composed herself quickly, folding her hands in front of her and giving each of them a hostess's smile.

"Hello, honored guests. It is my duty to inform you that the dining car is currently undergoing some scheduled maintenance and will be locked for the next thirty minutes."

"The track curved and I can't get a clean shot," Lief said, shrugging his bow up onto his shoulder. "If we hurry, we can catch up to him."

"We need to get through!" Nieve shouted over the wind. "Open the door, we're in a hurry!"

The crew member continued smiling blithely. "I'm afraid the dining car is now locked for the duration of the scheduled maintenance. It will open to allow passage in thirty minutes' time."

"We can't wait that long," Lief insisted. "We weren't informed of any maintenance or locked cars aside from the half hour before dinner. It's urgent that we be allowed through to meet up with our friends at the front of the train."

"For the time being, you may wait inside the lounge car," the server suggested, wearing her patience like a mask. "But the dining car is now locked. I'm afraid passing through will not be possible."

"I'll get it open," Nieve growled, starting forward. The server's eyes went wide as she lifted her hands defensively.

"Wait," Lief said, digging around in his pockets before showing the conductor's badge. "We have this, can we go through now?"

"You can't," she said quickly. "These locks are enchanted—no one can get through. If there is an emergency great enough to warrant forcing the door open, the brakes will engage and many passengers could be injured, not to mention it would set us behind schedule by several hours. I'm afraid you're going to have to wait."

"What about the maintenance?" Mason asked, gesturing with his free hand. "What if they need additional supplies? There has to be a way to get inside."

"We have an enchanted device that is able to send food and other objects from the galley to the dining car directly," the crew member advised. "But even if you used it to teleport yourself, you would still be stuck inside the locked car."

Lief sighed in frustration, running a hand back through his hair as his eyes scanned the roof of the train. He had to be looking for Sa'rhi, but the Controller had long since passed beyond sight. "Sa'rhi must have planned this somehow. Come on, guys, we can't get through here."

"But Rose and the others!" Mason protested.

"Our target is getting away!" Nieve shouted.

"There's nothing we can do except contact them," Lief said, shrugging helplessly. "And I'm worried about keeping that out here in the wind too long. We need to get it inside."

He pointed to the crate tucked under Mason's arm, cutting off further protests. A silent snarl curling her lips, Nieve yanked open the lounge car door and held it for Mason and Lief to pass by. She shot a final glare over her shoulder at the roof of the train, wishing she could give chase. Grudgingly she acknowledged that this had been Sa'rhi's plan all along: leading them away from Hane and the others in order to trap them on the wrong side of the dining car. Sa'rhi had probably already dropped down off the roof to stroll leisurely through the cars, knowing he couldn't be followed. Nieve hated smug villains—she was going to make him eat the top of his walking stick when she caught him.

"I'll call the others and tell them everything," Lief said, a finger pressed against the metal shell curled around his ear. "Is there anything else you two discovered while I was recovering the crate?"

"Just that he's not afraid to use bystanders to get in our way." Nieve eyed the crowd beyond the doorway, noting that by now most of them had stopped dancing, with many catching their breath or massaging sore feet. "At least we got the snake back, so it's not a complete failure."

"Did we?" Mason asked, testing the weight of the crate. "Lief, did you check inside?"

Lief's face went visibly pale. "I didn't have time. Don't tell me . . ."

Mason glanced around cautiously before turning his back to the passengers, using his body to shield the crate. Nieve crowded in shoulder to shoulder with Lief as Mason carefully pried open the top of the crate, just enough to peek inside. Nieve groaned and rolled her eyes. Lief covered his face and shook his head.

They may have recovered the crate, but they had failed to recover the snake.

CHAPTER 12

HANE

Wavewalker (leg mark), Citrine

And that," Rose murmured, eyes hidden behind the red and yellow lenses of her goggles, "is the last piece of the auxiliary engine in place. Ow!"

She yanked her hand back, shaking it hard against whatever gear had pinched her this time. All Hane had learned from observation was that fixing a train engine wasn't just complex, it was painful, too.

"Is it ready to take over for the main engine?" Odette asked anxiously, hovering just over Rose's shoulder. "The main gear shaft is starting to shimmy and I'm afraid if we don't take the main engine offline soon, the parts we made won't be enough to fix it."

"I know," Rose groaned, sitting back on her heels. She lifted her goggles to her forehead, revealing an oblong patch of clean skin in the center of her soot-caked face. She took a long draught of water from her canteen before swiping her mouth with the back of her hand. "They have to prime this one before they switch over entirely, right? Tell the engineers to send someone down to make sure it's all oiled and properly fitted before starting it up."

"Are you feeling all right?" Hane asked her. "If you need to take a longer break, I'm sure one of the engineers can take over for a little while."

"I just need a minute," Rose replied, twisting her back from side to side before reaching for a hand up. Hane pulled her to her feet, her knees and joints creaking and complaining from the amount of time she'd spent huddled over the engine, sometimes contorted into awkward positions as she removed certain parts and replaced them with others. Rose ground both fists into the small of her back and leaned backward, wringing a few more pops out of her spine. She coughed and cleared her throat before taking another sip of water. "The trouble with lung marks: constant dry mouth."

"While you're on your feet, I'd like to slip away for a minute and check the crew cabins," Hane suggested. "I only made it through the first car on your last break. Do you think I'll have time to get to the second car while you—"

Hane stopped just as Odette and Rose froze in place, listening to the sudden and urgent voice coming through their communication devices.

[Prickles, it's me. We found the Magpie, but he bolted.] Though the communication spell was heard inside Hane's head rather than their ears, they still detected a breathless quality to Mason's voice. [He said the Assassin went after you guys a while ago. Have you seen him?]

Rose looked to Hane before answering, correctly interpreting their headshake as a negative. "No, it's been quiet here so far. We've got our heads up now. Is there anything else you can tell us?"

[Too much for now; we're chasing him down. He's headed back to the Keepsake cars. I'll let you know if anything happens.]

"Got it, we'll listen for you." Rose waited a moment in case there was a further transmission. Odette didn't wait: she scrambled to the ladder leading up to the control room above the engine, shouting over the roar of the furnace for someone to come down and prime the auxiliary engine. Hane slipped their tonfa out from under their tunic, scanning the Assassin's possible points of entry. The engine car was unique from the other cars, with a glass-windowed cabin full of levers, control panels, and a multitude of communication devices elevated above the engine itself. Hane had likened it to the helm of a ship, only without any means of steering. Odette explained that usually at least two engineers worked the controls and communications, while another pair kept an eye on the engine and the coal furnace, but Rose had ordered everyone out of her way as she worked, cramming all four engineers up in the tiny cabin above the engine.

The engine car was also the only car Hane observed without an open space around the coupler. Instead, the side panels of the engine car extended back and over the front of the coal car, with a rattling iron grate over the coupler. The passage was easier to negotiate while carrying buckets of coal to the furnace, but the constant rattling of metal on metal combined with the roar of the furnace made the small space nearly deafening. Odette had offered both Hane and Rose little balls of cotton to stuff in their ears, but Rose's goggles had a feature to mute the noise and Hane used a perception spell that filtered constant background noise. It didn't completely deaden the sounds, but it was better than nothing.

The good news about the mostly enclosed engine space was that the Assassin could really only approach from one of two places: either they would drop down through the porthole from the control cabin, or they would have to come down the passage that skirted the coal car. There were no other ways to get inside the engine room.

Unless they could teleport, of course.

Enhance Sight, Hane thought, sharpening the only sense that could be of any use down here. The vibrations of the rail ties made it impossible to sense movement, and the smells of engine oil and smoldering coal would overpower any scent that would give away a human presence. Enhancing their hearing would be more of a detriment than anything, with all the rattling, roaring, and screeching of metal on metal. They couldn't even truly put their back up against anything as the furnace took up the space just past the ladder and the constantly churning engine lay bare and open on both sides. Even the floor was unreliable, with Rose's tools and spare parts scattered about, but she was already scraping those together into piles and fitting them back into their designated holsters.

An engineer descended the ladder so quickly that they must have simply slid down the handrails rather than using the rungs. Hane spun, ready to strike, but held back as they recognized the engineer. Odette looked as anxious as a canary in a room full of cats, her glasses glinting brilliantly in the light of the furnace as she tried to peer in all directions at once.

"At least we know to expect him this time," Rose muttered, hurriedly rolling up a tool pouch. "Assassins don't just use poison-coated weapons, they can use shadows and death magic, too. Oh, I need to adjust my goggles. Unless you managed to catch a glimpse of his shroud last time, Hane?"

"No." Hane didn't have a spell for that, and they hadn't fought the Assassin long enough to assess how powerful he might be. "Maybe we should move into the open. If his goal is sabotage, we don't want to fight him in here."

"All primed up," the engineer declared, wiping his hands on a grease-stained rag hanging from his belt. "You want us to cut power to the main engine?"

"Not just yet," Rose replied, a bit of hesitation in her voice. "Can you work up to splitting the power between both engines? We need time to deal with something before we can get to work on the main engine."

The engineer cast a doubtful look over at the hard-chugging mass of gears and shafts that made up the main engine; even Hane could tell something was wrong with it by the way the gears wobbled and bounced against their fittings. But trying to fix it now made them vulnerable. At least taking some of the strain off the main engine might help it last long enough to get through the fight.

"We'll keep it up as long as we can," the engineer promised. "Let us know as soon as we can take it offline—we've only got a partial staff here today, thanks to Squatch skipping his shift, so it's harder to make fast changes. And I really don't like the look of that gear rack."

Rose muttered darkly under her breath in Caelish, quite possibly a curse on all gear racks everywhere—whatever a gear rack was. She finished securing her tool pouches to her vest and leggings, then shoved the crate containing all her modified bronze gears out of the way before standing up and dusting off her hands.

"There was some mention of moving the battleground?" Rose asked as the engineer returned to the cabin above. "I think it's a good idea. I will absolutely lose it if he splashes my beautiful new parts with that acid of his."

"We can head up to the crew cars," Hane suggested. "Most of the cabins are empty, so there are fewer bystanders. Still not a lot of space, though."

"Better the empty crew cars than the passenger cars," Rose agreed. "But if he comes over the roof again, he could bypass us completely and hit the engine."

"Is the engine their target?" Hane asked. "I thought they were only trying to detach the rear cars to steal the Keepsake cargo."

"This engine was definitely sabotaged by someone," Odette spoke up, sweat glistening on her forehead and cheeks. "It's normal for this scenario to include malfunctions, failed enchantments, and missing tools and parts, but this is more extensive than that. The enchanting runes here aren't just worn out or incorrect; they've been intentionally worn down to fail. One whole toolbox of tightening wrenches was tossed overboard after being accounted for in the supply log. And there's far too much grit mashed between the gears for an engine that was serviced only a month ago, according to the maintenance logs. I think it must have been done by a crew member, which lends credence to the theory that the Magpie and their team reside in one of the crew cabins."

"I was hoping we'd have time to slip my peep-coil under the locked doors, but at this rate, I'll be lucky if I have time to fix the main engine before that"— a stream of ugly-sounding Caelish—"gear rack shatters." Rose's hands rested on the rows of knives sheathed along her belts. "Maybe we can knock a few doors down during the fight. For space."

"If we're going, we need to go," Odette suggested, checking a pocket watch. "We don't have a lot of time until—"

Hane lost the rest of Odette's statement as an undulating shadow flickered at the edge of their field of vision. Without the Enhanced Sight spell, they most likely would have missed it. Hane pivoted on the ball of their foot, sinking low into a lunge, crossing their tonfa in a guarded position. Glass shattered, shards and droplets spraying outward from the X of Hane's tonfa.

They lowered their face and braced themself, noting the direction the glass had been tossed from.

Odette gasped and shrieked, multiple small objects tumbling from her hands to roll along the floor. Her spell spheres? Were they armed, or had she dropped them accidentally? Hane didn't have time to wonder as the shadows shifted and seethed in the red light cast by the forge. They caught the glint of light along curved glass and moved on instinct, tossing both tonfa into one hand in order to carefully catch the glass orb mid-flight. By some miracle, the glass didn't shatter on contact, allowing Hane to lob it back in the direction from whence it came. It vanished as it broke through a veil of shadows, but Hane heard it shatter against the floor.

"Stop throwing things at my engine!" Rose shouted, flinging three tiny knives up at the low ceiling. "If any of that is acid, I'll feed all of you to the furnace!"

The knives hit the ceiling with hollow-sounding plinks, then burst into light, shooting out brilliant beams that slashed away the veil of shadows. Hane only caught a flicker of movement before the light seared their eyes, making them flinch and back away as they quickly canceled their Enhanced Sight spell. They wished Rose had thought to tell them about the light-knives earlier, but then again, she probably hadn't known about Hane's perception spell, either.

"You can't have fixed it already!" Hane's eyes were watering too much to see who spoke, but since it wasn't Rose or Odette's voice, that only left the Assassin. "The boss said there weren't enough tools and parts on board to fix it. That the train would need to reroute to the nearest station for repairs."

"Well, if that's what you were counting on, your boss's math was wrong," Rose countered. Hane blinked rapidly, fighting to clear their vision. "We're not letting this train stop until we arrive at—" She stopped suddenly. "Odie, where is this train going?"

"Mount Everlake," Odette replied, a slight tremble in her voice. "It's mostly a seasonal destination, for fishing, hiking, and relaxing, but the altitude offers unique benefits for certain crafts and experiments, such as—"

"And you're just a couple of vacationers who just happen to be combat trained as well as engine mechanics?" the Assassin sneered. Hane lowered their arm, squinting through their lashes in order to locate their opponent. He was crouched defensively with his back to the coal fire, a short sword dripping green liquid held crosswise in front of him. "We already know you were hired by Keepsake to protect the shipment. My boss is making a deal with your team right now. We can all just walk away right now and leave everything the way it is until we work things out."

"I think your boss's deal was rejected," Hane supplied, rolling both tonfa by their grips. "Our team already contacted us, saying they've given chase. I'll allow you to leave here, if that's what you wish, but if you try to stop us from fixing the engine, we will subdue you. That's a promise."

"Look, we don't have to go a second round here." The Assassin straightened partially, flipping his short sword so the end pointed back along his elbow. "Let's wait it out, have a nice little chat while my boss works it out with your team, and then we can—"

He lunged suddenly, his free hand reaching for Odette's neck. Hane saw her eyes go wide with panic, her mouth dropping open in a silent scream as she backpedaled toward the whirling gears and pistons of the main engine. Rose shouted a warning, but in the space of a blink, Hane saw her hesitate between protecting Odette or protecting the engine. The Assassin's hand was inches from Odette's throat when Hane exploded into motion, shifting their center of gravity to the heel of their foot as the engine room seemingly rotated around them, with the main engine becoming "down" from their point of view. Gripping the side rail of the ladder, Hane slammed a kick into the side of the Assassin's face, spinning him off balance and sending him teetering toward the engine. Completing their spin around the ladder, Hane grabbed the collar of the Assassin's tunic and yanked him backward sharply. The breath left his chest in a violent burst as he landed flat on his back in front of the furnace. Hane cut their gravity spell, reorienting instantly to land on top of the Assassin, one foot pinning the wrist holding the poisoned blade, the other knee digging into the meat of the Assassin's shoulder. Bracing the tip of one tonfa against the floor, Hane swung the other one up, intending to deliver a knockout blow across the temple.

"Wait, wait!" Rose shouted. "I can use him if you keep him conscious. Hold him down while we tie him up."

They rarely hesitated when they were certain which course of action was the safest—and rendering the Assassin unconscious was most definitely the safest option at the moment—but as they'd already had a few of their assumptions proven wrong so far, Hane hesitated to deliver the knockout strike. Just as they decided it was smarter to err on the side of caution, Hane felt the sting of something sharp pierce their neck. A needle? Hane shifted their weight just enough to look back at the hand trapped against the Assassin's side to confirm their suspicion. A thin hollow tube was clasped in the Assassin's hand. Such weapons usually only held a single shot, but if that shot was coated with poison, that was all it was needed to get the job done. And Hane's vision was already blurring.

Hane would have warned Rose and Odette to stay back, but before they could get the words out, the Assassin surged up beneath Hane, displacing them easily as their blood began to slow and their mouth went dry. Hane fell back on their shoulder and rolled once, stopping dangerously close to the auxiliary engine, which had been steadily turning faster and faster as it worked up to pulling half the train's weight. Hane let their eyes fall closed, fingers twitching around the grips of their tonfa before loosely falling open.

"Hane!" Odette screamed. "What did you do to them? Hane, get up! Get up!"

Rose cursed darkly, using a few of the same words she spat about the gear rack. "Reshing Assassins. I should have seen that coming."

"It was close," the Assassin agreed, almost amiably. "I was afraid it was going to be a double knockout. I guess I should thank you for saving me."

"Are they okay?" Odette asked in a trembling voice. "You carry antidotes, don't you? Please, you can't just let them die!"

"Yeah, I got it right here." Hane heard something slosh within a small container. "Here, I'll let you administer it. Just get out of my way."

Hane grit their teeth against shouting out a warning. Luckily, Rose beat them to it.

"Don't touch it, Odie!" Rose commanded. "It's a common trick, coating the outer layer of a vial with poison, claiming it's an antidote. It's easy for the ones with leg marks to do."

"But if it is an antidote . . ." Odette's voice sounded closer, as if she'd taken a step toward the Assassin. Hane focused on their breathing while staying as still as possible. As long as the Assassin was still talking, Rose and Odette weren't in too much trouble.

Yet.

"Don't worry, I don't have a leg mark." The Assassin had to be grinning to sound that smug. "Here, I'll show you. It's a hand mark, right here!"

The Assassin moved suddenly, throwing their hand out toward Rose. Odette screamed, something hissed like parchment torn in half, and Hane rolled up to their knees, whipping both tonfa in a sideways strike against the Assassin's left leg. One gave off a hollow-sounding "crack" as it connected with the Assassin's hip bone, but the other connected with a wet "pop" that made even Hane grimace: a dislocated kneecap wasn't something that could be walked off. The Assassin only had enough time for one horrified glance down before they crumpled to the floor, glass shattering beneath their weight.

"Was that the poison?" Hane asked, leaping to their feet. "Or acid? What broke?"

"No, no, it wasn't his, it was mine." Odette had a hand clasped to her chest, her shoulders heaving as she caught her breath. "He landed on one of the spell spheres I dropped earlier. Stay back while it takes effect." She blinked owlishly, focusing on Hane as if noticing them for the first time. "Are you all right? Were you just faking?"

"No, he definitely got me." Hane held both tonfa in one hand in order to reach up and pluck the needle from their neck. They grimaced as a hot line of blood leaked out to soak into their collar. At least the black cloth would hide it. They tossed the needle into the furnace before pressing their fingers to the wound. Luckily it wasn't too deep, but it would need to be healed. Without their dimensional bag with them, Hane didn't have access to their supply of healing potions, nor their first aid kit. They had a single roll of bandages tucked away in a pocket, but with the Assassin groaning and thrashing on the floor, it didn't seem there was enough time to apply them. "I'm wearing a charm that negates toxins. The poison still affected me, but only for a few seconds. I didn't mean to scare you."

"I'm glad you're all right," Odette said breathlessly. "I was afraid of what Nieve would do if we got you killed."

Hane shrugged. "We're not actually that close; I'm sure she would have been fine. What trap did he activate?"

"One of the confusion ones," Odette replied, manipulating the runes. "They have a short amnesiac effect, then there's some lingering disorientation. He'll be back to normal in about five minutes or so, but um . . . did you break his leg?"

"Just his knee, I think," Hane confirmed, tucking their tonfa beneath one arm in order to roll up their sleeve and check on the string of beads looped twice just above their elbow. It was a bit of treasure earned from their last climb in the Tortoise Spire and part of the cut they'd taken from the team's returned treasure. Unfortunately, the white, pearly beads were all turning gray, their magic nearly spent. Hane would have to bring the item to a Diviner to see if the magic would refill itself, or if it required an Enchanter in order to function again. In the meantime, they would have to be more careful around the Assassin—assuming he had any more tricks up his sleeve. "The pain is incapacitating, but temporary: once it pops back into place and he gets enough rest, he'll be fine. It'll take no time at all if the Magpie's Guardian knows any healing spells." Hane glanced over at Rose, realizing she had been quiet during the exchange. Her tunic and vest were coated in a white powder that dusted the floor and most of the train's main engine. "What happened? Are you okay?"

"Yeah, I'm fine," Rose grumbled, clapping her hands together, puffs of white powder erupting with each clap. "That was my bad. I should have just let you knock him out. Sorry for getting you poisoned."

Hane shook their head. "I could have ignored you, so the fault is mine. What is all of that?"

"Safety salts." Rose grimaced as she scraped the toe of her boot through the layer of powder dusting the floor. "He conjured a jet of what I assumed was acid, so I dumped a bunch of neutralizing salts on the engine. And now there's even more grit in the engine, which is just . . . great."

"It's better than the acid, right?" Odette said sympathetically. "And most of these pieces are coming out anyway."

"Yes, but it's going to be a pain unscrewing everything with all this extra grit on it," Rose sighed. "The good news is that most of it can be washed off with water once the engine shuts down, but that means carting tubs of water down here, because I don't have that many water mana crystals to burn through."

"If water is all you need, I can supply it," Hane offered. "Before that, though, we should tie up the Assassin and disarm him."

"No, the first thing we need to do is to deal with that wound on your neck," Rose said sternly, crooking a finger at Hane. "Come sit here and I'll get it cleaned up with my first aid supplies. You'll still want Lief to take a look at it later. Odette, you start stripping the Assassin of his weapons for now, but go carefully."

"I know, I know." Odette was already pulling on a pair of light blue gloves made of thick leather and probably spelled to protect her hands in some way. "I wasn't all that scared, you know. I mean, I was definitely worried about Hane, but I dropped those traps on purpose. I was hoping he'd step on one sooner."

"He's well-trained in silent, steady movement," Hane pointed out, obeying Rose's order and taking a seat on the floor in front of her. They kept their hand over their neck as she rummaged through an inside pocket of her vest. "When he moves, he barely lifts his feet from the ground, using a sliding motion rather than stepping. He kicked a few of the spell spheres, but he wouldn't have stepped on one."

"I didn't notice that," Odette admitted, kicking away the short sword first before crushing the hollow tube beneath her heel and sweeping it out of the Assassin's reach. She rolled him onto his back, making him groan and gag as she detached pouches and weapons from his belt. "I should have thrown a tangle-trap at him, but I was afraid the ropes would get caught in one of the engines and either cause a malfunction or just, um . . ." Odette's upper lip curled as if she were picturing something distasteful. "You know what? Never mind. I just want everyone to stay safe around the engines."

Rose snorted as she shook a small vial of liquid. She held it out for Hane to see. "Cleansing alcohol. Your charm probably took care of that already, but I'd rather be overly cautious than not cautious enough."

Hane nodded, accepting the treatment and removing their hand from the injury. The liquid felt cold, but it smelled like any ordinary cleansing solution.

"Want to wash that away for me so I don't waste any of my own water?" Rose requested.

Easy enough: Hane conjured a palmful of water and splashed it against the side of their neck.

Rose held out two more items for Hane's inspection. "Gauze. Bandage. I'm going to be tying this around your neck now."

"Thank you for showing me, but I've already agreed to let you bandage it," Hane informed her. "The quicker the better, please."

"Fine, fine," Rose muttered, pressing the gauze over the wound. Hane moved to hold it in place, but Rose knocked their hand away. It must have stuck to the water or the blood because it stayed in place as Rose started to loop the roll of bandage around Hane's neck. "You just seem like the type to be suspicious of people. Tell me if I make it too tight."

"It doesn't make sense to be suspicious of anyone this early in the climb," Hane explained. "It's only near the end when people start thinking about how the treasure should be split up and who earned their share and who didn't."

"That's very logical of you," Rose said, adjusting the bandage as she looped it over itself. "Sounds like you've been through it a few times."

Hane kept their silence, turning their head minutely to test the tautness of the bandage.

"That shouldn't be an issue for us," Odette said, currently in the process of tugging the Assassin's boot off. His body slid along the floor with each tug, making it difficult to remove. "The phantom vault on the next floor should contain more than enough to satisfy each of us, whether we're looking to accumulate wealth, power, or prestige. There should be no reason for any-one to turn on the others." She paused a moment as she loosened the top of the boot around the Assassin's calf. "Unless more than one person wants the same treasure. I suppose that could be a problem."

"How do you know another delving team hasn't beaten us to the vault and emptied it?" Hane asked, hoping Odette wasn't about to refer them to her ludicrously long spire document. "This is a relatively low floor, and even if there's a trick to opening it, someone may have discovered it already."

"It's a possibility, but I don't think it's likely." Odette finally got the first boot free of the Assassin's foot and started working on the other. "I won't know for sure until I can map out the next floor, but it's not as simple as finding a hidden key to unlock the phantom chamber; I doubt anyone who isn't actively looking for the Vault of Shadows could open it by accident, and no one in my research team has made the connection between the labyrinth vault and the Vault of Shadows yet."

"What happens if someone did get to it before us? Would we just find an empty room where the treasure used to be?" Rose asked, securing the bandage with a careful knot. "Done. Is it too tight? Can you breathe?"

Hane twisted their head from side to side, testing their range of motion while ignoring the pinprick of pain beneath the gauze. "It's fine, thank you."

"If someone did manage to open the Vault of Shadows before us, then the labyrinth vault would no longer grant access to the phantom chamber," Odette explained, answering Rose's earlier query as she tugged at the heel of the Assassin's boot. "That's why the chambers are all so hard to study. Once they're opened, the entry portal moves to another—ow!"

As the Assassin's boot popped off his foot, a glass vial tumbled free and shattered on the floor. While Odette's eyes were still going wide with fright, Rose cast out a handful of white powder and Hane conjured a jet of water at the shattered glass and mystery liquid, washing the mess away and into the auxiliary engine. Rose gave them a disgruntled look before focusing on Odette.

"Did you get cut on the glass? Have you been poisoned?"

"I . . . I don't think so?" Odette checked her fingers in the light radiated off of Rose's daggers, still stuck through the ceiling. "I can't see any punctures in the gloves. I think I was more scared than anything."

"Check your hands anyway, just to be sure," Hane advised, tugging at the bandage around their neck as they stood up. "We already know he uses poisoned needles, and a puncture that small might not be visible on leather. Rose, can you help me finish stripping him down?"

"Just a moment." Rose was already working on a new project, her medical supplies still cluttering the floor. Flashes of light reflected off a series of thin metal wires as Rose wove them through and around each other in a complex pattern. "I need to finish this before he comes all the way around."

The Assassin was moving with a little more purpose now, his vocalizations less moans and more like the confused utterances of someone waking up after a night of liberal inebriation. One long, loud groan, then he rolled onto his side, clutching his injured knee. Hane followed the motion, working quickly as they loosened the cuffs of his shirt to remove a bracer of throwing needles. The Assassin peered sidelong at Hane, his gaze barely focused but quizzical, as if trying to place where he was. While a confusion spell was meant to hit hard and fast, there were ways to overcome it if the victim recognized the spell. Hane worked quickly, divesting the Assassin of hidden weapons, vials of poison or acid, and a secret pouch containing tiny vials labeled with numbers: possibly antidotes to the Assassin's own poisons. Hane tucked that pouch away in a pocket, thinking it might be useful if Odette had accidentally poisoned herself earlier.

"Why does my leg hurt?" the Assassin groaned, panting as he grasped his knee. "What happened to me?"

"You fell over a tripwire. You nearly fell right off the train," Hane lied, searching for more hidden weapons.

"Do I know you?" the Assassin asked Hane blearily. "You look familiar."

"We're working together," Hane informed him, patting down his sides a little quicker now that the Assassin was fighting the confusion spell. "The Magpie hired us to help steal from Keepsake Treasuries, remember?"

The Assassin struggled to look around, gritting his teeth against the pain in his leg. While he didn't seem too concerned about Hane's unabashed rummaging, the Assassin tensed when he caught sight of Rose and Odette. "Who are they? What are they doing?"

"Oh, uh, the boss hired us, too," Odette said unconvincingly. "We were, um . . . we're sabotaging the engine."

The Assassin looked skeptical. He started to reach for something on his person, then stopped, his head swaying woozily. Hane checked for whatever the Assassin had been reaching for, but found nothing. Either it was well hidden, or Odette had found it earlier. All told, it was quite the impressive pile of weapons and poisons they'd removed from the man; Hane regretted not bringing their dimensional bag with them to help carry it all.

"I was hired as the team medic," Rose said, rising from her hunched position. Something metallic gleamed in her hand, though she kept it partially hidden as she approached cautiously. "Setting that knee is going to be painful, so I'm just going to slip this around your wrist. You won't feel a thing."

She took hold of his arm as she spoke, moving quickly and decisively as she clasped a bracelet of gleaming copper, silver, and gold wire around his wrist. The bracelet wasn't complete yet, excess wire protruding from both ends of an opening just wide enough to fit around the narrowest part of the Assassin's wrist. Rose began muttering to herself in Caelish as she quickly began twisting the bracelet closed.

"Wait, stop." The Assassin tugged at his arm, but Rose worked through the motion, twisting and whispering faster. Hane gripped the man's shoulder and elbow, bracing him from behind to keep him as still as possible. "Stop, no, I don't know you. Let go!" The Assassin twisted around to squint over his shoulder, this time recognition lighting his face. "I know you! You don't work for the Magpie! Let go, or I'll kill you all slowly! Let go—"

"There!" Rose hopped backward, releasing the Assassin's arm just as his attunement-marked hand began to shimmer with a noxious-looking liquid. "Stop resisting immediately. Don't fight, don't use magic, and don't remove the bracelet."

The Assassin fell still instantly, his face twisted in a rictus of disgust. When Hane backed away, he made no attempt to grab them.

"A control bracelet?" Hane asked, raising an eyebrow at Rose.

She shrugged as she pulled her goggles off, adjusting the lenses as she spoke. "Yeah, so? This is easier than tying him up and carrying him to the brig, or wherever. And he can be useful."

Hane didn't disagree; in fact, they were having a hard time coming up with a suitable argument against the use of control magic on a spire construct. They certainly would have objected if such a thing was used against a teammate, but this had to be better than killing the Assassin outright. Right?

"Hane, I need you to rinse the powder off the engine," Rose directed as she knelt beside the Assassin. "I need to set his knee so he can be of use to us. You, stay still and don't struggle, or this is *really* going to hurt."

With the last part spoken to the Assassin, Rose set to work fixing his knee while Odette kept herself between the Assassin and the equipment that had been stripped from him. She gripped the hilt of the poisoned short sword in her hand, but the way she chewed her lower lip made Hane wonder if she could bring herself to use it. On Rose's order, Hane held a hand out over the main engine, conjuring a steady stream of water to rinse away the safety salts Rose used to protect it from acid. The train's main engine had been gradually slowing down, while the auxiliary engine was churning faster and faster. At a glance, they appeared to be moving at the same speeds, though that was hardly Hane's area of expertise. The Assassin sat upright with his hands braced behind him for support, grimacing as Rose pressed her hands against either side of his knee.

"That's dangerous, you know," Hane informed Rose in a low voice. "The longer he's under compulsion, the better he'll get at fighting it."

"It's a temporary fix," Rose agreed. "The imbue won't last all that long, but the compulsion isn't weak; Dream mana has a low conversion differential to Coercion mana. It'll hold until we can get him somewhere secure."

"That's not all I'm worried about," Hane said, speaking softly as their conjured water splashed over the churning engine. "Compulsion requires a person to follow orders, but it doesn't exclude independent actions entirely. An order for him not to fight us doesn't mean he can't find other ways to harm us, or himself."

"Yeah, I'm not worried about that." Rose smirked, amber eyes glittering maliciously as she glanced up at them. "I order Brick around, remember? I know exactly how people try to subvert clear instructions. I'll be fine."

"Can I see the bracelet?" Odette asked, crouching behind Rose to avoid the spray of the water sent up by the spinning gears of the engine. "If I can memorize the pattern, I should be able to use a tracking spell to locate him as long as he's wearing it. As long as the pattern is unique enough."

"Should be unique," Rose said ruefully, being far less gentle with her patient than she had been with Hane. "I was working quickly, so I made a few mistakes in the pattern. Hey, you— What's your name?"

The Assassin's throat and jaw worked silently for a moment as he fought the compulsion to answer. "Ellis."

"Ellis, good, thank you." Rose nodded curtly. "Hane, stop rinsing the engine and come over here. I need to wrap Ellis's knee, but if he makes one false move, kill him: he's not that valuable to us. Ellis, hold your hand out for Odette so she can see the bracelet. And hold still while I wrap your leg. Don't speak, either."

As far as Hane could tell, the instructions were good ones: they definitely seemed like something Rose would have said to an obstinate sibling a time or two. Though as petulant as Mason could be around his sister, Hane imagined he still would have found a way to confound Rose despite the clear direction.

Odette crept forward cautiously, eyes flicking toward the Assassin as if expecting him to break free of the compulsion at any second. When the bracelet was just inside arm's reach, she reached out and cupped her hands over it without quite touching the Assassin.

"Identify Pattern: Assassin Shackle," Odette whispered, her eyes falling closed. Hane stayed on alert, ready to defend in case the Assassin discovered a way to defy Rose's orders. Luckily, Odette's spell ended before Ellis could take any actions against her. "Thank you."

"Okay. So once we're finished here, Ellis, I need you to—" Rose froze in the middle of looping a bandage around the Assassin's knee, cocking her head to the side. Hane heard it, too: Lief's easygoing voice coming through the communicator with an update.

[Pardon the interruption, but we have a situation.] He didn't sound winded, as Mason had earlier. Was that a good sign, or a bad sign? [The Magpie tricked us into thinking he was heading to the Keepsake cars, then doubled back along the roof of the train. We think he's heading to you. Are you all safe?]

"Oh, yes!" Odette spoke for the team, her head ducked as she activated the device on her ear. "There was a situation, but we have it under control right now." Hane suppressed a chuckle; Odette probably hadn't meant it as a joke, but the Assassin certainly was "under control" for the moment. "Thank you for the warning. No sign of the Magpie yet. Are Nieve and Mason in pursuit?"

[No, unfortunately the three of us are stuck on the wrong side of the dining car.] Lief didn't sound frustrated as much as he sounded ruefully amused by the situation. [We think the Magpie arranged to have the car locked down outside of its normal routine. The locks are time-activated and mana-powered, so we can't get through right now. I believe the Magpie isolated us from you for a reason, so stay vigilant.]

Odette glanced around nervously before responding. "Understood. We'll take precautions. Please make contact after the dining car opens up."

[Got it. We'll be there as soon as possible.]

Odette nodded, her hand dropping from her ear in order to unravel the knotted cord of rings from her belt. As she spoke, she freed a single ring and slipped it over her middle finger. "We need to secure this room. I have a ring for mental clarity, but depending on how strong the Magpie is, it may not be enough."

"My protection is pretty good," Rose said, messing with something on the side of her goggles. "But there is a possibility that the Magpie's orders could overrule the compulsion bracelet, which means Ellis won't be our friend for long."

The Assassin sneered at her, still holding obediently still as Rose tied off the bandage around his knee.

"We should run," Hane counseled. "We could leave instructions for the Assassin to ambush the Magpie to buy us some time."

Rose shook her head as she adjusted the goggles over her face once more. "You hear that whine from the auxiliary engine? It's not meant to take the full weight and speed of the train for very long. The new parts will keep it going for a while, but if I don't get the main engine working soon, both engines will die before the next significant elevation change. I'll have Ellis help me to speed up the process, but I need one of you to tell the engineers to cut power to the main engine. I can't do anything until it stops running."

"I'll do it," Odette offered, rushing to the ladder. "I need to set a trap over the portal anyway. Nonlethal!" she added hurriedly, in response to Hane's aborted protest. "It's just a snare trap. It won't hurt, even if the Magpie throws one of the engineers down first."

Hane internalized a sigh, accepting that there were no good options for avoiding another fight in this cramped space. The best they could do was prepare for the worst. "I'll watch the rear, in case the Magpie comes up that way. Odette, can you consolidate everything we pulled off Ellis and move it out of the way? It might be wise to toss the poisons into the fire, unless they'll explode."

The Assassin twitched at that, earning a sharp glare from Rose. She gave the knot a malicious twist before demanding he tell Odette about each and every poison pulled off his person before she burned it. Hane left them to it as they tucked themself into the shadows at the back of the car, waiting and watching for the next possible intruder.

It wasn't a pleasant wait, sitting at the back of the car where the rattling and metallic screeches were loudest, but the only way to reach the engine was by going through the coal car—either over or around it—and from here, Hane would see an approach long before they could be seen. And as awful as the din was, Hane had to admit it was a stroke of luck considering their opponent was a Controller: the harder it was to hear a command, the less effective a mind-control spell was. As long as the Magpie wasn't Emerald level, at least.

The coal car was covered by a secure tarp that flapped constantly in the wind, and while the back and sides of the car were quite high, the end near the engine was secured with only a waist-high gate, making it easier to shovel out buckets of coal to feed the fire. The only path around the coal car was a narrow walkway on the outside of the car, exposed to the wind and billowing white steam clouds spewing from the engine. The walkway was too narrow for people to squeeze past one another, so helpful signs directed people to either side based on the direction they were traveling: to the engine or away from it. Just to be safe, Odette had set traps at the ends of each walkway, with the intention of removing them once the engine was fixed. Hane eyed the flapping tarp above the coal car, wondering if it counted as the roof of the train or not before deciding it was safer to simply assume that it was.

What if I don't touch the roof? Hane wondered vaguely. *If it was raining, I could move and fight freely without ever touching the roof itself. I could use the steam from the engine, too . . .*

A flicker of movement cut off Hane's musing, making them go still with anticipation. Was it just the wind whipping at the tarp again? Or had someone just jumped down from the roof? Out of the corner of their eye, Hane checked on their teammates, finding Rose and her tamed Assassin hunched over the main engine that continued to slow down as the whine of the auxiliary engine pitched louder and louder with each passing minute. Odette was farther back and harder to see, but presumably she was taking care of the weapons and poisons stripped from the Assassin. Neither of them appeared to be watching the entrances to the car, making them perfect bait for an opportunistic villain. Hane firmed their grip around their tonfa and waited.

The center of the tarp over the coal car dipped low in the center, a sudden weight bowing it inward so steeply that the sound of the wind whipping against it was changed entirely. Still, Hane remained still and silent: even if the weight was caused by a person and not a spell or an object, they would have to enter the engine room to be a threat, and as bright as it was outside, anyone stepping inside the engine car would need time to let their eyes adjust. That was the best time to strike: Hane would see their opponent perfectly without being seen themself. They just had to hold. Patience. Patience . . .

The weight that bowed the tarp moved suddenly, like ripples seen beneath the surface of a lake, one, two, three, nearing the front of the coal car, then suddenly the tarp sank in deep over the gate, giving Hane the briefest glimpse of crouched legs before the person sprang upward, leaping from the tarp to the top of the engine car.

"Above!" Hane shouted, darting toward the ladder in the center of the car. "He's here, it's—"

Rose and Odette both looked up through the portal to the control room just as shouts and stomps sounded from above. Glass rained down through the opening in the ceiling, making Odette shriek and cover her head. Rose frowned darkly before she glanced back at Hane, a furrow of her eyebrows asking if they had this. Hane nodded: yes, they would handle this. Rose's job was to fix the engine; Hane's job was to protect her.

A shadow darkened the portal to the cabin above, making Hane skid to a stop just shy of the ladder. An unfamiliar face peered down at them, smiling merrily beneath the brim of a green newsboy cap. He waved once before squinting and making a motion as if he was counting. Hane could see his lips moving, but with all the noise of the engine, they couldn't hear a word. A mind-control spell didn't necessarily need to be heard to take effect, but Hane still counted it as lucky that between their Diminish Sound spell and the grinding whine of the engine, the effectiveness of any spoken command would be significantly weaker than intended.

Rose spoke sharply, Hane hearing her voice more than her words. A quick glance showed the Assassin clasping his hands over his ears, his head ducked low so he couldn't see his boss peering down at him. Most likely, Rose was attempting to protect her compulsion spell from having to compete against a stronger one. If the Magpie wanted to give the Assassin an order, he would have to come down the ladder to fight.

The Magpie sighed dramatically and shook his head at the cowed Assassin, then shrugged nonchalantly. Hane braced themself, waiting for the

Magpie to jump down the portal in order to wreck the engine, as the Assassin had attempted to do, but instead, he stepped smoothly out of sight, shadows shifting from movement up above. What was the Magpie doing?

Odette shouted, wide-eyed with alarm. When Hane only stared blankly at her, she stumbled forward, clasping their arm and shouting into their ear.

"We're speeding up!" she shouted, pointing at the auxiliary engine. "Too much more, and the engine will crack right down the middle! It can't maintain this speed for long."

Hane bit back a curse, glaring up through the ceiling. That was a far simpler solution than coming down for a fight. The Magpie had likely mind-controlled the engineers into increasing the train's speed. They had an idea, but they didn't want to shout it to Odette and tip off the Magpie, nor did they want to release their perception spell and let their guard down. Using hand signs common among experienced climbers, Hane asked a silent question.

"Can you understand me?" Hane asked, moving their hands slowly so Odette could follow.

She bit her lip anxiously, then nodded once.

"Can you slow the train if I lead him away?" Hane continued in hand-speak.

Again, another nod. They would have felt better if she would sign an answer, but it wasn't odd for someone to recognize more signs than they themself could make.

"Tell Rose," Hane signed. Odette's eyebrows lifted higher, forming a questioning furrow. By now, Hane could hear the strain of the auxiliary engine not just in the high-pitched whine but in the grind and clank of the gears Rose had so painstakingly replaced. There was no time to hesitate: Hane pointed at Rose as a directive to Odette then darted beneath the portal to the control cabin. From this angle, they could see the spell spheres stuck to the ceiling so that anyone dropping through would activate Odette's trap. While they had anticipated the usual two spell spheres and thought to avoid them, Odette had placed four this time, evenly spaced like the cardinal directions of a compass. That made the gaps in between even more narrow, but climbing the ladder to remove the traps made them far too vulnerable, either to attack or for a mind-control spell. There was nothing for it: Hane had to squeeze between the gaps in Odette's trap, and fast.

The Magpie will be expecting an attack, Hane rationalized as they eyeballed the distance and the space they had to aim for. *So I need to make an entrance he can't anticipate.*

Raising their hands above their head like a diver, Hane coiled transference mana tighter and tighter in their feet, ankles, and knees. The Magpie was just casting a glance down through the portal when Hane sprang, twisting vertically as they passed through Odette's trap, then curling into a ball to rotate midair.

Gravity Shift, Hane thought, spinning the world counter to their own rotation, so they landed in a crouch on the roof of the cabin. The Magpie must have crashed through a window in order to break in here, as evidenced by the glass shards coating the floor and the minor cuts on the four engineers manning the controls. The engineers didn't react at all to Hane's abrupt entrance, but the Magpie had taken a swing with a short staff capped with something the size and shape of a goose egg. Hane caught the look of surprise on his face as his follow-through pitched him off balance. Hane released their gravity spell in order to drop down on top of the Magpie and shove him through the portal, where Odette's trap waited.

Hane landed perfectly, one hand clasping the Magpie's shoulder as they rotated and shoved, pushing away quickly to land on a control panel of some kind. Unfortunately, the thief named for a bird seemed to have catlike reflexes that helped him recover his balance enough to stumble around the portal, rather than fall through it. He pivoted on the ball of his foot, baring his teeth in a mocking grin.

"Stop!" the Magpie commanded, the word distant and soft through Hane's self-impaired hearing. They felt the push of compulsion against their consciousness, but as prepared as they were for it, the suggestion was easily ignored. Hane leapt, swinging a tonfa through an overhead strike, intent on knocking the Magpie out cold. They felt a minor thrill as the thief's lazy arrogance turned to wide-eyed surprise, but as Hane swung the tonfa down, the Magpie blocked with his short staff held crosswise in both hands. A normal staff should have broken, which meant this odd-looking stick was actually a weapon.

Now that Hane could see the Magpie clearly, there was something vaguely familiar about him. Had they passed him on the train during their reconnaissance? Hane thought they would remember if they had, but they couldn't think of any specific instance where they might have seen this individual before.

"Protect me!" the Magpie shouted before Hane could break away. "Don't let them hurt me!"

The engineers turned as one, forcing Hane to defend with one tonfa while seeking to strike the Magpie with the other. It didn't seem as if any of the engineers were attuned, which made fighting them fairly easy, even if it was four on one—five, counting the Magpie, though he didn't seem especially combat proficient.

He thinks I won't hurt the engineers just because they're mind-controlled, Hane realized as the Magpie faded back, attempting to lose himself in the mix. *He's just delaying until the engine breaks; I need to end this quickly.*

With a roll of the wrist and a tight check on their own strength, Hane rapped an engineer on the temple with a tonfa, laying them out cold. The Magpie's jaw dropped as fear finally crept into his eyes. Hane noticed one tight swallow before the Magpie changed tactics entirely: leaping out the broken window in an attempt to run away. The compulsion to obey the Magpie's last order remained, however, and two engineers grabbed hold of Hane's arms as they attempted to give chase. Unwilling to struggle uselessly, Hane used their Burst spell to send the engineers flying away from them. The delay did serve one purpose, however: it reminded Hane that they couldn't follow the Magpie across the roof of the train.

But I can still catch up, Hane thought, tracking the Magpie's fumbling scramble across the coal car's tarp. Without the time to figure out exactly where Odette's trap was, Hane grabbed the nearest engineer and dropped them through the portal. Thick ropes sprang into being, entangling the unfortunate engineer, but also slowing their fall to the engine room's floor. Hane dropped through after, casting one quick look around to make sure everyone was okay.

"Slow the engine!" Hane shouted to Odette before lighting off after the Magpie. Maybe they could catch him before he made it onto the roof of the first crew car. The wind was with them and one good, strong jump should take them the length of the coal car's walkway.

Except that as Hane burst from the gloom of the engine room into the brilliant sunlight dazzling the exterior of the train, they realized the track was curving. Sharply, too. And at the speed the train was going, an ill-timed leap could be fatal.

Undeterred from their pursuit, Hane vaulted over the trap Odette had placed earlier and raced along the walkway, hands skimming the rails for balance. The Magpie was just scrambling onto the roof of the first car as Hane arrived at the coupler, and while they could have jumped and grabbed the thief's ankle, they held themself back. Barely. Curse the stupid no-roof rule in this scenario! They could run along inside the car to keep up, especially since the crew cars were the most likely ones to be empty, but the Magpie had fooled Nieve's team by doubling back once already, and Hane couldn't leave Rose and Odette undefended against a Controller.

Which really only left one option.

Hane looked to either side of the train, assessing the rush of sheer cliffsides and windswept tree branches to the right, and the wide, open nothingness of the left. Grimacing in open distaste, Hane peered over the left rail.

The valley was so far below, it looked more like a landscape painting than a deadly fall. Hane shook their head and sighed, resigning themself to what needed to be done.

"I hate this," Hane muttered, barely able to hear themself as they climbed up onto the brass rail. From here, they could just make out the Magpie atop the train car, moving cautiously with the wind at his back. Hane leapt, shifting gravity once more so that the side of the train became "down," leaving nothing but open air to their left. They moved cautiously at first, getting used to the feel of the windows beneath their feet and the wind streaming all around them. They sped up gradually, keeping close enough to the top of the car to keep an eye on the Magpie without touching anything they considered to be part of the roof.

This doesn't count as running along the roof, right? Hane asked themself, leaping across the void between two cars. *I'm outside the train, but not on top of it. Odette said spells don't count, right? I could blast them over the edge . . .*

But the mission brief had said "capture," and a fall here from either side was likely to kill him, so Hane held back. The Magpie would tire eventually and Hane could beat him to whichever platform he might attempt to enter through, even if that meant breaking a few windows in the process. They could afford to simply chase for now and wait for the right opportunity to strike.

The only trouble was remaining oriented in this sideways gravity without missing a step or a jump. Hane was used to short reorientations, from up to down and back again, usually in bursts no slower than most people could turn a somersault. Maintaining a gravity shift on the side of a moving vehicle was a new and challenging experience. They would have preferred to move cautiously and slowly until they became accustomed to their orientation, but they didn't have that luxury right now.

Only a few cars along the train, the Magpie's pace began to flag. He wore an expression that was both impressed and frustrated each time he peered over the edge of the roof and found Hane still doggedly pursuing him. It was hard to say if the Magpie was getting tired from all the running and jumping, or if he had an actual plan in mind. Unless he had planned for some contingency that included being trapped on the roof of the train, the only logical conclusion to this chase in Hane's mind was the Magpie's surrender and subsequent blackout via tonfa strike: Hane wouldn't be foolish enough to allow the Magpie a single word, lest he attempt another compulsion spell.

By Hane's estimation, they had reached the first of the general passenger cars, though they hadn't been keeping an exact count as they both kept an eye on the Magpie and suppressed the slight feelings of motion sickness brought on by the prolonged gravity shift. This was actually the first time Hane had used this particular spell on the outside of a moving vehicle, and it seemed their body was having trouble acclimating to both the movement and the strange orientation. They would keep going because they had to, but Hane had to admit that they'd be grateful once this chase was over.

Even at that thought, the end came unexpectedly: Hane felt the shudder of the train through their feet before the screaming whine of steel grinding against steel registered in their ears. The brakes. Odette must have engaged the brakes.

Hane slid to a stop and crouched down against the side of the train, casting a spell called Double Gravity twice. The pull of the "ground"—or rather, the side of the train—quadrupled, making Hane's entire body too heavy for them to move even a finger, but at least when the train jerked and bucked beneath them, they only swayed with the motion, rather than getting tossed off.

The Magpie wasn't so lucky.

As the train slowed sharply, the Magpie fell hard, landing face-first on the roof before sliding toward the back of the car. If he screamed, the wind stole it. All Hane could do was watch as the Magpie scrambled for a handhold before slipping over the end of the car—hopefully onto the platform below. Though it was hard to say how lucky that was, as the train's cars shoved forward into one another, held back only by their couplers. When the squeal of the brakes ended, Hane released their gravity spell and tried to run to the edge of the car, but after only a few steps, the train shuddered again, and Hane barely finished casting Double Gravity before the brakes screamed again.

Odette must be attempting to slow the train by applying the brakes on and off again, Hane rationalized. *Makes sense, since something this big can't slow down all at once. I just wish I was inside the train instead of outside it.*

It took two more cycles of screaming brakes for Hane to make it to the end of the car, like an inverted game of leaping lily pads. When Hane finally tumbled around the edge of the car and ended their Gravity Shift spell, their head spun woozily. They gripped the brass rail of the gangway, waiting for the dizziness to pass. Their limbs and extremities trembled with exertion, their stomach made its questionable status known, and the chill from the wind made them shiver, but for all that, they only allowed themself three full breaths before they pushed all that away and searched out the fate of the Magpie.

It was possible he had fallen from the train entirely; Hane couldn't believe he had planned for this exact contingency, so it was entirely possible the Magpie was dead at the side of the tracks, but since that option didn't require any follow-up, Hane considered the next possibility. Since the Magpie wasn't here on either of the gangways, he must have ducked inside the train car—but which one? Hane peered through the closer door's window, then strained to peer through the window of the next car. Chaos reigned in both cars, with passengers and luggage alike tossed from their seats each time the train lurched against the brakes. The flurry of activity made it impossible to figure out which car the Magpie might have ducked inside.

They've doubled back once before, would they do it again? Hane thought, looking back and forth between the two cars while holding fast to the rail. *Or would they keep fleeing toward the lounge cars and the Keepsake car? Which way?*

At more of a guess than a deduction, Hane leapt the gap between cars and ducked inside the car closer to the end than the engine. By Hane's estimation, there were more potential hiding places among the general population in this direction, considering the numerous passenger cars, lounge cars, and private cabins. It was the way Hane would have chosen if they were the one fleeing, and one way seemed as good as another at this point—assuming, of course, that the Magpie wasn't already dead.

The train kept lurching at intervals, but the stretches in between grew longer and longer, with the braking periods becoming shorter over time. Hane hoped that meant that Odette was bringing the auxiliary engine under control so it wouldn't break before Rose had time to fix the main engine. Hopefully the compulsion spell over the engineers had ended by now and they were able to assist Odette, rather than hinder her. For the sake of their teammates' safety, Hane decided they would only search two cars ahead before doubling back to check on them. It wasn't worth leaving Rose and Odette undefended if the Magpie had, in fact, doubled back again.

Enhance Sight, Hane thought, sharpening their gaze to quickly pick out the Magpie amidst the ashen-faced passengers, who scrambled to gather belongings and loved ones before the next dreaded lurch hit the car. Hane's hearing was still dampened, which was probably a good thing considering how many passengers seemed to be shouting or crying over the squeal of the brakes. It didn't look as if anyone was too injured, but Hane wouldn't be surprised if one or two of them had broken bones in bad falls. Hopefully no one had been passing between train cars the first time the brakes engaged.

No sign of the Magpie in the first car Hane checked, and the second car was no less riotous than the first, making it a longer search than it would have been under normal circumstances. Just as they were considering going back to the engine car, a face peeked through the porthole of the rear door, as if checking to see if the coast was clear. Hane saw the Magpie mouth a curse before he leapt to the next platform. Hane stumbled over an open trunk in the walkway as they started to run, losing sight of the Magpie for precious seconds. By the time they burst into the next car, the Magpie stood in the center of the car, looking windswept and ruffled, but no less superior than before.

"Kind passengers," the Magpie announced, grinning broadly. "The person chasing me is a bandit! Stop them and—"

Someone clapped a hand over the Magpie's shoulder, spun him halfway around, and punched him across the jaw.

"Hane!" Mason grinned and waved, still holding the Magpie's shoulder as he staggered and groaned, both hands pressed to his face.

"Mason," Hane greeted, nodding formally. It had taken everything in them not to let their gaze give Mason's presence away while the Magpie attempted to orate. "Step aside. I don't want to hit you when I knock him out."

"We need to question him," Mason said, shaking his head. "Don't worry, Nieve and I have protective spells against compulsion."

"Others don't." Hane gestured as if they meant the passengers, who were gawking at this mid-aisle performance, though they really meant themself. "Move."

"We need to know where the sn—" Mason cut himself off. "We need him to tell us where the stolen cargo is."

"Move." Hane advanced, rolling their tonfa into a reverse grip. "I'm not debating this."

"I'll tell you!" The Magpie's words were barely audible through the hands clasped to his mouth. "I'll tell you where it is!"

Mason gave Hane an apologetic look as he stepped between Hane and the Magpie. Hane tried to look past him, searching for their other teammates. Surely Nieve could knock this thief out with a single blow—if only she were here.

"Start talking," Mason demanded. "Or I let my friend in black back there rattle your skull."

The thief called the Magpie slumped in defeat. There was resignation in his eyes as he lifted them to meet Hane's gaze. "I thought that you, of all people, would understand."

Hane remained silent and still, tonfa ready to swing. Despite that, the words still resonated with them. Who was this person? What made him think Hane would understand?

Sighing heavily, the Magpie's gaze dropped. "There's a safe in the luggage car. I only have half the combination, though. Ellis has the other half."

"Rose has the Assassin under a compulsion right now," Hane informed Mason. "If he's not lying, we can get the other half easily."

"What's the combination?" Mason asked, giving the Magpie a shake.

"It's written down! It's in my pocket."

"Get it," Mason growled. Over his shoulder, he asked: "Is my sister okay? I didn't have a chance to—"

"Look out!" Hane lunged as the Magpie pulled something from an inside pocket that certainly was not a piece of paper. At first, Hane thought it a pale rope, or an enchanted whip of some sort, but horrified realization had them reversing their leap sharply as they understood what it actually was.

It was the snake.

The Magpie had had the snake on him the whole time.

And he had just released it in a car full of already panicked passengers.

"Strike!" the Controller ordered while Hane and Mason were still staring dumbly at the white-scaled snake. When it lifted its bone-crested head and hissed at Hane, they reacted without thought, flinching as they cast Burst to fling the snake away.

"No, no, we need it!" Mason lunged, catching the snake across his arms even as he craned his head back in fear or revulsion. The snake coiled around his forearm, black tongue tasting the air as Mason extended his arm out as far from his body as he could. The quick thinking in grabbing the snake was good, but in doing so, he'd released the Magpie. As Mason struggled to subdue the angry reptile, the Magpie made his getaway.

"Out of the way!" Hane shouted, trying to push past Mason. "Everyone stay calm, the situation is under—"

A sharp hiss and a loud Caelish curse word brought Hane up short. They looked back in time to see the snake rear back from a strike, its fangs retracting to the roof of its mouth.

"Did it—"

"Nope, didn't break the skin," Mason said, grimacing as he tried to figure out a safe way to contain the snake. "I'm fine, go after the—" Mason flinched twice more as the snake struck his bare arm. On the third strike, dripping fangs dug beneath the skin, latching on tight as a line of blood traced the curve of Mason's arm.

Hane hesitated, staring after the Magpie before turning back to Mason. "I can't leave you. Not after you've been bit by a venomous snake."

"Can't let him get away, either." Mason's voice was strained as he drew a stone rod from his quiver. It stretched and grew, taking shape even though Mason never took his eyes off the snake. "This is the good kind of venom, right? I'll be fine; just make sure he doesn't get away."

Hane hesitated, irritated at themself for being irritated. They knew what the right decision was in this case, but that didn't make it any easier. "I'm staying. At least until Lief gets here."

"He and Nieve aren't far behind." The stone rod in Mason's hand took the shape of a box, with tiny diamond-shaped holes along the sides like a wicker basket. His upper lip curled in disgust as he tried scraping the snake off his arm and into the stone box. The viper struck twice more before Mason managed to shape the stone box closed around it. Sweat dripped down Mason's forehead in heavy rivulets by the time he sat down across the aisle, giving Hane an exhausted grin. "See? No problem."

Hane debated, looking after the Magpie and estimating how far he could have gone by now. "Will that box hold if you pass out?"

"Yeah, but I'm fine," Mason assured them, waving them off. "Go on. Go capture the bad guy. I'll just sit here and . . . wait."

Hane crouched down beside Mason, setting a hand on his shoulder. The Transmuter's skin was already cold, the whites of his eyes turning the yellow of old parchment.

"Just rest," Hane said softly, making sure to hold Mason's gaze as they drew something from one of their hidden pockets. "I'm going to call Lief and tell him to get here fast, okay? Just concentrate on breathing and on keeping the snake safe."

"Yeah. Yeah, I can—yeow!" Mason's shout sent ripples of cries throughout the passenger car. The people inside the nearest cabin jumped as Mason slammed his head backward into the cabin door. "What in the name of the goddess—did you just stab me?!"

"Yes. Sorry. Not sorry." Hane hopped over Mason's sprawled legs as they slipped the tiny stiletto blade back into its hidden pocket. "Breathe slowly; the blade is poisoned."

"You what? Come back here!" Mason lunged after Hane but missed as Hane skipped out of reach. Mason groaned and sagged to the floor, curling around the stone snake crate. "Ugh, what did you do to me? Hey! Don't just leave me here!"

"I won't," Hane promised, releasing their pent up frustration over not being able to chase after the Magpie. This was more important—doubly so if they'd guessed wrong. "I'm just going to contact Lief and then I'll let you berate me all you want. Just stay right there and focus on breathing."

"Not like . . . I can do . . . anything . . . else," Mason muttered, voice getting weaker. He slumped onto his side, pulling the snake crate in toward his chest protectively. His breathing was ragged and rapid, blood still trickling down his arm. He really needed to stay awake, but his eyes were falling shut. Hane kept an eye on Mason as they felt for the activation rune on their earpiece.

"Attention Lief, this is Hane calling to report an injury. Assistance required immediately."

In the brief silence that followed, Mason seemed to deflate as his limbs went limp, his head dropping heavily toward the floor. Hane started to conjure a splash of water to wake him up when Lief's voice sounded inside their head.

[Hey, Hane, can you tell me which car you're in? And if you can, tell me about your injury.]

"It's not mine, it's Mason's," Hane explained. "We were in pursuit of the Magpie and he ordered the snake to attack. We're in one of the passenger cars near the front of the train. The snake is safely contained now, but the Magpie got away from us. He might be heading back toward you right now."

[He was bit by the viper?] Lief's tone was one of surprise and urgency. Hane imagined him picking up his pace as he made his way through the train. [I'm on my way. The dining car unlocked when the brakes started jolting the train. Listen, Hane, this is very important, but it's going to sound strange. I need you to find some sort of toxin or poison and get Mason to take it immediately. There's a chance that—]

"Already done," Hane interrupted. "I carry a blade coated in barbroot concentrate. Will that work?"

[It should. Good thinking! Barbroot isn't lethal and it should tie up the purifying venom. Hopefully.] There was a pause and when Lief's voice returned, it sounded slightly winded. [Nieve and I are on the way; just keep him awake and stable until we get there.]

"Got it," Hane confirmed. They waited a beat before figuring all that needed to be said had been said. Gingerly, they approached Mason and crouched down beside him. "Lief says you need to stay awake. He's on his way."

Mason grunted a reply. "I hate you."

"I'm okay with that," Hane said, settling in beside Mason. "Do what you need to do to stay awake. I'll wait with you until Lief gets here."

"What about . . ." Mason gasped for breath, his bald pate gleaming with sweat. "The Magpie?"

Hane shook their head. "That's not important right now. You need to focus on breathing and staying awake." Hane thought for a moment, considering ways to keep Mason awake. "Teach me some Caelish. You must have some colorful words to describe your current condition, and I'd like to know what Rose keeps calling the gear rack."

Mason's next gasp sounded almost like a laugh. Hane listened with one ear as Mason translated a few choice expletives while keeping their eyes on the far car door. It was a shame they'd let the Magpie get away, but they would have felt worse about leaving Mason in a vulnerable position on his own. All they could do now was wait.

Wait and hope the Magpie had the misfortune to run into Nieve while fleeing.

NIEVE

Champion (mind mark), Citrine
??? (heart mark), Sealed

I'm dying," Mason moaned from his bed. "The Wavewalker poisoned me. Avenge me, Prickles!"

"No," Rose said calmly from her perch on the top bunk. Despite Mason's thrashing and moaning just below her, she was determinedly examining each item taken from the Assassin and sorting them into piles that only seemed to make sense to her. She adjusted one of the lenses of her goggles as she squinted at a poison dart needle before placing it in a specific pile to her left and selecting another confiscated item from the mound to her right. "It's your own meatheaded fault for thinking a venomous snake bite could be harmless. You're lucky I wasn't there: I would have used a lethal poison."

"Why does everyone hate me?" Mason whimpered, curling onto his side and clasping himself around the middle. "I've been bit by two different animals already! I deserve some sympathy."

"There, there," Lief said, only slightly pedantically. He twisted a soaked cloth into a bucket of water before folding it neatly and placing it over Mason's sweaty brow. He sat on the floor beside Mason's bed, frequently checking his condition with diagnostic spells. "Hane did the right thing: without a toxin to combat, an ivory-crowned viper's venom will search for something else to purify. In most cases, it targets the highest concentration of metal in your system. Do you have any idea what life is like without iron in your blood?"

"I'd lose some weight?" Mason guessed weakly.

"You'd die, meathead," Rose called down. "Iron is necessary for the blood to carry oxygen. You can't live without it."

Mason muttered something Nieve couldn't quite make out, possibly uttered in Caelish. She stood with her back against the cabin door, giving her a vantage point that encompassed the whole room. Odette sat at the foldout table under the window, no fewer than three notebooks open and spread out in front of her. She held a pen in both hands with one more tucked behind her ear. Her expression was pinched in concentration as she added notes and drawings to various pages.

Hane was perched on the cabin's desk, right beside the stone crate containing the recovered ivory-crowned viper. They hugged one knee tight to their chest while the other dangled over the edge, looking a little worse for wear than usual after a fight. They weren't feeling guilty about stabbing Mason, were they? Lief said Hane had probably saved Mason's life. Not that Mason seemed at all thankful. After Odette explained that the Assassin had been taken to the train's brig, Hane fell silent, their dark eyes darting from speaker to speaker as the only indication they hadn't fallen asleep.

"Why do you even have a poisoned dagger?" Mason asked, directing the question at Hane. Then to Lief: "And why haven't you healed me yet? I'm dying!"

"I could purify the toxins out of your blood with a light spell, but it would probably hurt just as much as the venom does," Lief explained. "If we wait it out, the venom will purify the poison and both will pass through you safely. I'm monitoring your condition closely, and I can tell that the process is working, so let's just let it work for now."

"Don't most climbers carry poisoned weapons?" Rose asked, sifting through the mound of the Assassin's tools, as if looking for something specific. "Once I sort through this mess, we'll each have four or five poisoned weapons to keep."

"I don't want any," Mason groaned petulantly. "And I definitely don't want to be poisoned again!"

"As amusing as it is to listen to a full-grown man cry like an infant, we do have a few important things we need to discuss," Nieve reminded everyone, crossing one boot over the other at the ankle. "Now that we're all here and more or less alive, we should figure out what we're going to do about the Magpie."

"Capture him, obviously," Lief said, draping a second cloth over the rim of the water bucket before looking up at Hane. "You don't look well. You didn't get bit, too, did you? I wouldn't put it past you to stab yourself, but you should let me check your condition if that's the case."

Hane shook their head, hair falling forward of their face. "I'm fine. Some spell aftereffects, that's all. Not worth taking your attention away from Mason." Hane tilted their head slightly, hair parting just enough that they made eye contact with Nieve. "The Assassin said the Magpie offered you a deal. What was it?"

"Sa'rhi said he'd give himself up peacefully if we allow the Keepsake cars to be disconnected from the train," Nieve explained briefly. "Now, I'm all in favor of a fight, don't get me wrong. But if there's some weird reason why this is a good idea, I wanted to make sure everyone knew about it."

"I don't understand," Odette said, using a pen to point to the little snake crate Mason had shaped out of his stone rods. It looked like a stone box, with no obvious opening save for the tiny diamond-shaped air holes along the sides. "Why would the Magpie surrender after stealing the Keepsake cargo?"

"He wouldn't; he's lying." Lief sat back and wiped both hands with a damp cloth. "He's a Controller, remember? We can't trust anything he says, or have faith in any bargains he makes. Just because he says he'll surrender peacefully doesn't mean he won't peacefully ask a guard to free him after he's been locked up. It's not a risk we should consider taking. Hane, at least let me heal whatever's underneath that bandage on your neck."

Hane touched the bandage looped around their neck. "It's mostly healed by now. A simple regeneration spell would be more than adequate. What I don't understand is why the Magpie would offer to surrender in exchange for the snakes. How does the theft benefit him if he's in jail?"

"It's about the snakes," Mason groaned, rolling onto his back with a dramatic flop. "He thinks he's an activist, or some kind of hero. Wants to set the snakes free so they don't live their lives in boxes every day, getting milked for venom until they're dried up."

"That actually sounds really compassionate," Hane said, sounding surprised to admit it. "Can we do that? Release the snakes in exchange for the thief's surrender?"

Lief snorted as he wrung out another soaked handkerchief. "No, we can't. We were hired by Keepsake to protect that cargo. And we can't trust him anyway; he's obviously lying in order to escape with the prize."

"Is he, though?" Rose mused without stopping her efforts to sort the Assassin tools. "Consider the following: a person with a noble cause and money to spare becomes a vigilante, protecting a population that cannot speak for itself, such as animals. While the noble cause may remain unchanged, the money begins to run out because pure altruism rarely turns a profit. This results in less funds to pay compatriots, fewer means for carrying out the cause, and no resources to care for the endangered population. What recourse might a vigilante seek?"

Rose paused, goggles flashing as she looked around the room. Nieve panicked internally as the gaze fell on her: she wasn't even sure she understood the question, much less the answer.

"A platform from which they can share their beliefs," Rose finished, sounding slightly exasperated as she picked up the next weapon from the pile. "If the Controller is taken into custody, he will be given a trial. Yes, it is more than likely he will be imprisoned for his crimes, but he gets to speak his piece on animal exploitation, which helps spread his cause. It's almost like a retirement plan: if he's out of money anyway, might as well go to jail where he'll be housed and fed, and continue to share his cause with anyone who will listen."

"Whether that's the intention or not, it doesn't change the mission," Lief pointed out. "All we need is to finish this scenario and move on to the next floor. There's no question here: we protect the shipment and we catch the criminal, just as we were hired to do. End of story."

"We were hired to capture a target," Hane reminded him. "There was no mention of protecting cargo of any kind. The snakes have nothing to do with us, so it should make no difference whether they get stolen or not."

"It might even be better if they do get stolen," Rose muttered. Her eyebrows lifted as everyone looked up to stare at her. "What? It's evidence of a crime if the shipment goes missing. What's the incentive to confess if a crime doesn't actually take place? We don't know if Keepsake has a case against the Magpie; allowing the cargo to be stolen means Keepsake can charge the Magpie, and the Magpie can confess in order to spread their message."

"You know," Nieve said slowly, thinking it through. "Wouldn't it be easier to accept a surrender than to fight while protecting bystanders and minimizing damage to the train? Not to mention we'd be conserving our strength for the next floor."

"I'm disappointed, Nieve." Lief shook his head. "I didn't think you were the type to avoid a challenge."

"Oh, I don't mind the challenge," Nieve returned. "If you guys want it to be a fight, I'm happy to stand on the front line and take the heavy hits. But it's the tactic of—resh, I don't know the translation, but Sage says it all the time. It's about taking the easy path now to save your strength for harder trials down the way."

"Work smart, not hard," Mason summarized, one arm thrown over his face to block out the light. "I could get on board with that. Don't really feel like working hard right now."

"Plus it would give us time to work on some side quests," Rose pointed out. "Never mind working out a cohesive plan for dealing with the rockslide tomorrow."

"Oh yeah, I forgot about that," Nieve mused.

"So we're in agreement?" Hane asked, looking around. "We'll allow the shipment to be stolen in exchange for the Magpie's surrender."

Lief shook his head, for once looking more sour than amused. "I don't agree. Even if it's not part of the mission brief, that cargo belongs to our employer: Keepsake Treasuries. I think it's a secondary objective, and protecting it will most likely earn us an additional reward at the end of the scenario."

"I'm . . . kind of in alignment with that," Odette agreed hesitantly. "Secondary objectives are pretty normal, and if it wasn't meant to be part of our challenge, then why would we be linked to it through our employer? And just . . . more than that, Cure is a life-saving medication. Aren't human lives more important than a few snakes being kept in captivity? I mean, the snakes get fed, they don't have to worry about predators, and I don't think they're treated badly, they're just . . . used."

"And that makes it okay?" Hane challenged. "Because they're not physically abused, it's okay to keep them in cages their whole lives? Why do you get to judge which life is worth more than another? A snake's life is valuable to the snake, just as your life is valuable to you."

Nieve felt her jaw drop slowly. Was this really Hane? Hane arguing? Hane acting passionate about something? During their last climb, Hane had offered advice and guidance, but they never disagreed with the team to this extent. They hadn't balked at killing monsters or fighting the humanoid simulacra of the spire. What was this? Was there some deeper meaning here that Nieve had missed?

"You eat meat, don't you?" That odd question came from Rose, who was apparently interested enough in the conversation to push her goggles up onto her forehead and stop playing with the Assassin's toys. "Like chicken and beef and fish?"

"At times," Hane admitted defensively. "And I see the point you're making, but it's different. People need to eat and meat is a natural part of our diet, in moderation. But we don't need to manufacture Cure at a rate that requires dozens of snakes to live out their lives in laboratories. Cure isn't even entirely necessary if you know what type of snake bit you. Even if you don't, most clinics can safely mix two or three antivenins in order to treat common venoms. Climbers like Cure because it's a simple solution, but not everything needs to be simple. If you don't know the type of toxin you've been affected by, you can ring out and an Acolyte will treat you."

"Yes, and I'm sure that would be a popular suggestion among climbers if it mattered at all." Lief rolled his eyes, making no effort to hide his irritation. "I can't believe I actually have to say this, but listen: this is a scenario. It's not real. There are no snakes. There is no lab. No actual Cure production. There is no moral dilemma here, there is only finishing the challenge so we can get to the next floor. Preferably with more treasure in hand than we entered with, which is why I think it's best that we deliver both the imaginary thief and the imaginary cargo at the end of this imaginary train ride."

"Take a dive off the side of the cliff and tell me how imaginary that feels," Hane snapped. "The scenarios are real to the beings inside them, and I find myself in alignment with the Magpie's intentions. I want to let the Keepsake cars go in exchange for the Magpie's peaceful surrender."

"Looks like we're voting," Lief said with a bemused sigh. He glanced around the tiny cabin, taking in Odette at the window, Mason and Rose on the bunk beds, and Nieve at the door, something cold in the glitter of his gaze. "Does anyone else feel strongly about freeing a few snakes?"

A tense silence followed, punctuated by creaky mattress springs and the wind whistling past the window. As much as she wanted to make friends with Hane, Nieve simply didn't feel too strongly either way. Snakes weren't cute, like kittens and bunnies, and as a climber, she recognized the need for catch-all cures, even if she couldn't afford a real bottle of Cure herself. And looking at it another way, these white snakes reminded her a little of her favorite eel dish back in Dalenos. Would they even be having this conversation if these were eels instead of snakes? Or would Nieve have already tucked a napkin into her vest as a bib?

Odette shrunk in on herself, looking ashamed as she voiced her opinion. "I'm sorry, Hane, but I'm here for treasure, and I think turning over both the cargo and the Magpie gets us the better reward. I'm with Lief."

"I am, too," Rose decided, her expression still thoughtful as she said it. "Leaving aside the fact that none of this is real, I don't really think it's wrong to use animals for the betterment of people, as long as it's done humanely. The pitch gets far too steep when you apply that same logic to animals raised for meat, or horses used for transportation, or dogs used for hunting, and I don't want to travel down that slope."

"Ugh." Mason groaned dramatically as he pushed himself up to sit on the edge of his bed, swiping at Rose's dangling legs when she nearly kicked him. "As much as I would love to side with you, Hane, and wave goodbye to that car full of snakes, and then maybe toss that one over the side of the cliff,"—he gestured angrily at the crate on the desk—"my thinking is that since Keepsake Treasuries is both our employer and the owner of the shipment, that the entire challenge is turning over both the Magpie and the shipment. I think doing anything less will result in a subpar reward."

Hane's expression was grim, but they nodded as if accepting Mason's rationale. Glittering black eyes tracked across the room to land on Nieve, who startled as she realized she'd suddenly become the center of attention.

"Oh, I don't really care," Nieve said in response to all the silent stares. "It sounds like we have a majority anyway, and I don't mind taking the Magpie and his goons on in a fight."

"Great!" Lief smiled cheerily, his dark mood from earlier clearing as if it had never been there to begin with. "So, for tomorrow, I propose that we lure the Magpie into a controlled situation, possibly with crew members dressed as passengers so as not to start a genuine panic. We'll tell them that we've agreed to their terms, and when—"

The hiss of an object scraping across a wooden surface stole the team's focus, forcing Lief to turn around and scowl at Hane. With one finger on the corner of the stone snake cage, Hane dragged the crate closer to themself before picking it up and stepping smoothly off the desk. The sudden silence felt taut, like the moment before a sword leaves its sheath. Everyone seemed to be holding their breath as Hane stepped in front of Nieve, holding the snake crate in both hands before them.

"Move," Hane ordered flatly. "I'm leaving."

"Wait, wait!" Odette cried, half rising from her chair. "I'm sorry it didn't go your way, but we still need you. You're not—you won't ring out over this, will you?"

Nieve watched Hane take a deep breath, visibly calming themself down before answering. "No. I won't ring out, nor threaten to do so in order to manipulate the group's decision. You may continue to rely on me to do my part, but I don't wish to be a part of this discussion any longer."

"Where are you taking that?" Nieve asked, nodding to the makeshift snake crate. "Are you planning on setting it free?"

"No, I'm planning on returning it to the Keepsake car later on tonight," Hane replied, shouldering past Nieve to get to the door. "I'll have the easiest time getting it safely through the car window. It's the practical decision."

"Okay." Despite the coolness of Hane's words and actions, Nieve still felt that something wasn't quite right as the door to the cabin slowly rolled closed behind them. The tense silence remained until she heard the soft click of the door from the next cabin over.

"A bit childish, sulking for not getting their way," Lief commented in a soft tone. To Nieve, he asked, "Are they just soft-hearted, or is there something else they found triggering about this scenario?"

"I don't really know," Nieve answered honestly. "We don't know each other that well. They weren't this upset when—" Nieve's voice caught, the backs of her eyes stinging unexpectedly. Grief squeezed her heart, asking how she could have mentioned her last climb so casually it was almost callous? Sage had said that grief would come in waves, and it seemed Nieve was caught in a surge of it right now. She squeezed her eyes shut against tears and breathed deeply through her nose. "Three of our teammates died on our last climb. Hane didn't know them as well as I did, but they didn't seem as upset by that as they are right now."

"Odd," Rose commented, canting her head to the side. "There are some people who think it's wrong to kill the simulacra within the spires and that climbers are little better than murderers and tomb robbers who deserve to meet their ends, but that doesn't seem to be the case with your friend."

"I should . . . I should go talk to them, shouldn't I?" Odette asked, glancing around nervously. "I'm the team leader, so I—I guess that's my job."

"No, I'll go," Nieve offered, waving Odette's suggestion away. "They know me better; they might feel more comfortable telling me what the issue is. Just, whatever the plan for tomorrow is, make sure I get to fight Sa'rhi head-on, okay?"

"I think that's something we can all agree on," Lief replied, earning a few approving nods. Rose had already returned to examining the Assassin's tools and Odette looked immensely relieved that she didn't have to be the one going to talk to Hane. Mason looked as if he might have passed out at some point, lying on his back with one arm across his face to block the light. Hopefully sleep took away the pain of the toxins warring against one another within his bloodstream.

Nieve half expected Hane to have feigned going to their shared room in order to sneak away and find a shadowy corner to brood in. Instead, Hane was perched on the upper bunk, back pressed against the wall that adjoined Rose and Mason's room. They didn't look at all surprised to see Nieve as she stepped inside the room. A quick glance around showed that the snake crate had been set on the desk, a tiny black tongue flicking through the diamond-shaped air holes.

"If you wanted to listen in, you could have just stayed," Nieve pointed out, mystified by Hane's behavior. They had always seemed so cool and calm before; she was at a loss for how to deal with this sudden passion. "We need you, you know. You and I are the combat experts."

"They wouldn't need us to be combat experts if they accepted the Magpie's bargain," Hane retorted, tone sharp. They leaned forward, bracing their elbow on their knees, switching their language from Valian to Artinian as they spoke. "If it makes no difference to you, then you could have chosen to back me up."

"You're mad because I didn't side with you?" Nieve asked, also speaking Artinian. "It wouldn't have mattered; everyone else was against it. From the start, this was always more of a delve than a climb. Can you really blame them for choosing the option with the greater potential for loot?"

"Yes, I can!" Hane hopped down from the top bunk, apparently too agitated to stay still. "I can blame them when the price of treasure comes at the cost of suffering. If there's an option that allows those beings to go free, then we should take it. Isn't that what your previous team would have done?"

Nieve froze the wave of grief before it could crash down on her, hardening her heart the way Frost Form hardened her skin. "Only warning, Hane: don't you dare try to use my old team against me."

Hane's glare was fierce, but Nieve set her jaw and met it straight on. Hane was a good fighter, but if it came to an exchange of blows in a space this small, there was no doubt that Nieve would come out on top. It was hard not to feel like a bully, though: standing toe to toe with Hane like this exaggerated how much taller she was than them.

I don't want to intimidate them, I just want them to be reasonable, Nieve thought, trying to find a way to defuse the situation. *What would La—no. What would Sage do?*

After a moment's consideration, Nieve stepped aside, leaning back against the desk so that the path to the door was clear. She folded her arms over her chest while maintaining her glower. She'd made the first move; Hane would have to make the second. Hane fleetingly considered the door then the window before dropping down onto the edge of the lower bunk. They still appeared alert and wary, but less defensive somehow.

"I didn't mean to use them against you that way," Hane finally said, eyes darting away from Nieve's. "But it was a tactless thing to say and I'm sorry."

"Thank you," Nieve replied curtly. "And for the record, you're probably right. Lani was always championing the underdogs' causes, and Emiko was as soft-hearted as a climber could be. If Sage was here, he probably would have taken your side, unless he Saw something that made it a bad idea."

"And if Sage wanted to free the snakes, you would have argued against the team on his behalf," Hane pointed out, keeping their tone low. "But because it was me, you said you didn't care either way."

Nieve shrugged. "Sage is a Seer; there's almost always a deeper reason behind his decisions. And I know Sage better than I know you: I know what he thinks is important, even if I don't agree with him. It might be different if you were willing to meet me halfway and help me understand why this is important to you, but I really don't get it. I've seen you fight and kill inside a spire before, and it didn't seem to bother you then."

Hane looked distinctly uncomfortable, shifting their weight a few times before answering. "Sometimes the only choice we're given is kill or be killed. And I've made my peace with killing to survive. But the few times that we're offered a choice to save someone just for the sake of saving them, shouldn't we take it? If we accept that our actions here have no consequences, then what's the point of minimizing casualties and collateral damage during fights? What stops us from just grabbing all the passengers and crew and dropping them over the cliff so they don't get in our way later?" Hane's hands curled into fists that trembled. "Why do you care about protecting the beings that appear human, but not the ones that appear as monsters or animals? If the argument is that we should protect the cargo because those snakes aren't real, then it follows that we can massacre the passengers on this train indiscriminately, because they aren't real either."

Put that way, Hane's logic sounded solid. There was something unsettling about it, but Nieve had trouble refuting it. Why couldn't this have been a topic of conversation during the trip to Caelford? Sage was way better at these types of debates than Nieve was.

"I don't know why it's different, but it is," Nieve said with a shrug. "Look, you're thinking too hard about this. These are the goddess's trials; they're meant to be difficult in more ways than one. Yeah, it might be easier to kill all the passengers to open up space for a fight, but that's not something the goddess would approve of us doing. By protecting and saving lives despite the inconvenience, we not only earn Selys's favor but a greater tangible reward as well. So if one choice is more likely to get us better treasure, then that's the choice Selys wants us to make for ourselves."

"So the goddess sanctions the suffering of animals for human convenience?" Hane challenged.

Nieve threw her hands up. "I don't know everything, Hane, I'm just telling you how I interpret it. And I don't really think the snakes milked for venom are suffering, anyway. Just like Odette said, they're fed and cared for, and in exchange they get juiced every couple of days. What's so bad about that?"

Hane's eyes narrowed, their expression hardening. They let a beat of silence go by before speaking. "It's a very small jump from using snakes to make Cure to forcing a gateway crystal's consciousness into a weapon."

A jolt shot through Nieve like a lightning bolt: how could she have missed the connection between the snakes' rights and Chime's rights? Snakes might not be considered intelligent, but in terms of being "alive," they were at least relatable: they ate, they slept, they breathed, and they mated—all things Nieve could relate to personally. Gateway crystals did none of those things, and they still lived, still had desires and motivations and more magic than any Emerald-level attuned. Was a gateway crystal's "life" more valuable than a snake's simply because they could make their desires known? If the snake could talk and opted for freedom over providing the ingredient for Cure, would it be wrong to continue to keeping it in captivity?

Nieve's head was starting to hurt. She didn't like feeling confused; it made her feel as if people were laughing at her. And that, in turn, made her want to hit things. She needed this conversation to be over.

"Chime is real because they exist outside the spire," Nieve rationalized. "The snakes in this scenario aren't real, even if they think they are. If we happen across this exact same situation in real life, I promise I will help you free those snakes, or whatever the living cargo happens to be. But right now, all that matters is keeping the peace with our current teammates, and maybe earning some treasure along the way. Can we just focus on that, please?"

Hane's shoulders dropped as they looked away. "If you can rationalize choosing the wrong course of action inside a spire, how can you be sure you'll choose the right one outside of it? Even if this scenario is an illusion, we're real, and the choices we make are real. You can't be different out there than you are in here."

"I can," Nieve said firmly. "You know I love to fight, but the only time I'd ever fight anyone outside the spire is within a regulation dueling match. I don't go out searching the wilds for monsters to kill, I don't hunt, I don't even fish. I help my grandmother with the garden, I help my brothers find apprenticeships, I volunteer at the temple, and if I see something that isn't right, I do something about it. I've stopped thieves, broken up bar fights, and helped put out fires, because I know those are the right things to do, not because I'm expecting some kind of reward for doing them."

"It's easy when the situation is clear-cut like that," Hane pointed out. "Who wouldn't put out a fire, or stop a thief? You learn who you are in the murky gray areas, not in the bright light of day."

"I know who I am outside of the spire, Hane," Nieve replied harshly. "It sounds like you're the one who doesn't."

Silence filled the room until the air felt thick with it. Nieve knew she wasn't wrong, but Hane believed they were right, too. No one was going to win here. There would be no consensus, no victory. No new bonds of kinship between teammates.

Maybe I should have sided with them earlier, Nieve thought, knowing it was far too late now. *It wouldn't have changed the outcome at all, but I could have made an effort to connect with them. This is why I shouldn't be a team leader: I don't think of these things until it's too late.*

Just as before, Hane stood slowly, this time the way to the door was clear for them.

"I can leave if you want me to," Nieve offered. "This is your room, too. You shouldn't have to go."

"I'm leaving," Hane stated simply. "Don't look for me. I'm fine on my own."

Nieve sighed, shoulders sagging as she gave up. "Fine. Just be careful."

The warning was unnecessary, but if Hane took offense, they didn't show it. The door rolled slowly back into place, the latch clicking softly behind the unknowable Wavewalker. Maybe it would be different if she could laugh with Hane, or if they could share a meal together and just simply talk to one another. If she just understood where Hane was coming from . . .

Nieve rubbed her forehead with a hand, squeezing her eyes shut to clear the burgeoning headache behind her eyes. She was going to have to fix this somehow, but she didn't know where to start. She couldn't put Hane in a headlock the way she would Sage, and she didn't have the right way with words to smooth it over with an apology. Finding some sweets to leave out for them just seemed childish and more likely to earn their ire than their forgiveness. Why was it so difficult to just get along with Hane?

A sound like the hum of a plucked string sounded in Nieve's mind just prior to Chime's voice speaking up: <My life is more important than a snake's life. Is it not?>

Nieve grimaced, resisting the urge to jiggle her foot in frustration. Goddess, but she wished Chime hadn't been able to hear that entire conversation! She felt guilty enough over Hane; now she had to feel guilty for Chime.

"Yeah, I think it is," Nieve said, speaking aloud to the empty room. "I mean, if there was some weird challenge where I had to choose between saving you or saving some rare snake, I'd choose you without a second thought." A thought occurred before Nieve could block it out entirely; in an attempt to hide it from Chime, she tried changing her focus back to Hane and the way they had stormed out of the cabin.

<It is a relief to know you feel that way,> Chime answered. <I find myself more in agreement with your argument than with Hane's. A snake lives but a short time and individually has little intentional impact on its environment and does not form lasting attachments to others of its kind. I do not understand the empathy Hane feels toward creatures such as these.>

Nieve's first instinct was to agree—here was the argument she had been searching for but couldn't find earlier!—but then a very Sage-like thought entered her mind, and as much as she wished to, she couldn't ignore it.

Chime, you're an ancient being connected to realms of magic that I can't even fathom, aren't you? Nieve spoke the thought in her mind for the sake of caution. The pleasant tinkling of bells seemed to agree with Nieve's assessment. *That means you've been around longer than humans have existed on Kaldwyn, right? Was there ever a time that you, or maybe the other gateway crystals, sort of saw us humans as . . . snakes? With short lives and limited magical abilities?*

Chime's initial response was a low hum, one Nieve hadn't heard them make before. It sounded like a thoughtful noise, or perhaps hesitance. <I have a greater understanding now of Hane's argument, and for that I thank you. Perhaps it is selfish of me to consider my life more worthy than that of a snake, or that of a human. But my relief upon knowing you would choose my life over that of a snake's is still reassuring to me. Do you feel that is wrong of me?>

"No," Nieve replied, still ordering her thoughts. Philosophical conversations were certainly not her strength. "I think every being values their own life and the lives of their kind above the lives of others. I don't think that's wrong, it's just . . . survival, I guess. I think it's rare for someone to place an equal value on all lives, like Hane does. But they choose to climb the spires, which inevitably requires taking lives, so . . ." Nieve sighed in frustration as she ground the heels of her hands into her temples. "I don't get it. I feel like I'll never understand them."

<I fear I will be no help on the subject,> Chime confessed to a sweetly sad tune. <Might I ask you something? Earlier, when you said you valued my life over that of a snake, I sensed deep hesitation from you. What was that in regards to?>

"Ugh, sorry. I didn't mean for you to hear that." Nieve rubbed her forehead, wishing she had a drink at hand. Or at least some food; all she'd eaten so far was a single breakfast pastry. Actually, that wasn't a half bad idea. "Can I set you down for a minute, Chime? I want to change before I go get something to eat."

<Of course.>

After peeling off her boots, Nieve set the slim crystalline shard down on her pillow. She didn't need to change for lunch, but she needed an excuse to be alone inside her own head for a minute or two. Most of the time, it was easy to forget that Chime could hear her thoughts throughout the day, but when they spoke directly, Nieve preferred a bit of distance. Not to lie, exactly, more to organize her thoughts and responses so she didn't say anything she didn't mean. Her off the cuff responses were often interpreted as rude, and while friends like Sage understood her, Chime and Hane were still learning to appreciate her gruff method of communication. And based on her disastrous conversation with Hane just now, it was past time for Nieve to start rethinking her usual approach to conflict.

She moved slowly as she changed, unlacing the side of her protective leather vest before hanging it over the back of the desk chair, then tossing off the shirt underneath. A brief search through her bag turned up her only other shirt, slightly wrinkled, but at least it smelled fresher than the one she'd been wearing. After shaking it out and pulling it on, Nieve found a mirror inside the standing wardrobe and fixed her hair, tightening her headband and arranging her bangs to fall rakishly over it. Finally, she collected her boots and sat on the edge of the bed, careful not to jostle Chime as she tugged her right boot on first. Before pulling on the left boot, Nieve scooped up the crystalline shard, fitting it inside the hidden pocket that kept the crystal shard pressed against her ankle.

"Okay, so here it is." Nieve spoke as she laced up the boot, feeling the cool crystal press against her skin. "It's not right and I feel pretty bad for thinking it, but . . . you remember that final fight in the Tortoise Spire, right? The place where we discovered you?"

<Yes.>

"Well, I thought . . ." Nieve hesitated, guilt stalling her confession. "I thought that if Hogame had offered me the choice between saving you and saving my teammates . . . look, I'm sorry, it's completely pointless for me to even consider. I just . . . I miss them. I loved them."

A mournful sound, like soft rain falling in waves. <I believe I understand you. It is hard to choose the life of a stranger over the lives of loved ones. Especially if you consider that if this piece of my consciousness were to fade, I would continue to exist in the other fragments of my self. That is not to say I would not mourn the loss of those memories, but I can see how less value can be attributed when compared to the lives of three loved ones.>

"I still feel bad for thinking it," Nieve admitted. "Finding your pieces and making you whole again really is important to me, and nothing can ever change what happened to my friends. I just . . . I want you to feel safe with me. I'm not like the human who treated you like you were just some piece of treasure they collected. I wouldn't trade you away like a piece of loot."

<I sense that from you,> Chime stated. <You are the tenacious roar of a glacier, forever marching forward, unstoppable and undaunted. You do not yield easily. It is your strength.>

That actually sounded kinda cool. Nieve couldn't help but grin at the comparison.

<Another question, if I may,> Chime continued, tone a bit cautious now. <Just as glaciers contain hidden depths, I sense a deep longing within you, and a frustration tied to a sense of time. You worry that something will happen before you can reach your goal. Will you tell me either your worry or your goal? If possible, I would like to grant you a boon that may help once I am whole again. Considering such a thing will help me pass the time as I wait.>

Nieve grimaced at the question, standing up and tapping the toe of each boot against the floor, as if adjusting the fit of her boots. She focused on checking for her room key in her pocket, and on moving her war hammer from her sword belt to her equipment belt. She hung her sword belt from the bedpost, hoping it wouldn't be necessary for the space of a meal. When there was nothing left to do before leaving the room, she exhaled slowly, tamping down feelings of grief and homesickness.

"You can't help me," Nieve said when she felt steadier. "Sorry. What I need isn't related to ancient magic or even more power. I just have to make it to the top of a spire and meet the goddess. Before . . ."

<Before?>

Nieve set her hand on the door latch, willing herself to remain cool and calm despite the anxiety caused by Chime's entirely too personal question. She definitely needed to hit the bar tonight after her guard shift; maybe she'd even convince some of her new teammates to join her. That way, she wouldn't be a hostage to the curious entity who couldn't help but hear her thoughts.

"Before I'm out of time."

CHAPTER 14

HANE

Wavewalker (leg mark), Citrine

"Hey, we missed you yesterday, pal," Lief said with a false cheer that grated on Hane's nerves. "Odette said she caught up with you earlier. Are you clear on the plan or do you need me to go over anything?"

"No." If they had questions, they would have asked Odette. The only thing they really wanted to ask was why Lief was their partner on this particular part of the mission, though in actuality, they knew why: Lief, and probably some of the others, no longer trusted Hane to fulfill their part of the assignment faithfully ever since the argument the day before. Hane couldn't even deny that they were tempted to allow the thieves to steal the two Keepsake cars from the train in order to set all the rare snakes free, but going against the team's consensus would be a mark against their record as an independent climber. As much as they disliked the decision, they would abide by it.

"Did you get any sleep last night?" Lief asked, his easy smile absent from his eyes. "Nieve said you weren't in the cabin when she went to bed last night, which means you must have slipped in through the window later. That's an interesting trick, by the way: walking along the side of the train rather than using the roof."

Hane chose not to answer. They had slipped in through the cabin window in order to catch a few hours of unbroken sleep, but it had required inching along the side of the train facing the cliff side, rather than the valley, made all the more harrowing in the dark of night. At least they had remembered to unlock the window from the inside before returning the stolen ivory-crowned viper to the Keepsake cars. It had only taken the flat of a knife wedged beneath the sill to get the window to pop open.

"I'm only asking because you seem tired," Lief continued, his tone as light as if they were old friends having a casual conversation. "If you're not up for this, there's still time to come up with a new—"

"I'm fine," Hane said sharply, cutting a glare over at Lief. "I'm not going to sabotage the mission. Stop watching me like you expect me to betray the team."

"You can't really blame me, can you?" Lief shrugged as he sidestepped a piece of luggage protruding into the aisle. The train's crew had been through the first luggage car and attempted to set it to rights as much as possible, but with the upper luggage rack broken, much of what had been in the first car had been moved to the second car, making it far more crowded than it had been on previous visits. "It wouldn't be the first time someone decided they knew what was best and acted on it against the majority vote. And it's not like you or Nieve have much of a reputation here in Caelford, which makes it seem as if you have less at stake here than the rest of us."

That wasn't worth responding to. It didn't matter where Hane was; they weren't going to jeopardize their reputation as a climber. Especially since they might need to join another team if this attempt to find Chime's missing piece didn't pan out. That was the rationalization they'd come to the night before: that Chime was worth following through on a decision they didn't necessarily agree with.

The back of Hane's neck prickled uncomfortably: Lief was making no effort to mask his critical stare.

"What brought you and Nieve here all the way from Dalenos in the first place?" Lief asked, sounding more skeptical than curious. "It just seems . . . odd. Especially considering how neither of you speak Caelish."

"What does that make you?" Hane countered, shifting the wooden crate they carried to the side so they could open the door to the outside. They had to avoid looking at the panel that hid the secret compartment, as well as the marks that indicated the height of Odette's tripwire trap, making navigating the narrow space all the more difficult. "You claim to have been to most of the spires of Kaldwyn. Doesn't that make you odd as well?"

"Ha! I guess that's fair." Lief leaned past Hane to hold the door open, allowing Hane to step over the trap without dropping the wooden crate. "I like the travel more than I like climbing, but I've gotta earn money for train tickets and food somehow. And healers usually have an easy time finding teams to join." Despite his smile, Lief's eyes seemed strangely cold as he followed up on his earlier question. "So what prompted you to suddenly leave your Tortoise Spire and set out for Caelford?"

It was none of Lief's business, but saying so would only make them seem suspicious and the last thing Hane wanted was for someone to start digging through a lie and turn up the truth.

"Left too many bodies in the Tortoise Spire," Hane said grimly, the train's slipstream tugging at their hair and clothes. "The last climb just got to be too much."

"Ah." At least Lief responded the way Hane had hoped he would: awkward and apologetic. "I . . . have some experience with that as well. I'm sorry you lost someone."

It left Hane feeling dirty, using Nieve and Sage's grief to stave off questions about their reason for leaving Dalenos, but the death of a colleague was something almost every experienced climber could relate to, and few cared to have their trauma drawn out into the light. It was a safe answer, and not entirely a lie, so it was justified.

"Can we get on with this now?" Hane asked pointedly. "We don't have a lot of time."

"Yes, right, the rockslide. Um . . ." Lief hesitated, glancing over at the tattered remains of the gangway outside the sealed-shut door of the Keepsake car. "How do you intend to cross? Should I hold onto the crate and pass it to you, or—"

"No, it's no trouble." Hane eyed the distance, shifting the crate in their arms as they prepared themself for a change in gravity. "Watch my back?"

"Oh, I'm watching," Lief said, far too lightly. At least he wasn't trying to pretend everything was okay after yesterday's argument; Hane preferred the honesty of open mistrust.

Gravity Shift. Hane twisted as the world shifted around them, keeping the crate level as they reoriented to land feet first on the sealed door of the Keepsake car, softening the impact on the crate as best as they could.

"That really is quite a trick!" Lief called over the roar of the wind. "If you ever need a spell to help with—"

Lief cut off as a shadow swung down from the roof of the train, hanging from their knees in order to hold a blade to Lief's throat. Hane had to pivot on the balls of their feet and crane their neck in order to look back, as the luggage car was now "up" by their orientation.

"Relax, he's going to be just fine." The Assassin. Of course it was the Assassin. Hane sighed as they sat back against the door, cradling the snake crate to their chest. "As long as you—"

Hane didn't wait for the Assassin to finish his ultimatum—they heaved the crate across the gap between the cars, adding extra force with a transference-aided push. The Assassin barely had time to shout in surprise as he reflexively covered his face with his arms. Lief ducked, protecting his head as the crate exploded into splinters. Hane leapt back to the luggage car, reorienting gravity the right way around while freeing a tonfa from the harness beneath their vest. One strong crack against the inverted Assassin's knee had him crashing down to the gangway, where Lief was ready with a boot on his neck and an arrow to the string of his bow.

"My knee, again?" the Assassin howled, writhing in pain as much as he could. "It took Squatch all night just to make it stop hurting!"

"The Assassin did get free of the brig. Huh." Lief seemed mildly amused as he drew back the string of his bow, keeping an eye on the pain-wracked Assassin. "Who was betting on that? Rose or Mason?"

"I don't know, I wasn't there," Hane reminded him, clinging to the ladder set against the side of the train. Using a mirror provided by Rose, Hane checked the roof of the train. "I don't see anyone else coming. Shouldn't he have activated Odette's roof traps?"

"Some Assassins use a spell to lighten their footsteps," Lief said, making a face. "I think it's similar to water-walking, except it uses umbral mana instead. If his feet didn't touch the roof, then the traps wouldn't activate."

"You utter fools!" the Assassin cried, struggling against the boot on his neck. "Do you have any idea how much that snake was worth? You could have bargained with it, and I would have happily taken it off your hands! You just threw a fortune away!"

"Sounds like this one's not all that loyal," Lief snorted. "Let me guess: you're in it for the cash, not the cause?"

"The crate was empty," Hane explained, dropping down from the ladder. They freed a coil of rope from Lief's belt and knelt down on the brass grating to bind the Assassin's ankles. "I returned the snake you stole last night. And you used one of these valuable snakes as a projectile first, remember?"

"We even stole this little gem of a trick from your boss," Lief said cheerily. "Sorry to say he got the better of us yesterday. Where is he hiding today? C'mon, be a friend and tell us so we don't have to go looking."

The Assassin refused to answer, though he did thrash against the cord Hane looped around and between his ankles.

"Careful," Hane warned, using a knee to hold the Assassin's legs still. "Just because we took all his toys yesterday doesn't mean he's harmless today."

"Yes, thank you, the blade at my throat was a good reminder of—" Once again, Lief was cut off abruptly by an attack, except this time it came from a direction neither Hane nor Lief had considered: from beneath the train itself. One moment, Lief stood perfectly steady, the next a slim, glowing platform appeared beneath his boots and lifted rapidly, spilling him over the rail of the gangway and into the unforgiving cliff face. Hane leapt over the prone Assassin, throwing themself against the rail in an effort to catch Lief and pull him back to the safety of the platform. Lief dropped the arrow he'd been holding and managed to grip a vertical rail as he fell, making it easy for Hane to grab the front of his vest and haul him back from the whipping wind and the lashing tree branches.

"Thanks," Lief gasped, once he got his feet on the gangway again. He was still on the wrong side of the railing, but at least he wasn't in danger of being smashed against the cliff side anymore. Still holding onto each other for dear life, Hane and Lief glanced down along the side of the train, looking for the source of the attack. Hane groaned as Lief laughed. "Looks like you're not the only one who can walk along the side of the train, Hane!"

This had to be the Shaper Nieve had fought earlier: there weren't many attunements that could create magical constructs real enough to serve as a walkway along the outside of a moving train. He didn't even have to worry about disorientation the way Hane did, just the occasional tree branch that extended too far forward. A shiver through the brass grating alerted Hane to movement by the Assassin, but they couldn't very well turn around and finish tying the Assassin up while Lief hung over the side of the rail facing down an enemy who could attack from a distance. Even as they thought it, Hane saw the Shaper lift a hand in preparation of a spell.

"Look out!" Lief shouted, seeing something over Hane's shoulder.

"Look out yourself," Hane warned, bracing their stance and shifting their center of gravity low. "Try to relax your legs."

"My—whoa!" Lief shouted as Hane pitched their weight backward, dragging Lief forcibly over the rail and out of the way of the Shaper's attack. Perhaps that was part of being a good teammate, but the next tactic was slightly less so: Hane rolled to their back, planting a foot in Lief's stomach and kicking, sending Lief crashing into the Assassin. The chorus of grunts and the rattle of the brass rail confirmed that neither combatant had toppled off the platform, allowing Hane the freedom to deal with the Shaper. They flipped onto their stomach, grabbed the brass rail support, and hauled themself forward, staying low to the ground so as not to make a target of themself. Peering around the side of the train, Hane confirmed the Shaper's location before turning their hand palm-out and casting Burst like a cannonball. The Shaper took the hit in the chest, stumbling back along his conjured walkway, looking more surprised than hurt. When he spotted Hane lying flat on the gangway, he scowled and jerked his hand upward. Hane felt something beneath them lift them bodily from the platform.

I need to practice more with aimed Burst spells, Hane thought, springing to their feet in order to kick off the rising conjured platform. A somersault landed them on the rail, one hand gripping the vertical support for balance. *My hand-cast spells aren't powerful enough, but a Burst through my shroud is too diffuse for situations like this.*

The Shaper was already lobbing another spell at Hane, but they stepped back off the rail and out of sight of the Shaper. While it was possible to strike blindly with magically constructed objects, the Shaper risked hitting his own teammate that way. If the Shaper wanted to hang back and play it safe, the most prudent course of action was to deal with the Assassin first.

Lief was fending off the Assassin's knives using his bow as a staff weapon. The string had either snapped or been cut; Hane wasn't certain when that had happened, but by the way Lief guarded and twirled the staff, he was clearly no stranger to fighting this way. Perhaps the bow was even enchanted to be used defensively, which seemed wise considering how most bows were only effective when used at long range. But while it was enough to keep the Assassin from striking him, Lief wasn't able to gain any advantage, either.

"Did you knock him off the train?" Lief asked, tossing his hair out of his eyes in time to notice Hane slipping both tonfa free of their harness.

"No, he's on his way." Lying might have caused a blow to the Assassin's morale, but Hane didn't want Lief to be caught off guard when the Shaper showed up. "We should finish this first."

"Finish?" The Assassin cackled. "I haven't even started yet."

He hurled one blade at Lief's face, making the Biomancer yield one step in order to swing his bow around and knock the knife down to the tracks. In the same motion, the Assassin reached into a cloak pocket and revealed four glittering throwing needles clenched between his fingers. Hane stepped in front of Lief, using Burst to send the needles spinning away into the slipstream. Another sweeping motion from the Assassin and his free hand now held a rounded globe full of liquid, but as the Assassin drew his arm back to throw it, he grinned and let it fall through his fingers, on a perfect trajectory to shatter against the coupler.

"No!" Lief shouted, leaning out to swipe at it with the end of his bow, but that only put him off balance for a sudden jerk of the train to cause him to stagger and miss. Hane grabbed hold of the door handle in one hand and Lief's elbow with the other, keeping the team's only healer from pitching headfirst off the gangway. All Hane and Lief could do was watch in dismay as the globe of acid shattered around the coupler. The Assassin shouted triumphantly as the liquid sizzled and hissed, noxious green steam rising rapidly enough to cloud the reaction. As Hane got Lief steady on his feet again, the wind whipped the veil of steam away, revealing the coupler still intact, but with an ugly layer of gray-green foam encasing it like some sort of fungus.

"What the—" The Assassin appeared puzzled, frowning down at the coupler. Before he could recover, Hane rushed him, smashing his wrist with one tonfa while guarding with the other. Lief backed away, dropping to a knee in order to restring his bow. Hane continued defending, preventing the Assassin from grabbing another acid globe for a second attempt on the coupler: Rose's counter-concoction that coated the coupler would only work the first time. Subsequent attacks were likely to corrode the metal and cause the cars to separate.

Lief stood up, sweeping his bow wide enough that the end of it snapped against the luggage car door with two hollow thuds. He then spun it into firing position while grabbing an arrow from his quiver. Hane prepared to leap out of Lief's way when a flicker of the Assassin's eye betrayed his accomplice. Internalizing a sigh over the complaints they would hear later, Hane twisted one tonfa through the Assassin's arm, pinning it against the train before shifting their weight to one foot and swinging their other leg through a wide, sweeping kick to move Lief out of the way of the Shaper's attack. The intent was to push Lief up against the door of the luggage car, but rather than hearing the crash and rattle Hane expected, Lief cried out as he fell through the open door, landing hard inside the luggage car.

Well, that was unintentional, even if it was mildly amusing. It wasn't as if Hane could lose any more of Lief's trust at this point, and he would be sure to complain to the rest of the team, but as long as the mission was carried out, they would probably get over it.

There wasn't time to peek inside the car to check on Lief, not as spear-shaped magical projectiles shot across the gangway, but Hane wasn't too worried about him, anyway. A fall like that shouldn't leave much more than a bruise or two, and Lief was a healer, after all. Hane ducked under the Assassin's arm, thrusting him in the way of the oncoming projectiles.

"Gerrett, stop!" the Assassin shouted, trying to shield himself with the arm Hane wasn't currently twisting around behind his back.

Hane felt two impacts through the Assassin's body before the magic-made spears burst into sparkling splinters of light, a hoarse shout of apology coming from around the side of the car, where the Shaper had hidden after casting his spell. The Assassin's shroud had likely taken most of the impact of the spears, so he probably wasn't too damaged, but recovering from the hits made him unsteady enough that Hane was able push him forward and shove him through the still-open door of the luggage car.

"Crate that one up for me, Lief!" Hane shouted as they bounded past the door and up onto the safety rail. The Shaper, just peering around the side, pulled back sharply, throwing his hand out at Hane. He must have conjured and hurled something, but Hane had already noted the Shaper's position along the outside of the train and was spinning around the vertical support, dodging the projectiles before landing on the gangway and springing through the open doorway. Moving too quickly to register how the fight was going between Lief and the Assassin, Hane pushed through luggage crates and containers to get to the interior wall approximately where they had last seen the Shaper. A deep breath, then a strong Burst straight through their body at the wall, hard enough to dent the steel and rattle the rest of the car ominously. Hearing the supports for the upper luggage racks creak and groan, Hane leapt backward to the open aisle, watching for falling boxes or bags before checking in on Lief's fight.

Which, unfortunately, wasn't going as well as Hane had initially thought.

"Hey," Lief said weakly. The Assassin had Lief's own bow looped around his neck, pulling it tight enough to choke off his breathing. "I feel like we've been here before."

Hane sighed and tapped a foot impatiently. "You should have told me that you were this bad at combat before we teamed up for this."

"What—this is your fault!" Lief sputtered, one hand pushing back against the bow to alleviate some of the pressure. "You threw me through the door!"

"Shut up!" the Assassin shouted, one knee digging into Lief's back so he couldn't slip free beneath the bow. "You! Go unhook the cars or else your friend here gets to know what it feels like to have the blood boil in his veins!"

"I didn't know the door was open," Hane replied, ignoring the Assassin's threat. "And any experienced climber should know how to roll with a fall. There's no reason you shouldn't have been back up on your feet and ready to fight in seconds. I thought you were a professional!"

"Oh, I am," Lief assured them. "Everything would have been just fine if you hadn't pushed me through the trap across the doorway!"

"I didn't—" Hane stopped looking toward the door. Yep, there were the shattered remains of Odette's spell spheres. Which trap was that one again? Hane nearly groaned aloud when they realized that Lief was wrapped in a coil of heavy rope from the waist down to his ankles. He probably could have freed himself given a bit more time, but then Hane had gone and thrown the Assassin at him before he had the chance. "I apologize. It wasn't my intention, but this is my fault."

"While it doesn't improve our situation, I do appreciate the apology," Lief said, his voice strained as the Assassin yanked hard on the bow.

"Stop talking!" the Assassin barked. "Go separate the cars right now, or—"

"I'm going, I'm going." Hane lifted their hands in exasperated surrender, giving a wide berth to the irritable Assassin and the half-bound Biomancer.

"Thanks for giving me the excuse. I'm the one who wanted to take your boss up on their deal."

"Yeah? Woulda made things a lot easier if you'd said that from the beginning," the Assassin growled. "And what happened to Gerr-rr-rr—"

The Assassin started to stutter, his body spasming as his eyes rolled up in his head. Lief gagged as the staff of the bow jerked against his throat several times in rapid succession. He managed to get both hands on the bow and push it far enough away that Hane was able to pull it out wide so Lief could drop and roll away from the shuddering Assassin. Lief collapsed to his hands and knees, gasping for breath as the Assassin continued to shake and spit. Hane jumped back out of the way just as the Assassin dropped to his knees hard, then fell flat on his face, revealing Rose standing behind him with a bloodied wedge-shaped blade in hand.

"Sorry, Lief," Rose said, using a cloth to clean her knife. Little arcs of purplish lightning danced along the steel, hissing and sparking as Rose scraped the blood from it. Behind her, the hidden door to the empty, secret compartment Odette found days ago was still hanging open: Rose had gotten here hours earlier in order to coat the coupler with neutralizing powder, then hid herself inside to wait for a signal from Lief or Hane to launch a sneak attack. "I know that probably stung, but it was the only option that didn't permit a 'if I go down, I'm taking you with me' sort of situation."

"Oh please, don't worry about it," Lief said, smiling weakly as he pressed a hand to his own throat. He tugged lightly on the thin chain of a necklace before tugging his shirt collar up over it. "Hane's been throwing me around all day, I see no reason why you shouldn't get in a hit or two."

"I was trying to protect you from the Shaper. Both times." Hane knelt across the Assassin's back, holding his hands together while Rose looped a cord around them. "Are you okay? Any blood-boiling effects we need to know about?"

"Fortunately, he was stupid enough to touch me long enough that I was able to confuse his mana sources." Lief straightened up, clearing his throat a few times. "He may have thought he was secreting poisons through his skin, but it was actually only water. Lucky he didn't realize it, or I might actually have been in trouble. Does someone want to help untie me?"

"No, but if you hurry up and get that rope off, we could use it over here," Hane replied. The Assassin's muscles were still twitching, one leg jerking arrhythmically. "What spell did you hit him with, Rose?"

"It's just a lightning imbue I use to stun opponents." Rose tied off the cords around the Assassin's wrists before pulling another length of cord from inside her vest and sitting across the Assassin's legs. "My knives are all imbued with something: poison, fire, ice, shadow. It's part of the reason it takes me so long to get ready at the start of every climb, imbuing all these tiny things." Rose tossed her curls out of her eyes long enough to study the dent in the far wall. "What did you do to the Shaper?"

"Hopefully knocked him off the side of the train," Hane answered, glancing through the open door to the gangway and the Keepsake car beyond it. Normally, the doors rolled closed on their own, but Rose had wedged this one open after Lief signaled her. "But he could have created handholds for himself, or conjured a platform to catch him as he fell. I should go make sure—"

The Shaper must have been listening from outside, because just then he stepped into the doorway, breathing heavily and greatly disheveled: clothing torn, leaves and twigs caught in his short hair, and the glint of mad fury in his eyes. When he raised his hand palm out, Hane leapt in front of Rose and Lief, crossing their tonfa high in front of themselves and shaping their shroud to soften whatever blow was coming. They waited, braced and coiled, but the hit never landed.

"No, stop him!" Rose shouted. "Hane, quit being valiant and do something!"

"Resh it, I can't get a clear shot!" Lief writhed, trying to get his legs under him as he fumbled for his bow. "Hane, move!"

Hane jerked their head up from behind their crossed arms, searching for the problem. They found it almost immediately: rather than attack, the Shaper had created a magical construct of a door, thick and opaque, to block the open doorway. Hane surged forward, slamming their shoulder into the magical wall hoping the impact might break it, but no such luck. They took a step back, doubled their personal gravity, then cast Burst in a head-on attack, hoping to shatter it. The construct refused to so much as shiver.

"He's going to uncouple the cars!" Lief shouted, scrambling in the aisle. "Rose, can you blow the door?"

"Only if you want us all to lose our hearing," Rose said grimly, shaking her head. "Explosions are for outside use only."

"Hane—"

"I'm trying." Hane searched for the seams of the magical construct, little spaces like cracks they could push transference mana through to vibrate the construct apart. Low level Shapers or ones with little practice often left such gaps in solid constructions, but unfortunately, the spell was flawless, leaving no convenient veins for Hane to channel mana through. Failing that, they cast Burst again, then once more, spending high concentrations of mana in the hopes of creating a few cracks that would eventually shatter. They felt time running out like blood gushing from a wound: how long would it take the Shaper to sever the cars? Were the cars already separated? How long did they have before the Keepsake cars began to slow down, opening too much distance between themselves and the train?

"Get out of the way!" Lief shouted. Hane glanced back over their shoulder before leaping clear: Lief was partially free of the trap-rope, his bow raised and sighted for a shot. It must have been some struggle to rise to a firing position, what with Lief's hair disheveled and the collar of his shirt stretched wide, revealing the glint of a necklace chain. Rose held one of Lief's arrows, her hand cupped around the steel tip, muttering rapidly under her breath before thrusting it at Lief. Hane dove out of the way as Lief fired.

The arrow impacted the center of the magical construct, but it made no sound at all. In the space between heartbeats, Hane saw a swirling nexus of violent mana peel away from the arrowhead in tight spirals, somehow both dark and colorless at the same time. The ripples of magic tore a perfect circle straight through the center of the magical barrier, too small to walk through, but wide enough for a lithe Wavewalker to negotiate.

Void magic, Hane realized, taking a step back before diving through the hole in the center of the wall. *Must have been one of Rose's imbues. I didn't know void mana could be replicated.*

Once outside, the first thing Hane took note of was the coupler, which had, indeed, been broken. However, the thick, dangling chains that served as back-up to the coupler were still holding strong and serving to keep the Keepsake cars connected to the rest of the train. It would cause trouble if the engineers had to brake for some reason, or if a downward slope caused the Keepsake cars to run up on the luggage car, but at least for now, the cars were still connected. The second thing Hane noticed was that the Shaper was nowhere in sight. They pressed themself flat against the wall next to the door, protecting their back as they searched out the Shaper.

The gangway felt bigger than usual, owing to the flat ground on either side of the tracks. The train still followed the curve of a mountainside, but due to the frequent rockslides of this area, the ground around the tracks had been cleared and flattered, allowing for the occasional tumbling boulder to roll to a stop before impeding the tracks. The drop to the valley below looked less steep with the shoulder of earth between it and the tracks, though Hane had no doubt it was still a lethal distance to fall. If someone was planning on jumping off the train safely, this would be the place to do it.

Why couldn't we have been hired as Magpie's crew? Hane wondered, leaning quickly around the corner of the car to search for the Shaper. *We could have finished this already and no one would have objected to setting the snakes free.*

There was no help for it now: the team had spoken and as much as they might want to, Hane wasn't going to simply allow the cars to break free of the train. It wasn't worth it when they considered Chime, fractured and powerless, waiting for the day when they would be whole again. Keeping their reputation clean was necessary in case future climbs were needed in order to find Chime's missing piece.

There! Sound from the roof of the Keepsake car. Hane shrank back minutely before acknowledging that there was nowhere to go. The only comfort they could take about being caught out in the open was that the Shaper was in the exact same predicament atop the Keepsake car. Actually, the Shaper seemed to be in slightly worse condition as he jumped into view, balancing precariously on an injured leg. His focus kept his back to Hane the entire time, making him a vulnerable target for projectiles: too bad Lief wasn't out here with his bow.

By the new injury on his leg, Hane could only assume this opponent didn't have the same ability to avoid Odette's roof traps as the Assassin had: the way blood ran in a single, thick line down the Shaper's calf made it look as if he'd been gored by one of the snake-catches carried by the Keepsake guards. The spell he'd cast so abruptly was likely to seal the hole in the train's roof the same way he'd sealed Hane, Lief, and Rose inside the luggage car.

Once the immediate concern was dealt with, the Shaper turned around, frowning when he noticed how close the Keepsake car still followed the rest of the train. The frown deepened into a scowl when he noted the heavy chains still keeping the cars connected, then the scowl deepened even further when he noticed Hane on the luggage car's gangway. The Shaper pointed, snarling a word Hane couldn't hear over the wind. Rather than wait and find out what it was, Hane darted to the far side of the gangway before jumping onto the brass railing, then leaping the open space between the two cars, grabbing the rungs of the ladder beside the door of the Keepsake car.

The door was still sealed, the gangway entirely ruined by both the Assassin's acid and Rose's explosion, but the ladder was still sturdy enough to bear Hane's weight with the added benefit of making it difficult for the Shaper to see them. This would be over in seconds if Hane could only ascend to the roof, but with that out of the question, they had to get creative. As the Shaper leaned out to try and cast a spell at Hane, they freed a tonfa from their harness and fired a concentrated Burst spell through it. The Shaper quickly ducked out of sight, narrowly avoiding the spell.

It won't be long until he figures out he can cut the chains without dealing with me first, Hane realized, glancing back at the luggage car. The Shaper's door still covered the open doorway, sans the hole in the middle carved away by Rose and Lief's void-charged arrow. They hoped the others were all right, and not currently fighting with the Assassin or anyone else from the Magpie's crew, but they couldn't spare too much concern at the moment. The chains looked strong, but they wouldn't hold forever, especially not if the Shaper managed to drop a guillotine blade over them.

Rather than wait for the Shaper to attack again, Hane reoriented their personal gravity as they spun around the corner of the train, landing in a crouch that made the side of the car their new "down." From here, their shadow was hidden within the shadow of the train, but Hane could watch for the Shaper's shadow long before they came into view. Hane's vague plan was to wait for the right moment and blast the Shaper clean off the roof with a Burst spell, with absolutely no contingency in place for protecting the connecting chains. Before the Shaper could come into range of a Burst spell, a tapping sound from under their feet nearly sent them springing clear off the side of the train.

Hane frowned, their attention drawn downward through a window into the Keepsake car. One of the guards stared quizzically through the window at them, using the polearm Rose identified as a snake-catch to make the rapping sound Hane heard. A new plan coalesced so suddenly that Hane was already acting on it before they could think it all the way through, motioning for the guard to hurry up and open the window.

The roof might be out of bounds, but the ceiling wasn't.

Hane watched the Shaper's shadow approaching the edge of the car as the guard opened the window from inside the car. The train's slipstream would have made Hane's words inaudible, so they didn't speak, only reached in through the window and silently requested the snake-catch by pointing and gesturing with a curl of their fingers. The guard hesitated a moment, glancing back at their superior for confirmation, before pressing the staff into Hane's open palm. The Shaper's shadow was nearly at the edge now; in a moment he would look over and find the chains unguarded. It took a shift of their position to get the angle right, as well as a twist of spatial reasoning to figure out the Shaper's position from Hane's irregular position, but once they figured it was close enough, Hane slammed the end of the snake-catch up into the ceiling from inside the train car, earning a resounding metallic thud that caused the Shaper's shadow to leap and spin around. Hane quickly reversed the snake-catch out the window and slid over to be within reach of the roof. The view was dizzying as they briefly looked "down" across the short expanse of steel to the endless hazy blue-green emptiness beyond it. The Shaper was already spinning around again, realizing the ruse a moment too late. Hane swept out with the snake-catch, using the spiral twist on the end to hook the Shaper's ankle. Catching him mid-movement, Hane whipped the snake-catch sideways, using a touch of transference mana as a little added thrust. The Shaper pitched forward, landing hard on his shoulder before tumbling out of sight.

Hane raced to the edge of the car in time to see the Shaper create a platform where the gangway would have been, catching himself before he fell onto the chains he had been attempting to break. Rather than give him the chance to recuperate and try again, Hane swung the snake-catch through a wide arc, aiming for a knockout strike. The Shaper managed to create a shield between himself and the staff as he recovered from his fall. Even though the shield shattered on impact, Hane still hit it hard enough that the snake-catch rebounded off of it, sending pain and vibrations running up Hane's arm. They dropped the snake-catch in order to shake their arm out and reach for their far more reliable tonfa.

The Shaper scrambled to his feet and jumped from his magically constructed platform to the brass one on the luggage car. A sharp wave over his shoulder sent magically conjured spears shooting toward Hane, distracting them long enough that the Shaper waved aside the barrier he'd constructed to block entry to the luggage car and darted inside. Hane kicked off the Keepsake car, reorienting gravity to land feet-first on the gangway and tackle the Shaper before he could attack Rose or Lief. The transition from the brilliant daylight to the shadowy darkness of the luggage car left Hane temporarily blind as they slammed into the Shaper from behind. They could only hope their opponent was equally blinded and that Lief and Rose weren't in the line of fire.

The Shaper snarled, twisting halfway around in order to slam his elbow into Hane's temple. Hane hung on for two hits before letting go and backing away a step, feigning pain and disorientation as they slipped a tonfa free behind their back. Unfortunately, the Shaper wasn't lured in by the act and instead fought his way forward, wading through crates and luggage trunks as if trying to escape. Hane took the moment to recover their sight and look around for their companions.

An arrow shattered against the far door, drawing the Shaper up short in his staggering race to the head of the car. Hane located Lief perched dead center of the car seated in one of the middle racks of luggage, already setting a fresh arrow to the string of his bow. He smirked as the Shaper spun around to face him, a magically conjured shield held aloft in front of his hand.

"Relax," Lief advised in a falsely cheery tone. "If I wanted you dead, I wouldn't have missed. Wait right there for just a moment."

"Where's Ellis?" the Shaper asked, pivoting so that the shield protected him from both Lief and Hane. "What'd you do to him?"

"All in good time," Lief replied lightly. Though his eyes and his arrow never left their target, Lief's next question was clearly directed at Hane. "What happened? Are the Keepsake cars still with us?"

"For now," Hane reported. "The coupler broke, but the chains are holding."

Lief seemed slightly disappointed but shrugged it off easily enough. "I'm sure we can find a way to fix that. Can you take him?"

"I can," Hane confirmed, freeing the second tonfa. While they wouldn't look over to confirm, they heard a small rustle near the hidden smuggling compartment. Maybe it was Rose awaiting her opportunity to attack, or maybe it was the Assassin struggling against his bonds, but either way, Hane wasn't about to give up the secret of the hidden compartment to the Shaper. "Don't shoot me."

"No promises." The lilt of Lief's words made it sound as if he was teasing even if he wasn't. "We're running out of time here, so if you take too long, I'll shoot first and heal later."

Had it really taken that long? It seemed scarcely minutes ago that they passed through this way carrying an empty snake crate, but then again, they knew they hadn't had a lot of time to work with from the beginning. Best to end it quickly, then. Holding their tonfa behind them, Hane leaned forward and raced to the front of the car, the stacks of luggage turning into little more than blurs along the aisle. Just as they got in range of the Shaper, they dropped into a slide, ducking beneath the shield and swinging for the side of the Shaper's knee. The strike was dead-on, but before it could connect, the Shaper's shroud thickened until it felt like Hane's tonfa was moving through mud, taking momentum out of the swing. By the time it connected, the Shaper only winced before lashing out with a kick. The Shaper's heel caught Hane in the shoulder, sending them crashing back into the crates beneath the lowest luggage rack.

"Where is that reshing Assassin?" the Shaper demanded to know, backing up toward the door as another arrow shattered against his shield. "Why did we even bother springing him if he was just going to be this useless? I shouldn't have to do everything by myself."

"I'll take you to him right now if you surrender," Lief offered, though his light tone was undercut by the slow draw of his bowstring. "It's not like you can just run back to your master claiming the job is done when the Keepsake cars are still connected to the train."

"I don't believe I said I was finished just yet." The Shaper backed up a step, still holding his shield up against Lief's arrows. Hane attempted to crawl out from beneath the luggage rack, but a swipe from the Shaper's free hand sent a luggage crate spinning into them. Another backward step put the Shaper within reach of the car door. "It's all the same if I sever this car from the train. Even better if there's anything valuable hidden within all this drek." The Shaper groped for the latch on the door, refusing to take his eyes off Lief for even a second. He grinned when he found it. "There's just the small matter of finishing off the two of you, then—"

The Shaper's eyes went wide before he cut himself off, his sudden panicked expression nearly humorous save for the horror of the moment. Hane had watched him approaching Odette's trap across the doorway with mounting anticipation, mind scrambling to recall which type of trap this one was. It wasn't until the floor fell away and exposed the rapid blur of the rail ties that Hane remembered it was a trapdoor. The Shaper's scream split the air, making it seem almost as if he hovered in midair a moment longer before he began to drop. Hane turned away before they could see anymore than that, humming loudly to themself to block out the noises coming from beneath the car.

"Well, I, for one, feel very lucky that that wasn't the trap you pushed me into," Lief said, swinging himself down from the luggage rack. "Rose? Are you all good?"

A crate pushed away from the wall, seemingly under its own volition, until Rose stepped out from behind it. "Probably better than you two. Did I hear what I think I heard?"

"We can't leave this open like that," Hane observed, creeping around the edge of the square opening in the floor carefully. "It's right in front of the door. A crew member could fall through if they came back here to check on something."

"Maybe Mason can fix it later." Lief stepped up to Hane's shoulder, hand upraised in an offer. "Are you hurt?"

Hane assessed their injuries, finding little more than scrapes and bruises. "Not bad. Are you both okay?"

"Yeah, we got the Assassin tucked away nice and safe." Rose hooked her thumb over her shoulder, indicating the hidden smuggling compartment. "I gotta say, I'm impressed how you got through that opening in the Shaper's wall so quickly. It was actually bigger than I expected it to be, considering how small my void crystal was, but you jumped right through it like an acrobat."

"That's the sort of challenge I'm used to," Hane said, shrugging off the compliment. They eyed the large hole in the floor doubtfully, the ties of the track a shadowy blur. "I'll go find Mason and see if he can come back here to fix this. Maybe he can do something about the chain keeping the cars together, too."

"You don't have time for that," Rose said, checking a pocket watch. "The others haven't checked in yet, which means—"

"The rockslide," Hane recalled suddenly, a sinking feeling in their gut. "How much time do we have?"

"Not enough." Rose closed the top over her watch with a sharp snap. "You can get there in time, can't you?"

"I can." Getting there wasn't the problem. Stopping the rockslide without Nieve and Mason to help . . . that was another question entirely.

"Tell me what you need," Lief offered, hand still outstretched in an offer of aid. "I can help you push your limits, or reroute your mana pathways to make it more efficient for the spell you need. Biomancers aren't just healers, you know."

"I know." Hane hesitated, considering their options. "I need access to more transference mana. As much as I can handle. And—" Hane made a face, hating the next request they had to make.

"And?" Lief asked, delicate eyebrows finely arched.

"Something for motion sickness," Hane admitted ruefully. "Changing my gravity on moving vehicles has a disorienting effect on me."

"That's no trouble." Lief's voice was carefully polite as he placed his hand on Hane's shoulder. They had expected a joke or a tease, but Lief sounded distantly professional, as if concentrating on his spell work. "Both effects will be temporary. I'm lowering the threshold of your safe mana limits on transference and increasing the rate at which you recover mana. You'll feel a rebound effect as soon as you release it all, so make sure you're somewhere safe before you run out of mana."

"Thanks for the warning," Hane said dryly. Hopefully they could at least hold the rockslide off long enough for Nieve and Mason to come help. The two of them were positioned closer to the center of the train anyway, so they didn't have as far to go as Hane did. "The roof is still off-limits, right?"

"I'm afraid so," Lief replied, dropping his arm as he stepped back. Hane prepared to leap the open gap in front of the door when Lief spoke again. "Hey, I know you really wanted to let the thieves get away with the cargo. It says a lot about your character that you didn't just let it go when you were fighting on your own back there."

"Thanks." A prickly, uncomfortable feeling made Hane feel itchy between their shoulder blades; this was one of those social conventions where they were supposed to say something nice back, right? "I really did miss the signal to open the door back there. I never meant to throw you through a trap."

"Eh, at least I was luckier than the Shaper." Lief's grin looked a little dark. "Are you sorry you tossed me into the Assassin before that?"

"No," Hane replied shortly. "That one was intentional."

Lief barked a laugh as Hane leapt over the hole in the floor to get to the door. Outside, they braced themself with a deep breath, preparing for the shift in gravity that would allow them to run along the side of the train. If time truly was running short, they didn't have the time to barrel through cars full of passengers.

As for getting somewhere safe after they expended all their mana to stop the rockslide . . . well, that was a problem for later.

NIEVE

Champion (mind mark), Citrine
??? (heart mark), Sealed

Shh, shh!" Odette hissed, as if the outer door rolling shut wasn't loud enough to alert any of the passengers in their private cabins. She held her arms out, blocking Nieve and Mason from advancing any further into the car, holding so still Nieve couldn't even tell if Odette was breathing or not. After a moment, she exhaled, letting her arms drop to her sides. "Okay, Nieve, go guard the far door, Mason stay on this one. Don't let anyone through until I finish checking the rooms."

"I can't believe Hane got the combat assignment and I'm here on guard duty," Nieve grumbled, making no effort to dampen her footsteps as she crossed the car, passing by the closed and locked doors of private cabins. She folded her arms petulantly as she thumped her back against the door, blocking the view through the door's porthole. "They could be fighting the Magpie right now and I'm missing it."

"The others promised to call if that was the case," Odette said, standing with her palms out toward the first door along the aisle. "And you asked for the assignment with the highest likelihood of facing the Magpie in combat, remember?"

Nieve made a face and slouched against the door, frustrated and bored and perplexed. She'd been so riled after her conversation with Hane that she'd been afraid of snapping at her temporary teammates, which wouldn't have earned her any sympathy. Slipping away for some time alone had probably been the right decision at the time, but after learning her assignment for the day, she'd regretted it.

The plan was for Odette to use detection spells on each of the private cabins in turn, in the hopes that the three of them could corner the Magpie and take him down without much of a fight. Failing to find the Magpie within any of these rooms, the plan was to head down to the crew cabins at the head of the train and repeat the experiment. Nieve had a few issues with the plan, not the least of which was the fact that the Magpie might not be in any of the closed rooms, but in fact could be targeting the Keepsake shipment at that very moment. It certainly didn't help that Odette's detection spell seemed to take a very long time and had to be recast at every single door. If they didn't find the Magpie soon, Nieve might just start shouting for him to come out and face her already.

At least Mason was looking better than he had the night before. A little wan, perhaps, but that could be from missing dinner and only drinking a weak tea for breakfast; he hadn't felt up to eating anything more substantial. But he was steady on his feet and appeared to be in his usual good humor, grinning at Nieve from across the car. He lifted his eyebrows as their eyes met, making a motion with his hands that put one fist in the center of his opposite hand: an invitation to play a well-known game.

At least that's something to do, Nieve thought, mimicking the gesture. Silently, Nieve and Mason tapped their closed fists twice against their palm, but before Nieve could make her move, the latch behind her clicked, giving her just enough warning before someone tried to pull it open. She spun around, pressing the heel of her hand against the door to stop it in its tracks before she recognized the person on the other side of the door. Easing off on the door, Nieve let it roll open just wide enough to lean against the frame, blocking Odette from sight.

"Oh, hello, honored guest." The conductor looked surprised to find Nieve in the doorway, but he covered it quickly with a polite smile. "I had thought to find you in your cabin."

"I was on my way to the—wait, were you looking for me?" Nieve asked, confused. Was he going to ask her about the wine sample? She didn't want to tell him that she'd given it away.

"Yes, in fact." There was something off about the conductor's smile. Or maybe it was his eyes. They looked distant, somehow. Out of focus. "I must request that you accompany me to the dining car. Another honored guest is waiting to make your acquaintance."

Nieve frowned as the pieces fell into place: the only guest who would make such a request was the Magpie. In that case, this poor conductor was most likely under a mind-control spell at the moment. At least she wasn't too worried about him attacking her. Nieve leaned back inside the car, shooting a look over her shoulder at her teammates.

Mason stood at Odette's side, one hand on her shoulder and rousing her from her spell. Her eyes looked wide behind her glasses, lower lip clamped between her teeth. After a moment, she gave a shaky nod, approving the change of plans.

"All right, let's go," Nieve agreed, letting the door open wide. "It's okay if my friends come, too, isn't it?"

"Of course!" the conductor agreed readily. "But do hurry. Our honored guest does not wish to be kept waiting."

"I bet," Nieve muttered, grinning to herself as she followed along behind the conductor. She held the sheath of her sword in her off hand, tracing the wrap around the hilt with her thumb. Finally! A chance to actually *do* something instead of standing around waiting for Odette to finish her spell. Nieve hoped it was about to be a fight—she really needed to vent some frustration before it overwhelmed her. Hitting things always made her feel better.

Odette caught up to her on the way through the next car, latching onto Nieve's arm and whispering quickly. "You have to let me check for traps once we get there. And then we should make a plan. You might have to, um . . ." She trailed off, biting her lip as she shot a guilty look over at the conductor.

"Don't worry about that," Nieve assured her. "I can handle him. But make your spell fast, okay? Because I am itching for a fight right now."

Odette nodded and dropped back, following close on Nieve's heels. She seemed nervous about going into a fight, which was odd, considering that this was a spire scenario. Nieve glanced back to check on Mason and was reassured to see him holding one of his stone rods, tapping it against his palm in a manner that seemed almost threatening. He shared an anticipatory grin with Nieve, clearly looking forward to whatever happened next. At least he seemed prepared for a fight, even if Odette wasn't.

"Right through here, honored guests," the conductor announced as the four of them reached the exit to the private lounge. He held the door open, allowing Nieve and Mason past, but Odette hesitated, looking back at the food counter in the lounge car. Nieve paused in the middle of stepping over the gap between gangways, looking back at Odette.

"Everything okay?" Nieve called.

"Um . . ." Odette hesitated, then shook her head. "I'm not sure. I think so. Maybe."

The conductor released the door as Odette stepped outside, looking anxious to keep moving. After helping Odette across, Nieve blocked the space between the rails, barring the conductor from following.

"Let's wait just a moment," Nieve advised as Odette crouched down outside the door to the dining car. "My friend here wants to make sure it's safe before we continue."

"Safe?" The conductor chuckled unconvincingly. "Of course it's safe! Why, there's no place safer to my mind. Let's not keep our guest wai—"

The conductor cut off as Mason clamped a hand around his shoulder, holding him in place.

"Let's just hang out right here," Mason suggested, his grin more threatening than friendly. "This won't take long."

The conductor shuffled and fidgeted, anxious but ultimately helpless as Odette whispered spells under her breath, her eyes half closed as she examined whatever her Analyst spell revealed to her. Around the two-minute mark, he began to fret, insisting that the guest had wished for them to return "with all haste" and that he feared they were taking so long that the guest might have left already. Nieve didn't think the Magpie would give up so easily, but as the fifth minute ticked past, Nieve found herself just as anxious to kick down the door and get this battle started.

"Okay," Odette said, rubbing her hands on her pants as she stood up. Then again: "Okay."

Nieve only gave it half a beat before asking: "Okay, what? Is the Magpie in there? Can we go yet?"

"Ye—n—wait." Odette held up a hand, adjusting her glasses with the other. "I can't say if it's the Magpie or not, but my spell revealed two attuned individuals inside the dining car."

"That sounds like them. Let's go!" Nieve started forward, only to find Odette obstinately blocking the way.

"There are new traps since yesterday," Odette declared, arms wide-flung, as if Nieve couldn't move her if she wanted. "And I need to ask him a question." She pointed across the way at the conductor.

"Me?" His eyes opened wide in surprise. "Why me? What could I possibly tell you except to hurry along?"

"The wine bottle that was on display in the lounge car has been moved," Odette stated. "It's in the dining car now. Why?"

"Oh, well, that's quite simple." The conductor looked almost relieved. "That's a very rare bottle of wine, you know. We display it first in the private lounge car for our more discerning guests, but we move it to the dining car for the middle of our journey so that all passengers who wish to may view it. It was gifted to our train by—"

"That Twisted Root place, yeah," Nieve finished. "What does the wine bottle have to do with anything?"

"It's one of the traps inside," Odette explained. "It's behind the counter, but it's protected. If you try to move it, the car will lock down and we'll be stuck inside until the start of dinner service."

That sounded highly unpleasant. Especially if the dining car was any-where near as busy as it had been the past few days. Nieve made a note not to go anywhere near the wine bottle.

"Is that it?" Mason asked, still holding the conductor back from crossing the gangway. "Or is there anything else we need to look out for?"

"A few things, actually." Odette ticked off traps on her fingers as she recited them. "The last window on the left-hand side of the car can be popped out of its frame, and rungs outside the car will take anyone escaping up onto the roof. I believe that's the Magpie's chosen escape route, but we can't use it because—"

"Because of the roof," Nieve interrupted, rolling her eyes in frustration. "Of course."

"Right," Odette agreed. "You remember the cabinet full of sample wines, right?"

"I thought that was in the lounge car?" Nieve asked, frowning at the car behind her.

"The dining car has one, too," Odette confirmed shortly. "You need to know that if you try to force it open, you'll get zapped by a lighting spell. It's not deadly, but it won't tickle, either. There's a stasis spell on the tip jar, a trip-wire that will release the dinner cart and send it rolling down the side of the car, and a three-legged chair."

Nieve waited a full breath before realizing that was the end of the state-ment. "A what?"

"A three-legged chair." Odette's glasses flashed with reflected sunlight. "If you sit in it, it'll fall over."

Nieve looked over at Mason, wondering if she was missing something. "And that's . . . it?"

Odette looked confused. "What else would a three-legged chair do?"

"I don't know. Eat you?" Nieve tossed her hands up in an exaggerated shrug. "How is a three-legged chair a trap?"

"Because it—it falls over," Odette said weakly. "Maybe it's not important, but my spell revealed it, which means I have to tell you about it. If I didn't tell you, you could report it in my climber recommendations and ruin my reputa-tion as an Analyst."

"I'm not going to—" Nieve shook her head. "I'm just confused how that's a trap, that's all."

"It's the same thing as setting a bucket of water over a door jamb and shouting to your sister that you have something fun to show her," Mason explained through a conspiratorial smile. "It is a trap, but it's more for a laugh than about hurting anyone. Is that everything, Odette?"

"Everything I saw," Odette agreed before gnawing anxiously on her lower lip. She drew a breath, shoulders hunching defensively around her ears as she shot a glance at the conductor before hurriedly looking away once more.

Nieve got the message. She pulled her arm back, holding it just behind her back. "Mason, you're going to want to stand back."

"Oh no, you don't have to—" Odette interrupted herself with a scream as Nieve twisted at the hips, throwing what looked like a powerful punch at the conductor's head. He only had a moment to appear surprised before ice cold water splashed against his face, making him sputter and cough. Odette sagged to the brass grating, her knees weak beneath her. "Bless me, Tsab, I thought . . . I thought you were going to hit him."

"What? No!" Nieve laughed. "There's a few sure ways to break a compulsion. A knock on the head is best, but the shock of cold water usually does the trick just fine. I didn't think you wanted me to hit him."

Odette cupped her hands to her chest in relief as the conductor looked around wildly, grasping the brass rails as his mouth worked soundlessly.

"What happened? How did I get here?" Water dripped from his chin, soaking into his dark blue uniform. He shivered violently before wrapping his arms around himself. "Why am I wet?"

"Don't worry about it," Nieve assured him. "You probably don't want to be here for this. We're about to confront a passenger inside the dining car. You'll want to go the other way."

"A confrontation?" The poor conductor looked confused and angry and cold. "But why would you—ah!" His expression brightened at once. "Would this have anything to do with your interest in the Keepsake Treasuries cars?"

"It does," Mason confirmed with a nod. "But we don't want to put you in harm's way, so you'll want to head back into the lounge right here."

The conductor steadied himself before wringing out his cap and setting it back on his head. "I believe I will join you," he said firmly. "If there is a criminal on this train, I have the authority to detain them."

Nieve started to argue, but stopped when she felt Odette's hand on her arm. "Wait, we can use him. Nieve, you can resist compulsion, can't you?" Odette continued after Nieve confirmed that she could. "Okay, good, because I only have one of these." Odette selected one of the enchanted rings strung along her knotted ribbon. "This is enchanted for mental clarity and should offer some protection against mind-control spells, but just to be safe, Nieve should be the one who confronts the Magpie, and Mason should focus on protecting the bystanders. Once the fight starts, the conductor and I will focus on clearing the car of passengers before I assist you both however I can. Just watch out for my spell spheres, okay?"

"Okay," Nieve agreed, just about bouncing in anticipation. "You ready, Mason? I'll walk straight to the end, like I'm just passing through, then we'll come together around the Magpie before they can mind-control anyone. Sound good?"

"I like it," Mason agreed cheerfully, clearing the coupler in a single step. He paused just long enough to slip Odette's ring over his littlest finger, frowning when it stuck on his second knuckle. He flexed his fingers, then shrugged, as if figuring it was good enough.

Mind of Ice, Nieve thought, activating her own defenses against mind control. She reached for the latch, steeling herself with a breath as she reviewed the plan in her head. It was a good plan, one that minimized casualties as well as mind control victims. Mason was good as her backup, but she was the warrior here: she'd knock that Magpie out so fast, he wouldn't know what hit him.

So of course when Nieve strode inside the dining car, full of confidence and swagger, the plan hit an immediate hiccup: the train car was empty.

Well, almost empty.

Nieve stopped short just inside the doorway, Mason bouncing off her back with a muffled protest. She held her arm out as a barrier as she scanned the car once more, in case she'd missed something. Resh, but she hated last minute plan changes, especially when she was the one who had to change them!

"Mason," Nieve whispered, never taking her eyes off the Magpie. "Can you tell if anyone else is in here besides the ones we see?"

"Yeah, wait." By his tone, it seemed Mason was taking this as seriously as Nieve was. He muttered a spell under his breath in Caelish, staying just behind Nieve in the doorway. "I can use air mana to check for breath. If there's anyone hidden in shadows or invisible, I'll find them."

Nieve nodded, her eyes still locked on the lone figure seated at the food service counter. While they weren't entirely identifiable as the Magpie, especially facing away as they were, Nieve certainly recognized the man leaning against the far door as the Magpie's Guardian. The rest of the dining car was hauntingly empty: polished tabletops pristine and gleaming in the light through the windows, every chair neatly tucked in, not even a crew member behind the counter. Just the Guardian and presumably the Magpie: two people with attunements, just as Odette's spell had predicted.

The only other person in the car sat on a barstool, a teacup held in both hands, legs crossed at the ankles. His hair was longer than it had seemed yesterday, but then again, Sa'rhi could have tucked it under his newsboy cap yesterday. Today he wore an olive-green fedora, the brim of which further obscured the facial features Nieve sought to confirm that this was, in fact, the Magpie and not just a decoy. The white, ruffled blouse hid most of the upper body shape from Nieve's angle, though a brown leather waist cincher hinted at an unexpected gender. Cream colored leggings disappeared into calf-high riding boots, although heels that high would be impractical on actual horseback.

"Are you sure that's the Magpie?" Mason asked, echoing Nieve's own doubt. "Because I gotta say, if this car was full of people, I would not have picked that one out as the guy we met before."

"We know he's good at hiding in plain sight," Nieve said, second-guessing herself. "The Guardian is definitely the same one from the luggage car."

"Yeah, I recognize that one," Mason confirmed. He squinted over Nieve's shoulder, staying behind her like she was a human shield. "I'm just saying that if I'd been in any condition to visit the lounge last night, I would have bought him a drink and never thought it might be the same person who ordered his dog to bite me."

"Yeah." Nieve nodded in solidarity. "I'm pretty sure I would have done the same."

"I can hear you, you know." At least the voice was familiar, even if the person at the counter didn't look at all like the Magpie Nieve had seen before. Sa'rhi turned around on the barstool, hooking their elbows over the counter as they leaned back. "Are you coming over here to discuss terms? As you can see, I've ensured that our conversation will be kept quite confidential."

"Hey." Mason tugged Nieve back as she started forward, whispering quickly in her ear. When he let go, she turned around and shook his hand.

"You're on." A wide grin on her face, Nieve sauntered forward, one hand hooked around the hilt of her sword. "Hey, so, before we get started, how are we supposed to refer to you right now?"

"Ah, so respectful of you." Sa'rhi smirked as he crossed one leg over the other. "For now, I would like to be addressed as a woman. I try to make my preferences known by my state of dress, but I don't mind the occasional non-gendered pronoun in case you're ever uncertain."

"Thanks for clearing that up." Damn, but head-on, that ruffled shirt plunged *low*. Nieve had to look back at Mason in order to clear her head of distracting thoughts. "You did that spell, right? The air one? Is anyone else here besides the goon and the girl?"

"Huh? Oh, yeah. Hang on." Mason shook his head before making a rolling motion with his hand, as if he was feeling threads of air flow through his fingers. Nieve felt grateful that she wasn't the only one distracted by the Magpie's overnight transformation. "No, I can't sense anyone else's breath in here. It's just the four of us for now."

Nieve acknowledged him with a nod before turning around again to face the Magpie. Odette would probably put her plan into motion soon, although as to how that would play out in a car devoid of passengers, Nieve couldn't say.

"So?" Sa'rhi asked, swinging a dangling ankle. "Has your team decided to take me up on my very generous offer? I'm happy to submit to capture right here and now if you can confirm that my partners got away with the Keepsake shipment."

"Nah, we're not going to be confirming anything," Nieve replied, striding to the center of the room, one hand on the sheath of her sword. "The plan was to lie to you so you'd come peacefully and not put the passengers at risk, but since you've already gone to the trouble of clearing the room for us, I'd hate to waste it by not starting a fight."

Sa'rhi chuckled throatily. "I appreciate your honesty. I assure you, I would have known if you were lying."

"I figured as much." Nieve caught herself eyeing the plunge of Sa'rhi's ruffled blouse again and shook her head to clear it. "Do you mind settling a bet first? See, my friend thinks you're using illusion magic, but I can appreciate the boost of a good corset."

Sa'rhi actually laughed at that, white teeth flashing against painted red lips. "Sorry, darling, but I don't give up my secrets that easily." Her eyes seemed to sparkle with mischief, a coy smile curling her lips. "If you really want to know, you'll have to earn it."

"Oh, darn," Nieve replied, not bothering to hide her own grin. Movement from the side of the room caught Nieve's eye: the Guardian flexed his shoulders, the vertebrae of his neck popping as he stretched his neck to either side. "Is your friend over there going to interfere once we get started?"

"Yes, I'm afraid so." Sa'rhi sighed deeply before sliding off the stool, one hand lazily twirling her weighted walking stick like a baton. "I do wish we could have settled this another way. You know I'm just going to escape so I can free the vipers, don't you?"

"I know you're going to try." Nieve dropped her weight into her knees, casting Frost Form with a quick thought. "If you can beat me, I might even let you. But that's not going to happen."

"Pity." Sa'rhi stood like a dancer, weight centered over the balls of her feet, walking stick held slightly behind her. "Are you sure you wouldn't rather *stand aside*?"

Nieve felt the push of the command against the frozen barrier surrounding her mind, but it failed to penetrate. Probably just a test command, then, just in case Nieve had been foolish enough to begin without first shoring up her mental defenses. Nieve only smirked as she held her battle-ready stance, waiting for Sa'rhi or the Guardian to make the first move.

"Fine, then," Sa'rhi said, sighing heavily once again. "Squatch, clear a path for us."

Nieve caught movement out of the corner of her eye but refused to take her eyes off of Sa'rhi—she'd been hit by that weighted walking stick one time too many to let it out of her sight. Her sword cleared the sheath with a subtle hiss, turning almost of its own accord to parry the walking stick with the blunt side, rather than the sharpened edge. Sa'rhi's eyes glittered gleefully, as if she had been looking forward to this fight as much as Nieve had.

Something crashed against a distant wall, clattering to pieces as it shattered. The Guardian shouted a challenge as he grabbed a dining chair and hurled it across the length of the car, forcing both Nieve and Sa'rhi to leap out of its path. Nieve rolled up to her feet amidst the neatly arranged dining tables, accounting first for Sa'rhi and second for the Guardian before sparing a moment to check on Mason. The thrown chair splintered against a wide, round stone shield, shaped to fit Mason's forearm exactly. He kept his head and shoulders ducked behind the shield, presenting as small a target as possible as he drew another stone rod from the quiver on his back, reshaping it into a javelin even as he hefted it back for a mighty throw. The Guardian hurled another chair before Mason could loose his stone javelin, then charged the length of the car in the wake of the second projectile. Nieve ducked the ricocheted splinters while casting an ankle-high Ice Wall spell across the car's central walkway. The wall shattered as the Guardian tripped over it, falling hard enough to rattle the stacks of cups and dishes behind the counter, but at least it gave Mason time to take cover amongst the dining tables.

Nieve never heard the car door open, but a distressed cry from the doorway caught her ear. The conductor stood just inside the door, hands clasped to his face in horror as he stared down at the splintered remains of the two thrown chairs.

"Oh my!" He seemed paralyzed with horror, the wooden splinters keeping him transfixed. "We don't have any extra chairs to replace these, and the Everlake station doesn't keep furniture! What am I going to do?"

"Watch out!" Mason dove in front of the conductor, shield lifted high to block the next incoming projectile: the Guardian ripped up a chunk of ice from Nieve's low wall and hurled it as he scraped himself up off the floor. The conductor let out a high-pitched scream before ducking behind Mason and covering his head as shards of ice rained down around both of them.

Nieve cursed under her breath, shooting a wary glance over at Sa'rhi. It was bad enough protecting a civilian in the middle of a fight, but having a

Controller in the mix made it even worse. At any given moment, Sa'rhi might order the conductor to attack her or Mason, splitting their focus from the real fight while attempting not to hurt the innocent mind-control victim. By the smirk on Sa'rhi's face, she was thinking along the same lines.

"I had a thought!" Mason called, keeping his shield up as he urged the conductor back against the wall to cut down on angles of attack. "How about you take the big guy and I'll take the sweet little lady over there? That sounds fair, right?"

"Ha! I'll just take them both," Nieve replied, rolling her wrist to flash the blade of her sword. "Just keep an eye on our friend there and stay back."

Mason saluted her with a stone rod as he backed the conductor into a corner of the dining car. To the conductor's dismay, Mason ripped a table up from the anchors that kept it rooted to the floor and flipped it onto its side as a barricade, hunkering down behind it for protection. Nieve moved into the center of the car, her sword held low and wide as she watched both the Guardian and the Magpie at once.

"I really did intend for this to end with me turning myself in," Sa'rhi called, adjusting her hat so that it tipped at a quirky angle. "But since you're not willing to deal, I'll just have to escape with the cargo. Maybe next time I'll get the opportunity to tell my story. Although, I can't say that I'm upset to have the opportunity to free those vipers myself."

"Don't worry, you're not going anywhere," Nieve informed her with cool confidence. "You'll get the chance to tell everyone how you're just saving innocent little animals and drum up some sympathy for your—" Nieve realized she'd been distracted by Sa'rhi adjusting her corset and very nearly missed the chair thrown at her by the Guardian. She blocked with her arm, feeling more frustrated than pained thanks to her shroud and her Frost Form spell. "Will you stop throwing things? Break too many more chairs and we're all going to have to take our meals on the floor, Dalenos style."

"Yes, please stop!" the conductor begged, cowering behind Mason. "I must ask that you be considerate of our other guests!"

Nieve almost laughed, but an angry scowl twisted Sa'rhi's delicate features.

"You think I care if a few people have to sit on the floor to eat their dinner?" Sa'rhi demanded to know, swinging her walking stick around hard enough to shatter a bar stool. "Those same people who have no respect for the suffering of animals at the expense of their own comfort? No, they can eat standing up, sitting down, or not at all for all I care. My only concern is freeing the ivory-crowned vipers before they endure any more torture." She whirled around, pointing the marbled top of her walking stick at the Guardian. "What are you just standing around for? Get rid of them!"

By the way the Guardian obeyed instantly, Nieve guessed that Sa'rhi used a spell to control him. That was common for Controllers in Nieve's experience: their lackeys would allow themselves to be mind-controlled in order to fight uninhibited while the Controller stayed away from battle as much as possible. Nieve managed to pivot in time to catch the Guardian's punch against the flat of her blade. She had to brace the end with the knuckles of her opposite hand and rapidly reinforce the blade with ice in order to keep it from breaking. As powerful as Nieve was, a trained Guardian would almost always be stronger, which meant she had to fight smarter, not harder.

Not her favorite style of fighting by a long shot.

Nieve tested her strength against her opponent by rooting her feet to the floor with ice and shoving her weight into her braced sword. There was no sign the Guardian felt Nieve's added pressure at all, and as the ice began to chip and flake off the blade, it became apparent that the sword would break before the Guardian broke. The ice around Nieve's ankles shattered at a thought as she spun her sword, breaking it away from the Guardian's fist. She faded back among the tables and chairs, encouraging the Guardian to wade in after her while keeping one eye on Sa'rhi at the counter. As if entirely unconcerned with the outcome of the fight, Sa'rhi stood with the walking stick braced across the back of her neck, one hand on each end as she watched the fight begin between her goon and Nieve. She looked smugly unconcerned, as if the outcome of the fight was of little consequence to her. She was likely waiting to make her move, but what would that move be? Would she try to flee? Would she jump into the fight wielding her little walking stick? Or would she order the conductor to attack Mason when he least expected it? This was usually where Nieve would rely on Sage's foresight to warn her of unexpected avenues of attack, making her feel even less sure of herself than usual. She would still win—of course she would—she just felt as if she was fighting at a bit of a disadvantage.

Trusting Mason to keep an eye on Sa'rhi and the conductor for the time being, Nieve turned her entire focus over to the Guardian. He shoved his way through the tables and chairs that Nieve kept putting between them, freezing a table in place when the Guardian attempted to pick it up and throw it. For one heartbeat, Nieve thought the Guardian was going to be foolish enough to keep tugging at the table after she'd frozen it, giving her an opening to attack, but then he snarled and chopped his arm down the center of the table, breaking it in two. He hurled one half of the tabletop at Nieve before continuing his unrelenting chase. Nieve ducked the soaring half-tabletop and picked an opening at the intersection of four tables, widening her stance and keeping her balance low. She couldn't help but grin as the Guardian advanced on her, dragging a chair behind him like an oni with a club.

The Guardian stopped just outside of sword reach, swinging the chair up and over his head, intent on a downward smash. Nieve waited until the chair reached the highest point of the swing, legs only inches from the train car's ceiling, before exhaling slowly, channeling a spell from her mind mark to her heart, where it rolled down her arms to affect the space around her.

"Freeze," Nieve commanded, simply and softly, her mind giving the spell its shape. First—and most importantly—ice sprouted from the ceiling above the chair, crackling and fracturing as it spiraled outward, growing to encase the chair's legs and seat in a hastily formed stalactite. The Guardian didn't realize the chair was lost to him until he tried to throw it: the chair stuck fast to the ceiling, leaving the Guardian to stagger under the weight of his own momentum. Nieve lunged with a slashing strike across the Guardian's chest, but even though her hit landed true, the Guardian's shroud absorbed enough of it that even where Nieve's blade found skin, it failed to penetrate and draw blood. She had to shift her weight into her heels in order to avoid the Guardian's meaty paw grabbing for her shoulder. If the Guardian got ahold of her, the fight was as good as over. As long as she stayed mobile and out of reach, she had a good chance of winning.

Luckily, she'd coated the floor with a thin layer of ice when she'd stolen the Guardian's chair from him.

As Nieve glided backward with ease, the Guardian attempted to chase and fell to a knee instead. A sharp grunt of pain, then the Guardian drew a fist back, intending to punch straight down and shatter the sheet of ice underfoot. A subtle shift in momentum, then Nieve was charging forward, her sword drawn back for a vicious jab that might actually draw blood if it landed this time. The Guardian saw her coming and tried to scramble out of her way, the ice impeding his traction. He managed to shove himself backward in the nick of time, but as Nieve skated past him, she reached out and grabbed the back of the closest chair, an easy flick of her wrist sending the chair spinning across the icy floor to crash into the scrambling Guardian. There was a shout and a crunch, sending up splinters as well as shards of ice, hiding the Guardian from sight long enough for Nieve to check on her surroundings.

Sa'rhi had walked the length of the food service counter, saying something Nieve barely heard the tail end of to Mason. By the way Mason smirked and raised a javelin over his shoulder, Nieve guessed it had been a failed attempt at a mind-control spell. The sunny expression on Sa'rhi's face didn't waver even as Mason hurled his javelin—except when it left his hand, it didn't fly toward the Magpie.

It was flying directly at Nieve.

Instinct took over, compelling Nieve to sink down in a low spin, the javelin just catching at her ponytail as it sailed past her head. As the Guardian attempted to clamber out from beneath a table, Nieve kicked another chair his way as she rose from her spin. Piercing the ice with her sword for an abrupt stop, Nieve leveled a threatening glare at Mason.

"I—I didn't mean to—" Mason looked horrified by his own actions. He glanced back at the cowering conductor behind him, as if thinking the other man had somehow affected his throw. "I meant to throw it at her, I never meant to attack you!"

"Mistakes happen," Sa'rhi said, sultry voice thick with mirth. "Why don't you try again?"

Mason clenched his hand into a fist, yanking it away from his quiver. Whatever Sa'rhi had done to him, she hadn't taken over his mind. Not completely, anyway. Which was good, because the Guardian had given up on trying to climb to his feet and was instead hurling chairs and broken pieces of tables at Nieve from his spot on the floor, forcing her to duck and dodge and spin to avoid each projectile. She managed to send a few more chairs spinning his way, but each one was returned with twice as much force behind it. The friction was beginning to wear the ice thin, while splinters and shards of cracked wood coated the floor. Nieve double-checked that the chair nearest her had four solid legs before stepping onto the seat, and from the seat to the center of a dining table, setting her sights on Sa'rhi near the food counter.

Before Nieve could spring off the table and capture the Magpie in a flying tackle, Sa'rhi seemed to divine what Nieve was planning and vaulted the counter with one hand, ducking low behind it so Nieve couldn't tell where she was. She had an idea of where Sa'rhi was headed, though: the one window rigged for a quick escape onto the roof.

"Mason, block her exit!" Nieve shouted, pointing to the far corner window.

"Got it!" Mason slid the shield off his arm, shifted his stance, and flung his arm out wide as if he were hurling a discus. Unfortunately, instead of sailing diagonally across the car to the far window, the shield-turned-discus was flying directly at Nieve's midsection. With no time to dodge, Nieve managed to jab the tip of her sword into the wood of the table, bracing it so that when the shield smashed into it, it clanged loudly and bounced off, leaving little more than a painful vibration in the bones of Nieve's hand and wrist as well as a deep scratch along the table's surface. She glowered at her teammate as she shook her hand out.

A yelp sounded from the terrified conductor. "Please don't mar the tables! Think of the other guests!"

"I don't know what's wrong," Mason said, wide-eyed as he shook his head. "I wasn't aiming for you, I swear it just—"

"It's called Hand-Eye Confusion." The voice, unmistakably Odette's, came out of nowhere. Nieve frowned and looked around but failed to spot Odette anywhere. "It's a spell that targets both the mind and body, making it harder to control your actions. Everyone hold on to something!"

Nieve rocked herself backward, attempting to overturn the table she stood on to use it as a shield. Unfortunately, with the legs rooted to the floor, it refused to tip over. She jumped down and ducked beneath it just in time to hear a sound like breaking glass. White fog billowed out from the center of the car, spreading quickly to all four corners, too dense to see through and thick enough that it muffled sound. Nieve could hear the scrape of movement over shattered ice and the crunch of breaking wood, but nothing beyond that.

Detect Water, Nieve thought, casting the spell that usually allowed her to sense voids within a bank of fog. Unfortunately, whatever this cloud was made of, it wasn't water, effectively leaving Nieve as blind as everyone else. Maybe Mason had a little better clarity with his ability to sense wind and air, but all Nieve could truly sense was the ice she'd conjured along the floor, as well as a few pitchers of water behind the food service counter.

The sounds of scraping and heavy footsteps across the floor were coming closer, and though the fog muffled the sound, Nieve could hear the belabored breathing of moderate exertion as whoever it was stumbled and groped their way through the fog. Most likely it was the Guardian, attempting to find her while they were both equally disadvantaged. Through her Detect Water spell, Nieve could track the lurching progress by the ice melting along the floor, giving her an estimate of where the center of mass would be in order to land an attack blindly—but a sudden wave of doubt and insecurity held her back, keeping her cowering beneath the table.

Really? She was doubting herself now? Why now? It was a fight! A good one, too—this was where she should feel at her most confident! She wasn't outnumbered and none of her teammates had suffered any grievous injuries, so why did it feel as if she had worms crawling around in her guts?

Is it because I can't see? Nieve wondered, trying to find the source of her anxiety so she could quash it. *The person coming toward me could be Mason; I know he can take a hit, but he's still not at his best after yesterday. And Odette . . . I don't even know where Odette is in all of this.*

Panic flared like a match struck in the darkest of night.

How can I protect someone when I can't see them? Nieve wondered, her breath growing rapid and shallow. She scanned the thick, white clouds for signs of movement, or a shadow that could be an opponent or a teammate.

Fear felt like a ball of ice lodged within her throat, restricting her breath and preventing clarity of thought. *What if the Guardian is going after Mason instead of me? What if Sa'rhi finds Odette? What if I let another team die because I couldn't protect them?*

Fear rooted her feet to the floor, holding her frozen even as a shadow loomed ahead of her, coming closer through the fog. Friend? Foe? What if she attacked and killed one of her teammates? How would she ever make it to the top of a spire if she killed a comrade?

<It is not the companion who blares like a trumpet, nor is it the one who whispers like a breeze among the reeds.>

Nieve jolted as Chime's voice sounded within her mind, a tiny yelp escaping her mouth. The looming shadow paused, oriented, then continued on a more direct path toward her. Nieve ducked out from beneath the table, firming her stance and swinging her sword up into a guard position, certain now that the shadow must belong to the Guardian.

Thanks, Nieve sent back to the ancient entity hidden within her boot. She sidled to one side, clearing an avenue of attack for herself. *I didn't know you were paying attention.*

<You are welcome,> Chime replied simply. <I try not to interfere when you are busy, but I sensed your distress and thought I might be able to help.>

They had at that, but Nieve didn't have time to express her gratitude. She sunk low into her knees, trying to blend in among the unmoving tables and chairs within the fog, allowing the Guardian to wander closer and closer, his arms outstretched before him as if he were groping his way through the fog. She waited until he was nearly on top of her before bracing her foot against a broken tabletop and kicking it away, sending it skidding into the Guardian's knees. She'd hoped to bowl him over, but even though he staggered, he didn't drop. Instead, the table split in two, each half spinning off crazily while splinters rained back on Nieve as she charged through the wreckage to engage her opponent.

"Clear this fog!" a low voice commanded. Nieve felt a tug at the edges of her mind, a stronger compulsion spell than before but still not strong enough to penetrate her Mind of Ice. Not that there was much she could do to clear the fog, anyway: it wasn't made of water, which meant she had no spells capable of shaping it.

The Guardian, however, seemed compelled to obey the order despite Nieve standing directly before him, her sword poised to strike. Through the haze of the fog, Nieve saw him stoop and grope around before straightening up, something heavy in his hand. She grabbed for it just as he pulled it back, preparing to throw it through the closest window.

"No, you don't!" Nieve got one hand on the chair, rooting her feet to the floor with ice as enhancement mana surged within her muscles, foolishly engaging in a contest of strength with a Guardian. She managed to reverse her one-handed grip on her sword and jabbed the elongated hilt into the Guardian's stomach hard enough to make him grunt and wince. "We've caused enough damage to this room already, don't you think? We don't need to start breaking windows, too."

"Fine." The chair was released so quickly that it nearly dragged Nieve down as it fell. A hand clenched around the front of her leather vest, the ice rooting her feet shattering as he yanked her off the floor. "I'll just throw you out the window."

All the movement during their scuffle thinned the fog surrounding them, so as the Guardian turned toward the window, Nieve caught a glimpse of the blue sky over the hazy canyon far below. She gripped the Guardian's forearm, digging her fingers into muscle as hard as iron when something hit the window with a hard "plonk." The Guardian looked up as a shadow fell over them, his confused expression forcing Nieve to twist within his grip to look back over her shoulder through the window.

A slim black-clad figure perched outside on the window looking in at them—no, that wasn't quite right. The figure seemed to be looking *down* into the car, crouched on the other side of the glass like a spider. It would have been more troubling if Nieve weren't already familiar with Hane and their general disregard for the laws of gravity.

"What is that?" the Guardian asked, nonplussed. Not that Nieve could blame him: how often did people stroll along the outside of trains?

Hane cocked their head to the side as if puzzled, then pointedly tapped their wrist as if they were referencing the time. And then, just as suddenly as they appeared, Hane was bounding away again, heading toward the front of the train.

"Oh, right," Nieve recalled, firming her grip on the Guardian's arm. He looked startled, as if just realizing he was still holding her feet off the ground. Ice began to form along the Guardian's arm, sprouting from Nieve's hands and twining up the Guardian's shoulder. Nieve smirked as the Guardian tried and failed to shake the ice off. "I don't have time to toy with you right now. So let's hurry this up, okay?"

HANE

Wavewalker (leg mark), Citrine

Wind whipped at Hane's clothing, tugged at their ankles, and stabbed at their eyeballs as they raced headlong against it. Their skin had long gone numb, but every muscle burned with a deep, acidic ache that would have slowed them down if it had been allowed to work in concert with the motion sickness caused by Gravity Shift. Luckily, Lief's spell combined with Hane's own keen perception kept their equilibrium from drifting too far afield. Although, it helped to stare only straight ahead without acknowledging the odd sideways tilt to the world.

It was hard not to consider the upended gravity when most of the passenger cars had end-to-end windows, giving Hane glimpses of astonished faces as they ran past. As much as they tried to ignore it, it was difficult when it so often looked as if they were stepping on people's faces, or on hands pressed against the glass. They could only hope the passengers didn't think them a bandit; a brief glance through the window of the dining car had shown that both Nieve and Mason were too occupied with their own fight to assist in preventing the rockslide, which meant Hane didn't have the time to stop and explain themself to train security.

The steam clouds from the engine were thicker now, indicating that Hane was nearing the front of the train. At the junction between the passenger cars and the crew cars, Hane tucked themself into a tight ball as they leapt, squeezing their eyes shut as they reoriented gravity around them. The resounding "plonk" sound confirmed their landing on the portrait window on the opposite side of the first passenger car before they even opened their eyes. They remained low and crouched, making sure of their balance before looking around. The space around the tracks here was still wide and flat on either side, with the cliff face a short distance away. Looking ahead, Hane could see where the sheer cliff ended and where the tracks would curve to follow the slope of the mountain. According to Odette's notes, the steep slope of the mountain opened up just beyond the sheer cliff wall, and that was where the rockslide would begin.

Is this the best place to be? Hane wondered, sitting back against the window to consider their position. *No, the best place would be the roof, but since that's out of the question, this is the only other place that offers a wide vantage point as well as mobility. It has to be here. For now.*

As Hane's muscles trembled and burned, an icy line of sweat dripped down the center of their back. Their heart was racing at almost the same speed as the train itself, thundering in their ears and making the space within their chest feel small. Hane focused on taking deep, slow breaths as they watched the head of the train follow the final curve before entering the rockslide zone.

I don't have time for doubt, Hane told themself firmly, watching the flex of the train cars as they chased the engine around the curve. *There's no one else here, which means it's up to me. None of this means anything if I let the train be derailed here.*

As the car ahead rounded the curve in the track, clearing the sheer edge of the cliff face, Hane touched the communication device on their ear, confirming it was still in place. If this all went wrong, they needed to be able to call the rest of the team quickly before activating their return bell. The drop on the opposite side of the tracks wasn't as steep as it had been, but a derailment would still send the train rolling end over end for far longer than anyone on the team could endure. Better to ring out to safety than suffer injury or death, but it would still be a waste of time, effort, and supplies if they couldn't at least be certain whether or not Chime's missing piece was in the vault on the next floor.

The cliff face ended abruptly, opening up to a steep hillside peppered with small bushes, clumps of grass, and even the odd wildflower dotting the red-orange dirt slope rising to a distant ridgeline. Using perception mana to sharpen their vision, Hane scanned the ridge, searching for a trace of the rockslide to come. Pine trees grew thick along the peak of the slope, overlapping shadows keeping the secrets of the ridge hidden from sight. It hardly seemed possible that there would be so many boulders up there that they might derail a train as large as this one, but Hane had been through enough scenarios to know that not every challenge followed the same rules that applied to life outside the spire.

They noticed the erosion of the hillside first: a drainage trench worn away by years of rain and snowmelt, originating from a single point high on the ridge before spreading out in a triangular shape that reached all the way down to the train tracks, nearly encompassing the entire curve of the track. Following the trench up to its point of origin, Hane saw it: a rotted pine log braced between two healthy trees like a dam. When a breeze rustled the heavy branches overhanging the hillside, sunlight gleamed off the crowns of heavy granite boulders, all resting precariously against that single sideways log.

Is there a way to reinforce that barricade? Hane wondered, glancing furtively along the side of the train. Maybe a Shaper could keep it stable until the train was clear of the danger. Or maybe a Summoner or Soulblade with the right type of contracts could create a stasis field around the boulders so they wouldn't fall. Perhaps a strong Transmuter could reshape the terrain so that the boulders rolled backward into the trees, rather than down the slope into the train, but Mason had already admitted he didn't have that much power or range. He could raise earthen walls closer to the tracks, or he could turn boulders into sand, but only within a range of twenty-five feet of his position, and that was a little too close to the train for comfort.

An Emerald Wavewalker with a heart or lung attunement might be able to create a gravity well above the ridgeline, strong enough to draw the boulders away from the slope, but that was beyond Hane's personal proficiency. Working with a force as powerful as gravity was difficult enough in the first place, and a leg attunement made it easiest to either change their own gravity or change the gravity of something they touched, and both of those were taxing spells. Without Lief's spell against motion sickness, Hane would likely already be near the limit of their prolonged Gravity Shift.

"It's all down to transference mana, then," Hane murmured, settling back against the side of the car and shaking out their hands. It almost felt as if they were lying down, looking up at the ridgeline like it was a storm cloud about to let loose. "Burst, don't fail me now."

The train's engine reached the apex of the curve in the track when the rotted log began to splinter. The spill of stones started small, just a few leaking out to fill the erosion trench, some piling against one another, others rolling down the hill gathering speed and momentum, but at sizes smaller than Hane's fist, they weren't of much concern. Hane saw the log split long before they heard the echoing "crack" that resounded off the distant canyon walls. The spill of small stones became a river. Then a flood. Then finally one half of the rotted log tore loose, rolling and bouncing erratically until it was flattened by a boulder as big as a cart horse. Rocks, large and small, began to spill through the dip in the ridgeline, sending up a cloud of red-brown dust as they churned up the hillside.

Hane released a slow breath, wishing one final time that they could have stood on the roof of the train for this. Concentrating on their ultimate goal of reuniting Chime with their missing pieces, Hane readied themself to meet this challenge.

"Enhance Depth Perception," Hane murmured, casting a high-level perception spell that would enable them to pick out the boulders closest to impacting the train. "Enhance Visibility of Movement. Diminish Sound."

The last spell was to mitigate the thunderous roar of the rockslide as tree trunks cracked and the very earth itself rumbled. There wasn't much Hane needed to hear out here anyway, and they'd often found that limiting one sense could cut out distractions to improve their overall focus.

Lifting a hand palm-out, Hane tracked the first and heaviest boulder to come within the range of their Burst spell. This wasn't the best means of dealing with a challenge like this and Hane knew it, but without any other means at their disposal, this would have to work. Drawing transference mana up through the pathways from the mark on their leg to the center of their palm, Hane predicted the course of the boulder and fired off a targeted Burst spell. The boulder careened off to the side, spitting out fragments like shrapnel and spinning like a coin. It didn't shatter entirely—it was too far away for Hane to hit it quite that hard—but the spin took enough momentum out of it that when it began rolling forward again, it listed to the flat surface Hane had blasted it toward and came to a stop. It was still a hazard, stopping as close to the train as it had, especially if another boulder crashed into it, but Hane didn't have time to consider it further: there were plenty of other boulders to blast and send spinning away.

They couldn't stop every single boulder from hitting the train—there were far too many coming way too fast to direct a Burst spell at every single one of them. Hane picked the largest targets, the ones with the potential to hit the train hard enough to lift the wheels from the tracks, blasting them into smaller stones, or reversing their spin to slow their momentum. As broken bits of rocks and smaller stones petered into the tracks, the train began to rumble and shake, making for a bumpier ride than Hane would have preferred, especially seated on the side of the train as they were. Accounting for the additional vibrations made it harder to aim, and each missed blast was wasted mana. Once, a melon-sized stone bounced over the track and between the wheels, the sound of coarse grinding setting Hane's teeth on edge despite the spell dampening their hearing. Sharp-edged stones shot up from the gap between two cars, two of them slicing through Hane's sleeve, another cutting a searing line of pain across their cheek. There was nothing for it but to double-down on the pair of rolling boulders Hane was trying to stop from impacting the crew cars just behind the coal car.

At least it was getting easier to hit the boulders as Hane's car approached the midpoint of the curve in the track. The ruptured dam was almost straight up the incline, meaning most of the boulders were coming straight on, though plenty of others jostled and bounced off one another, sending them in odd directions. One boulder caught on something—a root, maybe, or perhaps just a shallow plateau—and other boulders piled up behind it, forming something of a natural wall. Another boulder hit a bump that sent it shooting up into the air like a cannonball. It passed out of sight while Hane was dealing with more direct threats, but they kept an ear out, hoping against hope that the stone didn't punch straight through the roof of the train. Minutes passed without hearing the tell-tale crunch, leading Hane to assume the rock had flown clear over the top of the train and continued down the canyon slope unhindered.

I'm going to have to move soon, Hane told themself as their car finally rounded the top of the curve. They tried not to think about how many cars followed behind this one, or how much longer the rockslide might go on for, and they certainly didn't want to think about how many more spells they had before they began reaching past their safe mana limits. Better to consider the good they had done so far in stopping enough boulders far enough away from the tracks that they could actually afford to miss a boulder or two without jeopardizing the safety of the train and its passengers. Better even to think about how deeply they were going to sleep once this challenge was over; it hardly mattered whether the Magpie had been apprehended or not by now, Hane was far too exhausted to be of any further use until they were fully rested and recovered. The others would have to take care of the rest of the challenge.

Assuming, of course, that Hane survived this trial.

Hane pushed themself up to standing, directing Burst spells at incoming boulders as they made their way to the edge of the passenger car. It was awkward moving and casting that way, mostly due to the angle caused by their sideways orientation. If the roof was off-limits, was it really too much to ask for an outside walkway to stand on? That would have made this so much easier. Though Hane doubted that anything about this was meant to be "easy" in the first place. Too exhausted to sprint and leap to the next car, Hane checked the hillside for any imminent impacts before stepping off the edge of the passenger car and rolling up to their feet along the side of the next one. Gravity Shift could have accomplished the same effect, but right now, the fewer spells cast, the better. At least by now it seemed as if there were fewer and fewer boulders rolling down the slope: perhaps this wasn't as bad as Odette had made it out to be. Or maybe Hane had finally caught a break for once. Without questioning their good fortune too much, Hane picked up a light trot, thinking that getting ahead of the curve put them in a better position than moving continuously while casting their Burst spell.

They jumped a third gap between cars before they realized something was wrong. It was more a gut feeling than anything they saw or felt, but as they came to their feet on the thick glass of a passenger car window, they stopped and looked around, searching for whatever had triggered their sense of wrongness. A glance inside the car showed nothing unusual, just wide-eyed passengers staring back at them, wondering what possessed someone to go for a walk on the side of the train, or maybe panicking in the face of the rockslide. Hane hadn't touched the roof at all since exiting the train, but perhaps their extended stint on the outside of the train had triggered a scale in the challenge. That seemed unfair, as Hane had followed all the known rules, but then again, the spires had never truly struck Hane as "fair" before, so they couldn't ignore it as a possibility. But Odette had said that touching the roof usually added monster attacks, particularly of the flying variety, and so far Hane didn't see any. Could something be happening in a different part of the train? Or were the tracks blocked off up ahead? Were the Keepsake cars still attached?

It took far longer than it should have for Hane to realize they hadn't needed to fire their Burst spell in minutes. With their hearing dampened as it was, it seemed almost . . . quiet. The train still forged onward, the steady "thump-thump-thump" of the ties more than audible, but where was the rumbling? Where was the crash and tumult of the rockslide, or the sounds of shattering wood as the boulders tore through the tree line? Even the dust was beginning to settle, thinning into a gray haze rather than the red-brown storm that was nearly impossible to see through.

Is it over? Hane wondered, still feeling that something was amiss. *It couldn't be over that soon, could it? Half of the train is still behind the curve. Is this meant to lull me into a false sense of security? Or is there something else I'm supposed to be doing right now?*

Hane's hand was halfway to the communication device on their ear when they saw it: the reason the rockslide had halted. Two boulders as tall and wide as barn doors had wedged themselves between two sturdy-looking pine trees at the top of the ridge, forming a natural dam, just as the old log had done before them. But behind them loomed a boulder bigger than any others prior—it had to be double the height of the train, and by the way the pine trees were bowing forward, it didn't like being restrained.

Oh, no, Hane realized, watching in horror as the trench filled with rocks and pebbles acted as rollers for the paired boulders above them. The pine trees creaked and swayed, giving the impression of an impending second wave, more boulders piling up behind the one that almost seemed to stare back at Hane in bold challenge. Hane did some quick calculations, considering the mana they had already spent versus the size, weight and momentum of the immense boulder, quickly coming to the conclusion they feared.

I can't stop that. Hane looked back along the length of the train, searching for any sign of their teammates. *But it looks like I may have to.*

Nieve

Champion (mind mark), Citrine
??? (heart mark), Sealed

"You want to let go now?" Nieve asked sweetly.

The Guardian still held her leather vest in a twisted, white-knuckled grip, but rather than dangling helplessly, Nieve more or less clung to his forearm, holding herself up. He had only made it two steps closer to the window before her ice spell bound his feet and legs, rooting him in place. The ice continued to grow and thicken, encasing his entire body up to his shoulders, leaving only his head and arms free—for now.

Despite the imprisoning ice, the Guardian still seemed determined to carry out the Magpie's order to clear the obfuscating white smoke from the room by tossing Nieve through the train window. That was the trouble with mind control: the Guardian couldn't act on his own until the compulsion spell ended. Perhaps the Magpie would have canceled the spell if she could see the predicament of her lackey, but the white smoke filling the dining car was still thick enough to cloak both Nieve and her ice-bound opponent.

The Guardian bared his teeth in a scowl, his fist twisting tighter in her leather vest. Nieve grinned as she dug her fingers deeper into the Guardian's wrist, the ice beginning to creep down his opposite arm and up his neck.

"Are you sure about that?" Nieve asked him. "Because I can do this as long as you can."

The Guardian tipped his chin up like a man gasping for a final breath before being submerged in water. The ice climbed up to cover his chin, his jaw, his mouth, and still he held on, refusing to let go. Though it wasn't her preference, Nieve would have been satisfied with letting him suffocate in his icy tomb, but as the ice grew down his other arm, he suddenly flexed and jerked his shoulder, breaking chunks of ice from his shoulder and back. The motion overbalanced him, though, and with his legs immobile beneath him, he wheeled both arms frantically to keep from falling over. The wild arm movements loosened his grip enough for Nieve to tear free and land on her feet. No longer concerned about keeping a hold of his opponent, the Guardian began to thrash within the pillar of ice, tearing it apart to free himself. Nieve skipped away, avoiding toppled chairs and broken tables. The ice was never meant to hold the Guardian for long, but at least it slowed him down for now.

The white fog had thinned a bit, allowing Nieve to see the shadows of nearby objects as well as movement in the center aisle of the train car. Two people appeared to be fighting, and by their respective heights, Nieve guessed them to be Mason and the Magpie. Mason was wielding a long bo staff, likely shaped of stone, as so many of his weapons seemed to be, though Nieve couldn't make out that particular detail definitively. The shield on his left arm was smaller than before, less a round shield and more a buckler, but it was more than enough to block the strikes of Sa'rhi's weighted walking stick. At some point, the thief had lost her hat, but other than that, she appeared to be holding her own against Mason. Odette was nowhere to be seen, but the white smoke was still thick in the corners of the car and there were plenty of hiding places where she could be if her invisibility spell was no longer active.

Nieve wished she'd known about that little trick prior to beginning this fight: she often used ice to elongate her sword for greater reach, but that was unsafe when she didn't know where Odette might be.

A guttural roar and the sound of ice shattering pulled Nieve's attention back to the Guardian. He was free of the imprisoning ice from the waist up, but his legs were still encased—for now. Even as Nieve brought her sword up defensively, he swung his fist through a downward arc, punching the ice along his left leg. Cracks spread outward like the strands of a spider's web, though it didn't break until the Guardian flexed his knee and ripped his leg free. He wavered momentarily on his right leg before he found a foothold that allowed him to repeat the process on the opposite leg.

Detect Aura, Nieve thought, activating the spell that allowed her to see magical auras around people and enchanted objects. Various auras appeared around the car, but Nieve only had eyes for the Guardian's shroud: a high-level Guardian would have freed himself much quicker than this one. As she watched him break himself free, the color of his shroud flickered through a range of orange colors, most of them pale and watery with short flares of fire-orange. Assuming that he was using his full strength to break out of the ice, that put him at the low end of Sunstone, meaning he was nowhere near Nieve's own Citrine level. It didn't mean he wasn't dangerous, but it did mean

Nieve had a chance to subdue him without having to kill him. It probably meant a few bruises, but that was what a healer was for, right?

Nieve blinked her spell away as the Guardian kicked hunks of ice out of his way and turned to face her, his scowl made somewhat humorous by the chattering of his teeth. Nieve grinned and beckoned with her free hand, inviting the Guardian to come at her.

Rather than accept her kind invitation, the Guardian grabbed the leg of a toppled table, swinging the whole table up and over his head. Fearing that he was still following the order to clear the smoke from the room, Nieve conjured a thick wall of ice along the windows, praying to the goddess that it would be enough to protect the train from further damage. But instead, the Guardian twisted at the waist, hurling the table at Mason's unprotected back.

Nieve managed to shout a warning, but there wasn't enough time for Mason to dodge the flying table. He took the hit on his shoulder, a single cry of pain or surprise before he vanished from sight, crunched between the table and the food service counter. Sa'rhi laughed and saluted her goon with the top of her walking stick before striding toward the forward door.

"No!" Nieve started to conjure a wall of ice to block the door, but long practice as a warrior and a duelist alerted her to a surprise attack from behind: the Guardian wasn't going to give her the time she needed to cast her spell. It was all she could do just to get her arm up in time and reinforce it with enhancement mana before the Guardian landed a punch that sent her flying the length of the car. She hit the far wall hard, steel creaking and groaning around her, but she managed to stagger forward and place herself between Sa'rhi and the door with only a slight ringing sound in her ears.

Sa'rhi sighed and placed her hands on her hips, one foot tapping impatiently. "Squatch, I thought I asked you to clear a path, and here you've gone and hindered it. What are you going to do about it?"

"Coming right now, Boss," the loyal goon replied, wading through broken furniture to get to the central aisle. Sa'rhi smirked as she stepped out of the Guardian's path, giving him a clear line of attack. As Nieve settled into a defensive stance, she shot a glance sideways to look for Mason. His Stone Form spell was similar to her Frost Form for defense, so she wasn't too concerned for his life, but a broken bone could still be enough to end a climb early depending on how capable the healer was.

"I wouldn't count on him getting up anytime soon," Sa'rhi suggested, following Nieve's gaze. "When Squatch knocks someone down, they tend to stay down."

"Oh yeah?" Nieve grinned, spinning her sword with a roll of her wrist. "Then why am I still standing?"

"I expect that to be remedied in short order," Sa'rhi replied, sounding almost bored as she flipped open a pocket watch. "But if you could hurry it up, darling? Gerrett and Ellis have probably already disconnected the Keepsake cars and these boots are not meant for walking."

"I wouldn't count on that." Odette's disembodied voice again, causing Sa'rhi to spin around in a circle as she searched for the source. "The rest of our team is there to prevent that, and your Assassin is a bit of a pushover."

"Well, then." Sa'rhi faded back another step, eyes scanning the wreckage of the room from side to side. "I suppose I had better go and help them. Apologies, Squatch, but I need you to keep the path clear for me. If you end up being taken in, trust that I will find a way to break you out later."

"Got it, Boss."

"Good luck getting through me." Nieve said it to Sa'rhi, but she didn't take her eyes off the Guardian. "I can hold this door until—"

It was the sudden movement that caught Nieve's eye: Sa'rhi spinning on her toes and darting to the corner window rigged with an escape. Before Nieve could even curse, let alone conjure an ice wall, the Guardian charged straight down the aisle at her, a cocked fist held level with his head. Nieve managed to spin her sword so that the dull edge pressed against her forearm before crossing her arms in front of her chest and bracing for impact. Bracers of ice formed along her arms to protect her bones, but not fast enough to absorb much impact from the strike that sent her flying again. Nieve gasped as she hit the wall, her breath leaving her in a dizzying rush. Her knees sagged, but she caught herself by jabbing the tip of her sword into the floor and grasping the hilt with both hands, steadying herself until she could breathe again. She had to recover quickly as the Guardian was already following to land the next blow, but a sharp scream stopped them both as they searched for its source.

"Fire!" That half-strangled cry came from the far corner of the train car, where a few slim wisps of white fog remained. Nieve could just make out the top of a conductor's cap cresting the edge of a sideways table before she caught sight of the orange and yellow flicker through the remaining wisps of fog, blocking Sa'rhi's path to the escape-window. The Magpie staggered back from the blaze, one hand uplifted to shield her eyes.

"Hurry, put it out!" the conductor cried frantically. "S-somebody, anybody, please! The fire!"

"Why don't you put it out, then?" Sa'rhi suggested, a wicked smile overtaking her features. "Come on out of there and do your job. Or are you just going to hide there and let this whole train burn?"

Nieve growled low in her throat, furious that the Magpie would involve the innocent conductor in this mess, but before she could rush in to help, the

Guardian threw a heavy punch at her face. Nieve conjured an ice wall before her, blunting the power of the strike. Another punch shattered the ice wall, keeping Nieve pinned with the wall at her back. She quickly conjured another wall, hoping Mason or Odette might do something to protect the conductor, but she could only watch, helpless, as the poor crew member shakily rose from his hiding place, looking around for something to douse the fire with.

"No, don't!" Nieve shouted as the conductor vaulted over the table-barricade, racing for the food service counter. He barely paused as he grabbed a ceramic jug of water on his way to the window. Tossing a smirk over at Nieve, Sa'rhi stepped smoothly out of the conductor's path, waving him on ahead of her so he could douse the flames.

He swung the pitcher back before heaving it forward, a wave of water headed toward the base of the flames at the window. The splash came far too soon, as if the water had met an invisible wall, with most of it splashing back in the conductor's face. He appeared momentarily stunned before Odette appeared out of thin air, arms still outstretched to protect the fire.

"There you are, little shrinking violet." The Magpie's grin was pure malevolence as she whirled the walking stick in a tight circle. "I knew one of you was creeping around, hoping I wouldn't notice."

Odette stepped in front of the conductor, her eyes round and white with fear, but she reached for the spell spheres on her bracer regardless. As Sa'rhi cocked her walking stick back for a heavy blow, Odette flinched and screamed, little glass marbles hitting the floor like the sound of falling rain.

It was the perfect moment for Nieve to sweep in and be the hero, but before she could, her ice wall shattered, the Guardian charging through it with his fist cocked back for a heavy hit. She dodged the first blow, but the crater left behind in the steel wall of the train by the Guardian's fist didn't bode well for future hits. She needed to end this quickly in order to save Odette and find out if Mason was all right, but fights with Guardians were rarely over quickly.

As Nieve tracked the next wind-up and planned her next dodge, the wall-mounted cabinet caught her eye. Her first thought was to curse it for being in the way, but the moment she recognized it for what it was, a Sage-worthy idea popped into her head. Nieve redirected the Guardian's next hit with the hilt of her sword, bobbing and weaving as if trying to duck under the next strike. When it came, she waited to duck it at the last minute. Unsure of what would happen, Nieve dropped to a knee and rolled to the side, holding her breath to see if her plan had worked.

It was difficult to see at first—she had been expecting some grand explosion or something equally dramatic, but this trap was more subtle than that.

The Guardian remained standing, his fist firmly embedded within the wall-mounted lockbox of wine samples, his arms shaking with adrenaline. It didn't look as if he'd activated a trap, it only looked as if he'd taken a moment to pause in confusion, as if wondering how he'd missed such a close target. But then the shaking intensified, the Guardian's eyes going wide, wider, until his mouth fell open in a silent scream. Sparks fizzled and popped around his fist and the tangy scent of lightning hit Nieve's nose hard enough to make her sneeze. She shook her head to clear it as she straightened up, carefully stepping around the trapped Guardian.

"Hey!" Nieve called out, summoning her usual battle-hungry grin. "Good call, Odette. Consider this one yours."

"How very sweet of you," Odette said, a tremble in her voice as she shuffled backward, keeping herself between Sa'rhi and the conductor. Nieve must have missed part of a conversation, because the conductor had his fingers in his ears and his eyes on the ground. "I would be ever so grateful if you could take this one off my hands."

It seemed that the spill of spell spheres had slowed the Magpie down for the moment. As Nieve sidled carefully around the shock-trapped Guardian, Sa'rhi was cautiously toeing one of the glass marbles as if wary of a trap. The motion of the train made the little balls roll, shiver, and hop, spreading out what once was a cluster into a veritable minefield. Every step carried the risk of a spell sphere rolling underfoot, activating some unknown trap. Even if Sa'rhi didn't know the marbles were dangerous, she certainly seemed to suspect they were. She scowled at a small cluster that had gathered in front of the nearest exit before looking back at the opposite door, where there were far fewer spell spheres to step on.

"Try it," Nieve suggested tauntingly. She grinned as she stepped onto a chair, then up onto a table. Luckily, with his eyes on the floor, the conductor didn't seem to notice. "I'll stop you before you get halfway there. Not so tough without your goons, are you?"

Sa'rhi made a face as she looked over at her Guardian, held fast by the paralyzing lightning trap inside the wine cabinet. Varicolored liquids dribbled down the wall, collecting in a puddle beneath the Guardian's feet. No help would be forthcoming from that angle. And by the twist of her lips, it seemed she'd realized that she wasn't close enough to climb up on any of the furniture like Nieve in order to avoid the spell spheres. She tapped the marble top of her walking stick against her thigh as if considering her options deeply.

"Give up yet?" Nieve asked, turning the blade of her sword so it flashed in the light. "It's okay if you need me to knock you out first. I know that's a mark of pride sometimes."

"I'm not out yet." Sa'rhi's tone was flat and even now, no hint of playfulness or banter. She drew her foot back and kicked the nearest spell sphere, sending it whirling toward the food service counter. Nieve flinched, drawing her free hand up to guard her face against whatever possible trick or trap might activate. Odette made a sound that was half whimper, half scream as she threw herself backward, crushing the conductor up against the wall. The liquor shelves behind the counter rattled ominously, the display bottle of twenty-year-old wine wobbling precariously. Nieve didn't breathe again until it stabilized, undamaged.

The spell sphere shattered as it struck the counter, releasing a fine cloud of sparkling dust. When the dust cleared, a harmless coiled rope was left behind in its place. Sa'rhi smirked at the result, a line of tension easing from the set of her shoulders.

"A good bluff," Sa'rhi declared, kicking more spell spheres aside, clearing a space around herself. The little balls clicked and rolled, but none connected hard enough to shatter as the kicked one had. She looked up at Nieve, a cocksure grin on her face. "I'm afraid you've underestimated me. I don't need my goons to beat you."

"You sure about that?" Nieve nodded at the line of tables ahead of her, allowing her to make it to the far door without ever setting foot on the ground. "Even if none of those explode under your feet, I'll still beat you to the door."

"Will you?" Sa'rhi smirked before turning slowly to face Odette and the conductor, a flick of her wrist rolling the walking stick in her hand. "Don't. You. Move."

A thrum of power seemed to make the car vibrate, the spell spheres rattling ominously. Nieve braced herself against a powerful command, but she never felt it touch the protections on her mind. Dumbfounded, she looked around for the target of the spell, but then everything seemed to happen at once: spell spheres scattered at a swipe of Sa'rhi's boot just as she swung her walking stick through an arc, releasing it at shoulder height so that it shot away from her with the speed of a cannonball. She was running for the far door, kicking spell spheres ahead of her to clear her path, but as much as Nieve wanted to chase her down and tackle her to the floor, she couldn't. That weighted walking stick was on a collision course with Odette's face.

Time seemed to draw out longer and longer, giving Nieve time to see details she wouldn't normally notice: Odette's body trembling as she fought the compulsion that held her locked in place, wide fearful eyes squeezing shut as she braced for impact. The conductor, crouched behind her, was similarly motionless, a high-pitched whine emerging from his throat as his gaze flickered between the walking stick and the fire on the window. Spell spheres shattered and popped, shifting the debris around the food service counter, but nothing seemed to slow the Magpie down. There was no time and Nieve was the only one free to act. It should have been a difficult choice.

It wasn't.

Nieve dove off the dining table, dropping her sword in favor of freeing up her hands. Enhancement mana made her legs stronger, her reactions faster, so even as the marble-capped walking stick flew, Nieve flew faster. She couldn't intercept it in time, but maybe she could stop it. No, not maybe. She *had* to stop it.

A memory of her last climb came back to her—not of its tragic end, but a moment of pure panic, when her magic worked almost purely on instinct to catch a pendulum trap as it swung down to crush her teammates. She hadn't consciously cast the spell so much as she'd willed her magic to work the way she'd needed it to. She had that same need now, that same will to protect and defend. She knew what she wanted her ice to do; she just wasn't sure how to shape the spell.

In the end, she closed her eyes and pictured the desired end result. Her arms outstretched in front of her, leaping after the flying walking stick, Nieve thought the word that had saved her last time: *Stop!!*

Conjured ice extended from her palm, not shooting from it, but *growing* from it, crackling and flaking as it reached farther than Nieve could, catching the end of the walking stick and freezing around it. Once the ice gripped it tight, Nieve yanked her arm back, drawing the walking stick back as well. The sounds of crunching wood and breaking glass filled the cabin, distracting Nieve so that she landed with a stumble, the conjured ice from her hand cracking and breaking as she used her arms to steady herself. The walking stick dropped heavily to the floor with a hollow thud, the staff still half coated in ice.

Odette and the conductor still appeared frozen in place, but the crisis had been averted: Odette's face and round glasses were still perfectly intact. As she recovered her balance, Nieve pivoted on the balls of her feet, one hand reaching for her war hammer in lieu of the sword she'd dropped. She had an ice wall spell half conjured inside her head when she saw it wasn't necessary: Mason had tackled the Magpie as she ran for the door. He had her pinned on the ground, one of his stone rods pressed against the base of her throat. As she opened her mouth, Mason leaned more of his weight into the rod, making her gasp for breath.

"Good catch," Nieve called, feeling almost giddy with relief.

"You, too," Mason called back to her. "You got anything that'll keep this one from giving out orders?"

"I can freeze her mouth shut," Nieve suggested. "Watch out for her hands; some Controllers can take over someone's mind through touch."

"Thanks, but I know all about Controllers," Mason retorted. "I can create manacles for her arms and legs, but it's her mouth I'm worried about."

Odette made a noise in the back of her throat, something like "ah ah ah" to get Nieve's attention. The Magpie's final order still held her frozen in place, her eyes the only part of her she seemed to have any control over.

Mason looked back over his shoulder, seeking the source of the noise. Looking apologetic, he shook his head before returning his attention to the pinned thief. "Sorry, Odie. We can't take the risk of allowing her to speak. Are you sure you can't break it?"

Odette's eyes darted back and forth in an approximation of a head shake.

"Well, that fire's gotta go out anyway," Nieve said, picturing a wave in her mind. Now that she could observe the fire properly, a few things stood out to her: the fire hadn't spread at all, but remained entirely contained beneath the window that had been modified into an exit. There was no smoke, no burning odor, no blackened or cracking glass. All of that was strange, but Nieve didn't really put it together until after she unleashed a wave of cold, conjured water, sending it splashing over Odette, the conductor, and the fire in the corner behind them. Odette and the conductor sputtered and shivered, breaking free of the order to remain still, but the fire continued flickering merrily.

"It's an illusion," Odette gasped, chafing her arms with her hands. "From one of my spell spheres. I set it earlier when I was invisible."

"I'm alive!" The conductor patted himself down as if confirming the presence of his own body. He placed both hands flat over his heart and drew a deep breath, a look of beatific relief clear on his face. "Praise the goddess, I survived!"

"Sorry about the car, though." Nieve took in the carnage as she turned around. The fire might have been an illusion, but the broken tables and chairs were not. One wall of windows was still shielded by a wall of ice and a pool of water sloshed in the corner near the fire. Odette had to remind everyone to step carefully as not all of the spell spheres rolling about were harmless. It also didn't help that the Guardian was paralyzed by the lightning trap in the wine cabinet, tiny bolts of blue-white electricity dancing through his upright hair.

"Can I get some help here, Tails?" Mason called. "I don't want to let her up, but I need someone to hold her while I bind her wrists."

"Yeah, I'll—"

"No!" Odette's exclamation was punctuated by the snap of a pocket watch clenched within a trembling fist. "There's no time! We're already late as it is."

"Late?" Nieve asked, puzzled. "Late for—" As memory caught up, Nieve sighed and cursed, her brief respite already over. "Hane. The rockslide. Right. Are you sure you'll be okay here without me?"

Odette stooped to pick up a spell sphere and after a brief examination, she ran over to Mason and the Magpie. "Hold your breath," she ordered Mason before sucking in a lungful for herself. She smashed the spell sphere beside Sa'rhi's head before motioning for Mason to lift the stone rod from Sa'rhi's throat. Nieve backed away, holding her own breath as a pale, sparkling mist emerged from the broken spell sphere. Sa'rhi must have seen it too, but as the rod drew away from her throat, she gasped for breath on reflex. She struggled for a moment, attempting not to breathe, but then her movements grew slow, her body went slack. Moments later, Odette motioned to Mason that it was safe to breathe again.

"Looks like you do have it handled," Nieve said, answering her own question. She kicked through the rubble of splintered wood and chunks of melting ice until she found her sword and sheathed it.

"Oh!" The cry of dismay came from the conductor as he took in the utter carnage of the dining car. "I suppose we . . . we'll have to figure out something different for our evening meal."

Nieve snorted before she caught a sharp-eyed glare from Odette. Holding her hands up in surrender, Nieve turned and trotted for the forward door of the car, leaving Odette and Mason to clean up behind her. She cursed as she realized the train had already rounded the curve in the track that marked the beginning of the rockslide. Setting exhaustion aside, Nieve bolted through the next train car, hoping Hane could hold on until she got there.

HANE

Wavewalker (leg mark), Citrine

Even with Hane's hearing dampened, it was impossible not to hear the grind of stone against stone or the thunderous crack of splintering wood, each new creak and groan like the constant ticking of a clock. It was already hard enough to come up with a good plan using only the resources they had at hand, but the ominous sounds and the rapidly diminishing time made it impossible to think clearly at all. The only thing to do was act on the first plan that came to mind and make it work.

Hane only wished that their plan had even the slightest chance of succeeding.

By the time the mountainous boulder came within reach of Hane's Burst spell, it would be going too fast for their current mana pool to slow it down, or even redirect it somewhere else safely. They certainly didn't have enough mana to stop it. What they did have was a plethora of boulders stopped along the grassy stretch of flat land beside the tracks as well as the means of moving said boulders, giving them their one and only option for stopping the massive boulder at the top of the ridge—and hopefully all the smaller boulders that would come rolling down along with it. The odds of this working had to be close to zero, but all they really had to do was buy time until Nieve or Mason could get there.

Someone would come.

They had to.

One deep breath, then Hane was darting along the side of the train, using blasts of their Burst spell to push all the stopped boulders together, fitting them tightly against one another to form something of a wall. If neither time nor mana had been a factor, Hane would have taken care to overlap the boulders, so that hitting one wouldn't bounce the one behind it into the train, but in their current state, it was almost all they could do to ensure that they didn't hit a boulder with Burst so hard that it ricocheted off its neighbors and bounce backward. No matter what, they wouldn't be able to construct a wall long enough to protect the entire curve of the track, nor could they predict where the massive boulder might strike—too many previous boulders had taken odd turns for Hane to think the big one would roll down in a straight line. They could only hope the boulder would end up where most of the other large rocks had ended. If it went in an unexpected direction . . . well, Hane would come up with a plan for that if it actually happened.

Hane *really* hoped it wouldn't actually happen.

Using controlled Bursts and motion shaping, Hane managed to get most of the accumulated boulders into something resembling a low, multi-layered wall. It still didn't look like much compared to the Godboulder looming over the crest of the ridge, but it was all Hane could do to prepare. They couldn't focus too much on one single boulder anyway, not when each rolling stone held the potential to derail the train and send it toppling down into the canyon. They needed to come up with a secondary strategy for any boulders that managed to avoid the haphazardly constructed "wall" that only protected about a third of the train.

The two stones currently keeping the giant boulder at bay were shifting, slipping and spinning on the pebbles collected in the trench. One was slowly fighting its way forward of the other boulder, scraping bark from the pine tree that currently held it back. Before long, it would tear free and release a fresh torrent of boulders to deal with in addition to the big-as-a-house boulder looming just behind it.

Think, think, think, Hane urged themself, looking for some answer, some solution that would satisfy this particular challenge. Their eyes landed on the rows of stopped boulders scattered haphazardly near the tracks, forming a loose barrier around the apex of the curve in the track. They grimaced as a terrible idea came to them. *If I jump off the train, I can direct transference mana directly into the stopped boulders and shoot them at the ones rolling down the slope. It won't stop them, but if I can juggle them long enough for the train to get past, I can let them all roll down into the ravine below.*

Of course, then the question became: how would Hane get back onto the train afterward, but the longer they put off acting, the less time they would have to aim and fire the stationary boulders at the rolling boulders. Without questioning whether or not they had enough mana to pull off this harebrained scheme or not, Hane picked out their landing point among the stopped boulders, running along the length of the car to make the leap as short as possible.

Just as they coiled their legs beneath them, a crack like lightning snapped their attention up to the top of the ridge. One of the load-bearing pine trees split down the middle, raining down green needles and heavy branches that obscured the boulders at the peak of the erosion trench. As the tree toppled forward, a sound like thunder rent the air.

Hane cursed under their breath as they glanced back along the length of the train, trying to judge just how long it would take for the end to reach this point of the track. If they spent absolutely every last tick of mana in their body, they just might be able to keep the boulders bouncing long enough to let the train by safely. Afterward, there would be nothing else for them but to recover enough to use their communication device to let their team know they were ringing out of the spire. There was no point in staying if they couldn't get back on the train, and as long as Nieve kept going, there was still a chance that Chime's missing piece could be recovered.

"Hane!"

The sudden shout made them stumble just as they were about to leap, pitching forward onto their hands and knees, and disconcertingly staring straight down at the wheels spinning along the rails. For a moment, the sensation of motion sickness rose up deep in their gut before Lief's spell suppressed it, allowing Hane to sit up and look back over their shoulder.

Nieve stood on the gangway of the next car, leaning against the rail with her hands held out in front of her, as if she held back an enormous invisible pressure. A quick look up at the ridge showed an ice wall bursting out of the ground, growing wider and wider to stem the tide of stones. Hane sat back against the side of the train, feeling weak with relief.

Nieve looked disheveled and winded, her jaw clenched tight in concentration as her ice wall grew thicker and wider, collecting the new spill of boulders tumbling over the ridge. Hane could still see the rounded peak of the enormous boulder over the top of Nieve's wall, but she'd caught it before it could gain too much momentum. For now, the rockslide was contained. The Champion looked over, a triumphant grin on her face as she met Hane's eye.

"Sorry to leave you on your own! Capturing the Magpie took longer than expected."

Hane nodded, too tired to shout over the wind and the thunderous impacts of boulders striking Nieve's ice wall. If the Magpie was caught, then this challenge was all but over. It almost made fighting a rockslide on their own for so long worth it.

Almost.

At least now they could climb down onto the gangway and reorient their gravity back to normal. Whether or not they would need to be carried back to their cabin was another matter entirely. But before they could slip around the edge of the car to step down, a boom like a cannon shot echoed down the slope, covering the sound of Nieve's curses.

"I'm not strong enough over that much distance," Nieve shouted, her hands still up in front of her. "I can make a stronger wall closer to the tracks."

"Strong enough to cut the momentum?" Hane shouted back to her. "The faster they go, the harder they'll hit!"

Nieve's face twisted as her ice wall shattered, the massive boulder leading the downhill charge of what seemed to be an army of boulders that had spread out in a wide line behind Nieve's wall. Rather than coming down from one central point, the rock slide was taking up the entire width of the ridge, jostling and scraping against one another as they gained in momentum.

"Guess I'll have to try," Nieve called, her face lined with concentration. "Unless you have any other ideas?"

"Try to slow them down," Hane suggested. "Can you create more walls like the first one?"

"Maybe." A muscle clenched in Nieve's jaw as she picked a point on the slope and created a second ice wall. It didn't have time to grow as large as the first before the rockslide battered it to shards without the slightest sign of slowing down. Nieve conjured another wall, then another and another, always just ahead of the oncoming rush. About halfway down the slope, Hane could tell it was making a difference: each time the boulders met with one of Nieve's walls, they slowed a little, jockeying against one another, sometimes colliding and rolling to a stop. If Nieve could keep it up, it was possible that the rockslide might meet the rocks Hane had stopped at the edge of the tracks and simply stop, but there were a few issues that Hane could already foresee: first was that the largest boulder was now far out ahead of the others, hardly affected by Nieve's efforts at all. Second was the sweat dripping down Nieve's face in rivulets and the slight tremble in her outstretched hands. Nieve was powerful, but Hane had no way of knowing how much mana she had spent while fighting the Magpie, which meant her mana could run out at any moment. And finally, there was the fact that the boulders were no longer coming head-on toward Nieve's position—as the train continued along the track, Nieve was moving farther and farther away from where her ice walls were needed, and she'd already confessed a weakness over distance. There was no way Nieve could stop casting long enough to rush through the passenger car to get to the far gangway, never mind back to the height of the curve, where the majority of the rockslide would impact the train.

"I'll make one last one," Nieve said, shoving sweaty bangs off her face. "A heavy one, right at the tracks. That should work, right?"

"Try it," Hane said, trying to keep the doubt from their voice. "If that's all you have left, then give it everything you've got."

Nieve's jaw clenched, her lips pressed together until they turned pale, her hands steadying as she flexed her fingers. Then all at once, something changed: a worry line appeared between her brows; her shoulders seemed to shrink ever so slightly.

"Is there a better way?" Nieve asked, her eyes darting sidelong before focusing on the slope again. "Is there something else I could do? A better plan than mine?"

"I don't know, but you have to do something!" Hane shouted, the roar of tumbling stones becoming louder and louder. "Quickly! Before it's too late!"

"What if it's not enough?" Nieve asked, the point of impact growing farther away every second she delayed. "What if I make things worse?"

"Do you honestly think you'll make anything better by doing nothing?" Hane called back. "Create the wall! Now!"

Nieve steeled herself, though doubt was still present in her expression. Hane saw the beginnings of an ice wall shift and shuffle the lines of boulders they had pushed together into a barricade just beyond the train tracks. Nieve dropped her hands abruptly, eyes going wide.

"I can't," she said, shaking her head. "I might roll some of those stones into the train, and then it's my fault if someone gets hurt."

People were going to be hurt if Nieve *didn't* get her ice wall erected immediately, but Hane couldn't put that into words fast enough in a way that was encouraging rather than accusatory. And Hane was better at acting than coaching, anyway.

Tamping down exhaustion and the warning scream of their nearly exhausted mana reserves, Hane rolled up to the balls of their feet and pivoted to face the gap between passenger cars. Their muscles protested as transference mana coiled tight within their joints, but despite it all, Hane's leap to the next car was just as clean as any. Pain shot through the arches of their feet, their center of gravity wobbling in a way that was new and heart-stoppingly terrifying. They waited a single beat for the world around them to stabilize before surging to their feet, hoping to make it to the point of impact before the massive boulder beat them to it.

What they would do when they got there . . . well, that was still a work in progress. They could gather every bit of mana they had left in one final Burst spell, hoping to cut the momentum of the lead stones, but that was really all they had. And the aftermath of such a spell . . . Well, it wouldn't be pretty.

"Wait!" Nieve shouted, leaning over the brass rail to shout against the wind. "Look! Back along the train, is that—your sight is better than mine, do you see it?"

Hane had let the perception spell sharpening their vision fade in order to conserve mana, but they cast it again now, scanning the length of the train for whatever Nieve saw. There, close to the end of the train, just behind the curve in the track: someone had their arm extended beyond the gangway rail, their dark skin the only attribute Hane could pick out over the distance. Before they could hazard a guess as to who it was, the collection of stopped boulders began to wriggle and writhe, pressing tightly against one another as if huddling close for warmth. Slowly, the definition between each individual boulder faded and vanished, becoming one enormous stone wall rising higher and higher while following the curve of the train track.

"It's Mason!" Hane confirmed, dropping to a crouch to keep their balance against the rushing wind. "He's using the boulders to make a wall!"

As more boulders melded into the wall, it grew thicker, stauncher, but with that singular massive boulder in the lead, Hane couldn't make themself believe the wall would hold. Even if it did, the stones chasing along behind it would be more than enough to pulverize the wall and derail the train.

Maybe I can shape its momentum, Hane thought, desperately searching for a workable solution. *Maybe if I get close enough to put a backward spin on its rotation, I can slow it just enough that it won't break through Mason's wall.*

The real question was whether Hane had enough mana left for such a spell, but they didn't want to consider the answer to that just yet. What they needed to do was get close enough that whatever mana they did have left went into this final spell. And that meant moving right into the space where the boulder would impact the train if the wall failed to stop it.

Scraping together their last vestiges of strength and will—and a deliberate blind eye turned toward the consequences of this decision—Hane prepared for one final sprint along the side of the train. Except the moment they straightened up, their vision swam. The world spun drunkenly, space bending oddly as if they were peering through the curve of a bottle. They fell flat against the side of the train, too dizzy to scrape themself up. It was too late now, anyway; they wouldn't make it in time. All they could do now was grit their teeth and brace for impact.

Except . . . it never came. Just before the massive boulder reached Mason's stone wall, it exploded in a spray of sand. Hane tucked their face into their shoulder, afraid to let go of the train in case their Gravity Shift spell failed them. In the haze of the sand cloud, smaller boulders smashed into the wall, making it shudder and shake as web-like cracks appeared along the surface—but it didn't break. It didn't topple.

The stone wall held.

It was almost impossible to see through the clouds of dirt and dust kicked up by the rockslide, but with their sharpened vision, Hane watched the final boulder come to rest against the others corralled by Mason's wall just as the last train car reached the apex of the curve. They did it! As impossible and as fragmented as they were, somehow the team had come together in the nick of time to save the train and capture the bad guy. It was over. It was—

Hane's gravity reoriented itself with no warning, causing the "ground" that was the side of the train to drop abruptly out from under their feet. They scrabbled for a handhold, drawing on transference mana that just didn't seem to be there anymore. As their vision blurred and their stomach lurched, Hane could only think that this must be the "rebound" effect Lief had mentioned earlier when modifying their mana.

"I got you!"

Had the shout come a second later, Hane would already be attempting to use their return bell with whatever shreds of mana they could gather, but the confidence in Nieve's voice stayed their hand. Their sudden drop was stopped by something hard and cold and inclined, as evidenced by the way they slid backward, toward the front of the car. Arms and legs felt as weak as porridge, unable even to turn around and face the end of the platform of ice. Luckily, Nieve leaned over the brass rail to scoop Hane up beneath the arms and drag them back onto the gangway, where they sagged limply to the grate. Nieve smirked triumphantly as she leaned back against the opposite rail, elbows hooked over the sides.

"We got it," she said, something like astonishment in the slow shake of her head. Relief made her grin look goofy, softening her eyes as she caught her breath. "You okay? Are you hurt?"

"I think—" A flood of bile rising in their throat choked them into silence. Hane pitched forward onto their hands and knees, retching through the brass grate and onto the tracks below. Movement behind them was Nieve drawing in on herself to avoid the spray, but when the bout of illness ended, she offered them a sip from her own canteen. Hane appreciated the offer, but refused it, sipping from their own canteen to rinse the taste from their mouth. It took several tries to get the cap back on, the motion of the train making the gangway feel more like a raft in choppy water than a level surface. The world didn't spin so much as it appeared oddly distorted, as if they were seeing everything through a rippling layer of water.

"I think—" Hane tried to stand, but couldn't figure out which direction was up anymore. And the brass grating just felt so cool beneath them. It would be so nice just to lay their head down and close their eyes, just for a second. "I think I need a healer."

They heard Nieve's voice, but it sounded as if it were coming from far, far away. A sensation like falling, then the darkness between blinks. The next thing Hane knew, they were engulfed in peaceful darkness, lulled to sleep by the rocking and swaying of the train.

I'm in a bed.

Hane's first thought upon waking. They remained still out of habit, maintaining their measured breathing. What time was it? What day was it? How had they gotten here, and how long had they slept?

What was that noise?

A soft click, followed by the slide of something heavy. A door? Were they in the cabin they shared with Nieve, then? That made the most sense, as Nieve had been with them when they'd fainted. Feeling confident that they had at least identified the "who" and the "where," Hane blinked their eyes open, just as someone peered over the edge of the mattress. A startled gasp and a wide-eyed look of fear was all Hane had time to acknowledge before the intruder dropped out of sight, falling to the floor with a crash. Hane frowned: that wasn't like Nieve at all.

"Oh Tsab, you scared me!" Hane had to lean over the edge of their bunk to see Odette pick herself up off the floor, adjusting her glasses and straightening her tunic. "I wasn't expecting—No matter. Why are you still in bed if you're awake? Hurry, we need to go!"

"Tsab?" Hane repeated, voice rough from sleep. They coughed as they searched for a canteen. Whoever had put them to bed took their water and their tonfa, but left their boots on as well as their other hidden weapons.

"Tsab, you know." Odette opened and closed the cabin's cabinets like she was looking for something. "Byakko's warrior daughter. Ah, here. Is this one yours?"

Odette held up a canteen. Hane reached for it and drank greedily. They hadn't even realized they were thirsty until the first drop hit their lips, then they couldn't stop. How long had they been asleep? Hours? Days? Longer? Was everyone all right? Why was Odette here instead of Nieve? Nieve hadn't been injured, had she? A gasp and a cough had Hane feeling almost human enough to communicate with actual words. "How long was I out? What happened? Where's Nieve?"

"You've been out since this morning," Odette replied, which was less than helpful considering Hane didn't know what time it was. "Lief examined you and got you fixed up. He said you overreached and you got hit by a rebound after his spell ended, but he also said you'd be fine. Why can't I find your bag? Do you have it up there with you?"

Hane resisted the initial urge to check on their dimensional bag, then gave in; Odette wasn't an enemy, she was a teammate. Still, they kept their movements discreet as they checked the rolled up satchel they'd stuffed between the mattress and the wall their first day on the train. "Why do you need my bag?"

"*I* don't need it, *you* need it!" Odette's voice was high and strained, her hands fidgeting and restless as her gaze shifted around the cabin. "I know Lief said to let you sleep as long as possible, but now it's time to go. Do you need anything? More water? Clothes? Where is your *bag*?"

Odette's pitch wound higher and higher, a spring about to snap. Hane ran a hand back through their hair, assessing their condition with care. Joints and muscles felt a bit stiff, but that was easily explained by how long they had been asleep. No painful injuries even though they remembered that the rockslide hadn't left them unscathed. A touch along their cheek found only smooth skin, no laceration or dried blood. As they began moving and stretching, one of their tonfa rolled out from underneath their pillow—most likely a thoughtful gesture from Nieve, who always slept with her own sword in easy reach.

Hane covered a yawn before moving the edge of their bunk, swinging their legs over the mattress in order to secure their tonfa in the harness beneath their dueling vest. Odette continued to vibrate with anxious energy in the center of the room, as if she were trying to hold back another exclamation to hurry up.

"Where's Nieve?" Hane asked again, because Odette had failed to answer that question the first time around. Before Odette could answer, a disturbing realization occurred to Hane: Odette might be vibrating, but nothing else within the room was. They tried to look out the window, but the shade was drawn, blocking the view. "Why is the train stopped?"

"Because we're *here*," Odette said again, this time with an edge of frustration over her anxiety. "We have a little time right now because the train crew wants to keep the platform clear until the prisoners are handed over, but once that's finished, it's all over." Odette crossed the room to the window, pulling aside the shade. The light from outside was bright enough to make Hane's eyes water. They heard continued pacing as they blinked them clear. "Are you still hurt? Should I call Lief? Do you need help getting down? Please, Hane, we are *so* close to the Vault of Shadows and I have been waiting for so long to get back there! Tell me what you need so I can help you."

She still hadn't answered the question about Nieve, but at least Hane understood her nervous energy a little better. Everyone on the team wanted to get to the vault, but only Odette had spent a year studying it, figuring out its secrets, and buying a key that would allow a team to reach it quickly. It stood to reason that this discovery meant more to her than to anyone else. And at least she wasn't trying to hide her anticipation by feigning concern and kindness; as abrupt as this wake-up call was, Hane could appreciate the frank honesty over a veneer of concern and compassion.

But as much as Hane understood her desire to hurry up and move on, there were a few issues that couldn't simply be ignored in favor of haste. One of which was actually fairly urgent.

"What I need most right now is to use the bathroom," Hane informed her with a level voice. "After that, I'll need to eat. Unless you know if there will be time to eat on the next floor?"

"Um . . ." Odette hesitated, falling still only as long as it took her to come up with an answer. "No, probably not. You should eat before we exit this scenario, but food service on the train ended almost an hour ago. I have some rations I can share if you need them."

"I have my own." Hane leaned back on an elbow to free the satchel wedged between the mattress and the wall, shrugging the strap up over their shoulder before sliding down from the bed. "Any idea how long we have until they let us off the train?"

"I don't know. Soon?" Odette shuffled and shifted, looking as if she wanted to chivvy Hane along, but restraining herself—barely. "The others are probably all off already. Nieve and Lief were the only ones who could move the Magpie safely, and Mason and Rose were helping with the Guardian and the Assassin. The Shaper, um, he sort of . . ."

"I remember." That was a sound Hane wished they didn't have to recall so soon upon waking. Odette sidled past them to open the cabin door, looking back impatiently. Though they didn't mean to nettle her, Hane had a policy of never leaving food behind during a climb, and one of the room's cabinets was full of prepackaged snacks. Hane swept all of them into their bag while Odette made tiny noises in her throat, her lower lip pinched tight between her teeth. "What else happened while I was out? Is everyone all right?"

"Fine, everyone's fine," Odette replied, speaking quickly, as if to make up for the lack of forward motion. "You got the worst of it, but mostly because of the rebound Lief's spell caused. You're fully recovered, right? Mana-wise, I mean."

Hane checked their mana reserves as they patted themself down, making sure they had everything they needed. Both tonfa were now secured on their back, their water canteen hung from a stitched loop on their vest, and their dimensional bag had everything else they needed. Their boots felt a little loose from sleeping in them, but they could adjust that momentarily. Most importantly, they found their mana readily available and casting spells on themself didn't seem to trigger any exhaustion, aches, or extreme effort. They did err on the side of caution, though, only casting perception spells on their sight and hearing for now.

"I'm fit enough to continue," Hane assured her, brushing past to get to the door. "I'll feel better after I—"

"Oh!" Odette reached out to pinch their sleeve, falling still as a look of concern came over her. "Your sleeve is torn. I wish Nieve had told me; I could have mended it while you slept."

"Outside of a medical emergency, I prefer not to have my clothes removed." As Hane continued to the cabin door, Odette relinquished her hold on the fabric, seemingly reluctant to tear it further. "Thank you for the offer, but this shirt is still functional. There's no need for you to go to any trouble."

"It wouldn't be any trouble," Odette said, shaking her head fervently. "I'd like to fix it for you. Really, I wouldn't mind at all." She worried her lower lip as she followed Hane into the corridor. "I could try to stitch it while you wear it, if that's more comfortable to you."

It was not. In fact, it sounded decidedly less comfortable than simply handing the shirt over, but changing would take time, and if the rest of the team was already waiting on the station platform, Hane didn't want to make them wait any longer than they had to.

"Bathroom," Hane reminded Odette when she tried to follow them through the door. "Don't worry about my shirt. I usually wear them out in spires, anyway. Is there anything else I should know?"

"Oh, um . . ." Odette maintained her sulky expression until Hane closed the bathroom door, locking it with a deliberate click. They heard a loud sigh before she resumed speaking through the door. "Well, we caught the Magpie and their crew, as you already know. Nieve and Lief have been taking turns guarding the Magpie, making sure they don't use any Controller spells to get free. Rose had to fix some engine parts that got, er, *disturbed* when I was trying to slow the train down after you chased the Magpie off. She had Ellis, the Assassin, helping her whenever Mason wasn't available, but only while he agreed to wear the compulsion bracelet she made. I think he's trying to get a more lenient sentence by helping. Oh, the Guardian was actually an engineer on the crew before the Magpie recruited him, so he was the one responsible for sabotaging the engine and leaving all the spare parts and tools behind. He's still a little shaken up after Nieve tricked him into activating a lightning trap in the dining car. Lief has been confusing his mana pathways to keep him safe until we could hand him over to the authorities, but I don't think he was a threat after we subdued the Magpie. By the way, no one wanted to trust the Magpie in the brig, so we locked them up in my cabin. Lief moved his things into Mason and Rose's cabin, and I spent some of my downtime in here while you slept. I hope that doesn't bother you."

Hane never even noticed, so they couldn't really say it bothered them. Without enough time to fully bathe, Hane splashed water on their face before combing wet fingers through their hair. Examining their reflection in the bathroom mirror, they noted the cut on their face had been healed without leaving behind even the faintest scar. Someone must have washed the blood from their face as they slept, but there was still a crust of dried blood inside their sleeve. Rather than undress, Hane scrubbed at it through the tears in their shirt.

"Let's see, what else?" Odette continued, voice raised to be heard through the door. "Oh, I finished the trading sequence! I got a gold key at the end, but I don't think we'll need it this climb. It'll probably count toward our treasures."

"Did we get any other treasures?" Hane called through the door.

"Not really," Odette replied. "I think Nieve claimed the Magpie's walking stick. And then there's all the stuff we took off the Assassin. I can't think of anything else right now. We'll get most of our rewards once we get off the train. The porters will bring it to us in a luggage container. We'll probably also earn a bounty for turning over the Magpie. If you hurry, we can—"

Hane opened the bathroom door, causing Odette to squeak in surprise. "What about the snakes?"

Odette looked puzzled. "What about the—oh! They're fine. At least, as far as I know, they're fine. The Keepsake cars are still attached, and none of the shipment guards said anything about missing any more of the snakes than the ones we returned. The crew used something called a car-spacer to replace the broken coupler, since there was no way we could fix it while en route." She cringed sheepishly, eyes big behind her glasses. "I'm sorry. I know you wanted to set them free."

"I did, but that's behind us now." Hane shaded their eyes to peer out the window. There was no sign of the uniformed guards now and it looked as if passengers were being allowed off the train. Odette saw it, too, hopping anxiously from foot to foot as Hane rustled through their bag to find the snacks they'd stowed away. "Do you know if any of the traps are still active? Like the ones on the couplers, or the roof?"

"Uh, no, actually." Odette's brows furrowed. "I haven't had the time to check since we stopped. Why do you ask?"

Hane gestured to the platform. "I don't want to funnel through the crowd if I don't have to. I'd rather hop over the platform rail if I can."

"Oh! I think that should be okay?" Odette considered a moment. "We wouldn't have the benefit of a ramp, but it would certainly be faster to jump the rail onto the platform. It doesn't look that hard to do."

"I can help you, if you need it," Hane offered, leading the way to the rear door of the car. "There weren't any other issues after the rockslide? No complications or side quests?"

"We had to skip the one under the train. The one through the trapdoor, remember?" Odette adjusted the straps of her backpack before following. "That's never a large reward, anyway, so it doesn't matter. There was supposed to be a lost item quest, but I never found it, so maybe it didn't happen this time. You did the collection quest and I told you about the trading sequence already. No one attempted the dueling challenge, but I think that's for the best, considering how much damage was done to the dining car."

Odette drew a sharp breath as Hane leapt lightly onto the brass rail outside, testing their balance as well as their mana reserves before hopping down to the platform. The gap between the platform and the gangway wasn't huge, but it did appear deep. Odette leaned over the rail, eyeing the gap warily. Hane stepped in close to offer her a hand.

"What was the dueling challenge?" Hane asked, steadying Odette as she climbed over the rail. "I don't remember you mentioning it."

"Didn't I?" Odette frowned, wobbling once before a small jump and Hane's assistance landed her safely on the station's platform. "Oof, thanks. I swear I thought we talked about the duelist with the enchanted sword?"

That's right, Hane did remember hearing mention of a shroudless person walking around with an enchanted sword. They just hadn't thought much of the duelist since then. "It's just a straightforward challenge, then?"

"Most of the time," Odette agreed. "Dueling challenges are usually one-on-one with safety parameters in place. Sometimes they establish firm boundary lines, but I think for this one, the duel is just limited to the car the challenge starts in. After a climber initiates the duel, the duelist sets the terms, as well as the prize. If the climber wins, they get to claim the duelist's sword."

Hane blocked Odette's path, catching her eyes with their own. "Don't tell Nieve she missed a dueling challenge. She might go running off to find the duelist."

Odette covered a gasp, her eyes wide. "I'm so sorry! I should have explained that sooner. It's just, I guess I thought dueling challenges were in all the spires?"

"They might be," Hane allowed. "But I think our scenarios differ from the ones here. If Nieve and I decide to join another team here in Caelford, I promise I'll tell her about dueling challenges, but if you tell her she missed one now, it'll just slow us down."

Odette sighed heavily. "You're right. I should have been more clear at the beginning. When you tell her, please say that I'm sorry."

"Hey!" Nieve shouted at them from a short distance away. With her hand in the air, she looked like she was signaling a boat from a distant shore. "What are you talking about? Hurry up, we've got loot!"

Hane glanced around discreetly as they crossed the platform to meet up with the rest of the team. The duelist from the train was among the many passengers waiting for their luggage to be unloaded from the train, but they weren't close by; there was no doubt in Hane's mind that if Nieve found out about the dueling challenge, she'd attempt to tackle it right then and there. Better to keep the truth hidden for now; the vault on the next floor was the true objective anyway.

Surprisingly, the captain of the Keepsake Treasuries guards was just leaving the team as Hane and Odette approached. Recognizing them, he tipped his cap and thanked them again for their assistance before hurrying back to the Keepsake cars, where someone in a crisp suit appeared to be waiting for him. Possibly a higher-up from Keepsake, come to check on the goods as they were off-loaded. The item of greater interest was the small wooden box he'd left behind with Rose before bidding everyone fair travels.

"Do you want to open it, Odie?" Rose offered. "He said it was in gratitude for retrieving the two snakes that were stolen, as well as protecting the cargo."

"Oh, um, sure." Odette smiled nervously as she flipped open the clasp on the box and lifted the hinged lid. Inside the velvet interior were six tiny vials of clear liquid, fitted tightly into padded slots. Hane recognized the vials amid the collective gasps of their teammates: six vials of Cure. A fortune held between two hands.

"Wow," Nieve whispered, her jaw hanging open in shock. "I mean, just . . . wow."

"Not bad for a job well done, eh?" Lief grinned as he plucked one vial from the box. As he wrapped a bandage around it to protect the glass, he shot a smirk over at Hane. "Bet you're glad now that we didn't let those snakes get away."

"Not really." Hane waited until everyone else had taken a vial before selecting the final one for themself. "It does make me wonder what reward we would have gotten from the Magpie if we'd allowed the snakes to be stolen, though."

Lief rolled his eyes as he tucked the vial of Cure into the medical kit on his belt.

"I don't know what to do with this," Nieve admitted, still staring at the tiny bottle in her hand. "It would sell for a high price, wouldn't it? But is it better to keep it, in case I get poisoned during a climb?"

"Better to have it and not need it than to need it and not have it," Mason pointed out cheerfully. "I might sell mine, though. It's not like I spend a lot of time in spires or running around outside the city."

"Keep it on you for now, and if you don't end up using it by the end of the climb, I'll make you an offer for it," Rose informed her brother as she slipped her vial into an inside pocket of her vest. "If you break it or lose it, I'm taking an equivalent price from your cut of the treasure."

"What? Why?"

"Because stupidity should be penalized."

Mason replied archly in Caelish, making Rose snap sharply at him in kind. Whatever they said, it made Odette's eyes go wide and caused Lief to snicker. Luckily, the arrival of their "luggage" cut off the argument that Hane couldn't follow. Two porters hauled a large trunk off a rolling cart, advising the team to make sure everything was accounted for, as some luggage had "shifted" during the journey. Nieve reached for the clasp, but Hane blocked her with a hand. When she glared at them, they nodded at the others. Odette held both hands up at shoulder height, palms up, face turned upward, as if practicing a ritual of worship or prayer. Rose and Mason lifted their palms, too, but for them, it looked more like an obligation than any kind of reverence. Lief made a face before copying the gesture himself.

"I forgot about this," Lief muttered to Hane and Nieve. "It's quick, don't worry."

Hane and Nieve exchanged a look before tentatively raising their hands. Odette spoke to the sky in Caelish, with Lief whispering a translation for Hane and Nieve.

"We are thankful for whatever fortune we have earned in the eyes of Nao and Kota."

Rose and Mason dropped their hands the instant Odette ended the prayer, the two of them jostling one another to be the first to open the trunk. Odette appeared more solemn, lowering her hands slowly as she exhaled. It almost seemed as if her anxiety about moving on had left her, but then she checked her pocket watch and the anxious twitches and fidgets returned to her.

"Nao and Kota?" Nieve asked quizzically.

"Children of Byakko," Mason answered shortly, physically lifting his sister and moving her out of his way in order to open the trunk. "Supposedly, they're responsible for the fortunes of climbers. One of them is luck, the other is money, but I don't remember which is which."

Rose punched her brother in the side, wringing a grunt out of him as he flipped the lid of the trunk open. She made a face at him before explaining. "Nao bestows luck, either good or ill, and Kota bestows wealth, sometimes in gold, but sometimes by replacing gold coins with something worthless, like buttons or wood chips. They're both considered tricksters, though I doubt they actually have anything to do with spire treasures. Not directly, anyway. Rumor has it that praying before opening treasure chests makes it less likely to receive bad fortune. Most people just lift their hands, though. Odie's the only one who actually prays."

"I—it's—well—" Odette stammered, looking too embarrassed to focus on the treasure. "So I honor the children of our god beast. Is that really so strange?"

"A little," Mason said, no malice in his tone, just a statement of fact. "I mean, passing knowledge is one thing, but Jesserah said you collected all the prayer cards for each of them and papered your bedroom with them. And every time the Idol Time shop announces a new carving, you're the first to put in an order for one."

"That's . . . that's a hobby," Odette protested, but it looked as though she was blushing.

"You know more about Byakko's offspring than I do," Rose said flatly, her tone accusatory. "Anyone who knows more about something than I do is either an expert or a fanatic."

"I'm not a fanatic," Odette protested softly. She cleared her throat and adjusted her glasses. "Can we please just focus on the treasure right now? We still have a labyrinth to get through before we find the vault."

Hane's stomach grumbled at them, reminding them they hadn't eaten since they'd awoken, and that hunger would make navigating the traps and puzzles of a labyrinth that much more difficult. They stepped to the side and rummaged through their bag for the food they'd swiped from the cabin, watching silently as the others pawed through eagerly through the treasure.

"Elemental resistance rings," Rose said with a sigh, dropping an open drawstring pouch back inside the trunk. "I hate these. It's not like a monster is going to give anyone the time needed to put on the appropriate ring to defend against their specific elemental attacks."

"Oooh, let me see!" Odette scooped up the pouch, peering inside before spilling a few into her open palm. "Fire resist, got it. Teleportation resist, got it. Levitation assist, got it. Another poison resistance ring isn't bad. . . . Oh, hey, this one might be a shroud enhancer!" Odette pinched a ring between her fingers, squinting at it as she turned it from side to side. "Does anyone mind if I use this one for the climb? I'll put it back in the stash when we divvy up."

"That sounds pretty useful, but it looks too small for . . ." Mason trailed off, elbow deep in the trunk as he dug down to the bottom. "No way . . . that's not—it is! Dibs, sis, this one's mine!"

"What is it?" Rose asked as Mason raised a closed fist above his head. "You know the rules, Mason! You can't claim something until the team decides its value!"

Mason huffed and rolled his eyes, but he opened his fist, revealing a tiny jeweled egg cradled in the cup of his palm. Barely as large as a fingernail, the egg seemed to have been carved from marble, then decorated with patterns of gold and silver as well as lines of tiny pearls and diamonds. "I've seen these worked into rings and necklaces before. I need it for my craft."

"Oh," Rose said, but it sounded more like "ew." She adjusted the lens of her goggles before turning back to the treasure trunk dismissively. "I don't care enough to fight you for it, but maybe someone else does."

"Does it open?" Lief asked, leaning in close to examine the tiny egg. "Or is it solid all the way through?"

"I think it's solid." Mason held it up to the light before giving it a vigorous shake. "Why? You want it?"

"Just curious." Lief's smile appeared congenial, but there was something in the way he considered the jeweled egg that seemed . . . off. Like he wanted it, but didn't want to admit that he wanted it.

Why, though? Hane wondered, eating a sandwich that was just bread and cheese. If Lief was interested in the jewel, why wouldn't he just say so? Mason didn't have a greater claim on it than anyone else did, which made it fair for Lief to contest his claim. Or maybe Lief had mistaken the jeweled egg for something else? Regardless, the egg's value would still be counted as part of the total treasure, which seemed to be a pretty decent haul so far.

Hane finished the sandwich and tore open a package of wafer crackers. Nieve caught their eye as they popped the first cracker into their mouth.

"Didn't eat," Hane explained in between crackers.

"Yeah, I figured." Nieve shrugged. "I thought it was better if I let you sleep."

"It was the right choice." The crackers were good, but they dried out Hane's mouth. After a quick sip from their canteen, they nodded at the treasure. "See anything you want?"

Nieve shrugged, hooking her hands through her sword belt. "I usually prefer to sell my cut for coin unless there's something I need. I don't really need anything right now."

Moving as cautiously as possible, Hane tapped their heel against the side of Nieve's boot while making sure everyone else's attention was on the treasure. "Odette filled me in on what happened while I was out. Thanks for getting me back to the room."

Nieve's noticeable delay in responding indicated she'd understood the question beneath the comment: was Chime still safe? Hane could only hope the others were too distracted to notice.

"Yeah, don't worry about it," Nieve said finally, giving Hane the slightest nod. "Teammates look out for each other, right?"

Hane decided that meant Chime was well and safe, hopefully alert enough to tell Nieve if the team was on the right course for recovering their missing piece.

"Ooh, this is a pretty toy!" Rose's goggles were a mismatched red and blue, making her look slightly crazed as she held up a small ice pick from the treasure chest. "If I'm right about the enchantment on this, when the spike contacts any solid surface, it'll sprout ice and anchor itself like a handhold. If it's all right, I'd like to try it out for the rest of our delve."

"Any objections?" Odette asked, glancing around rapidly like a nervous sparrow. "No? Go ahead, Rose. Anyone else need anything? I'm going to send this back to storage, so if you have anything you need stored, drop it in now."

"Here." Lief jingled a heavy coin purse before dropping it heavily into the trunk. "Our reward from Keepsake for capturing the Magpie and their crew."

"I still have some of the Assassin's weapons," Rose said, patting the pockets of her vest until she found two medium-sized pouches to add to the cache. "Unless anyone wants a vial of unknown poison, or anything small and stabby?"

Nieve reached back behind her belt, fingers resting on the marble top of the Magpie's walking stick before shrugging and dropping her hand. Hane guessed that meant she was holding onto it for now.

"Nothing else?" Odette confirmed. With a heavy sigh, Mason leaned forward and dropped the tiny jeweled egg back into the trunk, most likely because it was the safest place for it—there were no guarantees that climbers would actually make it out of the spire with their treasure, which was why it was wise to pay a percentage to storage facilities for safekeeping. Some treasure was better than no treasure, after all.

Odette latched the trunk closed before labeling it with a tag written in Caelish. Mason crouched down to shape the metal edges of the lid and trunk together in a seamless line, making the trunk more difficult to open. Hane and the others backed away as Odette set a delay bell on top of the trunk, scurrying away quickly before she could be caught in the radius of the bell.

"Quick check!" Odette called with authority, stopping Hane mid-step toward the train station's exit. "Does everyone still have their location trackers? I don't want to lose anyone inside the labyrinth."

As Hane rolled up their sleeve to check, the others all reflexively touched the embroidered bands, confirming their presence. Mason flexed his bicep, Nieve held up her arm, Lief turned his wrist, and Rose tugged at the ends of the bow on the choker she'd tied for herself. Odette nodded firmly as Hane bared their arm, showing the proof of their ribbon band.

"Good! That's good." Odette smiled shakily, her hands trembling as she tugged at the strap of her satchel. "It's possible that we'll encounter combat as soon as we step through the portal, so everyone just stay close until we get a chance to evaluate the scenario and locate the vault. The plan is to avoid the main objective and any other side quests that occur. Our only goal is making it to the entrance of the phantom chamber. Any issues with that?"

Hane wasn't in complete agreement with that, but as most of the others shook their heads, they decided it was best not to start another fight. They could agree with avoiding any objectives that slowed them down, but they also wouldn't ignore any beings in peril or pain. Even if that meant taking on an escort quest on their own.

"Oh, Hane, here." Rose handed them an earpiece as Odette led the way to the arched exit of the train station. "I renewed the imbue on it while you were sleeping."

"Thanks." Hane's pace slowed as they secured it to their ear. The others passed by on their way to the gateway, leaving Hane and, for some reason, Nieve to bring up the rear. It was odd to see her trudging behind slowly, looking back at the crowd on the platform as if searching for something. She caught Hane's questioning look and gave a resigned shrug.

"I kept thinking something would happen with that duelist and the Citrine sword," Nieve explained, matching Hane's pace. Odette stood beside the gateway now, bouncing on her heels impatiently as she waited for them to catch up. "I thought he might be part of the Magpie's crew or something. Isn't it weird that we didn't end up fighting him at some point?"

"There were a lot of weird elements in this scenario for me," Hane replied evenly and honestly. "I didn't know the challenges varied so widely from spire to spire."

"Yeah," Nieve agreed with a wry smile. "I guess we're not planning on being here so long that we need to figure it all out, right?"

"Right." Hane nodded. "But at least now we know to expect differences in scenarios, rituals, and rewards from whatever spire we go to next."

"Yeah! Good thinking ahead." Nieve bared her teeth in a vicious grin as she cracked her knuckles, first one hand, then the other. "I hope you're ready for a fight, partner. I'll race you to the vault!"

Hane arched a brow back at her. "You really want to turn this into a race? You know I'll win."

Nieve chuckled and pressed her knuckles into Hane's shoulder. Strangely, Hane almost considered returning the gesture.

SAGE

Seer (hand mark), Citrine

???

Sage staggered as he missed his step, the world tipping at a precarious angle. The lurch in his stomach informed him that he was falling before his mind was able to process and respond accordingly. A graceless stumble kept him upright, but before he could take stock of his surroundings, the filtered sunlight pricked his eyes with tears of pain despite the long shadow that enveloped him. Sage blinked and rubbed his face, squinting as he searched for any familiar landmark that could tell him where he was.

Wait, why don't I know where I am? Sage asked himself, feeling panic slowly building in his chest. *Okay, just calm down, breathe, and try to think back.*

What was the last thing he remembered? Nieve? Yes, there was a memory of Nieve that felt strangely old, like a blank stretch of time filled the gap since he'd last seen her. Memories came back slowly, as if Sage was only just waking from a dream: his last clear memory was looking back at Nieve as she waved him farewell. Farewell? Wait, where had he been going without Nieve? Belatedly, Sage remembered receiving a formal letter from the Soaring Wings administration, emblazoned with a stamp of approval.

That's right, Sage thought, reclaiming control of his slowly racing heart by taking deep and even breaths to the beat of a four-count. *I applied for a Judgment at the Tiger Spire. Nieve came to the gate with me. So that means . . .*

Sage shaded his eyes in order to study the towering monolith behind him. He stood outside the Tiger Spire, barely twenty paces from the base. Fleeting images, voices, and even scents ghosted through his mind like the fragments of a shattered dream: memories of his recent Judgment. For the space of a breath, he thought he remembered a face, a laugh, a feeling of something damp in his hand. Or beneath his boot? He'd had to collect something, hadn't he? No, his mission had been to find something . . .

Sage shook his head, giving up on chasing down memories of his Judgment. Forgetting the trial of Judgment was normal; he hadn't retained any memories from his first Judgment, so it was only to be expected that he would forget the details of his second. The far more important thing was that he'd survived—and that he'd likely earned a second attunement.

Where? Sage asked himself, still measuring each breath with a slow count from one to four. *I can feel it if I focus. Please be a combat attunement, please be something that makes me stronger . . .*

He felt the flow of strange new mana types emanating from a source just over his breastbone. Sage placed a hand over his chest, focusing on his heartbeat as he attempted to discern the new attunement he'd earned. He felt a brief elation as he recognized the sturdy sensation of enhancement mana, the type of mana Nieve used to bolster her strength and toughen her skin, but that wasn't the primary mana type of his new attunement. No, the primary mana type felt somehow . . . sharp? Or acute, maybe. It wasn't hot like fire mana, nor heavy like stone mana. He took another breath, tasting the air on the back of his throat as strongly as if he sipped it through a straw. As understanding sunk in, Sage's stomach dropped precipitously.

No, Sage thought, hands shaking as he fumbled the buttons on his dueling tunic. He was mildly surprised to find the fabric damp to the touch. *No, it can't be. Not with this placement, not with my original attunement—*

"Greetings!" The cheerful call nearly caused Sage to levitate without the use of a spell. His heart pounding wildly, Sage spun around to find a stranger wearing a kind smile as well as the purple tabard of the Soaring Wings administration approaching him. As he steadied himself, Sage recognized the spoken language as Valian, despite the stranger's Caelish appearance. "Welcome back! I assume you just finished your Judgment. Is that correct?"

The man was tall, dark hair shaved close on the sides with scarcely an inch of tightly curled hair on top. His belt lacked the standard sword that spire guards wore, but instead held multiple canteens, a key ring, a pouch marked for medical aid, and a small booklet tucked inside a leather holder. His casual clothing marked him as an administrator, and as he seemed unsurprised to find Sage outside the spire's base, it seemed likely that his job was to find Judgment applicants upon completion of their trials. While Sage understood all of this at a glance, his confusion over the Valian greeting, as well as his uncertain panic over his new attunement, collided with an impact that rendered him temporarily speechless.

The administrator cocked his head to the side, his smile wavering minutely. "Do you understand me? I can switch to Caelish, if you prefer. If you need a different language, I'll have to call a translator over."

"No, I'm—" Sage stopped himself, suppressing the urge to explain himself to the stranger. "Sorry. I understand you, I'm just feeling a little disoriented right now."

"That's certainly understandable," the administrator assured him, smile brightening once more. "May I ask if you feel injured or in pain? I have supplies that can help, or I can take you immediately to the healing ward at the administration office."

"Oh, um . . ." He hadn't even considered that he might be injured—which likely indicated he was fine. Despite that, Sage took a moment to evaluate his condition. "I think I'm fine, actually. A few bruises and some general exhaustion, but that's it."

"Glad to hear it!" The administrator grabbed his notebook and flipped it open to a marked page. "You can call me Daveen. Since we only have three Valians currently undergoing Judgments, you must be Nathan, Gareth, or Heather." He turned a few pages, then looked up expectantly, smiling as he held a pen to a fresh page. "Which one are you?"

"Er . . ." Sage suppressed his frustration with a sigh. "I'm not Valian, I'm Dalen. My name's Sage—Seiji Hayden."

Daveen frowned, lips pursing as if to voice a protest, but then he gave his head a small shake and flipped back toward the front of his notebook. Sage fussed anxiously with his open vest, trying not to seem impatient as Daveen silently scanned his notes.

"Ah, here!" The administrator's face brightened as he tapped his pen to the page. "A Seer, right? Can I see the mark on your hand for confirmation?"

"Yes, of course." Sage hadn't even realized he was wearing gloves. The leather looked more stressed and worn than he remembered, making him think it had seen hard use during his Judgment. He stripped away the right one, baring the back of his hand for Daveen to see.

"Perfect, thank you." Daveen marked his notes with a finger while flipping back to a fresh page. He scribbled something quickly before squinting at Sage's Seer mark and making a brief sketch of it. Sage examined it as well, making sure it hadn't changed during his Judgment. Daveen beamed as he finished the sketch. "All right, now that I've confirmed your identity, we can get to the exciting part! Do you already know where your new mark is? Don't worry if it's somewhere private; I can take you to a pavilion with dressing rooms. I just need to see the mark to confirm your new attunement."

"It's just here." Sage tapped the center of his chest, a sour taste on the back of his tongue. "You, um . . . you'll recognize what attunement it is, won't you?"

"Yes, of course. I know all the basic attunement marks given by each of the spires. Don't worry if it's not a standard Tiger Spire attunement; that happens sometimes."

Sage swallowed tightly as he peeled his shirt away from his skin. He wasn't as nervous about baring his chest to a stranger as he was about having his suspicions confirmed. If he was right about the mana type he was sensing, then not only was this not the sort of attunement he'd hoped for, but its placement made it just about the worst possible attunement he could have received.

But maybe I'm wrong, Sage told himself, stretching his collar wide using both hands. *I'm probably overthinking this and getting myself worked up over nothing. It could be good. It could even be unique and special somehow.*

His hopes were dashed by Daveen's softly spoken "*Oh,*" and a furtive glance that skipped away from Sage's eyes too quickly. The scratch of Daveen's pen on the page filled Sage with dread. He closed his eyes to steel himself before peering down at his own chest.

"Controller," Sage pronounced solemnly, his fears confirmed. "That means the primary mana type is perception, isn't it?"

"That is correct," Daveen replied, his smile somewhat diminished as he tucked his notebook away. "The secondary mana type is enhancement, with umbral as the tertiary mana type at Citrine level. Congratulations! Earning a second attunement is quite an achievement."

Sage didn't feel accomplished; if anything, this felt like a step backward. Enhancement mana was great, especially as he learned to use it to strengthen his body and reinforce his shroud, but the perception mana was the magical opposite of mental mana—the primary mana type of his Seer attunement. Even worse, heart marks typically cast spells down through both arms, bringing the two mana types close enough to one another that they could combine to disastrous effect. Considering it in gruesome detail made his stomach churn unpleasantly. Sage released his collar and pressed his hand over his chest, as if hiding the mark could change the results of his trial.

"You don't need to look so grim," Daveen said bracingly. "Controller attunements can be used to great effect while climbing or delving. It may not have been your first choice, but once you get used to it, I'm sure you'll come to appreciate it. Can I see your return bell, please?"

Sage was already complying with the request before he hesitated, fingers curling away from the tiny belt purse near his buckle. "Can I ask why?"

"It's standard procedure," Daveen said. His smile was still wide, but his eyes appeared shielded somehow. "Due to the nature of the Controller attunement, I'm required to bring you to the Soaring Wings administration building and make sure you're properly registered. No worries, though, I'll return your bell to you once we've finished."

Sage groaned as he freed the tiny pouch from his belt, passing it over wordlessly. It made sense that administrators would keep a hold of return bells until the registration process was complete, otherwise new Controllers might run away and wreak havoc unchecked. The power to take control of another person's thoughts and actions was a terrifying notion, so it made sense that Controllers were monitored by the Soaring Wings; in fact, Sage had probably read that somewhere long before he ever considered taking a second Judgment in the Caelford spire. He'd just never believed himself to be the type of person who would earn such an attunement. But then, the Seer attunement had been a bit of a surprise, too, so maybe attunement selection was a more random process than he believed it to be. Otherwise, he didn't know himself as well as he thought he did.

Daveen opened the pouch to verify its contents before nodding and holding out an open palm in invitation. "I'll teleport us both to the administration building to save us the walk. If you'd like, I can set up a consultation between you and one of our Sunstone-level Controllers so they can give you some advice on using your new attunement."

"I'll think about it," Sage replied. He wanted to read up on the attunement first before committing to meet with a known Controller; someone who worked for the Soaring Wings was probably safe enough, but he wanted to be certain he could protect himself from being controlled first. The realization struck him as curious as he eyed Daveen's extended hand. "Aren't you worried I might try to coerce you into letting me go, or command you not to tell anyone about me, or something like that?"

"Not in the slightest." Daveen's false smile didn't falter. "Like most of the post-Judgment administrators here, I'm a Sentinel. It would take more than a Quartz-level Controller to break my guard."

For some reason, Sage found that comforting. While he found the idea of intentionally coercing or controlling another person repulsive, the only worse scenario he could think of was doing it by accident. Sentinels were particularly resistant to mind-control spells due to their strong mental fortitude: Sage doubted he could cast a compulsion on Daveen even if he knew the correct spell—which he didn't. He grasped Daveen's hand firmly, offering the administrator a weak smile.

"I should have said this sooner, but thanks for finding me as quickly as you did. And I'm sorry if I came across as rude at all." Sage ducked his head ruefully. "I was just disappointed by the mana types and placement of my new attunement. Like, was it even worth it to get a second one in the first place?"

A tiny furrow appeared between Daveen's dark brows. "What makes you say that? Even if you didn't get the one you wanted, earning two attunements is still a great accomplishment."

"I know. I mean, logically, I know that," Sage hedged, feeling his palm grow sweaty against Daveen's. "It's just that the primary mana type of my Seer attunement is mental, and now with the perception mana from my heart mark . . . I wanted a second attunement that could make me stronger, and now it feels like I'm starting from the beginning again until I learn how to cast spells without blowing my arm off."

"Oh!" Daveen actually looked surprised. "It's not that bad, actually. All you need is a good Biomancer to help keep the pathways from interacting. It'll take a few sessions, and there's still some practice involved, so it'll take some time, but it's not as bad as you're thinking it is."

Sage looked up hopefully. "Really? Instead of setting up a meeting with a Controller, can you set me up with one of the administration's Biomancers?"

"Ha! Sorry to get your hopes up, but rerouting mana pathways doesn't fall under the Soaring Wings' purview." Daveen shrugged apologetically. "But lucky for you, this city's peppered with practiced Biomancers. I can give you a list of some mana pathway specialists. I can't say it'll be cheap, but one session should be enough to allow you to practice with your Controller attunement without it affecting your Seer attunement."

While that was a little disappointing, Sage wasn't terribly afraid of the cost: saving his arm as well as his Citrine-level attunement was worth it. Maybe he could even request additional funds from Dalenos so he wouldn't have to miss any climbs. The government wanted to secure their agreement with the gateway crystal of Sound as soon as possible, after all. Maybe this wasn't as hopeless as he'd thought.

Daveen activated the teleportation spell on a specific key hanging from his belt, keeping a tight hold of Sage's hand. Resigned to his fate, Sage looked up at the spire once more before the spell carried him away.

At least once he finished registering his new attunement, he'd be able to see Nieve, Hane, and Chime again.

NIEVE

Champion (mind mark), Citrine
??? (heart mark), Sealed

The moment Nieve walked through the gateway, she felt as if she'd been struck in the nose by the Magpie's walking stick. Except this time, it was a smell that punched her, rather than a well-dressed Controller.

"Ugh!" Nieve pinched her nose closed, eyes watering as she tried placing her surroundings. "What is that? *Why* is it? Is it something we need to destroy? With fire, preferably?"

By the looks of it, the team had landed in an underground sewer, like the ones beneath the larger cities in Dalenos. This one looked far less maintained, however, with half-crumbled walkways lining the sides of a sludge-filled trench. Cracks in the walls and ceiling leaked foul-colored liquids, fuzzy algae grew outward from suspicious puddles, and somewhere up ahead, Nieve could hear the roar of rushing water. Behind her, where the gateway from the train station would have been, was only a large drainage pipe, blocked by a metal grate. No going back the way they came in, then.

"Why would there be a treasure vault here?" Hane asked. "I was expecting the labyrinth to be ancient ruins, or haunted catacombs. Maybe a castle under siege."

"Let's discuss that in a moment, shall we?" Lief asked, the delicate features of his face pinched in disgust. "I have a spell that can effectively turn off your sense of smell. Who would like me to cast that on them?"

The answer was everyone. On her turn, Lief pressed his fingers to the space between Nieve's eyebrows and when he drew them away, she was finally able to take a deep breath without worrying about losing her last meal. After scrubbing away the tears beneath her eyes, Nieve was able to fully concentrate on her surroundings, noting details she had missed before. The light came from narrow holes in the ceiling, each capped by a thick grate and too small to climb up through besides—well, maybe Hane could do it, but no one else on the team could. Symbols had been painted on sections of the wall up ahead, strange light patterns danced on the ceiling of an intersecting tunnel up ahead, and small objects floating in the sewage sometimes bobbed and scraped along the bottom of the trench, though looking at the sludge too long made Nieve's stomach churn, even though she could no longer smell it.

"Thank you," Odette breathed as Lief finished casting his spell on her. She inhaled deeply, then, inexplicably, sat down on the stone walkway, pressing her palms flat against the floor. "Okay, give me a minute to map this place. I can pinpoint the entrance to the labyrinth and find the best route to it. Watch out for monsters, okay? This might take a minute."

"I'm glad we didn't encounter anything right away," Mason commented, his arms tucked in close against his body. He seemed to be shying away from both the wall and the channel of sludge at the same time. Nieve almost laughed: served him right for not wearing a shirt under his dueling vest. "I can only imagine the types of creatures that live here."

"I'd like to return to Hane's earlier question about the vault," Lief requested, fastidiously adjusting the fit of his gloves as if he feared to touch a single surface in this dank underground setting. "Are we certain we're in the right place? The floors didn't change while we were on the train, did they?"

"Odie will tell us all of that in a minute," Rose assured him, moving ahead of the group in order to squint at something in the shadows. "I think I have a guess, though. Did anyone find anything in their pockets? Like a mission brief, or anything explaining why we might be here?"

As Nieve checked her pockets and pouches, she also checked on Chime with a roll of her ankle, comforted by the familiar scrape of the crystal shard hidden there. As the shuffling and rifling of pockets, pouches and bags ended, the answer to Rose's question seemed to be a resounding no. She only nodded grimly before drawing a hunk of quartz out of a vest pocket, holding it up as it began to glow.

"We'll probably run into a guide, or someone who can tell us what's going on, then," Rose surmised, the glowing quartz in her hand clearing shadows like old cobwebs. "But that's a symbol I recognize well enough to draw at least one conclusion from."

Nieve started forward, her shoulder jostling against Mason's. She expected him to respond with some playful shoving, and maybe a joke about going for a swim, but instead he dropped back to walk single file behind her. This time,

Nieve couldn't hold back a snort: for the first time since the climb started, she had no trouble picturing Mason as a young noble of a high house. Lief trailed behind, remaining halfway between Odette and the rest of the team while Hane cautiously held one foot out over the sewage, hesitating slightly before stepping out over the sludge. Interestingly enough, the grime seemed to clear around the soles of their boots, as if they were calling pure water together so as not to stand in actual sewage.

Rose's light illuminated a painted image on the far wall across the trench, stretching from the floor to the ceiling. Nieve recognized it as a tall, cylindrical hat, one she had only ever seen in history books depicting Valian nobles. It had a name, something like "tall-hat," but she didn't think that was exactly right. The painting on the wall looked unfinished: one corner of the hat was carved away like a bite had been taken out of it.

"I don't know what this represents," Hane admitted, walking across the sewage to the far walkway. "At a guess, I would say it marks the territory of a lawless entity. Bandits, perhaps? Or maybe a ring of assassins?"

"Worse," Rose said grimly. "That's the symbol of one of the biggest drug rings on Kaldwyn: the Ash Hats."

Ash was a powdered drug known to enhance the user's senses, like sight, sound, and smell. At certain concentrations (or blends, Nieve wasn't really sure) it was said to help people push beyond safe mana limits, too, but using it came with serious side effects, such as addiction, dizzy spells, extreme fatigue, and even death. More importantly, its use was banned from legal dueling competitions, so Nieve had never so much as considered taking it. She'd heard the stories though, of climbers seeking an edge to help them inside the spires ending up as little more than husks begging at the edges of dirty alleys—if they didn't die first.

So it came as a shock when someone snickered out loud.

Even more shocking was the fact that it was Hane. As everyone turned to stare at them, Hane clamped a hand over their mouth and visibly tried to contain themself. Even with no sound escaping, Hane's shoulders continued to shake with barely controlled mirth.

"It is a terrible name," Rose agreed, seemingly amused by Hane's fit of humor. "I think it was meant to be comparable to the symbol used by the notorious Wax Lords, the undisputed kingpins of wax manufacture and distribution. Their symbol is a golden crown half-melted into a puddle, making it easy to see the influence behind the dissolving top hat, but calling themselves the Ash Hats really does undercut the symbolism."

Hane clamped a second hand over their mouth, tiny snorts and giggles escaping despite their best efforts. It seemed the situation was only getting worse the more they tried to contain it, like laughter might explode out of them if they didn't release it soon.

"Do you need to take a moment?" Lief asked pointedly. "The name might be stupid, but ash users can be extremely dangerous in a fight."

Hane nodded, spinning as precisely as any ice dancer before gliding along the surface of the sewage, tucking themself into a shadowy corner before laughter echoed off the stone walls and iron pipes. Every time it started to die down, it started up again, surprisingly gleeful considering its source.

"Huh." Nieve shrugged as Rose looked to her for an explanation. "I guess bad puns really put the sugar in their tea. I didn't know they could laugh like that."

Rose's lips curved into a smile, warm eyes sparkling in the light from her quartz. "It's nice to know they can laugh. Everyone should have a soft side."

Was . . . was Rose flirting with her? Nieve felt her heart trip and stumble hard into her breastbone. She tried to play it cool with a confident smirk, but Rose's bronzed curls were so distracting and so *close*. "Yeah? So where's your soft side, then?"

"Oh, Nee-eh-vay." Rose reached up and patted Nieve's cheek before sidling past her. "You haven't seen my hard side yet."

Her curls bounced as she tossed her head, striding back up the walkway to where Odette concentrated on her Analyst spell. Nieve's throat felt dry as she watched her go, wishing that bulky canvas vest didn't hide so much of her figure. When she finally tore her gaze away, she found Mason watching her with laughing eyes.

"You don't know what you're getting into with her," Mason commented, tipping his head toward his sister. "I bet you two of my shares that all she's after is someone new to lecture."

"Then I guess it's a good thing that I have a lot of practice at pretending to listen," Nieve retorted, her blood still hot beneath her skin. The little thrill subsided soon enough, especially as Odette sat back on her heels, surfacing from a near trancelike state.

"I have the shape of it, if you all want to come in close," Odette called, her glasses low on her nose. "Good news: we're on the eighteenth floor, in the right place, and the vault is still here. The hard part is going to be getting to it without getting caught up in a fight between rival drug gangs."

Hane slunk out of the shadows to join the gathering around Odette, their mask still hiding the lower portion of their face, though their eyes still seemed to be smiling. Rose had resumed her usual stern, focused expression as she awaited more details about the challenge. That was a shame, but Nieve could wait. Spires weren't the best places for getting cozy anyway.

"So, it's not great, but it's not terrible, either. Take a look." Odette exhaled slowly, holding her hands shoulder-width apart with palms facing each other. Her knotted cord of rings dangled from one hand, where she wore the glowing metal band around her middle finger. "Display Area Map, distal view."

Just as on the train, a smoky image took shape between Odette's hands, though this time, Nieve didn't recognize the image as a map. Instead, it looked more like a depiction of a critter's underground burrow. Even when Odette used a small blue light to pinpoint their location, Nieve couldn't recognize the features of the sewer in the hazy map.

"Right now, we're on the first subterranean level, all the way at the top," Odette explained, gesturing with her chin as her hands encompassed the spell. "From what I can gather about this scenario, there's a war going on between several minor gangs and the Ash Hats."

Hane snorted loudly before clapping a hand over their mouth. Nieve chuckled to herself, taking amusement from Hane's odd sense of humor.

"I think the main objective for this setting is to ruin the drug operation going on here. Either that, or end the gang war somehow. Either way, that's not what we're here to do." A chamber near the bottom of the misty map flashed golden, indicating a secret. "My map of the labyrinth isn't reliable from here, but our target is somewhere around there. That's where we'll find the entrance to the Vault of Shadows."

"Are you familiar with this scenario for the labyrinth?" Lief asked her, something like concern in the lines of his forehead. "I'm curious why there's a vault in a sewer at all."

"Yeah, and why is this sewer system so deep?" Mason followed up, eyeing the map warily. "This doesn't look at all like the sewage system under Caelford."

"I'm curious how you know what the sewer in Caelford looks like," Lief commented lightly.

Mason rolled his eyes, apparently not in the mood for teasing. "Our sewers are more like stone tunnels that run underground; most aren't big enough for a person to fit inside. When it rains, they get backed up and as a Transmuter, sometimes I get asked to help clear them out." His nose wrinkled, despite his inability to smell. "That's not nearly as foul as this."

"In some ways, I actually prefer this to the crypt," Odette said. "The smell was just as bad, but the atmosphere was at least twice as creepy. Mason, I believe this setting is based on ancient designs of sewers, the kind that had to keep getting bigger in order to keep up with the growth of a city's population. And yes, I have read reports about the labyrinth appearing as a sewer, with a drug war as the narrative. The missions change, but essentially the directive can be anything from rescuing a law informant from the Ash Hats' headquarters, depleting the forces of both factions, or destroying the ash operation so the drugs can't be distributed. Most of those missions play out within the first three levels of the sewer, which are mostly straightforward to navigate, with a few exceptions." The top three layers of the map pulsed with a green light before it faded out. "These middle layers are where navigating gets tricky. The labyrinth changes continually and it's largely resistant to mapping spells. There should be hidden treasures, at least one big guardian monster, and a mana fountain, if we can find it. The vault"—the chamber near the bottom of the map flashed gold again—"would normally be the stash kept by the Ash Hats' leader. Presumably, drug dealers will accept payment in the form of valuable art, family heirlooms, or notable weaponry in exchange for a supply of ash. Items that are too hot to be resold are stored in the vault until it's safe to move them. But that's not what we're after, so that's not the vault we'll see when it's opened." Odette's expression grew pinched, her teeth biting deep into her lower lip. "At least, I hope not."

"Are you finally going to tell us how to open it?" Rose asked, tracing a path through the smoky map with a finger. "We're here now, we might as well all know the secret in case something happens to you."

At first, it looked as though Odette was going to refuse. Her lips puckered, her jaw clenched, her fingers twitched as if to curl into fists. A breath later, she shook her head, seemingly coming to terms that it was time to share the secret.

"We need to find two secrets hidden within the labyrinth." A murky brown haze enveloped the twisted mass of tunnels and passages from the fourth floor down to the golden room near the bottom. "One should be a very specific key to open the vault—not a normal key or even a golden key, but something unique to the door of the vault. I don't know what it will look like, but the most likely place to find it is in the lair of the labyrinth guardian."

Nieve grinned as she cracked her knuckles. "That sounds like a good chance to let off some pent-up aggression, eh, Hane?"

"I'll leave it to you." Hane sounded uncharacteristically easygoing, as if the laughter had loosened them up. "I don't have any aggression to vent just now."

Nieve resisted the urge to pull Hane into a headlock and pal around; she knew Hane wouldn't appreciate it, and it would only spoil their mood. She did flash a grin at them, though; it seemed they were both looking forward to the challenges ahead.

"What's the second thing?" Lief asked when Odette fell silent.

She released a sigh, eyes hidden by a reflection on her glasses. "It's hard to describe, but we need to find something like a hint or a clue in order to unlock the Vault of Shadows. The door will have multiple locks on it, and if we choose the wrong one, we lose our opportunity to open it unless we start over from the beginning—and by that, I mean, leaving and coming back. The clue should help us determine which lock opens the Vault of Shadows."

"What does the clue look like?" Rose asked, curious.

The furrow between Odette's eyebrows deepened. "I can't say for sure. It could be something in the environment, or it could be a phrase someone says to us, or a pattern based on the labyrinth itself . . ." She shrugged helplessly. "It's different in every scenario, and it could be anywhere. We just have to keep our eyes open as we go along."

"Will we know it when we see it?" Lief asked. "Should it be obvious, or can it be detected by a spell?"

"The last time I was here, I searched for it using my Detect Secrets spell after I found the vault," Odette explained. "Even after seeing the depiction on the vault door, I still couldn't detect it within the labyrinth. I think we're meant to search for it ourselves instead of using spells to find it."

Nieve glanced down at the embroidered band tied around her arm. Odette had described the pattern as a code, but no matter how she looked at it, it was just some pretty shapes and colors. If the hint for opening the Vault of Shadows was anything like the code on the bracelet, there was no way Nieve was going to recognize it.

"Will the clue have an aura?" Hane asked. "How will we know if we've found it, and not just something that seems like it might be a clue?"

Odette hummed thoughtfully for a moment. "I'm not sure about an aura, but I guess I don't think it's likely. The image on the vault door might help us narrow it down, though. In fact, one strategy might be to find the vault first and then search the labyrinth for the clue."

"Ugh!" Mason jumped suddenly, swiping something off his dueling vest, a look of pure disgust on his face. It looked as if something had dripped on him from the ceiling. "Odie, please tell me you have some trick or secret or anything to speed this up, because I am not spending a whole day down here."

"Day?" Odette, Rose, and Lief all asked the same question, expressions ranging from confusion to disbelief to amusement.

"The labyrinth will take much longer than a day, my friend," Lief said, patting Mason's shoulder as if consoling him. "And that's when you're not searching for hidden codes and secret keys before getting to the vault."

"I was here almost a week last time," Rose recalled, glaring pointedly at the river of sludge. "At least it smelled better then."

Mason glowered at his sister as if she'd kept this information hidden from him. She pretended not to notice as she cleaned the lenses of her goggles with a handkerchief.

"Okay, so . . ." Odette trailed off, as if expecting someone else to take over. When no one did, she sighed and continued. "A plan. Right. Um, let's go . . ." Her eyes narrowed slightly. A red line appeared within her smoky image, marking a trail from where they stood now and descending deeper into the sewers. It ended right at the beginning of the tangled, writhing lines of the labyrinth. "This way. If we follow this path, we should avoid any spaces large enough to house a gang, although we could still run into patrols. Let's get to the labyrinth as quickly as possible, then we can look for a safe place to set up camp before we go looking for our other objectives."

"Safe areas?" Nieve repeated. "Does that mean there are places where monsters can't go? Like mana fountains?"

"Finding a mana fountain would be ideal," Odette admitted. "They're really hard to find, though. On this floor, there are generally two types of safe areas: static zones and push zones. A static safe area means we can rest there as long as we need to. We can even set up a campsite at one as long as we can find our way back to it. Push zones are only temporary safe zones: if we rest for too long, the labyrinth will, um . . . encourage us to move along."

"Ah yes, I remember those push zones so fondly." Lief's grimace belied his dreamy tone. "If it isn't a monster that gets you running, it's an environmental hazard, like fire, or falling rocks." He cast a dismal look down at the bubbling sludge. "Let's hope for monsters, everyone."

Mason shuddered violently, making a sound almost like a retch.

"What's the rule for getting lost?" Rose asked. "Stay put, or go looking?"

"Stay put," Odette said firmly. "If you get separated or lost, find a safe place and wait. I can find anyone wearing one of my bracelets. If I get lost, I can find my way back to the rest of you by tracking your bracelets. The labyrinth won't stay the same after we enter it, so moving around after you're already lost is just going to make it harder to find you."

"What about treasure?" Hane asked, surprising Nieve. They weren't really here to collect treasure, they were here to find Chime's missing piece. "Are we just supposed to ignore it as we search through the labyrinth?"

"Mm . . . I'm not sure." Odette grimaced. "Probably not? I mean, I don't think it's smart to waste time carrying around a lot of bulky treasure, but at the same time, I don't want to miss anything really good. Maybe we could just . . . check the treasure we find? There's always a small chance that the vault's secret key might be somewhere else, instead of in the guardian's lair. I think it's best if we don't get greedy until we reach the vault."

Hane gave a one-shouldered shrug. "Works for me. Is there anything else?"

"No, I think that's—wait!" Odette's sudden shout made Nieve jump. She cut a glare back at the Analyst, but Odette had her eyes closed as she drew in a deep breath. "Detect Traps." The colors on the misty map faded out, leaving it all a hazy gray. Slowly, blushes of red began to bloom within the mist: most on the floor, some on the ceiling, others in the walls, and more than a few beneath the channel of sludge down the center of the tunnels. "I forgot to mention the traps. I'll mark the ones my spell reveals, but everyone needs to remain alert. There's always a few that are protected by anti-detection runes."

"The space around us looks clear," Nieve pointed out. "Nothing until we reach that intersection up ahead."

"Wait." Hane cocked their head. "Do you hear something?"

Every shuffle and rustle made by her teammates fell still and silent, breath held in anticipation. At first, Nieve heard nothing, but then, very distant and dim, she heard it carried along the river of sewage: voices. More than two, at least.

Nieve grinned. "Looks like it's time to fight, partner."

Hane chuckled behind their mask. "I'll be sure to stay out of your way."

"Ha! See that you do." Nieve set her hand on the hilt of her sword, then, with a look at the narrow walkway, the close walls, and the burbling sewage, she thought better of it and tugged her war hammer free of her belt. Twirling it once and catching it, Nieve looked back at the others, teeth bared in a vicious grin. "Let's go."

HANE

Wavewalker (leg mark), Citrine

"Hold on just a moment!" Odette caught the back of Nieve's tunic, her knotted cord of rings following the motions of her hand. "I need to take my ring off the cord so I can use it to mark traps."

Nieve looked back over her shoulder, flicking her eyes down at Odette's hand before glaring levelly at her. "If you mark the trap, won't the bad guys see it?"

"Well, um, yes, but . . ." Odette trailed off meekly, working quickly to untie the ring from its knot. Once she had it fitted on her finger, she wound the rest of the cord around her belt once more.

If Hane remembered correctly from Odette's map, the trap was on the opposite walkway, across the channel of sewage. Possibly a pit trap based on its location, but they couldn't know that for certain. There was another trap on the ceiling, but it was in the opposite direction from where they were headed, which was to the right of the sewer's first intersection. They weren't likely to trigger it, but it was good to keep it in mind anyway, just in case.

While the others all crowded around each other along the walkway, Hane walked comfortably in the center of the tunnel. Most of the sewage was water, after all, and they preferred the freedom of movement to crowding along behind Nieve. As much as they would rather avoid getting wet here, they had already resigned themself to the fact that any fight taking place here was more than likely going to cause a mess. At least they didn't have to smell it, thanks to Lief.

Lief . . . they still weren't sure how they felt about him. On the one hand, he was competent, experienced, and an excellent healer—all great qualities in a team member. But he was also uncompromising and dismissive, with something cold and calculating hidden behind his bright smiles. That didn't necessarily make Lief untrustworthy—plenty of climbers had personal agendas. Hane was guilty of that themself, as their only purpose for being here was to find Chime's missing piece. But there was just something that seemed . . . off about Lief. Something that made Hane want to keep an eye on him.

He's wearing his sword again, Hane realized, watching Lief from the corner of his eye. *I haven't seen him wear it since the first day on the train.*

While Nieve never went anywhere without her sword, it hadn't been the most practical weapon for a train, nor was it particularly useful here, unless she decided to freeze the channel of sewage. Even then, the ceiling was low enough to restrict a normal sword's reach, never mind one of Nieve's ice-sword extensions. It made complete sense for Lief to use his bow over his sword.

Nieve and Odette settled their argument over whether to attack first or mark the trap first by counting down to start at the same time. Hane drifted into position, sinking low into their knees as they drifted close to the middle of the intersection. There was a possibility they might be seen, but the shadows here were deep and most people tended to avoid looking directly at the sewage anyway. Up ahead, they could just make out about five or six individuals coming closer to the intersection where the team hid just around the corner. While the details were difficult to make out over the distance, their opponents all appeared to be humans, each carrying weapons of the blunt-instrument variety—possibly pipes or pry bars, or even tonfa like Hane's. They each wore formal-looking hats, too, which seemed wildly out of place in a sewer.

Nieve's fingers, held behind her back, counted down the attack: three, two, one. She strode out into the open, putting her back to Hane as she held the war hammer out at her side, flourishing it with a roll of her wrist. The voices of the gang members fell silent just as Odette pressed her hands out from her chest, exhaling a spell.

"Reveal Secrets," she breathed before swiftly turning to put her back against the wall. A stretch of floor on the opposite walkway flared an alarming shade of red, illuminating the boundaries of the trap. A quick glance back proved it not only outlined a trap on the ceiling, but at least one more trap on the side of the wall. Or maybe that was a secret alcove containing hidden treasure? It looked small to be a trap.

Whatever it was, Hane didn't have time to consider it further. By the ring of metal on stone, the bad guys were preparing for a fight. Mason sidled around Odette, standing just behind Nieve with one of his stone rods in hand. Odette, Rose, and Lief stayed behind the wall, safe but blind to the action.

Hane glided along the surface of the water—yes, they were determined to think of it as nothing more than water, because that made it easier to accept the possibility of being drenched—in order to flank Nieve. They hung back a little, though: they meant it when they said they intended to stay out of her way.

"You got two options," Nieve called out, her voice echoing ominously along the stone walls of the sewer. "You either toss those weapons into the canal right now, or I hold each and every one of you underwater until you let them go. Your choice."

"Hane!" Mason hissed, beckoning sharply. "Hane!"

Hane measured the situation first, counting five ill-prepared opponents carrying weapons of opportunity and wearing clothes more patched and ragged than any climber's favorite cloak. Nieve had held her ground against a general of a god beast—she could more than handle herself here. A light push of transference carried Hane closer to the others without leaving a ripple on the water.

"Hey." Sweat dripped down Mason's face. He wet his lips anxiously as he peeked around Nieve at the ragged pack of gang members. "You know I come from money, right? Like, my family is loaded and I do pretty well myself. So it's fair to say I can afford to pay you for protection."

"Protection?" Hane frowned. "You're worried about them? Didn't you fight the Magpie on the train?"

"Nah, I don't mean that kind of protection." Mason shook his head, eyes betraying him as he glanced down at the water and swallowed tightly. "But you have water shaping spells, don't you? Like, powerful ones?"

Hane gave him a deadpan glare, holding their silence.

"I-I mean—"

Rose elbowed him in the side sharply, rolling her eyes. "Get over it, Brick, by the time this is over, we'll all—"

A sound that wasn't a sound pressed against Hane's senses, alerting them seconds before a thrum of power made the water shiver. At the exact same moment, Nieve started forward along the walkway, headed toward the taunts and jeers of the ragged-looking gang members. Before Hane could call after her, the floor yawned beneath her feet, opening in a perfect circle of darkness that overlapped the sewage as well as the wall. They heard only a gasp as she began to fall, arms reaching out for something to hold onto.

Hane dove after her, heedless of the spray of water sent up by their unplanned push of transference. They fell flat over the walkway, reaching for Nieve's outstretched hand. Fingers brushed, but didn't catch. No matter, they had saved people from these traps before; now would be no different.

"Reverse Gravity," Hane called, pointing at Nieve as she fell. The shaping spell was meant to cause an object to change direction, meaning a falling person should then fall up. Unfortunately, this time it didn't work.

Not only that, but the hole was pinching closed.

"Move!" Mason ordered, dropping down beside Hane. The stone rod in his hand grew thin and long, stretching out toward Nieve. She reached for it as she fell, but the distal end crumbled and turned to sand before it reached her. "I can reinforce it, let me try again!"

"You need to shape the hole!" Hane shouted, already scrambling to jump after Nieve. If they jumped after her and caught her, they could reverse gravity directly—but only if the hole was still big enough for the both of them to fit through.

"I can't, it's not—" Mason pushed himself up onto his hands and knees, looking bewildered. "This isn't stone."

"What do you mean it's not—"

The sharp snap of a bowstring over Hane's head triggered an instinct to duck and cover. When they looked up, they found Lief standing between themself and Mason, a fresh arrow already set to the string.

"I hate to say this as a healer," Lief said grimly, loosing his second arrow. "But it's too late for her. We have to worry about ourselves now."

"No, it can't . . ." Odette stood just behind Lief, eyes wide as she watched the hole shrink. She cupped her hands to her mouth and dropped to her knees. "No, she couldn't—she can't—I didn't—"

The hole was no larger than a fist now, and Nieve had long since dropped out of sight. They would have to deal with that later, but right now, Lief was right: they had other things to worry about. Hane leapt to their feet, using a Burst spell to knock back a thrown pry bar.

"Mason, make a shield to protect the others," Hane ordered. "Lief, I'll need cover. Odette, if there are any other traps your spell didn't reveal—"

Odette screamed, the cry long and bloodcurdling, echoing endlessly down each intersecting tunnel before bouncing back at them, louder and more heartrending than the original. Her head bowed forward, then her hands were in her hair, yanking hard. Rose, ashen with fright, gripped Odette's wrists to keep her from injuring herself.

Hane turned away; there was nothing they could do for her right now.

Just as there had been nothing they could do for Nieve.

A familiar chill curled around Hane, sinking beneath their skin, numbing them from the outside in. They'd lost team members on climbs before; this wasn't any different. The only thing to do now was to survive.

Transference mana coiled beneath the soles of their feet propelled them forward so quickly that they stood within the circle of clumsily armed gang members within the space of a blink. One of them was so surprised by their sudden appearance that she dropped the lead pipe she'd been holding and backpedaled rapidly. Hane let her go as they ducked beneath the swipe of a baton, kicking the lead pipe into the trench before leaping up and sending a Burst spell out through their body in all directions. Metal clanged, stone crumbled, a splash swallowed a scream. Hane landed in a half crouch, assessing the damage around them.

Their Burst spell dented the stone wall to their right, one gang member fully collapsed, another fighting to stay on his feet. Two had landed in the water, which was sad for them: moving water was the first spell any good Wavewalker ever learned.

"Swift Current," Hane ordered, one foot resting on the water in the trench. A rushing roar, a burbled scream, and then the sewage was racing past the walkway, as if coursing for a distant waterfall. Coldly, they turned to face the gang member standing in front of the crater in the wall.

"The boss'll get you," the youth warned, hands shaking where he gripped the base of a weighted baton. "He'll send a squad to hunt you down! A real squad, with officers!" He gulped nervously, feet shuffling into something approximating a balanced stance. He held the baton as if he meant to swing it from the shoulder, rather than strike from the wrist. "Just you wait! The Ash Hats are coming for you!"

Hane faced down the youth with a silent stare, daring him to make the first move. The youth licked his lips nervously, then telegraphed his next move, sliding one foot forward as he shifted his weight. Hane watched the heavy swing come at them, waiting for the momentum to reach its peak velocity before catching the baton against their fingertips and sharply reversing the momentum. The youth's swing bounced back, throwing him against the half-crumbled wall again.

Grit crunched beneath Hane's feet as they stepped forward to lean down over the dazed youth. The baton had slipped from his fingers, clattering to the floor. Hane didn't even lift a finger to redirect its momentum, but silently sent a controlled Burst out from their heel, rolling the baton into the trench. The youth shuddered as he stared up at Hane.

Hane said softly, "Let them come."

The youth's eyes slowly widened with fear. He scrambled, attempting to get to his feet, but Hane used the momentum against him by grabbing the front of his shirt and tossing him into the still rushing water. A scream rang out as he was carried swiftly away. The gang member who had fled was no longer in sight, but before Hane went after her, they had to know if the gang member on the ground was passed out, dead, or faking. As they rolled the limp body over, they noted a broken arrow shaft transfixed through his shoulder. Clearly Lief had gotten this one before Hane did.

Footsteps on the walkway made Hane tense. They didn't relax even when they recognized it was only Lief.

A low, soft whistle. "That was a little dark for you, considering how hard you fought to save those snakes."

"I like snakes more than people." Hane gestured to the broken arrow. "Were you intentionally aiming for a nonlethal shot?"

Lief crouched down, holding a hand out over the unconscious youth. "I wasn't sure if we wanted them alive or not. If it makes you happy, I'll aim to kill next time. He's alive, but concussed. He won't be getting up anytime soon." Hane could feel Lief studying them as he sat back on his heels. "Are you going to throw this one into the sewer, too?"

Hane cut a glare at him before straightening up and looking in the direction of the runaway. "As long as he stays down, we can leave him. We need to get away from here before the other one returns with reinforcements."

"That's pretty cold for someone who just lost their teammate," Lief commented breezily, his face blank but his eyes sharp. "Or is that why you dispatched those foot soldiers so ruthlessly? Part of your grieving process, perhaps?"

The cold sank in even deeper, rooting like veins of ice deep inside the core of their being. They could probably catch up with the runaway even now, but that would mean leaving the others without a combat expert. The decision made, Hane turned on their heel and walked back to where Mason and the others waited.

"I tried," Mason said, emotion twisting the features of his face. "I tried to get her, I just don't know why the stone became so brittle."

Hane motioned for Mason to step aside. Odette was still collapsed just behind him, sobbing into her hands with Rose curled around her, patting her shoulder and speaking softly, but her eyes were still wide with horror, tracking up slowly to meet Hane's.

"It happened so fast." Rose shook her head in disbelief. "I didn't even realize she—it just . . . happened!"

Hane knelt down in front of Odette and took hold of her wrists, carefully but firmly peeling them away from her face. She hiccuped and gasped, her entire body wracked with sobs. If she tried to speak, none of it was in a language Hane could understand.

"Look for her," Hane instructed, keeping their tone low and level. In their experience, sometimes people could still function through shock if orders were kept simple. "That wasn't a normal trap. She could have been teleported somewhere else on this floor. You can locate her if she's here, can't you?"

Odette blubbered something before swiping her nose on her wrist. Rose thrust a handkerchief into her hand, nodding encouragingly. Hane focused on the coldness within them as they waited through Odette's sniffles and false starts.

"Y-you're right," she managed eventually, her hands still shaking violently. "That—that wasn't normal. Maybe . . . j-just maybe . . ."

Odette drew a deep, shuddering breath as she shrugged her satchel off her shoulder. When she failed to undo the knot holding it closed, Hane untied it for her. They found the enchanted locator device easily enough and pressed it into Odette's shaking hands. It took a few deep breaths, but eventually she managed to hit the right sequence of runes along the bottom before selecting the section of the grid containing Nieve's location tracker.

An arrow appeared on the glass above the square, and for the space of a single heartbeat, Hane dared to hope. But instead of pointing out a path, the arrow spun in a circle, never settling on one specific direction. After a moment or two, the arrow flashed three times, then faded entirely.

"What does that mean?" Rose asked, looking from the device to Odette. "Odie, what does that mean?"

"It's—it's—" Odette shuddered, the device shaking as hard as her hands were. Hane didn't need to interpret the desperate sob that followed to know what the disappearing arrow meant.

"But she could be on another floor, right?" Rose pressed, her voice rising incrementally. "She could be, couldn't she? And I don't just mean here, in the labyrinth, but she could have been teleported to another floor entirely. Or outside the spire. Right? Right, Odie? Right!"

"I—I—" Odette's hands shook so hard that she nearly dropped the device. After watching her fumble in trying to put it away, Rose snatched it from her grip and thrust it back inside of Odette's satchel. With a deep breath, Rose held Odette by the shoulders and locked gazes with her.

"Use your mapping spell," Rose ordered, tone tightly controlled. "You can do it, Odie. You can find her. Don't think, just do it."

Odette snuffled wetly, swiping at her cheeks before pressing her palms to the floor. She attempted the spell a few times, stumbling over the words before giving up and saying it in Caelish. The misty map of the sewers appeared between her hands again, but this time no parts of the map glowed gold or red, nor any other color. Hane focused inwardly on the cold seeping through their bones into the marrow within.

The misty map changed into stacked boxes, like the layers of a cake. It took Hane several minutes to realize they were looking at a cutaway portion of the spire, but only three floors at a time. Odette's brows pinched tighter and tighter, her breathing shallow and rapid as she searched the floors below, then the floors above. One final gasping sob and the image collapsed just as Odette did, sobbing and stuttering into her hands once more.

"What is she saying?" Hane asked Rose.

"She—she's saying . . ." Rose turned away and sniffled before firming her jaw and turning back. "She can't locate the pattern of the bracelet. But that's okay, because everyone knows that the accuracy of detection spells varies with distance. Nieve could still be okay. No—she *is* okay, I'm sure she is."

"Is there any way to search outside the spire?" Lief asked. "An experienced climber like Nieve would certainly know when it was time to use her return bell."

Rose listened as Odette gasped and sobbed, nodding as if the sounds were intelligible. "Odie says her spell doesn't work that way, but you're probably right: I'm sure Nieve is safe on the outside right now."

Yes. That sounded logical. Like something Hane should have thought of first. Except for a niggling voice in the back of their mind reminding them how their transference spell hadn't worked, and how Mason—so repulsed by the sewer water that he had attempted to bribe Hane into shaping the water away from him—had dove after her only to have his stone rod fall to pieces before Nieve could grab it. And why was the trap so strange in the first place? Not only had Odette's detection spell failed to mark it, but it had acted more like a portal than a pit trap. Would a return bell even work in a space like that?

Hane stood up, looking back the way the surviving gangster had run off in. "We can't stay here. We need to keep moving."

"No no no no no." Odette's words, while intelligible, were not promising. "Can't, we can't—" Her speech dissolved, sometimes into Caelish and other times into Valian, Artinian, and maybe even Cas, Hane wasn't sure.

"She says . . ." Rose craned down to listen, still patting Odette's back comfortingly. "I don't know all the languages, but it sounds like we can only continue . . . by boat?"

"I think it was 'without,'" Lief suggested. He stepped past Hane and knelt down in front of Odette, placing his hand on her bowed head. "Try to breathe. You'll pass out if you continue like this."

Odette made an attempt to suck in a deep breath, but then she coughed and sobbed and continued babbling in various languages. Rose indicated her surrender with a helpless shrug, but Lief nodded along as if he were following.

"She's saying we should give up," Lief announced to the group. "She doesn't think we can continue without Nieve." He grimaced as he hitched his bow a little higher on his shoulder. "I don't understand her reasoning, but I'm okay with continuing. Unless . . . Hane, can you continue? Or is this the end for you?"

Hane didn't turn back to face them. The most likely source of danger would come from the direction the runaway had gone. They couldn't let their guard down, not when they were the only real warrior in the group. As tragic as it was, this wasn't an uncommon occurrence for them: making the judgment call to continue after a teammate had fallen. Based on the brief scuffle earlier, logic dictated that the team continue until they encountered something too dangerous to attempt with only five people and collect as much treasure as they could along the way. But the uncertainty over Nieve's sudden disappearance scratched at Hane's numbed nerves insistently, demanding to be acknowledged. Lief was giving them an out; they could choose to leave right now and verify if Nieve was all right, but . . .

The others didn't know.

Nieve hadn't fallen alone.

She'd taken Chime with her.

For this climb to be worth anything at all, Hane had to find Chime's missing piece in that vault at all costs. If Nieve truly was gone—and hopefully she wasn't, but *if*—then at the very least, Hane had to retrieve the one teammate they could still save.

"We continue," Hane decided, still facing ahead. "I'm not as strong as Nieve, but I can keep you safe. All of you. So let's keep going."

A low, soft whistle, most likely from Lief. "Look at that, we agree on something. What about you two? Rose? Mason?"

A moment of silent sibling communication, then Mason was shaking his head. "I don't think it's—"

"We should keep going," Rose said firmly. She sniffled, but she swiped at her eyes impatiently. "I'm sure Nieve is fine. It's terrible that she's not here now, but she's strong, and she's competent, and she's *fine,* which is all the more reason for us to keep going. We'll just grab some extra treasure for her when we get to the vault, that's all there is to it."

"She isn't fine, Rose, she's gone!" Mason argued. "You didn't see it. How the hole opened up, and how the stone crumbled. How do we know that—"

Someone hissed sharply and Mason fell silent. Hane refused to look back.

"Anyone who doesn't want to stay doesn't have to," Hane stated. "But I plan to continue. Odette, if there's anything you've held back about the vault, you need to tell me before you leave."

In the blank space that followed, only the sounds of Odette's hiccuping sobs and the rush of the water broke the silence. Hane held their patience close, waiting for the others to come to their own decisions.

"If my sister's staying, then I'm staying," Mason grumbled reluctantly. "Goddess knows she'll cut me out of the loot-split if I leave now."

"You bet your baked-ham head that I will," Rose retorted. Her tone changed to a softer, gentler tone when she spoke to Odette. "What's it going to be, Odie? Want me to step away so you can ring out?"

"I—" Hiccup. Gasp. Cough, cough. Sniffle. "I just—I think—"

As she broke down into single syllable sobs, Lief frowned and shook his head.

"She's having a panic attack," Lief explained. "She doesn't have the capacity for rational thought or choice right now."

"Can you fix her?" Hane asked.

"I can treat the symptoms, but that really only drags the attack out longer." Lief didn't sound pleased by his own diagnosis. "She has to work through the attack herself, and that can take time."

"We don't have time," Hane replied. "The one who ran away will return with reinforcements. Stronger ones this time. It doesn't matter whether she chooses to stay or to go, she just has to choose."

"We can't send her back," Rose protested. "She's the only one who really knows how to open the vault."

"She's also the only one who can create maps and mark secrets," Mason pointed out.

"Well, she's not going to be doing any of that in the state she's in," Lief reminded them. "For her own safety as well as ours, it might be in our best interest to send her out of the spire."

"No." If Hane weren't so numb, they suspected they'd feel the beginnings of a headache. Odette's maps and trap-marking made navigating a labyrinth easier, but they weren't entirely necessary. The greater concern was that she was holding onto some final secret for opening the vault, and that would make this entire delve—and the loss of Nieve and Chime—pointless. "I'm not comfortable deciding for her. Let's find a defensible position and wait for her to recover."

"I'm sorry," Lief started, his tone arched and distinctly noble-sounding. "But it sounds like you're saying we need to walk through trap-infested sewers filled with armed drug dealers while defending a teammate who can't contribute to the team's survival when we're already down one teammate?"

"Yes." Hane cast the barest glance back over their shoulder. "I'll take point and scout traps and mobs. Mason, craft a shield and stay in front of the others. If I need you, I'll shout. Lief, you get Odette on her feet and keep her moving. Rose, take rear guard. Use the communication device if you need me to double back in a hurry. We'll follow the path down to the beginning of the labyrinth, but we'll look for an easily defensible position along the way so Odette can recover."

Rose and Mason exchanged a look, communicating silently with one another. At almost the same moment, Rose shrugged and Mason sighed, shoulders slumping in defeat.

"I can set my goggles to alert me of movement approaching from behind," Rose said, already adjusting the dials on the sides of her goggle lenses. "I renewed the imbues on my throwing knives back on the train, so I can hold my own for a little while."

Resigned, Mason drew a long stone rod from his quiver, only to be stopped by a motion from Lief.

"For lack of a better plan, I'll agree with you for now," Lief informed Hane. "But I have a slight change to make: have Mason carry Odette. Stone mana makes him naturally stronger, and I can bolster his strength and endurance with a spell." He smiled pedantically as he patted Mason's arm. "No offense, friend, but I believe I'm a better combatant than you are."

Mason started to protest, but one glance at the sewer water gave him enough pause to agree.

"Fine," Hane agreed as Lief cast his bolstering spells over Mason. Mason looked the part of a big and heavy bruiser, but Lief had far more experience as a climber as well as a fighter. Even if Hane had yet to see him draw his sword. "Just don't shoot me in the back while I'm fighting."

"I'll try," Lief replied with a charming smile. "But you do zip around rather quickly. If you dart in front of an arrow after it's already left the string, that's your fault, not mine."

"Noted." Arrows shattered easily; if Hane had to, they could knock a flying arrow off course using their Burst spell. They would probably be in more danger of Rose's imbued throwing daggers than Lief's arrows, all things considered.

"Do you remember which way to go?" Rose asked, strapping her goggles onto her head backward, giving her actual eyes on the back of her head. "It wasn't a straightforward path, and I didn't take the time to memorize it."

"Only parts of it," Hane admitted. They had hoped that Odette might at least be able to give directions, but by the way both Mason and Lief had to coax her into climbing onto Mason's back so he could carry her, it didn't look as if she was in a state to course-correct. There was no help for it: Hane would have to go by memory and mark the traps as they found them. Hopefully they would find a room to hole up in soon, so Odette could get back on her feet.

And when she did recover, hopefully she would choose to stay, rather than ring out before they reached the vault.

Hane heard noises from up ahead. By the way Lief pivoted, his bow dropping from his shoulder to his hand, he heard it, too.

"Let's move," Hane directed, looking back to make sure everyone was ready. Lief stood just behind them, bow and arrow in hand. Odette was draped over Mason's shoulders, her hands dangling loosely and her face turned into the side of his neck. Mason hooked his arms beneath her knees, leaning forward slightly so she didn't tumble backward, but he didn't look overly burdened. Rose was in the rear, the strap of her goggles across her forehead, a throwing knife held in each hand.

Hane's eyes lingered on the patch of floor where Nieve had disappeared. For the space of a heartbeat, they felt something . . . hot—no, *roiling*—at the center of their being. Before they could acknowledge it, the numbing cold overwhelmed it, sealing it up and locking it away. Hane turned back to the stone path ahead.

"Don't fall behind."

NIEVE

Champion (mind mark), Citrine
??? (heart mark), Sealed

This is a nightmare, Nieve thought, hair streaming above her as she fell. *This can't possibly be real. It can't.*

The space that engulfed her became endlessly black the moment the hole sealed itself shut above her, giving her one final view of Hane and Mason's horrified faces as she dropped. She couldn't see her hand in front of her face, couldn't feel the sides of the hole with her arms and legs, couldn't find the war hammer that had dropped from her grip when she groped for a handhold. The only way she could even tell she was falling was by the lurch in her stomach and the air rushing past her skin.

Freeze, Nieve thought desperately, trying to create an ice platform. But with nothing to anchor the ice to, it only shattered as she continued falling. With grim determination, she ripped the tiny pouch off her belt, the one that hung near the buckle. Even in the darkness, she managed to tug open the drawstring with her teeth and grip the return bell tight within her fist. Squeezing her eyes shut (though in the dark it made little difference), Nieve sent a thread of mana into the bell and shook, hard.

Nothing.

That was when panic truly set in.

All Nieve could think of was her encounter with Hogame in the Tortoise Spire—the general of flame and punishment who killed half her team for violating an unwritten rule. Return bells hadn't worked then, either, but on her life, she couldn't think of a single thing she'd done wrong on this climb. And it was only she who had fallen, right? If this had anything to do with that last fateful climb in the Tortoise Spire, wouldn't Hane have dropped through the floor, too? Or was she overthinking this? The trap had been strange, working differently than any other pit trap she'd ever seen before, but was that all it was? Maybe all endless pits were warded against teleportation; she'd never met any climber claiming to have survived a pit trap by using their return bell.

Frost Form, Nieve thought, preparing her body for impact, in case the ground ever came. She spread her arms and legs out wide, attempting to slow her fall. It was impossible to tell if it was working, though. *What else, what else? Maybe if I elongate my sword, I can find the sides of this—*

Nieve nearly gasped as she realized what she had forgotten.

"Chime!" Nieve shouted out loud, as well as within her mind. "Chime, are you with me? Do you know what's happening? Chime, talk to me!"

<Silence . . .> Chime's voice, thin and distant, the sound of bells ringing a mournful tune. <Overwhelming . . . silence . . .>

What happened? Nieve asked the question in her head, as panic and inertia stole her voice. *Chime, what's wrong? Do you know what happened? Can you tell me where we are? Chime?*

The sound of the bells died along with Chime's final word. A kick of Nieve's foot found the crystal shard still hidden within the secret pocket of her boot, but no amount of mental screaming was met with any sort of response. Which only left her to ponder the few words Chime had managed to get out.

Silence.

Overwhelming silence.

A cold sweat broke out over Nieve's skin. Swallowing tightly, she gave her return bell another hard shake, punching it with more mana this time in case the first time hadn't been enough.

No change.

It can't be Hogame, Nieve told herself, as if denial could make it true. *It can't be. This isn't his spire and I haven't done anything wrong, and—oh, goddess, is Sage okay?*

Before her panic could compound itself, there was a noticeable change in Nieve's falling speed: she was slowing down. It was difficult to judge as the blackness all around her gave no indication of depth or distance, but she felt it in the pit of her stomach and the tickle of her hair on the back of her neck. There was no wind, no updraft from below to explain the sudden decrease in her descent, but it was the first thing she felt sure of since the ground opened beneath her.

She could see no distant floor, no iron spikes waiting to spear her, no bleached bones of the climbers who had fallen before her, and yet, some alien sensation told her that the ground was nearing. Her rate of deceleration slowed to the point that she could almost be floating. Changing her position from spread-eagle to feet-first was a challenge, especially with no visual cues to tell her when she was upright, but when the ground finally manifested itself, she struck it with her heels.

Then promptly collapsed, shivering and shaking as she clutched at the ground, fingernails scrabbling at a surface as smooth as glass. Her stomach took its sweet time in deciding whether it would hold onto her breakfast or not before settling down. Only then did Nieve push herself up and look around.

The darkness was no longer absolute, though Nieve couldn't determine the source of the light glowing somewhere above her. She would have guessed it was light magic, except it seemed too diffuse, like sunlight filtering through fog. The ground was hard, smooth, and shiny, like metal, except it was warm to the touch. Not hot, like a forge, just warm. Comfortable. Nieve turned a circle, looking for something—anything—she could use as a landmark. Failing that, she shaded her eyes against the light and looked straight up, searching for the hole she'd fallen through.

"No, I don't think I can create a tall enough ice pillar to lift me that high," Nieve admitted out loud. Her words sounded flat, insubstantial, as if this chamber swallowed them as soon as they left her lips. It was rather unnerving, but then again, so was the silence. Nieve gave her leg a shake, hoping to jar Chime to wakefulness. "Hey! You there? I could really use your help right now."

Nieve counted ten heartbeats before giving up on an answer. After a final look around, Nieve pressed her hand over her locket, verifying its presence before inventorying her supplies.

Return bell? Yep, still clenched in her fist. She gave it one more shake before tucking it away inside its pouch and securing it to her belt once more. She had her sword, but her war hammer was lost. Had she dropped it outside of the pit trap? No, she thought she remembered holding onto it as she fell; it wasn't until later that she had released it. She glanced around once more, confirming its disappearance, then went back to checking her supplies.

Emergency rations? Check.

Medical kit? Check.

Canteen? Check.

What was that tucked through the back of her belt? Oh, right: the Magpie's walking stick. Well, an extra weapon was always useful.

Why did I agree to let Hane carry my things inside their dimensional bag? Nieve asked herself regretfully. *I don't have a bedroll, or a torch, or rope, or any of the things I need for a solo trek through a spire.*

It seemed logical at the time: Hane's dimensional bag was small and light, so it didn't get in their way while fighting and it could carry a lot more than

Nieve's backpack could. She'd thought that if they were separated, she could just ring out and the lack of supplies wouldn't be an issue.

Too bad neither of them had seen this coming.

On the bright side, Nieve had never been as organized with her gear as she could be, so there were a few surprising odds and ends tucked inside her belt pouches. Some of it was useless, like half of an unsharpened pencil and, for some odd reason, a whittling knife. But she also found flint, a compass, and a small glow stick Sage had given her years ago as a name day gift. It wasn't much as far as supplies went, but somehow she'd make it work.

She had to.

The only other option was unthinkable.

Detect Aura, Nieve thought, searching her surroundings once more, this time searching for signs of magic invisible to the naked eye. There was always a way out, right? The goddess's trials were meant to be overcome, after all.

The shift in the dark room's atmosphere wasn't something that could be seen, but Nieve felt it from the core of her bones to the rippled flesh on her arms and legs. A force as powerful as a predator, as inevitable as winter, as indomitable as a mountain. Nieve pivoted on the balls of her feet, drawing her sword in one smooth motion, searching the endless chamber for signs of movement. Fear gripped her by the throat, freezing the breath in her chest, but Nieve was no stranger to the cold. She kept her sword up, her stance strong.

Even if she couldn't win, Nieve wasn't about to go down without a fight.

A short distance away, the air began to glow with ephemeral light, steadily becoming brighter, bigger, reflecting off the polished floor bright enough to leave light scars on Nieve's vision. She held her ground, waiting for whatever it was to manifest itself. If this was the being that had brought her here, she would teach it better manners for the next time it stole a climber away from their team.

Frost Form.

Mind of Ice.

Ice Armor.

Ice sprouted over Nieve's shoulders, growing halfway down her arms, across her chest, and down her back, encasing her in a breastplate and pauldrons as tough as any steel. More ice grew from the ground, forming icy greaves around her legs. Her heart fluttered madly in her chest, the arrhythmic beat whispering the word "Hogame" over and over again as it pulsed through her ears. She set her jaw like her stance: solid and determined.

The eerie light appeared to be taking a form or shape, sketching a pattern that Nieve struggled to comprehend. She felt pressure in her ears, her skin tight beneath her icy armor, a metallic taste in her mouth. The sensation of magic—of raw, primal mana—gave the air an electric quality, setting her every nerve ending on edge. The light glowed the pure white of fresh snow, but patterns within the light seemed to gleam and flicker brighter than others, giving the impression of shapes within the brightening glow: stripes as hard as steel surrounded by soft, pure snow. Nieve squinted, trying to discern the pattern within the light, when suddenly it flared brilliantly, making a sound like the screech of metal so loud that she felt it in the roots of her teeth. She shielded her eyes with an arm, never letting her sword or her stance falter. When the brilliance dispersed, Nieve shaded her eyes, squinting into the brilliance.

Her sword hit the ground seconds before her knees did. The icy armor conjured for protection sloughed off in pieces, shattering as it hit the floor. With shaking hands, Nieve bowed down and pressed her forehead to the floor.

There could be no winning against Byakko, God Beast of the Tiger Spire. The only hope she allowed herself was for a swift, painless death.

"Nieve Yukihara." The voice boomed all around her, inside her head as well as throughout the empty space surrounding her. **"Long have I awaited the day when you would seek me out in my home den. Yet I did not expect to see you greet me in the same fashion as you did when first we met."**

Nieve's first thought was that this was all a dream, brought on by drinking the unfamiliar spirits of Caelford. But god beasts were said to have power even in dreams, and her grandmother had raised her to be respectful of visages and god beasts alike.

"Great One, please accept my sincerest apologies." Nieve spoke without lifting her head from the floor. "But I'm afraid we have never met before."

Nieve heard the click of claws against the unblemished floor. **"Of course we have met, Nieve, child of Emenike. How else would you have come to bear my mark of favor?"**

Something inside of Nieve's chest contracted sharply, making her gasp in pain. She fought back the urge to clutch at her locket. "Great One, I'm afraid I don't—"

"Rise, child." The imperious voice held a note of impatience, not quite threatening but demanding enough that Nieve scrambled to her feet without protest. **"We have much to discuss and I will not have one of my favored grubbing about the floor like some cowardly scavenger. You are a proud warrior, are you not?"**

I am. Nieve thought the words but could not speak them while beholding the magnificence that was the God Beast Byakko. While it was commonly taught that the god beasts of the spires could take on human shapes at will, Byakko wore the form more commonly depicted in religious texts: that of a great white tiger, seated neatly on her haunches, enormous white paws showing steel-colored claws longer than swords. Unlike the texts, Byakko's stripes were not the deep black of common tigers, but instead a brightly polished silver that almost seemed to fade into the pristine white of her fur, except where the light reflected off of them. Byakko looked down at Nieve with intelligent sky-blue eyes, the only spark of color that was neither silver nor white. Nieve knew the god beasts were big—at least, she'd always heard they were—but she'd thought Hogame was big. Byakko could have snapped Hogame in half with her teeth if she'd had the notion. She looked half as tall as the spire itself, though Nieve's awe could have exaggerated the god beast's size.

It wasn't just the god beast's size that made her formidable but the sensation of pure, raw mana that seemed to crackle invisibly throughout the chamber. Nieve could feel it prickling the hairs on the back of her neck, in the slow churn of her guts, and in the thrum of her heartbeat. Almost without thinking, she reached for her locket, but drew her hand away sharply when she felt it vibrate under her touch. It had never done that before! Was Byakko causing that? Or was it simply reacting to the dense concentration of ambient mana?

Nieve jumped at a sudden motion out of the corner of her eye: the silver tip of Byakko's tail switched slowly back and forth along the floor, itself as large as some serpents Nieve had fought and killed. She swallowed tightly and ducked her head, awe and fear trapping her tongue.

Byakko cocked her head to one side, sizing Nieve up. **"You have grown, young one. And you have become quite strong. I am glad to see that you earned an attunement that suits your abilities."**

"Thank you, Great One," Nieve managed, her voice low and coarse.

"But I am also disappointed," Byakko added, the tip of her tail lashing violently before settling back to its swishing rhythm. **"Why do you reject the gift I deigned to bless you with all those years ago, when you asked for strength? It was not a choice I made lightly, young one. I risked the recourse of the visages for granting you such power. I cannot say that I do not find it insulting that you have not seen fit to call upon my power even once in all your years of exploration and battle. Tell me, child: do you think yourself mightier than I?"**

"No!" Nieve wanted to prostrate herself again, but settled instead for a deep bow at the waist. "No, Great One, I would never put myself beside you, or anywhere even near you. I may be of Dalenos, but we revere and honor all visages and god beasts of Kaldwyn. If I have offered you any offense, Great One, I can only offer you my life to make up for it."

Byakko's paws rippled, silver claws clicking against the floor in staccato rhythm before falling still again. **"I would not have your life, little one. Not when deeds performed in my service have already taken so much from you. I would not have sought this audience had you not entered my spire, but since you are here, I thought it was past time that I asked you directly. Why do you reject my gift, child of Emenike?"**

Only after hearing the name a second time did Nieve connect it to her father. She had precious few memories of him before his death, and her grandmother had always called him "Niikei" when she wasn't calling him "that reckless fool." She had seen her father's name written on old climber logs, but much like her own, she'd never heard it pronounced the way it was meant to sound.

"Great One," Nieve began, cautiously drawing herself up straight. She pressed her hand to her breast, the lump of her locket beneath her palm. "Did you . . . know my father?"

A lash of the tail and a flick of an ear. Nieve felt her heart stutter in her chest. **"Can it be that you truly do not remember our first meeting, child?"**

"I . . . I'm certain I would never forget meeting you, Great One." Her locket was still vibrating with the intensity of a hummingbird's heartbeat. She could feel it pressed between her palm and her breastbone. "Unless . . . forgive me my presumption, Great One, but . . . when I emerged from my Judgment at the Tortoise Spire, I found that I had been gifted two attunement marks. This one over my heart . . ." Nieve felt the frustrated confusion the mark had caused her for years well up within her, despite her unadulterated awe of the being in front of her. She tamped it down firmly, giving it no outlet to show itself. However much grief it had caused her, it wasn't worth disrespecting a god beast. "Did you give me this mark, Great One?"

Byakko's tail lashed once before she turned away and yawned widely, pristine fangs gleaming around a curled red tongue. When she turned back, the fur around the ruff of her neck fluffed up before lying flat again. **"While humans commonly forget the trial of their Judgments, I had thought that in summoning you to meet with me, you might retain the memories of our encounter. Perhaps I ought to have spoken to Genbu before returning you to your trial; this seems within the realm of his petty sense of justice."**

The center of Nieve's chest felt hot, as if she burned from the inside out. The hand over her heart shook; she felt as if she could barely draw breath. Was this the answer? After so long without knowing? The mysterious mark on her heart . . . was a gift from Byakko?

Byakko's upper lip curled in a sneeze that was more sound than substance. The fur around her head smoothed itself flat, though it twitched once or twice as if hiding irritation. **"I suppose if you do not remember our meeting, you must have many questions for me. I will answer what I can, seeing how this is no fault of yours. Yes, little warrior, I am the one who gifted you that mark you bear on your chest."**

Nieve trembled, from the crown of her head to the soles of her feet. The years of questions, of fears, of hiding the mark from even her closest friends, keeping it sealed and locked away in case it was put there by some malevolence that Nieve couldn't even imagine. Her grandmother had tested the mark so many times, attempting to pinpoint its source, but the only thing she had been able to confirm was that it was a Paladin attunement with no connection to any known visage. And since Paladin marks were conduits for a being's power, Nieve's grandmother had decided to seal the mark just in case it linked Nieve to some fearsome evil, like the Tyrant in Gold or some ancient god of the old lands. She knew the words to unlock the seal—she'd asked her grandmother to confirm them before leaving Dalenos—but she'd always been too afraid to release the power and call upon the unknown entity bound to her through the attunement. At least, she had been until she'd come face to face with Hogame, general of flame and punishment within the Tortoise Spire, but by then, the words were a half-remembered prayer learned in childhood and in her panic and grief, and she couldn't recall them at the pivotal moment that she needed them.

Now that same surge of grief hit her again: if she'd been able to unseal the attunement back then—or better still, years ago—could she have saved her friends by calling upon Byakko's power?

If that was true, then she truly had failed her team. She could have saved them. If only she had known . . .

"Have you no further questions for me?" Byakko inquired, the rough purr-growl of a voice coming across as inquisitive. **"You had so many more for me during our first encounter. Are those memories returning to you now?"**

Nieve shook her head, unable to speak. The heat within her breast burned like a scorch of lava, guilt making her feel sick and weak and angry and weary all at once.

Why? Why hadn't she been brave enough to break the seal and find out the truth so much sooner than this?

"Do you wish to know about your father?" Byakko asked. **"Or your mother, perhaps? I did not know her so well as I knew Emenike, but she was a fierce woman. Much like you."**

Under normal circumstances, Nieve would have begged to hear more about her parents. When she was younger, she tried asking her grandmother about them, but she claimed it was too painful to speak of the daughter she'd lost, and that she had nothing kind to say about Nieve's father, so she refused to say anything at all. Over the years, Grandmother had let a few details slip, but not many. Over time, Nieve understood what her grandmother had truly lost: her prestige as a venerated climber, and the freedom of will that Nieve was now able to fully appreciate. When Nieve's parents died in the Tortoise Spire, they left three small children behind, the youngest of which had been little more than a babe in arms. The temple of Dalenos could have raised them as orphans, as it did other children of fallen climbers, but instead Grandmother gave up everything to take over parenting Nieve and her brothers. Her freedom. Her climbing career. Even her contracts. She had never been anything but loving and supportive of her grandchildren, but as a climber herself, Nieve didn't think it possible to give up so much without feeling at least a small amount of resentment and frustration.

"What can I say about Tsubaki?" Byakko continued musingly. **"She was an Illusionist, remarkably talented with an occasional habit of recklessness. It's always a loss when the bright ones leave us so soon."**

Nieve's free hand curled into a fist that shook. The hand on her chest curled inward on itself, nails scratching at the hardened leather vest she wore.

"Your father was a cunning man," Byakko said, seemingly unaware of Nieve's inner turmoil. **"He was a marvel to watch in combat, always so unexpected, so daring. There was a powerful charisma about him that made people want to follow him. Even when he decided to give up all the progress he had made here in order to follow Tsubaki to the Tortoise Spire, many of the people on his team went with him, just so they could continue to climb with him. He was a leader who would give his all for his team, just as they would give all for him."**

What did Nieve even remember about her father? His bright smile stood out the most in her memory, more than his eyes, more than the shape of his face. Just that proud, gleaming smile. And maybe his laugh: deep and hearty, with a thrumming vibration she could feel in her own body when he held her close. Sometimes she thought she remembered his clumsy Caelish accent mincing the delicate language of Dalenos, but it seemed more likely she was only remembering how her grandmother used to complain about his accent.

The silence drew out longer than a normal pause. Nieve looked up to find Byakko gazing into the distance, her tail lying in a lifeless arc on the gleaming floor.

"They died in my service," Byakko said finally, her blue eyes distant. **"Emenike and Tsubaki. Your father was one of my favored, and I had need of something I suspected had come to rest within the Tortoise Spire. When he and his mate were felled by the task, I took it upon myself to honor their memory by granting one request of their first child to attempt a Judgment. That was you, young Nieve."**

Nieve nodded stiffly. She accepted everything Byakko said as fact, but the words weren't really sinking in. Her parents had died so long ago that it was hard to feel any sort of connection to either of them. There was nothing she could have done for them. She didn't even miss them; not really, anyway. But she could have saved Aldis and Lani and Emiko.

"My intent was to allow you to choose any of the attunements typical of a Judgment from my own spire," Byakko continued. **"Or a treasured weapon from one of my collections. But upon our meeting, my mind was changed. Even as a child, you were fierce as your mother, confident as your father, and perhaps a touch arrogant, too. When I asked you what request you would make of a god, you asked only for a way to become stronger, so you could protect those you loved."**

Nieve's nose itched, causing her eyes to water.

"You had a warrior's heart even then, young Nieve." Byakko's voice seemed almost . . . affectionate. Not kindly, but proud in a way. **"I saw that the best way to aid you in your quest for strength was to grant you the ability to call upon my strength and make it your own. Though it is not typically done, I gifted you with that Paladin attunement over your heart, the one you have shunned and sealed away all this time."**

"I didn't know." Nieve's voice came out thin. Weak. She swallowed and spoke up. "I forgot everything about my Judgment after it ended. I walked out of the spire with a Champion attunement in the middle of my forehead and it never occurred to me to check for a second mark. When I found it later, I . . . I was afraid. I didn't recognize it, I didn't remember . . . anything." She could still picture the moment clearly: she'd just returned home, jubilant over her successful Judgment and accepting the accolades of her family before they went out for a celebratory dinner. She was changing out of her Judgment garb in the privacy of her bedroom when she saw the mark in a mirror. At first, she thought it was a joke—surely one of her brothers had drawn a rune on her mirror to mess with her. But when she realized it was no joke, she'd shouted for her grandmother. "My grandmother said that only a visage could grant a Paladin attunement. She had the mark tested by trusted friends and colleagues among the Soaring Wings, searching for a connection to one of the visages. When they couldn't say who granted it, Grandmother said we had to seal it, in case it was dangerous."

"**I suppose caution and ignorance may both be forgiven, considering Genbu's probable interference.**" Byakko's tail swept across the floor, curling neatly around her front paws. "**Stubborn old reptile. The world is changing faster than he can adapt. You have done well in choosing to climb the spire your father so favored.**"

"Oh." Panic had such a grip over her that Nieve barely twinged at the thought of lying to a god beast. "I just wanted to see it. My dad's spire. I don't know if I'll stay long."

An irritated twitch of the tail. "**Perhaps you will come to reconsider.**"

"Perhaps," Nieve agreed quickly.

Byakko nodded regally. "**Then let us consider the matter settled. I have my answers, and now you have yours. All that remains now is for you to remove the seal from my mark.**"

Nieve pressed the locket into her chest until she could feel the edges of it digging into her skin. "Do I have to?"

Byakko's chin tipped down, eyes sharpening to gleaming points. Nieve choked as she tried to swallow and backpedaled quickly.

"I-I mean, it's just—well, my grandmother is the one who sealed it," Nieve explained rapidly, sweat running down the back of her neck. "It's kind of . . . sentimental?"

"**Your grandmother yet lives, does she not?**"

Nieve nodded stiffly.

"**Then your argument is irrelevant. Remove the seal.**"

It was an order from a god beast: Nieve knew better than to refuse. Not that there was any good reason to refuse but her own self-doubt. But she could stall.

"How, um, do I use it?" Nieve asked, slowly withdrawing the locket from the inside of her shirt. "And what happens when I use it?"

"**You may invoke my name in order to call upon my strength and make it your own,**" Byakko explained, seemingly mollified now that Nieve held the locket in her hand. "**You will become stronger as you inherit the will of a true predator. You will stalk your prey until all have fallen before you. You will be more resilient to injury and you will feel less pain, but the longer you hold my strength within your body, the more it will exhaust you, so I encourage you to train just as you would with any attunement.**"

Nieve hesitated, flicking her fingernail across the seam of the locket. It hadn't been opened once since her grandmother clasped the necklace around her neck and cast the spell that sealed her heart mark. There was no going back once she unsealed it, not unless she made an unscheduled return to Dalenos before finding all of Chime's missing pieces.

"Will it bother you? Or weaken you? If I call upon your power frequently?"

Another soft sneeze, this time in a way that expressed some level of humor. **"Child, you could not take on enough of my strength to weaken me even noticeably. But in case it lessens your concerns, I can always refuse your request for my power."**

"Is there anything else I should know?" Nieve asked, still hesitating as she toyed with the locket. "Like, could I summon you directly, or speak to you through the attunement mark?"

"You do not have the ability to summon me, as if I were some common contract." That sounded a little high and mighty, but, well, she *was* a god beast, after all. **"The mark will only allow you access to my strength and predatory instincts for now. As you grow used to my power and as the mark itself grows, I may allow you to use spells on my behalf. You may attempt to speak to me through the mark, but that does not mean I will hear. And even if I do hear, I may not always answer. I have enough to keep me busy without responding to every prayer that invokes my name. However, should you ever find yourself at the mercy of one of my peers or even one of the visages, you may reveal the mark and state that you are under my protection. That should give you some small measure of protection, if nothing else."**

Would it have made a difference to Hogame? If she'd known back then, would Byakko's name and an invocation of her strength have been enough to protect her friends? She gripped the locket so hard that the engraved knots at the corners imprinted themselves into her palm.

"You still hesitate." Byakko sounded curious, rather than offended. **"Be not afraid, child. Only the source of the strength is mine: it is yours to wield as you will. You need not think of me as a guardian or a protector: your greatest strength has always been your own belief in yourself."**

"What if I've lost that?" Nieve asked suddenly, clenching her fist around the locket as she looked up to meet Byakko's eyes. "What if I'm not that arrogant child who believed she could save everyone anymore? What if I'm not strong enough to use your gift of power? What if . . . what if I'm no longer worthy of your gift?"

Byakko met her gaze evenly and calmly, blinking once before responding. **"During your Judgment, you told me of a wish you intend to ask of the goddess. Do you still hold that wish sacred today as you did back then?"**

Nieve felt the metal of the locket grow warm in her hand, a tickle of emotion that was neither grief nor anger nudged her heart gingerly. While she couldn't remember what she'd said during her Judgment, she had only ever had one wish. And if she had to crawl up a spire from the bottom to the top, she would do it, just see her wish fulfilled.

"Yes," Nieve whispered. "I still intend to see it through."

"Then you are still that person," Byakko said firmly, as if that settled the matter. **"Now. Release the seal, Nieve Yukihara, daughter of Tsubaki and Emenike."**

"Granddaughter of Mitsuki," Nieve whispered, turning the locket in her hand. She drew a deep breath, letting her eyes fall closed to better remember the incantation. "Four knots bind the seal/Magic within safely bound/I release you now."

The tiny click of the locket popping open seemed almost anticlimactic. Nieve waited to feel something—some change, some foreign new power flowing through her—but all she felt was empty, as if the incantation had drained her both magically and emotionally. She'd been wearing that locket—that seal—almost since earning her Champion attunement. She'd envisioned opening it to be some big, dramatic event, making the moment slightly disappointing.

"Good." Byakko nodded once in approval. **"This is the power you once sought for the protection of others. I grant it to you now as I granted it to you then; use it wisely, child."**

"Is it . . ." Nieve placed her hand over the center of her chest, the spot where her locket usually rested. "Is it really there? I can barely feel it."

"Because at the moment, it is nothing more than a speck in comparison to your Champion mark," Byakko replied. **"It will grow the same way as the first one did: with time and practice. But perhaps I can offer you some aid, in order to speed the process along."**

One massive claw-tipped paw slid forward and to Nieve's horror, the god beast took a step toward her, back arching and tail swishing as she rose. Nieve's instincts all screamed for her run, but awe kept her feet firmly planted. Byakko's head tipped downward and all Nieve could picture were those massive fangs enveloping her whole. But then, by some trick of the light effervescing off of Byakko's white fur, the tiger's size changed as it drew closer, standing only as tall as Nieve by the time they stood face to face.

"Show me your mark," Byakko commanded, no less regal now than she was when enormous. Nieve struggled with the ties on her leather vest before peeling it aside in order to tug down the collar of her shirt. There, centered directly over her breastbone, was the same mark she had seen in her reflection the day she'd finished her Judgment. Looking down at it now, she thought she recognized something of Byakko in the whorls of the Paladin mark, but before she could study it, the still impressively large tiger leaned forward, pressing a warm, velvet nose to the center of Nieve's chest.

The next breath Nieve drew felt fuller somehow, as if she had been breathing through a straw her entire life up until then. Mana she didn't recognize seeped into her blood, her bones, her muscles. She felt dizzy and clear-minded and weak and strong all at once. When Byakko took a step back, Nieve thought she might faint.

"Very good." As Byakko faded back another step, her form seemed to stretch and swell until she was the same size as when she first appeared. **"Your heart point is quite strong, so you should be able to handle that much of an increase with little trouble. Your attunement is still quite weak, but from now on, you must strengthen it yourself."**

"Thank you," Nieve gasped, still wondering at the new mana flowing through her. What mana types made up a Paladin attunement, anyway? The only way she could describe the sensation was as a cold, bright light. "I will become stronger. I promise."

"I have no doubt." Byakko looked strangely satisfied as she sat back on her haunches, silver-tipped tail curling around her paws once more. **"I suppose it is time I return you to your challenge. Take up your sword, young warrior."**

Nieve bowed as she retrieved her weapon, taking great care to keep the edge tipped away from Byakko as she sheathed it. Everything felt strange now that the seal over her heart mark had been broken. Like the sensation of taking up a normal combat weapon after training with a weighted one, or the feeling of brushing her hair after having it cut. She understood what had changed, but her body hadn't accepted it yet. What would it be like to use this new power? How would she continue to keep it a secret? Or . . . should she even keep it a secret?

"I have one more question, Great One," Nieve stated, bowing her head reverently. "If it's all right with you?"

"Speak."

"Thank you." Nieve struggled not to fidget. Her hands felt sweaty, her mouth dry. "You've made it clear that you wish for me to use this gift you've given me. Does that mean it's okay for me to tell people that I am a Paladin of the Great Byakko?"

A corner of Byakko's mouth twitched; Nieve didn't know if that was a good thing or a bad thing. **"I am certain that those close to you will come to know the source of your power and I am willing to allow that.**

However, I am a private being and I do not wish to be beset by petitioners requesting this same gift of me. I will not have you lie, but I would ask that you not share our connection widely and without reason. Is this clear to you?"

"Yes, Great One." That sounded like it was okay to tell Sage—good thing, too, since she'd probably need his help with training. She just had to make sure she didn't start bragging about it at bars after having a few drinks.

"Good." Byakko nodded sagely. **"When you are prepared to return, take up the tool I have returned to you. I do not know if we shall meet again, but if it comes to pass, I would be pleased to know that you have come to wield this gift in a way that is worthy of its cost."**

Nieve was still trying to puzzle out what Byakko meant about a tool before the understanding that this gift's "cost" were the lives of her parents. Her mysterious attunement had always been about making amends for a loss Nieve barely remembered. But clearly Byakko did.

She dropped to a knee to be respectful, but she looked up to meet Byakko's eyes. "If my parents died in your service, then I'm certain they did so with honor. If . . . if it ever does come to pass that we speak again, I think I'd like to hear more about my dad."

Byakko sneezed, one ear flicking twice before going still. Nieve hoped that meant Byakko was pleased by the request. **"I might enjoy sharing stories of Emenike at another time. For now, I believe it is time that I return you to your team."**

"Yes," Nieve agreed, though inwardly she worried that her team might have left the spire already, especially after seeing her fall through that strange portal. "And thank you again, Great One."

A final sage-like nod from the spire's god beast, then Byakko vanished in a reflected flash of light. Nieve blinked away the afterimage of Byakko's silver stripes, the wide, empty chamber seeming much darker now that Byakko was no longer here. As she waited for her vision to return to normal, Nieve tugged her leather vest straight, lacing up the side again to fit it snugly over her shirt. The locket wouldn't snap closed—not entirely, at least. She didn't need it anymore, not now that she'd broken the seal on her attunement. But it felt wrong to tuck it into a pocket, so she tucked it down the front of her shirt again. It was a gift from her grandmother, a precious reminder of her wish and her oath. She would sooner die than leave it behind.

"Okay, so . . ." Nieve looked around. "How do I get out of here, again?"

As if in answer to her question, a misty light began to pulse a short distance away—right where Byakko had seated herself during their conversation. Squinting into the faint light, Nieve saw the small shape of . . . something on the floor. She approached cautiously, circling to one side of it before laughing at herself.

"The returned tool," Nieve repeated, stopping to retrieve her war hammer. It was familiar as the one she'd dropped, but as she hefted it, the weight felt strangely off. Before she could examine it further, light flared around her, brilliant and searing, and subtly familiar.

As thrilling as it had been to meet a god beast—again—Nieve was grateful to be returning to her team now that it was over.

HANE

Wavewalker (leg mark), Citrine

I'm running low on knives!" Rose shouted, holding one of her leaf-shaped blades by the pointed tip, the blade pulsating with red and orange magic.

"I've got you covered! Jump!" Lief shouted, loosing an arrow that skipped just wide of Rose. It sank deep into the rounded gut of a gang member wielding a meat cleaver. Rose spun away to leap the gap in the grating that formed a rusty bridge over the channel of sewage. Hane saw her teeter precariously on the edge of the walkway before she threw her weight forward, landing hard on her hands and knees, graceless, yet safe.

"Mason's securing a room up ahead," Hane reported, rushing forward to help Rose back to her feet. "Keep going, you'll see it on the right."

"What about you?" Lief asked. He frowned as he reached for his quiver: only two arrows remained, and his second quiver was already empty.

"I won't let them see where we're hiding," Hane vowed, stepping in front of Lief. "Go on. I'll be right there."

The look Lief gave them was carefully blank. A look back at the mob chasing them gave away his calculations. "You know what they say about climbers who try to be heroes."

"Just go," Hane ordered, crossing their arms in front of them as they willed up a powerful Burst spell. They didn't risk looking back to make sure Lief followed their instructions; they had to get the timing just right on this, or else risk exposing the safe room up ahead.

"We'll hold the door as long as possible," Lief called, sounding farther away. "Use the communicator if you're still alive after we seal it up!"

With any luck, Hane would get to the safe room before Mason sealed the doorway. If not, well, the team was already fractured by Nieve's sudden and unexpected disappearance, and if they had to, Hane could survive alone inside a labyrinth. There was little hope of opening the phantom vault without the rest of the team, though.

Hane held their spell in check as more and more drug-makers and gang members spilled around the corner of the intersecting sewer tunnel. At a rough count, there were about twenty of them, all armed with better weapons than the first ragtag group the team encountered upon entering the sewer. The officers even had guns, but Hane had been careful to dispatch those first. It was impossible to look at the motley crew of grime-encrusted gangsters wielding knives, syringes, and shields made of steel grating and not think of how much fun Nieve would have had wading through the lot of them, cheerfully hacking them down with a blade made of ice. It wasn't an emotional thought—Hane felt too cold for that—but it did make them consider how much easier this all would have been with Nieve here. Maybe instead of running past the rooms full of grinders, furnaces, and beakers, the team could have destroyed the illegal operations going on here and maybe earned some treasure for their trouble. As it was, Hane and the others hadn't been able to stop longer than it took to recover their breath before someone was on their tail again.

One more time, Hane told themself, transference mana wound so tight within them that they felt the shiver of it deep in their bones. They couldn't spare an extra spell to stabilize themself; the recoil from this Burst would hit them hard, but that was part of the plan, anyway. They felt Burst swell to the point where they could no longer hold it, a pent breath waiting to be expelled. They leaned into it as they let the spell rip outward from their body in an arced radius, not simply slamming gang members and drug dealers into the stone walls, but hurling anything and everything not firmly attached to the ground, such as broken pieces of grating, parts of the crumbled walkway, and a spray of sewer water. The released spell tossed Hane backward like a yarn doll, rolling twice before they skidded up onto a knee. Before they came to a full stop, they were already casting their next spell, one hand held out over the surface of the burbling sewage.

Wave, Hane thought, sweeping their hand up and forward.

The current backtracked on itself, swirling once to gather momentum before surging forward, gaining height and speed as it rushed toward the scattered and dazed gang members. Hane didn't wait around to make sure it swept them all away; chances were good that at least some of their opponents would remain to chase them down, and they wanted to vanish before that happened. Luckily, thanks to their Burst spell throwing them backward, they were close enough to the safe room to duck inside behind the cover of the wave.

That was, if the door wasn't already locked from the inside.

Hane pounded a fist against the door hard enough to feel the sting through their shroud. "Let me in!"

They couldn't hear the click of a lock over the sucking sound of a near-empty drain, but the door opened by a crack, revealing the tip of an arrow held at eye level. Hane brushed it aside coolly as they stepped inside, glowering at Lief as he lowered his bow. Lief only shrugged mildly.

"As if you wouldn't have done the same," he muttered before dropping the arrow back into his quiver.

"Seal it," Hane ordered Mason, the one actually holding the door. "Shape the outside to cover it completely. We don't want them to know there's a room here."

"It's a nice idea, but if they live down here, there's a good chance they know where the door is supposed to be," Rose pointed out, pulling her goggles off over her head.

"True, but I'm hoping they get distracted by the rival gang that was coming up from the other end of the intersection," Hane replied, eyes searching the room for any obvious doors or alternate exits. Mason could always shape a way out through the stone walls, but Hane was more worried about any opponents coming in and catching them off guard. It was a small space, possibly once meant to store tools for maintaining the sewer. Now, it appeared to serve as a supply station for the Ash Hats, based on the crude artwork drawn in chalk along the walls. While far too small to serve as a hideout, the room was equipped with dusty medical supplies, some tattered bedrolls, canned foods, and glass jars of water. Far less savory was a mound of weapons hidden just behind the door, mostly made up of rusted pipes, crooked pry bars, metal grating, and bricks. More than half of them were crusted with dried blood. At least, Hane hoped it was blood.

The closet-sized space had no other obvious exits aside from the one Mason was reshaping to appear as an unblemished wall, but there was a small grate up near the ceiling. Despite their exhaustion, Hane used a gravity spell to get up to the grate, checking to make sure it was secure and that no one was hiding inside. It was more than likely a ventilation shaft, bringing in fresh air to these subterranean floors of the sewer. Hane judged that they could fit inside, but only just barely, so if there was anyone past the metal grate, they would likely have to be the size of a child. The grate was firmly secured to the wall, anyway, meaning that anyone trying to get through was in more danger from the team than the team was from them. Regardless, Hane made a note to keep an eye on it.

"Who's hurt and how badly?" Lief called out as Hane dropped to the floor. As they assessed their own condition, Hane visually checked on the others.

Mason was still at the door, sweat soaked through the top of his dueling tunic, but otherwise he seemed fine. Rose sat on the floor, muttering to herself as she rummaged through the pockets of her vest. Hane knew she'd been struck by some thrown object, but it was only by looking closely that they could see the welt rising over her right eye; otherwise her mussed curls covered the injury entirely. Odette huddled in the same spot where Mason had dropped her, curled around her satchel as she rocked her body forward and back, eyes glazed. She didn't appear injured, just . . . not entirely there.

"I'll take a regeneration spell," Hane requested when no one else immediately spoke up. "I don't think I need more than that."

Lief nodded, holding his hand out toward Hane as he directed the spell. "If we rest here long enough, I'll check for anything left over after the spell runs its course."

"Thank you." Hane could already feel the effects of the healing spell, soothing bruises, sealing cuts, and easing the aches from a prolonged fighting retreat. There were a few more serious injuries that would require stronger healing spells, like a knife cut that slipped just under their vest, and a few close calls where they had been grazed by bullets, but their clothing hid the bloodstains, and their shroud combined with the cold that had suffused them since Nieve's disappearance kept their pain level low. Hane sat down, putting their back to the wall where they could keep an eye on the ventilation shaft as they sipped from their canteen. On a perfect climb, Nieve would be here to keep watch while Hane shut their eyes for a little while. Having to remain alert all the time took its toll on Hane's senses as well as their nerves, but there was no remedy for it. Not unless someone else wanted to step into the role of the leader.

"I'm just a little scraped up," Mason said, still sounding winded from carrying Odette. Stone Form would have protected him from injury, but maintaining it for long periods of time must have drained his endurance significantly. Hane was actually impressed Mason had been able to keep up with all the running, climbing, and trench-leaping while keeping Odette safe from harm. Mason smiled weakly as Lief laid a hand on his arm, casting a healing spell. "Unless you've got something that can cure me of this sewer water stench?"

Lief chuckled softly. "I have a scented sachet in my bag, but I'd have to remove my anosmia spell from you if you want to smell it."

Mason made a face. "No thanks. Ugh, goddess, the first thing I'm doing when I get back is taking the longest, hottest soak in a bathhouse." He shot Lief a quick wink. "You're welcome to join me, if you like."

"If you're paying, I wouldn't mind tagging along," Lief replied, smiling back before turning his attention to Rose. She flinched away at a light touch on her brow before holding resolutely still, her expression sour. Lief sighed and let his hand drop. "I need to fix that before it gets any worse. Are you dizzy? Do you feel sick?"

"If anyone doesn't feel sick after running through all that *resh*, then they're the ones who need healing," Rose quipped, unfurling a leather roll full of tiny throwing knives. She set it down on the floor at her knee, slotting the daggers into the belt sheaths that circled her waist. "If you want to fix it, go ahead, just don't get in my way. I wasted all my imbued daggers on those pox-ridden, cur-mannered, scum-eating wastrels, and I'm already running low on mana gems. Brick! I'm going to need your help."

If Mason heard his sister, he didn't bother to respond. His eyes were closed, head tipped back against the wall, legs sprawled long in front of him, despite the small space. Hane wished they had the luxury of the same: a brief nap would feel so refreshing just then.

"Hold still," Lief advised Rose, moving behind her and setting his fingertips against her temples. "You'll feel a moment of disorientation, followed by nausea. Try to bear it, I'll handle that next."

With Mason asleep and Lief tending to Rose's injuries, it was up to Hane to check in on Odette's condition. By the way she kept rocking herself, eyes glazed and unblinking, the most merciful act would be sending her out of the spire to recover. But as she wasn't physically injured and her shock wasn't due to a spell of any kind, it seemed a bit cruel to continue on to the vault without her. If she remained unresponsive by the time the rest of them were ready to move on, Hane might call for a team vote, rather than make a unilateral decision on the matter.

With a heartfelt groan and a great deal of bone and cartilage popping in protest, Hane levered themself up to their feet and crossed the small store room to crouch down in front of Odette. She didn't react in any way, not even a spark of recognition or confusion in her eyes. Just that endless, blank stare.

"Odette?" Hane asked softly. "You really need to tell us if you wish to continue or not. We can't afford to keep carrying you here, it's a risk to your teammates."

Her gaze slowly tracked farther away, avoiding Hane's eyes.

"Odette." Firmer now, but still gentle. "I understand how much you wanted to make it to the vault. We can still get there, I'm sure of it, but we need you to help us open it. If you can't assist with that, then it's not worth it for us to keep protecting you."

"That's not going to work," Lief advised, kneeling behind Rose as he healed the welt on her head. "If you press her too hard, she'll just start panicking all over again. She needs time to get over her shock."

"We don't have time," Hane replied impatiently. "Is there anything you can do for her now that she's no longer hysterical?"

"Hane, I agree that it's a problem, but a shock state isn't something that can be rushed." Lief sat back on his heels, taking a quaff from his canteen as Rose stretched her neck to either side, vertebrae popping loudly. As soon as Lief set his canteen down, he reached out to clasp Rose's shoulder, presumably casting a regeneration spell as he had on Hane and Mason earlier. "I think the best thing we can do for her is to send her home. We can't keep dragging her along, hoping she'll get better. We're about to enter the actual labyrinth, aren't we? That's going to be a lot more dangerous than outrunning a few sewer-dwelling lowlifes."

"We might need her," Rose pointed out, still settling her replacement daggers into her belt. "I know she seems a bit scatterbrained, but as an Analyst, she's actually pretty shrewd. I wouldn't put it past her to hold something back about opening the vault." Rose looked back over her shoulder at Lief, eyes narrowing thoughtfully. "Do you have enough mana to fill a few shells for me? Light mana imbues are really helpful down here, but it's inefficient for me to make it myself."

"I can do that, just let me eat something first," Lief requested, groaning as he lowered himself to the floor. Catching Hane's glare as he tugged his canteen off his belt, Lief rolled his shoulders in a casual shrug. "Look, if you want to help Odette, find something to help her calm down. You could try talking to her about something unrelated to get her mind off things, or play a game or something."

Small talk? Games? Hane would rather crawl through the grimy ventilation shaft to an unknown destination. Or fall down the same hole that stole Nieve away. Either fate seemed preferable and far less painful. But Hane couldn't help but agree with Rose: if Odette was holding something back in regards to the vault, then they needed her to recover. Fast.

"Have you tried drinking any water since we got here?" Hane asked Odette. They reached for the canteen on her belt, moving slowly so she could stop them if she wished. As gingerly as possible, they tried to get her to take a drink. When the water ran down her chin, Hane shaped it back inside the canteen again, hiding feelings of frustration. "Are you hungry? Is there something you would eat?"

Odette shook her head slowly. It wasn't encouraging, but at least it was a response of sorts.

Rose pushed herself up, arching her back with a groan. "She said that sewing calms her down. You should check her bag for her embroidery. Maybe that would help."

That was a better suggestion than talking at her, and while searching through someone's bag—while they were still alive, that is—felt like an invasion of privacy, it didn't bother Hane nearly as much as attempting to make small talk. Odette even dipped her chin, eyes vaguely following Hane's hands. Luckily they had seen Odette working on her stitching before, or else they wouldn't have known what to look for. They found the embroidery hoop in a small pocket, a threaded needle woven through the stretch of empty canvas. Not really sure where to go from there, Hane pressed the hoop into Odette's hand. She stared at it a moment before slowly working the needle out of the fabric.

Hane twitched at gentle pressure on their shoulder. Lief smiled wanly before sitting down beside them, hand still resting on Hane's shoulder. "You've got blood dripping from the side of your boot. You should have told me you needed more healing."

"Rose needed your attention more than I did," Hane pointed out. Odette sat frozen, holding her embroidery hoop in one hand while staring at the needle in the other, as if she'd never quite seen it before. Finding that too disturbing to look at, Hane turned to check on Mason. He appeared to be awake but only reluctantly. Rose had their hands interlocked over a strip of throwing knives, likely directing a cooperative spell to imbue them. Mason muttered something about hurrying up so he could take a nap; Hane sympathized.

Hane felt the tickle of breath against their ear a moment before they heard Lief whisper: "She keeps her notes on the vault in the notebook with a metal cover that locks when closed. Do you see it?"

Hane twisted around, shooting Lief a poisonous glare. Lief only shrugged, unabashed.

"We both agree that sending her out is the best thing, both for her and for the team," he said, tone reasonable. "Just grab the notebook first. That way, we didn't waste our time getting here. I'll even help you pick out something nice for her once we get inside the vault."

He had to be kidding. Right? Odette might be in shock, but she was sitting right in front of them—there was no way she didn't hear Lief's whisper. But if she did, she didn't protest, nor respond in any way at all, her entire focus centered on the needle in her hand. Rose and Mason were close enough to have heard as well, but Rose continued muttering spells under her breath, imbuing her knives for the next fight. Was stealing from team members common among Tiger Spire climbers? Hane was no stranger to taking supplies off of corpses, but that wasn't the case here.

Hane resisted the urge to pull free of Lief's touch; they still needed their wounds closed, even if they found Lief's suggestion repulsive. "Odette isn't just after some treasure, she has an interest in the vault itself. If she doesn't recover soon, I'll agree to send her out of the spire, but I'm not going to steal from her."

Lief sighed theatrically as he rolled his eyes. "Do you ever get tired of being so high-minded all the time? You must have joined this team because you want something from the vault; what sense is there in letting the prize slip through your fingers now? Do you really want Nieve's sacrifice to come to nothing?"

Hane did jerk away this time, pivoting on a knee in order to face Lief directly. "Nieve wasn't sacrificed, she was lost. And I would rather lose out on a treasure than steal from a teammate."

The look in Lief's eyes was almost pitying. He scrubbed his palm against his leggings in a deliberate manner. "I'll never understand how someone as strong as you can still have scruples while delving for treasure. Being soft-hearted in a spire will get you killed, you know."

Hane declined to respond, maintaining their heavy glare. Lief stood slowly and gracefully, a false smile in place as he claimed an empty stretch of floor. With an exaggerated yawn, he put his head down on his satchel and closed his eyes. Equally disturbing as Lief's suggestion was the fact that neither Rose nor Mason deigned to chime in. Mason might prefer to simply go with the flow, but Rose always had an opinion to offer. So why hadn't she said anything? Of course, Odette sat close enough to overhear, too, but in her current state, Hane hadn't really expected her to say anything.

Unless . . . maybe that had been the point? Maybe Lief had only been trying to get Odette to snap out of her fugue? It was possible, but it still gave Hane an uneasy feeling that stirred the cold numbing their emotions to Nieve's loss.

A light tug on their sleeve: Hane looked over to find Odette pinching the tear in their shirt closed. Her embroidery hoop lay forgotten in her lap, colorful thread laying in a lifeless tangle on the taut fabric. Odette had threaded the needle using a spool tucked inside her utility bracer, holding it uncomfortably close to Hane's arm. Slowly her eyes tracked up to meet Hane's and for one instant it looked as if she might speak. But then she buried her teeth in her lower lip, gaze tracking back down to the tear in Hane's sleeve. A prick of light glinted off the needle, making it seem as if the thread itself sparkled. She didn't speak, but her intention seemed clear enough.

"You want to stitch it up?" Hane asked, keeping their tone low and even.

Odette's eyebrows rose incrementally over the rims of her glasses.

"Do you need me to take it off?"

Odette shook her head. She scooted closer, changing her grip on the needle before pinching the fabric together and examining it closely. Uncomfortable, Hane twisted away from her and took another sip from their canteen. A quick check on the ventilation shaft, then they dug through their bag for something they could eat quickly. If they couldn't sleep, then at least they had to keep their energy up. A quick check on their injuries proved most were closed, if still a bit tender. Food and water would help restore the blood they had lost during combat.

Movement across the chamber: Rose stood up and picked her way over toward Hane, stepping over the equipment she'd tossed out of her bag and pockets while searching for more mana crystals. She grabbed two blanks and sank down beside Hane, eyes flicking briefly over to Odette, whom Hane was steadfastly ignoring.

"Can you fill a few shells with transference mana?" Rose asked. "I got water mana from Brick already."

Hane nodded, waiting as Rose set the vessels down in front of them, then asked, "What effect does transference mana have on your knives?"

"I use it for a substantial knockback upon impact," Rose explained while Hane filled the first blank with transference. "I could also make the daggers fly faster, or curve when thrown to make their trajectory less predictable, but I like the knockback to widen the distance between myself and an opponent. It only works on one target at a time, though. I need to work on creating an imbue that tosses back multiple targets the way you do."

Hane didn't know what to say to that. They stayed silent until they finished filling both blanks. "Your aim is impressive. I don't think I've seen you miss."

Rose shrugged off the compliment as she unfurled a leather roll of fresh throwing knives. "I was never confident in close-quarter combat, and I didn't want to waste time practicing something I was never going to excel at. I was always good at darts, though, and I found that I retain knowledge better if I take breaks from my studies to do something physical. You seem really calm right now. Is that because you're certain that Nieve was able to use her return bell?"

The sudden change of topic without so much as a change of inflection made Hane feel unbalanced for a moment, though their silence didn't stop Rose from using one whole transference crystal on imbuing her throwing knives. They didn't want to talk about this; Nieve was either fine or she wasn't, and nothing Hane could do now would change that result.

"We weren't close." Past tense, because it slammed the door on hope. "She was a skilled climber, so if she could use her return bell, I'm sure she did."

Rose studied their face with the intensity she usually reserved for spells. It was unnerving, but the only other option was to turn and face Odette, which was equally unsettling.

"You're a hard person to read," Rose said finally, lips pursed and puckered. "You should work on that, when you see Nieve again." Rose tucked the second transference crystal inside her vest and started to stand, pausing before straightening her knees. "For what it's worth, I think you're right: Nieve would have been smart enough and fast enough to ring out. If you know what she wanted from the vault, I'll help you find it."

"Are we still doing that?" Mason asked groggily, covering a yawn as Rose picked her way back over her scattered belongings. "Because I have to tell you guys, I don't think it's worth it to enter the actual labyrinth unless we're sure we're going to make it to the vault."

"I don't think getting there is the problem," Rose commented, spilling a bag of blanks and mana crystals onto the floor. Hane couldn't identify all the mana types at a glance, but most of the crystals were fairly small capacity. Rose frowned as she poked through them. "I'm sure we could find a way to get inside the scenario's standard vault if we really wanted to. My concern is opening the phantom vault correctly. Did anyone happen to notice any clues painted on the sewer walls as we were running?"

Hane shook their head, ignoring the tug of Odette's needle through their sleeve. At most, they had noticed slashes of red paint through the black top hats that marked the territory of the Ash Hats, most likely a defacement by one or more of the competing drug gangs. Nothing else stood out to them while navigating the sewer tunnels by a half-remembered map while protecting the team and searching for a safe place to lay low. At that thought, Hane made sure to glance up and check the ventilation shaft once more.

"I feel it's probable that we'll find the vault before we find the clue." Lief didn't open his eyes as he spoke. "Odette did say the vault door might contain a hint in regards to the clue. The area around the vault should be a static safe zone, which means we can use it as a campsite while we search for the clue and the key."

"You make it sound like you expect the labyrinth to just open up and usher us safely to the end," Mason said, rubbing at his eyes. "Even if Odette can't create a reliable map of the labyrinth, she still has the spells to detect traps and sense if we're going in the correct direction or not. And it's not like the labyrinth is going to stay the same day after day when we're searching for the clue to open the vault: it's going to keep changing on us, which means we won't always find our way back to camp."

"Isn't that what you're here for?" Lief asked in a light tone. "These walls and floors are all stone, the locked grates are made of metal, and much as you hate it, the sewage is mostly water. You should be able to bend this labyrinth to your will, my dear Transmuter."

"Scaling." That whisper came from Odette, drawing all eyes at once. She didn't acknowledge the attention, but continued stitching Hane's shirt, brows tightly knotted over her glasses.

When it became apparent she had nothing more to add, Rose picked up the explanation. "Altering the shape of the labyrinth would add additional challenges, as well as increase the difficulty of the existing ones. Sometimes minor changes don't trigger it, but if you're talking about Mason creating a straight line to the vault, we're going to end up finding the lower levels flooded, or something equally difficult to deal with."

Mason shuddered. "If any part of this labyrinth requires me to go for a swim, I'm telling you right now that I'm going to ring out."

"But you can just shape the water around yourself," Lief protested. "After Hane, you're the most capable person to handle a water challenge."

"Nope," Mason replied obstinately. "I can live just fine with the portion of loot I've earned up until now. If you ask me to get in that water, I am going home."

"Let's not argue the point until it becomes a factor," Hane suggested. "Manipulating the labyrinth itself is only worth it if we know exactly where we want to go."

"Then what's your plan?" Lief asked archly.

Hane considered for a moment before answering. A soundless echo drew their gaze up toward the grate near the ceiling. "I think finding the labyrinth's guardian will be the easiest feat to accomplish. Once we know what we're up against, we'll know if it's something we can defeat without Nieve. If not, then that makes our next decision much easier."

"I can agree with that," Rose said, putting away all the items she'd dumped out of her pockets and pouches in her earlier haste. "Guardians are usually easy to find, so teams can choose to avoid them. Sometimes there's even a shortcut from the guardian's lair to the end point, but that might not be the case if there's a vault key in the loot cache."

"You really think we can beat it?" Odette's hands were still, fingers curled into the fabric of Hane's sleeve as if grasping for reassurance. "I . . . read so many climber profiles. I worked so hard to create this exact team. Each member of this team was chosen specifically for the trials I researched. Fighting the labyrinth guardian was Nieve's role. Can we really do it without her?"

Hane felt Lief's gaze boring into them, silently urging them to lie.

Hane refused. "It depends on what we find. If I believe we can handle it with the five of us, then I think it's worth continuing. If not, then I will agree to ring out of this climb with you, Odette."

Odette's eyes tracked up from the row of neat stitches sewn into Hane's sleeve. "Really?"

"I swear it," Hane agreed. "If we can't get the key from the guardian, then we can't open the vault, which means there's no point in continuing. But if we are forced to leave, please know that I'm willing to join you again if another opportunity allows us to delve into one of the phantom chambers here."

Odette's gaze wavered, grasp trembling where she clung to Hane's shirt. "This wasn't the plan. The plan was supposed to work. I need . . . I *need* to follow the plan."

Hane loosened her grip carefully, checking to make sure the thread was tied off before examining the stitching. The shirt had been ripped in two places, and while Odette had only had enough time to fix one of the tears, the stitches were neat and tight; if the thread had been black, it would barely have been noticeable at all.

"Don't worry about the plan," Hane assured her gently. "I'm from the Tortoise Spire, remember? I'm used to picking up the pieces after a plan falls apart, so all you need to do is follow me." Hane hedged, then added, "If you want to. You can still choose to ring out right now."

Odette swallowed tightly before glancing around at the others: Rose and Mason stared back with similar expressions of calculation on their faces. Lief simply looked blankly expectant. Again Hane found themself wondering if Odette or any of the others had overheard Lief encouraging them to steal Odette's notebook detailing the vault's secrets. They might have asked, but a very distant something tickled the edge of their perception, like a premonition: a sound that wasn't a sound, or a subtle change in temperature or air pressure. They couldn't say what it was, but their experience as a climber told them that something was about to happen.

Odette ducked her face low as she drew a shivery breath. "I'm sorry. About Nieve. I should have known that trap was there, it should have been marked by my spell, or—"

"It wasn't a normal trap," Hane interrupted, only half paying attention as they tried to figure out where the sensation of urgency was coming from. "It was a portal, most likely person-based, rather than location-based. A normal trap-detection spell wouldn't have caught it in time. Mason, can you unseal the door? Let's get ready to move."

"Why?" Rose asked, looking up from a spill of mana crystals and throwing knives. Most of her equipment had been put away, but it looked as though she was still working to imbue a few more weapons. "I thought we were resting here for a while."

"No, we were only hiding from the gangs temporarily," Hane corrected her. While the ventilation shaft seemed the most likely source of danger, Hane tried to keep their eyes on everything at once. Was there a false section of floor they missed seeing earlier? What about the balled-up bedrolls in the corner; had they checked to see if anything was hiding inside them? "Don't take anything from here unless you've inspected it for an aura. Mason, the door?"

"I'm getting there." Mason stretched and yawned widely. He eased an itch on his stomach, moving at a lethargic pace. "I was really hoping to get away from the gross water long enough to eat something. Are you sure we have to go now?"

Hane hesitated, suddenly uncertain. Were they being overly cautious? This storage room wasn't a safe area, like a mana fountain, but maybe it was secure enough for a longer rest? Odette had only just started recovering from her shock state; a little food and water would help her a lot if there was time for it. They should be fine as long as this was one of those static zones Odette had mentioned.

But if it was a push zone . . .

Surprisingly, it was Lief who weighed in on the side of haste, already on his feet and checking his equipment. "I think we should move on and establish a real base camp. Once we're inside the labyrinth, we won't have so many human opponents to face and we can actually start the part of this delve that matters."

Rose muttered darkly under her breath. "Fine, just let me finish these last couple imbues. I'm not as particular as my brother; I can eat while we walk. As long as we're not being chased by anything."

"I'll get started on the door," Mason groaned, body protesting with pops and creaks as he unfolded himself from his seated position. "I shaped the stone from the walls over the door to camouflage it. It's going to take a bit to move it all away again."

Hane thought to mention that they didn't have time for finesse, but they found themself distracted as Lief checked the quiver on his hip, fingers skimming the fletched ends of his arrows. "I thought you were nearly out of arrows, Lief. Did you have extras in your supplies?"

Lief laughed as he patted the quiver. "No, I found this while climbing the Serpent Spire. It's a quiver enchanted to regenerate arrows. It's a little slow, though, so it can take a while to refill. Neat, huh?"

It was neat. Hane wondered how high Lief must have been in the Serpent Spire to find a treasure like that.

"Um, Rose? Mason?" Odette shifted her seat to face them, her chin still tucked tightly into her chest. "Lief, you too. I am so sorry to have been a burden to you. Thank you all so much for keeping me safe until now. I promise, I will do everything I can to get us safely through the labyrinth and to the vault door."

"We've been relying on that since the beginning," Rose said, shrugging as she slotted the last of her knives into a sheath along her belt. "But since you are feeling better, is there anything else you need to tell us about opening the vault?"

Odette gnawed on her lower lip, considering deeply. Just as she drew a breath to speak, Hane felt it: a disturbing pattern in the air coming from the ventilation shaft, like wind blowing the pages of an open book, or the rustling of falling leaves.

Or the wingbeats of tiny insects.

"Something's coming through the vent!" Hane shouted, moving to stand between the vent and the others. "Mason, get that door open. Quick!"

Lief had an arrow to the string of his bow, sighting on the vent over Hane's shoulder. Odette squeaked and scrambled to shove her embroidery hoop back inside her bag before shrugging it on over her shoulder. Mason pressed both hands to the door, the sound of grinding stone pervading the tiny chamber. Rose dropped her pouch of mana gems and blanks as she tugged on the drawstring, small crystals spilling and rolling like marbles.

"Leave what you can," Hane instructed. "As soon as the door opens, we're out."

"This is all I have left," Rose protested, kneeling to scoop up the nearest crystals. "None of you have fire mana or lightning mana. I used up my only void mana crystal. Just give me a moment and I'll—"

"We don't have a moment." Hane felt their stomach drop as the first winged insect popped through the iron grate. A moth as big as Hane's palm fluttered silently up to the ceiling, wings whirring too quickly to make out any specific markings, though Hane thought they saw flashes of red amidst the downy gray. They hated fighting small creatures! This was worse than trying to catch the blink-bat, and at least as bad as fighting off the shiuni swarm from their last climb.

"But it's just a . . ." Rose trailed off, squinting at the insect. Lief cursed and lowered his bow, backing slowly toward the door. More moths followed the first one: two and then five, and then ten, then Hane couldn't see clearly enough to count the rest as they arrived. They remained clustered in the corner near the vent, but that was more than enough for a room this small: Hane's perception made their sight sharp enough to see the shimmering dust that drifted off their silent wings.

One moth perched on the edge of a half-rotted shelf, wings folding neatly against its back. Hane's suspicions were confirmed when the red spots on the lower wings formed a single crimson teardrop.

"Bloodsucking moths," Hane said, keeping their tone low. "That dust coming off their wings is a sleeping powder. We need to get out of this room now, Mason."

Mason made a dismissive noise. "That powder isn't strong enough to knock out a human. Those things usually feed on rats, right, Prickles?"

"Though technically correct, you're missing the larger picture." Hane was glad to see Rose moving with haste now, giving up on finding any more mana crystals as she stashed the pouch inside her vest. "Usually these moths hunt alone or in pairs, as one rat can last up to four feedings. We are currently in an enclosed room with maybe fifty of these things." She backed up until she bumped into her brother. "And I think there are still more coming. Get the door open, meathead. Now!"

Mason muttered a word Hane had thought meant "gear rack." "Fine! I'll just shape out the frame. That's—" As Mason put his shoulder against the door to shove it open, it stuck fast after only moving half an inch. Mason shook his head. "Sorry. I need to clear the hinges."

"Can you do anything about this?" Lief asked Hane.

Hane shook their head. "If I drench them in water, the dust washes off faster and puts us all to sleep before we can escape. I can tear them all apart with a Burst spell, but we'll still be breathing in the dust."

"Masks!" Rose gasped, searching through her pockets. "I can create masks to purify the air we—ah!" She dropped several pouches in surprise as something made the moths swarm like bees around a hive, wheeling faster and faster as more moths joined the throng. As Odette stooped to help Rose gather her things, Hane found themself holding their breath. If Mason didn't get the door open soon, they would use a Burst spell to break it down. The noise was sure to alert any nearby gang members to their presence, but that was better than succumbing to the sleep powder before being feasted on by moths.

The next time Mason shoved at the door, Hane and Lief leaned into it as well, stone cracking and breaking as they forced it open inch by ponderous inch.

"Which way are we running?" Lief asked, covering his mouth and nose with one hand while the other shoved at the door.

"Oh, I know!" Odette's gaze turned distant for a moment before she blinked them clear again. "The entrance of the labyrinth is close! There's a pipe that leads—"

"Is the pipe wet?" Mason demanded to know, cutting her off.

Odette looked conflicted. "Well, it's . . . you know, a small alteration in the floor outside the labyrinth shouldn't affect the challenge much. I'll take you to the pipe and you can reshape the floor so we drop down a level, okay?"

"Fine." With a final shove, the door was open just wide enough for a person to slip through. Good thing, too, because Hane could feel their senses going dull.

"Go," Hane urged the others. "I'll stay behind and—"

Use a Burst spell to kill the moths so they couldn't follow, but Hane didn't get that far. A veritable geyser of moths burst through the iron grate, dust scraping off their wings in a sparkling mist. Mason and Lief tried to get through the door at the same time, briefly getting stuck until Mason elbowed Lief back, sending him crashing into Rose. Two brilliantly red large mana gems fell from her grasp, clattering to the floor. As if that was a signal, the moths began a series of swooping dives directly overhead, creating a thick cloud of shimmering dust.

Recovering quickly, Lief raced after Mason, towing Odette along behind him. Hane would have followed, but Rose was groping along the floor after the mana crystals, a cloth handkerchief tied across her nose and mouth. They grabbed for her shoulder, intent on dragging her out if they had to, but before they could, Rose sat back on her heels to drop the pair of crystals inside the reservoir of what appeared to be a perfume atomizer. She gestured sharply for Hane to get back before pointing the atomizer up at the cloud of moths and crushing the bulb in her opposite hand.

A jet of flame erupted from the nozzle, incinerating the moths as well as the dust. A few more squeezes of the bulb reduced the grand majority of the moths to little more than ash.

"Go," Rose ordered, jerking her head toward the door. "I'll follow. There's more coming through the vent."

"Don't fall behind," Hane called, already slipping out the door. Sometimes the best thing to do was stand back and let other professional climbers do what they did best.

NIEVE

Champion (mind mark), Citrine
Paladin (heart mark), Quartz

Wherever the teleportation spell had taken Nieve, it hadn't returned her to her teammates.

Oh, she was back in the sewer, all right—and this time, she didn't have Lief to turn off her sense of smell. At least the sewage trench was empty, so the smell wasn't quite as fresh, but it was still deeply unpleasant. She'd already tried using her communication device, only to find it wasn't working, then she'd waited around a bit, just in case Odette was tracking her with that strange enchanted device, but when that got boring, Nieve set out to find the team on her own.

And she was pretty sure she'd just walked in a circle. And not once, either. She scowled at the rotted remains of a wooden crate in the crossroads of two empty sewer trenches. It could be a different rotten crate, but Nieve was fairly certain she'd been through this intersection before.

"Ugh, wake up!" Nieve shouted, stomping her left boot against the walkway. "I could use some of those magic senses of yours, Chime! C'mon, help me out here!"

She fell still, listening intently for any hint that Chime might have woken up, then groaned in frustration. Navigation was not a strong point of hers, but she couldn't be so bad that she kept coming back to the same spot over and over again.

Which meant this was a puzzle, and the point was to find an exit somewhere within this infuriating loop.

"What am I supposed to do here?" Nieve asked aloud, half hoping to attract a monster or two. At least then she could vent her frustrations on something. "Do I punch through a wall? Or the ceiling, maybe? Am I supposed to flood the channel with water from somewhere? Or follow a specific path to break the circle? What is it? Someone answer me!"

Her voice rose until the shouts echoed down all four corridors, the final word carrying on infinitely. Nieve stomped her foot one last time before crossing her arms over her chest, not pouting, exactly, just . . . brooding.

What would Sage do here? Nieve wondered. Then, with a quick head shake, she changed the question. *What would Hane do here?*

Sage, undoubtedly, would have already figured out the type of magic that was causing the tunnels to overlap and loop endlessly. Nieve tried using Detect Aura, but the few runes she'd found meant nothing to her, and the magic was so dense, she couldn't discern the different types that made it up, never mind how to break the loop. But Hane . . . Hane was a bit more like Nieve, in that they relied on their physical skills to problem-solve more often than their wits. Sure, Hane was a bit more intuitive than Nieve was, but modeling Hane's approach was more likely to yield results than attempting to emulate Sage.

Hane would . . . Nieve looked around, trying to guess at what her secretive teammate might do. Her gaze tracked upward until she was staring up at the cracked and leaking ceiling. *Hane would choose a different path, since the one down here isn't working.*

How did that help? It wasn't as if Nieve could walk on the ceiling. There weren't any openings in the ceiling, either; she'd looked for that already. So then if the answer wasn't up . . .

Was it down?

Nieve leaned over the trench, looking up and down it twice before dropping down into the empty channel. She grasped her hilt, looking around herself warily, checking to make sure she hadn't triggered a trap or lured a monster out of hiding. Long minutes of silence—aside from the steady drip, drip, drip of the leaky ceiling—convinced Nieve it was safe enough to proceed. Feeling just a bit proud of her own cleverness, Nieve skirted around the rotten crate and chose to turn left, following what would hopefully turn out to be a new path and a way out of this loop.

So it was particularly frustrating when, after rounding only two corners, Nieve found herself facing the same rotted crate at the same intersection once more.

"Are you kidding me?" Nieve shouted, stomping the remaining distance to the crate. "Of all the reshing challenges I could have run into, I had to get dropped right into a reshing puzzle that reshing loops around on itself, without a reshing—"

A rage-fueled kick shattered the remains of the crate into splinters, sending the blackened base spinning into a corner of the trench, where it squelched sickly upon impact. But that wasn't what cut off Nieve's rant.

No, that was the sudden reveal of a rusted iron grate covering an opening in the floor, hidden just under the disgusting crate that Nieve loathed with all her being.

"Sage better not ever find out about this," Nieve muttered, curling her fingers through the grating. "Not ever. Okay, one, two—"

Strengthening her grip with a pulse of enhancement mana, Nieve ripped the grate straight out of the floor and tossed it aside. The sides of the drain were dry, and light glimmered at the end of it, though Nieve couldn't make out much of the lower level. Shrugging to herself, she swung her legs over the edge and dropped into the drain. It was wide enough that she was able to press her back against one side and support herself with her hands and feet against the far side, lowering herself slowly to the bottom of the drain. She tried twisting around to look below herself, but couldn't see much of anything. She waited, straining to hear a sound or a familiar voice, but eventually she grew bored of waiting and simply let herself fall, landing feet-first in the dry trench below her.

This level of the labyrinth was dimmer than the one above it, cloaking the shoulder-high walkways in shadow, making scent the first thing that registered to Nieve as she waited for her eyes to adjust. The smell of the sewer level above hadn't been overly offensive, as the trenches were all bone dry. The worst smell was a mild sourness suffused with a wet earth scent. Not the worst smell ever, in Nieve's opinion. Certainly not as bad as when she had first entered the scenario. But now, the fetid stench of rot, musk, and sweat hit her hard enough to make her eyes water. The trench was still empty and dry—thankfully, as she had landed in the center of it—which meant the smell was coming from something other than sewage.

While it was purely a guess, Nieve felt confident the source of the smell had something to do with all the reflective eyes staring down at her from the shoulder-high walkways lining the trench. She held her breath, gripping the hilt of her sword as she slowly counted up the pairs of eyes surrounding her, blinking the hulking shadowy figures into shapes that she could recognize. They must have been just as surprised to see her as she was to see them, judging by how still and silent they were, but by the time Nieve could make out their forms against the shadows, the less fearful of her they appeared. In fact, most were beginning to snort and stamp their feet in a show of aggression, and by the sound of it, there were even more of them crowded behind the ones Nieve could see.

Nieve's mind labeled the creatures as "trash hogs," though she knew that wasn't entirely correct. While Sage could recite every monster's name, where they might be found outside the spires, what they ate (or what ate them), and any important physical or magical attributes, Nieve only retained the most pertinent information about monsters: kill them before they killed her. And while trash hogs (or whatever they were technically called) weren't the meanest or scariest of monsters, they weren't weak or defenseless, either. It didn't help that at a rough count, Nieve estimated there were more than twenty of them clustered on the shoulder-high walkways, all glaring down at her.

Just like pigs, these monsters were bulky through the chest, shoulders, and barrel, with short legs and snub-nosed snouts. Beady intelligent eyes gleamed a nefarious red in the low light, which Nieve thought might be different from normal pigs, but she wasn't entirely sure about that. She was sure that normal pigs were a good deal smaller than these were, and while pigs might have small tusks, the wicked-looking tusks on the trash hogs were long, curved, and terminated in vicious points that could rip open the side of a lion. They also had wide, flat skulls that resisted blades and bashing weapons, as well as short, bony spikes along their spine. They could move deceptively fast, charging opponents head-on to strike with their tusks.

But the worst thing about trash hogs—in Nieve's experience, at least—was their disgusting habit of rolling in filth. Sure, pigs might enjoy mud baths, but the sludge and fetid rot that trash hogs coated themselves with made for an incredibly disgusting fight. Nieve was already looking forward to taking a bath, and the fight hadn't even started yet.

Maybe I can kill them all with ice spears, Nieve thought, turning a slow circle, prepared to draw at any second. *If they stay up on the walkways, then it would be easy to keep my distance and just—*

As soon as she thought it, Nieve caught sight of a walkway that had crumbled into rubble, creating an easy path down into the trench where she stood. It might create a bottleneck if the trash hogs all filed down that way, but hog-monsters typically became frenzied once the fighting started, and Nieve didn't think their reluctance to jump down from the shoulder-high walkways would last for long.

The squeals and grunts started from somewhere in the back, then worked their way forward, until Nieve was surrounded by an echoing chorus, punctuated by the scrape of cloven hooves on stone. The nearest trash hogs shook their heads menacingly, light gleaming off their tusks. With the fight imminent, Nieve considered the terrain and reluctantly released her sword. The trench was just wide enough that Nieve could touch the sides with both arms outstretched, making it too narrow for her sword. And trash hogs were hard to kill with a narrow blade, as it took precise strikes to land killing blows. Her war hammer was much better suited to the task, but as she reached for it, the altered shape of the spike opposite the hammer—now three curved, wicked-looking claws—reminded her that she had a new weapon in her arsenal.

Nieve straightened up, breathing deep into her heart. Byakko had said Nieve could invoke her power by calling her name, right? What better time to test out her new Paladin attunement than now?

Stones clattered and shifted as the first trash hogs picked their way down the incline from the walkway, the coarse hairs along their back bristling straight up through layers of filth. For now, they were approaching cautiously, assessing an unknown threat, but soon it would be a veritable stampede, and Nieve meant to be ready for them.

"Frost Form," Nieve murmured, casting the spell she had faith and experience in first. She had no idea of what to expect when invoking Byakko's powers, and her stomach fluttered nervously at the thought of harnessing a god's power, but Byakko had been clear in her expectations. She had gifted Nieve this power for a reason, so she might as well get used to using it. Nieve released her breath slowly, focusing on the cold light centered just over her heart.

"Great Lord Byakko, please grant me your strength."

The moment she spoke the words, Nieve felt a foreign presence rise up within her, like a hunting lion emerging from the grass that hid it from its prey. She felt it stare her down with merciless sky-blue eyes, telling her to step aside and allow the beast to take control. It would have been easy to resist, especially if she activated Mind of Ice, a protection against compulsion and mind reading, but the presence within her carried the familiar scents and sensations of standing in Byakko's presence. And if Byakko was asking her to step aside, then Nieve would do so willingly.

Lowering her defenses to allow the predator to take control was harder than she expected, yet once she did, the effect was instantaneous: she felt it surge through the muscles of her chest, her stomach, her shoulders, her arms, even through her fingertips, curling them like claws rather than squeezing them into fists. Her legs felt powerful, coiling beneath her as if to propel her through a powerful leap; she felt the phantom sensation of a muscular tail lashing behind her, keeping her steady and balanced. Her senses sharpened: she could see as clearly as if the chamber was lit with pure light; she could hear every individual step and identify its location; her sense of smell could discern the difference between the musk-sweat and fear-sweat that coated the bestial monsters. If she'd had the presence of mind to consider it, she would have noticed that she no longer found the stench of rot to be offensive, but instead could pick out individual scents through the tear-inducing medley, but her focus narrowed to a specific train of thought.

Specifically, her focus was on proving her predatory superiority by tearing through these reeking sacks of meat.

A guttural squeal heralded the first true war-cry of the trash hogs, though it was quickly drowned out by the rush of a stampede. Nieve was in motion almost before the sound registered in her ears, charging the few hogs who descended down into the trench. She punched straight down onto the first one's skull, hearing a satisfying crack beneath the armor-like flesh. She caught another one with a knee to the ribs, caving them in as if they were no more than brittle sticks. The force of her kick sent the trash hog flying into the one beside it, both hogs hitting a distant wall hard enough to send spiderweb cracks up through the walkway. The one with the cracked skull was still on its feet, but barely, staggering sideways as it attempted to catch its balance. Nieve kicked backward with her heel, sending the hog skidding down the line of the trench on its side, plowing through mounds of debris and cracked stone.

This feels amazing! Nieve thought, a smile growing on her face. *Is this really only a Quartz-level attunement? How much stronger would I be if I'd raised it to Citrine?*

Her knuckles should have been sore after that punch, but instead she felt nothing but the urge to rip, tear, and devour the opponents in front of her. Her blood sang with the song of the hunt, her nose guided her more than sight, and the power flooding her body begged for an outlet. There were so many opponents here to prove her strength against, how good would it feel to defeat all of them one by one and stand triumphant above the carnage?

Trash hogs raced down the shattered walkway, jammed against one another so tightly they jostled one another as they charged, as if Nieve could be overcome through sheer force of numbers. Nieve's body hunkered low in an unfamiliar stance that felt right just then, a hunting cat coiled to pounce. A stillness fell over her, so absolute that she scarcely felt the need to breathe. Her eyes picked out a pattern that didn't translate well inside her head, but the force rolling through her urged her to charge, so she did. Instinct screamed for her to flex her claws, to rake and rend, and while a distant part of her mind recalled the small fact that she didn't actually have claws, the urge was too powerful to ignore. Ice formed along her forearms, extending over her hands into long, icy dagger-like claws just as she slammed shoulder-first into the solid wall of hog flesh.

Afterward, Nieve would only remember flashes of the battle that followed, small moments that stood out in perfect clarity as if captured by a

Diviner. She remembered the feel of her ice-claws slicing cleanly through a trash hog's hide as if it were barely more substantial than a swatch of silk. She remembered a broken-tusked hog leaping off the walkway to crush her, only for Nieve to catch it mid-leap and hurl it into a cluster of other trash hogs. She remembered a severed pig's ear spinning through the air, drops of blood glittering like rubies as they fell. And while she remembered seeing the trash hogs scream and squeal, grunt and howl as she tore through them, the only sound she remembered was the steady thump, thump, thump of her own heartbeat in her ears.

She wouldn't remember the hoof that broke one of her toes through the top of her boot, nor the tusk that ripped through her leggings to score a long, bloody cut along her thigh, nor the way she threw her head back and roared so fiercely that a few of the trash hogs turned and fled, scattering down different trenches in their blind terror. She would never remember reforming her ice claws as they chipped and broke, just as she would never remember unconsciously licking at a splash of blood that landed on her face.

What she did remember was the silence that fell when the final trash hog lay twitching in its death throes at her feet. There was an unsettling feeling of confusion as she looked around for her next opponent and found only little heaps of mana crystals where the felled hogs had met their ends. As blood dripped off the tips of her ice-claws, she felt something urge her to lick them clean. Instead, she shook her arms out, willing the ice to fall away in brittle chunks, and even that took a force of will she wasn't used to needing when releasing a spell. A distant sound, echoing down the empty trench, made Nieve twitch and spin, nose flaring to catch a scent as instinct urged her to chase down more prey, to feel their lifeblood drain through her teeth.

And with that disturbing thought, Nieve decided she was finished using Byakko's gift for now.

She struggled with releasing the spell, unable to form the words to an incantation, or even to straighten up from her unfamiliar fighting stance, but after a few failed attempts to resume control of her body, Nieve activated Mind of Ice, cutting off her connection to Byakko's gift.

The aftereffects hit her all at once: her lungs suddenly ached for air, her muscles trembled with exhaustion, and her visual acuity vanished so abruptly that she felt plunged into darkness. A queasy sensation filled the pit of her stomach, making her seek out a clean place to sit down, but before she found one, her knees buckled beneath her, dropping her where she stood.

The chamber seemed to spin around her as she caught her breath, cataloging injuries as they made themselves known to her. The broken toe was nothing; she could bind it to the next toe and ignore it until after the climb ended. The cut on her thigh was of higher concern, but it only bled sluggishly. She could wrap a bandage around it over her leggings and keep it iced until she found the others; if it became a large enough problem, she could always sip one of the healing potions she kept in her medical kit. From the waist down, she felt like a bruised piece of fruit. Her throat felt strangely raw, the small bones of her hands and wrists felt shivery and frail, and a sudden light-headed sensation made her feel faint. As her vision tunneled out, she curled her head into her knees and focused on nothing but breathing. When her vision finally cleared, she pulled her canteen off her belt and took a long drink before splashing a palmful of water over her face.

I wish I had taken that warning about exhaustion more seriously, Nieve thought, finally catching her breath. *I'm glad no one was around to see that.*

<I saw it.>

Nieve's arm jerked at the unexpected toll of Chime's voice in her head. She scowled as water from her canteen spilled down the front of her vest.

Oh, are you finally awake?

<I was not asleep; my consciousness fled this vessel to escape the over-whelmingly threatening silence I felt earlier,> Chime retorted. <I returned to share some good news with you, but I hardly recognized your mana signature at all. I thought my vessel had been stolen until I was able to find traces of your thoughts within that . . . power.>

Was it that bad? Nieve asked, her throat too sore to speak aloud. Why was her throat so raw? Had she been shouting as she fought the trash hogs? Or growling, maybe? She wished she could remember the experience more clearly. *Why didn't you try talking to me sooner?*

<I did try.> Chime's tones were short, sharp, and clear. <You did not hear me until you freed yourself of that spell.>

Well, that was worth remembering. Had Nieve missed hearing Chime because theirs was a mental presence, rather than a physical one? Would she have heard a teammate if someone had been there with her? Maybe she should hold off on using her new attunement until she could do some more research on it.

Actually, that sounded slow. Maybe she'd just keep experimenting on her own for a little longer, at least until she reached Carnelian level with it. How hard could it really be to learn a new style of combat?

Did you say you had news? Do you know where Hane and the others are? Nieve asked, finally feeling recovered enough to push herself up from the floor of the empty trench. The carcasses of slaughtered trash hogs had all dissolved into small mounds of mana crystals, and while Nieve couldn't carry them all, she did start toeing through the piles, looking for any unique or especially large crystals to claim as treasure. *And what do you mean that you fled your vessel? Could you always just leave it anytime you wanted?*

<Ordinarily, no.> The sound of Chime's voice was comforting, giving Nieve the sense that she wasn't all alone inside the Tiger Spire. <That was what I wished to share with you: the piece of my self is very close. So close that when I tried to escape the overwhelming sense of power, I was drawn to my other self, my other consciousness. I know where I am, and I have information to share about my surroundings.>

That's great. Nieve crouched down, momentarily distracted by an oddly colored mana crystal that she couldn't identify. Shrugging, she slipped it into a pocket, along with the others she'd thought to grab. *We must be close, right? The vault is supposed to be somewhere in this labyrinth.*

A few long, drawn-out bell tolls made Chime seem thoughtful. <Not so close now as we were when you were falling . . .>

When we *were falling.*

<But as I have come to understand these structures, physical distance is more of an illusion than an accurate measurement,> Chime concluded. <More importantly, what you should know is that I am not alone.>

Of course you aren't, Nieve replied, kicking through more gem piles. She stopped when a stone slab shifted underfoot. She stomped on it a few times, confirming a hollow sound. *You're with me, aren't you?*

<That is not what I mean. And yes, the space beneath you is a hollow void.>

Keep talking, I'm listening. Nieve felt along her belt, searching for a tool that would help her move the square slab of stone in the floor. She was surprised to find the Magpie's walking stick still tucked in the back of her belt, but she doubted the marble top would hold up well if she bashed it against the stone slate. Instead, she selected her hammer with its three new curved spikes and tried to work them into a crease between the stone and the rest of the floor, thinking she could pry the stone up.

<What I mean to say is that my other vessel is not alone in the chamber you seek,> Chime explained, the tolls of their voice coming faster and faster as they continued. <There are other entities similar to myself within that room. Not exactly like me, mind you, I sensed nothing of another gateway crystal within that space, but there do exist several entities bound within objects, such as I am. Many are dormant, but the ones I was able to speak with do not appear to have been sealed to their vessels through force, as was my initial fear upon meeting them.>

That's good, isn't it? Nieve scowled as her clawed hammer only managed to scratch thin lines in the stone slab, rather than lifting it up. She growled in frustration before spinning the haft in her grip and smashing the slab with the blunt end, hoping that whatever was hidden underneath wasn't fragile enough to break. *That means that whoever bound you to the crystal sword didn't get a chance to pass on their technique.*

<While it proves nothing with certainty, it is a comforting discovery,> Chime agreed. <However, what I feel I must warn you about is the presence known only as The Eyes.>

Nieve had to get down on her hands and knees to reach into the hollow and pluck out the larger pieces of stone in order to find the hidden object beneath. *That sounds creepy. Do you know what object that one is bound to?*

<The Eyes are the only presence that moves freely about the chamber,> Chime explained. <I have never seen them, save for their eyes, burning like cold flames against the total darkness that dwells in the room like a living thing. I believe they are some sort of guardian for the treasures you and your companions seek.>

Nieve paused in the middle of groping through the broken bits of stone at the bottom of the hollow. *Odette didn't say anything about a guardian.*

<I was similarly surprised,> Chime intoned. <Which was why I thought it relevant enough to share.>

Thanks. Nieve's hand closed around something small and metallic: an iron key, meant to open a door somewhere in this reshing labyrinth, no doubt. *I'll pass that on to the others when I find them. Maybe Odette doesn't know about the guardian.*

<One more point of interest, which my other self did not know until our consciousnesses were joined,> Chime said, as if separate consciousnesses were a normal occurrence. <But the presence of The Eyes strongly resembles the silence that caused me to flee my vessel as you fell. It is a great deal lesser, but similar in nature, if not in truth.>

What does that mean? Nieve asked, pocketing the iron key as she straightened up. *Similar in nature, if not in truth?*

<The power is the same, but not the same,> Chime said, as if that meant anything at all. <It is the same manner as a flute may mimic a birdsong, but birds will still know the truth of its nature.>

The same, but not the same, Nieve thought as she turned to look down each empty trench. *Maybe a spire guardian gifted with Byakko's strength, or maybe one of her children watches over the vault's treasures. I'll have to ask Odette if she knows anything when I meet up with the others.*

If she ever met up with the others.

Hey, Chime, Nieve thought. *Are you able to sense Hane and the others? I need to find them as soon as possible.*

<Allow me to try.> Nieve heard a long, steady note drawn out like a ringing in her ears. <It appears that my senses are still limited by proximity. At the present, I do not perceive any familiar life forms nearby, but I do detect several sources of magic, some of which shiver with the whisper of secrets.>

"Well, that's something at least," Nieve muttered. Her voice sounded rough and her throat felt dry and scratchy. She took another sip from her canteen as she switched back to mind speech. *Can you point me in the direction of the most powerful magic source? That's probably where I'm supposed to go next.*

The pensive sound that followed was less like chimes or bells and more like crickets singing on a warm summer night. <Were this my own challenge, I would be able to guide you past every obstacle and see you safely to your destination. Though I can sense the flow and concentrations of mana here, I fear my inexperience might lead you into peril.>

Great, Nieve thought, scattering a mound of crystals with a swipe of her boot. *Guess I'll keep wandering through this sewer aimlessly until I run out of rations and I'm forced to ring out.*

<Surely it is not as hopeless as that,> Chime urged. <No matter how vexing traversing a labyrinth may be, the determined will always find a way out. And quite often the creators of such challenges incorporate hints to guide beings to their destination. Surely you have some experience in navigating settings such as this one.>

I've been in mazes before, sure, Nieve replied, casting Detect Aura as she turned a circle, searching for something that might tell her which way to go. *But never alone. Sage was the one who was good at puzzles and predicting paths; I just went where he told me to go.*

<Did he never explain to you his method of navigation? Did you learn nothing from watching him?>

Nieve huffed, setting out down a randomly selected tunnel, stomping footsteps echoing off the stone walkways. *I didn't always have the time to sit around and watch him. Most of the time I was fighting something to give him time to gaze into the future, or read the wind, or do whatever it was he did.* Nieve touched the iron key through her pocket. *Once, he said that if there's a key, then there's a door. So, I guess I'm looking for a door, then.*

Chime fell silent for a while, leaving Nieve alone with her echoing footsteps. After a while, she paused and created an ice pillar beneath her feet, lifting her up to walk along the walkway rather than down the center of the trench.

<I do not wish to share the secrets of my challenges with those who have yet to take them,> Chime said slowly. <But as I have already offered you a

prize worthy of completing my trials, I suppose it does no harm to tell you the secret of my own labyrinth challenge.>

You don't have to tell me; it probably wouldn't help anyway. Nieve flinched as she realized the thought came across too harshly. *I mean, your challenges aren't likely to have anything in common with the goddess's challenges, right?*

<Perhaps,> Chime allowed. <When I create a challenge such as this, I do not hide the objective behind opaque walls and barricades. The challengers at my shrine are able to see the finish from the start.>

Nieve's step slowed as she attempted to picture such a maze. *Doesn't that make it way too easy?*

<Not at all!> Chime's tones actually sounded hurried and excited. <The challengers may see the terminal point of the maze, but it is far from a straight path to reach that point. I shape my mazes out of pure sound magic, so that any who blunder on blindly would be deafened by the end. But for those who go slow and listen with care, they will hear the barriers long before they come within reach of them. And for those even more astute in the ways of sound, there are musical keys that may be used to create shortcuts. I even lay a path that may be followed from the origin to the terminus if one has but the ability to detect the correct pitch.>

Wait. Nieve stopped, unable to focus on her surroundings as she listened to Chime's description of their labyrinth challenges. *Are you saying there's some invisible path I could just follow straight to the exit? Can you sense it? Or can you tell me what I need to do to reveal it?*

<If the pathway were one of sound, I could lead you along it easily,> Chime replied in morose tones. <There are many magic types here, some blended in ways that are unfamiliar to me. My thought was that, perhaps, with your experience in settings such as this one, you might be able to tell me what seems out of place to you. If we can locate a hint or a clue, perhaps we can work together to trace a path to the chamber you seek.>

Nieve made a face, setting her fists on her hips as she gazed around the dimly lit sewer tunnel. *Sage never told me about any invisible paths before. If it was something I could find with Detect Aura, he probably would have taught it to me. But he did talk about feeling for air currents, because they could be coming from an opening, like a vent or a trapdoor. Or a secret sealed behind a wall.*

<This seems plausible. Have you attempted this method yet?>

Nieve conjured a thin layer of water along her arms and hands before holding them out wide, feeling for the slightest brush of a breeze against her damp skin. After several minutes of waiting, Nieve gave up and flicked the water off her fingertips.

Nothing. I feel nothing.

<I see. Is there another technique Sage might employ in a situation such as this?>

"I don't know," Nieve burst out, charging forward at a reckless pace. "Maybe there are markings on the walls that could point me in the right direction, but even if there was a great big sign scrawled there, I couldn't read it. I could try listening for a clue, but if it was sound-based you would have told me already, so it's probably not that. Maybe I was supposed to chase down the trash hogs and see if they led me to a big door labeled 'escape.' I could still find them if it would do any good; they smell so bad I could probably find them with my eyes—"

Nieve stopped so suddenly she nearly over-balanced herself. Two ideas clicked together like puzzle pieces, but it still took a moment to discern the image they created. Feeling a little foolish, Nieve lifted her nose and sniffed the air. It reeked of sewage, refuse, and rot, and beyond all of that, Nieve could smell the musk of the creatures that made this portion of the sewer their home. But breathing deeper, Nieve found a scent she hadn't noticed before—a scent she wouldn't have noticed if it weren't so familiar: the clean, heady scent of petrichor.

<What does this mean to you?> Chime asked, sensing Nieve's actions and emotions as she turned a circle, sniffing the air deeply.

Everything here smells gross, Nieve explained, taking a few steps experimentally and sniffing again. Was the smell of petrichor just a bit stronger here? Maybe at the next intersection, she could determine which direction it was coming from. *The first thing the team did when we got here was use magic to dull our sense of smell. The stench was so overwhelming, all I could think about was making it go away. So if someone was going to hide an invisible path through a sewer . . .*

<They might choose to do so with a strong, clean scent!> Chime finished, catching on. <This is good thinking. You hold the scent; I will watch for secrets and deviations in the mana that surrounds us. Even if the scent does not lead us to your comrades, it is sure to lead us to the destination you seek.>

Let's hope so, Nieve thought doubtfully. *A wet smell could just be a wet smell and nothing more. But since it's our only clue, we might as well give it a shot.*

HANE

Wavewalker (leg mark), Citrine

"There, there, I see it up ahead!" Odette shouted, her hands cupping a compass spell. She sounded winded, but that was to be expected of anyone running full tilt to stay ahead of a swarm of bloodsucking moths. "That's the entrance to the labyrinth guardian's lair! See the copper pipes up ahead?"

Hane had been more focused on the increasingly alarming number of blackened scorch marks and deep gouges scratched into the stone walls, like the marks of a terrible beast declaring its territory. Whatever made those marks was most likely the labyrinth guardian, and any hint they could discern from the scratches might prove a valuable clue to defeating it and claiming the key to the phantom vault. Just past the marks was a veritable forest of gleaming metal pipes, some thick and vertical, others thin and winding. The guardian itself was secondary to the main objective of finding the key to the secret vault, which would be all but impossible if something wasn't done about the relentless moths pouring out of every air vent the team ran past.

"I'm nearly out of fire mana crystals!" Rose called from the rear of the group. Her face was soot-blackened, the lenses of her goggles gleamed an eerie orange. Even her bronzed curls were looking tarnished and harried. "Does anyone else have a plan to get rid of these things?"

"I do." Hane cast a begrudging look down at the water in the sewage trench. At first, they had tried helping Rose fight the moths, as even the weakest Burst spell was enough to shred their fragile wings, but the narrow walkways made it impossible to fight side by side, so Hane had stepped out onto the water. Hane's instincts had reacted faster than thought, putting them up on the ceiling just in time to avoid losing their leg to the longest pair of serrated scissors they had ever seen in their life. The water had thrashed and rolled as the narrow toothy jaws retreated, the only clue that it was a creature being the sullen pair of beady eyes that glared up at Hane before it swiftly vanished beneath the surface. The truly terrifying part of that experience had been the fact that whatever the creature was, it was immune to being detected by spells like Sense Water. After that far too close encounter, Hane had been too afraid to step out over the trench again.

But the encounter had given them an idea.

"When I call out, everyone stops running!" Hane instructed. "Mason, reshape the wall for overhead cover! Lief, shoot out the nearest ventilation shaft grate you can find! Odette, can you cast Cloak of Shadows to cover all of us?"

A slight pause, then: "Yes, but it would be obvious if I cast it here."

"That doesn't matter," Hane assured her. There wasn't much time; the team was drawing close to the forest of copper pipes now. "Rose, keep lighting up the moths until you're out of fire mana, then get under cover. I'll take care of the rest."

"Please," Mason gasped between breaths. "Please tell me you're not going to—"

"Now!" Hane shouted, spotting a ventilation grate in the ceiling that looked brittle from rust and age. As Hane skidded to a stop, Lief shrugged the bow off his shoulder, sighted, and loosed, his arrow punching straight through the rust-pocked grate. Even before the fragments of metal finished falling, more moths with blood-drop wings began filtering through, drawn by the noise. Hane checked to make sure that Mason was indeed reshaping the wall and stretching a stone awning overhead before crouching down and setting their hands on the surface of the water. They cast their shaping spell quickly while stalwartly telling themself they weren't absolutely terrified that a sawtooth-jawed monster might swim up and snap their fingers off.

The water directly below the open ventilation shaft churned and spun, drawing in water from all directions. Before the current could overflow onto the walkways, Hane shaped it to rise upward in a reverse waterfall, streaming water up into the now exposed ventilation entrance. Once the spell was in place, Hane backed up beneath Mason's stone awning and checked on the team. Rose had retreated from the cloud of moths, her face coated in ash everywhere except where her goggles protected it. She wore them loose around her neck now as she tucked herself against Mason's side, staring warily at the moths fluttering too close for comfort. Odette held her hands out in front of her, palms facing each other as she watched Hane with wide eyes.

"Now?" she asked, preparing to cast the shadow spell.

"Wait." Hane wanted to make sure this worked first. The trench down the center of the tunnel was rapidly emptying of water as Hane's geyser fed water up into the air shaft. They could hear the splash and patter of water finding exits through distant grates, pouring down pipes and walls as gravity took hold of it once more. The falling water that landed in the trench was caught up again in Hane's whirlpool before jetting up into the vents again in an endless cycle. And while they were hard to make out against the other detritus littering the sewer water, Hane saw thousands of tiny waterlogged moths being dragged along the current, giving them hope that their plan had been successful.

Hane stepped back beneath the protection of the stone awning as water began to drip off its curved surface. "Now, Odette."

Odette nodded and whispered something in Caelish, shadows twisting and writhing between her palms before they stretched and grew outward, enveloping the team in darkness. She was right about the spell being obvious: no semi-intelligent being would believe this to be a naturally occurring shadow, but the moths weren't actually all that intelligent. Hopefully any moths not caught up by the water running through the ventilation shafts would be drawn to light sources rather than the shadows that cloaked the team. And the farther the moths flew, the more likely it was that they'd be caught by the water draining through the ventilation shafts.

After long minutes of blackout blindness, with only the sound of falling water to mark the passage of time, Hane began to shuffle sideways, seeking the edge of the shadow spell. They didn't lift their feet—no, that was how people stumbled and fell when they couldn't see—but instead slid slowly along the walkway, placing one hand on the wall as a guide. The shadow spell ended two full paces from where they had been standing, but it took longer than that for Hane to peer out into the dimly lit sewer once more, searching for any remaining moths. Water still trickled down from the vents, but the sewer trench was empty now, save for a few puddles, mounds of rotten trash, and a few thrashing lizards with long, scissorlike snouts. Hane made a face as they drew back.

"Odette, you can release the spell." Hane made sure to shout so she could hear them. Movement that wasn't falling water caught their eye: a lone moth fluttering back toward them. Hane shredded it with a tiny Burst spell. "Some of the moths survived, but they don't have the numbers to be a threat anymore."

The shadows collapsed inward, pooling between Odette's palms before she pressed her hands together, effectively ending the spell. While the others peered around curiously, Mason pulled back against the wall, cringing in disgust at the water dribbling down from overhead.

"That was exactly what I didn't want you to do," Mason said curtly. "I'm making an umbrella for myself, and none of you are welcome underneath it!"

"I'm carrying your bedroll," Rose pointed out dryly. "Unless you want it to get damp, you're going to share that umbrella with me."

Mason made a face as he reshaped a stone rod into an umbrella with a long handle. Cleverly, he shaped it so the side closest to the wall remained flat, while the outer side was wider and more rounded. "Just give me the bag, Prickles. You know if we walk side by side, one of us is going to end up getting pushed into the trench."

"I wouldn't advise that, even as a joke," Lief commented. He searched his bag as he surveyed the emptied sewer channel. "Ignoring all the sharp and broken objects, as well as the treacherous footing due to algae and . . . well, let's just call it algae. Anyone who falls down there is going to have a tough time getting back up before they get eaten by the sewer lizards."

"Gavials," Odette said, peering over the ledge before drawing a silk cloth from the outer pocket of her bag. As she spoke, she wound the cloth around her head several times, tying it above her forehead with a knot that looked like a bow. "Aquatic, carnivorous lizard-monsters. They can bite through steel and when they're underwater, they're completely undetectable. Sorry, I didn't get a chance to check for hidden monsters while we were busy running from moths."

That wasn't as surprising as was the fact that everyone seemed to be covering their heads against the water dripping from the vents. Rose wound a scarf over her hair similar to Odette's, and Lief pulled an oilcloth cowl from his bag. The hood not only covered his hair, but the drape of the cloth covered his shoulders as well. Mason shouldered his sister's bag without letting his stone umbrella slip from his shoulder, despite the fact that he still stood under the stone awning. More to fit in with the others than anything else, Hane tugged the hood up from their collar. Along with the face mask they still wore, their eyes and hands were the only bare parts of them—and they expected to cover their hands before proceeding into the labyrinth guardian's lair.

"I think I know what type of monster is waiting for us in there," Hane said, nodding at the gleaming copper forest of pipes. "But in case I'm wrong, I'm going to go in first and check."

"Can we beat it?" Lief asked, faintly amused. "If it is what you think it is, I mean."

"No," Hane answered simply. "But we might not have to. All we need is the key for the vault, right, Odette?"

"Well, yes," Odette admitted, shuffling anxiously. "But it's not easy to find even after the guardian is defeated. It's not in the cache with the rest of the treasures, which is why most teams miss it."

"That works in our favor," Hane assured her. "As long as you think you can find it."

"I . . ." Odette bit her lower lip as she eyed the gleaming copper-pipe thicket across the near-empty trench. Her fingers traced the knotted cord of magic rings on her belt almost unconsciously. "I have some ideas?"

Hane turned to Lief. "Do you have anything that can enhance her ability to locate secrets? Maybe sharpen her perception, or something like that?"

"Oh, I have something better." Lief grinned. "Analyst spells rely heavily on mental mana to locate hidden secrets, but the mind is easily distracted in dangerous situations like this, which makes it possible to miss things. I have a spell that intensifies mental focus, allowing Odette to cast stronger versions of her spells than usual. The downside is that she'll have less awareness of what's going on around her, meaning she could potentially step in the way of an attack by the guardian, or even one of us."

By the alarmed expression on Odette's face, she didn't seem too keen on the idea.

"Let me explain the plan and then you can decide if it's worth it, okay?" Hane requested. Odette nodded shakily. Hane gave a cursory check of their surroundings before motioning the team into a huddle. "We don't need to defeat the guardian, and we don't need the treasure cache. All we need is to buy enough time for Odette to find the vault key. Mason, can you confirm if those pipes are actually copper or some other metal?"

"It's all copper," Mason said miserably. "I can tell just by looking. Precious metals are my specialty."

"Good," Hane replied. "That means it'll be easy for you to change its properties, right?"

Mason gave an offhanded shrug. "I wouldn't call a metal shaping spell like that easy, but I can do it. Depending on how much metal you need me to change, and what property it is you need altered."

"I'll go in ahead to distract the guardian," Hane explained, pulling their dimensional bag around so they could rifle through it more easily. The deep, parallel gouges, the blackened scorch marks on the walls, the copper pipes . . . each of these were clues, and Hane had enough experience to piece them together to form a picture. But this was a different spire than they were used to, so it paid to remain cautious. "Listen for my call, just in case I'm wrong. But if I'm right, we should be able to claim the key by sacrificing the treasure cache. Can we all agree to that?"

After a round of muttered agreement, Hane motioned for everyone to lean in close, speaking softly so as not to be overheard. Just in case.

Moments later, Hane was sliding stealthily between gleaming copper pipes, staying low and tight to the shadows as they made their way to the center of the copper thicket. Unlike the rest of the sewer, this area was bright—almost too bright, as if the pipes were polished daily. They wore the gloves enchanted for stealth, but only hoped the labyrinth guardian couldn't smell them, or else any precautions they took would be in vain. They had seen clothing and enchanted items designed to suppress an individual's natural scent before; perhaps they should look into adding such an item to their stealth gear the next time they had the chance.

Spotting an opening between the copper pipes, like a clearing in a forest, Hane froze and searched for signs of movement: a twitch, a breath, a shadow, anything at all. The utter stillness of the open area ahead made the hairs on the back of their neck prickle uncomfortably. Spire-honed instinct screamed that this was a trap with a hair trigger. Hane drew back in order to look up, where the copper pipes threaded through the ceiling. Overhead was a natural blind spot for most beings, and if this guardian was a feline of some kind—as Hane expected—it seemed natural that it might seek a high vantage point.

The ceilings here were high—far higher than the normal sewer tunnels. Thick pipes, large enough to hide an entire team behind, rose from the floor in straight columns, while thinner pipes followed curves and angles, twisting this way and that as if they had been fitted in wherever they could. Copper fittings, valves, gaskets, and knobs would make climbing the pipes easy enough, but the smooth metal and reflected light made navigating the copper jungle treacherous. Hane estimated the ceiling here to be nearly three stories tall, making it nearly impossible to see what might be lurking far overhead. As leaping would draw more attention than Hane wished to attract, they began scaling the pipes, hand over hand, while sticking as close to the shadows as possible.

About ten feet above the ground, Hane found a dense patch of shadows between two horizontal pipes, giving them a vantage point from which they could peer down into the clearing. There were three steel cases of buttons, levers, and flashing lights, possibly control panels for whatever flowed through these copper pipes. The guardian's treasure cache was possibly hidden inside one of the control boxes, but Hane thought it was more likely under the square steel panel that was bolted shut in the center of the floor. Hopefully the vault key was somewhere else—somewhere higher up—because the floor would be lost to them by the end of the fight.

There! The reflection of a spark drew Hane's eye up and to the right. With all the curved and shining metal, it took a while to find the source of the reflection, but it confirmed Hane's initial suspicion. They had set the correct plan in place. All that was left was to follow the plan.

I hate this plan.

Hane finally located the labyrinth guardian stretched out atop a wide horizontal pipe, half hidden against a gleaming reflection bright enough to leave light scars on Hane's eyes. It was counterintuitive to hide where the light shone the brightest, but for a creature composed entirely of lightning, it made a great deal of sense. The beast wore the shape of a large cat, which appeared to be half dozing, eyes nearly shut as it splayed comfortably on the pipe. Its features were difficult to discern against the searingly brilliant element that made up its body, like lightning given form. The only detail Hane could truly discern was that the lightning beast was far larger than any predatory analogue outside of the spire.

Is it a lion? Hane wondered, trying to make out a mane through the flickering white light. *Or is it a leopard? A panther?* They shook their head at themself. *It doesn't matter; the strategy stays the same. It might actually be a good thing that Nieve isn't here; it would have been a poor matchup, but she probably would have insisted on fighting anyway.*

They were stalling and they knew it. Hane slithered backward off the pipe and into the shadows, mentally preparing for their next move. The others were waiting for a signal; Hane meant for the lightning cat to give it to them.

With a show of trepidation, Hane squeezed between two pipes and leaned into the open space containing the control panels as well as the potential treasure. They made a show of looking around before stepping cautiously into the clearing, moving slowly as if expecting an ambush. Keeping their head down, they made a sudden rush to the square panel set in the floor, sliding down to a knee to search for a handhold. A passive perception spell alerted them when the lightning cat moved, but even forewarned, Hane barely managed to avoid the lightning strike. They dove to one side, coming up to their feet in a roll as the bolt of lightning resumed the shape of a large, predatory cat sitting in the center of the steel floor panel, lashing its jagged lightning bolt of a tail.

Seated on its haunches, it was about as tall as Hane was, with sparks of electricity rippling over its hide. Distinct features were still difficult to parse due to the brilliance of its elemental body, but judging by the rough shape of the head and ears, Hane guessed it more closely resembled a leopard or a jaguar than a lion, but without the spots for reference, they couldn't be sure which it was. Not that it mattered: both cats were stealthy, powerful, and deadly. Hane gave up trying to identify it in favor of remaining alive.

"My apologies," Hane said, taking a step backward. Not all monsters spoke, but most seemed to understand. When they chose to. "I can see now that this is your treasure and it would be wrong for me to take it from you. If you allow it, I'll leave you in peace."

It was a speech that had worked a time or two in the past.

Hane wasn't so lucky this time.

They just managed to dodge the lightning cat's next leap, but barely—Hane had to jump without the luxury of picking a place to land and ended up tripping over a series of pipes running along the floor. The cat moved so fast, it didn't even appear to coil before it pounced, its entire body elongating into a single sheet of lightning that arced from one spot to the next. Hane was fast, but not that fast. Luckily, the hints leading to the copper thicket had been enough for Hane to prepare for just such a challenge.

The lightning cat stood on all fours, head hunkered low on its shoulders as it arched its back to rub against a series of copper pipes, making a crackling sound from its throat in a parody of a purr. Hane scrambled to get clear of the copper pipes as lightning jumped from the elemental cat to travel up and out along the copper pipes, making the open space at the center of the room the only safe place to be. Having anticipated Hane's dive for safety, the lightning cat beat them to the center of the room.

Reverse Gravity, Hane thought quickly, reorienting to fall up toward the ceiling. They managed to grab onto a pipe not currently conducting electricity, spin themself around it, then fall into an upside-down crouch in order to watch the lightning cat. The beast seemed confused at first, as if wondering where Hane had gone. It lifted its nose and sniffed the air once before turning to train its white-eyed gaze up on Hane once more.

Well, at least I have its attention, Hane thought, resigned to following out the next part of the plan.

What followed might have been described as a "merry chase through a copper maze" if either Hane or the lightning cat were moving at a speed that could be easily tracked by the naked eye. In anticipation of exactly this scenario, Hane had requested another boost from Lief, enhancing their speed and agility. It still wasn't enough to keep up with a being that could move almost as fast as light, so in order to stay one step ahead of the beast, Hane used gravity spells to change direction, altering their own personal gravity to fall faster or slower in order to throw the lightning cat off their trail.

The next time the lightning cat attempted to electrify the copper pipes, the lightning fizzled and died without twining up the length of the pipe, as it had the first time. For the first time, the cat showed something close to human intelligence as it eyed the copper thoughtfully. A lash of its tail sent a second lightning bolt flashing across the room to strike a different pipe, yet the same thing happened again. Not to be deterred, the cat looked up toward the ceiling and hack-coughed a lightning bolt at a pipe near the ceiling. This time, the lightning ranged out along the copper for several yards before it flickered and died. Seemingly satisfied, the lightning cat blurred into a column of white light as it leapt straight up to the perch where Hane first noticed it. A silent, level stare informed Hane that the cat was not amused. Lips peeled back in an electric snarl right before the beast hack-coughed a thin lightning bolt at them with deadly accuracy. Hane felt their hair stand straight up as they dodged, trying to keep to the open area as much as possible.

I need it to chase me, Hane thought, dodging another whipcrack of lightning. *The plan doesn't work if I can't lure it back down to the ground.*

Hane couldn't chance a look around to check on their teammates, not while dodging lightning bolts and avoiding the steel panel of the floor as well as the copper pipes surrounding the little clearing. They felt a steady ache growing at the backs of their eyes from all the light flares and reflections around the room. Maybe they should have thought to ask Rose for her goggles: the colored lenses might have dimmed the glare somewhat.

And thinking of Rose, Hane did have one trick up their sleeve. They just had to wait for the right moment . . .

In the space between attacks, something struck a metal pipe hard enough that the lightning cat looked sharply away from Hane, searching for the source of the noise amid the copper pipe maze. Hane took the opportunity to slam a Burst spell into the steel floor panel, earning a low rumble of thunder from the lightning cat as it returned its focus to them. It spat a jet of lightning directly at the panel, forcing Hane to dive clear of the sparks. The steel control panels rattled and popped as the lightning arced between them, but the copper pipes refused to carry even a single spark. Seemingly frustrated with its troublesome prey, the lightning cat began spitting balls of lightning at Hane rather than trying to strike them with bolts. The lightning balls moved a little slower, but when they came in contact with a solid object, they burst into smaller lightning bolts that fired off in all directions, making them harder to dodge. Trusting in Mason's ability to manipulate the conductivity of metal, Hane leapt into the network of copper pipes, ducking, dodging, and sliding to avoid the far-spreading attacks. A sound split their concentration for a moment, and as they searched for the source, the lightning cat pounced. Hane threw themself sideways at the last minute, reversing gravity in order to hide beneath the pipe the cat now sat upon.

Heart hammering in their chest, Hane spotted Odette twisting a pipe valve open with great effort: she leaned her shoulder in as she pushed, putting as much torque into it as possible. Did that mean the key was inside that copper pipe? Or was it just a misleading secret? Hane could get the valve open with a punch of transference mana, but that would lead the lightning cat to Odette—the exact thing Hane had been attempting to avoid throughout this entire encounter. Was it time to use the surprise Rose had cooked up for them? Or was it better to wait until Odette had the vault key in hand?

With a growl that sounded like distant thunder, a lightning-paw tipped with metallic claws reached around the curve of the pipe, catching briefly at Hane's shoulder before they could twist away. The claws didn't break through their shroud, but a shock of lightning jolted Hane hard enough that their head jerked back against the bottom of the pipe. Sparks and light scars swam across their vision, making it difficult to see the next paw groping blindly after them. If Hane ended their gravity spell and dropped to the ground, the cat might notice Odette and chase after her instead—a situation Hane needed to avoid at all costs. But rolling from side to side to avoid the massive paws of lightning wasn't going to work forever: eventually the cat was going to try a new strategy.

At least it's only toying with me, Hane thought bitterly, pushing up on their elbows and toes to arch their back away from the sparking paw. *Maybe it's not hungry, or maybe it's bored. Maybe it doesn't think I'm a threat because it thinks I'm alone. Whatever it is, I need to keep its focus just a little while—*

A crack of thunder so close by that Hane felt it vibrate through their very core made the copper pipes sing in resounding harmony. Lightning flashed in an outward radius from the cat, and while the copper pipe still refused to carry the charge, the lightning slammed into Hane with the force of a violent wave, shocking their system and cutting off their gravity spell. Hane fell hard, hitting a crossways pipe that kicked the wind out of their chest before they hit the ground. Before even drawing a breath, Hane shoved transference mana into their shroud, hoping it would be enough to toss the cat off their back when it landed on them.

"Hane!" Odette half stumbled over copper pipes bolted to the floor. Hane barely managed to discharge their shroud by the time she reached out and shook their shoulder. "Are you okay? That looked like it hurt!"

Hane still couldn't breathe, the ache in their empty chest almost as panic-inducing as the cat's unexpected absence. Where had it gone? Why hadn't it followed Hane down after knocking them off the pipe?

"I saw what happened," Odette said, helping Hane up. "It was going to stab your leg with its tail-tip. Lief got it with an arrow that—well, I'm not sure, but the arrow did something." She gasped as white light flashed off her glasses. "Oh no! It's after Lief, he's—"

Hane finally managed to choke down a single breath before pushing Odette away and leaping after the lightning cat. Lief had picked a vantage point almost two stories off the ground, where two pipes intersected, forming a nice wide perch just far enough away to get off one clear shot. With dark spots clouding their vision, Hane couldn't make out the details of the struggle, but it looked as if Lief had been pressed back against the vertical pipe, the cat's jaws locked around the midpoint of Lief's bow as he braced it by the ends. Hane landed in a sideways crouch along one pipe before launching themself forward, coiling transference into a compact ball at the heel of their foot. They landed a hard kick against the cat's side, transference ripping through the creature's form, peeling off stripes of lightning and staggering the beast long enough for Lief to firm his grip and attempt to twist his bow free of the cat's jaws. Instead, thunder roared again, leaving Hane deaf in its wake. They never heard Lief's bow snap, but they saw the look of horrified dismay plain in Lief's eyes as he held one half of his bow in either hand. As sparks began erupting off the cat's hide, Hane leapt off the pipe, diving for the ground. They rolled up to their feet on instinct, spinning around to search for the cat, but the moment they did, their vision swam and their stomach rolled. They felt something impact their shoulder, but as they jerked away, the pressure remained, following them insistently until they realized it was only Lief's hand.

Lief's lips were moving, but Hane couldn't hear a thing, still deaf from the roar of thunder. Sound began returning slowly, but as their stomach settled and their vision cleared, they realized Lief must have been healing them. It took them a moment to feel steady on their feet, but at least they recovered before the cat did. It still clung to the pipe overhead, form flickering between solid and ephemeral.

". . . slowed it down," Lief was saying, a hand still on Hane's shoulder but his eyes never wavering from the large cat on the transverse pipe. "It's going to be angry when it recovers."

"You mean it was only playing before?" Hane asked, their own voice distant in their ears. They shook their head to clear it, just as the cat did the same on the pipe above. It glared down through slitted, sparking eyes; the hardest thing just then was to avoid looking for Odette to see if she had the key yet. Instead, they gave Lief a brief glance, checking for any obvious injuries. "Looks like you're going to have to actually use that sword for once."

Lief looked surprised, one hand brushing the pommel of his sword. "I can't."

"What?"

"I can't, it's—" Lief shrugged, all traces of humor vanished from his face. "It's broken. It can't be wielded."

"Then why—"

Hane couldn't finish the question before the lightning cat leapt at them. A shove with transference sent Lief rolling in the opposite direction from them, forcing the cat to choose between targets. Luckily—or perhaps unluckily—the cat pursued Hane, giving Lief a chance to run and hide. Hane hoped he made it safely back to Rose and Mason, but the immediate issue of dodging the lightning cat's attacks took precedence. Just as Lief had surmised, the cat was angry now, throwing off sparks constantly as a hiss crackled through its fangs, knifelike claws swiping with surprising reach. There was no advantage to fighting it at close range—or any range, really—but without knowing where Odette was within this tangle of copper piping, Hane's options were limited. The cat lunged for their throat: Hane cast Burst outward from the center of their being, and while it wasn't as powerful as the kick earlier, it still staggered the cat's form long enough for Hane to dart to one side and reverse their gravity.

The lightning cat recovered in short order, giving chase by leaping from pipe to pipe, chasing Hane as they "fell" up toward the ceiling. By varying the amount of mana into the active spell, Hane was able to slow or speed their upward motion, causing the cat to miss its attacks and strikes. When their feet finally touched the chamber's ceiling, the cat spat an angry crackle at them, tail lashing in frustration as it paced just below them.

"I have it!" Odette stood in the center of the open space below, her shout drawing Hane's attention as well as the lightning cat's. That didn't diminish her excitement, though: she beamed as she clasped something tight within her fist. "I found it! You can—"

Odette broke off with a scream as the cat morphed into a solid sheet of lightning, pouncing on Odette faster than Hane could even blink. They released their gravity spell, but even a doubled gravity spell wouldn't help them reach the ground in time. Instead, they grabbed the special imbue that Rose prepared for them and hoped it would be enough.

The fist-sized globe was heavy—far heavier than a glass orb of sand ought to be. If this worked it would signal the others to start the next phase of the plan. If it didn't . . . well, Hane hoped the others would at least have enough time to ring out of the spire for safety. The cat would likely kill them before they could reach their own return bell.

Hane doubled the globe's gravity, then doubled it once more before releasing it and halving their own gravity. They still fell, but slower now, giving them a chance to watch the effects of the magically imbued globe. The cat whipped its head up toward Hane, spitting a lightning bolt that struck the falling globe, releasing sheets upon sheets of sand as it shattered. The crackle of a hiss, then all was lost to sight beneath the swirling sand cloud.

With a short burst of transference mana, Hane lost themself amid the copper pipes, keeping to the edge of the spill of sand so it wouldn't crunch underfoot. Holding their breath so the beast wouldn't hear it, Hane crouched down low, pressing both palms to the floor as they watched the sand settle.

The brilliance of the elemental beast seared through the veil of sand. When it cleared, Hane saw that every step the cat took forged the sand into glass. It snuffled wetly, head turning this way and that as it searched for its prey. Sparks scattered along the sand, leaping off the beast in tiny arcs, like stones skipped from the shore. It was hard to be certain but Hane thought the beast already looked slightly smaller than before. Sand was the natural opposite of lightning, but even with as much as Rose had been able to pack inside the glass orb, it was barely enough to inconvenience the cat, never mind ground it.

"Hey."

Hane flinched, surprised to find Odette standing over them. Apparently their hearing wasn't fully recovered yet. She crouched down beside them in order to whisper.

"I've got it." Odette opened her fist, revealing a black glass orb with a sparkling white core. Hane would have taken it for a treasure rather than a key, which was possibly the reason why no one had opened the secret vault up until now. "Any changes to the plan?"

"I don't think so." Hane kept their eyes on the lightning cat while continuing to cast their spell. "How did you manage to avoid the guardian? I thought it got you."

"I used a mirror projection from one of my spell spheres," Odette whispered. She tucked the orb key away in an inside pocket of her vest. "What one spell sphere sees, the other projects as an illusion. I knew I wasn't going to beat a lightning beast on speed alone."

Hane nodded, waiting for the moment when Mason's spell would take effect. It was gradual at first—just a few more grains of sand, slowly soaking up the water Hane conjured. The shift occurred suddenly, sand and water mixing and churning as the stone floor dissolved into quicksand, the lightning cat screaming in a surprised roar of thunder. Hane jumped to their feet, catching a look of trepidation on Odette's face before they scooped her up against their shoulder, casting the spell Null Gravity to make her light enough to carry despite their fatigue, then bolted away through the forest of pipes. The cat roared torrents of thunder as arcs of lightning rippled outward, but the metal failed to conduct it, giving Hane the time they needed to plot a safe course through to the end of the copper forest.

"Oof!" Odette gasped and wobbled as Hane set her down just outside the entrance of the guardian's lair, restoring her normal gravity as they released her. She grinned triumphantly at the others as she caught her breath, gasping the words: "I got it!"

"So it worked?" Mason asked, leaning heavily on his stone umbrella. Sweat beaded along his forehead, his posture hunched almost as if pained or ill.

"It definitely surprised the guardian, but I don't think it—"

"Run!" Rose screamed, cutting Hane off. A bolt of lightning lanced out of the copper thicket, narrowly missing Hane before hitting the opposing wall and blasting the stone into blackened rubble. Mason's stone umbrella shattered as he dropped it to create a stone bridge over the empty sewer trench. Hane stayed behind until the others were all across, then leapt the gap just before a second lightning bolt would have struck them in the chest.

"I thought the quicksand would hold it!" Mason shouted, waving the others ahead of him while he caught his breath.

"If the quicksand was enough to defeat it, we would have stayed to collect the treasure!" Hane shouted back. "We've weakened it and slowed it down, but that's it."

"Is anyone hurt?" Lief called back over the roar of thunder and pounding footsteps. "Odette? Hane?"

"I'm fine!" Odette gasped, casting a spell between her hands as she ran. "Left! Mason, hurry!"

Lief skidded at the edge of a walkway, one hand touching down as he sharply changed directions. As Hane rounded the corner, movement at the bottom of the trench caught their eye: gavials. A pack of them. Or a flock? School? Whatever a group of gavials was called, Hane didn't miss the gleam of their black eyes, tracking them just as assuredly as the lightning cat was.

"Here!" Odette shouted, stopping so suddenly that Rose ran into her. The two of them teetered precariously on the edge of the walkway. Rather than stop, Hane somersaulted over the gap to the opposite walkway, using a light push of transference mana to keep them from falling into the trench. Mason and Lief steadied the women as they each caught their breath.

"What's here?" Mason asked, looking side to side, then up and down. "I don't see any—"

A roar of thunder preceded the lightning bolt that ricocheted off a corner and bounced between the walls of the tunnel. Hane and the others hit the ground, covering their heads until the danger was past.

"We can't outrun it," Odette said, scraping herself off the ground. Hane saw her pat her inner pocket, a brief look of relief softening the fear in her eyes. "We need a shortcut, and this is the best place for it."

"A shortcut," Lief repeated dubiously. "You mean we're going to alter the labyrinth? I thought you said that would trigger a difference in scaling."

"Yes, but we can't just keep running blindly," Odette explained shortly. "We need distance from the guardian, and I can find the shortest path to the vault. I know it's risky, but we can stop and rest as soon as I find a static safe zone."

As Hane stood up to leap the gap once more, they felt a tingling sensation in the muscles of their legs, back, and core. The rebound effects of Lief's agility spell: they had pushed too hard while evading the lightning cat's attacks. It was only a matter of time before they exhausted themself, as they had on the train. And this time, there was no Nieve to carry them back to safety.

Nieve.

Hane closed their eyes for just a moment, tugging the icy feeling of numbness closed around them once more.

"Speed over caution for now," Hane decided. The rumblings of a storm approached, the distance between peals of thunder becoming shorter and shorter. If it was a choice between fighting the guardian now or facing an unknown opponent later, Hane would roll the dice on the unknown opponent: there was no winning against such a beast with this team. "Where should Mason make the shortcut?"

"Down," Odette said. "Ideally we want to drop straight through the bottom of the trench right here."

Right here? But there was no right here. Peering over the edge of the walkway only showed slick algae, broken glass, and even more hungry gavials. Their wiggling, belly-dragging gait might have been humorous if it weren't for those sinister-looking jaws that were at least half as long again as their bodies. The bottom of the trench showed no signs of a drain or a pipe or anything that indicated "down" as a direction.

"No!" Mason protested, shaking his head vigorously. "No way! I'm not going down there even if there weren't any—"

"Ears!" Rose shouted, holding something glowing and smoky over her head. Hane clapped their hands over their ears just as Rose lobbed the object into the center of the trench. A breath-held silence, then suddenly a blast that tossed Hane against the wall. Rubbing their shoulder, they swept a transference spell through the smoke and debris, sending it in the direction of the lightning cat. Across the trench, Rose covered her mouth with a handkerchief, leaned over the edge of the walkway to peer down, then jumped.

"Prick—Rose! Dammit!" Mason added some more language about what sounded like a "gear rack" and punched the ground before setting his jaw and jumping after her. Lief and Odette looked more hesitant—especially as the gavials stunned by the blast began to recover their senses.

"Of course my bow is broken," Lief sighed, shaking his head. "That would have been useful."

Hane drew a tonfa as they sized up the situation. The hole from Rose's explosion dropped straight through to the next layer of the labyrinth, but the details of the lower floor were difficult to make out through the smoke. They hadn't heard a splash, though, so hopefully that meant the ground was solid beneath the hole. A few of the gavials had been killed in the blast, but most just looked angry and injured. Hane sent a blast of transference through the end of their tonfa when one seemed interested in following Rose and Mason, flinging it backward and away from the hole.

"Jump!" Hane shouted, just as a lightning bolt pierced the cloud of smoke and debris. "I'll cover. Go!"

Lief shrugged, then leapt, a grimace on his face as he braced for impact. Odette hedged a little, looking as if she wanted to drop down into the trench before falling down the hole. Hane fired three more shots of transference to keep the small but terrifying monsters from diving through the hole. A crackle of light and an ominous thrum of power made them stop and look up: the lightning cat had just rounded the corner.

"You need to go!" Hane shouted. If it weren't for the key in Odette's vest pocket, Hane would already have jumped by now, hoping Odette would follow while accepting the loss if she didn't. They were already cloaked in the chill of loss; what was one more? But the key was the entire purpose of this mission; they couldn't leave her behind now. "Odette, jump!"

Odette's lower lip turned white beneath the pinch of her teeth. She eyed the hole one final time before taking off her glasses and leaping, legs flailing as she clutched her glasses to her chest. Hane didn't wait for her to finish falling: they jumped right after, twisting in midair to fire transference through their tonfa at a gavial that leapt after them, like a fish swimming upriver. When had these scissor-jawed crocodiles learned to jump?

To avoid landing on top of Odette, Hane slowed their fall enough to take hold of her shoulder and move her out of their way. Without bothering to check their surroundings, Hane watched for more gavials attempting to follow, sighting along their tonfa like the barrel of a gun. The sides of the hole began to grow inward, stretching toward each other to pinch closed. When the needle-like snout of a gavial appeared over the edge, Hane fired a jolt of transference at it, driving it back. By the time the hole had narrowed to little wider than a fist, brilliant light seared Hane's vision, driving them back a pace. They heard the low rumble of a thunderous growl just before the hole closed entirely.

Hane fought the urge to sag in relief. Just because they'd evaded one threat didn't mean they were out of danger just yet.

"Is everyone all right?" Hane called, still blinking light scars from their eyes. "Odette, do you still have the key?"

"I have it," Odette confirmed, leaving her glasses askew in order to pat her pocket. "Give me just a moment to conjure my compass arrow again."

"—covered in slime, so all the nasty stuff you blew up is stuck to me!" Mason appeared well enough to yell at his sister, who steadfastly ignored him as she adjusted the lenses of her goggles. "I don't have to follow you, you know. I could just let you die in here."

"And then what?" Rose asked simply. "Aid Jesserah in her bid to be the heir? You know she'll cut you off the instant she has what she wants."

Lief stared up at the ceiling wearing a pinched expression. "I'm not really sure that's going to stop—"

Something struck the ceiling hard enough that dust rained down from the portion Mason had just sealed. The silence was immediate and absolute, as everyone first looked up, then at each other. Hane shook off their exhaustion and quickly surveyed their surroundings. While it was clear they were still in a sewer, this was the cleanest room they had seen by far, save for the algae-covered debris that had fallen through the hole caused by Rose's explosion. Square-shaped with thick, short pipes protruding through the walls at even intervals, each pipe was capped with a wheel valve and a spigot. A long table along the far wall held various instruments and glass tubes, like a laboratory. Opposite the table was the only door. Hane prayed it wasn't locked.

"I know which way to go," Odette said, gasping in fright as the guardian hammered at the ceiling again. The arrow between her hands pointed to the wall behind the table of laboratory supplies, opposite the exit. "We need to go that way."

Mason gaped at her. "You want me to continue tearing a path through the labyrinth? You know what kind of penalty we'll get for that!"

Odette screamed as Hane scooped her out of the way of a large chunk of ceiling that would have crushed her. Tiny sparks of lightning danced through cracks in the ceiling. She recovered quickly after drawing a single, shaky breath.

"I know, but we can't stay here," Odette argued. "We can lose them on the way to a safe zone, but we have to move fast enough to outpace the guardian, and for that, we need to reshape the labyrinth!"

Mason hesitated, looking first to Rose, then, unexpectedly, to Hane. "You can keep us safe, can't you?"

Hane considered the cracks in the ceiling, the potential consequences for modifying a spire challenge, and the rebound of Lief's spell already weighing down their limbs so that even breathing felt like it required extra effort.

"We need to make it somewhere safe, fast," Hane said decisively. "Forget about finding the vault for now; focus on finding a place where we can recover with as few modifications to the labyrinth as possible. Once we're safe, we can discuss whether we want to risk further scaling, or take our time for safety's sake. Okay?"

"Okay." Odette nodded firmly, staring hard at her spinning compass arrow. "Going through that wall is still the shortest path. I can't detect a mana fountain, but I think I know where a temporary safe zone is."

Mason blew out a breath, shaking his head as he held his hand out toward the indicated wall. "I really hope you all know what you're doing."

So do I, Hane thought, feeling the exhaustion of overworked muscles tug at their limbs like a doubled gravity spell. It was harder to ignore the pain and push past it when they were already suppressing their grief over losing Nieve and Chime, as if they could only actively forget one sensation at a time. Given the choice, Hane would rather collapse from exhaustion than give in to grief: they could recover from being exhausted, but grief took far longer to recover from.

The ceiling cracked, dust and lightning raining down from the center of the room. Mason beckoned everyone through the shaped opening of the wall with a strong gesture, silently telling them to hurry up. As he reshaped the wall closed behind them, Odette took the lead, holding her spinning compass arrow in front of her. For once, Hane was content to follow, hoping their body would hold out long enough to reach the next safe zone.

Nieve

Champion (mind mark), Citrine
Paladin (heart mark), Carnelian

Nieve groaned as she stretched stiff muscles, bones and joints popping in a chorus of complaints. Her head hit something hard when she tried to sit up; it was only then that Nieve realized she had no idea where she was or how she'd gotten there.

"Where—" Nieve rolled, shielding her eyes as she attempted to get her bearings. She was still in the sewer, which was both good and bad, but somehow she'd ended up inside a little shelf dug into the stone wall, high above the walkway and the empty sewer trench. She blinked in surprise. She didn't even remember deciding to take a nap. Or had it been more than a nap? It was impossible to tell how much time had passed since . . . Nieve blinked blearily. Since when?

<You seem to be you again.>

"Ugh . . ." Nieve groaned, cupping her face in her hands. "What happened? Why can't I remember?"

<You used that strange new power again,> Chime stated in matter-of-fact tones. <I suggested that you wait until we found your companions in case something should happen to you, yet you insisted.>

Yeah, that does sound like me, Nieve thought grudgingly. Her entire body felt cramped and pained as she eased herself to the edge of the window-like shelf she'd fallen asleep in. A twinge in her elbow informed her that she'd been swinging a weapon recently and failed to ice herself afterward. A bruise in the middle of her back was the Magpie's staff, which seemed to have embedded itself into her kidney while she slept. A thousand other little pains made themselves known as she swung her legs over the ledge, ducking her head in order to look around. *What was I fighting?*

<Kobolds,> came the simple reply. <We came upon a small group of them. You decided to stop and fight, as you thought it might be an opportunity for treasure.>

Memories came back in bits and pieces. Nieve remembered tracking the scent of petrichor through the labyrinth until it became obscured by the musky scent of damp fur. Kobolds—humanoid monsters that stood about waist-high with animal-like features—had been carving a tunnel through the side of the empty trench. While Sage might have been able to identify the exact species of kobold, Nieve only remembered seeing gray skin and rodent-like facial features. Much like the trash hogs earlier, Nieve labeled the monsters as sewer-kobolds in her mind and decided it was safer to attack them before they attacked her.

Just kobolds? Nieve wondered, poking at a blood-soaked hole in her leggings. *That hardly seems worthy of calling on Byakko's strength.*

<That is what I said,> Chime said, sounding just a bit miffed. <However, you stated that you wished to practice with your new power, believing yourself to be close to new strength. You also seemed to believe the presence of kobolds indicated a treasure cache of some kind.>

Treasure? Nieve cupped her aching elbow, conjuring a sheath of ice around it. One of the special abilities of kobolds was their ability to sniff out hidden treasures, though what a kobold considered to be "treasure" wasn't always actually valuable. Once during a climb, Nieve and her team recovered a small locked chest from a kobold den, only to find it full of shiny buttons. *Did I get any treasure?*

<No.> Chime sounded grim. <You took an injury that sent you into a rage. You slayed all who stood before you, then chased down the ones who fled. Afterward, you were exhausted and injured, yet you did not return to your senses. Instead, you climbed into this outlet and fell deeply asleep.>

Nieve didn't remember any of that, but she didn't doubt it either. Through the hole in her leggings, the injury appeared to have been made by a spiked weapon, like a pickaxe—typical of kobolds. There were other injuries, too, but most were scratches or bruises. Her broken toe ached fiercely and when she checked the cut on her thigh from fighting the trash hogs, the scab cracked enough to seep fresh blood. Giving up on her leggings as a lost cause, Nieve checked her leather vest, feeling for the locket beneath it.

Calculating the cost of replacing her leggings, refilling her medical kit, and the healing potion she was now reconciled to drinking, Nieve found herself wondering if it had been worth it. Fingers still clumsy for sleep, she loosened her chestplate and peeled back her collar in order to look down her shirt. It took a bit of maneuvering to find enough ambient light to see clearly, but when she did, Nieve grinned to herself.

Yes. It had been worth it.

Her new Paladin attunement, so simple in comparison to her Champion attunement, had gained a new marking. After recovering from her last fight, she'd advanced from Quartz-level to Carnelian. Normally, it took months of training to strengthen a new attunement, but as she'd expected, Byakko's boost had pushed it right to the threshold, making it a short jump to the next level.

<Are you concerned about this new power?> Chime asked as Nieve secured her leather vest once more. <You are already quite strong; I do not see the purpose in giving up your control for fights you could win otherwise.>

It's training, Nieve argued. *This attunement is far behind my Champion attunement, and the only way to catch up is to train with it. And the more I use it, the more I'll learn to control it.*

The sound Chime made was hard to describe: perhaps something like grains of sand blowing across a rocky plateau. Whatever it was, it sounded doubtful. <I agree with you in theory, but I believe this to be hazardous. You and I are alone, and I have no ability to assist you, heal you, or even speak with you when you are in that state. I feel you are being reckless.>

Yeah, probably. Nieve reached up to fix her hair, surprised to find it in the same topknot it had been in for days. She smiled, thinking of Sage, then felt a pang of grief as her thoughts moved on to Emiko, then Lani. Before moving on, she downed half a healing potion, saving the rest for later. While her aches and pains diminished, she nibbled on jerky and a mix of dried fruit and nuts. Feeling slightly more human, she slid off the stone shelf and dropped to the walkway below. She inhaled deeply, filtering the scents of dry decay, rusted metal, and her own offensive body odor for that pure scent of clean, wet stone. After only a few deep sniffs, she coughed, her throat feeling raw. She couldn't find the scent of petrichor; how far off track had she gone in chasing down the kobolds?

<I can lead you back the way we came,> Chime offered, likely sensing Nieve's inability to locate the scent she'd been following. <I only request that if we come across more enemies such as those, that you fight them normally, without the use of your mysterious new power.>

I can agree to that. Despite the healing potion, her throat still felt raw, as if she had been screaming for hours on end. Talking aloud made her feel less alone, but just then, it was easier to simply speak mind-to-mind with Chime as she followed the gateway crystal's directions. *Is there anything else I've forgotten that might be important?*

<I can see that you have recalled the moments leading up to your decision to use your new power.> While it wasn't a surprise to know that Chime could read at least part of Nieve's thoughts, it was still an uncomfortable feeling. Rather than call out directions such as "right" or "left," Chime used small pings of sound to guide Nieve back to where she had lost the scent of petrichor. <I have informed you of all you have forgotten. Will you tell me how you came by this power? When you are under its thrall, I hear the battle song of steel against steel, the rhythm of endless marching, and a chorus of screams by those felled in battle.>

A chill went down Nieve's back at the last. She loved the thrill of battle, of victory, but duels seldom ended in death, and cutting down spire constructs didn't qualify as killing in Nieve's mind. Although Hane's argument about saving the snakes on the train had her thinking differently about that now.

I'm . . . not really ready to talk about that power yet, Nieve admitted, knowing full well that Chime could see her thoughts. They probably already knew more about the source of her Paladin attunement than their question suggested. *I'd prefer to explain it when we meet up with Sage again. And Hane. I owe it to the both of them.*

Again, that sound of dry wind and doubt. <If the opportunity presents itself, I will tell neither Hane nor Sage of this new power, unless it becomes relevant situationally.>

That sounded fair. If Nieve lost control while using her new attunement, at least Chime would be able to explain it to the others. Though she hoped it wouldn't come to that.

After only a few more twists and turns, Nieve detected a whiff of petrichor leading down a southern corridor. She came to a stop, considering whether it was worth it or not to continue backtracking for a potential kobold treasure.

<I sensed that tunnel was quite deep, with many twists and turns,> Chime informed her. <I cannot say for certain that there is no treasure, but can you assure me that it will be worth the time and potential danger to go and find out?>

No, Nieve admitted petulantly. *Probably not.*

The conversation lagged for a time as Nieve followed the faint scent through the labyrinth of the sewers, pausing only to inhale deeply at intersections to make sure she chose the correct path. The only sound besides her own footsteps was the ever-present sound of dripping, despite this section of the sewer seeming quite dry. There weren't even puddles in the empty trench. Every so often, Nieve spotted a kobold down an otherwise empty tunnel, but as soon as the kobolds spotted her, they quickly scurried away. Kobolds tended to be cowardly in single combat. Once, she heard the snuffling grunts of a trash hog, but the smell of petrichor led her down a different path.

To stave off boredom, Nieve searched for hidden secrets and treasures along the way. Whenever she passed a door, she leaned in to listen, testing the knob to see if it was locked or not. Sometimes she'd throw the door open and check inside if it seemed safe, but aside from a few abandoned supply stores, she found nothing of note. It seemed the drug gangs' operations didn't extend this deep into the sewer system. Maybe it was because of the monsters, or maybe it was because of the smell. Either way, it had been a long time since Nieve had seen any crude paintings on the walls.

The petrichor scent took her down a dead-end tunnel, ending just over an iron manhole cover. Nieve slammed an enhancement-reinforced heel into the center of the cover until it dented, making it easy to lift it and toss it aside. A strong scent of petrichor billowed out of the opening before it was consumed by the scents of rot, rust, and age. The hole looked as dark as the one Nieve had fallen through when Byakko took her, but at least this time there was a ladder set into the side. After a brief pause for a drink of water, Nieve swung her legs over the edge, gripped the ladder, and began her descent.

Climbing down was easy at first: each rung was equidistant from the last, making it easy to find toeholds even though the space was too narrow to look below her. The rust of the rungs offered a textured grip, so her hands didn't slip. But after only a few minutes, Nieve lost sight of the light at the top of the ladder, and the darkness became absolute. She tried looking down for the exit but saw nothing but blackness, making the distance impossible to discern.

This is fine, Nieve told herself, continuing on determinedly. *It's still just one foot in front of the other, right hand, left hand, repeat. There has to be a bottom to this shaft at some point, and I don't need light to find it.*

Still, a little light would be welcome. If only to watch out for traps or ambushes. At least she could still smell the faint trace of petrichor on the air; otherwise she might have beaten a retreat and looked for another way to go.

As the time wore on indefinitely, Nieve's mind began to wander. First, she thought of how much easier this would be if Sage were here: he could have cast a light spell to illuminate the shaft, and possibly even predicted the time it would take to reach the bottom. Nieve's new Paladin attunement possessed light mana, which meant she had the ability to create orbs of light as Sage did, but this was hardly the time to stop and experiment with new spells. Thinking of Sage brought up memories of Emiko and Lani, which made the darkness feel all the more ominous in Nieve's grief. Determinedly, she redirected her thoughts to Ren and Wyle, both alive and happily retired. Wyle probably could have simply teleported to the bottom of this shaft, while Ren could have used one of his contracted monsters to light the way ahead. For challenges like this one, he usually called upon a cute-looking firefly-spider that would dangle above the team on a thread of silk like a living lantern. When Nieve told her grandmother about that contract, the retired Soulblade had scoffed and rolled her eyes; Grandmother Mitsuki preferred to bond only the most ancient spirits of Kaldwyn, rather than the monsters of the goddess's spires.

Her grandmother had told her stories of the spirits of Kaldwyn—the beings and entities that predated the arrival of the Goddess Selys and her Soaring Spires. As a child, Nieve found the stories thrilling and tantalizing, dreaming of the day when she could take her Judgment and begin her career as a climber. Later on, when she listened to her grandmother tell those same stories to her brothers, Nieve felt the undertones of regret and loss, and read the sadness on her grandmother's face. If not for her parents' untimely deaths, Mitsuki would be a climber still, with all her contracts and her treasured climbing companions. She had given up so much in taking over for her daughter and son-in-law and raising their children for them, yet she never complained—except about Nieve's father from time to time.

Nieve couldn't imagine what it would be like to give up her dreams because of someone else's failure. She didn't think she could be as strong and selfless as her grandmother, putting the needs of others before her own desires. She certainly couldn't imagine doing so with the grace her grandmother displayed. The only situation Nieve could see herself giving up her climbing career for was if something happened to her grandmother and she had to take care of her brothers. Because of course she would—who wouldn't do at least that much? That wasn't as likely now as it had been back when she first started climbing. Danil, the elder of the two, was old enough now to take care of Ryoji himself, so long as Nieve sent home plenty of money from her spire climbs. But goddess willing, Grandmother Mitsuki still had plenty of good years left ahead of her.

Nieve froze in her descent, tilting her head to one side. She heard . . . music? Soft and distant, though she couldn't tell if it came from above or below. The tune was simple, plucked on the strings of a harp, or a koto. It was an odd sound to find in a sewer. Odder still was the fact that the tune seemed almost . . . familiar.

Chime, is that you? Nieve asked, afraid her voice would echo in the narrow space. *Are you singing or something?*

The tune faded out, replaced by Chime's ringing tones. <I did not mean to distract you. I heard it as an undercurrent of your thoughts and thought it might be comforting to you.>

Nieve frowned as she resumed climbing. *I don't know that song. Grandma doesn't play the koto.*

<Perhaps someone did,> Chime commented. <It is assuredly a song from your memory. I do not forget a song that I have heard, and this one is new to me.>

Nieve huffed out loud, stopping to shake out her arms. She peered down into the endless dark, bracing her back against the opposite wall. *How much farther? It feels like I've been at it for hours.*

<This space is ringed in secrets and magic,> Chime informed her. <I believe it is what you might call a shortcut.>

"Rather long shortcut," Nieve muttered, resuming her descent. She tried to keep her mind blank by focusing on her physical exertion. Nostalgia had no place inside a spire.

It came as a surprise when Nieve's feet finally hit solid stone. She staggered before regaining her balance and sniffing the air. The darkness hadn't ended at the bottom of the ladder, but her nose informed her that this was still a part of the sewer: a thick, green, slimy scent all but hid the delicate trail of the petrichor.

"Glow stick," Nieve muttered, patting her pockets. "Where did I— got it!"

Nieve rarely had a chance to use the enchanted glow stick, gifted to her by Sage on her name day some years ago, so it took her a minute to remember how to use it. It was shaped like a pencil but thicker: a ceramic rod topped with a glass gem. She felt along its length for the indent over the activation rune. When she found it, the sudden flare of light was so bright she flinched away from it.

"Ow, ow, too bright! How do I . . ."

It took a good couple of minutes squinting through the light to make out the runes on the side of the stick. Eventually, Nieve figured out that twisting her fingers beneath the glass orb could narrow the light into a beam that could be pointed ahead of her to light the way. Another rune adjusted the brightness by tapping on it. After finding a setting that allowed for a wide beam bright enough to illuminate the way forward, Nieve lashed the glow stick to her belt in order to keep her hands free. A final inhale confirmed the scent of petrichor, hidden beneath the earthy smells of mildew and decay.

Even with the light, Nieve moved cautiously, testing the ground ahead of her and stopping to sweep the light up, down, and side to side. It seemed she was in a long stone corridor, the walls close enough that she could reach out and touch both sides simultaneously. These weren't the smooth, Transmuter-sculpted walls of the upper levels, either. No, these walls were made of fist-sized stones that gleamed wetly in the light of Nieve's glow stick, yet when she touched them, they felt dry. The mortar between the stones felt old, flaking away at a gentle touch.

I don't like this at all, Nieve thought, more to herself than to Chime.

<I can hear a wider space ahead.> Was it Nieve's imagination, or did it sound like Chime was fearful, too?

The narrow corridor ended abruptly, Nieve's light spreading diffusely to illuminate a much wider chamber, similar to the tunnels above, but older. Creepier. A barred-off drainpipe was blocked by vertical iron bars, rather than a mesh grate, giving the impression of a dungeon more than a sewer. The trench down the center of the tunnel looked as if it held only black ankle-deep water, as still and placid as the surface of a mirror. The sheer number of spiderwebs dangling from the ceiling and stretched across corridor openings made Nieve draw her sword and cast Frost Form on herself. Setting her jaw stubbornly, she set trepidation aside and followed her nose, keeping both eyes open for traps and monsters. It would take an overflowing cache of gold coins and jewels to draw her away from the invisible trail of petrichor—and considering the possibility of mimics, perhaps even that wasn't enough to pique her interest.

A scuttling sound as Nieve approached an intersecting tunnel. She covered her light with her hand and froze where she stood, sword held out from her side. She waited until the sound was just ahead of her before uncovering the light and lunging forward with her sword. The spider was as large as a hunting dog, mandibles clicking wildly as the light gleamed off a hundred flinching eyes. The encounter was over quickly, as Nieve's sword transfixed the spider from head to thorax. When the body didn't dissolve immediately, Nieve swung her sword over the sewer channel, giving it a firm flick to cast the body off. She heard a splash as it fell, but she didn't linger: where there was one spider, there were bound to be others.

A long moan echoed along the tunnel, carried by the walls and the thin layer of water. Something squelched. Something scraped.

Something was coming.

I am not afraid, Nieve told herself, pivoting to face the source of the ominous sounds. *I am Nieve the Champion of Dalenos, the Paladin of Byakko. I am not afraid of monsters lurking in the dark.*

An alarming clamor rose with Chime's voice in Nieve's head. <I feel compelled to remind you that you are alone here. While I do not doubt your battle prowess, I believe this to be one of the times when discretion may be the better part of valor.>

You think I should run away? Nieve settled into an offensive stance, breathing deep into her heart. *Where's the discretion in putting my back to a monster in the dark? Better to kill it before it kills me.*

<And if you cannot?> Chime asked. <You risk damage and destruction of both of our vessels if you are vanquished here.>

Then I better not lose, Nieve thought, reaching for the cold light centered over her heart. Chime continued to protest, but Nieve pushed her awareness of them back into a corner of her mind in order to focus. Whatever this squelching, moaning monster was, it was no cowardly kobold. Calling on Byakko's strength made her reckless, it was true, but now that she'd advanced to Carnelian, she had an idea: what if she only called upon a tiny thread of Byakko's gift? Just enough to strengthen her sword arm, and maybe lend clarity to her sight. If it worked, then perhaps she could use her improved sense of smell to help follow the thin trail of petrichor through all the other scents of the sewer. She covered her thoughts in layers of ice thick enough to skate on, protecting her mind against the control of the predator. "Lord Byakko, I bid you grant me the strength to vanquish my enemies."

As she waited to feel the surge of strength in her body, the heightened senses of a born predator and the rushing thrill of the hunt, the moans and shuffling splashes drew closer. The glow stick's ray of light gleamed off of something in the sewer trench, but before Nieve could make it out clearly, something struck the walkway with force, making the stone shiver beneath her feet. Stone cracked and crumbled, splashing loudly in the water of the trench. There were smaller impacts and crashes from all around, creating confusing echoes amid the settling stones. It seemed the very ceiling was caving in around her until the body of a large black spider crashed to the ground at Nieve's feet. Honed warrior's instincts had her slashing the creature's head off before kicking its thrashing body into the trench. As the spike of adrenaline ebbed, a terrible thought occurred to her. Clenching her jaw so tightly that it made the crown of her head ache, Nieve pointed the beam of her glow stick up at the ceiling.

Thousands of gleaming eyes stared down at her.

Dozens—if not hundreds—of wolf-sized spiders clung to the ceiling, heavy bodies pressed flush against the shadows of the corners and corridors. The few that moved appeared to be securing their footing; the majority held perfectly still. Were they waiting to attack? She was all alone in the dark and completely outnumbered; Nieve was used to the aggressive spiders of the Tortoise Spire, which would keep on attacking despite loss of limb, and sometimes even after losing their heads. These silently staring Tiger Spire spiders made her break out in a cold sweat.

It was only then that Nieve realized that her invocation had failed.

Clearing her throat and putting the creepy spiders out of her mind, Nieve breathed into her heart and tried again. All she needed was a thread of power;

the meanest amount would be enough to see her through this safely. She shouldn't need to give up control of her mind for that much. "Great Lord Byakko, I request the aid of your strength. Guide my sword arm to strike down my foes!"

A splash that was more like a plop, followed by another, and another. Slowly, the creature shuffling along the trench oozed forward, Nieve's weak beam of light illuminating bits and parts before the whole.

Her first impression was of a mudslide during a rainstorm, spilling over itself in gleaming, wet waves. But then she saw the hands—or arms, perhaps, as there were no distinct digits to discern—gripping the walkways on either side, as if they were railings. The rough-hewn head and shoulders rose far taller than Nieve stood, though still not high enough to scrape the ceiling, where the spiders clustered together, tight and silent. The lump that served as the creature's head held only shadowed eye sockets and a round, gaping mouth through which the moans escaped. It showed no reaction to Nieve's light, but stopped just short of the twitching spider corpse Nieve had kicked into the trench. As she watched, the mud-arm resting on the opposite walkway melted as mud pooled around the spider's body. Shapes like thick fingers formed, lifting the bulbous body from the ankle-high sewage, but just as the mud-monster craned its head down to its hand, the spider dissolved into a handful of mana crystals, which only glittered for an instant before sinking into the mud. The mud-monster stared a moment longer before whipping its head back and bellowing loud enough to make the very stones tremble.

Nieve gulped, once again forced to acknowledge that her spell to invoke Byakko's strength through her Paladin attunement had failed.

"Byakko," Nieve started weakly, resolutely holding her stance. She didn't want the full flood of Byakko's power, not when it might urge her to fight the spiders as well as the mud-monster. Just a little strength, just a small boost, that was all she needed. "Greatest God Beast Byakko, please—" The monster was groping around in the trench, as if feeling around for another spider. "Please grant your Paladin the strength she needs to fight."

The mud-arm resting on Nieve's walkway shuffled forward. The monster was moving again.

And Byakko's power failed to manifest once again.

<Run,> Chime whispered.

Nieve ran.

Her light illuminated hundreds of eerily still spiders clinging to the ceiling, but so long as they remained out of her way, Nieve decided to ignore them. She nearly tripped headlong over a dead spider, flipped over on its back with its legs curled inward. After a brief stumble, she shoved it off the walkway to splash in the water below. Behind her, the mud-monster bellowed again, the sloshing shuffle turning into a squelching rush.

"Ice wall!" Nieve called, casting a hand out behind her. She pictured a thick slab of ice transecting the tunnel, floor to ceiling, wall to wall. As she glanced back to make sure it formed the way she meant it to, the mud-monster crashed against it, shattering the wall with as little effort as Nieve brushing aside a cobweb. "Resh!"

The glow stick's wan light jumped and bobbled with every step; with no time to check the air for the scent of petrichor, Nieve ran on blindly, searching for a likely place to hide. She scanned the walls for doors, for pipes, for shelves—anything she might use to hide herself. Maybe if she walled herself off behind a shield of ice, the monster would ooze right past her. It seemed a slim hope, but what else could she do?

Even if the mud-monster doesn't get me, the spiders will, Nieve thought, hopelessness drawing tight as a noose around her neck. The light on her belt bounced as she ran, alternatively illuminating the walkway, the trench, and the spiders clustered on the ceiling. *I guess I'm lucky the spiders didn't team up with the mud-monster and—*

Nieve skidded to a stop, the shape of a plan catching her by surprise. The mud-monster's sloshing footsteps didn't slow, but as she directed her light up at the ceiling, the spiders seemed to cower from it. Perhaps the spiders were more afraid of the monster than Nieve was—and if that were true, then there had to be a reason for it.

"I know I'm going to regret this," Nieve muttered, swallowing tightly as she sheathed her sword. She wanted both hands available to cast this spell.

<I know what you plan to do,> Chime said in a whisper of wind through reeds. <I do not object, but I beg that you consider an escape route before you follow through.>

This is exactly why no one relies on me to make the plans, Nieve thought, spinning on her heel and casting Freeze on the walkway, covering the stone with a thick sheet of ice. Turning back to face the monster, Nieve held an image of ice conjuration in her mind before sending the magic through her heart pathways and out through her arms. "Ice pillars!"

The water in the trench cracked as it froze, columns of ice shooting up from the center of the channel one after another to crash—hard—into the ceiling above. Spiders skittered and screeched, knocked loose from their perches as the ice impacted the ceiling. The darkness was suddenly alive with clicks, clatters, and the mud-monster's bellows as it gave chase. Nieve didn't wait to verify the effects of her spell: she kicked off the walkway and hunkered low into a speed skater's stance, praying the ice would protect her from any floor traps along the way.

The spiders in her path either fled in the same direction as her—away from the mud-monster—or attempted to climb back up the wall to the safety of the ceiling. Nieve ignored the ones she could, but for the ones that got in her way, she ripped her war hammer off her belt and knocked them aside without stopping. Some hissed menacingly as she skated past; one even reared up on its back legs to shoot a net of sticky webbing at her, but Nieve collapsed her knees to slide beneath it. She swept one leg out from under her, putting a slow spin on her slide in order to climb back to her feet without losing momentum. The moans and bellows of the mud-monster faded out, replaced with sickly crunches that made Nieve's skin crawl, but she didn't slow her breakneck pace down the icy pathway. At a four-way intersection of corridors, she created an ice bridge to continue on straight.

<Wait!>

Nieve skidded to a stop, though her heart continued racing on ahead of her.

<I sense the whisper of a secret. There is a passage hidden in the wall of the trench, I am sure of it.>

Through winded breaths, Nieve tried to catch the scent of clean, wet stone on the air, but the thick scents of mud and mildew made her guts churn, then the taste of bile obliterated her sense of smell entirely.

How sure are you? Nieve asked, trying to gauge the distance between herself and the mud-monster by the crunching sounds of snapped spider limbs.

<I am certain,> Chime said firmly. <I sense the same susurrus of the dark chimney you descended to reach this place. Even if it is not the most correct path, it may lead you someplace safe.>

Nieve hesitated, sweeping her light in every direction: along the trench, down the intersecting tunnels, and up to the ceiling. The hairy, round bodies of the spiders were plain in the light, but they were not stationary. To the contrary, the spiders appeared to be fleeing deeper into the tunnels. The sounds of crunching and clicking still emanated from the direction of Nieve's flight.

"Fine," Nieve sighed heavily. "If it gets me away from the mud-monster, then let's go. Ice Armor!"

As she jumped down into the trench, ice grew up from the soles of her boots and twined up her legs, stopping just short of her knees. While it didn't completely protect her from the foul-smelling pitch-black water, at least her feet were protected from anything lurking in the ankle-deep sewage.

"It's not far, is it?" Nieve asked, feeling the trench shiver beneath her feet. She made a face as she edged around a grimy humanoid skeleton, half collapsed in the trench. "Because if that monster finishes its meal, it's probably going to come looking for me, and I don't know if there are enough spiders left for me to do that trick again."

<Very close,> Chime assured her. A soft pinging sound drew Nieve's attention to the left side of the trench. <Here. What do you see?>

"A door," Nieve murmured, jabbing it with a sharp punch to confirm that it wasn't a mimic pretending to be a door. In all this darkness, she didn't feel certain that anything was what it appeared to be. When it didn't snap at her, she tried the doorknob. Locked, of course.

A bellow echoed down the waterway, powerful enough to send ripples up the central channel. Nieve briefly considered trying to punch her way through the door before realizing that if she did, she couldn't then shut it behind her. Though how much protection it would provide against a hungry mud-monster was a different consideration altogether.

<How is a mechanism such as this usually opened?> Chime asked.

"By force, if necessary," Nieve muttered, rattling the door to take its measure. "Unless I can find a—"

She slapped herself on the forehead before searching her pockets for the iron key she'd found earlier.

The hinges groaned as she shouldered the door open. Try as she might, the lock refused to release the key, so Nieve snapped it off and dropped the flat end into the water at her feet before slamming the door shut. She conjured an ice wall in front of it as a barrier, then, as an afterthought, conjured a second ice wall. The floor was slick beneath her ice-boots, water sloshing around her ankles with every step. The ceiling was only as high as the walkway, forcing Nieve to crouch as she crept forward. The air felt close and stale, leaving Nieve too breathless to sniff for petrichor. The glow stick showed nothing but black water and grimy walls. Nieve breathed through her mouth and kept her hammer at the ready.

The floor rose at a gentle incline, forcing Nieve to stoop lower and lower to keep from scraping her head on the ceiling. Eventually, she left the inky water behind, but if the slope continued to rise, soon she would be reduced to crawling. The passage came to such an abrupt end that Nieve nearly missed the opening to her right.

Sweeping her glow stick from side to side, up and down, Nieve stepped cautiously into the open chamber. It appeared to be square-shaped and fairly large, though it was hard to be sure when most of her view was blocked by tiered stairs leading up into shadowy darkness. A pathway circumvented the stairs, allowing Nieve to walk around the obstruction taking up most of the space, but instead she kicked the ice off her boots on the lowest step and began to ascend.

"I'm getting tired of all this darkness," Nieve griped, comforted by the fact that her voice didn't echo far. "It's not that I'm scared, I just like to see whatever it is I'm fighting."

<This place does not sing of battle and blood.> Softly tingling bells accompanied the statement. <I sense the notes of peace and growth here. This may be a safe place to take a short rest.>

"That might be comforting if I could see anything," Nieve grumbled. She huffed as she climbed the stairs, cursing each time a shadow made her stumble. By the time she reached the top, her chest was heaving for air, a stitch in her side doubling her over until she eased it with a stretch. As much as she longed to roll onto her back and simply rest, she brushed sweaty bangs back over her headband and looked around, checking for obvious threats and traps before taking another step.

Her beam of light illuminated a plain stone floor, revealing no patterns or tiles. The walls and ceiling were too far for the light to reach, with deep pockets of shadows seeming to swallow the thin beam whole. Nieve walked forward warily, certain that a room like this must exist to fulfill some sort of purpose. It didn't seem to be a mana fountain, but then again, how could she be sure unless she could see clearly?

Her boot struck something solid, jostling her broken toe hard enough to make her curse vibrantly. After brushing tears of pain from her eyes, Nieve swept her arm through the space ahead of her, feeling around for whatever she'd walked into. Whatever it was, it felt relatively sturdy but slim. It wasn't until she swept her light over the top of it that she recognized it as an unlit torch.

It took a bit of rummaging and a great deal of cursing to find her flint and light the torch—again, a simple thing she knew how to do but rarely had the chance to do herself. Maybe on the way to the next spire, she'd spend some time refreshing herself on the basics. That or keep Sage within arm's reach throughout the rest of the journey. He always knew how to do stuff like this. The flames caught slowly, illuminating a wide square platform surrounded on all sides by descending stairs. Looking down from the height of the platform, the soft luminescence revealed four more unlit torches, each at a corner of the stairs.

"Oh, this is a puzzle I know!" Nieve searched for a stick, or for anything that might help her light the other torches. Finding nothing, she drew her sword and cut the end off one of the long tails of her headband. After looping it around the end of her sword, she lit the cloth from the torch, then set about lighting the other four torches.

Some torch puzzles required climbers to share the flames in a specific order; other times the flames would die out rapidly, unless all the nearby torches were lit quickly enough. Solving a torch puzzle might reveal a hidden treasure or a secret passage, or trigger a fight. This time, none of those things happened. Disappointed and more than a little weary, Nieve climbed to the top of the platform again and turned a circle, taking note of the doorway she'd entered through as well as an opening in the opposite wall—hopefully the path forward. Exhaustion weighing heavily on her, Nieve sat down beside the torch, setting her sword within easy reach. As long as there was nothing else to do here, she might as well take a well-earned break.

Nieve took her time washing her face, hands, and feet with sweet-smelling soap and conjured water, taking care to check her injuries for signs of infection. The healing potion had worked its magic on the cut on her thigh, as well as her other scrapes and bruises, but her toe was still painfully broken, and she'd accumulated a few new wounds that she didn't remember receiving during her flight from the mud-monster. A fresh loop of bandage resecured the toe to an unbroken one, effectively splinting it. Her other injuries weren't worth wasting a healing potion on, but she made sure they were cleaned and covered. Afterward, she broke into her emergency rations and made herself a meager meal. The room was so quiet that her every bite seemed to echo on forever. Physically exhausted but not tired enough to sleep, Nieve stretched out on the square platform to rest, her arms folded behind her head.

"Why didn't the spell work?" Nieve asked the emptiness. A mural of the night sky was painted on the ceiling, allowing her to imagine she was outside, rather than hundreds of feet underground. "It worked every other time I cast it. Why did it fail that time?"

<Were you trying to use it differently?> Chime asked.

Nieve shrugged. "Most attunements work that way. Sure, casting ice spells is easiest, but I can use enhancement spells as well as water spells. Shouldn't the Paladin attunement work the same way?"

<I do not know,> Chime replied. <I have come to learn much about the magic of your goddess, but the power you now hold is new to me. I am not currently able to assist you in this matter.>

Nieve covered a yawn. She rolled to one side, popping the vertebrae of her spine before rolling to the other side and repeating the stretch. She didn't mean to rest for long; she just needed the ache of exertion to leave her body before pushing on again. The temptation to use her return bell was strong—she could just leave and meet up with Sage, and wait around for Hane. She felt certain they wouldn't give up on reaching the phantom chamber, even if they thought her dead from a pit trap. She tugged on Odette's embroidered bracelet, tried using her earpiece, then collapsed on her back, staring up vacantly at the star-painted ceiling.

<I sense power here,> Chime said softly. <It is subtle, like a secret, but one that must be deciphered rather than discovered.>

Do you always need to speak in riddles? Nieve asked, too tired to speak aloud. *My brain already hurts from coming up with that plan to distract the mud-monster with spiders earlier. I don't have the mental energy to try and understand you right now.*

Chime was silent so long that Nieve wondered if they had fallen asleep. Just as Nieve was cursing herself for letting Hane carry her bedroll, Chime piped up again. <Would you mind describing the room as you see it? Not the dimensions so much as the details I am unable to discern.>

Yeah, sure. Nieve covered a yawn. *There's a lot of stairs leading up to this . . . stage thing, I guess. Or a raised platform, at least. It's not like there's any place for an audience to sit for a play or performance. I lit four—no—five torches around the chamber, but I didn't see any hidden chambers open up, or any treasure magically appear. There's a doorway opposite the one I came through. That's really it.*

<What else do you see?>

Stars, Nieve replied, staring up at the mural. *Not real stars, just painted ones on the ceiling.*

<Is it normal to find such things in a place such as this?>

You mean inside a spire? Yeah, there's always weird stuff like that. But in a sewer . . . Nieve hedged. *I guess not? It's not like I've spent any time in underground sewers before this.*

<I see. Is there any significance to the stars on the ceiling?>

I mean . . . I guess it's kind of pretty? But why bother making a room in a sewer pretty? Nieve scowled up at the painted stars, resenting the fact that she had to work this out on her own. Sage probably would have spotted anything important as soon as the torches were lit. Nieve didn't even know what she was looking for. *Maybe this is a safe room? I don't know if there's a way to tell if it's a push room or a . . . what did Odette call it? Stasis room? I had to use a key to get in here, so hopefully it's the kind that lets me rest for a while.*

That still didn't explain the stars on the ceiling. If they referenced some local Caelford constellation, Nieve wasn't going to recognize it. She did try rolling her head from side to side, trying to find something she recognized from all the moon-viewing festivals her grandmother had dragged her to over the years. Without getting up, she walked her heels to one side, rotating her body to give herself different perspectives of the painted sky.

Oh, that one is Lord Byakko, the god beast of this spire. Nieve traced the lines of the constellation with her eyes. *This is probably some sort of tribute to her, right? Recognizing her rule over the spire, or something like that?*

<Perhaps,> Chime allowed. <But perhaps there is something more as well?>

Nieve sighed, seriously considering the idea of making camp for a good, long rest. But as Hane had her bedroll in their dimensional bag, the idea of sleeping inside a spire without a sentry or a sleeping bag wasn't an inviting prospect. Focusing on the starry ceiling was as good a distraction as any at the moment.

Since there's Byakko's constellation, the three aspects should be there as well, Nieve thought, letting her eyes go soft in order to pick out the biggest stars. *There, that's the Forge, the constellation representing the aspect of metal and creation. And then there's the Kha'an, the aspect of fertility or child-rearing. That leaves the aspect of sovereignty . . .*

Nieve yawned twice before rubbing her eyes and giving up. *I don't see it, but there's supposed to be a third constellation called the Crown. It represents the aspects of leadership and guidance. I think the legend tells of Byakko granting the first queen of Caelford the right to reign over the affairs of humans, or something like that.*

<Does it mean something that the constellation is missing from the painting?>

Yeah. Nieve gave up on trying to remain awake; she'd been pushing too hard for too long, and her brief respite earlier hadn't refreshed her as much as she would have liked. Wishing she wore a cloak that could be used as a blanket, Nieve reorganized the bags on her belt, stuffing her medical kit full of bandages, handkerchiefs, and a clean pair of socks so it could function as a decent pillow. *It means whoever painted this forgot it. Or maybe it's there and I'm missing it. I always hated moon-viewing parties. They're always just dark enough that my fingers or toes get stepped on by strangers.*

Nieve stretched out on the floor again, fluffing her makeshift pillow before rolling to one side, her knees drawn up close for warmth. Sleeping alone wasn't exactly safe, but neither was exhausting herself before she could find the others. Hopefully Chime would warn her of anything dangerous before it got too close.

<Forgive me for pressing,> Chime said. <But does the aspect of sovereignty have any personal meaning for you? I only ask because I sensed a slight change in the tune of your thoughts as you remarked upon it.>

Really? Nieve yawned as she thought back. *I can't think of any personal meaning; I barely remember learning about the constellations back in my pre-Judgment classes. Except . . .*

<Yes?>

It actually has nothing to do with the aspects or god beasts or constellations, so it's probably nothing. Nieve checked the weapons on her belt by habit, making sure she could draw one easily if she woke up surrounded by monsters. *Back when I was learning to speak Valian, I kept confusing the words "rain" and "reign." I used to think Caelford's monarchs had some power over the weather.*

An old memory surfaced, bringing nostalgia and embarrassment with it: Sage laughing uproariously while Emiko tried to explain what it meant for a monarch to reign. Nieve still hadn't fully understood afterward, but she had managed to knock a glass of cold tea into Sage's lap during a break in lessons, which had made her feel a little better.

Even though the memory pricked at her heart, it brought a sensation of warmth along with it. With one hand resting on the hilt of her sword, Nieve let her eyes fall closed and fell asleep with the music of her friends' laughter in her ears.

HANE

Wavewalker (leg mark), Citrine

"Almost . . ." Odette cupped a spell between her hands, brows furrowed in concentration as the misty compass arrow whirled and blurred. "It's close, it's so close."

"Look out!" Mason stepped in front of her just in time to block the spray of shrapnel from a clay disc explosion. Hane shattered another two discs before they could explode, blowing them to powder rather than shards. The clay discs camouflaged perfectly against the floor, walls, and ceiling, making them entirely undetectable until they floated up to about shoulder height before spinning rapidly and exploding into sharp-edged projectiles. As far as Hane could tell, the discs activated whenever anyone stepped within a certain distance of them. The clay shards were sharp enough to cut flesh and puncture armor, but overall Hane preferred these mindless objects over the more clever monsters they'd been fighting up until now.

"Not to rush you, Odie, but you really need to hurry up," Rose urged, scraping up the mana crystals left behind by an exploded disc. One wobbled up from the floor ahead of her but collapsed before it could begin to spin, a thrown knife cutting through its center. "We're all running low on weapons and mana, and if we can't make it to the vault, we at least need to find a static zone for an extended rest."

"I would kill for a mana fountain right now," Mason muttered, shield-slamming a clay disc before it could burst. Rose scurried to collect the mana crystals that landed between his boots. "Or a shower. Or a hot spring. I'd settle for a river in winter if it meant I could wash up and feel clean again."

"I just want to change my clothes," Lief remarked, hanging back from the trench. He'd reached for his bow a few times since the guardian fight, each time making a sour face when he remembered it was gone. "But that's probably a futile gesture until we put this putrid place behind us."

"Got it!" Odette shrieked, turning on her heel with a purposeful stride. Hane caught her collar before she could step off the edge of the walkway, something she'd tried to do multiple times before while focusing on her spinning arrow. "It's there, Mason, make the hole there!"

Mason cursed under his breath as he first shaped a stone bridge over the canal of sewage. He looked back to make sure Hane was ready before stepping forward, as the spinning discs never missed an opportunity to assault anyone crossing over the trench. Hane stood with both tonfa pointed outward and gave Mason the nod. Mason set his chin determinedly, ducked his head and bolted across.

Hane cast Burst through their tonfa, giving the spell more accuracy and control by compressing the spell to a narrow trajectory, firing at each clay disc as it revealed itself. After Mason went Odette, Lief, then Rose, who kicked the few mana crystals that landed on the bridge to the far side of the canal in order to collect them. When Hane was the last one, they leapt and twisted in midair, kicking off the ceiling to land on the far side without creating a target of themself. By the time they got there, they were the last to descend through the hole Mason shaped in the floor.

"It's here," Odette said, anticipation giving her voice a breathless quality. The compass arrow reflected off her glasses, still spinning wildly in all directions. How she could discern anything at all from a spell like that, Hane couldn't begin to guess, but as long as it worked, they had no cause to complain. At least with Odette focused on directions, Hane was free to keep an eye on their surroundings and watch for threats.

They turned a slow circle, surveying the new labyrinth level as they tucked one tonfa away—they preferred to keep one hand free so they could grab Odette before she walked into the canal. This floor didn't look that much different than the one above it, nor the ones above that. A dark green moss grew along the stone walls here, giving a sense of deepening shadows and time out of mind. The water wasn't nearly as murky or congealed as the other levels, but the black-glass appearance of the surface filled Hane with a sense of foreboding. They were tempted to try their Sense Water spell, but since it wouldn't help them detect the presence of gavials, it was safer to simply consider all water as hazardous to climbers' health.

"I think . . ." This way Odette trailed off as she took a few tentative steps in one direction, then stopped to chew on her lower lip. She turned around, took a step, then shook her head and reversed direction again. "We'll have to go through the walls to make it before the labyrinth changes. Here, Mason, follow me."

"Before we start reshaping the maze to our advantage, why don't we find another safe zone?" Hane suggested. "If this is the final level, the challenges are likely already difficult enough without beginning them as exhausted as we all are now."

"You want to stop right now?" Odette asked, taking her eyes off the spinning arrow long enough to shoot an incredulous look over her shoulder. "Why would we stop now? The vault is so close, we're nearly there! We can rest after we collect our rewards."

"Pfft, rest, who needs to rest?" Mason asked with a liberal helping of sarcasm. Despite his cynicism, he shaped an opening through the section of wall Odette indicated. Once the way was clear, he slouched against the wall, drinking from his canteen as he expounded his point. "I mean, it's not like we had to outrun a lightning cheetah while dodging scissor-toothed mini gators—"

"Crocodiles," Rose corrected. Oddly, there was no follow-up after that. She'd seemed quiet for a while now, but she was probably just tired. They all were.

"Then there was that long passage filled with poisonous gas, that wasn't stressful at all, right everyone?" Mason continued, following the others through his constructed doorway last, so he could close the opening behind himself. "At least we didn't end up stumbling into a kobold mining operation—oh, wait, we did, didn't we?"

No one took the bait; the wounds were still too fresh. The poison gas pipe hadn't been so bad: Rose created pure-air breathing masks for everyone with Mason's assistance, so it was only scary at the beginning. The mining operation, though . . . that had been troublesome. Hane imagined that any group willing to fight through scores of kobolds would be richly rewarded with treasure from the dig, but as lean as they were on combat professionals, Odette suggested they try to sneak around. It had almost worked—until they were spotted and had to outrun hundreds of tiny pickaxes as well as explosive fire magic used for mining. The one blessing of that level was that the sewer trenches were all dry, so Mason couldn't whine about his clothes getting wet.

"Oh, but then we had that lovely little jaunt through the garden, that was relaxing, wasn't it?" Mason recounted with relish, voice echoing off moss-covered walls. The team walked single file behind Odette as she followed the directions of her compass spell. "I can feel my strength returning just by picturing all those vines and lily pads, and the brightly colored frogs that definitely weren't spitting poison at us. And such pretty flowers, too! Remember those, Odette?"

The jungle floor had been misery: the ropelike vines didn't cut easily, but they could lash like whips, or twine around body parts to drag victims away. Odette had nearly been swallowed by a yellow-orange flower as wide as Hane stood tall. With jungle-like growth covering the walls, the ceiling, and even the water, Hane hadn't been able to safely land on any surface for longer than a breath. Just remembering it set their heart to drumming loudly in their chest.

"And who can forget that delightful slide?" Mason's false cheer took on a bitter undertone. "The one I didn't even have to slide down myself, because my loving sister tripped me into it headfirst. Who wouldn't feel well rested after that?" He cut an ugly sneer at Rose as she stalwartly ignored him. "It's a wonder I don't climb more often, honestly."

Actually, the slide had been the least of their trials, but they had nearly lost Mason over it. To get down to the next level, Odette had said they had to slide down an algae-slick pipe with a bit of water running down the center of it. Mason had pitched a fit, threatening to quit if they didn't find another way. Rose, with a characteristic eye roll, asked if she could have a moment alone with her brother. As the others backed away, she'd somehow managed to trip him and shove him down the slide before following closely after. While Mason clearly hadn't forgiven her for that, it seemed the two of them had reached some sort of agreement before Hane and the others caught up. No one had been hurt on the slide, but their clothing was certainly worse off for it.

As annoying as it was to listen to Mason recount the trials of the labyrinth, Hane sympathized with his frustration. Ever since fleeing the labyrinth guardian, the longest break they'd gotten was five hours in a push zone, and that time had been divided up among healing, eating, sleeping, and guard duty—and they'd been lucky to catch that much of a break. Most of the other push zones they'd stopped at had only allowed them to rest for twenty minutes to an hour before some hazard or attack hurried them along. It was a grueling run even for Hane, and Mason was far from an experienced climber. And based on this delve, it didn't seem likely Mason would be joining any more climber teams anytime soon.

"There's no point in stopping when we could be at the vault in less than an hour," Odette announced, slowing to a stop. "As long as the labyrinth stays in its current shape, there's a tunnel that can take us directly to the antechamber, but if it changes, it could still take us days. I just need to find . . . yes! It's that way." She pointed to a corridor across the trench. The angle made it difficult to see down, though from Hane's perspective, it appeared darker than most of the other ways they could have chosen to go.

"Fine," Mason sighed, giving up his veneer of cheer. "But if I don't see the vault in front of me in half an hour, I don't care what is going on, I'm lying down and going to sleep. I can't even picture what sort of treasure is worth all of this."

Rose rolled her eyes but withheld the expected biting retort. It almost seemed as if the two of them had traded roles, with Mason taking on the biting, talkative personality while Rose became more withdrawn, offering only a few words when it was necessary. It was a refreshing break from the bickering, but Hane was getting a little tired of Mason's whining. At least Rose's monologues were vaguely useful at times.

Hane watched the water as Mason formed a stone bridge across the canal. Usually whatever was hiding beneath the surface took the opportunity to attack the moment someone started to cross, and as this was a new level, no one knew what to expect this time.

Mason waited a beat before setting a foot on his bridge, then paused again, waiting out the inevitable attack. Just as he started to cross in earnest, Hane saw the ripple of movement beneath the water.

"Back!" Hane shouted, the word lost as water sprayed outward from the trench, Mason yelping as he covered his face and head with his arms. The spray of water yielded to reveal a long, slick-looking tentacle, with short spines along the medial ridge and pale gray suckers on the underside. Hane directed blasts of transference mana at the thick base of the tentacle near the surface of the water, but that didn't stop the lithe tip from curling around Mason's forearm. It started to drag him forward into the trench, but Lief and Rose braced him on either side, pitting their weight against the tentacle's strength. Mason screamed for help as he dug his heels in and reeled backward, though his panic seemed to be more sewer-water induced than pain-induced. Their Burst spell ineffective, Hane looked for another way to assist. They weren't heartened by the stirring of the water on either side of the tentacle.

"Hane, take him!" Rose shouted, leaning bodily into her brother's chest as her feet slipped on the stone walkway. Hoping she had a plan, Hane replaced her, standing with their back to Mason's chest. When the tentacle gave a mighty tug, Hane pushed back with an equal amount of force, wringing an airless grunt out of Mason's chest. Rose moved determinedly toward the tentacle gripping her brother, but Hane's focus was stolen by two more tentacles erupting from the surface of the water. One was whip-thin, only as thick around as Hane's wrist, and while it looked weak, it moved quickly and unexpectedly, curling and coiling back on itself before lashing forward to grab at wrists, ankles, or anything it could find. It darted at Mason's ankle, but Rose slammed her heel down on it, making it yank back on itself. The other new tentacle was as thick as a tree trunk, and what it lacked in mobility, it made up for in strength. As it reared back like a bucking horse, it struck the ceiling hard enough to shake stones and metal piping loose, then rolled to the side, shattering Mason's stone bridge.

Rose shouted a warning just before Mason tumbled backward, Lief and Hane crashing down on top of him. The end of the tentacle had been neatly severed, the end coiled around Mason's arm going limp as the injured tentacle retreated to the water. Mason retched as he scraped the tentacle tip from his arm, massaging the welts left behind by the suckers.

"Garrote wire?" Hane asked Rose as they picked themself up from the walkway.

"Never leave home without it," Rose replied, holding up a razor-thin wire connected by a pair of wooden dowels.

"Can we get past them?" Odette asked, cowering far back against the wall, her compass arrow still cupped between her hands. "If we don't hurry, the location at the end of the tunnel will change!"

Lief shot her an exasperated look before faking a gracious gesture. "After you, my lady."

Odette gnawed on her lower lip, anxiety warring with trepidation.

"We should proceed with caution," Hane advised, dancing around the twining little tentacle while keeping an eye on the larger one. "I've dealt with octopoid monsters before, but never in an environment like this. We need to determine if this is one creature with different tentacles, or three creatures each with their own tentacles, or if the tentacles are independent constructs of—"

Rose pressed something between her palms with a sharp snap, then rolled a small canister into the trench. "Ears!"

Hane barely managed to cover their ears before an underwater explosion shook the walkway, spraying water everywhere in a veiling mist. Mason moaned pitiably, his eyes squeezed shut as he flicked water off his hands. Rose sighed in exasperation before grabbing his wrist and towing him forward.

"Bridge! Now! While they're gone!" Rose ordered.

Edges of the walkway crumbled underfoot, but at least the tentacles had withdrawn; Rose was right—now was the time to hurry.

"Let's go!" Hane urged, leaping the trench while Mason was still shaping a new bridge.

"Go left!" Odette shouted. "We need to get—aaah!"

Odette screamed as a thin coil of tentacle grabbed at her from behind, catching the strap of her satchel. She struggled to pull away, keeping a tight grip on her bag.

"Let it go!" Hane shouted, almost in unison with Rose.

"I can't!" Odette shrieked, pressing away from the tentacle without giving up her grip on the bag. It was behavior Hane expected from an inexperienced climber, not a veteran and team leader like Odette. They understood not wanting to part with climber gear, especially anything expensive or irreplaceable, but most climbers understood not to bring anything they couldn't afford to lose.

Odette, it seemed, was not one of them.

Before she could be dragged into the water, Lief rushed in wielding a small hunter's knife, severing the bag's strap. He grabbed Odette's wrist and hauled her across the bridge, refusing to let go until both of them stood with the rest of the team.

"Th-that way," Odette said weakly, clasping her bag to her chest as she pointed. "It's close, we just—oh!"

Odette's bag slipped, making her fold in half to hold onto it. Rose rolled her eyes before spinning Odette around to tie the two ends of the satchel strap together. It wasn't pretty, but it was functional. "Next time we tell you to let it go, you let it go."

"R-right." Odette trembled so hard that her glasses slipped to the end of her nose.

"More tentacles," Hane called out, motioning for the others to get back. "Stay close to the wall and—"

"Aah!" This time it was Rose's scream that echoed off the moss-covered walls. Hane only caught a glimpse of a large stone-colored something that she struggled to get off of her head when four tentacles burst from the trench, writhing, grabbing, and smashing everything within reach.

"Rose!" Mason grabbed a stone rod from the quiver on his back, its width doubling as he swung it back over his shoulder. He shouted a word Hane didn't recognize, but it caused Rose to freeze in the middle of her panicked frenzy. Mason swung the rod sidelong, batting the creature off of Rose's head, though it took her headscarf with it in its teeth.

"Camouflaged attack lizards," Lief commented mildly. "Yes, that's what's been missing this whole time. Camouflaged attack lizards."

"Can you do something about them?" Hane called, attempting to deal with the tentacles. The tiny and medium-sized tentacles were easy to trick into knotting themselves up, but the tree-trunk tentacles were a problem, smacking into walls and pipes with enough power to crack them. One pipe in the ceiling screamed as it released a thin stream of steam.

"I'll use Detect Life," Lief said, one hand on Rose's shoulder to heal the scratches left behind by the lizard. "That will at least give us some warning before they leap. That's all I can do without my bow."

"Too bad you didn't bring a functional sword," Hane groused, holding both tonfa in one hand for an extra-strength Burst spell. They knocked a heavy tentacle off course before it could slam into the walkway ahead of them.

"Watch out." Rose said it flatly, without inflection or emphasis. Hane barely caught sight of another canister rolling toward the edge of the walkway in time to clap their hands over their ears. The tentacles fled once more after the explosion created a spray of water and echoed the crack of stone breaking. When Hane could see again, Rose was standing in the same spot, her back to the rest of the group, arms limp at her sides. A bit of stone crumpled beneath the toe of her boots. Her shoulders rose and fell with a deep breath. "I was wrong; we shouldn't have continued without Nieve. This challenge would be so much simpler with some ice mana."

Hane had been struggling to avoid thinking the exact same thing. Nieve conjured bridges of ice faster than Mason shaped bridges of stone, and ice could lock the tentacles in place, or even dice them into curry meat. And Nieve wouldn't shrink and shy from every splash of water, she would have barreled straight on through, heedless of the muck and the risk. But those thoughts weren't helpful; Nieve wasn't here and wishing she was wouldn't change anything.

"We might not be facing this particular challenge if she were here," Lief pointed out, eyes scanning the ceiling and upper walls. "If we had another combat specialist, we could have stood our ground and fought, rather than running from everything."

"This is it," Odette said as the team arrived at the mouth of the shadowy corridor. Walkways framing a channel of dark water disappeared into darkness, making it look longer than it was. "The destination can still change if we don't hurry."

"Above!" Lief shouted, pointing at the ceiling. Hane directed a Burst spell upward just in time to blast a lizard into the far wall, but by the sound of dismay that escaped Lief's mouth, it seemed the worst was far from over. "Oh my, that's a lot of lizards that no one else can see. Odette, you're certain that's the way we need to go?"

"Yes." She nodded firmly, chin raised resolutely. "And fast."

How much faster could any of them go? Hane was used to long runs, but this one was grueling even for them. They felt that if they stopped to catch their breath, they'd simply collapse. A challenge like this one was meant to be tackled slowly, with the team moving from safe area to safe area, collecting treasures and rewards along the way to stay heartened. But that became impossible after Nieve . . .

Cold, Hane whispered to themself. *Numbing cold. Don't think, don't feel. There's nothing I can do for her now, and everyone else is relying on me.*

It was worrying that the memory of Nieve kept surfacing no matter how much they attempted to lock it away. That trick had always worked in the past, allowing Hane to focus on saving as many people as possible, rather than dwelling on those already lost. There was no changing the past—they knew that to be true. They couldn't allow themself to be distracted by grief, especially not now when they were running low on stamina and magic. Not now, when others were relying on them.

Not now, and not ever.

"Okay, I can only do this once, so don't expect it again." Lief stepped up to the edge of the walkway, facing the shadowy depths of the corridor. "Don't go right away, give it a three-count first."

"Why would—" Hane stopped as Lief's body began to glow. They turned away, shielding their eyes as the light grew in intensity, burning in a brilliant aura around Lief. One hand cupped to shade their eyes, Hane squinted down the illuminated corridor. Several hundred yards long, it terminated in a dead end, with the walkway doubling back on itself to come up the far side. A large tunnel was set into the wall about six feet above the walkway, covered by an iron grate. It looked to be a drainage tunnel, perhaps for overflow, or perhaps to fill this level of the sewer. Whatever else it was for, this was the most direct path to the phantom vault.

The scrape of a footstep—Hane held their arm out to block Odette's way.

Odette made a frustrated noise. "We have to go! It can still—"

Right then, the reason Lief had asked them to count to three first became clear: stunned lizards dropped from their hiding places, bulging eyes wide as they crashed down to die on the stone walkway, or splashed heavily into the water. After long, tense moments of what felt like waiting out a storm, the heavy thuds and loud splashes stopped.

Lief sagged, resting his hands on his knees as he caught his breath. Mason grabbed Lief's arm and hoisted it around his neck, half lifting Lief off his feet. "I got you, let's go!"

Rose and Odette were already running full pelt down the walkway. Hane lingered just long enough to make sure Mason could keep pace with Lief before following after them. Several thin tentacles speared through the surface of the water, suckers latching low onto the stone wall like tripwires. Rose leapt each one like low hurdles while Odette slowed down to step over the first one. It snapped free from the wall, attempting to curl around her ankle, making her scream and kick at it uselessly. Hane leapt and pinned it beneath their heel while wondering how Mason and Lief were going to get past this new obstacle. The question was rendered moot as one of the thickest tentacles yet emerged with a splash, its shadow engulfing both Mason and Lief beneath it.

"I have— I have—" Odette fumbled with the spell spheres on her bracer, several clattering to the ground before she found the one she was looking for. She threw it hard, bypassing the tentacle to hit the opposite side of the trench. The sphere shattered, releasing an ice spell that froze part of the trench solid. As the tentacle thrashed to free itself, Lief and Mason hurried past, stepping over the tentacle Hane had trapped beneath their foot.

Ahead, Rose jumped up and grabbed the lowest part of the grate that covered the tunnel, bracing her feet against the wall as she tugged. Rust flaked off beneath her hands, but the grate didn't so much as budge. She dropped down to search her pockets while Hane cleared the tripwire tentacles for the others.

"I have acid somewhere . . ." Rose muttered, the contents of her pockets rattling. "You know, Brick, this is the exact reason I ask you to train your crystal mark, because—"

"Watch out!" Lief shouted, pointing out something over Rose's head. He and Mason both started forward to push her away, but the uncoordinated movement made them stumble, teetering far too close to the edge of the trench. Rose leapt backward, avoiding the falling lizard, but stumbled right into the waiting arm of a tentacle. Her scream spun out long and thin as something small tumbled from her fingers to land on the walkway.

"Rose!" Mason shouted, reaching out as if he could grab her. Lief plunged his knife through the lizard's back before it could camouflage or attack, while Odette scrambled along the ground on her hands and knees, groping after shadows. "Hane!"

"I'll get her." That's what they said, though they weren't sure how they were going to do it. The tentacle arched itself up high, dangling Rose like a piece of bait. It was fortunate she hadn't been dragged under the water, but doubtless an unknown number of tentacles lurked beneath the surface, waiting to snatch up any would-be rescuers.

Still, Hane was prepared to try. Picking out their path ahead of time to avoid watchful tentacles, Hane coiled, preparing to jump—only to be stopped by Odette grabbing their sleeve.

"Here! Rose's acid." Odette pressed a tiny vial of liquid into Hane's hands. "Use it to make an opening in the grate."

"But Rose—"

"We'll do what we can, but this is the best way to make sure most of us survive," Odette said in a rush. "And you're the fastest climber, so it's up to you to open the path."

She turned away with authority, shouting orders to Mason and Lief. A part of Hane knew they should hesitate—that they should insist on rescuing Rose first—but that was the kind of thinking that got climbers killed. And Hane was, first and foremost, a survivor.

The cross-hatched grating was easy to climb, despite being wet and rusty. They didn't realize how caustic the liquid in the vial was until they removed the cork with their teeth, the acrid aroma perforating their mask to burn the inside of their nostrils and make their eyes water. Holding the vial far away from themself, they dabbed just a tiny droplet on the grating, which immediately began to hiss and steam. They didn't need a large opening, just something big enough for each team member to crawl through. With that in mind, Hane chose their acid points carefully, using as little acid as possible.

Once Hane had four connecting lines of steaming iron grating, they climbed higher along the grating, feeling for a toehold in the middle of their would-be opening. Curling their fingers through the grating, Hane swung their leg back and kicked the grating while at the same time releasing a Burst spell through their foot. The acid-scored lines snapped off cleanly, the small section of grating falling with a clatter inside the tunnel. Hane let go with one hand, swinging around to look back at their teammates.

A section of wall had been reshaped into something like a fist, gripping the tentacle stalk around the middle. The end holding Rose flailed wildly to free itself, cracking the stone faster than Mason could reshape it. Whatever Odette's plan was, it was clear Rose had her own: from Hane's vantage point, they saw her raise a small weapon overhead before swinging it down into the fleshy appendage that gripped her. The tentacle snapped backward as ice sprouted from the puncture wound, growing into a ring that rapidly spread to coat the entire appendage. When the tentacle released her, Rose dangled one-handedly from the ice pick she'd claimed from the train's treasure cache.

Mason shouted something from the walkway. Hane tensed as Rose coiled her feet against the icy surface of the frantic tentacle. They forgot to breathe as she kicked off, ripping the ice pick free as she tried to angle her fall toward her brother.

She wasn't going to make it.

Hane reached out, straining to shape Rose's motion to carry her farther and slow her fall just enough so her weight wouldn't drag both herself and her brother into the dark water below. Mason caught her in his outstretched arms, pulling her bodily into him as he backpedaled into the wall. Before he could set her down, a trove of new tentacles burst through the surface of the water, causing Mason to hold his sister up in front of him as a shield against the spray. Rose elbowed him to break his grip, standing sturdily on her own two feet before tossing another explosive canister into the canal. The tentacles withdrew as the resulting explosion rattled the iron grating Hane clung to.

"Hurry!" Odette screamed, clinging to the lowest section of grating. Lief must have lifted her to reach the cross-hatching. Hane climbed down to help her through the opening. Lief came next, then Rose, followed by Mason.

They were safe.

For now.

Rose looked pleased with herself for some reason, batting Lief's offer of healing away as she twirled the ice pick in her hand. She caught Hane's eye and smiled sadly. "Nieve would have appreciated that, I think."

A pinprick of heat in the center of their chest threatened to melt the block of ice that numbed them. Hane swallowed tightly, pretending to scan the darkness for traps and threats. Rose barely even knew Nieve, yet her loss was clearly on Rose's mind. It wasn't as if Hane had forgotten Nieve—they just couldn't think of her now. And if they put off thinking about her long enough . . . well, if the past was any indicator of the future, they would forget her entirely before long.

Something about that thought made the pinprick of heat burn brighter, bringing a touch of pain with it.

"Uh, guys?" Mason's voice quavered. "Is it supposed to be doing that?"

Looking back, Hane felt their stomach sink. The water frothed and churned like a pot about to boil. Hane thought it was movement below the surface, but quickly realized it was worse than that—much worse.

"The water level is rising," Hane said grimly. "We can't stop here, we have to keep going."

"Are you sure?" Mason asked, a whining twinge in his voice. "Won't it take a while for the sewer to flood before the water reaches the tunnel?"

"It's just a little farther," Odette insisted, taking leading steps into the deep-set shadows of the tunnel. "The vault is at the other end of this tunnel. We can rest when we get there."

Lief sat with his back pressed against the curve of the tunnel, his pale complexion tinged with gray. "I want to get to the vault as much as anyone here, but I need a break. We all do."

"But—" Odette protested, brows pinching tight to wrinkle her forehead.

"We can do both," Hane said, speaking over her objection. "We need to stay ahead of the overflow, but we don't have to rush just yet. Let's conserve our energy as much as possible and try to recover some mana. Can we all agree to that?"

By the grumbles that followed, Hane assumed the others would have preferred a real rest, but one glance at the rising water was all it took to urge them back to their feet. At least at a slower pace, they could all eat, drink, and maybe recover a little mana in the process. There wasn't much talking beyond the sharing of food or requests for healing, which Hane took as a sign of general exhaustion. Lief and Rose each revealed enchanted light sources, holding them out to light the way ahead.

Slowly, the ache drained from Hane's limbs and their breath returned to normal. They ate the packaged food from the train and drank deeply from their canteen. They even refilled the others' canteens with conjured water, but only enough for a few gulps. Odette didn't use a spell to illuminate traps, choosing to call them out instead as she found them; Lief declined to cast any unnecessary healing spells in favor of recovering his mana. It was the right decision; Hane wasn't even using any perception spells to enhance their senses. Better to save their mana for later, when it was needed.

Hane couldn't be sure how long they walked in silence, but the tiny hum of a distant vibration shivered the ground beneath their feet. They paused, extending their senses to locate the source of the vibration. When they looked up, they found the others all staring back at them.

"What is it?" Lief asked, resigned.

"The water. It's reached the tunnel now."

"Look, look!" Odette cried, pointing ahead. "Put the lights out, I think I see the end! Look!"

Rose covered her light with her hand and Lief tucked his behind his back, proving Odette correct: the end was in sight.

Unfortunately, the end was blocked by yet another rusty iron grate.

Hane's exhaustion pressed in on them, their body voicing its protests with pops of cartilage and creaking joints. Alas, there was no other option. "Run. We need to get to the grate before the water catches up to us."

They felt slow and clumsy at first, like weights had been strapped to their feet. Their only relief was seeing the others bounce off one another as they forced tired limbs back into motion. But what started as a slow, uncoordinated jog quickly turned into a full blown sprint as a trickle of water caught up to them, growing wider and deeper with every step. The whispery sound of air flow was replaced by the roar of a rising wave: the tide was coming in fast.

The water surged to calf height, and while Hane was able to stand atop it, the others were forced to slow down, lest they slip. Hane ran ahead, charging the grate with their shoulder and a Burst spell. They bounced off the metal and fell back with a splash.

"Mason, do something!" Rose urged. "Make it brittle, or turn it into a softer metal. Anything, just do it fast!"

"Whoa!" Odette was swept off her feet as the current ran faster, spilling out through the grating to the room beyond. She struck the grate with her feet and used the cross-hatching to pull herself up. "I can see it! I can see the vault! It's right there, just—just—"

She stretched her arm through the grate as far as it would go, straining as if hope and desire would pull her through. The room beyond looked like an actual room, with a tiled floor, rounded pillars, and arched doorways on either side. Twin lines of statues marched from the center of the room to frame a relief set into the wall opposite the tunnel. Only it wasn't a relief: it was the vault door, depicting a scene etched in whorls of gold, silver, and copper. The surge of water pressed Hane against the grate, along with the others. It really was so close, almost in their grasp, yet still so far away.

"Rose, do you have more acid?" Odette asked, scaling the grating to stay above the rising water level. The force of the water was heavy, but not overwhelming. Not yet, anyway.

"No, and even if I did, it wouldn't work with all this water." Rose was pressed flat to the grating, her brother behind her with his hands braced wide as if protecting her from the current. "I have plenty of files on me, but I don't think we have the time for that to work."

"Mason, I'm going to help you channel metal mana," Lief coached. "Just focus and—"

"I'm trying." Mason shook his head, hands shaking where they gripped the grating. "I'm too tired, I can't focus. It's just—it's such a strong metal."

"Make it brittle," Hane encouraged, nodding as Lief ducked low to press his hand against Mason's crystal mark. "I'll break it, I just need you to weaken it first."

Water rushed against Hane's back, making it difficult to push away from the metal grating. The tunnel was nearly half full with the water level still rising. If there was one small blessing here, it was that the water appeared relatively clear, or at least void of any detritus present in most of the sewer trenches. Breathing wasn't too much of an issue yet, but it would be soon if Mason couldn't change the state of the iron. Hane scaled the grating as high as they could, scanning the room beyond while they waited for Mason's spell to take effect. Even without it, they would attempt to break through the grating using Burst if the water climbed up much higher.

The statues lining the room beyond the grate appeared to be naga—humanoid monsters with serpent tails rather than legs, as well as scales and fins on the human half of their bodies. Each stone carving held a long spear, tipped with actual steel rather than carved from stone. They appeared to be guarding the entrance to the vault, an impressive construction that reached from the floor to the ceiling. With the water pouring over and around them, it was difficult to make out the specific images on the vault door, save for the image of a golden sun at the top center. Could they even bring themself to ring out now, as close as they were to the vault?

As close as they were to Chime?

"Hit it!" Mason called, spitting out water as he spoke. "Hit it hard!"

Hane wound transference mana tight throughout their core: they hadn't thought they had this much in reserve, but then they realized Lief's hand was pressed to their back, more than likely assisting with the spell in some way. Rather than release Burst widely, they focused on creating targeted blasts through their hands and feet, all braced against the iron grating. The first Burst spells rattled the grate hard. The second caused a few sharp snaps. Over the roar of rushing water, Hane heard the gasps of those about to submerge, and only then did they realize the water was up to their neck. It would have been better if they could strike or kick the grating, adding momentum to their Burst spell, but the pressure of the water made that impossible. Drawing as deep a breath as possible, Hane prepared to cast their last Burst spell. If this didn't work, they would have to find a way to signal the others before ringing out, despite the object of all their desires right in front of their eyes.

The metal beneath Hane's hands shivered—not from the water spilling through it, but from something else. A vibration, or perhaps a sound? Hane thought they heard a distant ringing, but submerged beneath the rush of water, they couldn't be sure. Perhaps Mason was still trying to weaken the metal, and Hane was feeling the effects of the spell. Whatever it was, it was now do or die time: either the metal had to give, or the team had to give up on the vault.

Water surged and crested over Hane's head as they struck with their final Burst spell, giving them the unique feeling of tumbling weightlessly along a current. What happened? Had the recoil of their spell knocked them backward into the tunnel? Sense Water told them they were no longer close to their teammates, and the confusing rush made it difficult to perceive their location. There was a loud scrape of metal on stone, a gentle bouncing sensation, and then, miraculously, the pressure of the water vanished. Hane found themself still clinging to a broken section of iron grating in the center of the room containing the vault, where only inches of water accumulated before washing out through the arched doorways. Hane let their head rest on the floor as they drew breath after breath, relieved to find they could still do so. When they could lift their head, they did a quick headcount. It looked as if everyone had survived.

"I—" Odette coughed and shivered. "We made it. I can't believe—can't believe we got here after—after everything. We just . . . just ."

"Catch your breath, Odie," Rose advised, lying on her back as she followed her own advice. "We still have to figure out the riddle or the hint or whatever. We can afford to rest for . . . for just a minute."

Mason made a doubtful noise, something that was half squeal, half cough. "I'm not sure we can." Mason pointed to the nearest naga statue as the others turned to stare at him. "That's not real stone. And I think—oh. Oh no."

Hane didn't want to look. Nor did they wish to stand and fight, nor run away and find a safe place to hide. They just wanted this to be over already.

But wishing didn't make it so.

Hane scraped themself up off the floor just as the first naga statue cast off its stone exterior and came to life, hissing through needle-sharp teeth as it attacked.

NIEVE

Champion (mind mark), Citrine
Paladin (heart mark), Carnelian

Nieve's knees were beginning to ache, and her back felt bowed like a fishing pole. She longed to stand up straight, but the smell of petrichor had led her into an empty bronze pipe, more suited for crawling than for walking upright. While she refused to crawl, Nieve had briefly considered coating the bottom of the pipe in a layer of ice and sliding along on her belly. It would have put her in a poor position to defend herself if attacked, but the more aches and pains set in, the more she considered doing it anyway.

"How much farther?" Nieve asked, flinching as the bronze hummed her voice back at her. She knew Chime would hear her even if she spoke within her mind, but more and more Nieve found herself missing the sound of her teammates' voices. Speaking aloud didn't offer much comfort, but after feeling alone for so long, she was willing to take whatever little comforts she could find.

<I am afraid I cannot be sure,> Chime replied. <By the resonance, I would judge it to be quite long, but magical constructions are often inaccurate in the way they convey sound. And there is always the chance that external forces may act upon the construct to lengthen or shorten it, making any estimate I provide unreliable.>

Nieve slowed to a stop, sweeping the light of her glow stick as far ahead as possible, then turning to look behind her. She sniffed the air deeply, finding only the tang of the metal and her own sweat-and-leather odor.

<What is it?> Chime asked, likely perceiving Nieve's confusion. <I sensed no obstructions in the resonance created by your voice, but my perception may not be reliable in this place.>

"I lost the scent," Nieve murmured, keeping her voice low enough that only the nearby bronze fittings hummed a response. "How is that possible? I know I followed it in here."

<Was there a turnoff, perhaps?> Chime asked. <I sense nothing of the sort, either through sound or through magic, but that does not mean it is impossible.>

"I didn't see a turnoff," Nieve said, moving awkwardly to avoid hitting her head. A spasm in her low back made her think longingly of her return bell, but as long as she had come this far, she might as well continue until she either found the others or was forced to give up. Before retreating back along the bronze pipe, she set her hands on her knees and rounded her back a few times until it popped. Sighing as she eased the tender spot, Nieve retraced her steps along the pipe, stopping every so often to sniff the air.

As luck would have it, she found the scent after only a few yards, stronger than she remembered it being, but as she continued to follow it, the scent became fainter and fainter. Frowning, Nieve turned around again, finding the scent stronger until it ended abruptly.

"What the resh?" Nieve asked, frustrated. "It just stops. Why would it just stop? There's no way to turn, no trap door above or below, no switch or torch or—"

She cut herself off, squinting as she played her light over the bronze beneath her feet. A quick glance around her and along the length of the pipe in both directions, then a solid stomp with her boot. There was no difference in the sound here than anywhere else, but there was a faint discoloration to the bronze here, as if a new metal panel had been welded to the original pipe.

<Is it a secret?>

"I think . . ." Nieve trailed off, seeking the seams of the welded metal. It had been expertly patched, but now that she knew what to look for, she found the telltale lines indicating a difference in the metals of the pipe. "I hope I'm right. If this doesn't work, then I'm all out of ideas."

Standing up carefully, Nieve pressed her palms against the sides of the pipe for balance, then slammed her heel down into the center of the discolored metal. The resounding echo made her flinch, but the metal patch dented significantly. She adjusted her grip on the walls and kicked again, breaking one seam of the weld cleanly. Pausing to stretch her back, Nieve found the scent of petrichor even stronger than before.

Nieve grinned as she lifted her boot again, reinforcing her leg with a surge of enhancement mana. "I think this is it!"

Before she could strike, excited tinkling noises filled her head.

<I hear voices! Human voices!> Chime's tone twittered like birds on a bough. <It is too far for me to sense any mana signatures, but I believe we are catching up!>

"Catching up?" Nieve muttered. She crouched down low, cocking her ear toward the opening in the pipe. "I thought the smell of petrichor was a hint to lead us to the vault."

<Perhaps the others have already arrived at the vault,> Chime rationalized. <I believe I recognize the voices, but I do not wish to set expectations prematurely. I do hope that we have found Hane and your other comrades. I have been . . . concerned for them.>

The hesitation in Chime's voice meant something, likely emotional, but Nieve couldn't focus on that just then. Through the crack in the pipe, she heard the sounds of battle: metal clashing, stone cracking, water rushing, all amid hoarse battle cries and grunts of pain.

Hurry! Nieve urged herself, jumping to her feet. *If it is them, they might need me.*

Steadying herself against the sides of the pipe, Nieve drove her heel down with purpose, snapping the welded plate free. The resulting crash echoed wetly; heavy plips and plops of water fell from the ceiling to collect in about an inch of water in the rounded tunnel below. Nieve peered through the opening first, checking for traps and enemies before dropping down. The tunnel appeared to run at an angle with the pipe she'd emerged from, and while the water raining from the ceiling wasn't exactly fresh, it didn't seem putrid either. One end of the tunnel was brighter than the other, and while it was hard to be sure with all the dripping water, Nieve thought the scent of clean water on dry stone was coming from the same direction as the sounds of battle.

Though her every instinct urged her to rush to the end of the tunnel and dive into the fray, Nieve forced herself to move slowly and keep her breathing soft, keeping to the shadows as she crept to the edge of the tunnel. She hadn't survived this long on her own inside a spire just to die foolishly now. The closer she came to the end, the more certain she was that she heard Mason's distinctive booming voice and Rose's terse orders, though amid the echoes and splashes, the words were hard to make out. Hugging the shadows of the tunnel's end, Nieve surveyed the scene carefully, making sure this truly was her team and not simply an illusion meant to fool her.

The room beyond looked something like a fancy antechamber, with smooth round columns supporting the ceiling, and at least one arched doorway that Nieve could see. Something like a painting adorned the far wall, and the floor appeared tiled in various colors, though the pattern was impossible to make out through several inches of water, broken hunks of stone, and pieces of metal grating. She could barely make out distorted reflections on the surface of the water, giving her the impression of something large and possibly reptilian. The smart thing to do would be to assess the situation and try to figure out what and how many opponents battled just outside the tunnel's opening, but when a familiar figure clad all in black slid across the surface of the water mere feet from where Nieve stood, she realized she couldn't wait any longer. Drawing her sword, Nieve leapt over the jagged remains of the torn grate, splashing down in the room beyond with a feral roar.

"Hane!" Nieve spun a quick circle, keeping her sword high and defensive. The monsters were all naga, a species familiar enough to fill her with a sensation of relief: she knew how to fight naga. She spotted most of her teammates—Hane whirling around to face her, eyes wide over their face mask, Mason fending off blows behind a round, stone shield, Rose tucked between her brother and the wall, goggles masking her expression—but the pillars and doorways and the frothing splash of water made for a chaotic battlefield. She was still looking for the others when the water pulled sharply at her ankles, nearly yanking her off her feet. Nieve rooted herself to the floor with ice as she cast Frost Form on herself. One naga hurled a spear at her, thinking her trapped, but Nieve only swept the spear aside with her sword before conjuring a path of ice before her. Two running steps took her into a glide, the butt of her sword braced by her off hand. She transfixed the naga right where his humanoid torso met his scaly, serpentine tail.

A shadow's flicker of movement, then Hane appeared beside her, finishing the naga off with a sharp blow to the head with their tonfa. There was a wild look in their eyes as they searched Nieve's own.

"Nieve, is it—are you really—"

Nieve grinned as she clasped Hane's forearm, sending a thought to Chime, hidden within her boot.

<We have returned,> Chime said in warm, resonant tones. <It is good to see you, Hane of the riptide.>

Hane's expression was impossible to see beneath the mask. They blinked twice rapidly before pulling their arm free of Nieve's grasp in order to catch a spear strike in the X of their tonfa. Nieve lunged past them, driving her sword into the naga's stomach. His powerful tail swept a wave of water into their faces, giving him the cover he needed to retreat swiftly.

Hane locked gazes with Nieve briefly. "Are you hurt? How's your mana? Can you fight?"

Nieve laughed as she parried an attacking naga's spear thrust. "It's good to see you again, too, Hane. I'm a little tired, but I can fight."

Hane put their back against Nieve's, arms and shoulders in constant motion. For a moment, the two of them fought without speaking. When Hane spoke again, there was a ragged quality to their voice. "We've been on the move since you vanished. We haven't had more than a few hours of rest since we lost you."

That was startling. Hane was usually so cautious—why take such risks when the team was already short by one frontline fighter? Sleep was necessary for the body to recover—both physically and magically. If the others had been pushing through the labyrinth that whole time with no rest, they had to be almost completely exhausted by now.

A glance around confirmed this. Mason was neither transmuting his stone rods into javelins nor attacking. He braced his stone shield against his shoulder and leaned into it, holding off the attacking naga. Rose's cheeks were ashen beneath her heavy goggles. She panted as she leaned back against the wall, occasionally reaching up to pat her pockets as if she knew they were empty but hoped otherwise. Hane's clothing looked as if it had been ripped, stitched up, then torn again, and while they seemed as agile as ever, Nieve recognized their tightly controlled movements from their fight against Hogame. If Hane wasn't out of mana, they were at least conserving it as much as possible.

The battle was chaotic enough that Nieve was only able to search for Lief and Odette while trading blows with two naga attempting to flank her. Water splashed up her back, closing like a fist in her hair to yank her backward. Frustrated, she froze the watery grip in her hair, dealing with the excess weight rather than the tug. There had to be a naga spell caster in here somewhere, but they were likely cloaking themself with an illusion spell. She could use Detect Mind to locate them, but the splashing, churning water rendered that spell useless at the moment. She could barely find her own visible teammates in all of this; the spell caster would have to wait.

Nieve feigned a strike at the naga on her left before flipping her sword in her grip and jabbing behind herself, landing a solid strike on the other naga. As the two of them hissed and circled back, Nieve whipped her hair out of her eyes and resumed her search for Lief and Odette, the two team members she had yet to confirm as safe.

There, under the painting on the wall: Lief stood with his back to a corner wielding a stone bo staff to knock away spear tips. His jaw dropped as he saw Nieve, but he shook off his surprise quickly to wave her over. Nieve left one of the naga bleeding out in the shallow water as she picked her way carefully over rounded rocks and dropped spears. She stopped one naga gliding through the water on a trajectory to break Mason's shield by rooting his tail in ice. The naga stumbled to a stop, falling flat before twisting around to jab his spear at the ice encasing his tail.

"It's good to see you!" Lief said, smiling as Nieve swept aside his two opponents. "Are you hurt? I can heal you while you fight."

"I drank a healing potion earlier, so I'm fine. Where is—" Nieve cut herself off as she found the answer to her question. Odette was crouched on the floor behind Lief, rocking back and forth with her hands clasped over her face. Was she injured? Had she been targeted by a mental spell? Why hadn't Lief fixed her already?

"Ah, I'm afraid she's having another panic attack," Lief said, following Nieve's gaze to Odette. "But your arrival might be enough to fix that, so long as you're able to help clean up this . . . mess." His gesture encompassed the chaotic battle, the lackluster spells, and the violent current of the water. "We're not at our best at the moment."

"Hane told me." Nieve grabbed her hammer in her free hand, spinning it in her grasp to whip the clawed end across a naga's chiseled abdomen. "Sorry to leave you guys on your own, but I'm here now. I'll take care of it."

"What do you need?" Lief leaned his weight against the bo staff, one hand extended in offer. "More strength? Access to more enhancement mana? Mental agility?"

Nieve sidled away, eyes scanning the battlefield for where she would be most needed. "I'm fine. Keep an eye on Odette for me."

Lief sighed heavily as he twirled his bo staff back into a defensive position. "I look forward to hearing about what happened to you later."

Nieve nodded, already wading into the fray. Lief's offer was tempting, but she worried about his spells interfering with her ability to invoke Byakko's strength. She still didn't completely understand her Paladin attunement, or why it sometimes worked a little too well, or not at all. She preferred not to use it at all, but judging by her teammates' lethargic offense, it seemed likely she would have to.

<I can sense the spell caster you seek,> Chime whispered in a ringing tone. <They cannot hide from me.>

Nieve grinned. *Where?*

She didn't attack the spell caster immediately, even after Chime showed her where he was—attacking an invisible opponent head-on gave away the element of surprise. Instead, Nieve swept through the battlefield pricking and poking naga with her sword. She wasn't attacking so much as she was drawing their attention away from the others. One unfortunate naga was impaled on several stone spikes jutting out of the wall near Mason and Rose, and another was floating face-down in the ankle-deep water, knocked unconscious from a head blow. Nieve counted at least four more attacking naga as she made her way close enough to the spell caster that she could attack without drawing attention. She allowed one of the naga to push her back on her heels until the caster was within striking distance.

Everything seemed to happen at once: Nieve swung her hammer out wide, feeling scaled flesh yield as she struck the invisible spell caster, but before she could follow through with a clean kill, Hane was caught mid-leap by the haft of a naga spear, sending them flying right at her. Nieve managed to react quickly enough, catching Hane before they could slam into a wall—or worse, a spear—but the distraction cost her as the now-visible spell caster hissed threateningly. The water on the floor churned like a vortex, powerful enough that Mason, Rose, and Lief were swept off their feet. Nieve rooted herself to the floor with ice as Hane struggled free of her grasp to stand on their own. With the water moving as fast as it was under their feet, Hane looked as if they struggled to keep their balance.

"I'll get Odette," Hane called over the rush of the water.

"I've got the others," Nieve confirmed. She swung her boot back, intending to kick the spell caster in the gut hard enough to interrupt their concentration on the whirlpool spell, but before the kick could land, the spell caster melted into the water, reforming a short distance away. Another hiss through needle-sharp teeth and the force of the vortex increased, eating away at Nieve's icy anchor.

Across the room, Nieve saw Hane perch on the side of the wall and pull Odette to her feet. She'd been clinging to the colorful metal relief set into the wall, which Nieve had mistaken for a painting. Hane had to pry her fingers loose before hoisting her effortlessly up to a shoulder and bounding away, leaving Nieve to wonder if they truly were exhausted or if they'd dipped below their safe mana reserves to manage the rescue.

She didn't have time to wonder for long as she fended off a naga's spear thrusts. Something struck her ice-anchor hard enough that she nearly lost her balance, giving the naga an opening. Before she could recover enough to parry, a wave rose up and slammed into the naga's side, staggering it off balance. Not bothering to question her luck, Nieve spun her blade point-down to attack whatever it was she felt clinging to her ice-anchor. Luckily, she looked before she stabbed: it was only Mason, coughing as he fought the current to stand. Unable to lend a hand as the naga quickly recovered, Nieve turned aside spear attacks as Mason grabbed hold of her belt in order to haul himself up. By the time he gripped her shoulders to steady himself, Nieve had dispatched the attacking naga and was searching for the others amid the chaos.

Mason coughed so hard that he almost lost his balance again, nearly knocking Nieve down, too. When she could spare the chance, she rooted one of Mason's boots to the floor with ice—rooting both feet would be dangerous in case he had to move quickly. He looked grateful as he used his free foot for balance. His next cough sounded like "Rose" but anything else he said was lost to the roar of the water and the clash of metal and stone.

"I'll get her," Nieve promised, twisting around to cave in a naga's skull with the blunt end of her war hammer. "But first we need to do something about the spell caster. Don't you have some water spells you can use?"

"The current's too strong." He let go of Nieve's shoulder long enough to draw a stone rod and shape it into a shield, blocking a strike from the haft of a spear. Rooted as she was to the floor, Nieve couldn't turn fast enough to counter, but she did extend a lance of ice through her hilt as she reversed her jab. She felt the resistance of a hit right before the ice-lance snapped off. Hopefully that was painful enough to take that naga out of commission for a while. "Nieve, Rose can't swim."

That new tidbit sent Nieve's mind skipping like a stone, never settling on one thought long enough to truly register. What was the point of teasing Rose now, in the middle of battle? Wait, no—he'd said it because of the water. But the water was only ankle high; swimming wasn't necessary right now. Oh, wait—the water was rising. She hadn't noticed it, but the water level had risen from her ankles to just below her knees. No wonder it had been so difficult for Mason to stand. Even a strong swimmer would have difficulty fighting this current—and Rose couldn't swim at all.

Nieve cursed. "Where is she?"

"I lost her," Mason admitted miserably.

"We need—" Nieve looked around, accounting for two of the spear-wielding naga nearby. The spell caster was far beyond striking range, poised at the center of the vortex. He held a blade of polished abalone shell, forked tongue flicking through his teeth in a promise of death for anyone swept before him by the current. The only remaining spear-wielding naga had Lief pinned against a pillar, which he'd used to brace himself against the whirling current. Rose was nowhere to be seen.

I need to do it, Nieve thought, feeling the prick of cold, sharp light in the center of her chest. *There's no time—the only way to find her before she drowns is to use the hunter's heightened senses and speed.*

"I have to let you go," Nieve told Mason, keeping her voice steady against her nerves. "Find Hane, they'll keep you safe."

Mason swallowed audibly before releasing Nieve's shoulders to stand on his own. It appeared he was using Nieve's trick to anchor himself, but with stone rather than ice. He shot her a final look full of pleading. "You'll save her, right?"

"I will." Breaking and reforming the ice around her ankles, Nieve moved away from Mason, searching the churning water for any sign of Rose. When something struck her leg, Nieve reached down to grasp it, but it was only a broken section of metal grating, stirred by the current. The naga, with their powerful serpentlike tails, moved easily through the ever-rising flood; they ducked behind pillars to hide from sight before cutting across the floor in rapid, gliding attacks that had to be turned aside before they could land. As fast as the current was flowing, Nieve's conjured ice froze in chunks that bobbed along the surface, rather than rooting tails to the floor. Out of the corner of her eye, Nieve saw one distant spear-wielder fix his slit-pupiled eyes on her before diving beneath the surface, all but invisible beneath the current.

"I won't find her in time in all of this," Nieve growled, doubling the ice-anchor rooting her feet to the floor. As much as she hated the lack of control, she needed the hunter's instincts—she had to find Rose before it was too late. She centered her focus on her heart mark and surrendered control, praying that the spell would work this time. "Great Lord Byakko, please lend me your aid. I need to protect my friends."

The fear that the power wouldn't come was quickly extinguished—as was her fear, her pain, and her compassion. Foreign strength flooded her body, acuity sharpened her senses, and a predator's mindset took over. When she invoked the spell, her intention had been to find and rescue Rose. Now her only objective was the hunt.

Awareness like a premonition directed Nieve's attention behind her, below the surface of the water. Her enhanced vision picked out movement that would normally be masked by the frothing current: the diving naga swam up behind her, drawing its spear back for a thrust at her legs. Faster than thought, Nieve slammed her boot down on the spear mid-thrust, pinning it to the ground. A smarter being would have let go and swam away, but this one yanked at his spear to free it. Nieve dispatched him with a single downward thrust through the base of his neck.

Another warning flared at the edge of Nieve's field of vision: Lief slipped while defending himself, and in order to keep from being swept away, he'd dropped his bo staff to cling to the pillar he'd braced himself against. Pale eyes squeezed shut as the naga angled his spear for a killing blow. Nieve reacted with reckless abandon, hurling her hammer end over end to crunch through the naga's skull. Before it broke apart into mana crystals, Nieve caught the stunned expression on the naga's face as it toppled backward.

Huh, a distant part of Nieve's consciousness noted. *That was a left-handed throw with a newly modified weapon. I don't think I could do that again even if I used my right arm.*

Lief peeked out beneath his lashes, looking pleasantly surprised to find himself both alive and unharmed. Just as Nieve expected from a professional climber, he recovered quickly and picked out a target of his own: the spell caster. He raised a hand toward the naga in the center of the vortex, face pinched in concentration. The naga screamed, eyes bulging, finned head-crest flaring as it gesticulated wildly. While there was little immediate change, it felt as if the current abated. Nieve slogged through it, cutting across the whirlpool to its center. She was halfway there before she realized she wasn't consciously controlling the ice anchoring her feet: it broke and reformed automatically without conscious thought.

Nieve wasn't yet within sword's reach when the caster lunged at her with his wicked-looking abalone knife. An odd sensation—something like falling, but slowly—took hold of her, guiding her movement just enough that the blade slid harmlessly past, bringing the naga within arm's reach. She caught the scaled forearm in a clawlike grasp, nails digging in deep instead of a close-handed grip. Slit-pupiled eyes filled with rage as the naga hissed, baring its teeth—but that was a feint. The real danger was the powerful tail, whipping through the water to cut Nieve's legs out from under her.

And then the naga just . . . stopped. No tail swipe, no knife slice, no needle-thin teeth sinking through her flesh, not even the subtle movement of breathing. The naga was frozen solid in mid-motion, scaly flesh ice cold beneath Nieve's hand. It wasn't the rough-hewn ice block Nieve normally used to trap foes—no, this was delicate spellwork. A fine, clear layer of ice coated the naga's body, nearly invisible except for how close she stood. Sea-green eyes darted wildly behind the film of ice, the only part the naga that seemed capable of moving.

Is that something I could learn to do on my own? Nieve felt as if she was watching herself from a distance, unable to move, or speak, or even stop herself. She wasn't even sure how she managed to use her Champion spells through her Paladin attunement: no incantations, no pointing, hardly any thought and the spells just *worked.* Impressively, at that.

With the spell-casting naga neutralized, the swirling water ebbed sharply, the whirlpool collapsing in on itself. At the center of the room, where Nieve stood with the frozen naga, the water had only been knee high, but near the walls it had risen close to the ceiling. Now, gravity set in with violence: waves crashed into counter-waves, ramming into each other as the water level sought equilibrium. Nieve was ripped off her feet and slammed into a wall hard enough to feel it crack around her, but not hard enough to hurt. Stubbornly, she kept a grip on her sword and held her breath until the pressure pinning her to the wall abated and her boots hit the floor. She spat out a mouthful of water and assessed the new battlefield.

The water rushed out of the room through doors on opposite sides of the room, seeking the path of least resistance. While the rapidly lowering water level was the desired outcome, the uncontrolled rush of the current was once again making it difficult to stand, much less move. Nevertheless, Nieve pushed off the wall, leaving an indent of herself in the stone as she slogged forward.

There was still one more naga to kill, after all.

As if feeling Nieve's predatory gaze, the final naga glanced back over his shoulder, saw her approach, then dove beneath the water. He couldn't hide—not entirely—but he was faster in the water than Nieve was, so she waded to the center of the room and awaited her chance. She was only distantly aware of her teammates as her mind had assigned them the label "not prey," and as such they were nearly beneath her notice. She knew Mason stood in the tunnel she'd entered through, which was set higher in the wall than the doorways to either side, making it a good vantage point to watch for hazards in the water. Lifting her nose to the scents carried by water-stirred air, Nieve could tell that both Hane and Odette were somewhere in that tunnel as well, possibly hiding farther back. Lief had been washed into a corner near the recessed wall carving, hands pressed against the walls to anchor himself as he caught his breath. The one person Nieve couldn't locate by sight or smell was Rose—a fact that would have been more worrisome if Nieve had any control over herself. As it was, Nieve only cared to search for the remaining naga, intent on hunting it down as the final threat to her life.

The water level dropped below knee height across the room as the final naga finally surfaced, a sinister grin on its face as it hauled Rose out of the water by her hair. He lifted her high enough that any attack Nieve attempted would strike Rose first. Rose hacked and gasped, hands clawing at the naga's arm, legs kicking blindly. She was blessedly alive, but by the threat of the naga's teeth near her throat, she wouldn't be for long.

Nieve met the naga's gaze steadily, gauging the threat. The naga understood he only lived as long as Rose did, so rather than rip out her throat with his teeth, his tail lashed at the water, propelling himself backward toward the nearest exit. Something new emerged through Byakko's borrowed power—something Nieve didn't recall feeling when she'd called upon the power previously. There was a sort of heat that bloomed low in her stomach, a desire—a *need*—welling up in her chest that was somehow focused on Rose.

The distant part of her mind that was still Nieve tried to convince herself that it was a glimmer of recognition, the desire to protect a fellow teammate. That wasn't quite it, but at the very least she took comfort that her predatory instincts didn't label Rose as prey, or even as expendable. She was important, somehow. Rose could not be harmed.

Champion Nieve might have negotiated to let him go as long as he left Rose unharmed.

Paladin Nieve didn't negotiate.

She held her sword out to the side, holding the naga's gaze to make sure he watched as she released it. Before it could splash down into the draining water, Nieve launched herself forward off an angled block of ice conjured beneath her feet, turning her leap into something akin to flight. The naga, still watching the sword fall, failed to react in time, either to defend himself or to harm Rose: Nieve's fist crunched into the left side of his face, her other arm held out to catch Rose as she fell. The naga wobbled, partially stunned and probably dying. To help him on his way, Nieve whipped the Magpie's weighted walking stick from her belt as she spun a tight circle, cradling Rose against her chest as she slammed the marble cap into his temple. He dissolved into a pile of mana crystals before he finished crumpling to the ground.

"It's really you!" Rose gaped in wide-eyed wonder, one arm curled behind Nieve's neck to hold herself up. Her curls were a sodden mess, her clothing and equipment were soaked through, and she was probably cold, possibly even hurt, but all Nieve could focus on was the scent of her—forge fire, molten bronze, and a hint of something sweet, like vanilla. A need like hunger—urgent and all-consuming—rose up like a flush of heat from the pit of her stomach to fill her chest, her throat, her face. Carnal images filled her mind as the roar of her heartbeat obliterated all other sound. With the last naga dead, the hunt was over; why not enjoy the spoils of war?

No! The innermost part of her rebelled, weakly at first, but insistent and stubborn. Nieve fought to regain control of herself, grasping for the power of her Champion attunement to free her mind from the predator's grip. *No, stop! What good is having the strength to protect my team if I turn into the predator? This is not the power I want!*

Slowly, she felt the power of the beast drain out of her, bit by bit, as if it were reluctant to leave her. When Byakko's strength left her entirely, Nieve swayed on her feet, physical and magical exhaustion hitting her all at once. Her earlier thoughts about Rose made her sick to her stomach, making her feel watery, pale, and unworthy.

"Nee-eh-vay?" A cool hand cupped Nieve's cheek. Rose's voice was soft and concerned, her touch gentle. When she blinked her eyes open, she found herself staring into warm amber eyes, scant inches from her own. Before she could speak, the little furrow between Rose's brows smoothed as she leaned into Nieve's shoulder, wrapping both arms around her tightly. "I'm so glad you're all right! I thought you were— I mean, I'd hoped you had—but you're here, and you're safe! Thank the goddess, Nee-eh-vay, I am so relieved."

"Yeah," Nieve's voice sounded rough in her own ears, gravelly and low. She cleared her throat and tried again, one hand patting Rose's back awkwardly. "I mean, thanks. I'm glad you're okay, too."

"Rose!" A splash, followed by running footsteps. A hand clasped Nieve's shoulder, pulling her back a step. Mason stole his sister away in a tight embrace. "I looked, but I couldn't find you. What happened?"

"I'm a little more curious as to what happened to Nieve," Lief called out, jumping down from the elevated tunnel set into the wall. He turned back to help Hane lower Odette to the floor before continuing. "But I suppose the professional thing for me to do is ask if anyone needs a healing spell right now."

Nieve checked herself for injuries beyond the trembling exhaustion that had settled deep within her bones. One shoulder felt deeply bruised and her broken toe ached like a tiny, distant scream. She lost her balance reaching for her canteen, so rather than fall, she plopped down on the ground. No more than puddles remained of the conjured flood that had once threatened to fill the room, but as wet as she was, Nieve hardly noticed as she drained her canteen in long, needy gulps. When she gasped for air, Hane crouched in front of her, holding out her sword across their hands.

Nieve smiled weakly as she grasped in by the hilt. "Thanks."

Hane nodded. They lingered a moment, eyes searching hers before they stood up and turned away. A sweeping motion with their hand sent the water peeling off the stone floor like egg white scraped from a skillet. That was good: an emotional reunion was more than Nieve could handle at the moment.

"I need the crystals," Rose said through a cough. She pushed away from her brother and swayed on her feet. Alarmed, he held her by the shoulders until she regained her balance. "I'll collect them later."

"Nieve?" Odette approached cautiously, eyes wide and red-rimmed behind her glasses. She knelt down with her lower lip pinched between her teeth. Timidly, she reached out to touch the embroidered bracelet knotted around Nieve's arm. "I searched for you. I . . . I did. I swear to you, I did."

"I believe you," Nieve said, pleased to hear her voice returning to normal. She took the metal communicator off her ear and handed it to Odette. "This stopped working, too. Oh, and Lief's smell spell. I guess the hole I fell through nullified magic, or something like that."

"Did you pass through a void space?" Lief asked, sounding interested. "Did any of your other enchantments stop working? Did you check your defensive spells? What about your weapons?"

"No, all of my enchantments came out okay. Only the imbues and spells failed." Nieve leaned back against a pillar, letting her eyes fall shut. "Sorry. I'm exhausted."

"We're all exhausted," Hane called from a distant corner of the room. Were they still shaping away the water? Why bother? Everyone was thoroughly soaked already, a few puddles hardly seemed to matter. "We should take a long break and rest up. It'll give us a chance to catch up."

"No, no!" Odette protested shrilly. "The vault is right here! We're almost finished!"

"We don't need to set up a campsite," Lief said, laying down an oil cloak before sitting down on it. "But we do need to eat and recover for at least a little while. It's not as if we know how to open the vault, anyway."

Odette sighed heavily, shoulders drooping. "I know you're right, I just . . . I've been waiting for this moment for so long."

"Wait a minute." Nieve frowned as she followed Odette's longing gaze to the metallic relief set into the wall. "Is that the vault? The entrance to the phantom chamber? It's right there?"

"Odette led us to it." Hane didn't look up as they continued shaping the puddles to flow out of the room. "We modified the labyrinth to get here faster, increasing the scale of the challenges. I—" A falter, a pause, a deliberate turn away from Nieve and the others. "We didn't expect you to return."

"I would've thought the same thing in your place," Nieve replied, shrugging off the exaggerated rumors of her own death. She smiled in thanks as Mason retrieved her war hammer for her. "Sorry you guys had to press on without me, but at least we're all here in one piece, right?"

"Yes, and I am intrigued as to how you found your way here without the guidance of an Analyst," Lief said, setting out packages of food, bandages, and various potions atop his oilcloth picnic blanket. "Let's trade stories while we recover for a while, shall we? The vault isn't going anywhere while we're sitting right here."

<Have care,> Chime whispered as Nieve agreed along with the others. <If you seek to protect your newfound power, you will have to leave certain portions of your story untold.>

It wasn't just Byakko's gift that Nieve had to hide, but Chime's assistance as well. As she dug through her sodden satchel for rations to share, Nieve prepared a few quick lies, with apologies to Chime and Hane; she would tell both of them the truth as soon as they rejoined Sage outside the spire.

Rose sat down beside her, still soaked to the skin, but smiling warmly as she offered Nieve a woven basket of small green fruit. Conflicting feelings of attraction and shame made Nieve's skin itch as she accepted a single fruit and suppressed the urge to inch away. This close, she could still smell the sweet vanilla of Rose's perfume, making her hungry for something other than food. To distract herself, Nieve focused on the scent of petrichor suffusing the room: was that a result of the naga's flood? Or was the smell so strong here because this was the vault's antechamber?

"So?" Lief asked, giving Nieve an encouraging smile as the rustling of bags and other comforts faded as the others settled down to rest. "What happened? And how did you make your way here?"

"Right, yes." Nieve put on a grin she didn't feel, injecting false confidence into her lie. "So I guess that hole was some sort of portal, because it transported me to a different part of the labyrinth . . ."

HANE

Wavewalker (leg mark), Citrine

"Well?" Odette's sharp voice held a note of impatience, making Hane flinch. Had she asked them a question? They hadn't been paying attention. "You must have some thoughts of your own by now."

Hane snapped their attention back to the vault door, studying the metallic relief once more. They had started off listening to Odette as she pointed out the possible locations for the glass-orb key, but then their attention had wandered to Nieve's peculiar explanation of following a scent through the labyrinth, and now they couldn't remember a single thing she'd said. "Sorry. I'm afraid that my experience from another spire might lead me to the wrong conclusion in this matter."

Odette huffed, her arms crossed over her chest as one foot tapped against the tile floor. "Okay, then which impression would you choose if this was the Tortoise Spire? We might be able to eliminate a few possibilities if we look at it that way."

Resh! Hane had been hoping she'd let it go. They honestly hadn't put much thought into the relief at all; they were only standing here because sitting with Nieve and the others was too uncomfortable at the moment. Unfortunately, Odette seemed dead set on figuring out which depression might unlock the secret chamber, rather than allowing Hane time to parse their feelings.

Not that there should be anything to parse, right? They should be feeling relieved that Nieve and Chime were both alive and well and had found their way back to the team. And they *were* relieved. Really.

So then, why was that relief buried beneath layers of guilt and remorse?

While it was rare for a climber presumed dead to return to life, Hane had seen it happen before. Most often, they didn't discover the mistake until they exited the spire and found out that the endangered climber had managed to use their return bell in the nick of time. It was far less likely for a presumed-dead climber to catch up to their team within a spire, but it had happened once or twice. Hane always handled those situations the same way: with an apology, an explanation, and an expression of relief over their return.

So why hadn't they been able to summon the exact same sentiments for Nieve's sudden and unexpected return? Granted, they had been a bit distracted by the battle going on at the time, but instead of anything remotely grateful or welcoming, Hane simply summed up their situation as if her return had been anticipated. The others barely knew Nieve, yet Rose had greeted her with a tearful hug, genuinely grateful that she was alive. In the aftermath of the battle, each member of the team expressed similar sentiments. Mason punched her in the shoulder, grinning as he proclaimed her too tough to die, while Lief teased her about being spat back out after the spire attempted to swallow her whole. Odette, still struggling with her anxiety at the time, had asked multiple times if it really was Nieve, then broke down tearfully, begging Nieve to believe that she had attempted to search for her by her embroidered bracelet.

And Hane?

Hane had decided it was more important to dry off the floor than tell Nieve how relieved they were to see her again. At first, they thought it might be easier to face her after everyone settled down to recover and eat, but by then it just felt awkward; the rest of the team had moved past it, making it feel wrong to bring it up again. And so rather than join the team for some shared food and rest, Hane lingered nearby, pretending to study the vault door while attempting to process why Nieve's return felt different from any other climber's return.

"Hane." Odette carried the crack of a whip in her tone. "Are you well? Should I ask Lief to check you for a head injury?"

"What? No. Why?"

"You seem distracted." Odette dipped her chin at the metallic relief set into the door of the vault. "I count six possible locks where the guardian's key could go. If we guess wrong, we don't get another chance. I need you to focus and tell me what stands out to you."

Hane silently scanned the vault door again, looking for anything they had missed on their first few passes. The central figure was a humanoid with wings, which potentially made them a visage, an ancient monarch, or a monster; as the clothing appeared Caelish, Hane couldn't begin to guess who or what it was meant to represent. The winged person wore a crown, but it had been painted over by a black top hat, claiming the vault as the property of the drug operation on the upper levels of the labyrinth. Carved images surrounded the figure on all sides: above was the golden sun and to either side the relief depicted clouds. The left cloud leaked silver raindrops, the right cloud was lanced with a golden lightning bolt. On the figure's left-hand side, there was a forge with a tiny golden flame inside. To the right, distant mountains were etched with silver veins running through them. Two animals sat at the figure's feet: an opalescent cat to the left, and an obsidian racing dog to the right. Hidden within each of those images was a barely noticeable indent perfectly sized to fit the black glass orb taken from the labyrinth guardian's lair. But which one was the right one?

"I'm not sure. Maybe the top hat is a clue?" Hane suggested without conviction. "I'm not familiar with the local history, or what cultural significance any of these images might have."

"I suspect the defacement of the image is meant to be a clue for less observant climbers," Odette replied, shifting her weight to tap the other foot. Perhaps the first one became tired. "If it is a clue, it's only in reference to the scenario vault, not the phantom vault."

"Is this image meant to represent a specific event or legend?" Hane asked, barely stopping themself from looking over their shoulder as Nieve and the others laughed loudly. "Or maybe we're supposed to connect one of the images to the figure in the center? Is that supposed to represent a specific person?"

"The staff in her hand marks her as a queen," Odette said, pointing to the odd symbol atop a long staff. "But the wings likely denote an ancient queen, before our nation became Caelford. Not much of that history has survived, and this doesn't look like a depiction of any of the stories I've heard."

Hane glanced back over their shoulder, watching as Rose handed Nieve her communication device, the imbue fully restored. "Rose seems pretty knowledgeable. Maybe we should ask her?"

Odette slammed her heel against the floor, twisting at the waist to call back to the others. "Hey, since we've all had a chance to rest, do you think we can try opening this vault now? It's only the whole reason we came on this climb, after all."

"Oh, calm down, it's not going anywhere now that we're here," Rose replied, the words softened by a smile. The Architect seemed particularly high spirited ever since Nieve's return from the dead. Even as she spoke to Odette, her eyes were on Nieve's face. "Besides, we never found the hint, right? It's unlikely we'll figure out the correct lock unless we find it."

"There's no harm in taking a good look," Lief said, pushing himself up to his feet. "It would be nice to finish this climb today, wouldn't it?"

Nieve shifted her seat before gathering up her pouches of shared food. "Can't hurt to try. I wouldn't hate to get back to sleeping in a real bed after all of this."

"Oh, well if that's what we're working toward, then I'm in." Rose leaned her shoulder against Nieve's briefly before gathering up her own supplies. Oddly enough, Nieve didn't reply in kind; she looked deep in thought with her lips pressed firmly together and her eyes down as she tied off each of her little bags.

Mason, asleep on the flat of his back, remained dead to the world with one arm thrown over his face to block out the light. He snorted and snored at the scrape of Nieve's and Rose's boots on the floor as they stood.

"You said this wasn't a depiction of a local legend or myth, correct?" Lief asked, adjusting the strap of his bag as he approached. His mouth pursed as he eyed the relief. "What about the forge? Isn't that a reference to one of the larger festivals of Caelford?"

"It's also an ancient tradition," Rose added. "From long before we were called Caelford."

"So is that it, then?" Nieve asked, hanging back a bit. She seemed distracted to Hane. Was she disappointed they hadn't hugged her upon her return? Should they try that now? They might, if they had any idea of how to initiate such a gesture. And maybe they were wrong, anyway. How awkward would it be if they tried to hug her and Nieve refused?

"Why the forge over the mountains?" Odette asked, pointing out the silver veins depicting ore-rich stone. "There's nothing to craft if you don't have the raw materials."

"If we're going back to the beginning, then why not the sun?" Lief squinted, as he eyed the golden sun skeptically. "It looks like that gilding is meant to come off."

"It is." Hane had checked that earlier. "The obvious keyhole in the center is a trap. The real keyhole is hidden under the sun. But that would open up the scenario vault, not the phantom chamber."

"We can get this, I know we can," Odette insisted, undeterred. She crouched down, eye to eye with the pearlescent cat. "That guardian we fought was kind of a cat. Do you think that was meant to be a hint?"

"It was a lightning cat," Hane reminded her. "It could just as easily be the lightning cloud."

Odette huffed as she straightened up, squinting at the cloud. "You're right. I hate it, but you're right. Ugh!" She stamped a foot, hard. "I don't want to spend days searching the labyrinth for the hint! Why can't it be simple, just this once!"

"The crown is missing." Nieve said, shouldering her way forward for a better look. Her face seemed curiously thoughtful, as if it meant something to her. Or was she reacting to a hint from Chime? Hane longed for a private moment along with Nieve and Chime almost as much as they longed to solve the riddle of the guilt twisting their stomach into knots.

"The crown isn't missing, it's just painted over," Odette said with a touch of impatience. "And that can't be a hint to open the phantom chamber, that's just the symbol of the Ash Hats."

"No, wait." Nieve's whole face screwed up, as if thinking was a physical process. "The crown *was* missing. Look, the forge, and there in her hand—that symbol on the top of her staff is the Kha'an, isn't it?"

"Yes, but the queen's staff has always been topped with a Kha'an, that doesn't help us figure out who this is supposed to be," Odette replied.

"Do you know something?" Hane asked Nieve.

"I don't . . know." She hesitated, squinting at each image in turn. "The missing aspect was the Crown . . . the Crown is the symbol of sovereignty . . ." Nieve gasped so loud that it made Odette and Lief twitch in surprise. "Rain! It's rain! Up in the corner, it's the rain!"

"Wha—no!" Odette protested. "That makes no sense! How can it possibly be rain?"

"You found something, didn't you?" Lief asked with a knowing smile.

"Yeah, I found this secret room with a mural on the ceiling," Nieve said, speaking with more confidence now. "It was just of the night sky, but the stars were painted in specific constellations. I found the Forge and the Kha'an—oh, and Lord Byakko, obviously. But the Crown wasn't there; it was missing, just like it is here."

"It's not missing; you can see it very clearly under the paint," Odette said impatiently. "And what does the Crown have to do with rain, anyway?"

"It's the symbol of her sovereignty," Nieve said, as if that solved everything. Hane was relieved to see they weren't the only one bewildered by that. That pinched look returned as Nieve struggled to explain. "You know, the constellations? The aspects? The crown represents a monarch's reign. Like rain!"

Hane stared. Blinked. And very carefully tried not to laugh.

"You're basing your hypothesis on a homonym?" Lief asked, skeptical. "Those words are only the same in Valian. This is Caelford. If that's the clue, why frame it in a non-native language?"

"Look, I don't know. I don't even know what that word means. But I'm sure it's supposed to be the rain," Nieve insisted. "The god beasts speak all languages, don't they? So why can't the hint be in Valian?"

Lief started to say something then stopped himself, smiling in bemusement. "I don't really have an argument for that. Shall we take a vote?"

"We're not voting on—" Odette was cut off as Rose spoke up from the back of the group.

"I think Nieve is right," Rose announced coolly. "She obviously found the clue we were meant to find, and if the clue is Byakko's aspect of sovereignty, then I vote we try the lock near the rain cloud. Brick?" She raised her voice as she called out her brother's nickname.

"Wuh?" Mason grumbled sleepily. He rolled onto his side and yawned. "Yeah, what Prickles said." After a bit of adjusting for comfort, he appeared to fall back to sleep.

"If it doesn't open, we don't get another chance," Odette reminded everyone. "We would leave empty-handed. Worse than empty-handed, considering all we went through to get here."

"Then we should trust Nieve and pick the rain cloud," Hane advised calmly. "I believe her when she says she found the clue."

"But the clue could be interpreted in other ways!" Odette insisted. "What about other constellations? Did you even look for—"

"You know, I think she might be right," Lief said, unexpectedly. "I don't doubt that the mural she found was meant to be the clue, and the more I think about it, the more the missing Crown constellation and the painted-over crown seem like hints to me."

Odette huffed and flailed her arms. "Okay, but rain? Really?" She turned around, a helpless look on her face as she met everyone's gaze. "It's just . . . I can't be wrong about this. Not now. Not when it's right—it's right—"

She brushed the carved figure's wings with her fingertips, opposite hand holding the glass orb in a grip that shook. Rose eased past Nieve to stand in front of Odette, resting one hand on her shoulder.

"I know this means more to you than the rest of us," Rose said patiently. "You've put more effort into learning the secrets of this phantom chamber than anyone else, and you're afraid that if we make a mistake that the vault's location will change before you can find it again. But even if that happens, you still made it this far. You can write up your findings for future researchers to study. And we're all still young in our climber careers! There's no reason you can't find it again. And I promise I'll be with you the next time you say you found it."

Odette still looked unsure. A trickle of blood ran down her chin from a bitten lip. Very gently, Rose eased the black glass orb out of Odette's hand, waiting a beat to see if she would protest. When she didn't, Rose turned and took Nieve's hand, turning it palm up to place the orb in her grip.

"You're the tallest," Rose said, the flash of a wink suggesting something else. As her touch lingered, Nieve appeared to stiffen, holding rigidly still.

Rose smiled as she released Nieve's hand. "Of course, if you're wrong, you'll never convince me that you're not a meathead."

Nieve chuckled nervously, tossing the orb once before catching it. "Really? You're all going to trust me on this?"

"Of course," Hane said softly, though they didn't think she heard amid the chorus of agreement and at least one loud snore.

Nieve stepped up to the vault door, scanning it studiously once more. Remembering their conversation on the train, Hane wondered if Nieve was doubting herself, even after navigating a troublesome labyrinth on her own, discovering the vault's secret, and saving all their lives from the naga statues come to life. How could she still be doubting herself after all of that? There weren't many who could survive alone inside a spire; Hane knew that from personal experience.

Setting her jaw stubbornly, Nieve held the orb up to the image of the rain cloud, pressing it against the barely noticeable depression in the relief. At the last second, Odette lunged at her, shouting "No!" as she grabbed Nieve's arm, but too late: the orb clicked against the metal of the door, the inner light pulsing steadily before flaring brilliantly. Odette's breathing became fast and shallow as she trembled from head to toe. The precious metals adorning the relief flickered and gleamed, becoming brighter beneath the glare from the orb.

Then, slowly, the vault door ground open, sliding into a recess within the wall.

A collective gasp sucked the air from the room; Hane found themself holding their breath along with everyone else gathered at the vault door. A rustle from behind was Mason finally sitting up and looking around for the source of the noise.

"You got it open?" Mason asked, surprised. "How do you know it leads to the right vault?"

"It's a portal," Odette whispered. The vault door opened to shimmering blackness, flat and infinite at the same time. "This is—this is!" Rather than finish the thought, Odette darted through the doorway, vanishing from sight.

Lief shrugged, hitching his bag higher on his shoulder. "Last one in gets last pick of the treasure." He ducked his head and stepped through.

Hane waited for Nieve to step forward, but she hesitated, glancing sideways to meet their gaze. For a moment, it looked as if she wanted to say something, but then Rose clasped her hand, grinning girlishly as she tugged Nieve after her.

"You did it! I'm so impressed." Rose's smile made her look younger somehow, and even better rested than they knew her to be. She'd been dragging as much as anyone, yet now she seemed exuberant and fresh. "I guess you're not a meathead after all."

"Ah, maybe." Nieve's chuckle sounded hesitant. "I probably just got lucky, that's all."

"Let's go take a look!" Rose bounced on the balls of her feet as she tried leading Nieve forward to the portal. "This is what you came here for, isn't it?"

"Yeah." Nieve looked over at Hane. "It is, isn't it?"

Hane nodded, unsure of what Nieve was trying to communicate to them. Or even *if* she was trying to communicate something. She'd seemed slightly . . . off ever since she'd recovered from the fight. Or maybe Nieve was completely normal and Hane was the one who was off—it wasn't like them to be distracted by emotions during spire climbs.

Nieve definitely swallowed tightly before allowing Rose to tow her through the portal. Just as their linked hands passed the threshold, Hane heard a loud scramble behind them.

"Wait, Prickles!" Mason stumbled, catching himself against a pillar as Nieve disappeared after Rose. He yawned as he trotted after her, shooting a grin at Hane. Not wanting to be left behind, Hane stepped through the same time as Mason. As long as they found Chime's missing piece hidden within the vault, it would all be worth it—the complicated trials, the injuries, the frustration, the grief, and even the guilt.

And then maybe they could take just a little time for themself outside the spire to figure out what had changed since their final climb in the Tortoise Spire.

Two steps carried them through the portal, the inky blackness clearing to reveal—

Nieve's ponytail, complete with red headband tails. Although now that they stood behind her, Hane noted that one tail had been cut shorter than the other. Had they missed her explanation for what happened to it?

Nieve glanced back with an uneasy smile, stepping to one side so Hane could see past her. The others all stood within the threshold of the phantom vault, staring and assessing, as if wondering where to start. Odette quivered from head to toe, her hands clasped over her mouth. Mason and Rose clasped each other's forearms, squeezing tightly as their gazes zipped around the shadowed room. Lief quirked his head to one side, lips pursed in a considering manner. And Nieve . . .

Nieve looked confused.

But maybe that was the right reaction, considering the state of the vault. This was no royal treasury, boasting each treasure's storied history on a neatly lettered plaque. No, this looked like a rich miser's attic, which perhaps began with an organizational system that broke down over time. The shelves along the walls looked haphazardly laden, with weathered books placed beside—or on top of—glittering gems, golden flatware, and dusty mirrors. An old-fashioned wardrobe was so overstuffed that the doors couldn't contain the spew of coat sleeves and shoes. A broken grandfather clock stood at an angle, the glass-pane door hanging open.

Shadowy alcoves lined the walls offset from one another, adding depth and mystery to the treasures that spilled into those spaces. In one, Hane spotted a dusty wine rack stretching nearly to the ceiling, yet it only appeared to contain four or five bottles of wine. A yellowed shroud hung limply over one corner, a single red eye crying a tear of blood stitched in its center. Another alcove contained a row of barrels, most of which appeared sealed, but at least one appeared to be full of carved stones. Or maybe they were bones; Hane didn't look too closely.

In the main chamber of the vault, Hane saw what appeared to be pieces of disassembled furniture leaning against one another, with a stack of framed wall portraits right beside them. There were glass display cases and pedestals, but they appeared to have been used for storage, rather than display purposes. And even then, there were still mounds of small items scattered throughout the room, just sitting in heaps on the floor. The closest mounded collection appeared to consist entirely of feathers, ranging from long black flight feathers to soft, gray down, with an occasional splash of a bright blue and brilliant red. Were each of the feathers valuable somehow? Or was the challenge here to sift out the pearls from the sand?

Lief nudged a small wooden box with the toe of his boot. It released a few strangled, tinny notes of a song before clicking brokenly then falling silent. He blinked at it once before raising his eyebrows. "This is . . . not what I was expecting."

"We are in the right place, aren't we, Odie?" Rose asked, unsure. "This isn't what I'd expect of a gang leader's vault either, but . . . are we even in a vault? Or did we end up somewhere else?"

Odette didn't appear capable of speech: her glasses fogged over as tears leaked down her cheeks. Hane couldn't tell if she was overjoyed or on the verge of another panic attack. While everyone else turned to Odette, awaiting an explanation, Nieve's eyes roamed the room critically, seeming to inspect each shadowed corner. Despite the ambient glow that seemed to come from everywhere and nowhere at once, the chamber was oddly dim. Shadows shifted and whispered along the walls and in the crevices behind pieces of furniture and mounds of oddities. Did she suspect an attack? Or was she simply conversing with Chime? Hane longed to ask if Chime could sense their missing piece within this cluttered chamber; finding the crystal shard would alleviate at least one knot of tension held tight within their guts.

"Wait a minute," Mason said, taking two hesitant steps forward. "Prickles, do you see that? The pendant inlaid with white, yellow, and rose gold?" He pointed to a chest laying open on its side, a spill of small gems, beads, and shards of broken glass gleaming between the lid and the latch. "We've seen that, haven't we? That's the symbol of—"

"Of House Haleem!" Rose gasped. "I've only seen it in the family portrait at the palace! I heard it was lost when the family went into decline. You don't think that's the real—"

"Wait!" Nieve caught Rose's arm as she started forward. The urgency in her voice had Hane sinking into a half crouch and searching the shadows as well. Had she seen something? Or was Chime sensing something? Rose frowned over her shoulder, tugging gently to free her arm. Nieve held on, her eyes still roaming, her jaw firmly clenched.

Sharpen Senses, Hane thought, scouring the shadows for signs of movement. Failing that, they cast Sense Water, seeking sources of water within the room. Aside from the water in their teammates' canteens, the only other source of water was a thin, silent trickle hidden somewhere in the depths of the chamber. If the trickle collected within a vessel or pool, Hane couldn't sense it at all.

"What are we waiting for?" Mason asked in a loud whisper after several beats of silence.

"Perhaps Nieve's time alone in the spire has made her cautious," Lief suggested lightly. "I've already searched the room for life and—"

Lief's words died in a strangled yelp. Hane pivoted, drawing both tonfa at once. Before they could find the cause of Lief's sudden silence, they found their path barred by Nieve's arm. Looking up to follow Nieve's gaze, Hane finally saw it: a disembodied pair of silver, slit-pupiled eyes. Fear seized Hane's chest, making it difficult to breathe. The eyes seemed to narrow at the corners, either in amusement or malice; Hane couldn't guess which without a face to go with the expression.

"Odette." Nieve's voice was hard and brittle, flecked with unforgiving frost. "Tell us everything. Now."

"I . . ." Odette's voice was breathy, awed, her gaze locked on the floating eyes, hovering closer to the ceiling than the floor. "I . . ."

Rose gasp-screamed, reeling back so suddenly she crashed into Nieve before ducking behind her to hide. Mason shouted wordlessly in alarm, one hand reaching back for his stone rod quiver. Nieve held a hand out before him, just as she did for Hane. Only then did Hane realize that Nieve had yet to reach for a weapon of her own.

"Odette." Nieve's tone was so cold, it was a shock she didn't breathe steam. "Did you know? About the vault guardian?"

Odette shivered from head to toe. A tiny gasp may have been an attempt at speech, but she gave up, shaking her head slowly, tears gleaming on her cheeks.

"Ah, so you expected me."

The voice was a whisper, clearly audible, yet soft as a misty rain, slippery like silk over satin. Hane blinked, casting Enhance Vision on themself. Was it their imagination, or was there a faint shadow around the pair of floating eyes?

"So few know to expect me that I have come to enjoy the surprise," the silky voice continued. "Too many think to rush and take that which is not theirs. It is my pleasure to inform them that even the oddest of rewards come with strings attached. And I, myself, am quite fond of strings."

The shadowy outline was becoming clearer, though Hane's perception spell didn't seem to be the cause: the being was coalescing itself out of the room's shadows, taking on form, shape, and substance. Hane's stomach dropped drastically as certain characteristics became evident. Like pointed ears on the crown of their head, and a long, lashing tail. Catlike features on a humanoid form, guarding the vault of a god beast.

Hane could put those pieces together, but they didn't like the image they formed.

"Oh," Rose whispered softly. Then again: "Oh!" She took a tentative step forward, eyes wide, her hands open and bared. "I—we—humbly request your forgiveness. We did not expect to find—"

Odette finally broke from her stupor, something like a joyful sob escaping her mouth as she wrenched her hands free of it. "I just—I can't believe it's really you! After all this time, I—" Her lips continued moving, but her voice died. Another tiny sob, then she tried again. "I've wanted to meet you for so long, and now I—I don't know what to say! I feel like such a fool."

The shadowy figure seemed to smirk. "You know me, then?"

"Oh, yes!" Odette said eagerly, like the star pupil of a class. "Child of god beast Byakko's third bearing, commonly known as the Glass generation, you are said to be the fifth of a litter of four, coalesced from the shadows of your siblings: Heshet of the Pristine Sands, Anshaa of the Obsidian—"

"Name, Odie!" Rose hissed without taking her eyes off the shadow-being. "Tell us their name!"

"Oh!" Odette looked shaken to her core. She pressed both hands over her heart, one on top of the other, then bowed from the waist. Not a full incline, but still a steep angle. "I am honored to stand in your presence and offer you the seven greetings of deepest honor, Sheuket of the Wandering Shadows."

"Sheuket," Rose whispered, mimicking Odette's gesture with her hands to her heart, but only dipping her chin slightly. Mason copied her one-handedly, the other hand still reaching back to grasp a stone rod. Rose elbowed him in the ribs, making him drop it back into his quiver.

"Are we in trouble?" Nieve demanded to know. Boldly, she took a step forward, putting herself in front of the team like a bulwark. Fearless and stalwart, she met that eerie silver gaze straight on in challenge, just as she had when confronted by Hogame of the Tortoise Spire. It confounded Hane how she could doubt herself and her strength when she was always the first to step up against an unwinnable challenge. "We opened the vault using the key and the clue hidden in the labyrinth. We didn't cheat or break any rules. If we've entered a forbidden space, I request that you allow us to leave immediately. Unharmed."

The shadow-being seemed fully coalesced, human-shaped but for their cat's ears and the long sleek tail behind them. No longer filmy and transparent, a velvety black obscured all their features but their eyes, as if they only existed as a silhouette. Their feet never rested on the floor as they maintained their unsettling hover, one foot kicked back at an angle. Their tail, switching mildly behind them, trailed off into faint shadows at the end, while the rest of their form filled in completely opaque. From head to toe, they appeared only as tall as Hane, but size hardly counted in the matters of god beasts and their kin.

Sheuket cocked their head to one side, silver eyes narrowing on Nieve. "You have the means to be bold, I see. Fear not: you all have leave to enter this place, else you would not have found it. I am only here to ensure that no more is taken than what is due."

"What does that mean?" Lief asked. He stood firm as the silver gaze ticked over to him. "Are you this vault's guardian?"

"I am," Sheuket agreed silkily. "While any item within this vault may be claimed as a treasure, it is my duty to ensure that no more is taken than has been earned. Choose wisely, little friends, for if you try to take more than the value of your efforts, you will find me a less accommodating host."

"Forgive me, honored Sheuket," Rose said meekly, holding up her hand in question. "How do we know what we've earned? What metrics evaluate our efforts? I would never wish to offer any offense to you or your great Mother, but what would happen if I overestimated my worth, or underestimated the value of one of your treasures?"

"Ask," the shadow-being replied simply. "Each of you may ask of me three times if what you wish to take from here is worth the price you paid to reach this place. If I judge the items worth your efforts, you may choose to leave immediately, or you may pick out more treasures and ask again. If I judge that you have taken more than is fair, you will have the opportunity to balance your yield. If, after a third time, you still have more than I judge you to have earned, then you will leave with nothing." The shadowy tail tip lashed sharply as silver eyes narrowed. "I warn you now that if you attempt to steal from the Vault of Shadows, there will be no place that you may hide where my shadows cannot find you."

"So not only do we not know what any of this stuff is worth," Lief said, waving a hand toward a collection of empty glass jars displayed neatly on a shelf. "But we also don't get to know how much we've earned? This is like a shop with no price list, and all we have to spend is foreign currency with no exchange rate. Isn't that deliberately skewing the odds that we'll undervalue our efforts and take less than our due?"

The crinkling at the corners of the silver eyes seemed to indicate a smile. "Clever human. These are the treasures accumulated by Mother's youngest children; what need does she have to give them up at all? Make your choices and be grateful to leave this place with what you can."

Lief shrugged, smiling ruefully. "It was worth a shot. Are there any other rules we should know before we go pawing through your vault? Anything we're explicitly forbidden from taking?"

The shadowed head shook slowly from side to side. "The only things you may not take are those which you did not earn. Go forth and seek your desires."

"You don't have to tell me twice." Lief started forward before pointing to a stack of disassembled furniture leaning against the wall. "Can you tell me if any of that is made of black poplar?"

Another slow shake of the head. "Answers are treasures in and of themselves, human. If that is what you wish, you will count it among your yield."

Lief pulled a face before smoothing it with a bland smile. He traced a finger along the wooden frame of a standing mirror before wandering deeper into the vault, stopping to examine a stack of framed paintings. Oddly, he seemed more interested in the frames than the portraits, keeping one hand pressed against the hilt of his sword before moving on to study the wooden beams and planks of deconstructed furniture. Mason hesitated a moment longer before easing away from the doorway to go and claim the symbol he'd spotted earlier. Rose spoke a word of thanks in Caelish before setting her own path through the vault, one that took her unerringly to a small hill of books. Odette held back, her hands twisting anxiously in front of her.

"My only request is for knowledge, honored Sheuket," Odette managed tremulously. "I wish to know you—not the legends and the stories, but *you*. If that is not too bold to ask."

The head tilted slowly, eyes narrowed in evaluation.

Odette's expression melted from hopeful to confused to horrified in the space of a breath. With a little shriek, she drew her bag off her shoulder and dropped to her knees, trembling hands fumbling the knots that held it closed. "A gift! I-I need to offer a gift first. What do I—oh!" Odette drew out a tangle of ribbons and string, looking dismayed at the mess. "Gifts made by hand are preferred, right? I, um . . . I make bracelets for my friends, but these are all—oh! J-just a moment, please . . ."

While there was no spoken response, the eyes relaxed as if in interest or, at least, acceptance. While Odette worked on separating the embroidered ribbon bracelets, Nieve sidled away, jerking her head at Hane to follow. As Lief, Rose, and Mason were already sifting through the vault's treasures without the guardian's objection, Hane trailed behind her, keeping an eye out for crystalline shards along the way.

The vault was no less chaotic further in than it was near the door. In fact, the deeper into the vault they went, the larger it seemed to be, with blind corners hiding pockets of treasures and trash alike. In some places, similar objects had been mounded together, like seashells of varying shapes and hues, or dusty instruments clumped around an unstrung harp nearly twice Nieve's height.

They passed by Rose, muttering intently to herself in Caelish as she sorted through the stacks of cracked and yellowed tomes. Hane hoped she didn't intend to go through the entire pile: the mound was big enough to ride a sled down.

Farther in, Mason knelt among three small treasure chests, flipping each one open in turn. The first held glittering gems, all different sizes and colors. The second held tarnished and battered jewelry, some hopelessly tangled, others missing the gems from their settings. The third box was inexplicably filled with cream-colored sand. Mason looked perplexed as he tipped the chest to one side, looking for anything buried within. Just as Hane passed by, Mason jumped up with a shout, calling out to his sister excitedly, the only slightly recognizable word being "lumenite." Hane recognized it as a prized metal but didn't know its worth off the top of their head.

Lief waved lazily as Hane and Nieve sidled past, barely taking his attention off a handsomely carved wooden chest with amber inlays set into the design. Despite a few scuffs and a lot of dust, it looked exactly like the sort of thing that would be found in a noble's home: unnecessarily ornate for the mundane purpose of general storage. But if that was what Lief had come to claim, then that was his business, not Hane's.

Nieve kept looking around as if unsure of where she was going; seemingly by coincidence, she turned into an alcove near the back of the vault—the same one where Hane had sensed a trickle of water. As she paused to study something gleaming and golden along a cluttered display case, Hane pinpointed the source of water: hidden at the back of the alcove was a beautifully carved alabaster fountain. The font head was a roaring tiger, the fangs gleaming with a lifelike quality. The water arced from the back of the tiger's throat, landing in a shallow basin below. Even standing this close, Hane couldn't sense the water collected in the pool, and when they tried manipulating the water with a simple shaping spell, they felt a heady, swimming sensation. They blinked and backed away: now was not the time for disorientation. When they looked up, Nieve was examining something with a golden honeycomb pattern on it, her expression thoughtful as she turned it over in her hands. When she caught their eye, she shrugged ruefully.

"We should look like we're picking out stuff to keep, right?" Nieve whispered, almost sheepishly. "What do you think this is?"

Hane didn't have the faintest idea of what the honeycomb object might be, but that was entirely beside the point.

"Did you know?" Hane asked, voice scarcely above a whisper. "About the guardian?"

"Yeah. Ch—*they* told me." Nieve tapped the toe of her boot on the floor, indicating Chime. "Odette never mentioned it?"

Hane shook their head. It suddenly dawned on them that they were more or less alone with Nieve, and now that the tense atmosphere created by the vault guardian was somewhat lessened, Hane's guilt came back in full force, making their eyes skip away from Nieve's. Should they say something now? Apologize for being so abrupt earlier? Ask forgiveness for leaving her for dead? Justify their actions as logical? Or should they just forget about it and hope the twisting nausea went away over time?

Before the silence could draw out too long, Nieve took them by the shoulders and drew them close against her in a brief but tight hug. Upon release, she kept her hands on Hane's shoulders, standing at arm's length from them.

"I'm sorry for this, but we should talk for a minute," Nieve whispered, carefully emphasizing the word "we." "I'm really glad that you're safe; I was worried about all of you."

The embrace was . . . uncomfortable, but not altogether unpleasant. That said, they were grateful it had been brief. Moreover, they thought they understood the intention behind the gesture: in order to hear Chime's voice, contact with Nieve was required. That was confirmed as Hane recognized Chime's ringing tones inside their mind.

<It is good to be at your side again, Hane.> Chime's voice, but changed somehow. There was a lightness to it, joyful, even. <Nieve requested I speak with you so that we not be overheard. Is this acceptable to you?>

This is fine, Hane replied before leaping straight to the point. *Do you sense your missing piece here?*

<Yes!> Chime, usually so steady and even-toned, sounded excited. <We are close. So close, in fact, that my consciousnesses have merged and I have recovered enough of my power to assist you in finding me.>

That would certainly help. The piece of Chime hidden within Nieve's boot was long, but narrow and entirely transparent, except when the light passed through it just right. Hane suspected that some of the shards might be even smaller, and finding one tiny, nearly invisible object in all of this would take more time than was normal for picking out treasure.

"We'll have to pick a few other things, too," Nieve whispered. "It would be weird if we only took a broken crystal shard, right?"

Hane nodded. "That shouldn't be difficult." There were bound to be plenty of useful enchanted items in here that could prove functional as climbing tools. And even if they didn't find anything they needed, the treasures here would still fetch a good price when sold.

<I will use my recovered power to have the crystal shard emit a sound,> Chime explained in both of their minds. <Only the two of you will be able to hear it, and only as you are connected to me. Please do not be alarmed if I fall silent for a time after; this use of my power will come with some cost.>

Understood, Hane thought.

Nieve smiled briefly before releasing Hane's shoulders, the two of them moving cautiously around the scattered treasures to stand at the edge of the alcove. From here, they had a good vantage point of most of the vault, which should help them once they heard Chime's magical sound. A bit nervous, Hane leaned in close to Nieve, uncertain how to initiate physical contact. As if she understood, Nieve grinned and braced her elbow on Hane's shoulder, pretending to lean against them.

"Where do you want to start looking?" Nieve asked.

The phrase must have been a cue for Chime because scarcely a moment later they heard a crystal clear ring echoing faintly, like the sound of silverware striking a crystal goblet. Hane remained perfectly still as their eyes tracked the tone to its origin: somewhere between a cluster of cracked vases and a stack of dusty chairs.

"I think we should look—" Hane started pointing in the direction of the sound but froze before completing the gesture. While Rose, Mason, and Odette seemed completely oblivious to the magical tone, Lief cocked his head to the side sharply, frowning in the direction of the noise. Hane chanced a look up at Nieve, finding her similarly startled.

Perhaps it was only a coincidence: anything could have caught Lief's eye, after all. Chime said only Nieve and Hane would hear the tone, so there was no reason to think Lief could have heard it. But as Lief knelt down to brush aside shards of pottery and a tattered shroud, Hane felt nerves flutter wildly in the pit of their stomach. What would happen if someone else happened to find Chime's shard and claimed it as a treasure? Chime would know better than to say anything—hopefully. But how would they get the shard back to complete their quest? Trying to buy it would seem suspicious, but the thought of stealing a piece of treasure from a teammate went against Hane's principles as a climber.

But wait, why would anyone want to claim a broken piece of crystal as a treasure in the first place?

Before Hane could think that through, Lief held up something pinched between his fingers—something the size of a toothpick. Hane felt Nieve stiffen beside them, as if preparing for a fight. Hane elbowed her just as Lief noticed the two of them staring. He smiled his easy smile as he straightened from his crouch, shaking his head dismissively at his finding.

"It makes you wonder, doesn't it?" Lief asked, turning the object so that it glinted in the light, casting prismatic rainbows on the nearby wall. "How do all these strange and broken things end up inside a god beast's vault in the first place?"

"They are brought here," Sheuket answered unexpectedly. The vault guardian casually finished tying off an embroidered bracelet around their shadow-black wrist, pausing to admire it for a moment before continuing. "Mother charges each of her young to contribute new items to her secret chambers before they may be allowed to journey independently. While the young ones are restricted to search within the spire, many of the elders are permitted to visit Mother's shrines to retrieve the gifts offered in her name. Is it so curious that—"

The child of the god beast stopped suddenly, silver gaze darting down to the colorful bracelet around their shadow-dark wrist. Their opposite hand twitched as if to reach for it, but stopped just as suddenly as it started.

"Do not touch, do not resist." Odette finished repacking her satchel, slinging it over a shoulder as she straightened up with her tracking device in hand.

The guardian's bracelet seemed to shudder and pulse—or maybe it was Sheu-ket that trembled. "Do not speak, do not use your magic, do not move unless I order you to."

Odette adjusted her backpack and pushed her glasses up her nose before seeming startled to find everyone staring at her, eyes and jaws agape. She shrugged meekly and offered the team she'd assembled a shy smile.

"Good news, everyone! Looks like you can take as much treasure as you'd like after all."

NIEVE

Champion (mind mark), Citrine
Paladin (heart mark), Carnelian

Everyone started shouting at once.

Rose, wide-eyed with horror, cried, "What have you done?"

Mason, reeling back until his shoulders hit the wall, asked, "What happened to Odette?"

Lief, throwing his hands out defensively, shouted, "I'm not one of them, I didn't know! I swear it!"

Nieve could only stare, dumbfounded as the guardian dropped subserviently to one knee. Sure, it had been a little suspicious that Odette hadn't mentioned a vault guardian, but nothing could have prepared Nieve for this. Placing a child of Byakko under a mind-control spell? Was such a thing truly possible?

While Nieve was still struggling to comprehend just how powerful someone would have to be to mind control a child of a god beast, Hane whirled into motion. A flicker of silver was all the warning she got before Hane slipped a knife the size of her little finger beneath the bracelet tied around her forearm. The point of the knife dimpled her skin but didn't break it: the bracelet fell away neatly. Before Nieve's bracelet could hit the floor, Hane punched the knife through their own sleeve and twisted before reaching beneath the fabric to cast away their own severed bracelet.

Lief, standing the closest to them, caught the motion and mimicked it, tearing his own bracelet off while shouting to Rose and Mason. Mason snapped his cleanly by flexing his bicep in a way that made Nieve envious. Rose, looking stunned, pulled the bow out of the ribbon she'd tied around her neck.

"Odie, what are you doing?" Rose asked plaintively, the bracelet dangling limply through her fingers. She shook her head in disbelief. "This isn't you, I know it's not. Please, just—just end the spell and beg forgiveness, then maybe we can all leave here alive."

"Oh no, you don't have to worry," Odette assured her, smiling too brightly. She set a hand on the kneeling guardian's head, petting it like a cat. "Look, they can't break the compulsion; the spell is far too powerful, which means they can't hurt any of us. Don't you see how great this is? We don't have to worry about following some arbitrary rule about how much treasure we can take!"

"Odette, you need to stop this," Mason ordered fiercely. "This isn't what we signed up for; we're not supporting you in this."

"Where did you find an enchantment powerful enough to bind a child of a god beast?" Lief asked curiously.

"*That's* your question?" Hane demanded sharply.

"What?" Lief looked around at the others, shrugging indifferently. "I'm not saying I approve, but you can't tell me that's not impressive magic. I mean, look at it! Who would suspect something that small was actually enchanted with a mind-control spell?"

"Where I got it isn't important," Odette said firmly. "All you need to know is that the guardian has been safely subdued so you can pick whatever treasures you want. Isn't that great?"

"No!" Nieve shouted, finally finding her voice. "When Lord Byakko finds out you did this, she's going to eat you. No excuses, no justifications, because you will be *dead*. You know that, right?"

"Oh, don't worry about that," Odette said with a casual nonchalance that sent a chill down Nieve's spine. "All the phantom chambers are sealed with layers of protection, most of them controlled by this kitty right here." Odette patted Sheuket's head, the guardian holding unnaturally still at her side. "Byakko can breach those layers if she wants to, but I highly doubt she will. But just in case . . . Sheuket? Veil this room against intrusion, sight spells, and communication spells. I don't care to be interrupted while we sort this out."

The tip of the shadow-being's tail twitched violently, but otherwise Sheuket held perfectly still. Shadows as black as night stretched out from beneath them, coating the floor, walls, and ceiling in velvet darkness that seemed to swallow both light and sound.

"Okay, I'm done with this," Mason declared, starting forward with purpose. "Take off the bracelet, Odette, or I will."

"I wouldn't." The singsong tone reminded Nieve of her grandmother chastising one of her brothers. "Have you ever seen one of Byakko's children in a rage? They might attack all of us indiscriminately once they're freed."

Mason's step faltered. Nieve's heart skipped a beat as she remembered the outcome of fighting a god beast's general.

But this time, she had an advantage.

"Do it, Mason," Nieve said, touching the attunement that linked her to her father's patron god beast. She wouldn't allow this to happen. Not again. "Sheuket won't attack you, I promise."

Mason hedged, glancing back once before shaking off his trepidation and starting forward again. "Right. The rest of us haven't done anything wrong, and we'll be forgiven if we free them. Last chance, Odette, I'm warning you."

Odette frowned, stepping forward to place herself between Sheuket and the others. "Is the reward not enough? If you like, I can have Sheuket take us to the Vault of Otherwordly Metals, the one chamber said to be filled with rare and mythical metals and gems. Think of the works of art that you and only you could create with such a resource!"

Mason was tempted, Nieve could see it in the way he slowed his step, then he determinedly shook his head. He placed a gentle hand on Odette's shoulder, meeting her eyes with a pleading look. "Please stop this, Odette. You're a friend, and I don't want to hurt you."

It should have looked intimidating: Mason stood head and shoulders taller than Odette and his attunement made him naturally stronger than any-one else, except for Nieve. And yet, all Odette did was sigh heavily.

"I don't want to hurt you, either," Odette said. "But you're not giving me much of a choice."

"Mason!" Rose screamed suddenly. "Get back!"

"What?" He looked back, puzzled. "She's just an Analyst, what can she—"

"Sheuket," Odette stated simply. "Protect me."

The shadows deepened so suddenly that Nieve felt as if she were falling endlessly once again. She reached out for Hane, more to have something to hold onto than anything else, but at some point after severing her embroidered bracelet, they had vanished. Steadying herself against the broken grandfather clock instead, Nieve ripped her claw hammer off her belt, holding it slightly behind her. If at all possible, she'd rather not attack one of Byakko's children, but she also didn't wish to be caught unprepared if Byakko's child attacked her. No, the best way to end this quickly would be to summon Byakko herself.

Nieve ducked her chin but kept her eyes up and her war hammer ready. She pressed her free hand to her heart, feeling the pulse of the cold light within her Paladin attunement. "Great Byakko," Nieve thought, focusing on the attunement itself rather than invoking it. "Please, hear my prayer: one of your children is in danger and they need your help right now. Send aid imme-diately to your Vault of Shadows."

As she awaited a response, the absolute darkness grew colder, sending a stark chill up her spine. A nearby crash had her casting Frost Form over herself while keeping her breath soft and listening for her teammates. She heard voices and shuffling sounds, but the darkness swallowed them before she could orient herself toward them. The air seemed heavier, weighing on Nieve's shoulders as well as within her chest. Why did she feel tired all of a sudden?

Mind of Ice! Nieve set her mental defenses against a potential sleep spell, but it did little to help. It felt as if the shadows of the vault were a physical presence, pressing against her nose, mouth, and throat, making the simple act of breathing that much harder.

"Forgive us, Sheuket, please!" Rose shouted, sounding frantic and desperate. A sliding shuffle and a series of hollow thuds, like several small objects striking the floor. Nieve moved slowly toward the sound, one arm stretched out before her to feel for Rose and her other teammates. "We had no idea Odette planned this, or else we never would have joined her team! Please, if you can fight the compulsion at all, we can . . ." Rose cut off, her breathing labored as though she was struggling to breathe. "We can he . . . we can help . . . "

Her voice trailed off, leaving Nieve groping blindly through the dark. She heard a soft thud as something dropped heavily to the ground. With no sound to follow as a guide, Nieve fell still. Breath came slowly, as if filtering through layers upon layers of wool pressed tightly over Nieve's face. Swallowing her fear and ignoring her panic, Nieve shuffled forward, hoping she was heading in the right direction.

"Rose?" Nieve called, each breath a precious commodity. "Rose, where are you?"

Small objects underfoot felt like books, sliding easily beneath Nieve's boots. She huffed out a breath she couldn't afford to lose as she stumbled into the waist-high pile of books Rose had been searching through earlier. Groping through the dark, Nieve lowered herself to a knee, shoving books aside until her hand found something warm and yielding: Rose, collapsed as if fainted.

"No, no, no," Nieve whispered, inching forward on her knees. She set her hammer down to lift Rose by the shoulders, propping her up as she felt for a whisper of breath. "Not again, Lord Byakko, please not again! I'm begging you, Great Byakko, please aid your—"

"Nieve."

Nieve reacted violently, swinging her elbow back toward the unexpectedly close whisper. As she connected, the only thing she was sure of was that it wasn't Hane who had spoken her name: they would have harmlessly redirected her strike, while this person staggered backward, crashing into something that fell with the sound of shattering glass.

"Goddess resh it, Nieve, it's me! You have detection spells, don't you?"

Oh, yeah. Nieve blinked, casting Detect Mind on herself, giving her the ability to see warped auras around sentient beings. While the darkness was still absolute, she could clearly see a distorted patch of space in the circle of her arms, as well as another just over her shoulder. She heard the sounds of flimsy wood splintering as whoever it was stood up.

"Don't hit me again," Lief warned, his steps scarcely making a sound as he came closer. "We're being suffocated by the shadows; I'm trying to help you breathe."

"Rose is unconscious," Nieve explained, trying to shift so Lief could find Rose in the darkness. "Heal her first."

"I'm going to keep you from passing out first." Fingers caught in her hair before Lief's hand found her shoulder. "You're our warrior, aren't you? If Sheuket gets serious, we'll need you to defend us."

"If Sheuket gets serious, there won't be anything I can do about it," Nieve replied. Breathing still felt slow and heavy, but gradually the feeling of light-headedness left her, as if the little air she could breathe was functioning more efficiently than before. "How did you find us?"

"Detect Life, remem—oh, wait. You weren't there for that." The hand on Nieve's shoulder lifted. A touch grazed her arm before settling on Rose. "I can sense the aura of living beings. Not that it's much help in a place as cluttered and hazardous as this vault."

"Can you find Hane?" Nieve asked.

"Hane found me already." Lief sounded focused, though Nieve couldn't see what he was doing. "I think Mason must be shaping the air he's breathing; he's still conscious for now."

Nieve pressed the back of her hand to Rose's cheek, feeling for breath and warmth. "We should ring her out so she'll be safe. We should all ring out!" Nieve looked around, squinting into the darkness as she searched for more distorted patches of darkness. "Quick, find Hane and Mason and tell them—"

"That's not going to work." Lief's flat tone quashed Nieve's flare of hope. "These shadow barriers aren't going to let us teleport out of here any more than they're going to let us call for help. Vaults are normally shielded to prevent theft, and on Odette's orders, Sheuket made them even stronger."

Not again, Nieve thought, helplessness solidifying in the pit of her stomach like a cooling chunk of lava. *This can't be happening again. I need— Chime!* She reached out mentally, feeling for the gateway crystal's consciousness. Chime wouldn't be hindered by the darkness; perhaps they could find a solution that didn't require fighting Odette or Sheuket. *Chime, can you hear me?*

I need to know where Odette is. Or if you can sense the child of the god beast, tell me where they are.

No response. Not that it was unexpected, Chime had warned her that using their power would leave them weak. Nieve had hoped Chime might retain enough consciousness to at least communicate mana signatures to her, but clearly that was too much to hope for.

"What about Odette?" Nieve asked, barreling through despair. "Tell me where she is, and I'll find a way to force her to end the spell."

"I know where she is, but I wouldn't go near her. She ordered Sheuket to protect her, right?" Lief sounded grim in the darkness. "If we try attacking Odette directly, we'll end up fighting for more than just air." A rustle of fabric, the creak of boot leather. Nieve thought she heard the pop of a cork followed by short, quick gulps. "I have a better idea, but first: How do you feel, Nieve? Dizzy? Sick? Can you stand?"

"I think I'm . . . yeah, I'm fine." Breathing was difficult, but the ache in her chest was gone, and she didn't feel disoriented when she shook her head. "Is Rose going to be okay?"

"She's using less air than both of us while unconscious, so she's fine for now," Lief assured her. "Listen, Nieve: I have a spell that can counteract compulsion, but I'm not sure it'll be enough to overcome an enchantment strong enough to compel a child of the god beast—especially with the ribbon tied around their wrist. I'm going to try anyway, but I need you to be ready to protect me if it fails."

Nieve nodded before realizing Lief couldn't see her. "I'll be ready. If Sheuket appears, I just need to get the bracelet off of them, right?"

"Yeah." A sardonic tone laced Lief's words. "I'm sure it'll be that easy. Tell me when you're ready."

Nieve shifted Rose in her arms, feeling the brush of curls against her upper arm as she gently laid her down on the floor. Feeling carefully, she folded both of Rose's arms over her stomach to avoid stepping on them. Only then did she grope after the haft of her hammer and rise, drawing her katana with her right hand. "I'm ready."

"Okay." A long, strained inhale, then a shuffle of feet. "Get ready. One, two—"

Nieve didn't hear "three" as the radiance that burst outward from Lief was almost bright enough to sing. She shut her eyes tight before she realized she could see despite the glare—maybe Lief had adjusted her vision in addition to fixing her breath in anticipation of exactly this. The light cast back the nearby shadows, revealing Rose lying peacefully at their feet. As Nieve turned a circle, watching for Sheuket, she spotted Mason crouched behind a table turned on its side, one arm up to block the light. Near the entrance of the vault, she saw Odette reeling backward, her hands over her eyes.

Odette! Feral instinct made her lips twitch into a snarl. It wasn't the hunter that whispered in Nieve's mind, but a cold, flickering rage. She hefted her hammer back, considering her left-handed throw earlier and wondering if she could replicate it now without invoking Byakko's power.

"Sheuket, make them stop!" Odette screamed, her back hitting the wall. "Save me! Protect me!"

Before Nieve could swing her arm through the throw, a figure appeared in front of her, black as the night and deep as velvet. An arm bearing a colorful bracelet swept her hammer aside effortlessly. Silver eyes darted at Nieve's sword, as if daring her to swing sidelong, but she hesitated, the sword trembling in her grip. This wasn't Hogame, an entity of judgment and flame; Sheuket hadn't meant any harm to Nieve or her team, and even though she doubted her sword would even leave a scratch on them, she was loathe to attack the child of a god beast—specifically the god beast who granted her the attunement centered over her heart.

Lief darted beneath Nieve's sword arm, one hand outstretched before him, determination in the clench of his jaw. Instead of going for the bracelet, Lief lunged at Sheuket's chest. The being's form faded to insubstantial shadows but still remained faintly visible as Lief's hand sank into the incorporeal chest up to his wrist. His eyes hard, light flared white-hot from his palm, filling the shadow until all Nieve could see was a thin outline of a cat-being around searing bright light.

A scream like a caged animal echoed from every corner of the room as the form erupted, spraying shadows like knives in all directions. Nieve managed to knock Lief back and block Rose bodily, cutting blades of shadow slamming against her shroud and armor, but failing to drive her back. Darkness enveloped the vault again, but after blinking away the light scars on her vision, Nieve found it wasn't as absolute as before: she could actually see her own feet on the floor, and a sideways shuffle found Rose close by, still asleep or unconscious but breathing shallowly.

"Rose!" A crash, a curse, then more crashing. "Nieve, Lief! Where's my sister?"

"Mason, here!" Nieve reached for her glow stick before remembering she'd tucked it away inside a pouch. "Rose is okay. She's asleep, but she's all right. Can you follow my voice?"

A groan to her right: Nieve looked over to see Lief sitting up on the mound of books. As he reached out to steady himself, a stack of books shifted and went skidding across the floor.

"Did you get them?" Lief asked woozily. "They were solid for an instant—I felt it. Did you get the bracelet?"

"No." Nieve grunted as Mason collided with her in the dark. She struggled to direct him to Rose without releasing either of her weapons. "I thought you had them."

"It wasn't enough." Lief cradled his forehead in one hand, eyes squeezed shut. "Ugh, that took a lot out of me. I can either try to fight the compulsion again or keep everyone healed up; I can't do both."

"Rose, wake up!" Mason said, hunched over his sister's form. "Is she hurt? I can't tell—"

A cold wind stirred Nieve's hair, and an eerie laugh like *kekeke* made her flesh crawl. She turned her back to her teammates, squinting into the shadows as she searched for the source of the sound.

"You have done well, shining Biomancer." Sheuket's silken voice seemed to emanate from the vault itself. "Not so well as I had hoped, but you are only human, after all. If each of you can be just as clever, perhaps you will survive this." A silence sharp as fangs. "Most of you, that is."

"Stop talking!" Odette screeched, fear stark in her voice. "You're still under my control, Sheuket! The enchantment isn't that weak. I order you to kill everyone still standing!"

Lief scrambled off the mound of books, sending the tomes sliding every which way as he tumbled to the floor. He gestured frantically at Nieve, but before she could figure out his meaning, the shadows ahead of her sharpened and coalesced, becoming three parallel blades that slashed through her shroud, impacting the leather of her armor as well as her skin toughened by Frost Form. Another set of shadow blades struck from behind, staggering her forward. Mason and Lief each grabbed one of her wrists and yanked her to the floor as another set of blades swept past.

"They're resisting her orders," Lief hissed. "Stay down and they won't attack you!"

"Until she changes the command," Mason said miserably. He hefted Rose into his arms while staying low on his knees. "What do we do? Should we try ringing out?"

"It won't work," Lief said. "Odette issued specific orders about the barriers on this room. Unless Byakko or one of the visages feels like dropping in for a visit, no one is getting in or out."

A pang like grief and lost faith struck Nieve with the force of a battering ram: if Byakko hadn't responded to her prayers by now, then she likely hadn't heard them. She might still be able to invoke Byakko's strength through her

Paladin attunement, but what good would the blind fury of a predator be against a shadow entity such as Sheuket?

Wait, Nieve thought, an idea striking like lightning out of a clear sky. *I don't need to defeat Sheuket; I only need to force Odette to release the spell. And even if that makes Sheuket attack me, then at least they won't be focused on anyone else.*

I can protect them!

"Lief, you said you can sense Odette, right?" Nieve whispered hurriedly.

"I can, but—"

"No, listen," Nieve interrupted. "Hane and I are your combat specialists; we're the ones who can end this. Take Rose and find somewhere to hide." She cast around blindly, the shadows impenetrable if she tried looking more than a few feet in any direction. "There's a corner alcove with a water fountain somewhere near the back; you'll be out of the way there. Now, point me at Odette."

She saw the reluctant look that Lief exchanged with Mason, but in the end, Lief helped her orient on the barely visible aura belonging to Odette. Motioning for the others to wait, Nieve stood tall, striding forward determinedly as she struck the blade of her sword with the flat of her hammer, a sharp, clear tone tolling outward.

"Odette!" Nieve shouted into the darkness. Shadow blades screamed at her from the side: she twisted and cut through them with a blade coated in ice. "Was capturing Sheuket your plan all along?" Nieve spun the haft of her hammer in her grip, hooked claws swiping through another set of shadow blades. "Tell me why! What good could possibly come from kidnapping one of Byakko's children?"

"I see no reason to answer that," came the startlingly calm response. "You may have weakened the compulsion, but I still have the upper hand here. The matters of the Tiger Spire don't concern you, foreigner, so I'll make you a deal: claim whatever treasure it was you came here for, and I'll allow you to leave."

Nieve snorted, tracking Odette's voice through the shadows. "As if I would! You hired me to be the team's defender, didn't you? That's what I'm going to do, even if that means defending them from you!"

"Then you'll die with them." The location of Odette's voice had changed. Nieve oriented on the new source while grimly watching the shadows for signs of movement. "Sheuket, I order you to—aah!"

Odette's voice rose sharply in a cry as the sounds of a scuffle broke out. A roar like an ocean wave, then splashing footsteps across the stone floor. Nieve sensed water lapping at her boots as she parried another shadow-strike. She had just enough time to grin and think *There's Hane!* before she heard the plink of glass marbles splashing and cracking on the floor. She groaned aloud as she remembered the effects of Odette's spell spheres.

"Better watch your step, Wavewalker!" Odette shouted furiously, her voice now coming from somewhere behind Nieve. "You haven't seen all of my traps yet, and I'm not as weak as you think I am!"

"I never thought you were weak." Hane's voice came from the ceiling, nearby as if they stood right over Nieve's head. "And because I know you're a strong opponent, I don't intend to hold back. So if you're being forced to do this, now would be the time to tell us. It'll be too late after I kill you."

A bitter laugh made the room feel colder. "I chose this mission, but failure will still cost me my life, so don't think your threats frighten me at all. I came here prepared to do what needed to be done. Is it so easy for you to turn on a comrade, Wavewalker?"

"Is it really so easy for you?" That deep voice could only belong to Mason. Somehow he was closer to the source of Odette's voice than Nieve was, though he should have been on the opposite side of the room from her. Or maybe she was more lost in the dark than she thought she was—hadn't she passed this standing mirror once before? "My sister and I have known you for a long time, Odie. We took classes together, attended the same festivals, our parents are close—you've even been to our home! Our sister is one of your best friends! How could you do this to us?"

"Your sister Jesserah was the one who suggested I invite Rose on this climb in the first place," came the simple response. "And don't think we're friends just because we walk in the same social circles; it's not as if you ever bothered to—"

Odette's voice broke off suddenly as a crash resounded through the dark. Nieve ducked instinctively, finding something solid to set her back against— not that it made much of a difference against shadow-strikes, but deeply ingrained fighting tactics were hard to ignore.

"Nieve."

Another urgent whisper spoken so close to her ear sparked a second thoughtless reaction: she slammed her elbow up and back before she recognized the voice as Hane's. Luckily, Hane had prepared for that: Nieve's blow slowed as it met Hane's shroud, then rebounded somewhat gently, as if her arm had been caught and forcibly slowed. Hane didn't wait for an apology, nor did they offer one, but continued talking rapidly as soon as Nieve relaxed.

"I need a thick layer of ice over all the spell spheres she dropped so we can move safely," Hane explained. "You can do that using Detect Water, right?"

"Yeah," Nieve whispered back. "Yeah, I can do that. You can find her, right? Knock her out, or . . . something?"

"She's using Cloak of Shadows and some of her spell spheres project her voice," Hane explained. "I'm crushing the ones I can find, but now that she's dropped more of them, that probably won't work as well anymore. Tell me quickly: what did Sheuket mean when they said you had the means to be bold?"

Nieve hesitated, and not just because she was afraid of being overheard; Sheuket, at least, seemed to know of her connection to Byakko already. The heightened senses of a predator might help her find Odette, even despite Cloak of Shadows. But what about all the other side effects that came with Byakko's power? What if she attacked one of her teammates? What if she lost control and couldn't turn it off? Just thinking about the way she'd looked at Rose while under the influence of the predator's mindset made her insides squirm with shame.

"I can't explain it right now," Nieve said slowly. "I have this new power, but it's not . . . reliable. I can't control it very well; I might end up hurting someone."

Silence. Nieve wondered if Hane was still there. Then: "I know you don't want to hear this, but it may come to that. Unless you have a way to fight Sheuket directly, the only other solution is—"

Nieve hesitated, doubt warring with shame and grief in a nauseating, endless cycle. "I can't fight Odette. Not—not seriously. What if I hurt her? What if I—" Her breath choked off; she couldn't even say it. Odette's actions were deplorable and downright heretical, but Nieve wasn't an executioner. Subduing an opponent was one thing; sending the hunter after them was entirely different.

Another brief silence. Nieve twitched at a soft touch on her shoulder. "This fight is hard for me, too. It's like . . . like last time." That admission cost them; Nieve could hear it in the raw quality of their voice. In its own way, it was almost more startling than Odette placing a mind control enchantment on the child of a god beast. A long pause followed, wherein Nieve sensed Hane wrestling with some inner turmoil, then finally: "We survived the last fight. We'll survive this one, too."

Nieve caught Hane's hand as it withdrew from her shoulder.

"We won't just survive," Nieve promised. "This time, we're going to win."

Hane's hand slipped from her grasp, but they still hovered just overhead; Nieve could see them with her Detect Mind spell. A beat of silence passed before they spoke again. "Okay, Nieve. I trust you."

It was enough to make her feel as if Lief's spell had stopped working, the way it was suddenly hard to breathe. But then Hane vanished into the depths of the vault, leaving Nieve with a job to do.

This time would not be like last time.

Detect Water, Nieve thought, feeling for the puddle of conjured water seeping into the stone floor. The glass spell spheres were easy to sense as she knew their shape, size, and texture better than anything else currently resting on the floor. It wasn't enough to seal the marbles in ice—too much pressure on them would cause them to shatter and release their stored spells—so instead Nieve left a pocket of air beneath a thick film of ice. She might have missed a few of the scattered spheres, but it was the best she could do considering her limited visibility.

With that taken care of, the only thing left to do was choose her opponent wisely.

"Here, kitty kitty," Nieve murmured, scanning the darkest shadows with Detect Mind. She struck the blade of her sword with her hammer again, hoping the noise would make something jump, or at least draw the shadow-being's attention to herself. A shout drew her attention to a shadowy alcove—thankfully far from the one with the water fountain, where she hoped Lief was tending to Rose. Odette and Mason shouted at each other in Caelish as glass shattered and wood creaked and groaned. Something hit the floor with a hollow thud, followed by the sound of cascading stones.

Where was Sheuket? That was the true danger. If Nieve could keep their focus on herself, then she wouldn't have to worry about—

Odette raised her voice, shouting something that Nieve only understood a single word of: Sheuket. If that was the order Nieve suspected it was, then she had to find Mason. Fast.

Following the blob of distorted space as well as the rattling sounds of rickety shelving, Nieve darted through the vault's detritus, dodging anything she couldn't leap over. She ran as the shadows deepened and converged over the alcove hiding Mason and Odette, but she tripped over a rolled-up rug in the darkness, falling in an uncoordinated sprawl. As she pushed herself up, she saw Mason retreating from a series of angled sickle-like shadow blades, each striking one after another. The first cracked his stone shield, the second shattered it completely. Before he could shape a new one, a shadow blade caught him from shoulder to hip, shoving him back on his heels. He managed to keep his feet, but only barely. He caught the next shadow blade on his arm, shouting raggedly as it scored a clean hit.

Nieve grunted as she leapt to her feet, swinging her hammer and sword out wide as she conjured a wall of ice between Mason and the oncoming shadow blades. The sickle-shaped blades sliced right through it, chunks of ice thudding heavily to the floor. Mason shouted, taking a bad cut on his bare shoulder with his tunic taking the rest of the hit. His left arm dripped blood as he backed away, shielding his face with his right. Before the next blade could strike, Mason stumbled over a small treasure chest, falling hard, but mercifully missing the next few strikes.

Toppling a wardrobe that was in her way, Nieve dove in front of the next curved shadow blade, slicing through it with her sword. She stood over Mason, slashing and hacking at the blades as quickly as they could form, but even she could tell that she would run out of stamina far before Sheuket ran out of shadows.

I need Sheuket to focus on me! Nieve thought, spinning and parrying, slashing and guarding. *Mason isn't trained for this; he wasn't even supposed to be here. It's my job to protect him, but how do I—*

The shadows within the nearby alcove writhed and shivered before breaking apart into smaller pieces, scattering like a pod of jellyfish: Odette had to be hidden within one of those shadowy patches, but which one? Attacking the wrong one wouldn't do any good, but if she happened to pick the right one, she might end up killing Odette, which was the worst possible outcome. Assuming the compulsion was designed to outlast Odette, her final orders would remain in effect and the team would lose any means of control that might allow them to end this peacefully. If Nieve could find Odette, she could pin her down and threaten her enough to force her to end the compulsion, but between the shadow blades striking from all angles and Mason groaning and bleeding on the floor at her feet, Nieve didn't have the focus she needed to search for the barely visible warping of her Detect Mind spell among the fleeing shadows.

If only Sage was here, he'd use light mana to burn away the shadows, Nieve thought, her sword arm moving through a complex figure-eight pattern to cut through two shadow blades attacking from different angles. She faltered, missing her next swing as a sudden thought occurred to her: she had light mana now, too! The only problem was that she didn't know any light spells. She'd seen Sage conjure light orbs of different colors and sizes, ones he could carry in his palm, ones that could range out ahead of a team, or ones he could cast up at the ceiling to illuminate a room, but just because she knew it could be done didn't mean she had the ability to cast a spell she'd never practiced before. And with her shoulder aching from a blow she failed to block and Mason vulnerable to attack on the floor, the circumstances weren't ideal for practicing.

But there was one spell that might work—a simple one that she had already used earlier, back in the train scenario, when she'd infused her shroud with mental mana in order to connect with Chime. Light mana was still new to her, but the process for infusing a shroud with a specific mana type wasn't really a new spell; she was just drawing from a new source. And luckily, Nieve used her heart pathway often enough that moving mana through it was easy for her.

Sage would have called it sloppy and he would have been right to, but Nieve couldn't consider that now. Her Paladin attunement had grown slightly, making her somewhat reckless practice worth it. Focusing only on the light mana of the Paladin attunement, Nieve waited for the moment when her next movements swept her arms out wide, striking through shadow blades coming from opposite sides.

"Light!" Nieve shouted in her native tongue, drawing on the raw light mana inside her chest and sending it out through her shroud. It wasn't as concentrated and controlled as her ice spells, and it certainly wasn't the neat orb of light Sage could conjure, but dim light suffused her shroud, making it look as if her skin was glowing. It wasn't bright enough to affect the scattering shadows, but by reshaping her shroud over her arms and hands, Nieve managed to create two golden nimbuses of warm light, just bright enough to melt the fleeing shadowy patches one by one until the one cloaking Odette burned into nothing.

Odette shrieked in outrage, putting her back to the nearest wall as she scrabbled for a spell sphere on her bracer. Nieve grinned as she released her spell, her shroud flowing back to its natural shape to protect her body: Odette's bracer was nearly bare. Whatever trap or spell she'd wanted wasn't within easy reach.

"Kill them both!" Odette screamed. "No games, I want them dead!"

Nieve swept her sword through an arc parallel with her shoulder, extending ice over and past the tip of the blade, feinting at Odette's throat. Her true intention was to reverse the strike as Odette turned to run, severing the tendons in her ankles. She'd never kill a teammate, no—but immobilizing them so they couldn't hurt anyone else . . . that was a slightly grayer area. And if the pain was enough to force Odette into releasing the compulsion spell from Sheuket, then so much the better. But before Nieve's ice blade could extend far enough to be considered a threat, something pulled tight around her neck and jerked hard, yanking her off her feet. As she fell to the ground, Nieve dropped her hammer to claw at her throat. Her nails tore at the delicate skin, digging deep furrows along her neck, but failing to catch on whatever it was that pulled tighter and tighter with each strangled gasp.

A shadow noose? Nieve thought, feeling the skin dimple beneath an ephemeral rope. *If that's it, all I need is light mana to—*

All rational thought fled as the phantom noose jerked hard enough to roll Nieve onto her back. Breathless panic made her give up her grip on her sword to claw uselessly at her neck. Looking up at the ceiling, Nieve couldn't help but see the shadows condense into black, gleaming swords, each the shape of a hiltless katana, and all pointed straight down.

Not at Nieve.

But at Mason.

Nieve arched her back, kicked and thrashed, managing to roll onto her side as red clouds fogged her vision. Mason had propped himself up on something, one end of a bandage pinched between his teeth as he pulled it taut. His opposite hand held a wad of cloth against his shoulder, sweat beading his forehead as he concentrated on binding the wound. Nieve tried to scream, to gasp, to point and warn, but by the time Mason looked up, it was too late.

The shadow blades screamed as they plummeted down, sending up ribbons of blood. All Nieve could do was watch as Mason's jaw dropped open, his arms falling limp as his body slumped sideways. A thin trickle of blood spilled from one corner of his mouth, his eyes wide and staring.

No.

No.

Not again. *Never* again. She couldn't watch another team die—one was already too much.

She'd made a promise.

They had to win this time.

Choking down as big a breath as she could manage, Nieve squeezed her eyes shut and focused on the light mana of her Paladin attunement, drawing it into her shroud once again. It didn't need to be bright; it just needed to break the shadow noose around her neck—quickly, before her air ran out! Her lungs screamed against her held breath, but that almost seemed to help more than hurt: rather than exhale, Nieve visualized "breathing" light mana into her shroud, praying it would be enough.

Her first gulp of air made her dizzy, but she didn't let that stop her from pushing herself up into a staggering crawl. A black and red haze consumed her field of vision, but she didn't need to see to know where Mason was. She found his outstretched arm first and used it to guide her to his body. Ignoring the slick blood on her fingers, Nieve groped for her medical kit by memory, blinking furiously to clear her vision.

"Hang on," Nieve whispered, finding her full potion bottle. She used her teeth to rip the cork out, her free hand gripping Mason's jaw to turn his head and hold his mouth open. Despite the red-tinged haze still clouding her vision and the disorientation that begged for her to lie down just a little longer, Nieve poured a stream of potion down Mason's throat. Her hand trembled, spilling potion over his chin and down his neck, but she managed to get most of it into his mouth. He swallowed on his own, which was a good sign, but after a few moments his eyes fluttered shut and his head rolled limply. The potion half finished, Nieve poured the rest over the injuries centered on his chest and abdomen.

"I hope that's enough," Nieve whispered, her voice raw with ragged breath. She cast the empty potion bottle aside before reaching for the half-finished one in her kit. She took a sip for herself, then corked it and left the remainder in Mason's hand, pressing it close to his side. "Goddess protect you, Mason. The goddess . . ."

And me.

Yeah, it was probably heresy.

But Nieve had already been found guilty of that crime once before, anyway.

"Byakko," Nieve exhaled. "Aid your warrior."

The person who reached out to grasp the haft of the fallen war hammer as they stood and turned toward the sounds of battle wasn't Nieve. Nor was it Nieve who hooked her foot beneath the hilt of her katana, kicking it up to catch in midair. It wasn't Nieve who stalked into the shadows, full of grim purpose.

The hunter had come out to play.

HANE

Wavewalker (leg mark), Citrine

Hane narrowly avoided a guillotine blade of shadows by reversing directions and crashing into something tall that crunched and shattered around them. They shook shards of glass out of their hair before rolling out of the pile of fresh kindling and taking refuge under what they hoped was a table. Pressing their hands to the floor briefly, they conjured a small pool of water, then darted out and away, staying on the move.

The vault had grown so dark that Hane could barely see their hand in front of their face, but they were no stranger to fighting blind. They left puddles of water each time they stopped moving, mapping the walls, floors, ceiling, and even furniture so they could see it with their Sense Water spell. Nieve's patch of ice served as a landmark near the front of the vault, helping Hane orient the rest of the space around themself. It was easy to lose track of direction in the darkness—not just left and right, but forward and backward, even up and down. Before they could fight, they had to know where they were, as well as where their opponents were, without getting pinned down themself.

Unfortunately, as a shadow-being with catlike reflexes, Sheuket was even faster, and it seemed they could sense shadows the same way Hane sensed water. Thanks to Lief's attempt to break the mind-control spell, Sheuket was resisting as much as they could, but they still couldn't disobey a direct order. The moment Odette called for Hane's death was the moment they would no longer be able to move freely about the vault—and they couldn't risk direct combat with a being that didn't have to materialize in order to kill someone.

We won't just survive.

This time, we're going to win.

Winning had been the plan from the start: Kill Odette, free the shadow-cat-being, save everyone else. That was winning, right? Most climbers would have considered it a win, anyway.

Not Nieve, though.

No, for Nieve, only a perfect victory would do.

Hane just had to hope she knew enough not to stand between Odette and her fate, because no matter what, there would be no happy ending here for the traitor.

This time, we're going to win.

It was impossible. Nieve was hoping for the impossible, expecting the impossible, *believing* the impossible. Hane was practical. Tactical. Ruthless when they needed to be.

They were a survivor.

And yet . . . the moment Nieve said it—the moment she declared victory against the child of a god beast as well as someone powerful enough to place an effective compulsion over them—was the moment that Hane believed it, too.

They even had a plan: remove the bracelet from Sheuket's wrist, allowing them to take revenge on Odette themself. Simple, right?

Too bad it only worked while Sheuket wore a physical form.

How can I force them to take a physical form? Hane asked themself while running across the ceiling. They trailed one hand along the wall, leaving a thin trail of water to mark the boundary. *A light spell would work, but Lief exhausted himself earlier and Rose is unconscious. There must be something in here that produces light, but would a lantern or fire be enough?*

As they pondered the question, Hane nearly missed the shadow blade arrowing straight at them. Quickly releasing their gravity spell, Hane slid down the wall to the floor, the blade striking hard enough to sink several inches through the wall right where Hane had been. A splash of conjured water, then Hane was weaving and ducking through the items stacked along the wall, hiding from Sheuket and their shadow blades.

If only we'd had more time to explore the vault when we could still see it, Hane thought, darting behind a standing mirror in the middle of the vault. They paused, checking for shadow blades before sprinting to the far wall. *If only there was some way to know what each item in here does, or where to find it . . .*

Wait! There is someone familiar with this vault and the items in it! Hane splashed a hanging shroud with a handful of water before using Sense Water to pinpoint their location in the vault. *But where can I find them? If Lief really had them, then where are they now?*

Nieve said Chime told her about the vault's guardian, which meant Chime had to know other secrets of the vault as well. Perhaps they even knew what some of the treasures did and how they functioned, but the only way to be sure was to find Chime's missing piece.

They knew where Lief was: they'd seen him with Mason and Rose's unconscious form in the corner with the strangely silent alabaster fountain. Putting aside how they could ask Lief if he remembered the tiny crystalline shard he'd had right before Odette mind-controlled the vault's guardian without drawing suspicion, Hane reached out with Sense Water, finding the tiny trickle of water falling to the fountain's basin, and used it as a guide through the ever-changing terrain of the vault. Surely asking about a broken bit of crystal wouldn't be the oddest thing to happen to any of them on this climb so far.

As they rounded the corner of the alcove where they had so recently spoken with Nieve and Chime, Hane spotted someone crouched beside the fountain, seemingly staring into the basin. Hane crept forward, reaching to grasp their shoulder when Lief whirled around, throwing his arms up defensively.

"It's me!" Lief hissed through his crossed arms. "If you hit me, I'm not going to heal you!"

"I don't need to be healed." Hane searched Lief's tunic and belt with their eyes, trying to pick out a tiny crystalline shard hidden in a pocket, pouch, or sleeve. "Are you okay here? How's Rose?"

"Rose is recovering, she'll probably come around soon," Lief said, nodding at a figure laid out on a long trunk, a cloth folded beneath her head as a pillow. As he spoke, Lief reached inside the fountain's small pool, picking out the canteen he'd abandoned when Hane surprised him. He shook it off before holding it beneath the water to fill it. "Are Mason and Nieve okay? Tell them they need to come to me for healing; it's best if I remain stationary so I can be found in case of emergency."

"I'm sure they'll appreciate hearing that when they're bleeding out in the middle of the vault," Hane replied tartly. Lief's logic wasn't bad; it just wasn't practical, either. Injured people couldn't always retreat when they needed aid.

A brief search of their surroundings didn't reveal a tiny crystalline shard anywhere nearby. Had Lief dropped it in his surprise earlier? If so, then there was little chance that Hane would find it without help; even without the perpetual darkness, the floor of the vault was coated in a layer of scattered gems, broken glass, and shards of pottery. To cover their search, Hane asked: "What are you doing?"

"Attempting to revive Rose. Conserving my mana. Being a good healer." Staying low to the floor, Lief moved to Rose's side, pouring a little water from the canteen into her mouth before wetting a handkerchief and dabbing her face. She groaned fitfully, her brow furrowing as if in pain. "What are you doing? Shouldn't you be fighting a shadow monster right now?"

"Nieve and Mason are handling it; I need a moment to catch my breath." A lie, of course, but a believable one. "Are you sure that water is safe to drink? I checked it earlier and it's like no water I'm familiar with."

"I drank some myself before giving any to my patient," Lief replied, somewhat sharply. "It's not poisoned, and I didn't sense it affecting me in any way. Since it's locked away inside a vault, I figured—"

Rose sat up abruptly, the wet cloth falling from her forehead as she covered her mouth to cough. Or at least, her body went through the motions of coughing—the sound, however, was strangely muted, more like a huff of air than a hacking rasp. After a moment, she collapsed on the lid of the trunk, her head striking the wooden surface with force, but no sound. Hane stared, incredulous, as one of Rose's legs twitched, the scrape of her sole leaving a scuff in the dust, but no hiss of sibilance. Lief turned around, wide-eyed as his gaze met Hane's.

"Stealth potion!" they whispered at the same time.

"Go drink!" Lief ordered, pointing at the fountain. "Then get back out there. Even with a stealth potion, too many people in one place will attract unwanted notice."

"Right." Hane crouched beside the fountain and scooped up a small amount in the palm of their hand. Realizing how thirsty they were from leaping all around the vault and creating a map of conjured water, Hane's next scoop involved cupping both hands within the basin and lifting it to their mouth to drink.

As they sipped the cool water, they watched Lief tending to Rose, noticing that despite their close proximity, they couldn't hear Lief's whispered words, nor the rustle of Lief's bag as he searched for something. Rose rolled onto her side, blinking slowly as she asked an unheard question. As Lief leaned closer to hear, Hane sucked in a mouthful of air and choked.

There! On the floor between the trunk and Lief's knee: a toothpick-sized glimmering shard of crystal!

Lief turned to look back over his shoulder, frowning at Hane. "Are you okay?"

"Yes." Hane muffled a cough on their sleeve; they'd ended up spilling half the water down the front of their tunic. They swiped at their mouth with the back of their hand, then deliberately shuffled their heel against the floor. "Did you hear that?"

"No, but I can hear you when you speak." Lief looked briefly intrigued, then shook his head. "It's fascinating, but there's no time to study it. You should hurry, I'm sure the others need you."

"Wait." Hane needed a reason to get closer: if that shard really was Chime's missing piece, they couldn't just leave it to be lost once more. They scrubbed their wet hands on their pants, then crawled to the side of the trunk, uncomfortably close to both Lief and Rose, who looked dazed, but aware. "I have a plan, but I need help."

"You want light, don't you?" Lief guessed. "I already hit them with my strongest counter-compulsion spell and I can't keep wasting mana. Not if I'm going to keep everyone healed up."

"No, I understand." It was a struggle to keep their eyes up instead of looking down at the shard. Hane leaned in closer, reaching blindly for the shard they'd spotted from the fountain. "Just tell me this: can light mana force Sheuket to take a solid form?"

"Possibly. If the light is strong enough to cut off other shadows, and if Sheuket decides to stand in the beam of light for a while." Lief shrugged. "I wouldn't hang my life on those odds."

"We may have to. Forcing Sheuket into a solid form is the only—" Hane felt their hand brush against a tiny object, sending it rolling against the base of the trunk. They feigned a cough to cover their momentary distraction. "The only way to get the bracelet off their wrist."

"I still have blank mana crystals that can be turned into light crystals," Rose whispered, holding herself up on an elbow. "I can probably find a way to channel that into a ray of light, but it wouldn't last long, and as Lief pointed out, Sheuket can just move out of the light."

"So we need a way to light the whole vault," Hane surmised, trying to keep their movements minimal as they tried picking the crystal shard out of a crevice in the floor without the others noticing.

"No good," Lief whispered. "Something like a lantern on the ceiling will be too diffuse to force Sheuket into a solid form, but something focused would be too narrow; a simple step to the side and they'd be back in shadow form."

Hane pretended to think as they scratched at the shard with a nail, prying it out of the crack in the floor.

Luckily, Rose was actually thinking instead of just pretending. "What if we created a trap that wasn't so easy to sidestep? If Hane sets the trap, then they could lure Sheuket to it and be ready to grab the bracelet before they escaped?"

"You mean something like a light-landmine, or an explosion of light mana?" Lief asked. "Aren't there too many variables to rely on something like that?"

Hane sighed in relief as they pinched the crystal shard between their fingers, a familiar ringing tone filling the inside of their mind. They didn't think Lief or Rose heard their exhale, but they must have noticed Hane's movement because they looked to Hane almost in unison.

"What about reflections?" Hane asked, saying the first thing that came to mind. "There's a standing mirror in the middle of the vault, and there's plenty of glass and other reflective surfaces. Can we use that?"

Rose canted her head to the side thoughtfully. "Yes, I think that could work. We'd only need one strong light source that way, so long as we can get Sheuket trapped in one of the reflected beams. It wouldn't be easy to set up, though."

A frightful scream pierced the darkness, followed by a shouted command in Caelish that made Rose gasp.

"Mason," she whispered, collapsing as she tried to push herself up. "That *zakresh*"—something that sounded like "gear rack"—"just ordered Sheuket to kill Mason."

"Time's up on catching your breath, Hane," Lief said frankly. "Go find some mirrors and get them placed around the vault if you can; we'll work on creating a light source."

"And help Mason!" Rose requested, catching Hane's sleeve as they stood up. "Please, he's—he never should have been here in the first place."

"If he's with Nieve, he's as safe as any of us," Hane assured her, feeling the ends of the crystal shard prick their palm. "But I'll do what I can."

A quick gravity reversal, and then they were sprinting across the ceiling toward an adjacent alcove on the opposite side of the vault. A quick look around proved that the standing mirror they'd seen earlier—against all odds—was still upright and unblemished, despite being nearly in the center of the vault. They spotted Nieve on her feet a short distance away, hammer and sword whirling as she slashed through blades of shadows. Hane silently wished her luck before their view was obscured by the alcove's corner. They dropped to the floor with nary a sound, clutching their fist to their chest while reaching out for Chime's consciousness.

<Hane.> Chime's voice was barely louder than a gentle wind rustling leaves. <It is good to find myself in your care once more.>

I'm glad I found you, even if it was mostly luck, Hane thought, swiftly sorting through the mess of items on the floor. They considered a silver platter, but dismissed it when they saw how tarnished it was. *Can you speak to Nieve for me? Or can you connect our thoughts directly, so I can speak to her?*

<It is difficult to remain focused enough to speak to you right now,> Chime replied softly. <I fear I do not have the strength to connect the both of you right now.>

That, at least, was understandable: Chime had said they would be weaker after creating the sound to help find their missing piece.

Are you in pain? Hane asked the entity, fearing the response. Chime was their best chance to find mirrors and objects of power inside this vault, but they didn't want to guilt Chime into overextending themself.

<Not in the way you interpret it,> Chime replied mysteriously. <I appreciate your consideration, but I understand the urgency of the situation. I will do all I can to aid you.>

Thank you, Hane thought, relieved. *Do you know where—*

Before they could finish asking the question, the image of an old-fashioned hatbox appeared inside their mind. Hane spotted the item on a low shelf just ahead of them.

<I do not know all that is here, but I have been here long enough to have some knowledge,> Chime explained. Hane lifted the lid of the hatbox, finding the box itself empty but a pristine mirror on the underside of the lid.

This is perfect. Hane propped the lid upright within the box, then angled it carefully so Rose could hit it with a beam of light. Despite the detritus underfoot, so long as Hane stepped softly, their movement made no sound. Leaning around the corner of the alcove, Hane searched for the next reflective surface they could use to reflect a powerful beam of light.

Odette was screaming orders again, this time in Valian, but Hane couldn't pay attention to that right now; Nieve was handling the combat so that Hane could handle the plan. And Chime was already sharing an image of Hane's next target: a wardrobe with a mirror hidden inside one of its doors.

<This object is no longer where it once was,> Chime intoned. <If you cannot find it, I shall endeavor to provide another.>

I see it. The wardrobe lay on its side, the door hanging at an angle from a single hinge. Checking their surroundings carefully, Hane darted across the room, hoping the mirror hadn't shattered when the wardrobe fell.

A sharp tug freed the door from the hinge. One long crack bisected the mirror, but it would have to do. Hane looked back, sharpening their sight with perception in order to line the mirror up correctly. They would only get one chance with this: it had to be perfect, or else it wouldn't work.

"A clever ploy." A silky whisper right beside Hane's ear. They whipped a tonfa free of its harness, striking through the space beside them, but it only passed through harmlessly. "You seek to trap me in order to free me. An elegantly ironic solution."

Hane coiled into a crouch, pressing the fist containing Chime's crystal shard against their chest, their shocked surprise not entirely feigned. "I'm trying to help you. It was never my intention to fight you."

"A fact I will appreciate if you manage to release me from this spell." The silken purr was followed by two soft sniffs. "Ah, you found the Basin of the Whispering Waters! You truly are clever for a human, aren't you?"

Hane remained tense and alert; Sheuket didn't seem interested in attacking them just yet, but that could change at any moment. Moving their fingers carefully, Hane slipped Chime beneath the collar of their shirt, twisting the folds of their hidden mask into a pocket and pressing it flush to their collarbone. "If you let me, I'll take the bracelet off of you right now, Sheuket. I want to end this before anyone gets hurt."

"Would that I could," came the lamenting sigh. "But I'm afraid that time has already come and gone, silent one."

"What?" Hane asked sharply. "What do you mean?"

The only reply was a whispered *kekeke* on a breeze that made the hair on the back of their neck stand up. Swallowing back fear and bile, Hane leapt onto the fallen wardrobe, freeing the other tonfa from their harness as they scanned the shadows.

Where was Nieve? She'd seemed so close only a moment ago. Hane had seen her fighting fiercely yet calmly, standing her ground as she slashed apart Sheuket's shadow blades. But now, no movement disturbed the shadows; the only sounds were faint rustlings and the skittering of an object cast aside.

Hane coiled transference mana in the soles of their feet, preparing to leap, but the whisper of a different disembodied voice stopped them.

<Wait,> Chime whispered. <Do not go that way. Nieve is unharmed, but she is . . . different.>

Different? Hane asked, still poised to jump. *Different how?*

Before Chime could reply, something at the center of the vault began to glow. It wasn't the harsh light of Lief's counter-compulsion spell, but a golden nimbus that spread to encompass a figure as it slowly rose from its knees. Hane only recognized Nieve within the glow by her high ponytail and the uneven tails of her headband swaying behind her as she kicked her sword up into her hand.

Nieve? Hane wondered, staring in awe. *But she doesn't have light mana. Did she find an enchanted object, or a potion, or—*

Nieve's head turned in Hane's direction, her gaze so sharp and sudden that they felt their breath catch in their chest. They felt frozen in place despite the lack of ice magic. Nieve's eyes . . . they were—blue?

<She is . . . not herself,> Chime whispered as Hane remained pinned by the icy glare. <But she will not harm you. I think.>

What is wrong with her? Hane shifted their weight sideways, just to prove to themself that they could. What they couldn't do was take their eyes off

Nieve. A chill ran down their spine. *She isn't mind-controlled, is she? She's a Champion, she couldn't be . . .*

Before today, Hane wouldn't have believed that a human could mind-control a god beast's child, and yet, Sheuket was little more than Odette's puppet now.

No one was making it out of this alive if they had to fight both Nieve and Sheuket.

<It is not quite what you think,> Chime intoned. <But I fear she still may be dangerous to us.>

What does that—

"Are they dead yet, Sheuket?" Odette's voice, coming from the shadows. Nieve's cold stare broke away suddenly, orienting on something Hane couldn't see. "If Rose is still alive, bring her to me. She's more reasonable than—aah!"

Nieve's movement was almost too fast to track: one moment she was standing perfectly still in her faintly glowing shroud, the next she'd twisted at the waist and thrown her war hammer into a patch of shadows that swallowed it whole. Odette stumbled forward, shaking violently as she tripped over a padded ottoman, landing hard on her hands and knees.

"Kill her, kill her, kill her!" Odette screamed, covering her head as she cowered on the floor. "Sheuket, stop at nothing until Nieve Yukihara is dead!"

The moment Nieve looked away, Hane felt as though they could breathe again. They watched, helpless, as Nieve dashed for Odette's prone form, her sword tucked into her side for a single, powerful thrust. Hane's heart clenched within their chest. If she struck true, this nightmare would be over! But just moments ago, Nieve had said that she could never . . .

This time, we'll win.

At the last moment, a breeze like a resigned sigh stirred the shadows. Sheuket appeared between Nieve and Odette, their form shadowy and ephemeral, but the silver claws on their fingertips solid enough to catch Nieve's thrust and turn it aside as if it were nothing. Steel rang against steel as Nieve reversed her strike into a slash and Sheuket caught her blade with one hand while striking with the other. An open-handed swipe caught Nieve along her jaw, leaving behind a thin white line that failed to bleed. Through the dimly glowing shroud, Hane saw Nieve's eyes narrow, her lips peeled back into a snarl.

What's wrong with her? Hane asked Chime, slinking down into the shadow of the wardrobe. *If it's not a compulsion, what is it?*

<She has asked me not to discuss this matter with you yet,> Chime explained in hesitant tones. <She has assured me that she will tell you herself at a later time. But as far as I can tell, this . . . form does not harm her.>

Form? No, Hane didn't have time to consider that just now. Odette was picking herself up from the ground and backpedaling into the shadows. If Sheuket's orders were to kill Nieve and only Nieve, then Hane had an opportunity to move freely through the vault. The sooner they set up the mirrors, the sooner they could cut the bracelet off of Sheuket's wrist.

Despite the utter chaos that had displaced many of the treasures throughout the vault, the ornate standing mirror was still standing stark and obvious right where Hane remembered seeing it earlier. All they had to do was spin it around so that it faced the rear of the vault in order to catch Rose's beam of light. A quick check to make sure the way was clear, then Hane darted out to adjust the mirror, their footsteps silent beneath them.

"So you've come out of hiding?" Odette's voice spoke from somewhere so close that Hane startled and missed their step. They stumbled into the mirror, narrowly catching it by the frame before it could crash to the floor. "That's suspicious behavior, coming from you. What do you think you're doing?"

Hane tried to make it look like an accident as they spun the mirror around, getting it roughly oriented to catch a reflection from the wardrobe mirror while appearing to catch their balance after their stumble. It wasn't likely that Odette was actually close by, but if she noticed the mirrors, she would likely figure out the plan before they could set it into motion.

"You didn't think I forgot about you, right?"

Hane sank into a low crouch, their tonfa held out defensively at their sides. They kept their head up for attacks while discreetly searching the floor for the spell sphere Odette had to be using in order to project her voice.

"I knew you were the one I had to look out for." Odette's voice leapt away, coming from a distant corner of the vault now, farther away, yet still clear. "No name, no family, no history—it's like you simply appeared one day, a fully formed Wavewalker with a talent for climbing. What are you really? Why are you here?"

"You hired me." Hane cast their perception wide, seeking Odette's hiding place. She wasn't much of a threat—not as a combatant, at least. But she was smart, and the plan to trap Sheuket between beams of reflected light was fragile enough without Odette catching on to it.

"What I wanted was to hire a few high-minded, self-sacrificing, idiot warriors from Dalenos so no one would care if I left them behind to rot inside the Vault of Shadows. Nieve fit the part so perfectly, but you—"

There—the scrape of a footstep within a pool of shadows. Hane charged forward with a burst of transference, swinging their tonfa high, intending to scare rather than strike.

Stars broke out across their vision as something wet trickled down their face. The pain came afterward, sharp and all-consuming. Hane staggered, the vault tilting from side to side as one tonfa slipped from their fingers and clattered to the floor.

What just happened?

"You played the part of a fool so well at first that I almost didn't suspect you. Saying that you were going to walk on top of the train." A derisive huff, less a chuckle than a snort. "But you were far too good at vanishing into the background, always watching, always listening, just waiting for me to make a mistake."

Odette's voice echoed strangely, the words overlapping one another like the ripples from a handful of thrown rocks. Colors and lights still danced nonsensically across Hane's vision even after they attempted to clear it with a perception spell. Hane touched their forehead, fingertips coming away bloody. A head wound? How? No, wait—that was the wrong question. The real question was—

Odette stepped out of the nearby shadows, shaking her head as if disappointed. She didn't look any different from before, really. She still looked more like a scholar than a climber, more anxious than confident. She didn't seem capable of hiring five climbers in order to lure them to their deaths, all so she could betray the god beast of the spire.

"Were you trying to take it from me?" Odette asked, almost curious. "Was this about stealing the mission and the reward for yourself? Or did someone hire you to keep an eye on me?"

Hane didn't even bother trying to puzzle out an answer to that. They whipped their poisoned stiletto blade free of its hidden pocket and lunged.

And somehow ended up crashing headlong into the wooden wine rack, causing it to splinter and collapse, dust and bottles raining down on top of them as they tried to make sense of what had happened.

How? Hane asked themself, muffling a cough as they shoved splintered wood off their back. *How is she doing this? She's an Analyst! She can't be faster than me!*

As they attempted to orient themself, Hane realized they weren't just seeing double; they were seeing four times as many objects as they should be. Unless there really were four Nieves fighting four Sheukets.

The blood roared in their ears as the bottom of their stomach dropped out.

Shock, Hane realized dumbly. *I'm in shock.*

But why am I in shock?

No, that's not important right now. What's important is . . .

Wait, what was the important thing again?

Thinking was physically painful, like breathing in smoke from a raging inferno. But something important lurked within the recesses of that smoke, something vital to the survival of the team. They had to pierce that veil somehow, retrieve the thoughts hidden by disorientation and pain. But before that, they would have to figure out how to deal with Odette.

"Are you even with the Tails?" With their head injury, it was even harder to determine the direction of Odette's voice. It sounded as if it were coming from everywhere at once. "Or are you with the Wings? Haven? Are you some visage's hero? Who sent you to spy on me? What gave me away?"

I never even suspected you, Hane thought, struggling to find focus through their shock state. *I was too busy watching Lief, suspecting he might be the one to betray the team in the end. If I hadn't been so focused on him, maybe I would have seen the real danger.*

That was it. That was part of the answer. Was it something to do with Lief? Chime? No, that wasn't it, but they were close. Weren't they supposed to be doing something? There had been a plan, hadn't there?

Swallowing hard against the bile rising from their stomach, Hane reached out with their Sense Water spell. Everything was still out of focus, but only if they used their eyes. Focusing only on the landmarks of the pockets of water and on Nieve's conjured patch of ice, the nature of Odette's trick began to take shape.

"What about me?" Hane asked, their speech slow and slurred. Each word tasted like blood. "What gave me away?"

Without waiting for a response, Hane sank low into their knees, swinging their tonfa back behind them. This time, when the sensation took them, they recognized it for what it was: teleportation magic. They were moved from the alcove with the wine rack to somewhere near the mound of books Rose had been interested in. At least this time, they weren't halfway through using a transference-aided movement when they were teleported, making it a much less violent transition.

The question still remained: how was Odette forcibly teleporting them around the vault?

"Oh, catching on, are we? You are so unbelievably frustrating, you know that? I had to pretend I was useless and helpless for half the climb just so you would finally let your guard down."

It was a struggle not to vomit. Hane bent over double resting their hands on their knees as they fought off waves of nausea and dizziness. A constant ringing in their ears made them think they were on the verge of passing out, but as they caught their breath, they realized they were hearing the sounds of steel on steel. Hane managed to dive out of the way just as Sheuket and Nieve came within inches of where they'd been standing, trading sword strikes and clawed slashes. Pain jolted through Hane's shoulder as they landed, but it

actually seemed to clear their mind for one short moment as they scrambled out of the way of the two focused warriors. Sheuket's silver-tipped fingers raked sidelong across Nieve's leather vest, trailing silver blurs in their wake. Their hand withdrew from Nieve's weakly glowing aura, but not before Hane realized something important: while most of Sheuket's form remained as insubstantial as a shadow, their slashing hand was inky black and solid up to the wrist, becoming ephemeral only once they withdrew it from Nieve's shroud.

The shadow-being's form was solid inside Nieve's glowing shroud!

Before their shock-addled mind could connect that realization to their earlier thoughts, Hane felt the teleportation magic sweep them away again, dropping them from somewhere near the ceiling to crash down on a stack of paintings leaning against the wall. Canvas tore, wood splintered, frames slid beneath their hands and feet as they fought to stand up. The clarifying pain in their shoulder lessened, becoming small and distant. The haziness of a concussion returned, their half-formed thought over Sheuket's form trailing off in a dreamlike haze.

"Hane!"

They couldn't look. Couldn't even be sure they heard what they thought they heard: their name half hissed, half whispered.

"Hane!"

It was all they could do just to tip their head to the side, searching for the sound they thought was half imagined. They'd lost all sense of direction as Odette spun them round and round the vault, never letting them settle long enough to truly get their bearings. It appeared they'd landed near the alcove containing the Basin of Whispering Waters. Rose crouched nearby, hiding just behind the corner. She held her goggles by the strap, her expression tight and pinched. Her free hand beckoned for their attention. What did she want? Didn't she know that if Odette saw her, she'd be the one getting tossed around like this?

Hane tried to look her way without appearing to stare in her direction too long; the last thing they wanted was to give away her position. Rose looped the strap of her goggles around her wrist and tugged at it, mouthing the same word over and over. Laughter, maybe? No, that made no sense. Packer? No, but that seemed closer.

Rose tugged at the strap looped around her wrist and pointed at Hane, mouthing the word again. She cast about frantically for a moment, then tugged the goggles down around her neck, tossing the eye pieces behind her so that the strap looked like a choker. When she pantomimed tying a bow on it, Hane finally understood.

Tracker!

The tracking bracelets. Was that how Odette was doing this? But wait—they had discarded their location tracker the instant they saw that Sheuket was mind-controlled. It wasn't still stuck to them somehow, was it? They thought they'd cast it away from themself when they'd cut it off, but maybe it was stuck to their leggings, or beneath their boot?

Hane fought to get to their feet, swiping at their sleeves, their tunic, their pants, anywhere they thought the tracker might be. As the search yielded no results, Hane shot a discreet look at Rose and shook their head, pain blurring their vision as they did.

Rose's brows pinched in an expression of desperation and helplessness. Holding up her goggles so that the lenses caught a flicker of light, she mouthed a new phrase: "We're ready."

We? Who? At any moment, the teleportation spell would whisk them away again, giving them scant seconds to make sense of all of this. Looking around for any frame of reference, Hane spotted Lief in the alcove opposite Odette's. He had the hatbox mirror tucked beneath one arm and held the other extended out toward Hane, face pinched in concentration.

Regeneration spell, Hane realized, recalling how the pain in their shoulder faded earlier. *That's not going to fix my concussion. Why is he over there? I thought he was with . . .*

As Hane's addled mind groped after an answer that just barely eluded them, Odette's spell struck again, this time dropping them in the middle of a disgorged wardrobe. The spongy terrain of clothing, shoes, and hats making their knees go weak beneath them. Hard objects hidden beneath the mound of clothing made it impossible to stand; Hane attempted to crawl to the edge of the pile, buttons and lace catching at their clothes to trail behind them.

If this was my wardrobe, I'd be a very cross dresser, Hane thought, a bubble of hysterical laughter wringing itself from their throat. Then, with grim bemusement: *Oh, I'm more addled than I thought I was.*

"You think you're so clever, but I was watching you, just as you were watching me! That's why I never let my guard down around you!" Odette's voice was tinny and distant, but that made sense as it was likely being carried through a spell sphere somewhere. "You righteous Dalenos warriors are all the same! Big sense of justice, no common sense!"

Wait, what was that about letting my guard down? Hane wondered, kicking their leg free from a clingy shirt sleeve. *Was my guard ever up? I never even suspected . . .*

A fleeting memory of an embroidery needle and shimmering thread. Odette's tear-streaked face, far too close for comfort. The soft, repetitive tugs at their sleeve . . .

As fractured as their thought process was, Hane didn't question it: they grabbed the top of their sleeve and yanked, ripping the stitches clear of the seam. They didn't quite get it off before the next teleportation spell moved them again, but they were casting it away from themself even before they landed, something hard rolling under foot so that they toppled backward into a pile of cheap splintered wood in an alcove that reeked with the cloying scent of alcohol. Glass shattered beneath them, one shard digging viciously into their back, just above their hip.

"Sheuket!" Odette shrieked. "Why is she still alive? Hurry up, I have another one I need you to—"

Hane rolled onto their side, digging the shard of glass out of their back as they stumbled to their feet. With the pain came flashes of clarity: Light. Mirror. Sheuket. Bracelet. *Go!*

They darted from the alcove into the open space of the vault, sharpening their perception as they clutched the thick shard of glass tight within their fist. They remembered toppling the mirror in the middle of the vault after one of their violent teleportations, but maybe if they could find it, they could dig out a large enough piece to—

Hane skidded to a halt, jaw dropping open in dazed wonder.

The mirror—it was still standing! Unblemished, undamaged, unmoved even. But how was that possible? They were sure they had—

Hane squeezed their palm around the shard of glass, blood leaking through the fingers of their clenched fist. The how wasn't important right now.

One graceless stagger, then Hane gripped the standing mirror in a bloodied hand, pivoting it to face the tilted wardrobe mirror. Someone shouted just before a brilliant beam of light shot out from the fountain alcove, bouncing off the mirror Lief held, to the wardrobe mirror, to the standing mirror in the middle of the room, right where Nieve held her ground against the child of a god beast.

Sheuket hissed as the beam of light struck them through the core of their being, pupils shrinking into narrow slits against the harsh glare. Their form condensed into the stark blackness of a silhouette, one arm rising to cover their eyes, the other swiping out with silver-tipped claws in a blind attack.

Hane was already in motion, darting past the mirror, diving under Nieve's sword strike and evading Sheuket's claws as they flicked the shard of glass up between their fingers, pinched like a blade jutting up from their knuckles. They slashed at the band of colorful woven ribbons, feeling the glass catch and pull. For one breathless moment, they thought it wouldn't be enough—but then the threads parted and the bracelet slithered to the floor.

Odette's mind-control spell was broken.

Sheuket was free.

Too shaky to move out of the way, Hane watched the tip of Nieve's blade come closer and closer, as if to spear Sheuket through Hane. A blinding flash of silver and a bone-shivering metallic screech, then Sheuket held the sword trapped between their claws. Their eyes narrowed dangerously as Nieve strained to free it.

"It is over," Sheuket said, a note of finality in their tone. "Release her, or I shall end her."

Even with no idea who Sheuket was speaking to, Hane vaguely understood that whatever force held Nieve in thrall would not yield easily while their opponent yet lived. Nieve's face was contorted into a vicious scowl, her arms, face, and armor bloodied but unrelenting. Her shoulders and arms shuddered with the effort of attempting to free her blade. Sheuket's ears were pinned, their tail lashing with fury; they didn't want to kill Nieve, but they would if they had to.

"Nieve." Hane's voice came out as a croak. Their head throbbed, their body ached, their palm dripped blood steadily, but they pushed all of that back. Letting the shard of glass fall to the floor, Hane grasped Nieve by the shoulders, giving her a tiny shake.

"We did it, just like you said. We . . . we survived and we won. We *won*, Nieve. It's over."

Nieve's gleaming blue gaze wavered. She blinked. Her eyes fluttered shut, then her sword clattered to the ground as her knees gave out beneath her. That seemed like the thing to do, so Hane collapsed beside her, unsure if they were holding onto her shoulders for her sake or their own. All they really knew was that their vision was blurred and the fact that they no longer felt sick was a bad sign. "Nieve?"

A weary smile twitched at the corners of her mouth as her eyes flicked up to meet theirs. "Thanks, Hane. That . . . that helped."

She collapsed inward on herself, as if her bones had all gone soft. Her breathing slowed, her body trembling with exertion; whatever this new ability was, it certainly appeared to have its share of drawbacks.

Before Hane could ask Nieve if she needed any urgent healing, the shadows of the vault roiled and writhed, hissing like snakes as Sheuket turned their sharp, silver-eyed glare on Odette.

"N-no!" Something pale and hard dropped from her grip, clattering to the floor as she backed away from the shadow-being. Eyes wide in fear and disbelief, she pressed her back to the nearest wall and slid down to the floor, as if to sink directly through it. "I didn't—it's not my—please, you don't under—aaah!"

Shadows stretched from behind wall hangings, out from under tables, even through the wall behind her, taking the shape of grasping hands that closed tight around Odette's arms and legs, snaking around her body until she was bound tight, shivering and whimpering as genuine panic stuttered her breathing.

"I will have this one," Sheuket said as the shadows drew tight around her. "I trust there are no objections."

"You can have her!" Lief called from the back of his alcove. He must have set down his mirror as the beam of light no longer rebounded throughout the chamber. "We don't want her, right, guys? Let the nice vault guardian have the traitor so we aren't held responsible for her crimes!"

"I honor God Beast Byakko," Rose stated solemnly. "I will not defend anyone who sides against her or her children." She stepped out of her alcove, goggles dangling loosely in her grip, the lenses no longer emitting the powerful beam of light she'd imbued them with. The odd light of the vault grew steadily brighter, revealing the utter disaster that had befallen treasures and trash alike. Rose scanned the room critically, as if looking for something. She stooped and picked up a small ceramic and glass device: Odette's enchanted tracking device.

"This is how you were doing it, isn't it?" Rose asked, holding the device up. "The bracelets weren't just location trackers; you had targeting runes sewn into them that this device could act on. What were you going to do? Mind-control all of us if we didn't go along with you?"

"No, I—I never!" Odette protested. "I thought you would be happy! You could have chosen anything in here with no restrictions. Think of all the forbidden knowledge that you could have collected for your parent! You'd be the favored heir for sure!"

"You clearly don't know me as well as you thought you did." Rose squinted at the runes on the device before shifting it in her grip to pull her goggles on. After a few adjustments of the lenses, her lips tightened into a bloodless pucker. "No, this doesn't have the ability to place a target under compulsion. But a randomized teleportation spell . . . you've been planning this from the beginning. That's why you stitched a contingency targeting rune on Hane's sleeve. In case we took off the bracelets."

"Rose, please!" Odette sobbed, struggling against the grasping shadows. "You can't leave me here! Rose, we're friends! We went to school together, I've shared meals with your family! Bring me back, give me to the queen's justice, I'll admit to everything, please, please—"

"You don't get to say those words," Rose said coldly. "Not to me. You're nothing but a traitor who deserves whatever lies ahead for you."

"Please, you don't understand!" Odette begged. "It wasn't my fault, I was forced to do this! The people who made that bracelet, they're incredibly strong with contacts in every nation! In every *spire*! Please, please, you have to believe me!"

Rose watched Odette with a coldly blank expression as she let the device fall from her hands. "The only thing I believe is that you just contributed one more piece of strange treasure to the Vault of Shadows." She turned away abruptly, frowning as she scanned the vault critically. "Where is my—Mason!"

As she raced across the chamber, Hane was surprised to see Mason stretched out on the floor, not too far from where they sat with Nieve leaning against them. When did that happen? *What* had happened? They tried puzzling it out as Rose picked up a healing potion and attempted to pour it into her brother's mouth.

As Odette continued to plead and beg, a dark shadow stretched across her mouth, effectively gagging her. Tears rolled down her cheeks in a final plea for mercy before Sheuket flipped their wrist in a dismissive gesture. The shadows vanished at once, taking Odette along with them.

"She will be judged for her crimes," Sheuket said solemnly. "This is not the first attempted abduction to take place in Mother's spire, but she is the first to be taken alive. She may earn a reprieve if she gives up the organization behind these abductions—in a hundred years or so."

Sheuket turned a slow circle, training their quicksilver gaze on each remaining climber, silently passing judgment. The silence was that of a withheld breath, as each of them waited to find out if it would be their last.

"I will accept that you five were unaware of the traitor's intentions," Sheuket finally pronounced. "And I will forgive the theft of the Whispering Waters. This time."

Lief cringed noticeably, determinedly keeping his head low as Sheuket continued.

"However." Hane cringed as Sheuket's tail lashed angrily. "For your complicity in delivering the traitor here, I will inflict a penalty upon the rest of you. It is my responsibility to punish Mother's transgressors, after all."

Rose sniffled deeply, her back to the vault's guardian as she hunched over her brother's unmoving form. "Please, Great Sheuket, I beg you—"

"Call your mother here and let me talk to her," Nieve demanded hoarsely. She still leaned into Hane for support, but her eyes were sharp and clear as she challenged the child of Byakko. "Unless you want me to—"

Sheuket held up a shadow-dark palm, silver claws tucked out of sight. "That is not necessary. I have released the wards; you may choose to leave immediately, if that is your wish. However, if you still wish to claim one of my treasures, you may only claim one item each. For any who beg to differ"—silver eyes slashed at Lief, whose mouth had parted slightly in response to Sheuket's pronouncement—"I would have you know that I could send you from this spire with nothing at all and have this matter over and done with already. It is only out of gratitude to this young one for freeing me that I will allow you to linger long enough to select a single treasure."

Lief's mouth shut with an audible click as Sheuket directed a formal nod at Hane. That wasn't entirely fair, as everyone had played a role in freeing Sheuket, but far be it from Hane to correct the child of a god beast. Rather than argue, Lief picked his way across the vault, pausing to touch Hane's shoulder, then Nieve's, casting regeneration spells on each of them. He knelt down beside Rose, setting one hand on Mason's forehead and the other on his chest. After a moment, he met Rose's eyes. "He'll be fine once we get him to the Soaring Wings' healing ward. I'll keep him stable until then."

Rose whispered her thanks as she wiped tears from her eyes.

"My patience is already stretched thin," Sheuket stated, crossing their arms over their chest as their tail lashed like a whip. "Make your choices quickly, or I shall send you back with nothing. Mother must know what has happened here sooner rather than later."

"I claimed my treasure already," Hane admitted, pressing their hand to the front of their tunic, confirming that Chime was still hidden safely beneath their shirt. Even that small amount of movement hurt, but at least the only thing they had to do now was activate their return bell. "Thank you for your mercy, Sheuket."

Sheuket said nothing in return, but narrowed their eyes and dipped their chin once in acknowledgement. Hane was grateful they hadn't asked after the treasure they'd claimed; it would have been a strange thing to explain.

Rose cleared her throat delicately, trembling as she stood and faced Sheuket, head bowed with her hands folded over her heart. "If I may make a small request of you, Great One? My brother, he's—" She glanced down at Mason, unmoving beneath Lief's healing hands. Her next breath shook, but she steeled herself before speaking again. "With your permission, I wish to select one treasure on his behalf."

Sheuket's tail fell still, curled in the shape of a shepherd's crook. "I will allow this."

"Thank you," Rose breathed. After exhaling a shaky breath, she gazed around the vault before shuffling toward the scattered pile of books.

"Hey." Nieve's voice sounded rough. Her shoulder bounced against Hane's, making them grit their teeth in pain. "Since when did you get so cuddly?"

"Too tired to move," Hane admitted shortly. "Something might be broken. Definitely concussed. Still could throw up."

"Oh!" Nieve started to get up, a motion that jostled Hane terribly, but she collapsed just as quickly, her entire body quivering. "Resh it, I'm drained. I don't think I'm hurt, but . . ." Nieve grimaced as her eyes traced the clean slices through her leather vest and the lines of blood on her arms. "Maybe I am. I'll probably live, though."

"Glad to hear it," Hane joked without humor. "I think I'll live, too. At least until we make it to the healing ward."

"You better," Nieve said, weariness in her scratchy voice. "I owe you a meal for getting me to snap out of it. Thanks, Hane."

Hane let their head roll onto Nieve's shoulder, finding it easier to breathe that way. The two of them were awkwardly collapsed around each other, uncomfortably close, but Hane couldn't move without pain and Nieve couldn't move at all. Focusing only on breathing, Hane let their eyes fall closed and waited for the call to ring out.

"Your treasures," Sheuket hissed, tone undercut with impatience. "Claim them. Now."

"I can't even move," Nieve groaned, the fingers of her sword hand spasming violently. Hane felt her stiffen, but refused to open their eyes. "Hane, did you—"

<My consciousness has been safely recovered.> Chime's tones sounded far off, almost tinny in quality. Whether that was the gateway crystal's previous exertions, or a manifestation of Hane's exhaustion, they couldn't be sure. <I fear I shall sleep once we leave this place, but please know that I am truly grateful to the both of you for your efforts here today.>

I'm just glad we don't have to come back here, Hane thought wearily.

Me, too.

Was that . . . Nieve's voice? Inside Hane's mind? Or maybe it was a dream; they felt tired enough to be dreaming.

Lief muttered something under his breath about not being able to pick his own treasure while keeping Mason alive, but by the way he abruptly cleared his throat and changed his tone, Sheuket must have heard him. "I think I'll claim that mirror, if that's all right. It must be pretty special to still be standing when everything around is knocked over or broken."

That was strange, especially as Hane distinctly remembered knocking that mirror over. Or had that just been the concussion? Either way, they couldn't really bring themself to care that much.

"That is acceptable," Sheuket agreed. "Do not leave it behind. That's a stubborn one."

Now Hane was *sure* they were dreaming.

Hesitant steps approached, crunching over something like shards of glass before they shuffled to a halt. "Great Sheuket." Rose's voice, respectful and hesitant. "With your permission, I submit these two books as claimed treasures for myself and my brother."

A brief silence before a whisper of shadow answered her: "I deem these as acceptable. You may take them." Another brief silence, though this one felt somewhat ominous. "And you, warrior? Have you made your choice?"

"I don't know," Nieve said through a heavy exhale. "What's the best thing in here? Can I have that?"

"You may either have the answer to your question, or you may have the item. You may not have both."

Nieve made a dismissive noise in the back of her throat. Hane's sudden desire to pull away from her had nothing to do with the discomfort of physical contact. "Fine. Then I want the golden honeycomb thing I found earlier. I have no idea what it does, but it looked shiny. Should sell well, right?"

Silence, followed by a glint of gold. Hane peered through their eyelashes as the item Nieve requested appeared between the two of them. About the size of Nieve's hand, it was a six-sided object with golden hexagon shapes across its face, like an artist's rendering of a honeycomb. Nieve picked it up and turned it over, showing a flat side etched with runes Hane couldn't identify.

"The Six-Eyed Augur," Sheuket said solemnly. "May it lead you down better paths than the one that brought you here. Now be gone from this place and pray we do not meet again."

"Hey, it may not have been pretty, but we saved—oh. They're gone." Nieve tugged a tiny pouch off her belt buckle, tearing it open with her teeth to free her return bell. As she palmed it, Hane shifted, wincing as they reached for their own bell. Nieve's arm snaked around their waist, curling around them, the golden honeycomb held tight within her grip. "Don't worry, I got you. Everyone ready?"

"I've got Mason," Lief called. "Rose, do you have my mirror?"

"Got it!" Rose shouted. "Don't lose my brother!"

"I haven't lost him yet. On three, everyone?"

Hane pressed one hand over Chime's shard, tucked inside their shirt as the other hand curled around Nieve's belt, holding on through the countdown. They had no memory of the count reaching one, but they felt it as Nieve gave her bell a vigorous shake.

They trusted her enough to see that they made it to a healer. It was just too difficult to keep their eyes open any longer.

SAGE

Seer (hand mark), Citrine
Controller (heart mark), Quartz

Sage's right arm was still burning uncomfortably as he scanned the Soaring Wings' waiting lounge for an empty seat. Usually he preferred sitting at one of the reading tables, but the ache of his abused mana pathways demanded a more comfortable seat today, so instead he chose one of the plush couches. After setting his short stack of books down on the cushion beside himself, he rolled his shoulder and massaged his sore arm.

Maybe I should look into finding a more experienced Biomancer, Sage thought, grimacing as he soothed a knot of pain. *That would cost a lot more, though, and since I'm not sure how long Nieve and Hane's climb will last, I should probably try to be thrifty. And I'm sure this treatment is working, it's just . . . painful.*

It was only his third mana therapy session since completing his Judgment, and from the research he'd been doing, it would still take quite some time before it was safe to actually try using his new Controller attunement. Apparently it took time, effort, and no small amount of pain to alter an established portion of his anatomy. Luckily, aside from his morning sessions with his bargain Biomancer, Sage didn't have all that much to do lately.

He'd found Nieve's note when he returned to his hotel after completing his Judgment, and while she hadn't explicitly stated that she and Hane had left their return bell anchors at the Soaring Wings facility near the spire, it seemed the most likely option. And with nothing better to do than rest up after his mana therapy sessions, Sage spent most of his afternoons reading spellbooks in the Soaring Wings' lounge, waiting to see if today was the day when Nieve and Hane would return from their delve.

The waiting area was nicely furnished and usually fairly quiet, unless a returning team was passing through. In addition to the couches and plush chairs, there were tables surrounded by round stools and a small reading selection available in a singular bookcase. Up a slim flight of stairs to the upper level, a balcony encircled the perimeter of the room with more private reading tables and a low wall to allow people to watch for returning friends and family, but as anxious people tended to pace the balcony in endless circles, Sage found he preferred the downstairs waiting area better. There was even an attached outdoor courtyard where passing food vendors would stop to sell spiced flatbreads, roasted meats, and sweet honeyed yogurts.

For all those comforts, though, the wait was still nerve-wracking.

While Sage had grown familiar with some of the people who showed up day after day just as he did, most were as anxious about their teams and friends as he was, so the only pleasantries exchanged among them were small waves or familiar nods. The majority of the signs, lists of returned teams, and posted flyers on the walls were all written in Caelish, so he couldn't distract himself by perusing the boards, though he did check the lists of returned teams at a translator's desk daily. The provided reading selection was mostly written in Caelish, with a few books in Valian mixed in. So, after the first day with nothing but his worst fears to distract him from the tedious wait, he'd searched the city for a bookstore that carried spellbooks written in Artinian. While it wasn't safe to use any control-based spells yet, he could at least practice a few basic enhancement spells. He selected the book on top of the stack and flipped it open to a marked page, picking up where he'd left off the day before.

It wasn't so much that he minded waiting: the lounge was peaceful, and he had no real obligations to attend to, so it should have been relaxing. Unfortunately, if he allowed his mind too much time to wander, it always chose the darkest alleys to explore, making him relive the worst days of his life, or positing scenarios he'd rather not consider.

What if Nieve and Hane perish on the climb?

How long do I wait for them?

What do I do if they never come back? Do I try to find Chime's pieces without Chime? How would I even do that? Would I just go home? What would I do if I went back home? Work in my parents' shop? Do Emiko's parents still hate me? How would I face Ren and Wyle after losing Nieve?

Would I ever climb again?

Sage realized he'd been staring at the same page of his book for far too long without absorbing a word of it. He sighed and turned the page, thinking a fresh start might help. It didn't.

"Excuse me?" A young woman approached him, wearing the uniform of a Soaring Wings administrator, but with a pin that indicated she was either new or in training. She spoke Artinian slowly and with a heavy accent, but her speech was understandable enough. "You have been asking for updates on temporary team Greyhound 149, yes?"

"Yes," Sage agreed, his heartbeat suddenly leaping from normal to racing. "What happened? Did they return? Are they okay?"

"Most of the team has returned," the woman explained. "They report losing one to the spire and others are injured. I may take you to the healing ward now."

"Yes, thank you, yes." Sage's hands shook as he gathered up his books. Someone had been lost? Who? Nieve? Hane? Were they simply lost, or had they . . .

His heart beating high enough in his throat to choke him, Sage followed the administrator down the corridor he'd seen returning teams come through. He was desperate for answers, but at the same time, he didn't want to know. If he lost someone else to a spire climb . . .

No. It was unthinkable. Nieve and Hane had defied death before; surely they could do it again.

They had to.

Sage nearly fainted when he heard Nieve's voice coming from a room just ahead. He had to stop outside the room to swallow gulps of air and wait for the dizziness to pass.

"You may enter," the administrator explained. "But do not distress the injured while they heal, yes?"

"Yes," Sage agreed. "Thank you. For ah . . . just thank you."

He still waited a beat after the administrator walked away; his heart was pounding, his hands felt clammy. Nieve would make fun of him if he showed this much emotion upon seeing her again.

Finally feeling in control of his emotions, Sage rounded the doorway, knocking lightly on the frame to announce himself. He stopped on the threshold, confused to find an unfamiliar climber smiling as she spoke with Nieve at a patient's bedside. It was a shock when he realized the person passed out on the bed was Hane, looking somewhat tiny and vulnerable out of their usual black spire attire.

Both women had stopped talking at the sound of Sage's knock. The stranger had a hand on Nieve's shoulder, standing close to her side as she leveled an annoyed glare at Sage. Nieve, however, broke into a relieved grin.

"Sage!" Nieve tried to push herself up from her chair, but her arms trembled and she dropped back down heavily. She seemed in good spirits, though, as if she were only exhausted rather than injured. She must have spotted the concern on his face because she quickly added: "Don't worry about Hane; the healers came by already and said they'd live."

"Thank the goddess." Sage sagged against the doorway, feeling weak with relief. "Are you okay, too? You look . . . terrible."

Nieve must have washed her face and hands, but Sage could see a heavy layer of grime peeking out from the collar of her shirt and the edges of her sleeves. Her armor—worn but sturdy—had been slashed and shredded, coated in stains that Sage hoped weren't all blood. Or at least, not her own blood. Seeing her too exhausted to stand reminded Sage of how she'd looked after escaping Hogame in the Tortoise Spire; he hoped that whatever she'd endured hadn't been that bad again.

"Do I?" Nieve asked, grinning. "I smell even worse. Come over here and give me a hug."

"Is this your other teammate, Nee-eh-vay?" the stranger asked pointedly. She spoke Valian rather than Artinian, though her appearance suggested she might be Caelish. "Sorry if I'm interrupting, but you know I don't speak Artinian."

"Right, sorry." Nieve switched to Valian as well, sounding far less rusty than Sage expected her to be. Had she spoken Valian for the duration of an entire climb? "Rose, this is Sage. He's a Seer on my team and my oldest friend. Sage, this is Rose." Nieve's grin softened as she looked up at Rose, but then she blinked and quickly looked away. "She's an Architect on the team I just delved with."

Sage frowned, puzzled by Nieve's awkward transition. Rose looked a little worse for wear after just finishing a climb, but beneath the rumpled clothing, mussed hair, and smudged grime, it was easy to see she was a gorgeous young woman. She looked a bit severe, but that wasn't necessarily a deal-breaker for Nieve. And she had curly hair! Sage had seen Nieve kick people off their barstools in order to sit next to women with curly hair. And by the way Rose leaned over Nieve's chair to rest her hand on her shoulder, it looked like she was interested, too, so why was Nieve acting so reserved?

"Nice to meet you, Rose," Sage said pleasantly. "Thank you for looking after Nieve. I know she can be a handful."

Rose only replied with a thoughtful hum. The way she eyed Sage made him feel he was being evaluated. She smiled as she turned back to Nieve. "I only stopped by to return that hammer to you. Try not to leave it behind next time; I may not be there to clean up after you."

Nieve huffed a laugh, still avoiding eye contact. "Thanks. I'll try."

Rose lingered a moment longer, shooting a look at Sage as if hoping he'd go away. Any other time, he might have given the two of them space, but it had been far too long since he'd seen Nieve, and unless she specifically requested it, he wasn't going anywhere.

"I suppose I'll see you when we split up the loot," Rose said, hand trailing along Nieve's shoulder before she stepped away. "Unless you come and join me at the bathhouse later, eh, Nee-eh-vay?"

Was it Sage's imagination, or did Nieve just gulp?

"Yeah, maybe," she said, picking at a tear in her leather vest. "Tell your brother that I hope he recovers quickly."

"He will, but I'll tell him all the same."

Sage stepped aside, clearing the exit for Rose. He kept up a polite smile and started to bid her farewell, but as she turned to face the doorway, his jaw dropped. Unable to stop himself, he pointed at a book tucked inside Rose's belt. "What book is that? It looks ancient! Can you read it? I've never seen writing like that before."

Nieve chuckled as she leaned back in her chair. "Good to see you haven't changed, Sage."

"I can't fault a fellow scholar for their interest," Rose said, a hint of a smile at the corners of her mouth. She freed the book from her belt to display the cover and the incredibly detailed scrollwork. "I have no idea what book this is; I choose it for my brother. He collects rare metals and I think this inlay might be lumenite. The book itself is immaterial, so if you're interested, he might be willing to sell it after he removes the inlay."

"Wow, that really would be a treasure!" Sage agreed. Lumenite was such a rare metal, it may as well be mythical. Before he could ask if he might flip through it, he spotted the cover of the second book and gasped so hard that he choked on his tongue. "That—do you know what that says?"

Rose placed her hand over the book's cover defensively. "Yes. Do you?"

"Yes, it says—" Sage shook his head, correcting himself. "Not that I can actually read it, I just recognize the cover from my studies. That's one of the rarest books on all of Kaldwyn! It's—" He looked around quickly, lowering his voice to whisper. "Essence of the Spirit Arts, isn't it? I heard only fourteen copies ever made it here from the old continent, but no one's really sure because every time one surfaces . . ."

Rose's expression became hard and cold, mouth pursed as she hid the Spirit Arts book behind the lumenite scrollwork book. Sage shifted uncomfortably as he averted his gaze. Every time a tome of archaic magic surfaced, it promptly vanished into the ether again. While commonly believed to be the work of Wydd and their protection of forbidden knowledge, Sage thought it was just as likely that the books were hidden away in the vaults of the rich, stored as antiquities and treasures, rather than being put to use. Rose's intentions were none of his business, but Sage itched to ask her anyway.

"I should probably go check on my brother to see if he's woken up yet." Rose looked back over her shoulder, a smile lighting her face. "Farewell for now, Nee-eh-vay."

"Yeah, see you later."

Sage waited until Rose was far out of sight before raising an eyebrow and asking: "Nee-eh-vay?"

"Pet name," Nieve said shortly. "Not for you."

"Okay, okay." Sage held his hands up in surrender. "Are you sure you're okay? Because she seems exactly your type and she just invited you to meet her at a bathhouse. Is there something wrong with her, or . . ."

"No, she's perfect," Nieve said sullenly, slouching in her chair. "She's smart and gorgeous and competent and—"

"Curls?" Sage suggested.

"Curls!" Nieve agreed through a pained expression. "I know, and I like her, it's just . . ." Nieve shook her head. "There's a lot I need to tell you, just . . . not here."

"Sure. Whenever you're ready." Sage started to cross the room, intending to give Nieve a hug no matter how badly she smelled, but he drew up short, remembering that Hane was asleep on the bed. "Should we maybe, um, go somewhere else?"

"Oh, you don't have to worry about them." Nieve nudged the hospital bed with her foot. "They're only faking. Right, Hane?"

Lashes parted, revealing a dark-eyed glare. "I wouldn't have to fake-sleep if you weren't having uncomfortable conversations at my bedside."

"What do you want me to do about it? I couldn't just kick her out," Nieve retorted. By way of explanation, she added: "Hane's not allowed to sleep until a healer checks on their concussion. I'm still recovering myself, so I'm keeping them company." Nieve grinned as she held her arms open. "Come here, Sage! We missed you."

Unable to hold back, Sage rushed into his oldest friend's arms. The hug was brief, though, as Sage broke away with tears in his eyes.

"Ugh, you do smell awful! If you don't go to a bathhouse before the hotel, I'll push you in a river myself."

Nieve snorted. "I'd like to see you try." Leaning to one side, Nieve grabbed the arm of a chair and dragged it closer, patting the seat in invitation. "Tell us about your Judgment."

"Oh, it was delightful," Sage replied dryly. "It was a marshmallow eating contest, and Selys herself came down to offer me the attunement of my choice."

Hane snorted, which was only surprising because Sage wasn't sure he'd heard them laugh before.

"Ugh." Nieve rolled her eyes. "Can you at least tell us what attunement you got and where it is? I can see it's not on your face."

"No, it's—" Sage pressed a hand to the center of his chest, hesitating. "Okay, look, I don't want to go into the whole story right now, but . . ." A deep breath to steady himself. "It's a Controller attunement."

The admission was met with stunned silence. Followed shortly by loud, guffawing laughter.

"Controller!" Nieve laughed. "You got—oh, you don't even understand how funny that is! No, Sage, I don't believe it!"

"I'm glad you think it's funny," Sage snapped. "It's not even close to what I was hoping for, and the placement is terrible, but I'm working on it."

"The goddess must have a sense of humor!" Nieve roared. "Oh no, oh wait! Look, Sage, I got you something."

Nieve shifted in her seat in order to draw something from her belt. She swung it sidelong, stopping it just short of Sage's nose so that all he could see was his own reflection on a polished green orb. He scowled at her as he gripped it by the staff to see it properly.

"I pulled that off a Controller in the first scenario," Nieve explained, still grinning widely. "It's perfect for you! Whenever you use it, you should think of me, and remember that, no matter how many attunements you earn, I'll still always be able to put you in a headlock and drop you in the nearest lake."

"It's a pity that your attunement practically makes you immune to mind control," Sage said mildly, examining the staff weapon. It was heavier than it looked, suggesting a weighted core, but even with the marble knob on the top, it felt perfectly balanced in his hand. With a shrug, he stuck the staff through his belt. "This is mine now. You can't get upset and ask for it back later."

"I've seen Controller spells used to great effect on teammates," Hane said placidly. "I can make you a list of spells that I'm familiar with, if it helps."

"It would, thanks." Sage dipped his head, feeling abashed. "I have a lot of work to do before it'll be functional—conflicting mana types, you know—but I'm working on it. I'd appreciate any support you're willing to offer."

"Good luck with all of that." A brief pause, a flicker as their gaze darted away. "I'm glad you came out of your Judgment safely. Nieve was worried."

"It's good to see that you're all right after your climb. Er . . ." Sage hesitated, eyeing the blankets with sudden trepidation. "You are all right, aren't you?"

"Scrapes and bruises. I'm fine." Hane pushed themself up against the pillows. It was shocking how different they looked in the pale linen hospital robe, which seemed slightly too big for their shoulders. Lines of fresh bandages showed beneath the fold in the front of their robe, suggesting they might have more than simple scrapes and bruises. "We really could have used you on that delve, Sage. Your Sight would have made all the difference."

"Sorry I wasn't there." Sage looked from Hane to Nieve, assessing their injuries. "Was it . . . *really* bad?"

The look his teammates exchanged confirmed their answer before they gave it.

"It wasn't . . . quite as bad as last time," Nieve said gingerly. "But it got pretty bad. Worse in some ways, maybe."

"We didn't lose as many people," Hane explained plainly. "But the fight was almost as difficult. I think it would be best to discuss it at a later time."

"Yeah, sure, of course. Whenever." There was one question Sage couldn't wait to have answered, though. Looking around furtively, he leaned in and lowered his voice. "Did you find . . . them?"

"We did," Hane confirmed. After another quick check for anyone listening, Hane opened a closed fist, revealing a slim crystalline shard. It looked shorter than the piece recovered from the Tortoise Spire, only about as long as Hane's littlest finger. One edge was cut to a perfect right angle, as if this piece had broken off the ricasso.

"Wow, you guys did it!" Sage beamed at both of them. "Congratulations! You know what that means?"

"Drinks!" Nieve cheered.

"No," Hane said firmly.

Sage chuckled. "It means we can move on to the next spire. Did Chi—did *they* say anything about their other pieces? Maybe where they are inside the other spires, anything like that?"

"They were pretty exhausted at the end of the climb," Hane explained. "We should let them rest before we ask them."

"That's fine," Sage said agreeably. "We have a few options to choose from, so I thought it might be best to let—"

"Hey." Nieve sounded startlingly sedate for someone who had just shouted the word "drinks" in a healing ward. "I, um . . . I have something to tell you. Both of you. Just, um . . ." She turned to face Sage but cringed away from him looking almost . . . timid. "Just please . . . don't be mad at me?"

"Why would I be—" Sage stopped, dumbfounded as Nieve peeled off her leather vest and tugged down the collar of her shirt. His first instinct was to turn away—this was Nieve! Practically his sister!—but out of the corner of his eye, he spotted the bold, dark lines of an attunement mark. Taken by surprise, Sage leaned in to stare, his mouth slowly dropping open. "Nieve, is that—when did you—how long—why don't I know what that mark is?!"

"Is that the reason for your strange behavior in the vault?" Hane asked, stoic as always.

"Yeah." A dark flush in her cheeks, Nieve covered the mark up again and smoothed her shirt over it. "I don't want to go into too much detail about it here, but ah . . . I felt like I owed Hane an explanation for . . . well, you know."

Hane nodded, an understanding passing between the two of them that left Sage on the outside.

"And Sage, I—" Whatever she saw on his face made her fidget anxiously. "I didn't mean to hide it from you, okay? Grandma made me seal it because we didn't know what it was."

"Wait." Sage shook his head, trying to understand. "Wait, if it's been sealed, then—how long have you had that?"

"Since my Judgment?" Nieve's brow furrowed, her shoulders rising defensively. "I'm really sorry, Sage. I always wanted to tell you, but Grandma told me I had to keep it a secret. And since it was sealed, I figured it never really mattered, except . . ." An impish shrug. "It's different now. I'm . . . trying to figure it out."

"Okay." Sage pinched the bridge of his nose. Then repeated himself: "Okay."

It was a lot to process: his best friend since childhood had been hiding a specialized attunement from him for years! And while Nieve had no obligation to tell Sage everything about herself, that's how things had always been between the two of them. At least, that's how it had been for Sage: he'd never held anything back from Nieve. Maybe if he'd been the one to get a mysterious, unknown attunement, he might have done the same, except . . .

No. He knew himself too well: if he'd emerged from his Judgment with a second attunement, there was no way he would have ignored it as long as Nieve had.

"Sage?" Nieve sounded small. That was wrong: Nieve was never small. "I, um . . . I could really use your help? I don't know how to use it properly and it's a little . . . unpredictable. I was hoping that you could help me figure it out?"

Sage sighed, scrubbing a hand over his face. "Of course, Nieve. I'm just— surprised, I guess. Or shocked, maybe. But yeah, I'll do what I can to help." A quick glance at the door before speaking in a whisper: "Can you just tell me what attunement it is? I'll have to do some research."

"It's a Paladin mark," Nieve admitted, smiling sheepishly. "But it's a little . . . different. I'll tell you everything, just not here, okay?"

"Sure. Sure." That was probably for the best. But still . . . Nieve was a Paladin? Really? Sage had so many questions he wanted to ask. He suddenly felt impatient to get out of here and find somewhere to have this discussion in private.

An uncomfortable silence settled over the three of them. Nieve continued to fidget and shuffle nervously; Hane was simply quiet by default. Every rustle of the stiff hospital sheet seemed to drag on and on in the sudden stillness. Sage struggled to identify what he was feeling: a little upset, perhaps, that Nieve hadn't been honest with him, but at the same time he understood her reasoning. He was also curious and more than just a little excited about the idea of helping Nieve use her new attunement, but conflicted over whether or not that would take time away from working out his own double-attunement issues. And underneath all of that was just his gratitude that both Nieve and Hane were alive and well after a harrowing delve. Suddenly, it all just seemed like a lot to process.

Surprisingly, the one who broke the silence was Hane.

"You were saying something earlier about our options," Hane said. "For our next spire. What are they?"

"Oh, um . . ." That seemed like a safe enough subject to discuss. "Well, the quickest option is to head for Valia and the Serpent Spire. There's a train that goes directly—" Sage stopped, noting a look of distaste exchanged between Nieve and Hane. "What is it?"

"No trains," Hane said firmly.

"Not unless we can go on the roof," Nieve added with a chuckle. Hane very nearly smiled at that.

"Um, okay . . ." Confused, Sage continued. "Well, if it's not going to be the Serpent Spire, then we're choosing between the Hydra Spire and the Phoenix Spire. The Hydra Spire is closer, but I heard there's going to be a tournament in East Edria for a special gate key, or something like that. My translation of the announcement could be off, but I'm sure about the tournament part."

"What kind of tournament is it?" Hane asked. "Is it a standard dueling match? Or is it more like a series of competitions with multiple eliminations?"

"If it's a normal duel, I'm definitely doing it," Nieve declared. "It's been so long since I've entered a dueling tournament!"

"Something to keep in mind is that we'd have to travel past the Hydra Spire to get to the Phoenix Spire," Sage pointed out. "And travel through Edria is a little . . . complicated. Out of curiosity, I picked up some maps from a Way-agent. Wait, I think I have them with me . . ."

Sage was sure he'd brought the maps—he enjoyed plotting routes along them in between chapters of his spellbooks—but as he patted his pockets down, he failed to find them. After a few minutes of frantic searching, he remembered tucking them inside the cover of one of his spellbooks.

"Hold on, I know where they are." He had to bend over double to retrieve the books he'd tucked under his chair, then it was a matter of remembering which book he'd hid them inside . . .

"Excuse me." A warm voice speaking lightly accented Artinian from the doorway. Sage didn't look up, assuming it was a healer to check on Hane. "I didn't mean to eavesdrop, but did I hear you might be headed to Edria?"

"Hey, Lief," Nieve replied. For some reason, she dug her elbow into Sage's side. "Don't you look pretty. Did you wash up and change, or is that something your fancy new mirror does for you?"

A soft chuckle followed Nieve's bizarre question. "I was informed that I had to wash up before I could be released. In all good conscience, the healers couldn't allow me to leave covered in that much blood."

"I'm sorry," Sage said automatically, still sorting through the maps of Wayfarer stations for the one he wanted. "Were you badly—"

The words froze on his lips as he looked up. The stranger in the doorway was tall, with the pale skin and wavy blond hair of a Valian. His warm smile revealed perfect white teeth as well as good humor. His clothes looked expensive, as if they had been handmade just for him, all delicate fibers and complementary colors. He was standing still, but there was an elegance about him—his posture, his movements, everything. But what struck Sage the hardest were his eyes, sparkling with intelligence and vibrantly violet—Sage had never encountered anything like this man's eyes before.

This had to be the most beautiful man in the world.

Belatedly, Sage recalled that it was rude to stare. He coughed into his fist, trying to cover for his lapse. "Injured," he finished lamely, looking down at his maps again.

"That's kind of you to ask." Hard-soled boots crossed the room as Lief moved to stand on the opposite side of Hane's bed from Nieve and Sage. "I'm a healer, so most of the blood wasn't mine, thankfully. I'm Lief, by the way. Biomancer."

"Sage." Sage stood up to reach across Hane's bed, exchanging a Valian greeting with the newcomer. "I'm a Seer on Nieve's legacy team."

Lief appeared mildly surprised at that.

"I know, it's weird, but I'm Dalen, not Valian."

"Oh, no, I didn't assume that about you." Lief flashed that smile again. "I just had no idea that Nieve was part of a legacy."

"What do you want?" The harshly worded question came from Hane, surprising Sage for the third time since their reunion. The Wavewalker wore a hard look on their face, as if Lief were unwelcome. As Sage returned to his chair, he noted that Nieve seemed just as surprised by Hane's question as Sage felt.

"My apologies, Hane, I should have asked permission before entering." Lief didn't lose his smile even in the face of Hane's scowl. "Out of consideration, I'll try to keep it brief: I was planning on using the treasure from this delve to fund my trip to Edria, but, well. I don't have to tell either of you that our yields didn't quite meet expectations."

Nieve nodded and even Hane dipped their chin slightly. Sage was dying to find out what happened while he'd been waiting for Nieve and Hane to return.

"I was just passing by your room when I heard you three might be headed that way." Lief flashed a charming smile. "It's cheaper to travel as a group. Is there room for one more?"

"We might not be headed to Edria," Hane said, tone slightly harsh. "We might go to East Edria instead. Or Valia. Or we might stay here a little while. You should probably make your travel plans without us."

Nieve shot Sage a confused look. He shrugged helplessly, unsure of what was going on.

"I wasn't asking for a free ride," Lief said cajolingly. "I can't afford the full fare, but I can offer you all my assistance along the way. Free healing, boosts to physical strength and agility, or assistance with strengthening mana pathways . . ."

Sage perked up at that.

"Plus." By the confident flash of his smile, Lief had saved the best for last. "I speak Cas. Do any of you speak Cas?"

Hane's expression turned sour as both Nieve and Sage shook their heads. School had required that everyone learn at least one additional language, but Sage had been lazy and chose Valian, even though he already spoke it fluently thanks to his parents. It would have been better to choose either Cas or Cael-ish, but both Nieve and Emiko had chosen Valian, and Sage had just wanted to take the class with his friends.

"I'm in no hurry if you need time to decide where you're going," Lief continued. "But I could be ready to leave as soon as we divvy up our loot from the delve."

"We don't need—"

"Do you know how to keep conflicting mana types from interacting between two close-set attunements?" Sage asked in a rush, cutting over Hane's abrupt refusal.

Lief smiled warmly. "I do, but that sort of treatment requires multiple sessions over several weeks. Sometimes months. I'd be more than willing to assist you with that, if you'd help cover some of my travel expenses."

"I—" Sage cleared his throat. "We need him."

Hane cut him with a threatening glare. "I don't want to travel with him."

"Everyone stop and take a breath," Nieve ordered with authority. "Lief, give us some time to get back to you. We need to talk it over as a team. Okay, guys?"

"You're right, we should discuss it first," Sage agreed. As much as he needed the help of a Biomancer, Hane might have perfectly valid reasons for wanting to exclude Lief from their travels.

They just needed to be reshing good reasons to pass on free biomancy therapy.

Hane's eyes went tight before they looked away. "Fine."

"I appreciate your consideration of this matter." Lief's smile wilted minutely. "I hope to see you all when we meet to divvy up the spoils of our delve."

While he had to be talking mainly to Nieve and Hane, Lief's gaze lingered on Sage just long enough to make the tips of his ears burn. Just as Lief turned to leave the room, a healer stepped inside, asking for privacy with the patients. Sage hugged Nieve around the shoulders as he stood and waved a simple farewell to Hane before following Lief out into the corridor.

"Hey, ah, I'm sorry about all of that," Sage said, catching up with Lief's long stride. "I don't know about what happened between you and Hane, but I didn't mean to make it awkward."

"I'm not worried about it," Lief said smoothly. "Hane's concerns are justified; we did lock antlers a few times during the delve, but I don't hold it against them." He stopped and turned to face Sage, warm smile in place. "Do you mind if I take a look at your close-set attunements? Just in case your team agrees to let me tag along, I'd like to know what I'll be working with."

"Yes, of course." Sage stepped off to the side of the corridor, making space for others to pass. Lief took hold of his hand and wrist, eyes turning distant as Sage's skin prickled beneath his touch.

"Ah, that's a tough one." When Lief looked up, all Sage could think of was how close he was. And how his hand was beginning to sweat. "It'll take some time, but I believe we can work it out."

"Uh huh." Something twisted inside Sage's stomach. Fear? Nerves? Hunger? Was he ill? Regardless of what it was, Sage withdrew his arm by taking a step backward for distance. "I, um . . . thank you. For offering to help."

"Oh no, thank you." Pearl-white teeth in a perfect smile. "You're helping me too, after all."

Soaring Wings Climber Registry

Temporary Delving Team Designation: Greyhound 149

Name: Odette Keita
Attunement(s): Analyst, heart
Rank: Citrine
Status: Active Climber
Additional notes: Team leader/recruiter, proof of possession of a Floor 17 climber gate key. Delve objective: retrieve valuable treasures, conduct research to locate/confirm presence of a secret chamber known as "the Vault of Shadows." Current member of the organization Spire Secret Seekers, a research team dedicated to locating secret rooms, passages, vaults, etc. of the Tiger Spire of Caelford.

Name: Rose Oladele
Attunement(s): Architect, lung
Rank: Citrine
Status: Active Climber, Irregular
Additional notes: Warrants preferential treatment; potential heir to the Oladele family. No current team affiliation.

Name: Mason Oladele
Attunement(s): Transmuter, hand
Rank: Citrine
Status: Active Climber, Irregular
Additional notes: Crystal Mark of Metal (leg placement); warrants preferential treatment; potential heir to the Oladele family. No current team affiliation.

Name: Lief Valmont
Attunement(s): Biomancer, leg
Rank: Citrine
Status: Active Climber
Additional notes: Traveling climber-for-hire, originally from Valia. Spell focus on healing, purification, and mental protection.
Internal Information Only: [REDACTED]

Name: Nieve Yukihara
Attunement(s): Champion, mind mark
Rank: Citrine
Status: Active Climber
Additional notes: Current leader of Team Guiding Star Legacy registered in Dalenos; inherited the team "Guiding Star" from her parents (both deceased while climbing the Tortoise Spire). Team Guiding Star Legacy is officially on hiatus due to lack of members; Yukihara is currently registered as a climber-for-hire.
Internal Information Only: Special circumstances granted; lend reasonable assistance as requested.

Name: Hane

Attunement(s): Wavewalker, leg mark

Rank: Citrine

Status: Active Climber

Additional notes: Currently a member of Team Guiding Star Legacy (Dalenos), but also registered as a climber-for-hire while the team is on temporary hiatus.

Internal Information Only: Special circumstances granted; lend reasonable assistance as requested.

Soaring Wings Judgment Applicants

Applicant: Seiji "Sage" Hayden
Nation of Origin: Dalenos
Attunement (if any): Seer, right hand, Citrine level
Status: Active Climber
Additional notes: Current member of Team Guiding Star Legacy, also registered as a climber-for-hire while team is on temporary hiatus. Judgment application included a letter of approval for a second Judgment issued by the Dalenos branch of the Soaring Wings Administration, and Letter of Request with appropriate funds from the Spire Relations Division of the Dalenos Government.
Internal Information Only: Special circumstances granted; lend assistance as requested.
Status: Approved for Judgment
Results: Currently Ongoing

Attunements of Caelford

*Copied from Sage's travel journal;
notes in parentheses are from margin comments.*

Okay, I know I don't get to choose my attunement (or, at least, as much as anyone knows when it comes to Judgments, I guess), but since I went to the trouble of requesting a Judgment at the Tiger Spire, I figure it can't hurt to be familiar with the typical Caelford attunements. And maybe this list can help Nieve and Hane if they get the chance to join a climber team during my Judgment. I don't know about Hane, but Nieve gets forgetful when it comes to attunement functions and mana types.

Since I can only guess that my usual approach to solving challenges (carefully and methodically) is what earned me the Seer attunement, my plan is to try and be a little more aggressive this time, in the hopes of earning an attunement that can assist me in combat. So, essentially, I guess I'm going to have to try and think like Nieve during my Judgment. (Does Nieve think before she acts? I'll have to ask her.)

Just in case it helps, I'm going to list the typical Tiger Spire attunement in order of my personal preference. (Of course, there's always the minute chance that I might end up with a different attunement entirely, in which case I definitely wouldn't mind getting either the Guardian or Swordmaster attunements!)

Forgemaster: Forgemasters have superior control over metal, allowing them to move quickly even in full armor by subtly altering the armor's structure while they move. They also can strengthen or alter the properties of metallic objects.
Mana Types: Stone, Fire, Enhancement (Citrine level)

Transmuter: The Transmuter focuses on transforming materials into other types of materials, making it immensely potent at construction, as well as destruction.
Mana Types: Stone, Water, Air (Citrine level)

Sentinel: The Sentinel attunement emphasizes mental fortitude, providing superior resistance against mental spells.
Mana Types: Stone, Mental, Enhancement (Citrine level)

Illuminator: The Illuminator serves as a beacon of light and peace to all those around them, shielding allies against negative effects like fear and paralysis.
Mana Types: Light, Water, Air (Citrine level)

Analyst: Analysts are experts at discerning detailed information about how something works, such as the mechanics behind spells, items, and traps.
Mana Types: Mental, Umbral, Transference (Citrine level)

Biomancer: Biomancers are one of few attunements capable of safely influencing the inner workings of another person's mana. They specialize in altering the target's mana flow, potentially improving both mana capacity and increasing mana regeneration.
Mana Types: Life, Mental, Light (Citrine level)

Architect: The Architect attunement is capable of imbuing items with temporary magical properties. These tend to be stronger than permanent enchantments, but only last a matter of days. (I know this one has strong combat applications, but I worry about any attunement with perception as the primary mana type interacting with my mental mana.)
Mana Types: Perception, Umbral, Enhancement (Citrine level)

Controller: Controllers are specialists in mental compulsion, capable of forcing others to do their bidding.
Mana Types: Perception, Enhancement, Umbral (Citrine level)

PERSONAL CORRESPONDENCE

A letter to Nieve from her grandmother,
received the day she departed Dalenos.

My Darling Girl,

It has been one of my greatest joys to watch you grow in both strength and character, and though my heart breaks at the thought of you leaving home, please know in your heart that I am proud of everything you have accomplished, and everything that you will accomplish in the future. I know you leave home with a heavy heart for all that you have lost, but believe me when I tell you that all wounds cease to bleed in time. Trust in your strength and trust in yourself: do not measure yourself by what you have lost, but by what you have learned.

I pray you never face a fight such as the one that drove you from the spire of our home, just as I pray that you never need to break the seal upon your locket. But just as you requested, I have inscribed the incantation below, should dire need drive you to release your mysterious attunement:

Four knots bind the seal.

Magic within tightly bound,

I release you now.

All I wish for you, my darling child, is that you walk a path of worth for no one but yourself. To that end, you needn't fret about sending any of your treasures home to us; the boys and I can take care of ourselves. But should you wish to ease our hearts, I daresay we would all enjoy receiving letters of your adventures if and when you have the chance to write them.

Walk your own path, my child, but do so under the guidance and protection of the goddess, as well as those who came before you. Be brave and honorable, but above all, be safe. I pray you find what you seek.

All my love and prayers,
Grandmother Mitsuki

Acknowledgments

It's tough to start this on a positive note when looking back at the year I spent writing this book, since it was filled with so much loss and heartache. But while it was probably one of the worst years of my adult life, there were also so many things to feel grateful for, and that's an easy place to start. I am so grateful to still have my beloved greyhound, Chromie, at my side as I write this. This hasn't been an easy time for her, either, but she's been a great source of comfort and I hope I've been the same for her. I'm also grateful to the caring and wonderful staff at my local veterinary clinic. Saying goodbye is never, ever easy, even when you know it's the right choice. Thank you, Dr. Sharpe and Dr. Taylor, for being there for my family when we needed your support the most. I hope future visits will see more smiles than tears. And I am most grateful for my husband and partner, Andy, who navigated these stormy seas at my side with both grace and strength. Thank you, my love. Words will never be enough.

But another source of strength during these times came from you: the readers and fans who embraced *Crystal Awakening* with enthusiasm and welcomed me into Andrew Rowe's universe. I have loved every minute I have spent talking with fans of Andrew's works, diving deep into the magic systems, and admiring the fan works you all shared with me. Knowing that you all were waiting for the next installment of *Shattered Legacy* kept me focused throughout my ordeals, and provided me with something positive and productive to focus on. I can't express to you all how much that helped, but it truly did. I hope this second book has lived up to your expectations, because you all deserve nothing but the best.

I am also so very grateful to my publisher, Podium Audio, for allowing me the time I needed to grieve and to process. I put a lot of pressure on myself to always meet deadlines and exceed expectations, and when I can't meet my own high standards, I feel as if I am letting others down. The staff at Podium never made me feel that way and allowed me to take the time I needed for myself. Thank you, Victoria, Nicole, and everyone else at Podium whom I might have inconvenienced by pushing back the delivery date. I hope you all know how much that extension helped me, and I hope that you all are able to take the breaks you need for your own health and wellness.

Prior to writing *Crystal Awakening*, I was a self-published author who was used to handling every aspect of publishing on my own: from editing and formatting, to hiring artists and narrators, and even marketing and self-promotion. To be honest, I had no idea what I was getting into when I decided to self-publish my first book. Working with the teams at Podium has been both an honor and a dream! I wish I could extend my thanks to each and every one of you personally for all that you do.

Nicole, you and your team of editors taught me so much about the origins of words that I never knew before! As a lifelong learner (and a bit of a nerd), I truly appreciated these lessons. I can't wait to see what I will learn this time!

Leah, thank you for keeping me on target with the cover art! I definitely have a tendency to get swept away by details and lose sight of the larger picture. I can't thank you enough for bringing in Asur Misoa to work on the amazing cover art for both *Crystal Awakening* and *Phantom Chamber*. The both of you are far more talented than I could ever hope to be on my own.

And speaking of incredible talent, a huge thank you to Travis Baldree and Emily Lawrence for breathing life into my words as the narrators of the audio book! I could not imagine what these characters would sound like without your voices behind them. And of course, thank you to Marina and her team for all the work they put into creating the wonderful audio editions for *Shattered Legacy*. Reading has never been more accessible than it is today, and I just want to extend my appreciation out to every coder, programmer, engineer, and technician who make that possible. You all touch so many lives and deserve to be recognized for all your hard work.

One truly amazing team to work with has been the marketing wizards of Wunderkind PR. Elena, Brianna, Lisa, thank you so much for all the wonderful opportunities you found for me to talk about *Crystal Awakening* and my work as an author. I had no idea how much fun it could be to share lists of my favorite books, discuss the research behind my words, and just share my enthusiasm for this series. It's been amazing working with you and I can't wait to see what you find next!

I owe a huge debt of gratitude to the online communities of Climber's Court on Discord and Reddit. It's been such a joy to see my book enjoyed, discussed, and, yes, even cried over, but more than that, this community is such an amazing resource on Andrew's complex magic system as well as the lore, characters, theories, and helpful information. It's also just a welcoming and chill place to hang out and discuss other book series, television shows, video games, and anime. I'm especially grateful to the moderators and programmers who work tirelessly to keep the community a fun and safe place for everyone. From the first time I listened in on one of Andrew's moderated interviews on Climber's Court, I thought "Wow, I'd love to do that!" and this past year, you all made that dream come true. Thank you all so much for welcoming me into your amazing community!

Special thanks to all the experts and subject matter specialists who helped me learn and enriched this world and my characters with their knowledge! Thanks to Krista K. (aka Kritta) for creating all the wonderful art used in the chapter headers, as well as Nieve's locket in the appendix. You work so hard and put so much soul into your art, and it truly shows! Thank you, Janelle, for helping me understand different hair types and textures; that was so important for me to include in this novel! And thank you to Amy Reader-Lalor who taught me so much more than I ever knew about sewing, stitching, and weaving!

To all my wonderful, amazing, detail-oriented, and enthusiastic beta readers: This book would not be what it is without you! Thank you all for your honesty in your feedback, especially your corrections and concerns. What you do is so valuable for writers like me, and I appreciate each of you. A thousand thanks to Krista K., Nick "Ghost" Chevalier, Tobias Begley, Justin Green, Andrew Ritchie, Markus Kemppainen, Jonah L. L., James L. M. Wolter, Amy Reader-Lalor, Yvonne Etzkom, Brandon Yee, Rebecca Reeves, Izzy Trejo, Eamon, Alex W., and Matt P.

Of course, I can't overlook the support and love from my friends and family: thank you one and all for encouraging me to pursue my passion as a writer. Eamon, my brother, thank you for always being there to brainstorm fresh ideas and consider different approaches, and for your phenomenal world-building ideas. Seriously, you and I need to collaborate one day! I'll bring the characters if you bring the world and the magic. And my sister, Arielle. I knew you were the right person to come out to regarding my new gender-identity and pronoun preferences when your first response was: "I totally see this for you." It meant so much to me in that moment. It still does. Thank you so much for just being you. It really means everything to me.

And finally, to the two people who brought me into this universe and made this possibility into reality: Jess and Andrew, please accept my sincerest and humblest gratitude. Jess, I love you, and I appreciate you for always reaching out to check on me. You've been such a constant throughout this process and I have no idea where I would be without you. Thank you for everything you've done and thank you for everything you will do, because I know you're a part of this as much as I am. And Andrew: I'll never be able to thank you enough for inviting me into your universe and allowing me to contribute my own characters, lore, and hidden gems. I look forward to the day when we can enjoy a spirited conversation about anime and video games over drinks. The first round is definitely on me!

ANDREW ROWE

Andrew Rowe was once a professional game designer for awesome companies like Blizzard Entertainment, Cryptic Studios, and Obsidian Entertainment. Nowadays, he's writing full time.

When he's not crunching numbers for game balance, he runs live-action role-playing games set in the same universe as his books. In addition, he writes for pen-and-paper role-playing games.

Aside from game design and writing, Andrew watches a lot of anime, reads a metric ton of fantasy books, and plays every role-playing game he can get his hands on.

Interested in following Andrew's books releases, or discussing them with other people? You can find more info, updates, and discussions in a few places online:

Andrew's Blog: https://andrewkrowe.wordpress.com/

Mailing List: https://andrewkrowe.wordpress.com/mailing-list/

Facebook: https://www.facebook.com/
Arcane-Ascension-378362729189084/

Reddit: https://www.reddit.com/r/ClimbersCourt/

Also by Andrew Rowe

The War of Broken Mirrors Series
Forging Divinity
Stealing Sorcery
Defying Destiny

Arcane Ascension Series
Sufficiently Advanced Magic
On the Shoulders of Titans
The Torch That Ignites the Stars
The Silence of Unworthy Gods

Weapons and Wielders Series
Six Sacred Swords
Diamantine
Soulbrand
Book 4 (coming soon!)

Other
How to Defeat a Demon King in Ten Easy Steps

KAYLEIGH NICOL

As a hybrid fantasy author, Kayleigh Nicol has been both self- and tradition-ally published. A lifelong learner, Kayleigh draws inspiration from movies, books, video games, and anime as well as personal experience from many years of working with animals. After living in various regions around the United States (the Northeast, the Midwest, California, and Texas), Kayleigh has come to believe that a home is where and what you make it. Kayleigh identifies as a nonbinary individual, and while they do not consider feminine pronouns such as "she" and "her" entirely incorrect for their identity, their preference is for the use of non-gendered pronouns, such as "they" and "their."

You can find their blog at www.kayleighnicol.com, and follow them on Facebook and Twitter.

Also by Kayleigh Nicol
Sorcerous Rivalry
Mistress Mage
Mage Prince
Cursed Realm (coming soon!)
The Mage-Born Anthology

DISCOVER
STORIES UNBOUND

PodiumAudio.com